THROUGH THE ABYSS

SUPREME CREATION
BOOK 1

SIDNEY SON

Editing, design, and distribution by Bublish, Inc.

ISBN: 978-1-647044-32-9 (paperback)
ISBN: 978-1-647044-31-2 (eBook)

This book is dedicated to all the people that believed in me despite all the challenges in writing this book. It has brought great joy to my life and opened a new chapter for the future. Hopefully, with the help of God working through these people, I will be able to continue along this journey.

This is also dedicated to Karrie Allen, Johnny Suttles, Jimmy Haney, Jennie Son and the late Sidney E. Son Sr.

CHAPTER ONE

JONATHAN SLOWLY POPPED his eyes open and awoke from what seemed like a comatose state. After shaking his head around to clear the cobwebs and to get his bearings, he yawned as he stood up from the chair he had been sitting in. Pushing it aside, he was surprised to feel quite relaxed after his remote viewing session. Looking at the chair again, he noticed the name Broyhill on the back of the cushion. It was one of those padded, reclining office chairs on wheels. Jonathan thought aloud, "I'm gonna have to requisition one of these babies for my office at Wright-Patterson."

Feeling the need to get the blood flowing, especially in his legs, Jonathan bent quickly at the knees into a squatting position and then raised up. After several repetitions, he felt much more energized, especially after passing gas. "Yep, it's time to get outta here," he said.

He was in a small, dark room, which had an eerie red glow emanating from the neon lights that were aligned one foot below the ceiling along the walls—obviously designed to allow a person to maintain good night vision while providing just enough light to see. In the room was a small table, the chair he has been sitting in, and a half-empty can of soda. He grabbed the remaining beverage and chugged it down. "It's flat. Figures," he said aloud. Crushing the can in his powerful grip, Jonathan tossed it into the chair and headed for the doorway. He really didn't know how long he had been in here, but judging from the taste of that soda, it must have been several hours.

Grabbing the barely visible door latch with his right hand, Jonathan slowly turned the handle clockwise, until, with a click, he pushed the door ajar. Squinting, he slowly opened the door to prepare his eyes to adjust to the potentially brighter surroundings.

Standing there, several feet from the door, was a seven-foot-tall, reptilian-looking creature, who wore a silver, skintight, one-piece jumpsuit. Jonathan recognized him. It was Gilla, or at least that's what his human name was. His actual name was twenty-seven letters long and would require a person to be hooked up to about ten thousand volts of electricity just to pronounce part of it.

Gilla had a green scaly skin and a large head that resembled that of a lizard—a Gila monster to be more precise, hence the name. His vertically slotted eyes were ochre yellow and glowing slightly in the low lighting. They sat in two orbital sockets located directly in front of the skull. This beast was definitely a predator. No nose to speak of, just two small nares at the end of a long snout; his mouth, which contained upper and lower jagged teeth, was flanked by two fangs that hung like stalactites from a cavern ceiling. The tongue, which was bifurcated like that of snakes, and used much in the same way as a sense organ, was constantly going in and out of his mouth. It would extend out about six inches or so, only to swiftly be retracted back. When needed, however, the reptilian could extend it out several feet, especially when catching prey.

Jonathan had once jokingly grabbed Gilla's tongue once as it escaped from his mouth. Needless to say, the lizard was none too pleased and promptly grabbed Jonathan's right hand with his left. He then, almost simultaneously, moved his own scaly right arm behind Jonathan's trapped arm in an upward motion and grabbed his attacker's chin, being careful not to cut him with his claws. This demonstration was not meant to hurt his friend, but just to provide enough negative reinforcing behavior to stop this tongue grabbing habit before it actually became one. He then squeezed Jonathan's right hand firmly, which caused the immediate release of his sense organ. Gilla now merely moved his right leg forward in a sweeping motion behind Jonathan. The reptile now, while maintaining pressure on his opponent's arms, merely rotated his hips, performing a perfectly orchestrated hip throw takedown. It all happened so rapidly that Jonathan had no time to break his fall. He landed flat on his back with Gilla's hand on his chin and knee on his liver. Not only was the wind knocked out if him, but his pride was hurt. The scaly creature, having made his point, offered his fallen assailant a hand and helped him to his feet. Jonathan never grabbed Gilla's tongue again.

Gilla's head led down to a powerful, thick, well-developed neck, which flowed down to his shoulders. The V-shaped torso transitioned onto powerful, muscular appendages for both arms and legs. Each hand had a thumb and three fingers containing thick, curled claws that could easily rip and sever flesh. Surprisingly, however, they could also be quite adept for more delicate tasks. The feet, too, were similarly clawed, except for the big toe. Its talon was arched and significantly larger and longer. This was always, in particular, to be avoided in the event of a confrontation with one his kind, although in most cases it was purely an academic matter, since the average human would only last a few seconds anyway. The tail, while touching the ground and aiding with balance, could also be wielded as a powerful weapon. This creature was fast, strong, and was a killer. Born and bred. Luckily, he was friendly to humans and had always been a trusted confidant of Jonathan's.

"Thank God it's you, Gilla! I'm so glad you like to keep the lights low. At Los Alamos, those little triangular-headed fuckers would have it so bright it would have taken me an hour, with sunglasses, for my eyes to adjust." Jonathan whined.

Gilla responded in his slithery tone, "Yoush always sh pleashant when yoush comesh out from she glean shroom."

"Yeah, well, all that tachyonic energy in there just gives me a case of the red-ass and makes me want to fight. I wish those little gray bastards were here," Jonathan pined. "I'm feeling highly motivated and truly dedicated to stomping their little heads into a bloody pulp, until their big, black, soulless eyes come out."

"Capshion Johnm yoush makesh me hungray." Gilla hissed, with a gurgling sound rising from his stomach, much like spittle from Pavlov's salivating dogs. "Wesh basher gesh ousha here before wesh are caugsh. Ish almosh shime for sifsh change," Gilla hurriedly replied.

"Holy shit, I was in there longer than I thought. I'll tell you what I saw when we get back up to sublevel three. Just led the way," Jonathan concurred.

Walking with Gilla through the warm, dimly lit corridor toward the elevator, Jonathan's thoughts drifted back to the visions he had gleaned in the tachyonic chamber. He would discuss these with Gilla later to try and figure out what the best course of action should be. But, for now, he just needed to stop thinking and get out of this heat. The tachyonic room, although located almost a mile and half below the Earth's surface, at Dulce Research Facility, New Mexico, was unusually cool, probably due to the amount of energy dispersed by the tachyons traveling through the titanium shell of the room at nearly light speed. Outside the room, however, was a toasty 127 degrees Fahrenheit. Gilla, of course, loved it. His race had been living in the subterranean realm for eons. They were the original occupants of the planet—or that is their claim, anyway, which seems to have some validity to it.

As the story goes, millions of years ago the Reptilians lived above ground during the time of their earlier cousins, the dinosaurs. Even then they developed from hybridization with an avian species, which made them smaller but smarter, and their ancestors continued to thrive. The Earth was warmer then, with lots of herbivores for the carnivores. Their race developed as one with the Earth, in tune with her magnetic fields and internal pressures, and although not technologically advanced at the time, they did have a written language and lived as an organized society.

Then, around 65 million years ago, sensing something was about to happen, they fled underground. An ELE, or extinction level event, occurred when a large meteor struck just off the Yucatán Peninsula in Mexico. This is commonly called the KT extinction event. Almost all life on Earth was extinguished, but the Reptilians, thanks to their keen senses, had been preparing for decades. They had created vast underground cities with huge grow rooms that used tachyonic energy to cultivate a kind of blue-green algae that requires very low lighting. Although they are carnivores, the insect-like creatures that provide them sustenance thrived on the algae.

The Earth's surface was uninhabitable for thousands of years, first because of the subzero worldwide temperatures caused by the dust blown into the atmosphere from the initial blast, which blocked the sun's rays, and second because of the charred, barren, desolate landscape that was left after the thaw. Earth did slowly recover, but the Reptilians had already evolved and adapted to live underground, which is warmer than the surface temperature of today's Earth.

Therefore, the way many Reptilians see it, we are the aliens on this planet. The squatters. We were created much later than they, and this is their planet. Although much of the species is against humanity for this reason, no others are for man's destruction of Earth's environment. Gilla, as well as a few others, believe that with cooperation, both races of humanoids can work together to save Mother Earth and live in harmony. While some secret factions of governments have formal treaties with the Reptilian leaders, at present all interactions between species are strictly contractual in nature, with tension remaining high between the two groups.

Jonathan, being a realist and knowing firsthand the corruption of man, is highly skeptical of a working relationship with any species; humans cannot even work among themselves. That is unless, of course, there came some help by some divine intervention. He, however, has little faith in such a God, considering, his experience both of life and in the military. In his mind, no God would allow all this pain and suffering to happen to his creation. Humans are just another form of animal—or virus, more accurately—living on a host, using all its resources, then moving to a new host or area. At least, this was Jonathan's take on the human condition, for now.

Upon seeing the elevator, Jonathan asked Gilla, "How much time before shift change, Gil?" Both were walking at a fairly brisk pace. Gilla, barely turning his thick neck, which was not really designed to swivel on his torso, replied, "Sixsh minushes, Jonashan. Wesh will makesh in shime."

"Just barely. Let's hope no one has to catch a ride until we get to sublevel ten, or we may have to fight our way off this base," Jonathan bantered with a mischievous grin. He was still irritated by what he had gleaned in his visions, and the fact that he was sweating bullets wasn't helping to improve his mood. Gilla just continued, without a word or hiss, tongue darting in and out of his mouth. He knew Jonathan was a warrior who thrived on action and loved to fight. In fact, even though he was human and was physically much weaker, Jonathan could hold his own against any of his kind, especially if armed. Humans have the ability to improve synaptic firing through learned, repetitive skill. Reptilians' skill, on the other hand, was instinctual and was already at a maximum upon maturity. Man, being more intelligent, through training, can develop new neural pathways that, while not physically increasing their speed per se, did enhance response time. Nevertheless, Major Jonathan, as far as humans were concerned, was in a league of his own. Gilla had always sensed something special in his friend, something that separated him from any other *Homo sapiens* he had ever encountered. Yet he was unable to detect what exactly it was. Jonathan was an alien among aliens.

As they approached the elevator, Gilla pushed the up button with one of his claws, and the door opened. They moved purposely into the six-by-six-foot, stainless steel carriage, which had handrails on three sides and hand straps hanging from the ceiling. Gilla pushed the close-door button located on the digital control panel, which was to the right of the elevator doors. Tactilely entering the secret coded sequence, this due to the size of his talented hands, never failed to amaze Jonathan, and the elevator was off. The necessity of the handrails and overhead hand straps was quite apparent due to the speed at which the elevator traveled. The readout dial, which read in feet and levels, was clicking off 100 feet a second. Thankfully, the designer of this vehicle was insightful enough to put the car in a vacuum-sealed shaft, allowing the elevator to accelerate rapidly and ascend at incredible speeds. This frictionless environment reduced drag, which under normal conditions would have created enough heat to melt the elevator. Going down, however, was still limited by the effects of gravity, and could travel no faster than 32 feet per second per second, terminal velocity.

After a few moments, the elevator slowed as it approached sublevel twenty-one, the lowest level other than the tachyon chamber. They had traveled over 7,000 feet in just over a minute and a half. At this speed, stopping on different floors would have been impossible. The car's occupants, because of inertia and gravity, would be reduced to a crushed blob on the carriage's floor.

Jonathan knew that the inertia itself could be defeated with a simple electromagnetic gravity field, which would allow the elevator to travel exponentially faster, but that would make too much sense. No one has ever accused the military of being efficient.

"Ding, ding, ding," a bell rang as they passed levels. Twenty-one, twenty, nineteen. All was going well; it looked like they were in the clear, until "ding . . . ding . . . ding . . ." The elevator was slowing. Fifteen, fourteen, thirteen. It finally stopped at sublevel twelve.

Before the doors opened, Gilla reached into a pack he was wearing and pulled out a cloak, which he tossed to Jonathan. "Here, push shis on. Ish will makesh yoush invisible." Hurriedly, Jonathan obliged. "Gil, this thing is cool. I heard about these when I was at Groom Lake, but never had the opportunity to get hold of one. I hope this works," Jonathan whispered.

"Gosh in the she corner and besh quish," Gilla hissed. "Besh ready, jush is caseh."

As the gears of the doors groaned upon opening, another Reptilian and two Grays entered the car. The Reptilian's name was Rex and even though he was outranked by Gilla, he was not one to let an intrusion by humans at this level pass unreported. Humans were not allowed below sublevel ten under any circumstances. There were things going on down here that would probably cause a war with humanity if they were ever to get out. The two Gray minions to Rex had been named Trick and Treat. Rex had always been very fond of Halloween; it offered him the opportunity to mingle with the humans on the surface unabated.

The alien Grays, who stood no more than four feet in height, are the triangular-headed beings Jonathan had referred to earlier. They had large heads, proportional to their bodies, with exceptionally large, solid black eyes. The eyes are actually biomedical enhancements that allow the Grays to see in the dark. It is, in fact, the same technology that man obtained after one of their spacecraft crashed in Roswell, New Mexico, back in 1947. The bodies recovered, Grays, were studied and dissected. Some other inventions included fiber optics, lasers, Kevlar, night vision, and the transistor, which was given to Bell Laboratories; now AT&T.

The remaining features of their faces were unremarkable, with two small holes for a nose, a tiny mouth, and no ears, just holes. The body was very slim, supporting long, gangly arms. The hands had opposable thumbs with only two fingers. They did not speak out their mouths but communicated through telepathy.

They had once been similar to *Homo sapiens*, but they had sought to evolve into higher and higher creatures, through genetic manipulation and biochemical engineering, until they had virtually ended their species altogether. It had been determined, by removing all emotions and desires, to create peace among its members. With the adoption of a beehive mentality style or order, each member of their species would work toward a common goal, peacefully. One problem, however, was that there would always have to be a select few to issue orders and be in control. The evolved Grays had no wants, desires, or drive to do anything. They just did not care at all. The genetically altered beings also had another complication: they had stopped procreating, because emotion and the drive to survive and spread one's seed are so fundamental in the act of copulation that the Grays had become sterile.

The only means they possessed to continue their species was to clone copies of themselves. Clones, because they were not created from the necessity of life and the physical act of sex, had no soul. The leaders, having been removed for thousands of generations from the rest of their species, were now totally separate creatures. Taller, stronger, and having all the emotions of most humanoids; the genes they possessed, although being unaltered, would have regressed their species back millions of years, giving new generations an equal footing with that of the ruling families. They would sooner let the Grays die out and enslave another species than for that scenario to take place.

So they travel the universe, searching, studying, and experimenting for ways in which they can regain that raw emotion, which they so desperately needed for their race. Cloning, just like any replication process, gets worse and contains more errors each time it is performed. They did not have many generations left before their cloning would no longer produce viable life. It was for this reason, and the close genetic ties to *Homo sapiens*, that they came to Earth in the first place.

These two Grays, Trick and Treat, however, were Rex's slaves. This was a customary practice, especially because they really did not care anyway. Rex would just give them orders, and they followed, no explanation needed. They are highly intelligent and highly technological creatures. Even though they were Rex's minions, they were still part of the greater Gray collective and always kept in tune with the hive. Essentially, they were still under orders from their original leaders, for which reason they are never truly ever trusted.

Upon seeing Gilla, Rex acknowledged his presence and authority, hissed a few words in their native language, and quickly turned around and pushed for sublevel nine on the panel.

Luckily, Rex was too concerned with an experiment he and his minions were conducting on a new viral strain against humans to be aware of Jonathan's presence. Trick and Treat, though, did sense his presence by detecting his thought patterns. But since this was no concern to their master, it was no concern to them. They never acted alone or on impulse. Order. Life was about order, no matter what.

"Ding . . . ding . . . ding." then the door slid open. Once again, Rex turned and acknowledged his superior's presence and exited the elevator, closely followed by Treat. Trick paused, however, looking directly at where Jonathan was hidden, then at Gilla, and just as suddenly turned and joined his companions without incident.

As the doors closed and the tension dissipated, Gilla hissed a sigh of relief. Jonathan removed the cloak and slapped Gilla on the back. "That was intense, Gil. I'm glad Rex wasn't in his usual search and destroy mode. His little Gray turd noticed me though. I know he did, I could feel it."

"Yesh, bush shey had basher shings sho do shoday," Gilla uttered. Besides, Gilla had had a firm grip on the flash gun he was carrying in the small of his back, just above the tail.

"Hey, Gil, can I keep this cloak? It may come in handy one day." Gilla nodded with approval and a smile that only Jonathan could genuinely appreciate.

Jonathan hated the Grays. They caused mankind pain and suffering. Gilla suspected it was because of an abduction, or close encounter of the fourth kind, which may have happened to him as a child. It could be discovered through regression therapy and hypnosis, subjecting him to all the experimentation and torture they performed, but he would have none of it. Jonathan realized it was not the Grays' intention to cause humanly pain and suffering; we were just ants to them. They were merely testing and studying us, nothing personal. Though things, as Gilla knew, are never that simple when it comes to humans. Letting go of emotion in lieu of logic was not a trait that the human race, or Jonathan as an individual, were very proficient at.

Still, Gilla was endeared to Jonathan because of his spirit and his sense of honor. Many years ago, after a battle against one of his own, named Philoraptor, Phil for short; Gilla had been severely injured and left for dead. Jonathan, rock hounding near Mount Shasta, California, had found him barely alive just outside of an ancient lava tube. Though this was his first encounter with a Reptilian, and even though the stories he had heard about them gave him a little anxiety, Jonathan bandaged his wounds, gave him some antibiotics, and sat by his side for three days until Gilla was able to express his gratitude and thanks. Jonathan was then able to get him into the hands of some of his kind who were sympathetic to his needs. Gilla informed his savior that he had his life debt and would always be there for him, no matter what. Jonathan did not require such a reward, and that's not why he helped him; he knew that not to accept his service would be a great insult. But Jonathan had done something that Gilla would have never expected—he befriended him. Most humans, in Gilla's experience, would have used this life debt as an opportunity to have a slave, a bodyguard—or worse, a pet. But not Jonathan. He was a man of honor. He also vowed to help him track down and get his revenge on his attacker, Philoraptor, when the time was right.

Jonathan, standing up, pushed the panel button for sublevel three. "Let's get to the train and get out of here. There are a few things we need to discuss on the way to Groom Lake," Jonathan stated.

Gilla, with excitement, replied, "Jensh will besh shere! SSSSSSSS . . . yesh!" Jen was a female Reptilian Gilla had been hooking up with for years, and although Reptilians did not have relationships like humans, they did have the instinctual urge to procreate, usually on an annual basis, which was quickly approaching. Reptilians, although not normally mating for life with just one partner, have been known to be quite selective in choosing a mate, depending on the traits they are looking for in their offspring. Jen was, as Jonathan put it for him, "a USDA Grade A piece of ass." She had everything Gilla was looking for to further his line.

"Calm down, old friend. I know how you get when love is in the air," he said laughingly. "We have things to discuss first." Gilla nodded in agreement, with a humorous pouty sort of look.

"Ding, ding, ding . . . ding . . . ding . . . ding." The elevator had reached its intended destination, sublevel three.

CHAPTER

TWO

ARIELLA WAS IN the lounge, sitting in front of the porthole on the east side of the habitat. Although this was an incredible opportunity, for she had been among a select few even considered for the job, she was missing the surface. The warm feeling of the sun on her skin, the salty smell of the ocean air, the sounds of the Earth, the ones above the waves. Being 15,000 feet below the surface of the ocean, in the Mariana Trench, had its advantages; one being peace and quiet.

Ariella, while enjoying the company of others, could never be accused of being a socialite. She enjoyed the solitude that the abyssal ocean offered. It was like being swaddled by Mother Earth, an experience she had missed growing up, as her mother had died during childbirth. Her current view, when the lights of the habitat were illuminated, was like something out of a Jules Verne novel. Though only being one league under the sea and not 20,000, she was seeing what Captain Nemo would have seen, from the angler fish, using their luminescent lure dangling in front of their teeth-laden mouths as a fishing pole to attract prey, to transparent glass sponges and spicules floating aimlessly in the depth. Life flourished in the total darkness. Just outside of the porthole window was a three-foot-long sea pen growing out of the pelagic ooze that made up the shelf floor. Crabs and shrimp down here, as well as most creatures, used bioluminescence not only to lure food, but to attract a mate. A steady rain of decaying particles called detritus makes it look like it's snowing. "It really is quite beautiful," Ariella had told her colleagues on more than one occasion.

Other than the oddities of life, the Hab, as it was referred to, was nestled on a precipice in the trench, with a sheer fall of over 3,000 fathoms to its north. This room of the Hab had a huge twenty-by-six-foot clear aluminized window, a technology not available, anywhere, to the public. In fact, the Hab itself was classified Top Secret. Ariella didn't even know such a structure existed, or was even possible, until she had arrived topside over two months ago. She had dealt with the US government before, while doing research on the damage done to the atolls in the Maldives Islands, off the coast of India, after the December 26, 2004, tsunami that ravaged the Indian Ocean. Every time she and her research team headed south from their base of operations, the island of Addu, to study the ocean current changes, an unmarked Blackhawk would appear and inform them, by loudspeaker, that they had entered restricted waters and must leave at once. After numerous calls to the US embassy in Malé, which led to endless transfers and more questions than answers, Ariella finally called an old friend she had known while teaching at the University of California at Berkeley, near San Francisco. Charlie had worked for the government, building and repairing bases. Although Ariella was not normally inclined to contact ex-lovers, she was persistent. Charlie, on the down low, informed her of a secret US air base called Diego Garcia, located just south of Addu. She had never heard of it; no one had. Regardless, Charlie advised her to stay clear—way clear—of that area, lest she end up in a freak boating accident or become a victim of some sort of mysterious disappearance.

"Ariella, could you come to the command bridge; there is a communiqué from the San Francisco Bay Naval Shipyard. It's Charles Hargood," the squawk box echoed. Ariella walked over to the wall receiver, pushed the button, and responded, "Thanks, Justin. What is he doing calling me here? Doesn't he know this line is for official or emergency communication only?" She was mildly perturbed, not so much by his calling her, but because it reminded her of yet another failed relationship. Also, the last time they had spoken ended on a sour note. Even though she was happy with her crewmates, just hearing another voice, any voice, would do her some good. Still, she was not looking forward to this call.

"It's flagged top priority. It all looks official to me," Justin said. He was trying to ease her nerves and keep her calm; that was his job. Stress in this environment could easily lead to mania, which could endanger the entire crew. There was no quick getaway from here.

Captain Justin LaMarr had seen much in his naval career. Being a Navy SEAL on SEAL Team Two, had indeed offered him the excitement that any young man would have wished for. From missions in the Middle East and off the coast of Africa, to the islands in the South China Sea, he had traveled the world by the age of thirty. He was truly an American hero, though no one would know it, and he certainly was not one to brag. Justin LaMarr had an aura about him, a calm that a man only gets when he has seen death, up close and personal. At the age of forty, he was awarded the rank of captain, five years before it was expected, and although he knew he deserved it, he was incredibly happy and surprised, especially coming from a family who told him he would never amount to anything. After being commanding officer for SEAL training at "BUDS" in San Diego, Captain LaMarr was offered his current post, commander of the Deepwater Naval Observatory, the most advanced structure of its kind. It allowed for inhabitants to breathe regular air under normal atmospheric conditions, thus eliminating the need for decompression. Captain LaMarr accepted this position with honor and immediately went to work. He, of course, was offered the opportunity to choose the members of his team, a task he was more than qualified to do.

Justin was an intelligent, calculating leader who possessed the charisma needed to excel in any leadership position. He had studied all the personnel files and histories of his team members. Being very personable, especially with civilians, he had talked with Ariella at length on many occasions about various things, including Charles Hargood. Ariella, much like himself, was too career driven to be tied down to anyone for too long. However, she still dreamed that she might settle down one day, with the right man and under the right circumstances.

Captain LaMarr was under no such delusion; he knew he was a career frogman and would always serve the US Navy first and foremost, above anyone, including himself. The Navy had given him everything, and he planned on returning the favor for life. Therefore, with his current assignment and situation, he could not see anything that would resemble a healthy relationship, which is another reason why he remained single.

Ariella paused for a moment and took a deep breath. "Think," she whispered to herself. Charles Hargood was not a clingy sort of man, and he would not call unless there was a good reason, especially considering communication with the habitat was highly restricted. "But why?" she said aloud. Scenarios raced through her mind . . . "Nothing?!" Rather than working herself into a frenzy over an answer that she could not solve, she closed her eyes, dropped to her knees, and prayed. "God grant me the serenity to accept things I cannot change, the courage to change the things I can, and the wisdom to know the difference, Amen." She had learned the prayer from her father when she was a young girl; it had helped her many times before. Immediately, she felt better. "It always works," she sighed with a smile. Walking westward through the library toward the bulkhead door, it always amazed her how big this station really was. The designer not only knew the fact many people get claustrophobic in confined spaces, but also had the foresight to realize that assignments would likely last for long periods at a time. They paid close attention to room sizes and ceiling heights, putting in as many of the creature comforts as the scientists were normally accustomed to in their daily lives.

Reaching the steel bulkhead door, she grabbed the wheel and turned it clockwise until it stopped. Pushing the door, Ariella entered the submarine bay. This was an enormous area, considering where she was. A full 50 feet long, 24 feet high, it offered substantial room for all of the equipment and machinery needed for the assignment. The largest object in the room was the mini-sub call the PRIEST, Piloted Research and Investigative Electrical Submersible Transport. This manned sub could supposedly travel down to the depths of 40,000 feet, deeper than any known point on Earth. Roger Sealy, mechanic, computer geek, and technological all-around fix-it, insisted, jokingly, that the Navy called it PRIEST because "Every time you get into it, you better pray that the damn thing doesn't implode!" Though this was said in jest, Roger knew this was an incredible piece of hardware, with a pressure of over eight and a half tons per square inch at its reported maximum operating depth; the most minuscule problem could result in this twenty-foot-long vehicle being crushed into the size of a basketball.

Behind the sub was a gadget called ARES, Automatic Robotic Exploration Submersible; the US Navy loves its acronyms. This machine truly was a technological wonder. It used the closest thing to a true artificial intelligence that Ariella had ever seen or heard about. On its own, ARES was preparing to dive into the pool, which was at the rear of the bay, and continue its investigation deep into the trench. The fault line was opening up, causing the trench to expand. No one knew why; that is what they were here for.

Beside the pool were the nickel titanium zirconium exosuits, which contained the same material that the Sea Lab was made of. These allowed team members to explore the environment outside of the Hab for periods of up to seventy-two hours safely. The suits could also withstand incredible pressures, maximum depth unknown; however, it too was believed to be capable of over 8,000 fathoms. The exosuits were lined up on the rear wall, behind the exit pool, like a squad of robots, which they essentially were; a man could just get into one. Ariella did not know what particular kind of metal they were made of; surely it was something exotic. Everything here was state of the art, highly classified, and decades ahead of anything that Woods Hole Oceanographic Institute or the National Underwater Marine Agency, NUMA, possessed.

When offered this position, she wondered why the US Navy was in charge of the operation. What was really going on? Even having her suspicions, she came anyway. This was the chance of a lifetime, a true adventure of discovery. More is known about the moon and space than what is in the depths of Earth's oceans. In fact, more people have been on the moon than have been 2,500 fathoms under the sea.

Traveling through the submarine bay, she arrived at the opposite bulkhead, opened it, and entered the terrarium. Although she could have gotten to the stairwell quicker by taking a more diagonal route through the sub bay, she loved this place. All the plants—it was so unexpected for an undersea world. To Ariella, it was Eden. The terrarium, being even larger than the sub bay, supplied all the vegetables consumed in the Hab. There were nearly 100 rows, on different levels, growing everything from asparagus to zucchini, hydroponically nurtured, under temperature- and humidity-controlled conditions, with hundreds of grow lights. These plants thrived and provided an ample supply of nourishment for the crew. Fruits from apricots to watermelons were being grown on the upper level, accessible by catwalks, where the humidity was greater. In the northwestern end, in a separated section, there was even an apple tree, which required a certain number of days below freezing in order to produce fruit. A few plants, such as the roses and lilies, although not necessary, were just botanist Frank Gilmore's way of showing off. Frank had his headphones on, listening to music, while singing to the roses he was pruning. At the base of the rose bushes, he had planted flat-leafed parsley, claiming that the two plants worked symbiotically to nourish one another. Noticing Ariella as she walked toward the stairs, Frank smiled, and while rocking his head up and down, shot her a peace sign. She returned the smile, shook her head side to side, waved, and continued to the stairs. Normally, she would have stopped and talked with Frank. He was a pleasant man, a good soul, who seemed to be genuinely interested in her as a person. But she was on a mission to find out what this call was all about, and since Frank was busy "rocking out" anyway, no harm no foul.

The command bridge was in the upper level of this wing. Since there were no elevators, even though they had a fully equipped gym, walking the four flights of stairs at least provided a little exercise during their especially busy times.

Upon reaching the bridge, the automatic glass doors opened. The captain was in his chair reading a file marked Ultra Top Secret in big, bold, red lettering. Ariella always thought it kind of silly to advertise the fact that something was secret. Sort of like the brown bag laws for purchasing alcohol in the southeastern US—everyone knows what is in the bag. She always thought that the best way to hide something was right out in the open, without bringing attention to it. Now, although not usually being a nosy person, even she wanted to know what it said.

Lieutenant Steven Barett, whose family made and designed high-caliber assault rifles, was sitting at an LED screen monitoring the diagnostics and preparation procedures ARES was performing. Lt. Barett, also a SEAL, was not only a capable soldier, but was adept at all the computer, mechanical, and research equipment on board. He was young, smart, and quite handsome. Being a little cocky, Ariella loved to pick on him and flirt. She knew, however, he was too young for her. In her thirty-six years, she could at least say that every man she had been with, of which were only a few, had the potential of being "the one."

These were the only two people in the command center; something was definitely going on.

CHAPTER

THREE

ARRIVING AT THE transportation level, Jonathan felt a sigh of relief. Even though he has an Umbra security clearance, one of the highest, he was not supposed to have been in the tachyonic chamber—no human was. If not for Gilla, Jonathan would never have even known it existed. However, in the transit hub, he had no such problems. Humans, Reptilians, Draconians, Nordics, Grays, and Ebens all intermingled like busy bees, bustling to and fro, in order to get to their destinations. Here he was Major Jonathan Arlin Hawthorn II, Army Delta Force, five foot nine, 170 pounds of twisted steel and sex appeal. This was how he often referred to himself, particularly around others in the military. As such, he carried himself with confidence, which he innately had, although he did not consider himself superior to anyone. In fact, it was just the opposite; he was always telling others that they could accomplish anything if they put their mind to it. He did not feel he was special; little did he know.

"Hey, Gilla, wanna take the shuttle or the maglev?" Jonathan inquired jokingly.

Gilla hissed, "Would love sho gesh shome fresh air, lesh drive . . . hiss, hiss, hiss." He too had a sense of humor. At seven feet tall, nearly 400 pounds, and having an extra appendage, a tail, which highways shuttles and automobiles were not designed for, a drive through Nevada on the subterranean highway would have been torture.

Looking down at his watch, which was set to military time, Jonathan pronounced, "Zero six thirteen hours. We've got seventeen minutes to kill until the next train to Area 51 arrives. Why don't you go check and see if you can find out if Jen will be at S-4. I'll wait over on the bench," pointing at the passenger loading area.

"Shank you, Jonashon . . . good shinking." Gilla turned and headed to what could be best described as a phone booth, though that's not exactly what it was. Jonathan did not get bogged down thinking about the technology, or how it worked, if it had no practical application for humans, which this pseudo phone booth didn't. Besides, right now he had other things to think about.

After strolling over to the passenger platform, Jonathan sat on the unoccupied bench. Crossing his left leg over his right knee, he sat back and tried to relax, if only for a moment. Looking around, while stroking his goatee, he contemplated his vision.

What he saw in his visions were never clear enough to "do this" or "go there"; he had to always extrapolate from his prior knowledge and experience base to determine what they meant, which he was very good at. Still, he would wait until they were safely on the way before thinking too much about it, to ensure secrecy. Down here, your thoughts can be invaded, especially by Grays or Replicants, if you look like you have something to hide or are deep in thought. Jonathan found it useful to talk loudly and clearly, appearing to be open, or to repeat one of the mantras he had memorized to mask his thought.

At the present, "conjunction, junction, what's your function . . . and, but and or, will get you very far . . . ," a Schoolhouse Rock jingle that played on Saturday mornings during commercial breaks while watching cartoons, was churning in his head.

Chanting his mantra silently, almost automatically, Jonathan looked down the tunnel for approaching lights. The tunnel was vacuum-sealed at both ends of the station and only opened on train arrivals or departures. Using a combination of magnetics and compressed air, this allowed for it to be shot like a bullet through the Earth. It could travel at speeds of Mach 2, twice the speed of sound, although on this trip there were too many stops for them to achieve such speeds. Their destination lay due west, except for a slight northern trajectory going through Durango, Colorado; nearly 230 miles away. With several five-minute stops and taking into account acceleration and deceleration times, it will take them around half an hour to arrive at Groom Lake.

The Sub-Global Transit System crisscrossed the entire planet, connecting nearly every major city and many military installations throughout the world. There were hundreds of different routes, all hidden secretly hundreds of feet below the surface. The tunnels were excavated using a massive mole machine designed and manufactured by the Rand Corporation. This piece of equipment was not one of the "over-the-counter" models and was used specifically to construct this tunnel system. The borer was capable of melting rock using a nuclear-powered drilling disc, tipped with wolfram graphite auger bits. The tungsten-carbon mixture could withstand immense heat while being extremely durable. While the mole machines available to the general construction industry could tunnel 500 feet per day at best, this model could melt through rock at six miles per day. Additionally, instead of debris being removed and hauled to the surface via conveyor belt, the Rand Tunneler created such heat that the rock simply melted. What was left was a smooth, even, and round hole, which resembled obsidian. Jonathan, being among other things a geologist, had seen similar types of rock melting in the ancient megalithic structures of the Incas while on vacation in Peru. Some of the hardest rocks on Earth—quartz, diorite, and granite—proved no match for this machine. The major knew he was indeed part of a privileged few to be privy to the truth. He believed that if the general population had knowledge of how fragile and on the edge of slavery, or worse, eradication; the human race really was, there would pandemonium. However, what he had gleaned earlier started to make him doubt everything.

As Gilla approached, Jonathan snapped out of his mantra and raised both hands, palms up. 'Well . . . ?"

Gilla shook his head side to side and with his lizard smile spoke. "Shesh nosh shere yesh . . . shomorrow."

"All right," Jonathan replied, giving the thumbs up. "You deserve a little R and R and down time. When was the last time you molted? You want to look your best, old friend," he said with a wink.

"Shop ish Jonashan. Yoush know ish whash nosh long ago."

"I know, but it's just so easy sometimes and you're such a good sport about it. I gotta have something on you, you know, to keep you on your toes," Jonathan jested. "We humans may be smaller and weaker, but we can be quite crafty."

"I'll jush follow my nosh," Gilla returned the banter.

"Good idea. With that muzzle you could smell bullshit from a mile away," Jonathan volleyed back.

With that, the intercom announced in Eusshu, Gilla's language, in English, and in several other dialects, the approaching train, which would be arriving in two minutes. This line traveled east to west, from Savannah, Georgia, to San Francisco, California. On the East Coast, it tied into a perpendicular line that stretched from Key West to Nova Scotia. Similarly, on the West Coast, from Tierra del Fuego, Argentina, to Barrow, Alaska; at member countries, there were border stops or checkpoints. For other countries not part of the Global Federation, the train just ran right through, or more accurately, under. Not that it was possible for a country, any country, to bar its travel or secret activities, for that matter. The United States had tried that at Dulce, twice. Once in December of 1967, with the Gas Buggy test, setting off a twenty-nine-kiloton nuclear bomb underground to try and eliminate the Reptilians and Grays there, and again in 1979, when Delta Force stormed the facility. Both operations were catastrophic failures and nearly caused all-out wars. Since then, neither side not wanting war, they formed a working agreement. The Reptilians controlled the underworld; at least that is how it appears to be, for now. Jonathan was not sure anymore. Something else . . .

As the train approached, the glass partitions that sealed the tunnel slid neatly on tracks, disappearing into a slot in the rock. The passenger platform was not too crowded, it being a Saturday morning. Finding a private car was not going to be a problem. The approaching train slowed to a halt. It resembled a monorail one might see at Disney World, only sleeker looking, more like a bullet. The automatic doors opened. Gilla and Jonathan boarded.

Inside, it was quite spacious, with room enough for six humans or four Reptilians. The seats, made of the same fabrics as Gilla's suit, floated on a cushion of air molded to their occupants. There was even an option that accounted for Gilla's tail.

Although there were windows on both sides, each shuttle car was equipped with an electronic cloud that not only made the glass opaque if one wished; but it eliminated all sound and electronic communications from coming into or going out of the cabin. Also, it allowed for the occupants to converse without the threat of someone, or something, listening in on either their thoughts or conservations. No matter what mental or electronic means were employed, the cabin provided complete privacy.

Looking at the control panel, Jonathan turned on the cloud and proceeded to tell Gilla what he had gleaned in the chamber.

CHAPTER

FOUR

AS THE DOORS to the bridge opened, Captain LaMarr cut his eyes upward over his reading glasses toward Ariella. As he was studying the expression on her face, he nonchalantly closed the classified brief and placed it on the table. Seeing that she looked fairly relaxed, considering the situation, he felt a bit more relieved. Ariella could be quite a handful when upset.

Captain LaMarr, upon arrival, stood to greet her. "Hello, Ariella, good morning. Can I get you a cup of coffee?" he asked her while heading to the kitchenette. "A teaspoon of honey and French vanilla creamer, right?" He knew that she would accept his offer and how she liked her coffee; he was merely trying to break any underlying tension.

"Thanks, Justin, that's exactly what I need. Make it a little stronger than usual…please." Ariella smiled with appreciation. "Good morning, Stevie." She spoke in a playful tone, one that a woman uses when not getting the proper attention.

"Oh . . . hey . . . I mean, good morning, Miss Marconi. Just making sure everything with ARES is system ready. He's going deeper than he has ever been and I—" Steven was interrupted.

"Enough chitchat, Lieutenant. Stay focused on the task at hand. You know how ARES is—unless you reprogram him, once he's ready, he's gone. Check out all the diagnostics thoroughly. We don't want to lose him," Captain LaMarr barked, not even looking back at him.

"Yes, sir," Lt. Barett responded while giving Ariella a pouting face. He quickly returned his gaze to the LED monitor. He knew the captain was right. ARES cost over 5 million dollars. Losing him was not an option.

"What's going on, Justin?" Ariella's inflection left her question open-ended on purpose, testing to see if he would tell her either about the classified file or what ARES was doing.

"Not really sure. The communiqué came through requesting your response ASAP, so I called you." Justin grinned, avoiding the trap.

"That's not what I meant," she stated frankly.

"I know," the captain responded, expecting her reaction. "I'll tell you more when I can."

"Come on . . . aren't we a team down here? You watch my back . . . I'll watch yours?!" Ariella questioned.

"Of course, Ariella! I'm just not sure what to tell you yet. When I do, I will. Promise." He spoke sincerely.

"Okay, sorry, Justin. I know you will. I'm just a little frazzled with Charles calling and all." Ariella quickly turning her head to see Steven's reflection in the monitor, as he mockingly acted like he was crying. "Oh, you're so funny," she snapped at him with a sassy tone, but with a smile. It was exactly what she needed to lighten her mood. Captain LaMarr spun around to look at the young lieutenant, who quickly erased the expression from his face as if he had been innocent. He then glanced at Ariella and saw that the playful pecking had worked; she was starting to relax. So he let Lt. Barett get away with his witty banter.

Lt. Steven Barett was a good solider and a good man. He had consistently demonstrated grace under pressure in some pretty hairy conditions, especially as a nineteen-year-old in Desert Storm. He had a great work ethic, finishing his BS degree in computer mechanics, electronics, and programming after his two-year tour in the Middle East was over. Steven Barett possessed a levity about himself that endeared him to others, a trait that came in handy under tense situations when used properly. Captain LaMarr took notice of him back in BUDS several years ago, when he was CO and Barett was a SEAL candidate. Lt. Barett had just finished OCS, and in order to keep his spot and not miss his cycle at SEAL school, he had skipped his officer graduation ceremony.

Rich boys usually don't make it in such outfits as the Navy SEALs, Army Rangers, or Marines Force Recon. Coming from wealth, such as he did, most young men would never even have considered joining the military; they usually followed the family business or lived off their trust funds. However, after completing BUDS, Captain LaMarr had the privilege of meeting Steven's father. He instantly saw the pride and respect that the senior Barett had for his son and knew that Lt. Barett, though coming from a family with means, was not spoiled as a child.

Ever since that moment, Captain LaMarr had followed young Barett's career. When it came time to pick an assistant for this mission, although many men qualified, Justin picked the young lieutenant. He not only wanted to take Steven under his wing; he wanted someone with a little extra something special—that unknown factor that is not on one's résumé. Steven Barett had it. Thus far, Justin LaMarr could not have chosen better.

Ariella walked toward the captain, more relaxed than when she had first entered the bridge. These two men made a good team, almost like father and son, or so at times it seemed. Ariella, while enjoying the flirting with Steven Barett, liked Justin LaMarr . . . a lot. But she knew that it would never work; he being devoted to the Navy and she to her work. "In another life," she pondered silently.

"Here you go, ma'am, just as ordered." LaMarr handed her the hot mug of coffee.

"Thank you." Taking a sip, "Perfect, you're the best, Justin," she cooed, looking into his gray blue eyes, meaning what she said and not just referring to the coffee.

Justin saw that starry look in her chocolate brown eyes; he felt it too, and blushed just a bit. However, being as pragmatic as she, he knew this was going nowhere. It still felt good, though.

Trying to get back to the task at hand, he said, "I agree with what you said earlier, even though I have never met the guy; judging by what you have told me, he must have something really important to talk about. Something official.

So the way I see it, it's work related. Just look at it that way and you'll be fine," Justin said caringly, but matter-of-factly. He was not only trying to help her find the courage to initiate the call on her own, but also to defuse what was happening between them.

"You know what . . . you're right," Ariella exclaimed with confidence. She did realize what Justin had done and was thankful for it.

They both moved toward the table where the captain had set down the secret file and grabbed the communiqué from the fax machine. He handed it to Ariella. She noticed the file again, Ultra Top Secret, but she felt confident that Captain LaMarr would let her in on whatever was happening when he had determined what her role was to be.

Finding the number to contact on the communiqué, Ariella grabbed the headset, put it on her head, turned to the correct frequency on the radio, and just before hailing San Francisco Bay Naval Shipyard, hit the loudspeaker button; she wanted Justin to hear this. "This is Ariella Marconi for Charles Hargood. Say again. . . this is Ariella Marconi for Charles—" She was stopped by a woman's voice.

"Ms. Marconi . . . thank you for getting back so quickly. Mr. Hargood is expecting you. One moment while I transfer you to his office," the woman said pleasantly, but with a rushed tone.

"Thank you," Ariella said quickly. Her heart began to race.

Justin caringly motioned for her to relax, like this was no big deal. It was working.

"Ariella! Hey. Look, I apologize for calling, but there's an urgent situation happening in Puerto Rico. We need you!" Charles announced quickly and to the point.

"Oh . . . okay. What's up, Charlie?" Ariella was a little taken aback. None of the verbal barbs, snide remarks, or wisecracks she was used to, nothing. "What the fuck?" she thought to herself. This must be serious.

"Our new Puerto Rican Hab is starting to go offline. There has been some seismic activity and, well . . . we just don't know what to expect. We need someone who can handle any sort of . . . unexpected underwater situation, and with your mixed geological and oceanic background, along with your problem-solving skills, I told them that was you."

"Okay, Charles . . . fine, what do you need from me?"

"I need you in Puerto Rico." Charles said cautiously. He knew this was about to get ugly.

"Charlie. . ." Her upper lip started to curl. "I'm freaking 15,000 feet under the damn ocean, I've been working steadily, studying why this trench is opening up for two months, and I still don't know why in the hell it is happening!" She was full throttle now. "Now I'm supposed to just stop what I'm doing, surface, spend nearly a week traveling to the other side of the world, and then . . . oh God . . . go back under the fucking water. Why don't you just teleport my ass over there, for Christ's sake. Better yet, I'll just click my heels together and wish my ass to Puerto Rico!" She stopped her tirade after seeing the lack of encouragement in Justin's eyes instead of a scolding look, which she expected. She then paused, took a deep breath while still looking at Justin, and cracked a nervous smile.

"Ariella, I'm so . . . ," Charles started to say.

"No, Charles. I'm sorry! That was totally uncalled for. I'm just a little frustrated about all that's going on down here and . . ." She paused while turning a little red herself from embarrassment.

"Quite understandable. You have every right to be angry. Hell, you know I'd be pissed to be pulled a project that wasn't finished. So really . . . no need to apologize," Charles meaningfully responded.

"Are you sure there's no one else? What about George Felder?" she pleaded.

"No, they want the best, and regardless of anything else, the best is you. I'll stake my reputation on it."

"All right." She looked at the floor and sighed. "All right. What else can you tell me?" Accepting her new assignment, she had already begun to work on it.

"I wish there was more I could tell you, but that's all I've been told. Someone is keeping a tight lid on this." Charles was not being completely truthful, for he did know more. He was being cautious, though, because the line wasn't completely secure. "I can tell you that your security clearance is being raised to Ultra. I'm not really sure, considering the situation, what that means, but it's something," Charles explained. "Oh yeah, they're sending a guy over from Wright-Patterson. Let me see, a Jonathan Hawthorn. Yep, that's right."

"Were there any fatalities . . . that you know of?" Ariella spoke worriedly.

"Oh no . . . no. The base wasn't occupied. At least not when it first started going offline. It's all a little unclear, but no people were on board," Charles stated while rifling through some papers, checking for anything he had missed. "Your guess is as good as mine, but my money says it's occupied or will be by the time you get there."

"When will they be here to drop the bell for me?"

"Apparently, they weren't going to take no for an answer, because the ship left last night for your position. It should arrive . . . three p.m., your time. You know the military, pretty persistent," Charles finished, trying to lighten things up.

"Yep . . . but they also have the bucks, don't' they?" she added with a nervous giggle.

"You got that right. Look, Ariella, it was good to hear your voice, and again, I'm sorry about all of this, but I have to go. I know you'll get the job done."

"You're not going to be there!?" Ariella said with surprise.

"No, I have to go to Pearl and inspect the new sub pens. They've been expanding over there, and they need my ex-per-tise." Charles gloated.

"Okay, it was good to hear from you to. And, Charles . . . I'm sorry again . . . take care of yourself and stay away from the North Shore. You were lucky last time that surfboard only gave you a concussion," she added earnestly.

"I will," Charlie chuckled. "Take care, bye."

"Bye."

With that, the line went silent. Ariella looked up at the ceiling for a moment, pulled off the headset, looked straight at Justin, walked over to him, and grabbed his face with both hands and kissed him square on the lips. A short, affectionate kiss. She pulled her head back, looking into his dilated pupils, and said, "Thank you, Justin." He again blushed, because he knew what she felt and what she meant.

"If life had been different . . ." he daydreamed.

With a cute smile, looking down, she spun around and left the bridge. She had things to do; her ride would be here in eight hours.

FIVE

ARIELLA WAS SITTING on her bed, in her bathrobe, drying her hair. She had taken a long, hot shower to relax and go over the recent events in her head. The secret file, ARES, Charles calling, and her kissing Justin. She felt stupid. What was she thinking? It was so unlike her to be run by emotion. Even if she was a woman, she prided herself on making clear, rational decisions, and her kissing him was not one of them. She wanted to just stop thinking about it, but she couldn't. She couldn't stop thinking of him, with her, right now.

While lost in her thoughts, she cried aloud, "Oh, Justin!"

Suddenly, there was a knock on the door.

Justin LaMarr was also thinking over recent events. He remembered the kiss, to be sure, and loved it, but he was disciplined. He was thinking about her, however, or at least contemplating sharing the classified file with her along with the real purpose of this mission.

Captain LaMarr rarely asked advice from others, especially when making command decisions. But in light of recent events, he decided to confide in Lt. Barett to get his thoughts of these matters. Justin LaMarr needed a reality check, just to ensure he was not making a decision based on emotion.

Since Ariella's clearance was being raised to Ultra Top Secret, they both had heard of it and even though it was not official as of yet, but both officers felt confident that it was going to happen.

Additionally, she was a member of a team, his team. She had proven to be competent and trustworthy. Captain LaMarr felt she needed to know about the mission. Lt. Barett completely agreed, and told the captain he would have told her about the mission a long time ago. He felt too that she was an asset rather than a liability. Lt. Barett thanked Captain LaMarr for including him in the decision-making process. It was just one more stage of his development. Justin informed young Steven that he sensed he would be doing that and much more soon.

It was settled. Both agreed to bring Ariella into the fold. That, of course, fell under the captain's purview.

After looking at the results of the diagnostics for ARES with his lieutenant, Captain LaMarr grabbed the file stamped Ultra Top Secret and left the bridge. He was headed for Ariella's cabin.

Since his and Steven's discussion, Justin felt relieved. He was walking on a cloud, and it felt good. Maybe it was that he did not like keeping secrets from Ariella, or that he enjoyed sharing secrets—only when appropriate, of course—or that she had kissed him. No matter, he was not going to dwell on the why. He was happy it happened, it fed his ego, and even though he did not see it going any further than it had, he liked the affection. He would be lying to himself if he thought otherwise. "What man doesn't like being kissed by a beautiful, intelligent, fully developed woman?" he thought to himself.

Whistling the line from *The Good, The Bad, and The Ugly*, Justin opened the second-floor access to the terrarium.

Dr. Deborah Walker, MD, had just left the lab on her way back to the medical bay when she and Captain LaMarr crossed paths.

"Captain LaMarr," she drawled out slowly. "What, pray tell, has gotten into you?" Deborah's drawl was thick, from southern Alabama. "You look like you're happier than a pig in shit. Whatever it is, mamma wants some too." Dr. Walker teased.

"Hey, Deborah . . . nothing new, just having a good morning, that's all," he said while beaming.

"Yeah, right!" Deborah spat with a sarcastic tone. She had run into Ariella earlier and, being a woman herself, put two and two together.

"What do you mean by that?" Justin asked sheepishly. "Can't a guy just be happy?"

"Ariella is in her room, if that's who you're looking for." She was laying it on now, grinning ear to ear.

"How did you . . ." was all Justin got out before Dr. Walker continued.

"Just 'cause I got you by a few years, young 'un, don't forget, I'm still a woman." Dr. Walker pushed the door to medical and, while entering, waved, said, "Have fun!" The door shut behind her.

Being a typical man, a military one at that, Justin was clueless as to what Dr. Walker was actually inferring to. There had been women before, for sure, but they always seemed to conflict with his mission, which was to serve the US Navy. He was not, as he would admit, familiar with the female mind.

He continued on through the sub bay on the catwalk over the PRIEST, until he reached the lab. Turning toward the stairs, he waved to Robert Washington, a geophysicist, who was moving like a man on a mission. "Cap" was all he said, and while giving him a two-finger salute, continued walking toward Supply.

After ascending back up one level, Captain LaMarr approached Ariella's cabin. He paused, reconsidering briefly if this was the correct course of action, until once again he decided it was. While in the motion of knocking, he thought he heard moaning, and . . . his name. Too late, he was knocking.

<hr />

Ariella was confused, almost like she was in shock. She could not think clearly. "C—c—coming . . ." Holding her robe closed, she got up to open the cabin door, half expecting it to be Deborah, who she just run into after her shower, and opened the door. Standing there with the classified file held up in his hand for her to see, was the man she had just been dreaming about—right here, now, at her door, in front of her. She unconsciously let go of her robe.

Justin was not sure exactly what he had heard, but he was sure he heard Ariella say she was coming. Seconds later, she opened the door.

She was in her robe, right hand holding it closed. Her lips were red and full, pupils fully dilated, and skin flushed. She looked at him with mouth agape. She, at that moment, was the sexiest woman he had ever seen in his life. She dropped her hand, allowing her robe to open. He reflexively shook the file in his hand as he tried to speak, "I . . . I . . . ," was all he could get out. He was in a trance.

They both stood there, unmoving, for what seemed like an eternity; when in fact it was just over two seconds. Ariella, seeing that Justin was going to show her the file, could take it no longer. She grabbed him by his shirt, pulled him to her, and kissed him again.

After a heated embrace, he dropped the file to the floor and moved her backward just enough so that he used his foot to shut the door.

CHAPTER

SIX

AS THE TRAIN came to a stop at Groom Lake, directly below the airstrip, Jonathan and Gilla quickly exited the passenger car. They both had blank expressions on their faces, as one would get after hearing some shocking revelation.

Jonathan was several feet ahead of Gilla on the passenger platform when he spun around and said, "Gil, tell no one else of what we discussed, not even Jen. We can't afford for this information to get into the wrong hands." Jonathan cautiously looked around. "You're the only one I trust," Jonathan finished.

Gilla nodded in agreement, but then as a way to remind him of where they were and who might he listening, he started singing, "conjuneshion, juneshion, whash your funeshion . . ."

Jonathan smiled. "Thanks, buddy." He started his mantra.

Exiting the platform, Jonathan was looking around for transport. The Groom Lake Research Facility, part of Nellis Air Force Base, or Area 51, as it is popularly referred to, was enormous, more so underground than above. At the surface, some of the largest hangars and longest airstrips on Earth were clearly seen from great distances. The surface facility and fenced-in area covered more than 4,000 square miles.

Security was stringent, containing everything from motion and UV detectors to sound and thermal sensors. It even had ammonia sniffers that detected the gas, which is a by-product of protein digestion in all biological entities. In mammals; although most ammonia is excreted through the urine as urea, trace amounts are released during perspiration and respiration. These trace amounts are what the sensors were designed to detect.

Anyone getting close to the base would undoubtedly experience a flyover by an unmarked, black chopper. It would be quickly followed by men in trucks, dressed in civilian clothes, carrying automatic weapons, with authorization, as posted, to use deadly force.

While people still see UFOs, in a true sense because what is seen cannot be identified, around the base from time to time, the intense security is mainly for what's under the ground; a sprawling city the size of the state of Rhode Island, which fans out in every direction. It has everything: shopping malls, swimming pools, grocery stores, housing, a rapid transit system including a train, shuttles, and taxis, with thousands of miles of tracks and roads. It even has its own agriculture and livestock areas—essentially all the convenience of a modern city, except it was all underground and highly classified. At any given time, there were over 5,000 human personnel and half as many nonhumans living and working in one of the eight black project areas that made up the facility, each with a security clearance of Top Secret, the highest clearance that a project can have.

Holding up his hand, Jonathan was attempting to hail a transport; he whistled and then yelled, "Taxi," with a chuckle. Humans are such creatures of habit, even down here, he thought.

The transport driver, seeing a man and a large Reptilian step off the train platform, was waiting for the signal. It being the weekend and not many people needing his services, he was becoming restless and bored. With his foot poised above the accelerator pedal, he was coiled like a snake, ready . . . until . . . there it was. The hand went up, the unmistakable sound of a whistle, and the word "Taxi." He was off; like a funny car driver trying to set the track record in the quarter mile, he let it all out with reckless abandon. Seconds later, screeching to a halt, he lowered the front passenger window and greeted his potential fares.

"Hello, sirs," in a distinctive northern Indian accent, probably from Delhi or Uttar. "My name is Abhar; it would be my pleasure to serve you fine gentlemen on this most auspicious morning, thank you." Smiling and nodding, Abhar was getting out of the vehicle.

Jonathan, being impressed by the quickness, exuberance, and willingness to serve, said, "Abhar you appear to be a man in need of some excitement today. Are you the type of man who can get us to places quickly, without a lot of questions and . . . unnecessary attention?"

"Oh yes, sir, most definitely. I am your man," Abhar stated while bowing his head and spreading both hands out.

"Great! I'd like to procure your services for the rest of the day, let's say for . . . 500 dollars, with another 500 dollars at the end of the day. That is, if you do a good job. Does that suit you?" Jonathan pulled the cash from his pocket and counted it in the open.

"Excellent sir, a most generous offer. Whatever you need, Abhar will make it so."

"Perfect!" Jonathan motioned to Gilla. "All aboard the Abhar express."

Abhar was already running from his side of the car to the passenger's side in order to open the door. Jonathan and Gilla just cut a look at each other and grinned. Jonathan liked this Abhar fellow.

Abhar opened the door and guided Gilla to get into the back seat, while motioning Jonathan to sit in the front. Jonathan gave Abhar the agreed 500 dollars. Jonathan sat down, while the Indian man raced around to the other side of the taxi and looked for anything unusual. Everything was unusual, unless of course you were in New Delhi. Hindi prayer beads hanging from the mirror, the smell of sandalwood incense burning, multicolored Kashmiri seat covers, and a small bobble-headed doll of Vishnu, the supreme god deity and savior of Hinduism, which sat on the dash.

Abhar got in, closed the door, and politely asked, "Where to, sir, I will take you anywhere that is within my power."

"Well, we need to go to S-4, but I believe both my friend here and I could use a bite to eat. Any recommendations?"

"Oh, absolutely, sir. My cousin Rakish makes the best red curry duck with basmati rice in the entire underworld, yes, sir, I'll bet on that, I will," Abhar attested. Then, pointing at Gilla, "And for you, my fine Reptilian friend, I would recommend the Himalayan rhinoceros beetle, a mighty fine delicacy, if I do say so myself, and all the curried chicken you can eat," Abhar added with an expectant smile.

"Is your cousin's place . . . private?" Jonathan queried.

"Most definitely. He even has a private dining area with a cloud, if that is what you wish."

"That sounds splendid. Drive on, my new Indian friend." Jonathan had a feeling that running into this fellow was a stroke of luck.

Upon arrival at the eatery, Jonathan, laying his head back and cutting his eyes toward Abhar, asked, "Abhar?"

"Yes, sir?"

"You strike me as a man who can get things done." It was more a statement than a question.

"Oh yes, sir, I am a man of many talents and resources."

"I want you keep your ear to the ground concerning anything to do with the Marianas, Puerto Rico, and any recent ocean disappearances." Jonathan paused, and then continued, "Without, of course, drawing any attention to you or to us. Can I trust you to do that for me, Abhar?"

"Without question, sir. You need not worry; I would sooner eat cow than break the trust of an employer."

Jonathan being satisfied knowing Hindus do not eat beef, as cows are sacred, dismissed Abhar to his quest, while he and Gilla ate in privacy and comfort.

The food was sumptuous. Abhar was not exaggerating. His cousin Rakish's food could compete with any Michelin Star restaurant's cuisine on the surface. Even Gilla, who was normally extremely proper when eating around humans, was licking his plate with his forked tongue. After a glass of red wine, which Rakish said was imported from his family's private vineyard in Jamnotri, near the Tibetan border, Jonathan and Gilla, feeling completely fulfilled, rose to leave. Immediately, Abhar arrived, ran around the taxi, and opened the doors.

Jonathan stared to wonder if Abhar had been watching, waiting for them to get up just so he could rush over here and be punctual, or whether it was just a coincidence. Not sensing anything nefarious, however, as he was always right about these sorts of things, Jonathan decided he would watch a little more closely.

"I trust your meals were to your liking, my fine sirs," Abhar genuinely asked Jonathan, who started to speak, but was interrupted by Gilla, who was normally silent when other humans were around.

"Ish was magnifisho," Gilla stated like an Italian, putting his fingers together, kissing them, and then flicking them open after he spoke. Jonathan had a humorous look of shock on his face while addressing Abhar, laughing. "Yeah . . . whatever he just said."

Putting on a more serious face, Jonathan inquired if there was any information, as of yet, about what they had discussed earlier. Abhar informed him he had heard from a source that a few USOs, unidentified submersible objects, had been reported exiting the seas close to Puerto Rico, north of the island of Vieques, but that was all he had heard at this time. He assured Jonathan that if anything was abuzz, he would hear about it.

"What sources?" Jonathan asked.

"Oh . . . sir, I cannot tell you that, so sorry, sir. Just as your anonymity is important to you, sir, so it is with them. I will not break their trust, just as I am sworn to keep yours," he said apologetically.

"I understand. Stay on it for me, though, it's important." Jonathan smiled and patted Abhar on the shoulder. He admired a man of honor and principles.

As he and Gilla climbed into the cab, he barked, "To S-4, mi amigo, rapido!" Jonathan was in a good mood despite the situation. This Abhar fellow may prove his worth before it is all said and done.

Abhar hit the accelerator, pinning their heads to their seats. They were off.

CHAPTER SEVEN

AFTER ANOTHER SHOWER, Ariella was sitting on her bed, while in her bathrobe, drying her hair again! She was relaxed and calm, not at all worried about the time crunch she was now under. Two hours left, plenty of time, she thought. Usually, she would be frantic, running about like a half-crazed animal caught in a trap. Even the revelation of what they were really doing here could not penetrate the feeling of ease she was experiencing. She might have to do this more often, she noted.

Besides, she had some time to ponder this latest information on the way to Puerto Rico. At least she was going to get a little time topside, some fun in the sun.

As she dressed, she assessed her belongings. Luckily, she was not a high-maintenance girl and did not have a lot of what she called unnecessary stuff. She rarely wore makeup, and when she did, it was very little. She did have skin and hair products, as she was not above vanity, but all these along with other hygiene items fit into a small bag. All her clothes were easily contained in one medium-sized duffel bag. She would make quick work of getting her stuff together.

Captain LaMarr had returned to his cabin also after the shower. He ultimately did inform Ariella about the true nature of the mission and what the file contained. Although it did not seem that important to her at the time, since she was leaving, he knew she would analyze everything he had told her later. That was how she was built, a natural born problem solver. Also, she might be back soon; especially if whatever was happening in Puerto Rico got resolved soon.

Justin was feeling slightly uneasy about his actions—not in a physical sense or because of who it was with; he cared a lot for Ariella. It was that he broke a major rule for any commanding officer: Do not fraternize with subordinates. And even though Ariella was a civilian, she was still under his command.

Hopefully, this would all go unnoticed since Ariella was leaving in a couple of hours. He would miss her. However, if that were not the case, her presence could have complicated things. He looked in the mirror to check the scratches on his back. Smiling, he mumbled, "Yes, sir, you still got it." He put his shirt on and headed to the bridge.

The Hab was bustling with activity. Like ants, everyone was not only preparing for Ariella's departure, but for fresh supplies. Although the Sea Lab was fully stocked with all the food and necessities for many more months, the crew was actually waiting for delivery. Chinese, pizza, and everyone's favorite, McDonald's. Every crew member except Roger Sealey, who had a large supply of Red Bull and Hot Pockets, knew this type of food was horrible for the human body and preferred to eat healthy. They all, however, were willing to ingest a little MSG and other chemicals. It was not going to hurt them, much.

Even Lt. Steven Barett, who was the epitome of health and fitness, ordered three extra-large meat lover's pizzas, a large General Tao's chicken with four egg rolls, and a double quarter pounder meal, supersized, with a vanilla shake. He, along with several others, would undoubtedly be in a fast-food coma before the day was done.

Dr. Deborah Walker, while not immune to the seduction of fast food, knew what the repercussions would be. She raided the supplement closet in preparation for the inevitable assault that would ensue. She grabbed the Pepto Bismol, Tums, Zantac, and the all-important baby wipes. She was like a warrior gearing up for battle. Anticipating the effects of the food on her own digestive system, Deborah had already planned on premedicating with a few Zantacs about thirty minutes before the battle.

Upon leaving her closet, Dr. Walker was heading to the bridge to alert the captain, in case he didn't know, of what was going to happen to the crew after the glutinous feast. Not that she was above it—she ordered a nine-piece McNuggets meal, a PuPu platter with crab Rangoon, and a cannoli herself—she just wanted to make sure Justin was not expecting too much from his crew for the next twenty-four hours. Strolling along with dreams of crab-stuffed pastries smothered in duck sauce, she ran into Ariella.

"Well . . . what do we have here! You look like a woman who has just been properly bedded." Deborah smiled and winked at Ariella.

"Shh." Ariella put her finger to her lips, looking around. No one was there.

"So don't leave momma hangin'."

"What can I say but, wow!" Ariella blushed.

"I was hoping you would get to release some of that tension, it's just not healthy. And from the looks of it, you certainly did that."

"I have to admit, Deb . . . I feel wonderful, like a woman. I think I forgot what it felt like," Ariella stated with a gleam in her eye.

"Any regrets?" Dr. Walker said, noticing that gleam.

"Surprisingly, not really. We talked and are both taking it for what it is."

"And that being what, exactly?" Deborah's motherly instinct was kicking in. She cared for Ariella.

"An emotional overflow of powerful feeling that was shared with someone special," Ariella dreamingly stated, reflecting on the last several hours.

"Oh, hell no, honey! You ain't fooling no one with that bullshit! You have feelings for the man, I should know." Deborah threw her hands up. "Don't get me wrong, hon; he's handsome, in shape, commanding . . ." Even she started daydreaming herself of Captain LaMarr. "But he's married to the Navy, and until that relationship changes, I'm afraid he's given you all he can give," Dr. Walker said in earnest.

"What do you mean by that?" Ariella fired back.

"The memory of what seems to me like some real good sex, darling." She was blunt.

"It was more than that!" Ariella snapped.

"Of course, it was, sugar," she said, grabbing Ariella's hand with one of her own while massaging the top of it with the other. "You got to make love with a wonderful man you care about, and who cares about you. That's why it's so special. It had real, honest to goodness feelings. But if you have dreams of the future . . . I just don't want to see you get hurt. Memories are hard enough to come by, especially the good ones, darling." The southern lady was direct, in a charming way. Ariella knew she was right. But right now, she wasn't going to dwell on what probably would never be, and dream about what could be. The feeling was too good to spoil, at least for the time being. With a smile and an understanding nod, she admitted, "I know, Deb, but a girl can dream."

"It's always good to have dreams," she agreed. "But now it's time for some reality." With a devilish grin, Deborah put her arm around Ariella's neck. "Give me all the details, mamma'll take you to the bridge." The two women walked, giggled, and smiled all the way to the bridge as Ariella recounted the morning's events.

———

Justin arrived on the bridge with a lightness in his step and a smile on his face. Although the captain was not an unpleasant man, and was quite friendly, he usually did not grin or smile unless something was clearly humorous.

Lt. Steven Barett noticed the change in his mentor's demeanor immediately. He shook his head side to side while looking down and smiling. Captain LaMarr looked at him with an innocent grin and asked, "What's so funny, Steven?" knowing Lt. Barett sensed his good mood.

"You old sea dog. It's good to see you still have it in you," Lt. Barett snickered.

Acting shocked and surprised, although he was not, Captain LaMarr jokingly demanded, "What are you talking about?"

Lt. Barett held up one hand and made a circle with his finger and thumb, with the other index finger, moved in and out of the circle as if to signify sex. "You know, you and Ms. Marconi," he said with an approving nod and grin.

"Stow that shit, Lieutenant," Captain LaMarr commanded, but with a smile and a light tone.

"Yes, sir . . . Sir?"

"Yes, Lieutenant?"

"Permission to ask a question, sir?" Lt. Barett was not going to give up that easily.

"Yes, Lieutenant? Make it quick." He readied himself for what he knew was coming.

"How was it?" Steven looked like a kid, with a grin and his tongue between his teeth; he was expecting a response.

"It was incredible," the captain said in an authoritative voice. "Is that all, Lieutenant?"

Steven put his hand in a fist and brought his arm down like he had caught something. He was happy for his commander.

"Fair enough, Steven," he said nodding. "Fair enough. Let's make the final preparations for the dock-up. I want this to go smoothly."

'Aye aye, sir." Both men were now in a good mood.

Ariella and Deborah arrived at the command bridge to make final preparations for her departure, which was rapidly approaching.

Captain LaMarr was looking at the monitor, checking ocean currents, temperature, and pressure readings for the oceanic depths between 2,000 and 2,500 fathoms. All of these measurements had to be precisely calculated, not only to position the bell for its proper alignment with the docking chamber, but also to account for the pressure difference between the bathysphere, or bell, the airtight seals, and the docking chamber. This was critical; even a small gap the size of a grain of sand could cause a large swing in the pressure gradients between the bell and dock, causing a blowout. The bathysphere would essentially be launched like a missile from a silo. The dock chamber, although safely separated structurally from the rest of the Hab, would implode. Exit from Sea Lab X would then only be possible via propelling to the surface.

Lt. Barett was at the computer terminal and using a yaw stick to make small adjustments to the bell's course as it descended. It was almost to a depth of 10,000 feet and falling at almost 100 feet per minute. In just under an hour, it would arrive. At this time, he only had to make minor changes every several minutes, nothing too demanding. In the final ten minutes, however, he and Captain LaMarr would be rapt, making the minor corrections needed for a successful dock. Roger Sealy would be on the top floor of the east wing, monitoring the docking chamber both electronically and visually. But for now, Steven had only a minor role to play, which afforded him the time to see Deborah and Ariella just before they entered the bridge.

The two women had grins on their faces and were talking in a whisper, closely. Prior to the glass door sliding open, it appeared that Dr. Walker mouthed "Trust me" to Ariella. Steven Barett could read lips also, a talent he had acquired from always wearing earmuffs while firing weapons at his family's rifle range.

"Ladies," Steven said with his glowing smile.

"Hi, Steven," Ariella greeted him, still snickering at her and Deborah's last words.

"What are you two ladies so jubilant about?" Steven asked, already sensing they were rehashing the morning's sexcapades.

"Oh . . . you know, girl talk, sweetie." Deborah spoke before Ariella, who was not good at making things up on the fly. Lt. Barett could not help himself, he had to pick. It was just in his nature. "I can't put my finger on it, but there is something different about you this morning." Speaking directly to Ariella, he said, "Did you change your hair . . . no . . . did you get some unexpected bonus and are hiding it from us . . . or are you just that happy to be getting out of this tin can?" Steven asked, leaving her a way out, but baiting her also.

"Yeah, uh . . . well . . . it's going to be nice to get some sun." She was caught completely off guard. "I may even take a swim." The fish was nibbling on the line. It was time for Steven to set the hook.

"I thought you were going immediately from the USS *Reagan* on a Sikorsky to Guam and promptly hopping a flight to San Francisco, with an aerial refuel?

Let me check your itinerary in case I made an error. One sec . . . ," Lt. Barett said, taking up the slack and adjusting the drag, while drawing her in.

"Uh . . . uh . . . that won't be necessary. Thank you, Steven, I'll work it out when I get aboard the *Reagan*." She was turning beet red and little beads of sweat were forming on her upper lip and forehead. *He knows*, she thought.

"Are you sure? It won't take me but a few seconds, Ms. Marconi," he jibed while spinning toward the computer keyboard. "I can do it . . ."

"Don't you need to watch the monitor and the bell, Lieutenant Barett?" Captain LaMarr suggested. He had heard the whole conversation and felt it was time to throw Ariella a lifeline in order to save her form his young officer's banter.

"Yes, sir! Sorry, sir. Just trying to ensure that Ms. Marconi has a smooth transition to the surface and is clear on travel arrangements." Lt. Barett spoke in a professional tone. He let some slack out on his line and let his catch run with it.

"Dr Walker, Ariella." Captain LaMarr greeted both ladies with a nod. "I hope it's been a good last morning for you, Ariella. You will be missed," he said, looking directly into her eyes.

Deborah, who had sashayed over to the kitchenette to grab a cup of coffee, nearly spat it out when she heard the captain ask Ariella about her morning.

"Excuse me." Deborah covered her mouth feigning like her coffee was too hot and waved her hand over it.

Ariella was transfixed by every word Justin was saying, until all at once, and about the same time Deborah almost spat out her coffee, she realized what he had just said. Her eyes got wide as she wore a nervous smile.

"Lieutenant Barett," Deborah called, trying to get is attention, with no success. "Steven!" she said louder and with much more authority.

"Yes, ma'am?" he reflexively responded.

"Can you be a dear and help me tote some samples to the docking bay? Um?" She was trying to give the captain and Ariella a few minutes alone. It quite possibly could be the last chance they had, at least for now.

"I'd love to, ma'am, but I'm really not supposed to leave my post, unless . . ." Steven understood where Dr. Walker was going with this. He just threw his line in the water and jigged his bait.

"You go ahead, Lieutenant. I'll watch that for a few minutes," Captain LaMarr said, pointing at the monitor. "We still have about half an hour before things start to get serious." Captain LaMarr was on the hook.

"Are you sure, sir, protocol and all?" he reminded. He started reeling in the slack.

"I think for this occasion it will be fine. Don't you?" the captain asked, swallowing hook, line, and sinker.

"Yes, sir." Lt. Barett's hook was set. *Fish on*, he thought.

"This way, sweetie," Deborah said while motioning toward the door.

"Lead the way, Doctor Walker," he exclaimed. Steven reeled in his line to claim his prize. A fine catch, although not much of a fight.

CHAPTER ⟋ EIGHT

DURING THE RIDE, it was hard to relax and survey the underworld. Abhar drove like a man on a mission, which he had. Get to S-4. But Jonathan was beginning to wonder if getting his fares there safely was part of the plan. He and Gilla had been in a few dicey situations and fared well in most. This, though, was a different kind of anxiety, one of having absolutely no control. Jonathan had a grip on the "oh shit handle," and Gilla braced himself between the two doors with his long arms.

Abhar was oblivious to their discomfort. He was laser focused on the road, accelerating, braking, passing, and changing lanes, all while repeatedly laying on the horn. Jonathan had no doubt Abhar had missed his calling in life as a race car driver. Learning to drive on the streets of Delhi, India, a city with a population of 25 million, he was never challenged driving in the underworld. Traffic being light this morning, he was having a calm, pleasant drive, through most days were calm to him.

Abhar came to be in Dreamland, or Area 51, through a most fortuitous series of events. While on a Hindu pilgrimage in the Ladakh mountain range of the Himalayas, next to the Tibetan border, he was caught in a "whiteout" blizzard. He was trapped and nearly froze to death, when he was rescued by a monk who lived among the society of Green Men. There were evil men who were associated with the Indian Nagas, an ancient serpent race; the Alpha Draconians, one of three extraterrestrial Reptilian races; and the Grays. By practicing the occult and black magic, along with the help of these alien groups, they hoped to one day gain control of the universe.

This monk, who never gave his name, took him into the underground world of Patala, or snake world, and to the city of Shambhala. Abhar had suffered from frostbite but was miraculously healed, with no permanent effects. Concerned for Abhar's safety so near to the capital city of Bhogavati, where he certainly would have become enslaved, the monk snuck him on a maglev train in a supply car. Provided with the proper credentials to verify his job as being a freight handler, Abhar departed for parts unknown, with only the clothes on his back.

It was a matter of chance that the maglev was coming to America with a shipment of lodestone, a magnetic rock, which was used as an inexhaustible source of power in the new and improved tachyonic electro-gravitational motors. The old Kohler converters, as they were called, could not achieve the speeds necessary for intergalactic travel. By utilizing knowledge formulated by Townsend Brown and various equations from Einstein and Tesla, this newer technology was responsible for creating crafts capable of achieving superluminal, faster than light, speeds.

As they go in the classified world, once you have gained access to one city or base, you automatically have access to most others; that is, of course, if factions were not actively at war, another reason is to keep a watchful eye on those who do possess this knowledge. Everyone here was monitored, at least when relating with others from the outside world. Those who leak information are quickly discredited or terminated.

Abhar, having access to most general areas due to his job, could not actually get into the project areas in any underworld facility. His security clearance was Subastral, one of the lowest, at least for access to the underworld; it was still above Top Secret, though. He had been here for twenty-five years and at his present profession for twenty-one. In that time, he had worked all over the underground world. He loved the Groom Lake facility the best, though; it allowed him to hit Las Vegas occasionally for some gambling and to see some shows.

Being good at his job and being trustworthy had its advantages, at least for Abhar. With the aid of his connections, he was able not only to get his cousin Rakish here, but several other family members as well. The family worked hard and pooled their money together. In just ten more years, Abhar would be able to retire from this career and see the world once again, above ground. An added perk was that maglev trains were free to ride. Finally out of the traffic and on the open road, Abhar informed his passengers that it would take about twenty-five more minutes to get to the S-4 facility.

Wanting to know more about his resourceful driver, Jonathan questioned him about his heritage, how he came to be here, where he thought he would be at the end of his career, and so on. All of these things could reveal a lot about an individual, and Jonathan knew what information to look for. He was also beginning to see the value of such a man, not only now, but possibly in the future. Not many could have achieved so much with so little. Abhar appeared to have no formal education, military training, or auspicious introductions to the secret world. Though no one would ever expect it, Abhar and his family had amassed quite a fortune. Due to security, things cost more down here, but people also earned substantially more related to cost. In a normal year, it was not uncommon for Abhar to earn six figures a year driving his electric taxi, a nice contribution to the family pool. For his heritage, this was quite common. Abhar, upon retirement, would be able to travel in style; everyone chipped in for it.

Jonathan, while listening to Abhar spin the tale of his past, his family, and plans of the future, became a homesick, except there was no home to go to. He never knew his father and only very little about him. Johnathan Arlin Hawthorne met his mother Cathy in high school, and then he joined the military. That's all!

Cathy had him when she was seventeen and raised him on her own. She never had a relationship with another man, at least none that he knew of. She provided him with a stable environment; a great education prepared him for his life today. At times, it seemed she knew exactly what he would become. He learned to camp and hike; how to eat off the land; studied karate, kung fu, kendo aikido, and jujitsu; could fire any weapon; was taught to decipher codes—all the things that he used today.

Cathy worked two jobs, or at least he thought she did. He could never recall what she did, however. Tutors were hired to advance his studies in music, art, and academics. He excelled in sports, just as he did in everything. He graduated high school at the age of sixteen. He had already received a BS in geology before he entered West Point, the United States Military Academy, at the age of eighteen. There he obtained another degree in civil engineering and achieved the rank of cadet battalion commander, one of the highest-ranking seniors in the school. He joined the Army Rangers and later graduated from sniper school. After various deployments, missions, ops, and so on, he attended NC State while stationed at Fort Bragg and received his master's degree in both geology and geotechnical engineering.

Cathy had indeed prepared him, but for what? He was thankful; however, he just did not understand what her plan was for him. With all she invested in him, and in what he had become, there must have been a plan. He would never know, though. Tragedy had struck three years ago on a dark, winding section of the Pacific Coast Highway, in Northern California. Apparently, Cathy fell asleep at the wheel, lost control, and drove off a cliff into the ocean. Her body was never recovered. Although the official report suggested no foul play, Jonathan, who was out of the country in Iraq at the time, sensed that something was not right about her death. Every so often, he would ponder the report in his mind; it would come to him one day, he knew it. Thoughts, like food, took time to digest, especially on a subject such as this.

Regardless, her death, along with the loss of life he had witnessed in war, whether by his hand or others', had shown him how quickly life could be snuffed out without warning. It was truly a precious thing. After her departure, he was alone for the first time in his life.

Snapping out of the nostalgic haze he was in, Jonathan turned around and looked at his Reptilian friend. "Almost time, Gil," he stated with excitement. "One more day and someone is getting laid." He gave Gilla the thumbs up, while Gilla gave a positive hiss. Abhar too added a nod of approval. Even the lizard had got someone, Jonathan sulked.

Screeching to a halt, they arrived at their destination, miraculously in one piece. S-4 was another sprawling complex within the Area 51 perimeter. The facility was controlled by the United States Aerospace Command (USAC), a secret government entity with a black budget of close to a trillion dollars annually. It operates as the military and diplomatic branch representing mankind, at least for the United States.

USAC deals directly with the two current extraterrestrial, nonhuman factions in, on, or around the planet. The Galactic Federation of Light, benevolent alien entities, as well as several terrestrial groups, which seek to help *Homo sapiens* and Earth transition into the next stage of evolution and development.

Contrarily, the Draco, Orion, Gray federation are imperialists that wish only to manipulate, enslave, and destroy humanity. They are determined to make Earth their own, at any cost. Although the imperial federation is against humanity in general, with the assistance of the Federation of Light, neither side can gain a significant advantage over the other. Therefore, all species, from all sides, intermingle together in a "cold war" type of truce, for now.

Though all three kinds of the extraterrestrial Reptilians are malevolent toward humanity and work closely with the Reptilian races of terrestrial origin, many, like Gilla, were trusted allies of man.

S-4, although containing sympathizers from most of the known species, was predominantly occupied by humans. This was a technological playground, which would have any scientist salivating just for a chance to visit. Every resource and piece of equipment known to man, and many unknown, were at their disposal.

Since security was even tighter here than at the Groom Lake facility, requiring a minimum classification of Stellar or above to enter, it was one of the most secure places on Earth. Many areas were restricted to even higher classifications, while still others were so secret their security clearance level names were unknown.

Jonathan, however, had access to almost every area the United States controlled and many of the other races too. At times, with Gilla's help, he was able to gain access to areas he could not get into alone, and even some, such as the tachyonic chamber at Dulce, that he could never be cleared for.

The entire facility was constructed under a mountain, which had been carved out using the Rand Mole boring machine and molded to specifications using Keely vibration drills. These machines made quick work and initially had the cavity ready for building assembly in just under a year. Traditional tunneling and boring methods would have taken nearly a lifetime.

All structures inside the mountain could withstand a direct nuclear strike of up to 20 megatons without so much as a scratch. Each structure was also positioned on top of a system of springs, which would, if needed, absorb the blast shockwave of a direct hit or the tremors of an earthquake.

All told, the underground complex at S-4 occupied almost 18,000 acres, 26 square miles of planar space, with an average vertical clearance of almost 2,000 feet. This huge space was invaluable for the testing of antigravitational aircraft and other exotic technologies, secretly.

Jonathan, being thankful to be alive after the harrowing experience of the drive, looked at Abhar with astonishment as the driver spoke.

"Here we are, sirs, the S-4 facility as promised, safe and sound." Abhar reached into the center console and pulled out a device that looked like a cell phone and handed it to Jonathan. Abhar then instructed, "With this, Sir Jonathan, you may contact me at your leisure when you are ready to depart. Abhar will be there. Yes, I will."

Jonathan inspected the device. It was an ordinary cell phone with a peculiar-looking square mechanism protruding from the headphone port. "What is this?" Jonathan asked, pointing at the unknown object.

"Oh, you are very observant, sir, yes you are. That is an antenna and scrambling device, yes it is. My sister's husband designed it." Abhar was smiling, with pride as he spoke. "This device ensures that all communications with my clients, such as yourself, are always received and remain completely private, yes it does." Abhar was smiling and nodding his head as if a great revelation had just been uncovered, which, in fact, was true.

Jonathan gazed at Abhar with amazement, which was the intended effect, and said, "You are just full of surprises, aren't you, my Indian friend?"

Abhar was really pleased with himself now. "So, you are telling me that this little square gizmo here"—Jonathan was holding the phone and placing his fingers on the unknown part—"blocks all unwanted radio and microwave frequencies, probably with crystals, and prevents any third parties from listening in on our communications?"

"Oh, sorry, sir, I am unaware of how it actually works, only that it does. Oh, yes it does. My brother-in-law works at Wright-Patterson Air Force Base as a scientist there and has assured me of its capabilities. He has. I have used it many times without incidence, I have, sir." Abhar was looking down, sounding almost apologetic.

"It's okay, Abhar. If you say it works, it works. I trust your judgment," Jonathan said, looking at the Reptilian. "You have so far been the most resourceful individual I have met, anywhere, in a long while. I am lucky to have made your acquaintance." He meant every word.

Abhar's expression brightened as he spoke. "You are too kind, sir. I only hope to continue to serve you, sir."

"Of course!" Jonathan then continued with a series of questions. "Abhar, you said your brother-in-law works at Wright-Patterson? What's his name? That is, if you can tell me. I work there and may know him." Jonathan finished his questions in earnest.

Although Abhar was not a spy of any sort, he too had his ways of finding out information, especially on people. Being a part of the underworld for over twenty years, Abhar has made many connections all over the globe. Not only had he been checking into that information about the Marianas, Puerto Rico, and ocean abductions, as requested by his employer, he was also checking into Jonathan himself. It was a general rule Abhar always followed; know who you are doing business with. It was part of the reason he had been so successful and had remained alive much longer than anyone knew possible.

Abhar had determined his fare; Major Jonathan Hawthorn, did in fact work at Wright-Patterson Air Force Base in Ohio. His sources revealed that the major was a brilliant, honorable, extremely capable, and highly respected man in many circles, both terrestrial and nonterrestrial. He was one of the guys you wanted on your team in any situation. Even though there were some discrepancies in his records, which could easily be attributed to his high security clearance of Umbra, Abhar trusted and admired him. He always went the extra mile for one of the 'good guys.'

Jonathan was looking at Abhar, who was looking down, biting his lip as if pondering his next words. Slowly raising his head with a trusting expression, Abhar answered, "Yes sir . . . my brother-in-law does work at Wright-Patterson. His name is Haji Patel, yes, sir, it is. He is a fine gentleman and loves my sister very much."

Jonathan, with a look of surprise, answered, "You're shitting me! I know Haji. He's in the R and D department working on . . . oh hell, I'm sure you already know, spacecraft. He's awesome!" Jonathan paused for a moment, realizing the implications of the two being connected. "It's amazing how small the world really is." He did withhold, however, how well he actually knew the brother-in-law. He wanted to see Abhar's reaction.

Abhar was not surprised Major Hawthorn knew Haji; he had already uncovered where Jonathan was employed. It was good to hear others speak so well of a family member, though. Abhar made a mental note to contact Haji as soon as the opportunity presented itself.

"Oh yes, sir, considering all the beings among us, and where they all come from, oh yes, the world is very small, it is."

"Gil . . ." Jonathan howled at Gilla, who had been relaxing, especially since the end of the drive.

Since the humans had started talking, Gilla had been paying attention to everything that was said. He was especially attentive to Abhar—what he said, how he said it, and, most importantly, how it all tasted. Being a reptile had its advantages, one being that he could sense the pheromones being produced and released by reptiles and other creatures, particularly by humans. His bifurcated tongue acted almost like a nose does to a dog. With it, he could sense fear, dishonesty, excitement, essentially the gamut of emotions. He also liked Abhar, and thus far everything tasted fine, especially the rhinoceros beetle and curried chicken he had at his cousin Rakish's.

Gilla had been thinking of what Jonathan had seen in his vision, and of Jen. He needed a release, fast, and he knew it. Being a reptile has its disadvantages, also. His mating time grew nearer; it was harder and harder for him to focus on anything else. He knew his time of being useful was coming to an end.

"Did you hear that? Haji and Abhar are related. That's crazy, huh?" Jonathan questioned, smiling, while pointing at Abhar.

Gilla hissed, "Shas why shey smell she same sho me, hiss, hiss, hiss!" he responded in jest. The whole group laughed.

Abhar started to get out of the car to open his passenger's door when Jonathan stopped him. "Is there something wrong, sir, is there?" Abhar questioned with a perplexed look on his face.

Jonathan was looking around, and although nothing appeared out of the ordinary, he did not want his Indian friend drawing attention to him or Gilla by opening the doors and creating a production of it. He relayed his concerns to Abhar so as not to offend him, which his chauffeur understood. "Now, Abhar, if you could . . . I need you to call Haji for me and tell him that Major Hawthorn will be arriving in a few days. Here is a list of things he needs to have ready when I arrive." Handing Abhar the list, which he had written while sitting on the maglev platform earlier at Dulce. Jonathan had planned to contact Haji himself, but upon the revelation that Abhar was related and with the approval of Gilla's taste buds, trusted Abhar with this as well.

With a surprised reply he said, "Oh yes, sir, it will be good to hear from Haji again, yes it will. We have not spoken in a long while, no we have not."

Jonathan's response was quite shocking and caught Abhar off guard. Jonathan said, "You were going to call him anyway . . . right? To check on me?" Jonathan was testing him; he wanted to see his reaction. He wanted to see how much Abhar trusted him. Jonathan had no illusions that his driver already knew a great deal about him. Abhar was initially a bit nervous, but as he thought about what was just said, and who said it, he felt comfortable with just answering the question, man to man.

Abhar responded, in a calm clear voice, "Yes, sir . . . I was."

"Good answer, Abhar. Good answer. I knew I liked you for a reason," Jonathan said as he got out of the taxi. Gilla followed. Leaning back through the open passenger window, Jonathan said, "Make sure to stay on that other thing we discussed earlier, and, Abhar . . . I trust you." Jonathan's expression changed to a lighter one and so did his tone. "See you in a few hours. I'll buzz you," Jonathan said while holding his hand to his ear like a phone and walking away.

Abhar nodded with genuine respect. He raised the window, hit the accelerator, and was off. He felt good about Major Hawthorn. He would do as directed and call Haji immediately. As soon as he rounded the corner, he reached for the scrambler phone that was on his hip. As he brought it to his mouth, he spoke into it, "Haji Patel." The phone started ringing.

CHAPTER

NINE

JONATHAN, WITH GILLA at his side, made his way to the entrance of the installation. Jonathan was hoping that some more information would present itself concerning his recent inquiry. If anything new existed, he was confident in Abhar's ability to find it.

As they approached, one of the two sentries held out his hand and halted them. The two men wore desert camouflage fatigues and black berets. Both were young and muscular. Each stood close to six feet in height. These guards held M-4 fully automatic machine guns in their hands and flash guns on their hips, which was ironic because the holstered weapons were more much more powerful. However, this being a human-controlled facility and predominantly occupied by people, the M-4s provided more shock and intimidation value. Everyone was familiar with them.

Since the armor lux weapon looked like a black-lensed flashlight, it is commonly called a flash gun. It is, however, an incredibly powerful weapon and a useful piece of technology, acquired from the Grays. It has three distinct phases, with varying intensities at each level. The first phase, closest to the hand, was used to stun. The second phase was used to levitate objects or people;

intensity was varied according to size. The last knob, phase three, was all about business. It adjusted from paralyzing to vaporizing anything that lived, with no trace. The middle setting of the phase three caused temporary death for several hours. This was used as a neuralizer, which erased memories and allowed new ones to be implanted. When people are abducted, or have seen things they should not have, this is typically what happens to them.

The sentry on the right, a sergeant, barked, "Name, rank, and ID number, sir!"

Jonathan, wearing his camo pants, boots, and a light long-sleeved shirt, rarely wore his uniform down here. So he had nothing to distinguish his rank. While handing his ID to the corporal, who was on the left and reaching for it, Jonathan responded in kind, "Major Jonathan Hawthorn, US Army number 3659120, Sergeant." Both men, hearing his rank and authoritative tone, snapped to attention and saluted their superior officer. Jonathan snapped to, returned the salute, and ordered, "At ease, as you were, gentlemen." As the corporal ran the ID through the scanner, the sergeant pointed at Gilla and in an unsure tone asked, "What about him, sir?"

Jonathan smiled while pointing at the returning corporal, who went to the sergeant and whispered into to ear. Then he gave Jonathan a fearful but respectful look before returning to his post. The sergeant's demeanor changed as if he was talking to the president. He quickly said, while stepping aside, "Sorry, Major Hawthorn, for the delay . . . you gentlemen may pass."

"No problem, solider, good to see someone is doing their job around here," Jonathan said in his commanding military tone. He and Gilla passed the first security checkpoint.

The initial guard post sat just outside of a thirty-foot-high rectangular enclosure, which surrounded the entrance. Flanked on each side of the rectangle was an elevated gun turret that pointed directly at Jonathan and Gilla as they entered the boundary. The pharynx-style guns would automatically deploy if a breach in security occurred. At 50,000 rounds per minute, the spray of ammo would certainly cut anything it touched in half.

After continuing another 20 yards, the two arrived at a large, five-foot-thick, steel door. Being operated by the sentry post at the first security checkpoint, it was already slowly opening outward and continued to do so until it was four feet ajar. As soon as Jonathan and Gilla passed, it quickly reversed its direction to close again.

The door closed with an Earth-rumbling thud and the ten massive steel bolts mechanically clanged into position within the wall, securing the entry.

Just inside the entrance corridor, which was at least 40 feet wide and 20 feet high, was a band of light. This glowing ribbon encircled the entire room while emitting a wispy white aura, which dispersed throughout the area. This light source, while illuminating this part of the passageway, was used to eliminate unwanted pathogens before entering the complex. It used Rife Telefunken vacuum tubes and advanced optical analysis, computer-varied radio impulse frequencies, to selectively destroy pathogens instantly. This was another level of security, which would destroy any unauthorized intruder.

Jonathan, knowing that they still had to pass another checkpoint, just loved the redundancy of the military, and though not impossible, it was highly unlikely for anyone or anything to enter without permission.

As he and Gilla passed through the cleaner, which the band of light was often referred to as, they approached what was similar to a TSA airport checkpoint, except without people. A large digital readout flashed, "No electronics or weapons past this point." Then instructions followed indicating that all electrical devices were to be placed in one container and weapons in another. These were then sent through a tunnel, which scanned and removed unauthorized devices. Weapons were logged in and either stored or returned to the entrant, depending on security clearance. As posted, any electrical device that passed through the walk-through scanner would be rendered useless by a selective electromagnetic pulse. Individuals who had biomechanical enhancements were directed to a separate area in order to pass security. All individuals were categorized instantly by overhead laser scanners as soon as they entered the area, so there was no need for additional biometric identification devices at this checkpoint. Jonathan placed the flash gun, his .45 caliber Springfield XTM, the scrambler phone, and his personally encrypted cell phone in the proper containers. Both he and Gilla walked through the scanner, which acted like an MRI on steroids, toward the collection area to retrieve his possessions. Jonathan's credentials, unlike those of most people that entered this facility, allowed him the privilege of carrying his weapons. Even though he was merely a major, down here he had more clearance and authority than most generals.

As Jonathan collected his things, he turned toward Gilla and stated matter-of-factly, "See, I told you I was 100 percent human. I don't need any of that space age shit anyway," smiling as he holstered his pistol in the small of his back.

Gilla had accused Jonathan, in a not so jesting manner, of having been enhanced, due to some of the things he was able to do. Gilla just raised both arms, palms upward, and shrugged his smooth shoulders. He knew, though, that Jonathan was not being deceitful, for he could taste it, but felt he may have altered without his knowledge. Gilla knew about several times in Jonathan's life when he had experienced time discrepancies and déjà vu moments that were frighteningly descriptive.

Continuing down the arched hallway, so as not to allow anyone to view inside the actual complex, the corridor opened into a vast hangar area, which had been hollowed out of the mountain. It was one of the most immense continuous areas ever created by man, being two miles long, one mile wide, and 3,000 feet tall.

On the far west wall, over a mile away, were several different spacecraft hovering several feet in the air, effortlessly. The north wall housed the research and development laboratories and offices, while the east side, where Jonathan and Gilla entered, was solid rock. The southern wall, which was two miles long, contained a goliath hangar door that allowed for access to the outside world. The opening, which started at an elevation of over 500 feet from the pavement, was 1,000 feet long and 600 feet tall, allowing for enormous antigravitational craft to easily pass into and out of the hangar. The exterior of the door looked exactly like the mountain, so much so that a person rock climbing on the outside would never know the difference. It weighed so much that a harmonic sound generator and antigravity field had to be employed just to open and close it. Being made of a mixture of carbon steel, titanium, nickel, and cubic boronic nitride, the door was essentially indestructible.

Shortly after Jonathan and Gilla entered the open area, a tram car arrived to transport them to any destination within the installation. The hangar acted as a hub of sorts; everything branched out from the entrance. Jonathan told the driver, a short, plump, bald man with a curly mustache, to take them to the Applied Science Building, Geology Division.

On the way to the science building, Jonathan was enjoying the air blowing on his face. Air in the underworld is much cleaner than in the natural world. It was not only filtered, but there was no pollution, pollen, or other contaminants to lessen its quality. Ambient temperature remained at a constant temperature of 58 degrees Fahrenheit (14 degrees Celsius), with a relative humidity of 60 percent, which was a bit dry, but quite comfortable considering they were in the desert.

There were several trams moving about, carrying passengers to various locations; however, this was the weekend. Therefore, the facility only contained about 10 percent of its normal workforce. For some people, like Jonathan, there was no such thing as a five-day workweek. He had always adhered to a simple philosophy: if the time presented itself, he would take a vacation, usually something simple like camping in the mountains, fishing in streams, searching for gemstones, and hiking, especially to waterfalls, where he loved inhaling the ionic mist from the water as it fell through the air. Also, on occasion, he would go to the tropics, but only if he had a female companion to travel with. The islands were a romantic paradise; at least that is the way Jonathan Hawthorn saw them.

Most of the people scurrying about were maintenance and security personnel. Over toward the testing area, near the far corner of the hangar, it appeared that a crew was working to clean up some debris, which was undoubtedly caused by some experiment that had gone awry. That is how things worked here, at times, by trial and error. Most technology was cutting-edge, whether it was being reverse engineered from crashed spacecraft or stolen from alien entities. Some gadgets and science were actually given to the human race—why is still up for speculation.

Another tram approached from the opposite direction with several Etherians on it. Etherians, also gray in color, were not the Grays associated with the Draconian Reptiles. They originally came to Earth in the 1947 Roswell, New Mexico, crash. They had been around ever since, helping mankind through peaceful means. These beings were slightly bigger and had smaller eyes than their rivals. As they passed, their gazes were locked on Gilla, who was riding behind Jonathan. They did not trust Gilla's kind, with good reason, and would just prefer to have nothing to do with his race at all. There were a few, however, with whom Gilla had a working relationship.

At the present time, it was wiser and safer for them to continue on their way anyway.

As the tram moved along the row of the science complex, Jonathan noticed there were many lights on inside. When he asked the driver about it, the man turned, grumbled that they were renovating the physics building, and turned back around. It was obvious that he was not in the mood for chitchat. Most people do not like working on the weekend.

The tram ride, which was refreshing despite the rude driver, lasted several minutes, until they arrived at the Applied Science Building, Unit G, for Geology.

"Thanks, Buddy," Jonathan said as he and Gilla departed the tram. The driver, without acknowledging him, drove off. "What an asshole!" Jonathan said to Gilla while flipping the driver off to his back. Gilla just stared with amusement since it should be him losing his cool.

CHAPTER

TEN

WITH THE BRIDGE cleared except for Justin and herself, a vacant silence filled the room. Ariella could hear her pulse and thought for a moment that her heart was going to jump out of her chest.

It felt like an eternity, though it had been only a few seconds, since Lt. Barett and Dr. Walker had departed. All the different thoughts and emotions running through her head were making her dizzy. Without thinking, she ran over to Justin and laid her head on his shoulder. For a few moments, there was nothing but the warm, loving embrace she felt in his arms. Captain LaMarr then spoke softly. "Are you okay, Ariella?" He kissed the top of her head.

"No . . . I don't want to leave," Ariella pouted. She balled her hand into a fist, and like a hammer, hit him in the chest. "What the hell were you thinking asking me how my morning was?!" In a playful, sarcastic tone, she continued to scold him. "What was I supposed to say?!"

Justin broke in. "Yeah . . . I guess I boneheaded that one, huh?"

Expecting a better apology than that, Ariella was getting a little more heated now. "You can keep national security secrets, interrogate prisoners, command thousands of troops, sneak behind enemy lines to accomplish only God know what . . . kill ten men using just your thumbs, but you can't do a better acting job than that?!" Ariella's lower lip was quivering.

Justin LaMarr noticed when Ariella was angry with Charles Hargood, her tone was different and her upper lip quivered, not the lower one. She was truly angry then. Now it was merely deflection. He felt it too, the uncomfortable queasiness deep in his core. The difference, though, was that he has been trained to ignore his emotions. Right now, however, he did not want to. To break the mood, he replied, "Probably five."

"Five what?!" Ariella snapped.

Justin, while extending his arms, wiggled his thumbs. "Kill five men . . . with my thumbs."

Ariella froze, not knowing how to react. She just glared into his blue eyes. The care, understanding, and, most importantly, the strength in them, which was something she desperately needed right now, melted the iciness of her mood. She was not mad anyway, just anxious over the feelings she was having.

Looking at Justin, seeing how relaxed he looked with his silly smile, caused her to burst into laughter, which slowly changed into sobbing. She felt stupid, like a child.

Justin pulled her into his embrace and with his right hand brought her lips to his for a warm, tender kiss. He whispered, "I don't want you to leave either."

Other than a few beeps and clicks from the electronics and mechanics of the Hab, the bridge was silent. Justin and Ariella were standing embraced, rocking side to side. Ariella, using her left index finger, wiped the tears from her eyes. "I'm a mess, just look at me."

"You're beautiful," he said softly.

"Tell me what to do, Justin." She was looking at him with a fretful smile, waiting for an order. She knew what he was going to say before he spoke.

For the first time in her life, she was not only willing; she wanted a man to make the decision. Ariella did not trust men; her alcoholic father had broken her of that custom long ago. The years of abuse and broken promises made it nearly impossible for any man to break through her defensive walls, but Justin had. She trusted him and would do as he commanded.

"Ariella . . . we both knew how this was going to end before it even began. I too never thought this would happen. The feelings I have for you are real . . ."

Extending his arms and pushing her far enough away to look into her eyes, he said, "But, Ariella, you have to go. You've given your word." He let that sink in for a second before he continued. "You are a woman of truth and honor, with strong convictions. That's what makes you so special. But going against your beliefs now would curse anything we might ever have while burning a hole in your soul."

Ariella looked at him with reverence, knowing everything he had just said was completely true! She knew at that point that she was leaving, though the most important thing was not what he said, but how he said it. There was caring and love in his eyes. along with a warmth in his touch. She felt what he said and believed him.

Justin now spoke in a more commanding voice. "Do your duty, go to Puerto Rico, solve whatever problem they've got going on down there, and get your ass back here ASAP!" He paused, judging how she was digesting what he had just said. Ariella was in a trance, staring at him with her baby browns. He determined she was mesmerized by his voice, so he continued. "When you do, we'll see where this goes."

Ariella's heart was aflutter. The sternness but caring in his voice and eyes provided her with all the strength she would need to do what was necessary. She replied quietly, "Is that an order, Captain LaMarr?"

"Yes, Ms. Marconi, it is." He then dipped her, gave her a kiss, spun her around toward the door, slapped her on the ass and teased back, "Now get your shit and get to the docking chamber and I'll see you after I'm done here."

Ariella, following his orders, walked toward the exit. As she approached the glass door, she looked back over her shoulder at Justin, who was still fixed on her, and she said tentatively, "Everything is going to work out . . . I just know it is." Which was a lie, but she would hold on to that hope for as long as she could. "Thank you, Justin." Blowing him a kiss, she walked through the doorway. The glass door shut behind her.

Captain LaMarr stood there like a statue, contemplating everything that had just transpired. He had never really been in love before, so he was not sure what it was. His love had been the US Navy, and she was a jealous mistress. Seeing Ariella walk out the door, blowing him a kiss goodbye, gave him a foreboding feeling. All special forces are trained to use their instincts to evaluate situations in order to complete the mission. From his personal experiences, this sixth sense saves lives. Right now, though, he did not have the luxury of dwelling on such things; the bathysphere would be here soon.

Walking over to the monitor, which was tracking the bell's descent, Captain LaMarr checked its speed, the ocean currents, and made some adjustments with the yaw stick. His thoughts were a little cloudy. It must be all that coffee he had drunk earlier. He decided to visit the head; maybe with some relief, he would see things more clearly.

———

While walking to her cabin, Ariella was thinking about her life. She was thirty-six. Single with no children. Ariella's mother had died in childbirth and her father had passed over ten years earlier from cirrhosis of the liver caused by his alcoholism. She was alone except for her career, which usually was the only thing keeping her warm at night. She had always been a happy person, or so she thought. Ariella was not sure anymore. All she was sure of, though, was her refusal to have any sort of relationship that might resemble what her parents had. Undoubtedly, the scars of those relationships had contributed to her remaining single for this long. Everything she had done, every decision that led her to that very moment, was now in question. She felt utterly lost, unsure of her future.

Arriving at her cabin, Ariella looked around, making sure she was not forgetting any of her things. After she finished packing, she sat on the end of the bed for a moment of pause. A pleasant thought crossed her mind: what if all this was a dream . . . No such luck. The loudspeaker sounded and snapped her back to reality. "Lieutenant Barett, return to the bridge. Lieutenant Barett, return to the bridge. Captain, out." The words "Captain, out" stung her eyes. It felt as if he was telling her it was over, which, for now, it was. She drove the thought from her mind. Besides, she had a job to do in Puerto Rico with a Major Jonathan Hawthorn. Hopefully, he was competent enough to help her get done whatever it was they required of her, and quickly. Ariella thought, even though these things rarely worked out the way she wanted them to, that her luck was changing for the better.

"ETA for the bathysphere, thirty minutes. That's right, boys and girls; there is Chinese and pizza delivery at 2,500 fathoms. Get ready and bring your hungry. Barett, out."

Ariella was almost at the docking bay, which was located on the south wall of the rec room, when she heard music. Led Zeppelin's "Stairway to Heaven." How appropriate, she thought with a grin. Her mood was improving as she turned the corner to ascend the last section of stairs. Entering the rec room, the atmosphere was festive, with crew members enjoying the music and camaraderie. A laser, which was changing colors every few seconds, had been run through a beam splitter and radiated across the ceiling. Dr. Walker and Robert Washington were talking and drinking some sort of smoking beverage. Frank Gilmore, wearing a tie-dyed shirt and a Grateful Dead headband, was lip syncing enthusiastically to the song. Roger Sealy, though positioned at the south wall of the room monitoring the progress of the bathysphere, was also nursing a smoking beverage while toe tapping to the music.

Nancy Taylor, the resident chemist, was the first person to notice Ariella enter the room. After she had heard about Ariella's sudden upcoming departure, she immediately started making alcohol. Although strictly prohibited, Nancy felt it was necessary to break rules for this unexpected occasion. After tinkering in the lab for several hours, she had created in record time what her daddy called apple pie moonshine. It tasted like you were eating apple pie. This stuff was powerful too. One Solo cup of this 190-proof beverage would leave even the habitual drinker shit faced. She knew Captain LaMarr would not be too keen on having a crew full of drunks after just one drink, so she lowered the alcohol content to 80 proof, which was comparable to a good vodka. Nancy, being the barmaid that she was, decided to chill her creation with dry ice, which produced the smoke coming from the cups, while adding an air of mystery to the ambience of the room.

"Hey, Ariella," Nancy said, waving her hand while running over to greet her. Nancy and Ariella had also been close, considering she was one of three women on Sea Lab out of a crew eight. She and Ariella were the same age, had been awarded PhDs in their respective fields, were workaholics, and single. Nancy, after giving her a hug that nearly knocked Ariella over, pulled her by the arm toward the table full of drinks. "Sorry I haven't seen you this morning. As soon as I heard you would be leaving, I started preparing for your farewell party. Here," she said, handing Ariella a smoking beverage.

"Wow, you put this together with such short notice, for me?" Ariella was truly touched by Nancy's gesture.

"Well, it was nothing," she said with a pouting lower lip sticking out. "I'm going to miss you, Ariella . . . Now this is called apple pie . . . try some!" she said, pointing to Ariella's cup.

Nancy Taylor was exuberant, to say the least. She talked fast, especially when excited; moved quickly, and slept extraordinarily little, only a few hours a night. She was an odd sort of woman, which Ariella found to be endearing. Nancy was a genuine person; there was absolutely nothing fake about her. She wore no makeup, had no tattoos, no cosmetic enhancements, and told it just the way she saw it. Her parents, when she was a little girl, had her tested for Tourette's syndrome—the results were negative—and though she was slightly autistic, she was just brutally honest.

"So, what's up? How are you? Are you nervous about leaving? What will you be doing? Will you be back? How's your drink?" Nancy had to pause to breathe. Like a child waiting for permission to have a sleepover, Nancy waited for Ariella's reply.

Ariella adored Nancy. "First, thank you, Nancy . . . for this," waving her hand around the room. "My drink is fabulous; I love apple pie. Maybe you should have one." Ariella picked up a smoking red Solo cup and handed it to Nancy. Then, with a motion to her own lips, she coaxed her to drink.

Nancy, getting the hint, downed the whole cup and then continued. "Sorry, I made this super caffeinated coffee this morning to keep me awake. I was up all last night working. I just couldn't miss you leaving." Nancy grabbed another drink, and this time took a sip.

Ariella said with a calm smile, "I'm going to the Puerto Rican Trench. Other than that, I don't know why." She continued with a sigh, "I hope to be back soon, though, real soon. I have some unfinished business here." Ariella had not talked with Nancy about this morning's sexual escapades with Captain LaMarr, and considering the time frame, she felt it would be better left unsaid.

"Ooh, ooh, ooh . . . you mean with the captain, don't you?!" Nancy said. She then, bright-eyed, took a gulp of her drink.

Ariella, experiencing a bit of anxiety, finished her drink and reached for another. Although her father had been an alcoholic, Ariella drank occasionally, sometimes a little too much, but never took it to extremes. "Who told you?" she questioned Nancy.

Nancy with a giggle, "Everyone knows. News travels fast in the vastness of the abyss! I heard it from Robert this morning . . . congratulations, by the way. We all were betting on how long it would take."

"What?!" Ariella blurted out. "How long has this been going on?"

From behind her, the answer came from Frank Gilmore. "About a month."

"Frank," Ariella said with a cautious tone. "You won . . . didn't you?"

"Of course, babe. I not only understand the language of love in my plants, but in all of God's creatures," Frank stated with a satisfied grin.

Ariella was embarrassed, and it was starting to show. She could feel her face heat up and perspiration form in her armpits.

Frank noticed her awkwardness. "Don't worry, babe. We are all adults here and we all adore you and respect the hell out of the captain. No one did anything wrong. You can't stop nature, babe." Frank's demeanor and attitude could put a Tasmanian devil at ease. "I'm just glad the two of you finally did the nasty." Frank had such a way with words. "One more week and Steven would have won. That kid's got it all—the looks, the brains, the money, the charisma . . . I'm just glad he didn't win," Frank jokingly added. "Nancy, hit me again. Your daddy taught you well, that's some good hooch." He extended his cup to her.

Nancy smiled—she loved Frank—and handed him another smoking beverage. He bowed to her as he accepted her offering.

Deborah Walker and Robert Washington saw the gathering that was forming and made their way over.

"Well, what was your bet, Doctor Walker," Ariella asked with a slight irritation.

"Come on now, darling. I couldn't say anything. That would have disrupted the natural order of things. And to tell you the truth, sweetie, my bet was never; at least not on this voyage anyway." Deborah put her hand on Ariella's shoulder. "You know I just love you to pieces and I would never, I mean never, do anything to hurt you." Motioning for Ariella to look around, she said, "This is all for you; we love you." Deborah gave her a hug. Ariella responded in kind. Deborah had just reaffirmed what Frank and Nancy had told her earlier.

Everyone was smiling and having a good time. They were gathered around her; she was the center of attention. The thought of how much they all cared for her brought tears to Ariella's eyes. This had been an emotional day. She jerked back her tears of joy and with a smile said, "I—I—don't know what to say but . . . hell, give me another drink!" Everyone clapped and laughed. They were all happy that Ariella was starting to relax. She started to move through the crew and say her goodbyes. They all said they would miss her and hoped she would be back soon.

Besides the captain and Lt. Barett, Roger was the only one she had not spoken to yet. He, at present, was preoccupied monitoring the arrival of the bell, which was nearly here. One minute later, her ride arrived. Estimated time of departure, T minus twenty minutes and counting.

The activity slowed as the crew patiently awaited the captain's arrival. He had to give the final approval before the hatch in the docking chamber could be opened. After checking and confirming with Roger Sealy that the seal was intact, the order was given to remotely open the bathysphere's hatch. The docking bay was separated for safety. If the seal failed, only the docking chamber would be affected. The hatch opened without incident. After checking the readings on the sensors, the go-ahead was about to be given to open the dock chamber. Lt. Barett had performed perfectly, guiding the bell into position. Captain LaMarr had expected nothing different.

"Open the gates." The captain raised his hands and lowered them as if starting a race. He stepped back while Roger Sealy opened the air lock. With a slight pop, the dock chamber door swung open. Roger walked in and performed a visual inspection of the area. After being satisfied they were safe from implosion, he turned to the captain and gave the thumbs up.

Captain LaMarr, in a more serious tone, demanded, "Who made the booze?"

Nancy Taylor stepped forward, raised her hand, and wore a look of surprise on her face. She was taken aback, since she did not think the captain would have a problem with a bit of hooch. Everyone else too was standing with their mouth agape.

"Yes, Captain. I made it," Nancy sheepishly said.

"We have a problem . . . how is it that there is contraband in my Hab . . . and I don't have a drink in my hand?" LaMarr asked, trying to keep a straight face. There was an audible sigh as Nancy Taylor cracked a smile and saluted. "Sir, yes, sir, a drink coming right up, sire." She handed him a cup.

Captain LaMarr chugged it down and reached for another. A cheer was heard throughout the Hab. The captain, however, had no intention of finishing this drink. Someone had to stay frosty, and that someone was him. He did not mind and was happy for his crew. They all had been working hard. This was exactly what they needed. Realizing his job was not quite done, he called, "Mr. Sealy. Mr. Barett."

"Yes, sir," the lieutenant replied.

"Get yourself and Mr. Sealy here a frosty beverage, and you two please get this tin can unloaded. I'm sure everyone's anxious about their food. So be quick about it."

"Yes, sir, Captain," Lt. Barett said with a huge grin.

"Thanks, Cap." Roger gave his typical two-finger salute and turned to climb up into the bell.

"Eighteen minutes until departure, people. Let's make this a smooth transition." Captain LaMarr finished giving his orders.

Justin looked at Nancy and said with surprise, "Wow, this is incredible," pointing to the drink. He leaned forward and whispered in her ear, "Make sure that when the party is over . . . dump the rest." He winked at her but was entirely serious about discarding the leftovers. Besides, if they ever needed more, Nancy could make it again.

Nancy returned the wink with a smile. She admired Captain LaMarr and thought him to be a good leader. He had handpicked her, as well as the others, for this mission, even though she was quirky. She was thankful for the opportunity. Responding to the captain's last statement, "I will, Captain, you can count on me to dispose of this properly. Thank you for not getting mad. I didn't think you would. Some party, huh?" She paused before calmly and slowly saying, "And, Captain . . . Ariella is over there," pointing with her right index finger toward Ariella, who was standing beyond Dr. Walker and Robert Washington, staring directly at the captain. "Go get 'em tiger," Nancy said with a growl.

Justin LaMarr, rarely surprised, half expected the news of this morning's adventure was already common knowledge and thought it was not something he condoned—a leader should never fraternize with subordinates—but he was not ashamed of his actions. Being very adept at judging the feelings and emotions of others, he didn't sense any tension or negative judgment as a result of his actions. Therefore, he remained relaxed as he approached Ariella, knowing all eyes were on him.

Luckily for Ariella and Justin, the food started coming out of the bell and everyone scurried like rats to get their share.

Ariella spoke first, "Aren't you going to get your food?"

"I had takeout this morning," he said sensually.

She blushed a little. "How was it? Filling, I hope."

"Oh, it was . . .. but I don't ever think I could ever get too much. It was that good."

"I'm glad to hear you enjoyed it so much. Do you think you'll be ordering again anytime soon?" Ariella coyly asked.

"It all depends on how long it takes for the chef to get back into town." Justin continued his metaphor.

Ariella was beaming.

From across the room, someone said, "Kiss her already."

Both Ariella and Justin looked toward the voice and saw Frank Gilmore smiling, with both hands out with palms up. "What's the holdup, Captain? C'mon." Frank urged.

Captain LaMarr froze, and on this rare occasion did not know what to do.

Ariella pounced, grabbing his face with both hands, and kissed him square on the lips. She was totally out of character. It was exhilarating.

"Atta girl," Deborah said.

"Where's mine?" Frank Gilmore complained.

"Oh, Frank . . . come here," Ariella answered as she met him and kissed him on the lips also. Ariella felt so electrified she went around and kissed all the men and women on the lips, even Steven Barett, who had his mouth full with a double quarter pounder.

Her rounds being complete, she returned to Justin's side. She felt alive, Like a weight that had been on her for years had been lifted. She knew, no matter what the future held, she would never be the same.

As the bathysphere was now unloaded, Ariella was saying her last good-byes. Even though she felt positive, which the booze certainly contributed to, there was still an air of apprehension, a feeling she just could not shake. Ariella sensed that she would never see some of these people alive again. Looking around the room, she took a mental picture of each of their faces. This was how she wanted to remember them, just in case.

Turning to Justin, she stared into his eyes, looking for answers, she supposed. Though none were found, Ariella was pleased by what she did see. This man cared for her. She knew it.

Justin, looking back through her eyes into her soul, saw her fear. He was proud of her for facing her fear with the courage he knew she possessed. Justin was going to miss her, more than he knew at the time, for sure. But their separation would be good for them. They both needed time to evaluate their feelings and current situations.

As the couple stood there silent, they overheard the lyrics, "If I leave here tomorrow, will you still remember me," by Lynyrd Skynyrd playing in the background. Neither Ariella nor Justin could say what they really felt. They did not know how to. Instead, after waving goodbye to everyone else, Ariella kissed Justin again and said, "Goodbye, Justin LaMarr."

"Goodbye, Ariella Marconi," Justin replied. Ariella entered the bell and the hatch shut behind her.

CHAPTER

ELEVEN

WHILE STANDING OUTSIDE of the Geology Division of the Applied
Science Building, Jonathan was deciding whether Gilla should accompany him
in or not. Thinking it would be faster passing through security and getting the
information he was looking for alone, he asked Gilla to wait for him outside.
Gilla, not feeling he was much use at the time anyway, was perfectly happy
sitting on the bench, which was to the right of the entrance and thinking about
his upcoming rendezvous with Jen.

Jonathan approached the door alone and put his hand on the biometric
palm scanner. This device not only studied the individual's fingerprints, heart
rate, and temperature; it also cross-checked a person's electromagnetic field,
which is distinctive to each individual and species, with known unique values.
After a few seconds, a green light above the entrance lit up and the door slid
open. Jonathan entered what resembled a long foyer hallway. At the end there
was another sealed, impenetrable door. He entered the room and the door
behind him closed. Once again, sensors were aligned along the perimeter of
the room, which ensured that the only person to be admitted was the same
one who had passed the security check. The opposite doorway would remain

shut if an intruder or someone attempting to piggyback tried to enter without authorization.

Since it was the weekend and no guard was present at the building's security office, bringing Gilla would have required a person to physically let them through the office complex. Besides, Jonathan figured he would have found what he was looking for within a half an hour anyway.

Once successfully past the second door, Jonathan headed straight to the kiosk. Using his finger as a guide, he moved down the list of items until he came to records, third floor, and room 317. Though Jonathan was unsure of what he was actually looking for, he was confident the information he collected would be valuable. Since there were only three floors and needing to work his legs, he took the stairs.

Upon arriving at room 317, Jonathan removed his ID and ran it through the laser scanner. The door popped open with a click. Finding the nearest computer, Jonathan got to work searching the common databases for known sources of amber and amber-like substances.

One of the aspects of his vision was a tremendous chunk of amber-like crystal that appeared to be submerged under water. He knew amber, a diterenic isoprencid with the chemical formula of twenty carbon atoms to thirty-two hydrogens, was a fossilized resin. But he was surprised to find Puerto Rico and the island of Hispaniola were the only major deposits of the substance in the Western Hemisphere. Was it a coincidence that these two islands were along the border of the Puerto Rico Trench? Jonathan did not believe in coincidences. He was being sent there with an oceanographer named Ariella Marconi, who was presently some 15,000 feet under water in the Mariana Trench at Sea Lab X, to investigate some large anomaly. Could this be the crystal in his vision? The relatively high melting point of amber, 560 to 760 degrees Fahrenheit, an organic substance, and the location near thermal vents that are scattered along the trench seemed entirely plausible. The trench is in fact a highly seismic area where two tectonic plates meet. Could this amber-like substance be simply seeping out of the Earth?

Although Jonathan did not necessarily think what he saw was amber, it would be unheard of for a piece of this material to be as large as he envisioned. He sensed it was something similar. He began searching for any information pertaining to a biotic source of chemical seepage evolving from the ocean floor, which could possibly solidify to form the huge mass.

Delving deeper and studying opal, which was formed by diatoms or algae, and radiolarians or protozoa, he found it was, at times, similar in color to amber. Jonathan briefly looked at the petrographic records of rocks, but was still leaning toward some sort of organic substance that may have been altered by submarine volcanism.

Thus far, all this research could have been performed at the local university. Now, however, Jonathan was accessing information not available to the public. It required him not only to key in his nineteen-digit pass code, but to use voice recognition software to verify his identity.

After successfully logging in and punching of a few keys, Jonathan entered the Department of Defense website. Scrolling sown through the menu, he opted for the Department of the Navy, research and development, followed by HAARP, the High-Frequency Active Auroral Research Program.

Many people have heard of the large, high-energy antennae array located in Gakona, Alaska, and know that the site is controlled by the US Air Force. However, HAARP falls under the Navy's nonprofit MITRE Corporation, which oversees all the Navy's research and development programs. Raytheon Corporation specifically works on and maintains the HAARP arrays and related facilities. Working closely with the JASON Group, a super-secretive organization with the highest of security clearances that works on the fringes of science, these two entities control most of the HAARP arrays around the world.

The HAARP technology, which is highly classified, uses extra low-frequency (ELF) waves, Earth-penetrating tomography (EPT), and ionospheric high-power radio frequencies, some of which include communication with underground bases and nuclear submarines, selective communication transmission and disruption, location of hidden subterranean tunnels and installations, alteration of human mental and physical faculties, weather modification, and an energy beam weapon—indeed, much more than the public is led to believe.

Unknown to all but a select few who were involved in Desert Storm back in 1991, the millions of Iraq's Republican Guard that suddenly lost the will to fight and surrendered were directly affected by HAARP altering the enemy's brain patterns, although that was not what Jonathan was interested in. He was scanning through the section that showed usage dates and recent seismic and volcanic activity.

By using a magneto hydrodynamic generator to change thermal and kinetic energy into electricity, creating powerful magnetic fields, along with superconducting magnets and a Tesla magnifying transmitter, HAARP can propagate energy waves and aim them toward any fault line in the world, even ancient ones. The result is a purposefully targeted earthquake or volcanic eruption.

Jonathan had experienced this particular aspect of HAARP firsthand on one of his missions as a Ranger. He was part the 75th Ranger regiment, out of Fort Benning, Georgia. On March 2, 2002, Jonathan and his team were involved in a predawn raid against Afghani Muslim Al-Qaeda forces on the Philippine Island of Mindanao. At the time as the raid commenced, a 7.2-magnitude earthquake was directed at the rebel stronghold. Three days later, on March 5, Afghanistan was rocked by a 7.4-magnitude seismic event. At the time, though, Jonathan merely thought it a stroke of luck that an earthquake had occurred at the time of the raid; now he knew netter.

These events not only sent a clear message to the world, that the US would not tolerate states that harbor terrorists; it also showed the frightening power of HAARP.

Scanning through the site, Jonathan was especially eyeing the recent 2006 upgrade, which allowed for a magnetically driven pulse to be generated and directed through the ocean. He then cross-referenced the MITRE and Raytheon Corporations, the JASON Group, and Los Alamos National Laboratory's Blackbeard Team, which controlled the HAARP satellite network, to determine if the array had indeed been deployed. If so, that could possibly be the explanation for the expansion in both the Mariana and Puerto Rico Trenches and the formation of the amber-like crystal he believed was there.

After reviewing all available seismic activity and dated uses of the array, Jonathan determined that HAARP was not the cause of the recent phenomena. Not having much luck in the database, he decided to check one more site, just in case. Using the mouse, Jonathan entered the National Oceanic and Atmospheric Administration's network. He then pulled up the geosynchronous satellite data for both the Puerto Rico and Mariana Trenches.

There it was! Exactly what he was looking for! It was 30,000 feet below the ocean, near Puerto Rico, but there it was nonetheless. Even though he already knew the trenches were on the move and expanding, the hydroscopic photograph showed the amber-like substance, the crystal he had seen in his remote viewing session in the tachyonic chamber at Dulce, at the Puerto Rico site. Another similar object was located in the Mariana Trench. *I knew it!* he thought to himself.

Jonathan decided to print copies of the crystal at different sections and various magnifications for later scrutiny. Feeling a sense of accomplishment, he walked over to the laser printer and examined the photos. He was amazed at how realistic they appeared, as if he was actually there in front of this huge amber object. In his estimation, the anomaly was 500 feet tall, 250 feet wide at its base and nearly 50 feet thick. It was shaped similarly to a teardrop, much like that of drip-dried amber.

Satisfied with what he had found and the pictures he had produced, Jonathan grabbed a brown clasped envelope for the photos and a flash drive to copy the information he found. After putting the needed information on the drive, he erased the computer's search history, logged out, and exited the site.

As he was leaving the records room and walking toward the stairwell, he wondered how the crystal, the trench, and the rest of his vision tied together. It did not make much sense to him at the present. He would just focus on what was real, the amber crystal and his assignment in Puerto Rico. Although he knew more information was needed, time was starting to become a factor. He would have to enlist some help once he got back to Wright-Patterson.

Upon exiting the building, Jonathan noticed Gilla staring, eyes glazed over, out into the massive, cavernous space. Shouting, Jonathan said, "Earth to Gilla, come in, Gilla. Hellooo!" There was no response. Jonathan knew at that moment that his companion was finished being any sort of help, at least for now. "Gilla!!" He said even louder.

Gilla shock himself out of his dreamlike trance and answered, "Yesh . . . sorry Jonashun. I wash shinking of Jen. Hiss, hiss, hiss." It was a positive sign to see Gilla in good spirits. With many Reptilians, just before mating, they become territorial and violent. Gilla, being very mature, has learned how to focus his energies and remain peaceful, especially around humans, who posed no threat. Around his own kind, however, his instincts would override his logic. He too would become a vicious and dangerous animal. "Ish don'sh shink I'm much good shoo you righsh now," Gilla sincerely stated.

"That's all right, Gil. It's probably best we get you back to Groom Lake anyway. Then you can take a break, relax, watch some dirty movies so you can rub one out; you need to be at your best. Don't want to blow your load too soon, old buddy," Jonathan jibed.

"Yoush jush jealoush yoush nosh geshshing any," Gilla retorted.

"Damn right I am! I can't remember the last time I was with a woman. Hell, the way things are going, it might be a while; unless of course I pay for it, and that isn't going to happen," Jonathan complained.

"Yoush will be in sin cishy, hiss, hiss, hiss." Gilla jested.

"Very funny, dino breath. I hope you and Jen get stuck after you blow, so they'll have to cut your green dick out of her."

Gilla, knowing Jonathan's twisted sense of humor, just sat there and hissed amusingly, while Jonathan flagged for the tram. As the tram approached, they noticed it was the same short, plump, bald man who had escorted them earlier. "Fortune must be smiling on us, my friend," Jonathan said, looking at his green friend. After looking at the driver, who appeared to be miserable, Jonathan resisted the urge to berate the man for his rudeness earlier. At least he was getting out of this tomb today. "Take us to the front entrance," Jonathan directed as he and Gilla boarded. Without a word from their driver, they departed the science building.

Passing back through security was uneventful. The same two sentries on duty earlier jumped to attention and cut Jonathan a sharp salute. Jonathan returned the salute and told the soldiers to relax and try to enjoy the rest of their weekend.

Jonathan looked around as he was reaching for the scrambler phone. At the same moment and out of nowhere, Abhar's electric taxi appeared.

"Hello, sir. I hope you found everything you were looking for, yes I do." Abhar was reflexively coming to open the door when Jonathan held up his hand and halted his movement. Instantly, Abhar remembered what Jonathan had said earlier about drawing unnecessary attention.

After getting into the vehicle, Jonathan asked, "How do you do it, Abhar? You are always so . . . punctual." He was not really expecting a straight answer.

"Oh, sir, I am most fortunate, I am. I have always had a sense about different things, yes sir, I have. I have discovered that when I focus on a person, I become in tune with them, I do. I learned to use it back when I was a little boy," Abhar attested.

Jonathan, while expecting some mundane answer, was not surprised by Abhar's admission of possessing some sort of extrasensory perception. He knew when they first met that there was something special about the man. What did surprise him, though, was that Abhar was able to, obviously, tune into him without his awareness. He may unknowingly be a remote viewer, much more powerful than Jonathan, without even realizing it. If he could begin to capitalize on his gift, it might help provide some answers.

"Well, whatever it is you do, I like it. I'm glad to have you on my side." Jonathan was not offering him any information on his own ESP skills.

"Oh, sir, you are too kind. It is my duty to be prompt, it is. What kind of driver would I be if I failed at getting my passengers to their destinations in a timely manner or neglected their personal needs? Not a particularly good one, I would think. No sir, not good indeed."

"We need to get back to Groom Lake. I need to catch a flight out of Vegas and Gil here is going to hole up there and wait on his lady friend, who will be arriving tomorrow. It's about that time for him," Jonathan said, referring to Gilla.

Abhar, looking into the rearview mirror, offered, "Sir Gilla, my nephew Sanjay has a most economical inn that is very comfortable and most importantly"—Abhar was looking around as if he was about to reveal a secret—"it's extremely private. Oh yes it is. You and your lady friend can enjoy yourself without being disturbed, yes you can."

"Yesh, Abhar. Shank yoush!" Gilla responded.

"Very good, sir Gilla. An incredibly wise decision, yes, very wise. I can even pick your friend up when she arrives. I can, sir."

Gilla nodded his approval. He too really liked how Abhar operated.

"He likes you. It took days before he would speak a word to me. You've known him now, what, a few hours, and he's a regular chatterbox," Jonathan said, smiling. "Take us to your nephew's inn. We'll drop Gil off on the way."

With that said, Abhar pushed the accelerator to the floor, and they were off.

While getting Gilla checked in at Sanjay's inn, Jonathan said his goodbyes to Gilla and told him he would be sending someone he knew to meet him back at Los Alamos. "I'll see you back here before your guest arrives." Gilla was intrigued, but Jonathan wanted to leave him in suspense. He also asked Abhar if he could book him a flight out of Las Vegas to Nashville, Tennessee.

Jonathan not only changed his routes when returning to Wright-Patterson, his base of operations; he felt it necessary to take some time to gather his thoughts. Depending on traffic and weather conditions, he should have about a five-hour drive to process this new information.

"Oh yes, sir, I can most definitely do that for you. No problem, sir. I can do it as we drive there, sir. Yes I can."

Jonathan's eyes widened a bit; he was envisioning this pseudo-racecar driver trying to book him a flight while en route but decided just to go with it. "Abhar, did you get in touch with Haji?"

"Yes, sir. It was very good to hear from my brother-in-law, it was. He speaks very highly of you, sir, very highly indeed." Abhar again surveyed the area for eavesdroppers. "Everything you requested will be ready when you arrive, sir Jonathan, it will."

"Excellent! And the other thing?" Jonathan was referring to any further information about the trenches or USOs.

"No, sir, not as of yet . . . may I make a suggestion, sir?" he asked in a humble tone.

"Sure, what is it?"

"May I suggest that you keep the phone I gave you, yes, please do. At least, of course, until you get to Wright-Patterson. I would prefer to pass any information I discover directly to you sir, yes I would."

"That sounds like a hell of an idea, good thinking. I'm guessing you talked with Haji about me, right?" Jonathan smiled with an inquisitive grin.

"Yes, sir. Haji said that I should trust you with my life, he did. And that whatever you are now involved in is of significant importance, it is. If I may, sir Jonathan, I want to be of service to help you if I may, it is my karma, it is." He bowed.

"You don't owe me anything, Abhar."

"Yes, sir, I do . . . you see, sir, I owe a great deal for my life. A life that was doomed many years ago. I have never had a chance to fulfill my karma until now. It would be my honor and duty to assist you in any way I am able. Yes, sir, it would." He was looking at Jonathan with a serious stare.

Abhar's words had caught Jonathan off guard. First, he and Haji had always had a good, trusting relationship, but he was not expecting the glowing review he received. He never realized how much he was being analyzed. Second, he remembered how Abhar had told him how he was rescued by a monk and understood how karma worked, but he already had Gilla's life debt and now, apparently, Abhar's karma working with him as well. *What the hell is going on*, Jonathan thought. He was not one to believe in fate; however, it seemed like some greater force was at work here. "How about this, my Indian friend. You owe me nothing. What is between you and your karma is for you to decide. It would be an honor to accept any assistance you wish to offer." Jonathan reached out to shake Abhar's hand, which he did. "Thank you, my friend."

"The honor is all mine, sir Jonathan, all mine." With that said, they were off again toward the maglev station. Abhar was laser focused on the road, while Jonathan was lost in his thoughts. He was fortunate to have this man working with him. He had a lot of potential. While Abhar was busy booking the flight; Jonathan was considering how best to use Abhar's skills.

Abhar informed Jonathan that it appeared he would be able to leave Groom Lake on the normal afternoon flight out of Las Vegas and catch a flight to Nashville with a stopover in Denver. Taking into account the two-hour time difference due to time zones, he would arrive in Nashville at around 0600 hours tomorrow morning. He also took the liberty of reserving Jonathan a rental car, a V-10 Dodge Viper convertible. Abhar had remembered how Jonathan commented on how he liked the breeze on his face.

Jonathan was utterly amazed at the insight of his new companion. Although he would not have chosen to rent a sports car—he could be a bit conservative at times—he was glad Abhar had done so; he had always wanted to drive a Viper.

Before he knew it, Abhar was pulling into the maglev terminal, the same one where he and Gilla first met the Indian driver. The terminal was connected to the surface airport facility, where Jonathan was to catch his flight.

Using his instincts, Jonathan decided to go out on a limb. He removed the photographs from the brown envelop to show Abhar. "Abhar."

"Yes, sir?"

"Tell me what you think this is," Jonathan said as he handed him the photos.

Abhar shuffled through the pictures, studying each one carefully. "Oh, sir, it is quite beautiful, it is. But, sir, I do not believe I possess the expertise to offer my opinion as to what this might be, no I do not, sir," he said modestly.

"I don't care about that. Tell me what you think!" Jonathan said in a louder tone, but one of respect.

"Well, sir Jonathan . . . I do not know what it is or why it is there but . . ." Abhar was hesitant at telling Jonathan what he thought.

"But! Spit it out, Abhar. Whatever it is."

"Sir . . . I sense that this object is not from here, no, sir, not from here at all."

"What do you mean? Not from this planet?" Jonathan asked.

Abhar paused for a moment; then, seeing the impatience of his new friend, responded, "No, sir . . . I mean not from this universe. Sir."

A silence filled the cab briefly after this revelation.

Jonathan said with a surprised cry, "Abhar, this is where I'm going to. This thing is 30,000 feet under the water just north of Puerto Rico." He paused to let the significance sink in. "Find anything you can about this. Anything!" Jonathan said as he grabbed the photos and exited the transport.

"I will, sir Jonathan. Oh yes, sir, I will," Abhar answered in a hushed voice, realizing the importance of the situation. He felt honored that Jonathan trusted him with this information.

"Take care, my friend, and be careful. There's no telling what forces are at work here," Jonathan cautioned. "I'll expect to hear from you soon." He held up and showed Abhar the scrambler phone.

"Keep it close, sir, very close indeed."

Jonathan stepped back from the taxi and waved goodbye. Abhar was gone as fast as he had appeared. Jonathon walked over to the nearest elevator and rode it to the surface. He looked at the clock; it was 1510 hours.

After getting an orange juice at the concession stand, Jonathan headed to the one and only gate and took a seat. Waiting for his flight to board, Jonathan sensed his life was about to get a lot more interesting.

CHAPTER

TWELVE

THE TRANSITION FROM Groom Lake to Las Vegas went pretty smoothly. Even though there were daily flights to and from Area 51, as with all airports, at times there were delays. Jonathan abhorred standing still, wasting time. Unless, of course, it was his choice to be idle. Delays, such as traffic jams, airport layovers, or standing in endless lines, really irritated him. Movement—that is what he needed. So much so that on most occasions he would take another route, driving or flying. Although they would be longer, he did this just to avoid being inactive. He could be lazy just like anyone else; however, it was then the lion's choice to bask in the sun.

Thanks to Abhar, though, after landing at McCarran International Airport in Las Vegas, he had just enough time to visit the restroom and devour a sandwich from the airport deli before boarding his flight. Abhar was so resourceful that he not only got him on this booked flight at the last minute, but also somehow managed to reserve him a window seat. Although most of the flight would be at night and he would not arrive in Nashville until around midnight, it would still be light enough to look down at the Rocky Mountains as the plane flew thousands of feet above.

The sight of peaks from the air reminded him of how small he actually was in the big scheme of things. Not feeling like reading the airline magazine or doing its crossword puzzle, both of which he had completed on his last flight several weeks ago, he decided to see what was playing for the in-flight movie. Jonathan, not interested in what was showing, flagged down the flight attendant and purchased some noise-canceling headphones; he needed to think.

While he gazed at the billowy white clouds below, just over the mountain tops, his thoughts drifted back to the amber crystal. He did not know what its chemical makeup was or what it was called, but the name Firestone kept coming to mind. Besides being a brand of fire or any rock indigenous cultures used to make fire, such as flint or pyrite, Jonathan knew of no other stone with that name. He could not remember hearing the name, even in school, which he was sure he had.

And what of the other things he saw in his vision, apart from this Firestone amber crystal; there were people who seemed familiar to him, an environment that included unknown plants and what appeared to be someone staring back at him from the other side.

He was sure all these questions would be answered in time; unfortunately, that time was not now. At this instant, Jonathan wanted what he wanted, when he wanted it; although he had grown to know things very seldom worked on his time schedule, he still wanted them to. He was a work in progress. Switching gears in his head, rather than driving himself insane trying to solve an enigma at this time, he decided to focus on more concrete thoughts.

When he was at the computer lab at S-4, Jonathan had pulled up and printed the dossier of Ariella Marconi. It was always his standard operating procedure to review a person's bio before working with them.

Weary of looking out the window at the stark landscape while noting that the two other people in his row, a woman who appeared to be ten years his elder and her mother, were not interested in what he was doing and posed no threat to his privacy, Jonathan decided to examine Ms. Marconi's information.

Freeing his feet from around his backpack, which was wedged under the seat in front of him, he was able to maneuver enough to get it out onto his thighs. Even though he always packed light, a small suitcase and his backpack, due to his weapons, his carry-on-sized suitcase had to be checked in and TSA alerted to what it contained. Jonathan carried a host of personal security items, which would land him handcuffed in some small room answering questions for hours if he tried to get them through security.

These included: a Springfield XDM .45 caliber semiautomatic pistol, a Glock snub-nose 9 mm, five loaded clips for each weapon, 240 rounds of ammunition, a ten-inch Bowie knife, two pocketknives, a CRKT tactical lock blade folding knife, a Leatherman multitool, and his twin, T-handled mini-butt knives, which looked like decorations. He also had his flash gun packed away, but since it looked exactly like a flashlight, it would be overlooked. Moreover, once his weapons were recorded and locked, no one went into his bag again anyway.

The only other items in this small bag were a change of clothes, a jacket, his toiletry bag, an extra pair of Merrill hiking boots, and a folding machete. One could never be too careful.

Most of these things, however, would normally be on his person or in his backpack, which never left him. But on commercial flights, he had to follow protocol and check his weaponry just as a normal passenger would. He was not unarmed, though. In his front pocket, Jonathan carried a device that looked like a pen but could fire a vibratory laser beam at a distance of 50 feet, stopping a human heart. No one would ever suspect a thing, other than a heart attack.

His backpack was his survival kit, which alone weighed 10 pounds. It contained everything he needed for survival: several water purification methods and devices, six different ways to create fire and even a few different substances to keep it going, even on water, a full first-aid kit, fishing and sewing equipment, a compass, five 2,500-calorie energy bars, 200 feet of 550 parachute cord, and so on. Essentially anything he would need to survive and thrive in nature until he could get back to civilization.

Digging through his pack, moving his digital camera, his binoculars, and his half-eaten bag of trail mix, Jonathan pulled out the brown envelope containing the photographs of the crystal and the bio. He had been so intrigued by what he was seeing on the DoD website that he almost forgot he had copied her file. Jonathan had not looked at it yet.

Pulling out the document, he read the name, Ariella Talah Marconi. Marconi . . . that name sounded familiar. He continued, age thirty-six, date of birth, March 10, 1971. Single, no children, parents deceased, and no siblings. Five foot eight inches tall. Jonathan stopped there and skipped to the meat of the file, the history.

Ms. Marconi was a highly educated woman, with bachelor of science degrees in physics, marine biology, and geology. Interesting, he thought, since he too was a geologist. She had completed her master's by age twenty-one and a doctorate in geological oceanography by age twenty-four.

Her work history involved several places of note, such as the National Underwater Marine Agency, professor and researcher at Woods Hole Oceanographic Institute, where she received her PhD, and, most recently, dual employment at Scripps Institute of Oceanography at Point Loma, San Diego, and the University of California at Berkeley near San Francisco. It appears Ms. Marconi taught at Scripps on Monday and Tuesday, then flew out and taught at Berkeley on Wednesday and Thursday. She then hopped a flight back after Thursday's classes. What a workaholic, Jonathan thought, but so was he at times. That probably also explains her being single and having no children, he surmised. He noticed that her last relationship ended over a year ago, and he was not surprised that there had not been another. She was married to her career, or that was what appeared to be so from reading her file.

As Jonathan continued to delve, he understood why the name Marconi sounded familiar. Her great-grandfather, Guglielmo Marconi, invented the radio, or so the history books show, although Nikola Tesla had already patented several versions of the device at the time of Marconi's invention. Her grandfather and father were also famous physicists; however, most would never be privy to their accomplishments. The Marconi vortex dynamo, which was a spherical tank of mercury, along with a Van de Graaf generator, could produce extremely powerful electromagnetic fields, which canceled the effects of gravity on Mars. This worked with the Thule Tachyon Seven Drive to produce an electromagnetic-gravitational spacecraft capable of traveling the stars. In 1956, her grandfather, Antonio Vito Marconi, and father, Vito Giuseppe Marconi, were the two scientists in charge of the Vatican's Marconi Project. They had launched a manned disc-shaped object, with the improved Andromeda tachyonic propulsion system, from Argentina toward Mars. The mission was a complete success, and a base was established, all under a complete cloak of secrecy.

Jonathan remembered that Ms. Marconi began in physics, following in the family profession, but abandoned it in favor of oceanography. There was sure to be some juicy, hidden story underneath that decision. Flipping to the next page, Jonathan felt stunned. She was beautiful. Not in that model sort of way, but gorgeous nonetheless. Her Italian lineage was evident from her chocolate brown eyes, her thick, rich, dark hair, and her olive skin. She had a short, little pug nose, which was cute, and thick, full lips. While her face was not round, it tended more to the circular side rather than rectangular. Looking at her facial structure, Jonathan presumed her family was originally from north central Italy, around Bologna. She was blessed with a clear complexion and obviously had fared well during the teenage acne years. Pictures do not lie, for there was a pain in her eyes, something that bothered her greatly; Jonathan, who had his own pain, saw it clearly.

All of this, however, was not what left him so disoriented. He could not shake the feeling that he somehow knew this woman, or at the very least had seen her photograph before. Backtracking over what he had previously read—where she grew up, went to school, worked, traveled to—he felt it was highly unlikely that they had ever met; he would have remembered her. Nonetheless, he still was convinced he knew her. This was going to eat at him like a brown recluse spider bite, all the way to the bone. "Focus," he whispered. Nothing. "Shit!" he blurted out without meaning to. The elderly woman next to him was a little startled but settled down when Jonathan whispered, "I'm sorry, ma'am, forgive me."

Once again, rather than work himself into a frenzy, which he tended to do when faced with such dilemmas, he dealt with the facts and what he could evaluate from them.

Regardless of her obvious academic qualifications and practical experience under the ocean, he questioned why she was picked for such a highly secret mission. Her clearance had to be upgraded just for this assignment. Very peculiar. He wondered what forces were at work behind the scenes. And surely there must have been others suitable for the task at hand who already had security level Ultra. Maybe the powers that be were hoping to ignite the untapped greatness that had remained silent within her, especially considering her lineage. She was a Pisces, and Jonathan, from many personal experiences, knew how people born under that sign felt and acted. Lacking a natural confidence at birth, many times a Piscean would work at the task or goal with fervor, believing that they are inadequate. In the end, however, they wake up to find they are one of the best, if not *the* best, at what they do. They are also described as mystical thinkers, sometimes saying and coming up with things that are truly brilliant, while at other times the exact opposite. They needed grounding and the preverbal "kick in the ass" to get them to stop thinking and start doing, necessity being the mother of invention at times. All of a sudden, a humorous thought occurred to him—a water sign working in and under the water. Well, it made perfect sense; he was a fire sign who loved fire. He could already foresee the potential turmoil that awaited him with respect to her. Being totally opposite, verbal communication would be extremely important to establish trust. Luckily for him, his mother was a Pisces, as were many of the people he grew up around and who served with him. He really did understand their personalities and mannerisms; it was just getting them to understand his. They were going to be in her comfort zone, the water, and it was not like they were going to spend eternity together.

Hopefully, they would uncover what they needed to at the Puerto Rico facility, and he could get back topside and figure out what his vision was all about. Jonathan decided to close his eyes and concentrate on the significance of this Marconi woman and her pain. Maybe something would come to him. *Thank God for noise-canceling earphones*, he thought to himself as he drifted into a meditative state.

Jonathan woke to the sound of a bell. The captain was on the intercom talking to the passengers. "Ladies and Gentlemen," he said in a very deep husky voice. "We are on our final descent into Nashville, Tennessee. We should be landing in about fifteen minutes. Skies are clear and the temperature is 58 degrees Fahrenheit. Local time is 11:20 p.m."

As the captain continued, Jonathan alertly flagged down a stewardess, who was kind enough to get him a cup of black coffee. He was a bit surprised that he felt as rested as he did; he obviously needed a break because he had slept right through the stopover in Denver. His training as a Ranger afforded him the discipline to remain awake and still function at a high level after several days without sleep. He was thankful for shuteye since he would be driving through the night in order to get to Wright-Patterson Air Force Base.

As the plane landed and taxied down the tarmac toward the gate, Jonathan turned on his BlackBerry to check for messages. The visual voice mail indicated that Ms. Marconi was safely aboard the bathysphere, as scheduled, and should be boarding the USS *Ronald Reagan* by 0500 hours his time. The other message on his personal phone was from his secretary and friend, Ashley. She was checking in to see if he needed anything and what time he would be arriving. Jonathan grinned; she was truly one of his biggest assets, always asking the tough questions and keeping him in line. She too was a Pisces. He texted her a message telling her that there would be no need for her to arrive any earlier than normal and that he would be there when she arrived.

After dealing with his personal messages on his BlackBerry, he switched on and checked the scrambler phone without expectation; it had only been six hours since he and Abhar last spoke. Surprisingly, there was a message that indicated that an unidentified object, which looked like clear water with colored lights, was spotted diving into the waters near Guam, exactly over the Mariana Trench. No time stamp was on the message.

Jonathan highly doubted the Navy was the source of the sighting; it rarely was. For one thing, the Navy had a strict policy of keeping communications silent, especially when such things were witnessed, and second, most sailors, not wanting their next assignment to be above the Artic Circle, would never say anything at all.

The source did not matter, though. It was from Abhar, and Jonathan felt it was something even he would have had difficulty obtaining. One day, he would get Abhar drunk and find out how the hell he came up with this stuff. Jonathan sent him a simple text, "K, thx!" He would call him from Wright-Patterson when got to his office.

After grabbing his bag from the carousel in the nearly empty airport, Jonathan made his way over to the rental car desk. The clerk was watching the clock; he was apparently getting off at midnight. Jonathan was quickly served and given the keys to the rental, which was parked adjacent to the terminal and within walking distance.

There it was, a candy apple red, V-10 Dodge Viper convertible. Jonathan briefly thought he heard angels singing. All this baby needed to be track ready was some slicks. He climbed in, inserted the key, and turned on the ignition. The engine roared to life and produced a low rumble at idle. Goose bumps appeared all over Jonathan's body. "Oh my," he said audibly. *This is going to be fun*, he thought.

Checking and adjusting his mirrors and seat position, he familiarized himself with the machine. This car was fully loaded: heated and air-conditioned seats with separate temperature controls, a large navigation touch screen with GPS, weather, and premium stereo system controls. It also had a DVD player. Individual passenger and driver thermostat systems with seat memory. The six-speed gearbox was designed in linear style for accurate shifting. A digital display showed everything from individual tire pressures to estimated distance with remaining fuel at current consumption. The interior was tan leather, which was elegantly soft, and chrome trim. Jonathan was impressed; this was one of the most advanced and powerful vehicles in the public sector. This was really going to be a treat.

Even though it was a brisk 59 degrees, Jonathan opened the automatic retracting roof and cranked the heat to maximum. Sitting back in the race-style seat, he was surprised at how comfortable he was. Typically, high-performance sports cars, with their tight suspension systems, would beat the hell out the driver. Comfort was overlooked for performance. Jonathan was looking forward to the next few hours on the road. He threw the car into reverse and backed out of the parking spot. Shifting into first gear, he thought of Abhar and laughed. Popping the clutch, he tore out of the parking lot. Smiling, he was off.

CHAPTER THIRTEEN

PERHAPS THE TIME was not quite right; the two humans in question were totally oblivious to what had been happening to them all their lives. Orders were orders, though, and they would be followed.

Captain Rahzu looked through the translucent wall of his spaceship, Rah Jump Craft (RJC) 430, which was constructed of modified water and pure energy, in the lifeless blackness of this buffer universe. Sitting adjacent, in the next dimension, was Parallel Universe 431, which contained the Earth.

His kind, Dimerians, were responsible for creating this universe, as well as many others. Although Yahweh, from the House of Yah, formed this creation, Earth, with the WORD, the House of Rah had secretly been working undetected here for millennia.

Feeling uneasy, Rahzu called his commander, CheRahna, to the bridge. As her bright, silvery form approached, one normal for a Dimerian female, he could not help but think that this change of plans was a big mistake.

CheRahna, nearing her captain, who was displaying the evolved male's bright golden form, sensed his uncertainty. Even though she could not see any of his facial expressions—in elemental configuration they only had a humanoid outline—she knew that his forehead was furrowed, and he wore a grimace upon his face.

"Captain Rahzu, what seems to be the problem? I sense you are upset. I hope I have not failed you in any way?" Commander CheRahna, the lower-ranking officer, felt that she had not, but used it as an icebreaker to set her captain at ease. He sometimes could be tight-lipped about things, and she did not want to enter his mind to scan his thoughts.

"You have performed exceptionally, CheRahna. I will fulfill my duty and do as I am directed, but I question whether our new orders are the best course of action at this time," Captain Rahzu responded in a worried tone.

"What orders? And from whom?!" CheRahna asked authoritatively, in an irritated tone of her own. She and Rahzu had been given carte blanche and were allowed to make decisions at their own discretion when dealing with the humans; to date, they had been quite successful.

Not only had there been no hypnotic embolisms among the most prized subjects, but there had also been no Rah defections since they were placed in command.

Little did the humans know that many of the great figures of their history had actually been Rahs in disguise, manipulating and steering events for ages. Currently, there were no fewer than a thousand such impostors operating on Earth to ensure that Rah interests were being personally attended to.

Rahzu knew that she too would be upset. Neither of them liked or needed to be micromanaged. "Admiral YetziRah has ordered us to gather the human male number 99985 and the human female number 69552 for inspection and reimplantation."

Walking over to the amber-colored crystalline sphere, CheRahna pulled up the information on the human subjects. "It appears that the male's implantation device is malfunctioning, but that has always been a problem we've had with him. I still believe it has something to do with the unique electromagnetic field in which his body resonates, even if our technicians have never solved the glitch." Continuing her investigation, she noted, "Our spy working near the female reports that she has lost contact with the subject and a new operative would be needed to reacquire her . . . but that's all. Nothing out of the ordinary in the Earthling world."

Rahzu knew that everything CheRahna had just said was positively correct. Humans move, change jobs, and even die. Changing operatives is commonplace and unavoidable; it is actually good practice in any surveillance assignment to switch agents so as not to draw attention to themselves and blow their cover.

CheRahna continued as she moved in Razhu's direction, "They aren't scheduled for inspection for another four Earth years. I wonder what is going on." She was truly baffled by the new orders.

Rahzu stated with conviction, "I feel the same as you do, Commander; however, we both know not to openly question YetziRah about his orders. He answers only to the head of our house, Xanix Rah, who would never side with us to override this plan." Rahzu paused, thinking about what he had just said . . . others have been destroyed for hinting at less. He felt confident, however, that his candor with CheRahna was appropriate and would be kept private.

Without a word, pacing back and forth across the bridge, Rahzu finally broke the silence. "There has to be a reason why the admiral has ordered us to do this. He appears to have been right about choosing the proper hosts for the experiment. We can only trust he is also correct about this decision now."

CheRahna reluctantly nodded in agreement. She too had experienced YetziRah's wrath when she was on Dimeria in training. She would not dare a repeat performance of questioning his authority. "What are your orders, Captain?" Her speaking professionally signified her obedience, despite her lack of enthusiasm for the change of plans.

"We will send a cruise Rah with Lieutenant ShemRahya and Lieutenant Rahphila to gather the male. You may send another with Ensign RahKael and Lieutenant KaRah aboard to collect the female." Rahzu, looking out toward the portal, finished by saying, "Get Commander TamaRah here and have her contact her operative on Earth and find out where to best place the next asset in order to reacquire the human female after our inspection."

CheRahna was about to begin contacting her subordinates when Rahzu abruptly stopped her. He sensed that she had another course of action in mind. He respected her enough to hear her out, aloud. They had made an agreement long ago not to probe each other's minds or to read the thoughts that lay there;

it would make it impossible to work together. They had been a team now for over a thousand Earth years and had always worked well together. *No sense in fixing something that was not broken*, Rahzu thought. "What is it, CheRahna? Tell me your thoughts."

She was reluctant to say anything at first, even though she felt comfortable speaking her mind on most occasions to her captain, she could still see he was irritable and did not want his unpleasant feelings toward YetziRah to be directed at her accidently.

"Please CheRahna . . . speak freely. There is nothing you can tell me that will make me angry at you . . . I promise," Rahzu said in a calm voice.

"Well . . . judging by how displeased we were to hear the new orders, I just thought it might be a better idea if we gathered the crew and personally informed them a unified front could be important right now. Wouldn't you agree, Captain Rahzu?" She finished by showing her submission to him.

Rahzu thought for only a second, and then responded, "And that is why I am recommending you for advancement to the next stage of evolution. Your assessment of our situation is accurate, and your plan is the correct one. Well done, CheRahna." Rahzu was genuine with his words, and she could feel it. He was proud to have had her under his tutelage, but also knew she needed to evolve and deserved it.

"Contact the crew, Commander CheRahna, and give them instructions to meet us at the pleasure pool." Rahzu smiled as he turned back toward the crystal amber portal.

"Thank you, Rahzu," CheRahna said leaving the bridge. She really admired and respected her captain.

FOURTEEN

ΛS THE ƎΛTHYSPHERE rose, Ariella, feeling the effects of the alcohol, was extremely relaxed. Its ascent of 50 feet per minute afforded her approximately five hours of complete solitude within the vastness of the sea. Despite leaving, Ariella was beginning to get a little excited about her new mission.

Although not averse to change, she usually did not look forward to it, either. Maybe her giddiness was also due to the slight change in pressure between the Sea Lab and the bell. She giggled at the thought. It had been a fulfilling day.

Continuing to rise, Ariella gazed out the quartz glass porthole at the absolute darkness, and other than the dim lights of the bell's instruments, the nadir of the ocean offered nothing to see. Without warning, the side of the canyon wall, which was parallel to the bathysphere's ascent, lit up in a fabulous display of bioluminescent glory. "Wow! What is that?" she could not help saying out loud. Checking the depth, 12,350 feet, she tried to postulate what type of glowing organism lived this deep.

It suddenly came to her—there was apparently some type of crustacean from the suborder Natania, or shrimp, only much smaller. Ariella assumed that the creatures were using the cliff sides as a spawning ground and hatchery for their young.

Looking at their simple beauty, she reached for her bag, pulled out a pen and notepad, and started documenting what she was witnessing. Now her excitement was genuine. Ariella had encountered a new species, and she got to name it. This was a privilege; one could spend a lifetime in the ocean and never see something completely new. *Crangon ariellaeuscorum* had a ring to it. No one would ever forget me now, she thought. The common name, which came to her immediately, was the Barett crawler shrimp. After Lt. Steven Barett, who had a knack for crawling under her skin, in a good way. She penned that in for now, deciding not to devote any more time to that at present.

She diligently recorded everything she saw: the size, shape, color, or lack thereof, the social characteristics, mating habits, and so on. And though not an artist by any stretch of the imagination, she sketched a picture. All thoughts of Justin LaMarr, the Hab, and her new assignment faded away. This is what she lived for, her true passion, solving and witnessing the mysteries of the ocean.

Ariella was lost in her work when, most unexpectedly, she heard a low-pitched groan, followed by a bark and a deep whistle. *Could it be?* she thought while checking the depth gauge again—10,725 feet. Ariella rushed across the bathysphere with the excitement of a child who was first seeing Disney World, to look out the porthole that faced the void. She could see nothing. She switched on the exterior illumination, and there they were—three blue whales in all their grandeur. They were side by side, at various levels, staring at her and the bell. The largest, which had to be a male, must be over 140 feet long. It was the biggest specimen she, or probably anyone, had ever seen.

Ariella remembered that blue whales could dive to incredible depths, but no one would have thought to find them in the abyss. Unfortunately, even today, little is known about these majestic behemoths of the ocean.

Ariella was mesmerized. She felt like royalty as the whales danced and sang. By the sounds they were making, the delicate movements they were performing, and from what she had learned from studying them before, they were happily curious at her presence. *This is all for me*, she thought, an experience she would never forget.

After performing for about ten minutes, they exited the stage as suddenly as they had appeared, heading upward toward the surface. A little disappointed that the show was over, hoping for an encore performance she knew would not come, she quickly surmised that, considering the depth, they were probably in need of air.

Ariella closed her eyes and replayed the whale song in her head. *What a day*, she mused. She had experienced great sex, fell in love, had a party, caught a little buzz, named a new species, and watched the performance of a lifetime by nature's largest mammals. What would happen next?

Completely lost in thought, all concept of time eluded her. She was enjoying the silence and the peace that those on the surface world rarely, if ever, experience. Time melted away as she continued to sink deeper into her mind. Then, catching her completely off guard, the whales returned and began to sing their song once again. This time, however, it sounded more like a tragic play, foreshadowing a catastrophic event. She turned the lights back on; the whales were huddled very tightly together, a behavior signifying danger. The noises they made now were high-pitched and frantic. Ariella, looking out, could not see anything that was an obvious sign of danger. She was now becoming frightened, especially being 7,500 feet below the surface, totally alone.

Suddenly and without warning, the huge beasts crowded the bell. She had seen this before when one of their own was injured or sick. They were trying to protect her, but from what? Visions of a giant squid and Moby Dick attacking her in the minute bathysphere came to mind. "Come on, get a grip," she said aloud with a stuttering fear.

Ariella felt like a soccer ball being passed between players as the moved down the field to score. The bell was slamming into the sides of the whales; she was worried that all the jarring would cause a crack, making the bathysphere implode, crushing her like a grape.

As quickly as it began, it ended. Darkness, silence, an eerie calm. In an instant, a white light, so bright, shown through the portholes, causing Ariella to close her eyes. That was the last thing she would remember.

CHAPTER

FIFTEEN

ΛS THE CRISP, cool night air blew through Jonathan's short, cropped hair and around his neck, goose bumps developed over his entire body. He felt exhilarated by the evening's drive. He had only been on the road for a few minutes when he reached Interstate 65. While approaching the on-ramp, the heater, which was now starting to radiate the thermal energy from the engine, started to warm his legs.

It was the simple things in life that usually pleased him the most, but he had to admit, at this moment, he was more than content; he was ecstatic. Abhar was in for some sort of treat the next time they met; Jonathan would surely see to that.

There was little traffic on the road in the early morning hours. He was making good tome while only traveling five miles over the speed limit. He was enjoying this experience too much to be in a rush. If this was during the day, Jonathan would have been blaring the stereo on some alternative rock station, but then he would have had to drive at breakneck speed to match the beat.

Instead, he chose to listen to Art Bell and Coast to Coast Radio. As usual, Art was talking about ETs and UFOs, and the upcoming end of the world.

Little did people know how accurate he actually was concerning a great many things, such as Dulce, Los Alamos, the Roswell landing, and other secret sites around the nation and in space. Jonathan did not know for sure, but suspected that whoever was feeding Bell with this information was deeply entrenched within the breakaway civilization's organization. That person, if ever discovered and caught, would be filleted like a flounder, considering there really are secret bases on the moon, Mars, and various other heavenly bodies.

In the show this evening, interestingly enough, Art Bell was interviewing a woman who claimed to have been abducted by aliens multiple times during the course of her life. Jonathan knew this sort of thing happened quite regularly. She was describing déjà vu moments, missing time episodes, unexplainable wounds and scars, and a constant uneasiness that she was being watched.

A chill ran down Jonathan's spine. While not feeling as if he was being watched, since he was usually the one watching, or knowing of any unexplainable wounds or scars, which he probably would not have noticed anyway, he did, however, experience many of the other things the woman mentioned. Gilla also had always thought that Jonathan had been visited several times in his life, but could not offer any concrete proof.

Making matters worse, the woman claimed that her last abduction had taken place while visiting Mammoth Cave, Kentucky. Looking up at the next road sign, Jonathan noticed he was only five miles from the Kentucky state line and 55 miles southwest of Mammoth Cave National Park, which the interstate traveled right by. "You've got to be shitting me," Jonathan said aloud.

That little feeling, which developed deep in the pit of his stomach, was screaming at him to change routes, alter his course of travel, and avoid the area completely. His ego, however, would never allow such a thing. He was an indestructible badass, or at least that is what he was telling himself.

Looking directly at the display on the dashboard, the clock read 1:03 a.m. He was traveling 70 miles per hour. Right then, he decided that once he got closer to Mammoth Cave, he would put the pedal to the metal, throw caution to the wind, and see what this beast of a machine could do.

To ease his tense mood, though, he switched the radio station, which was playing a mix of classic songs from the sixties through the nineties. *This was a good change*, he thought. Not too much to spoil the drive, but just enough to allow the recent unpleasantness to escape from his mind while making time flow smoothly on the road.

He continued along his original route, mile after mile passing by. Jonathan was getting close, within 15 miles of the ill-fated hole in the Earth. He had already passed Lost Cave and was now seeing signs for Horse Cave and Cave City. Shortly after passing Horse Cave and Cave City, three exits ahead a brightly lit road sign signified the Mammoth Cave National Park off-ramp was approaching.

It was time, Jonathan thought. As the song "Danger Zone" by Kenny Loggins played on the stereo, he imagined being a fighter pilot in the Top Gun training program, flying an F-14 Tomcat. He tuned the volume of the music as high as it would go, as the song suggested, downshifted, and buried the accelerator to the floor. To his surprise, the tires squealed as his speed rapidly climbed from seventy mph to 115 mph. Shifting up, he continued to accelerate. The engine roared.

The wind was fierce, and ripples developed on his face. He probably should have pulled over to put the top up before he took flight, but it was too late now, he was committed. With the high beams on, the dashed white lane lines looked like one solid boundary. He was flying! Or that is what he felt like as the song reached its bridge.

Before he knew it, he was traveling down the road at 145 mph, which shocked him. The car handled much better than expected. It was definitely built for power. At this velocity, Jonathan quickly realized he was moving at 210 feet per second, or a mile in less than half a minute. Looking ahead, he could barely make out the little white dot. It was a large stork flying just over the highway and just below the height of the Viper's window. He applied the brakes, hard, making the vehicle swerve from side to side. His speed dropped rapidly.

By the time he was passing the mythical baby deliverer, Jonathan reflexively brought his right hand up to wipe off his face. "That mother fucker just shit on me," Jonathan yelled as he turned around to see the bogey behind him. Once again it had already become a small white dot. Turning around, not having both hands on the wheel, combined with the swerving due to the rapid deceleration, all caused him to lose control of the vehicle. Much like a jet fighter falling from the sky, it went into a flat spin.

As he slid down the highway, he could only hold on for dear life as he slowed. Finally, after what seemed like an eternity, the spinning stopped. Miraculously, both he and the Viper ended up on the shoulder of the road. Disoriented by his near-death experience, he staggered out of the car, only to immediately fall to the pavement. As he brought his head up, he noticed his enemy, his conqueror, the stork, approaching.

"That son of a bitch," he said while reaching for his Glock, which was in his shoulder holster. "Fuck you!" he shouted as he began wildly firing into the air. "Die, motherfucker, die!" He emptied the clip. Lowering his empty weapon, he fell to the ground again. Jonathan proceeded to finish cleaning his face of the milky white bird excrement, when suddenly the bird fell dead 10 feet in front of him.

Surprised that he had hit the animal, since he had not actually been aiming at anything, Jonathan crawled over to inspect his kill. No blood, not one bullet hole. "What the hell?" he mumbled aloud. He began to wonder what killed the stork, because it certainly was not his bullets.

Without a sound, a blinding white light surrounded him. He felt the warmth radiate from it. There was silence, except for the stereo playing "Rocket Man" by Elton John in the background. That was all he would be able to remember about this incident, at least for a while.

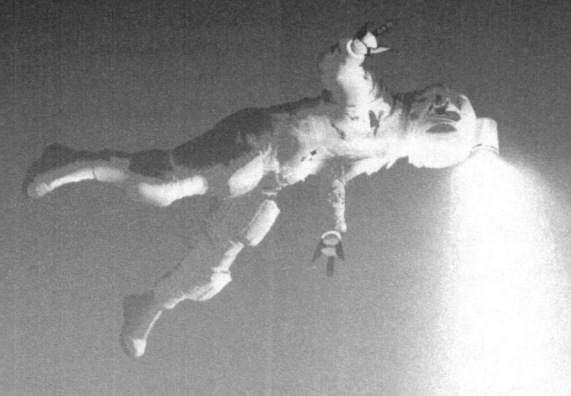

CHAPTER / SIXTEEN

AFTER THE MEETING, everyone went to their respective groups, Golds and Silvers. To ensure the orders were completed swiftly and without question, all the crew members, as suggested by CheRahna, were personally informed of the new mission.

Although contrary to how things were normally done, by presenting the new orders as a unified front, Rahzu and CheRahna felt that the crew was clear about their new assignment. While feeling a bit dejected initially, the captain assured them that their performances thus far had been exemplary, and the changes had no negative bearing on any of their records.

Captain Rahzu and Commander CheRahna, in their groups, were quickly surrounded by the crew members, who were eager to hear each other's individual orders.

The two normal Golds, who were around Rahzu, were Lt. ShemRahya and Lt. Rahphila. ShemRahya had been with Rahzu from the beginning, and his loyalty was without question. The two were instructed to take a cruise rah, travel through the amber portal, and collect human male number 99985, known as Jonathan Arlin Hawthorn II, and bring him back here to Rah Jump

Ship 430 as quickly and silently as possible. As usual, they were to disguise themselves as the Grays, which were aligned with the Reptilian race from Alpha Draconis.

Pulling Lt. ShemRahya aside, Rahzu whispered, "You are my most trusted confidant. I will tell you more when I can. Safe journey," Rahzu said, sending him and Rahphila on their way.

Understanding their assignments completely, ShemRahya and Rahphila departed without any further questions. As they walked toward the ship, they discussed the new mission freely among themselves, a practice Rahzu encouraged.

"Rahphila, I know that the orders came from YetziRah, but I wonder what could be so important for us to break protocol now, at this time," ShemRahya wondered.

"I got the impression that Rahzu and CheRahna were also kept out of the loop on this one. Something's up," Rahphila responded.

"You're right! Come to think of it, they put on a good show for us, being supportive and encouraging, but they too, didn't have the slightest idea what was going on," ShemRahya countered.

"All I know is that Rahzu would have told us what was happening if he knew. Maybe when we pick up the human, more will be revealed." Rahphila then bent down like a sprinter at the starting blocks. "Race you to the Cruiser Rah, winner gets to drive!" he challenged as he and ShemRahya broke into a run.

CheRahna was doing the same as Rahzu. She was among her Silvers, Ensign RahKael, Lt. KaRah, and Lt. Commander TamaRah; the latter two she trusted with her life. First pointing toward RahKael and KaRah, CheRahna explained that they were to gather female number 69552, one Ariella Talah Marconi, from her position on Earth. And just as Rahzu had instructed his Golds, bring her back to Parallel Universe 430 for inspection and reimplantation. They were, of course, to use their discretion so as not to bring unnecessary attention to the mission. They too were told to disguise themselves as Grays, which were controlled by the alien Reptilian race.

Ensign RahKael, who was a new addition for this assignment, stepped forward and posed a question. "Commander, why are we disguising ourselves as these disgusting little creatures"—pointing to an image that had been produced by a hologram—"when, after we have completed our inspection, we erase the human's conscious memory anyway?"

KaRah giggled slightly, not because it was a silly question, but because she too had asked it before.

CheRahna opened her hand, palm up, which signaled for KaRah to answer RahKael.

"We have learned, by working with humans for many years, that even though we can erase their conscious thoughts, their subconscious always stores and records everything it senses."

RahKael was interested, and nodded as KaRah continued.

"They have learned, through a process called regressive hypnotic therapy, to tap into this warehouse of information, which we have been unable to delete."

CheRahna broke in. "Unless, of course, we completely erase their mind, which would leave them a pathetic, drooling idiot. Most of the time, that would not suit our purpose."

Lt. Commander TamaRah joined the conservation emphatically. "Humans have what they call a soul. It is a force within that is essentially indestructible, which we don't fully understand. I have been working closely with humans for millennia, and one thing in our favor is that they are disconnected from this powerful inner force. At least most of them are." TamaRah walked over to the amber crystalline sphere to show RahKael more about some of the things she was referring to.

After pulling up examples of angels and demons, while showing a brief history of the human race, TamaRah informed RahKael of the importance of secrecy, especially when angels were nearby.

"Careful? What can any of these humans do to us?" Ensign RahKael asked in a sassy tone.

Commander CheRahna answered with a commanding and serious tone to show the importance of her next words. "There are forces on Earth that we don't quite understand. We do know that there are a few of these on the planet." CheRahna removed a tri-sword from its wall display, one of the few weapons that could kill a Dimerian. "This, as you well know, is something to be careful about. There are swordsmen on Earth who. if given this weapon, would pose a great danger to any of us." She put the sword back in its position of display on the wall, and then continued. "There are also other powers in Yahweh's creation that are elemental in origin." In a lighter tone she added, "I tell you of these things so that you are aware of them. The chances of you encountering anything that could harm you is slim. We value your contribution to the team and would not want any misfortune to befall you, RahKael." CheRahna patted her on the shoulder.

"Has any Rah died on Earth before?" RahKael asked.

They all bowed their heads, not in reverence, but in shame. TamaRah pulled up the Earth's globe on the amber sphere and showed RahKael a vast wasteland. As she explained, RahKael was engrossed in every word that poured from her.

TamaRah, looking away from the globe and facing RahKael, stated, "Long ago, two Rah agents, who were working on Earth, defected and turned against us. They began aiding Yahweh in his quest to remove us from his world. While this was largely successful, we still have a small presence there. We just don't operate in the open as we once did." TamaRah let a glint of nostalgia shrine through her pale silver form. "A powerful Silver named SaRah turned from us and was mistakenly caught in a nuclear blast of some sort, which eliminated much of our presence on the planet at the time. The explosion froze her essence in an atomized state of trillions of basic particles, which make up what is now called the Sahara Desert," TamaRah finished with disgust.

"I see the name of the wasteland resembles the traitor's name, except a few letters have been reversed," RahKael noted.

CheRahna explained, "When someone defects from the House of Rah, it is blasphemy for them to be associated with anything that is Rah. Their names are reversed for eternity to signify their betrayal." CheRahna could not go on. This history lesson was over. "Enough of this nonsense!" She was irritated at the embarrassing memories of the past, though none of them had anything to do with it.

"Lieutenant KaRah, Ensign RahKael!" CheRahna ordered.

"Yes, ma'am?" KaRah answered.

"Yes, Commander," RahKael responded.

"You two get the ship ready. I need to speak with TamaRah for a moment. I know you will make me proud," CheRahna finished with them on a positive note. "TamaRah."

"Yes, Commander."

"When you get to Earth, since you will be so close and this location is so secluded, have your agent meet you personally. Something is not quite right with all of this, and I don't want anyone listening in on your conversation. So don't use telepathy. Gather any new information on the human female, and most importantly, find out where she is moving to, so that we can get another agent in place ahead of her."

"You can count on me as always, Commander CheRahna," TamaRah guaranteed.

"I do and I will. Thank you, TamaRah. Be careful." CheRahna smiled at her as she left, walking to Rahzu's side of the room.

Already in the Cruiser Rah, RahKael asked KaRah, "I thought TamaRah said there were two Rah defectors? What happened to the other one?"

"He is still on Earth, working behind the scenes to thwart our plans and aid the humans in developing for their next stage of evolution." TamaRah said this most seriously.

"Where is he now?" RahKael asked with fearful concern.

"We don't know. He changes his appearance, language, and mannerisms so often we can never get a fix on him." TamaRah looked around as if telling a secret. "He is a very powerful Gold. He almost surely has a tri-sword. No one has actually seen him in over a thousand Earth years, but he's there. YetziRah is quite embarrassed about the whole situation; the traitors were his agents." She paused for a moment. "If I were you, I wouldn't go around talking about this to anyone."

"I won't. I hear YetziRah's wrath can be worse than death. Thanks for the advice," RahKael said.

As the Cruiser Rahs used their energy pools to levitate, Captain Rahzu directed them out of the hangar bay and into the void. Using the energy from the Rah amber crystal on board the RJC, an intense orange yellow beam blasted out from the ship and squarely hit the amber crystal portal. In an instant, the Cruiser Rahs were gone.

Rahzu and CheRahna looked at each other with a bit of trepidation, hoping, however, for the best.

CHAPTER

SEVENTEEN

THE FIRST CRUISER Rah that exited the portal was occupied by the Silvers, Lt. KaRah, Ensign RahKael, and Lt. Commander TamaRah. KaRah and TamaRah had been here many times before, but this was RahKael's first time to Earth, in Parallel Universe 431. She did not know what to expect, though she surely thought she would see something. Thus far, this world was absolute darkness.

KaRah explained they were under almost six miles of water and that the Earth's star was not strong enough to beam light to these depths. Since this was a secret mission and no artificial illumination would be engaged, other than the lights created by the ship's energy pools, KaRah switched on the display panel, which allowed them to see every detail as if they were in full sunlight.

"This is Earth?! Where are the humans?" RahKael asked with a disappointed shock.

"All the humans live above the water and must breathe air to survive. They can only come under the oceans with the aid of devices that supplement them with varying mixtures of nitrogen, oxygen, and other minute quantities of gases," KaRah briefly explained while plotting a course to intercept the human female.

"Politics. You know they don't tell us much. Go there, do this, but the humans are quite fascinating and fairly intelligent for being as primitively developed as they are," KaRah stated matter-of-factly.

While KaRah brought the Cruiser Rah out of the trench, she decided that the fastest rate of travel would be through the air. Also, the humans have sensors and vessels called submarines, which use sonographic waves to detect objects under the water, and though they were made largely of water held together with energy, the density difference would be detected. It would only be a matter of time. At least in the atmosphere, KaRah knew the ship could avoid instrumental detection.

Additionally, they would be traveling so fast, KaRah was not concerned with visual detection, especially since they were not traveling over populated areas. Even if they were spotted, the humans would call it a UFO, an unidentified flying object, and would just assume it was a Gray spaceship performing some sort of fly-by.

RahKael was excited that at the very least she was going to get to see something while on their way to pick up the female, though they would only be out of the water for a few minutes.

KaRah was talking with TamaRah, who was getting prepared to meet with her asset. TamaRah was informing KaRah that she needed just a few minutes, at most, to ensure that she was not only able to get the information they came for, but to properly reassign her operative. They then could make haste, grab the human subject, and return through the amber portal back to Parallel Universe 430.

As the craft rose from the water, RahKael could see the glow of the moon on the surface of the sea. Beautiful, she thought, as the ship rocketed off westward, toward the other side of the planet.

Within a minute, the sky was getting brighter as they continued traveling west. The darkness faded and gave way to a powerful, bright sunny day. Now in full daylight, RahKael saw the vast blue water of the Pacific Ocean as the ship flew overhead.

"Where is the land? I saw a little in the display earlier, but was that it?" RahKael asked in puzzlement.

KaRah grinned, largely out of amusement but partly out of annoyance. She responded, "Most of the planet is covered by water, RahKael, but there are very large areas of land. You saw them when you were looking at the planet back on Rah Jump Ship 430." KaRah paused for a moment, getting her composure together. "None of these land masses, however, are along our flight path,"

TamaRah, sensing the tension, looked at KaRah, then at RahKael. While still facing Rahkael, TamaRah spoke, "Hey, KaRah, what do you say we return to the portal by going the long way, over Asia and through Africa? It'll only add a few minutes to our time."

Even though the route was longer, it would place them over several highly populated centers. Since they would be going at such a high velocity, it did not matter if they were sighted. They would be out of the universe before even one of the human's flying machines could get into the air.

"What do you think RahKael? Would you like to see more than just some blue water?" KaRah asked while thanking TamaRah for the assist.

"Sounds like a plan to me! Great idea, TamaRah! Thanks, KaRah." RahKael was so pleased she clapped several times in rapid succession.

"Calm down, it's only a few minutes' worth of travel," KaRah said with a giggle.

"We'll record it all so you can watch later," TamaRah said while turning on the flight recorder.

Another minute passed and they had nearly reached their destination. Entering the ocean again, the Cruiser Rah began to dive. KaRah noted all the naval vessels on the surface and realized that they would be picked up on sonar, especially if they traveled rapidly. She knew a trick, however, that CheRahna had taught her. She would let the ship drift down, into the depths, while sending out harmonic frequencies that would mask the Cruiser Rah's presence. Plus, they had a way to slow down Earth time. Using the energy of the amber crystal, they were able to create a vortex that brought all ions to a virtual stop. Since they were elemental in nature, they could move freely once the device was deployed, as if everything were normal.

Once the human female was taken, this vortex would be left in her place to distort time locally until they returned with her. While experiencing a loss of time, in the real world the abductee would sense nothing.

Approaching the bathysphere, the crew of the Cruiser Rah noticed a group of large mammals surrounding the bell.

"What are those?" RahKael asked.

"They are called *Balaenoptera musculus*, or blue whales," KaRah informed her.

"Well, girls, I'd love to stay and chat, but I have to meet with my operative," TamaRah said while waving goodbye. Within a second, she disappeared. Dimerians could travel in several different ways without a vehicle. One way, which was called blinking, was a form of telekinesis. But instead of moving objects, the Dimerian would move herself. During the process, the dense body completely dissociates, and the only thing traveling is energy. Upon arrival at the destination, much like teleportation, the dense body is reformed from existing material at the location. There are several problems with this type of travel. While quickly activated, it can be detected by other Dimerians. Second, since one only teleports one's own energy, enough material must be present in order to reform. If enough silver were not present upon reforming, another material would have to be chosen. This could place the traveler at risk, especially when dealing with inferior materials.

Another way of travel was called expansion or flashing. Essentially what happens is that one expands infinitely large in whatever universe one is in. A destination point is chosen, then the Dimerian rematerializes at the new location. This method of travel is superluminal, or faster than light, and is typically used when traveling great distances. Although not as quickly initiated, one does not lose one's own properties and it is harder to detect using this form of travel.

On this particular occasion, TamaRah, while being very cautious about meeting with her operative with all of the activity on the surface, chose to "blink out" to the meeting site. No Dimerians would be looking here to sense her, and no human would see her materialize 30,000 feet at the bottom of the trench. Finally, ocean water contained vast amounts of silver, thus making reforming natural for her.

Quickly and only for a moment, TamaRah used telepathy to contact her agent for their meeting at the bottom of the chasm. After a few moments, they were face to face. TamaRah would learn all she needed to know from her trusted, very capable, Rah cohort.

Meanwhile, RahKael was fascinated by the whales. "What are they doing? It looks like they are playing with the object," she said, pointing to the bathysphere on the display.

"I believe they are attempting to protect her from us. They can sense our presence and somehow know what our intentions are. No matter, though. They can do nothing," KaRah explained while moving toward the amber crystal sphere.

Placing both hands on the crystal sphere, KaRah concentrated on the occupant inside the bell-shaped object and called the human female to the ship. She whispered, "Orth-itti-Rah," which meant stop the time for a Rah.

In a flash, a blinding white beam surrounded the bathysphere. As suddenly as it appeared, it was gone. Lying on the floor in front of the Silver was Ariella Talah Marconi, number 69552.

"Is she dead?" RahKael asked, wondering if they had accidentally killed their captive.

"No, she is merely unconscious. Let's get her to the life pod before she awakens," Lt. KaRah directed as she moved toward Ariella. With Ensign RahKael's assistance, KaRah placed Ariella in the life pod, which kept her in a state of suspended animation.

Looking back at the display at the whales, which were not moving due to the placement of the time vortex, RahKael thought how beautiful the beasts were.

At that same instant, TamaRah reappeared with a sense of accomplishment about her. "Everything go well?" TamaRah said with spirit. "Has the target been acquired?"

"Yes, TamaRah. No problems at all. How was your meeting? Everything a go?" KaRah asked while plotting a course for their departure.

"Of Course! Once again, my asset did a great job and provided reliable intelligence on the subject. We know where her next assignment will be and have already began getting another agent to that location to intercept." TamaRah responded to KaRah's question while she was too mesmerized briefly by the frozen whales. "Wow! This planet does have its perks."

"I'm glad things went as planned, TamaRah," KaRah said with satisfaction as the mission appeared to be going smoothly. "Okay, RahKael, get ready! We're going to quickly show you a different part of the planet on the way back."

RahKael jumped up and down, clapping repeatedly. An odd sort of behavior, KaRah thought, but she was young, and this was her first time on Earth—a treat for anyone. KaRah finalized the flight path through Southeast Asia, over Hong Kong, through the Himalayas on the Indian Plateau, across Africa via Cairo and over the Sahara Desert, the resting place of their former comrade, and ending in the Puerto Rico Trench. KaRah felt this would give RahKael a good representation of this planet. Once finished, the ship rose from the ocean rapidly and they were in the air. Minutes later, the ship entered the portal.

EIGHTEEN

WHEN THE SECOND Cruiser Rah exited the amber crystal portal, the Golds, Lt. ShemRahya and Lt. Rahphila, were all business. They both had been here many times before, so they had no plans to sightsee.

Even though the implantation device was not working properly in the male human host, they could still locate their quarry quickly because of the unique chemical makeup of Dimerian amber crystal.

ShemRahya immediately surmised that their destination took the ship over many densely populated areas. Although they were not really concerned with being sighted, their mission was a quick snatch and grab, and they would only be on this planet for matter of minutes, ShemRahya did not want to risk the possibility of running across large amounts of air traffic originating out of the places called Miami and Atlanta.

Thus, he altered the Cruiser Rah's trajectory so that they would travel up the eastern seaboard of the United States and then veer northwest once they reached the state of Georgia. Their final destination was in southern Kentucky at a place called Mammoth Cave.

As soon as their vessel hit the open air, ShemRahya spoke. "All calculations have been set. Do you have a bearing on the human, Rahphila?"

Rahphila, standing at the amber crystalline sphere, turned and responded. "Yes, ShemRahya. The human, Jonathan Arlin Hawthorne II, number 99985, is located at 37 degrees, 12 minutes north, 85 degrees 58 minutes west. Target is moving at ground level at a rapid rate of speed, approximately 250 feet per second, northwest," Rahphila replied with exactness.

"Splendid, Rahphila. It appears our subject is traveling somewhere in a hurry. Let's get over there quickly so we can see what he's up to," ShemRahya curiously instructed.

Several minutes later, the two Dimerians were hovering high in the sky above the area where Jonathan was traveling. They witnessed the bird evacuate its bowels and the subsequent spinout. Watching Jonathan stagger to his feet and fire his pistol blindly in the air, missing his target completely, both ShemRahya and Rahphila stared, dumbfounded, as the stork fell from the air, lifeless.

"Did you see that, ShemRahya? He killed the flying creature without striking it with his primitive weapon."

"I did . . . either the shock of the event caused the premature demise of the avian creature, or there is more to this human than we previously thought," ShemRahya pondered.

"Maybe that could also explain why his implantation devices keep failing so quickly," Rahphila added. "Do you think he has telekinetic powers?"

"Possibly, Rahphila . . . possibly. I have heard of some humans who possess such powers; however, I have never had the pleasure of meeting one." ShemRahya briefly paused while thinking. "I think we should collect the carcass of the dead avian, as well as our human subject, for further investigation. It may provide us with an explanation for this peculiar event." Walking toward the display, ShemRahya turned and asked, "Rahphila, did you record the incident?"

"Yes, ShemRahya. Just as I always do," Rahphila defensively replied.

"I figured that you had. It had more to do with me checking my thought process rather than questioning your attention to detail," ShemRahya said apologetically. "Sorry, Rahphila."

"Oh . . . okay. No problem then." Rahphila switched his demeanor back to a more helpful one. "Well, what's going through your mind then?"

"I am thinking that we should get back to PU 430 and perform an independent study on the human and the lifeless creature. If no explanation presents itself, then we will show the recording to Rahzu." ShemRahya then looked at Jonathan in the display, lying on the ground and studying the stork. "If we do solve this riddle on our own, we have done our due diligence and not saddled Captain Rahzu with another problem."

"Do you think we can show the recording to TamaRah, KaRah, and RahKael? It is pretty funny if you think of it," Rahphila said, catching ShemRahya off guard. Rahphila recently had seemed to develop a sense of humor.

"What has gotten into you, Rahphila? Seems to me that TamaRah is starting to rub off on you," ShemRahya approved.

"Just trying to lighten up. Become a more positive influence."

"Good. It's working. Let's get these two and get back. Once we've solved our little enigma, I think it would be a fine idea showing the Silvers the recording . . . is that agreeable to you?"

Rahphila countered, "Of course, I had no intention of asking the Silvers for help. I think you and I can figure this out. Besides, it wouldn't hurt our records either."

"No, it definitely would not . . . it's settled then. We need to grab the human and the creature and head back. I want to get there first. KaRah's always trying to take my parking spot," ShemRahya finished with a bit of humor of his own.

Rahphila grabbed the amber sphere, concentrated, and an instant later Jonathan and the stork were on board the Cruiser Rah. After putting him into a life pod, the Dimerians guided the ship back through the portal to PU 430.

CHAPTER

NINETEEN

AT HOME, ABHAR could throw off all his pretenses and just be himself. The world did not know the real Abhar Am, and that is the way he preferred it.

Keep your friends close and your enemies closer. He had learned that adage from a close friend long, long ago. But for that to be possible, it was necessary for him to continue his charade, at least for the time being. The façade was not so much for his safety, but for the people he called his family and friends. Abhar could take care of himself.

By the time he had arrived, his wife was asleep and his dinner was in the oven. He had gotten used to his life, the way he lived, the places he worked, and those few he chose to call his friends. Grabbing a bottle of wine from the cupboard, Abhar headed to the den for his recliner. His plan was to relax for a while before getting back to business. Luckily for him, he really did not require sleep, he was not made that way. Getting the corkscrew from the end table drawer, Abhar opened the wine. A fine tasting gewürztraminer from a small winery in Oregon. After smelling the cork, he placed the open bottle in the table to breathe.

Checking his PDA, Abhar reviewed the day's events. Earlier, he was glad to see that Jonathan had gotten his message. With the reply, "K, thx," Abhar thought about calling and talking to him personally; but since it was past midnight in Nashville time, he decided against it. He felt it was important for Jonathan to enjoy his drive and clear his head, or that is what he intended to happen. Looking at the clock, eleven p.m., Abhar quickly determined that it was one a.m. where Jonathan was right then.

After he poured himself a glass of wine, Abhar slowly took a sip. Allowing the aromatic flavors to enter his sinus cavity, he swished the wine in his mouth and took a slow breath. "Ah, excellent," he said aloud. He really enjoyed drinking good wine and had learned from experience that many times, the quality of vintage from the small wineries was far superior in quality to those of the more commercialized brands.

While enjoying his vino, he focused on other events happening around the globe. Abhar liked to be a man in the know. It was safer that way. Scrolling through the PDA further, he noted that the unidentified submersible object that he had reported to Jonathan earlier, had yet to resurface. Abhar knew what was in it. There was not much on the planet, or in the solar system, for that matter, that escaped him.

He had been monitoring the spy for some time. He was still trying to figure out what the end game was. Abhar was sure that the Cruiser Rah was going down to meet with the operative, but for what purpose? The answer would present itself in time.

Continuing to search through his list of contacts and monitors, Abhar began to pour himself another glass of wine when his PDA came to life as an alert went off.

The message was from his source at Sierra Bermeja, a secret base inside Mt. Cayal, located within the boundary of the Laguna Cartagena National Wildlife Refuge on Puerto Rico. This was the same source that had alerted him to the Rah presence just over an hour ago.

To Abhar's surprise, another Cruiser Rah was seen coming from the same depths as the previous vessel, except this one was heading up the eastern seaboard.

Just as he was about to relay this message to Jonathan on the scrambler phone, another alert came in. It showed the craft turn northwest, directly toward Mammoth Cave and Jonathan.

Abhar knew this was no coincidence. Instead of texting his current employer, he attempted to call him. The phone rang with no answer. "Damn!"

Abhar said aloud, dialing again. Still no answer. He suspected with the top down, the radio up, and Jonathan traveling at a high rate of speed, there would be little chance of his getting through. Eleven fifty-two p.m. Time was running out. Abhar could sense it.

All at once, it came to him, what the Rahs were doing. They were coming for Jonathan, just as they had done many times in the past. Though Abhar knew the Rahs would take Jonathan and there was nothing he could do to prevent it, he was about to put into action a series of events that would put Jonathan's life at risk.

Pressing a few keys on his PDA, Abhar was about to send a coded message to the scrambler phone in Jonathan's possession. This was not a message for him, but one for the phone. It contained a set of detailed operations which the phone was to employ at specified times in the future. He would first have to phone deliver a slight electrical shock in order to rouse Jonathan from his state of suspended animation, which he would most likely be under. Next, he instructed the device to set off a mini-electric magnetic pulse, to destroy the control device they would be implanting in him.

Pausing for a moment before sending his message, Abhar knew two things were about to happen. First, Jonathan was either going to live or die, depending on what the Rahs wanted him for. Abhar thought he knew his lineage, and if he was correct, Jonathan would survive.

Second, his signal would be traced, compromising his location and everything he had established here. Even though the EMP would render the phone useless, destroying all its electrical components, the Rahs' sensors would be monitoring all transmission frequencies and would be able to trace its origin.

He continued to pause. Eleven fifty-four p.m. He needed to decide, and fast. Once Jonathan was taken through the portal, it would be impossible for the commands to be received, and all his present planning would be for naught.

Two Cruiser Rahs, two trenches, two people about to be working on the same mission, the amber crystal portal, and the inevitable abduction of not only Jonathan, but his future mate as well. This was not just chance.

Finger hovering over the send button, he thought of himself. He had not exposed himself in a very, very long time. He was sure it was worth it, especially considering who he believed he was involved with. He pressed the send button.

He sat there in his recliner as the potential repercussions of what he had just done sank in. He filled his glass of wine to the top, drank it, and stood up. He looked around his home briefly, one last time. He was going to miss this place, this life.

"Sarah!" he called to his sleeping wife. "Wake up, darling, it's that time. We have to leave for our new home." Hearing his wife stir and answer obediently, Abhar went over to the fireplace mantel and removed a unique-looking sword from its display.

"It's been a long time, dear friend, a long time indeed." Grabbing the handle, he quickly whirled it in successive figure eight patterns before stopping it vertically, pointing straight up. Admiring the blade for a time, he lowered it and headed for the garage. Abhar was already packed and prepared for this day. His wife, Sarah, soon joined him. Everything was about to change as they left their home forever.

CHAPTER TWENTY

STANDING ON THE bridge, Captain Rahzu was reflecting on all the recent changes to his original assignment. When he first arrived in PU 430, his mission was one of surveillance and subterfuge. He and those under his command were to study Yahweh's creation while being the proverbial thorn in his side. Rahzu had enjoyed his command and what he and his crew had accomplished. His mission was clear and concise, with definite, achievable goals.

Now, he was being kept in the dark as to what the reasons were for the recent alterations in his assignment. No longer was he just to conduct reconnaissance and covert raids meant to destabilize or manipulate the planet's geopolitical system. Those days seemed to be gone forever.

The duties being forced upon him at present, included abduction, guerrilla-style attacks, and the apparent destruction of Earth. Surely, Xanix Rah and YetziRah knew that such actions would, if they had not already; cause Yahweh to be intolerant of their presence.

Rahzu was no fool; he knew that even though being more of a creator than a destroyer, Yahweh was not one to be trifled with and that not even Xanix Rah wanted his vengeance to befall him.

Breaking his train of thought, the first Cruiser Rah came back through the portal. As predicted, ShemRahya and Rahphila came back first; they only had to abduct the specified human male and return, while the female Silvers had to abduct their female and formulate new plans with the agent working on the planet.

After directing the two Golds to the hangar bay, Rahzu ordered them to be at ease until the other ship returned. No sense inspecting the humans one at a time; he did not like redundancy.

Waiting for the other ship to return, the captain continued to contemplate his current predicament. Slowly, an idea seeped into his mind. He walked over to the amber crystal and used it to pull up information on PU 78. Rahzu knew of the planet ET-Rah, which had been secretly created there and kept hidden from the Dimerian council. Though must members of the House of Rah were not privy to this information, Rahzu had been briefed about its existence. However, he had not been informed of any plans associated with it.

Using the database, Rahzu zoomed in on the planet's surface to investigate. He was looking to see what knowledge he could gain by accessing the files. Not much. It was noticed that more complex flora had spread over much of the planet and complex sea life was starting to flourish.

Suddenly, the answer came to him. How could he have been so naïve that he did not see it before? He knew what Xanix Rah and YetziRah were up to, or at least part of it.

At the very same time the epiphany came to him, the second Cruiser Rah containing the human female exited from the amber portal. As directed, it too headed toward the hangar bay.

Rahzu, feeling a little more relieved for at least having a theory about what his superiors had planned, was now able to switch his focus to keeping his crew and himself alive during these troubled times.

In the hangar bay, crews from both shuttles were waiting patiently for their captain. Before leaving the bridge, Rahzu had called for CheRahna to join him. Together, once she arrived, they made their way down to inspect the humans. Rahzu was not ready to share what he had discovered, not just yet. He wanted to let things percolate for a while to see if his assumptions were correct. He would confide in her when the time was right.

As the captain and commander entered the hangar bay, the crew ended their conservations and stood at attention to greet them. The life pods containing the humans were on display for inspection. After Rahzu finished looking over the humans, he inquired about the dead ciconine creature and why it too was brought here.

ShemRahya quickly told him about the incident involving subject number 99985 and the stork that he was going to have Science Officer Rahphila conduct some tests on to determine the reason for the avian's death.

Being proud of his lieutenant, Rahzu commended him for his swift thinking and proactive behavior. He also ordered the senior science officer, Lt. Commander TamaRah, to assist Lt. Rahphila with not only the investigation involving the mysterious death of the bird, but also the removal and reimplantation of the monitoring devices in the humans.

Although ShemRahya's thoughts were to have himself and Rahphila perform the evaluation on the stork, he realized, though, that he was still getting credit for his reasoning. Besides, ShemRahya wanted to coordinate with KaRah about the plan to return the humans. There were also some questions he had concerning certain transmissions he was noticing back on Earth, in PU 431.

Lt. Rahphila, however, was ecstatic that he would be working with Lt. Commander TamaRah. He had been spending more and more time with her lately and really enjoyed her company.

TamaRah too was pleased about her new assignment. She was glad Captain Rahzu gave the order for her to assist Rahphila; she was not ready to openly admit she had developed feelings for him, which is not normal for Dimerians.

Although Golds were male and Silvers were female, they did not procreate by mating. They merely created a son or daughter—once, of course, they had evolved enough. But TamaRah had concluded that her operatives on Earth, as well as herself, had all started to develop mannerisms common to humans. Having experienced many sensory pleasures of the flesh, such as taste, smell, and the feel of the warm sun or a cool breeze, she began to wonder what the act of love making felt like. She longed to experience everything that was human and wanted to share that bit of pleasure with Rahphila. She also sensed that he too was starting to acquire more and more human traits.

Rahphila walked up to TamaRah and motioned to her, saying, "Lead the way, Commander," in a playful, flirtatious manner.

"Why thank you, Lieutenant. That is quite gentlemanly of you;" replying with some coquettishness of her own.

Their behavior did not go unnoticed. Rahzu had seen it many times before. He had even experienced a bit of humanity himself, long ago. The jocosity of his lieutenant commander and lieutenant left him feeling a little nostalgic. However, he was the captain and could not indulge in such horseplay. Rahzu also knew, because many of his crew worked so closely with and among humans, that it was inevitable that a few of them would begin to adopt some human characteristics. His responsibility was, however, to not let things get out of hand. Thus far, it had not.

CheRahna too had witnessed the flirtatious behavior of the subordinates. She was not as understanding as the captain was about allowing the crew to toy with fleshly, human experiences. But it was not her command, and therefore not her decision. She would, however, monitor the crew's performance and behavior, and if necessary, would relater her concerns to the captain.

Commander CheRahna adamantly refused to have anyone associated with her defect from the House of Rah. If anyone did, she would personally and completely end that Rahan's existence. It was already embarrassing enough to be affiliated with the previous defectors.

Rahzu knew CheRahna would not like what they had just observed, and he knew why it bothered her so. But ruling with an iron fist was not his style, and it rarely proved to be effective. He was confident, though, that if things started getting out of control, she would be quick to inform him.

"Commander," Captain Rahzu said to get her attention.

"Yes, Captain?" CheRahna answered, slightly irritated over the situation.

Pointing toward TamaRah and Rahphila, Rahzu suggested, "Give those two a little latitude. But if it gets out of hand, I want you to take care of it. Can you do that, CheRahna?" he finished in a supporting tone.

"Yes, Captain Rahzu. I will do my best not to allow my personal feelings to interfere with my judgment, sir." She was a tad bit humiliated that her emotions were getting the best of her and that they were so easily noticed.

"CheRahna . . . you are the finest officer I've ever had under my command; and one day, hopefully soon, you will make a finer captain than I. However, you are not perfect yet, so don't be so hard on yourself. Dimeria wasn't built in a day. Oh, sorry, it was," he finished humorously to break the tension.

CheRahna stoically stood there for a second before she broke out in laughter. Rahzu was right as usual. She was thankful for his positive remarks, but had her doubts as to whether or not she would make as fine as a captain as he. "Rahzu, if I become half the captain that you have been for me and this crew, it would bring great honor to the House of Rah." Her silver form glowed a little brighter.

"Indeed you will, CheRahna. Indeed you will."

⌣

After the inspection was over, ShemRahya and KaRah quickly paired off and got down to business. Both being security officers, though they did laugh and joke some, they had to be serious. The safety of the entire Rah Jump Craft was, together, in their hands.

Theirs was a very odd arrangement. No other commanding officer split responsibilities so evenly as Captain Rahzu had with his security detail. He felt that the natural male reaction to situations was at times too tyrannical, while, on the other hand, the female lack of action, at times, was too liberal. Rahzu had personally chosen these two straight out of the Rah Academy quite some time ago. He got hold of them, as he often said, before they were overly influenced by a corrupt system.

All security issues were discussed, and a consensus agreed upon before any action was taken. That, of course, did not include those times when immediate action was required. This primarily dealt with planning and disciplinary actions.

On those occasions when the two officers disagreed, the one with a stronger affinity for their point of view won out. So far, ShemRahya and KaRah had only needed the captain to intercede on one occasion, and that was not over an impasse. The junior officers just did not know how to handle the situation.

ShemRahya and KaRah had talked, in detail, about the captain's insightfulness in regard to directing them to work together as one. It amazed them how well they performed their duties, which both took very seriously.

"How is the trainee coming along?" ShemRahya asked, sensing KaRah's annoyance.

KaRah, looking around carefully, was finally comfortable enough to release her frustration pertaining to the new ensign. "It's not her questions, ShemRahya. We all had them when we first got here." She paused while composing herself.

"It's her pompous attitude. She speaks as if she has all the answers. That everything we've been doing is wrong!" KaRah finished emphatically.

"Has she said as much?" ShemRahya questioned.

"No!"

"Then how do you know that is what she thinks?" He was aware KaRah could sense the feelings, thoughts, and actions of the younger, less evolved grayish silver female.

"Really!" She smacked him on the shoulder to relieve some of her anger. ShemRahya just laughed.

"Do you want to go to the hold and spar for a bit to release some more of that anger? A good sword lashing might do you some good." He was picking on her now.

"In your dreams, you might get lucky and get a hit in, but I doubt it," KaRah said sneeringly, though she was merely playing with him.

She knew that few could match ShemRahya's swordsmanship. Not even the captain, who had participated and won in the Dimerian Ring, could defeat him in the practice ring. If it was not for his active service here, in Parallel Universe 430, ShemRahya would have been a sure bet to represent the House of Rah in the Blade Wars. He was one of the few Dimerians who, with practice, she believed had a chance to dethrone the champion from the House of Yah, ZYah Zeh, God of the Blades.

"You know, her attitude will change, and she'll learn some respect, or it will make her careless, and it will bury her," ShemRahya said flatly. "It will all work itself out, you'll see."

"I suppose you are right. I'm betting that her attitude won't change, though." KaRah said matter-of-factly.

"Maybe . . . KaRah. On Earth, did you notice a weird frequency bouncing off your Cruiser Rah when you exited the water?"

"I did . . . why do you ask?" She was interested to see if he had a theory as to what it might be.

"I'm merely speculating, mind you; but I think Dimerian technology is tracking our movements on Earth," ShemRahya admitted. "But I have no proof."

"What makes you think it's Dimerian?" KaRah pressed for an answer.

"Well . . . any other signal that hits the Cruiser Rah is easily detected and interpreted. This wavelength, however, is so subtle, I only noticed it when I exited the craft to place a Rah crystal on a ley line. The power of the Earth along its energy grid apparently increased the intensity of the frequency, that was why I became aware of it. Since then, I have been paying close attention. It's always there . . . right when the Cruiser Rah leaves the ocean," ShemRahya finished, looking to KaRah for an answer.

"I picked up the same sort of signal today . . . let me correct myself. RahKael picked up the strange signal today." KaRah hated to admit that. "She came up with a theory that it was a Rah frequency, a very old Rah frequency, that we were noticing."

"Wow, that had to hurt, admitting that," ShemRahya prodded as he guarded himself preparing for a hit that never came.

"You'll never know," KaRah sighed.

"Do you think her theory is correct?"

"Unfortunately, ShemRahya, I do."

"If this is true and RahKael is correct, there is only one Rah that comes to mind capable of doing this," ShemRahya concluded.

"But he hasn't been seen or heard of for many, many years. Do you really think it is him?" KaRah asked, almost in shock.

"I don't know." She questioned his assumption.

ShemRahya told her of an ancient adage. "A true warrior always reflects weakness when he is strong; always attacks an enemy where the weakness lies; and the best trick of all is when a warrior lies dormant, making his opponent believe he is no longer relevant or even exists," ShemRahya said solemnly.

KaRah chewed on this idea for a moment before responding. "We should talk to RahKael about how and why she believes it's an ancient Rah frequency. Especially considering what you are suggesting."

"We better get up there then and have a talk with little miss know-it-all." ShemRahya could not help himself.

"Shut up! Let's go."

After bringing the life pods containing the humans to the area where they were to be examined, TamaRah and Rahphila flirtatiously conversed while working to remove the current monitoring devices from the human subjects.

These instruments were stealthily placed in a person's back, right between the shoulder blades. This particular area, which is one of the two main energy centers of the body—the other is located just below the ball of the foot—was used not only for supplying energy for transmissions, but, with all that bioelectrical energy, it made detection of the monitoring instrument virtually undetectable unless someone was specifically looking for it.

In the process of examining Ariella's chemical and electrical makeup, Rahphila made an unexpected discovery. "TamaRah, this one appears to be pregnant, and judging by the trace amounts of hormones being released, it just happened," Rahphila said with a grin.

TamaRah, working on Jonathan, asked quickly, "When . . . this week?"

"No, TamaRah, today."

TamaRah stopped what she was doing for a second and let her mind imagine what the human female must have experienced just a few hours ago. She wanted to know that feeling.

Rahphila continued, "And estimating by the amount of semen still in her vaginal cavity, it appears that she had coitus more than once."

Little did Rahphila know that this nearly caused TamaRah to go over the tipping point and flat out demand him to occupy a fleshly human body so she too could have sex. If she could already have had the discussion with Rahphila that she had planned to . . .

The thought left her mind, though, for now, and she finally removed the monitoring device from Jonathan. All the electrical circuits were melted. "Rahphila, bring your sexy body over here and look at this," partly being playful, mostly serious. She was perplexed. "What do you make of this?"

Looking at the device, Rahphila could clearly see it had been destroyed by some type of electrical force. However, he too was a bit confused by what could have accomplished this. "Look right here," Rahphila said, motioning for TamaRah to come closer, much closer. While pointing at what he had discovered, he stated, "You see here. These electrodes were slowly, over time, burnt by a constant energy. And these . . ." Rahphila turned his head to find TamaRah's face right next to his. He was not exactly sure what he was feeling at that particular time, but he certainly liked it.

TamaRah also liked being close to Rahphila and could sense his excitement. He attempted to continue what he was saying, "These . . . ah . . . have been fried by . . . some sort of . . . EMP . . . but much later . . . after the device was already ruined." He managed to finish his thought, with difficulty.

Though TamaRah was listening and still interested in finding out what had caused the instrument to fail, she was more interested in Rahphila. She threw her left arm over his shoulder and around his neck and asked sensually, "So you're saying"—while drawing on his chest with her index finger—"that you think that somehow, the human male's body initially fried the circuitry, hmm?"

Rahphila was flustered. This avalanche of strange but exhilarating feelings was almost overwhelming. He only managed to get out an "Uh huh."

"Well . . . let's put the bird in the scanner and . . . we'll wait to see what the cause of death was. Sound good?" She was about to explode from the anticipation.

"Okay . . ." He was nearly drooling.

TamaRah was building him up to pop the question. She had him right where she wanted him. "You enjoy eating food and drinking wine when in the flesh, right?"

"Sure," he said a little more clearly as he regained some of his composure.

"We have seen each other when we have donned the flesh . . . do you find this human form appealing?" At that very second, she materialized in human flesh, except she was completely nude.

While she rubbed one of her voluptuous breasts against his chest, causing her nipples to get hard, Rahphila was unsure of what was happening. Reflexively, he changed into his human form, nude also. Looking down, he quickly noticed that TamaRah's nipples were not the only thing getting hard. He was out of control and unsure what to do about it.

TamaRah, also looking down at his erect penis with her beautiful amber eyes, giggled and said, "Let's go back to my room for some privacy, and I'll show you what this is for." Firmly grabbing his hardness, she continued, "I want to experience what this human woman did this morning—for scientific purposes, of course."

"Of course . . . for science!" Rahphila realized that he wanted her, and he had for a long time. At this point, he would do whatever she asked.

Changing back into their respective Dimerian forms, they left the life pods and the scanner, which was evaluating the stork, for more exciting scientific research.

On the way to her room, TamaRah was recalling what the spy had told her about making love. When broaching the subject, even the asset would get aroused. She had experienced the pleasure that TamaRah had been fantasizing about. Now, finally, it was her time to make some memories, to have a story to tell. And with the one person she wanted to make love with. TamaRah could not remember the last time she was this excited.

CHAPTER

TWENTY ONE

ƎƎING IN A state of suspended animation, Jonathan dreamed of nothing. However, as soon as Abhar's encrypted phone began to stimulate him, his training kicked in and he sprang out of the life pod, which was programmed to open on movement, like a Jack-in-the-box.

All his Ranger training at Fort Benning, Georgia; his experience on covert missions in Bosnia, Kosovo, Afghanistan, and Iraq with the 75th Ranger Regiment; the secret raids and torture as a Delta Force solider; and his introduction into the secret world in which he now lives, all aided in preparing him for this moment.

Jonathan was locked, cocked, and ready to rock, except that he had no firearm. *Where am I and what's that awful taste in my mouth*, he thought. Not focusing on the taste too much, Jonathan was paying attention to the where. He had been in many hell holes all over the globe, and sometimes under it so deep it was sweltering, where one might think they were already knocking on purgatory's door. He realized he was aboard some type of spacecraft, but not like any he had been on or seen before.

Surveying his environment—one of the first things a soldier should do— he noted that while the ship's structure was an opaque solid, it resembled frozen water, but without the cold. The room he was in was large, at least 50 feet square. It had many pools of different colors—blue, green, yellow, orange and gray, to name a few. The largest pool, by far, was amber in color. The same color as the crystal.

Continuing his survey, he saw the capsule he had been lying in, as well as another, which he would inspect after he completed his scan of the surroundings.

One of the first groups of objects he noticed, other than the colorful pools, was the arrangement of weapons on the wall. Various slings, spears, bows, muzzle-loading pistols, and swords. There was even a gadget that appeared to be a primitive atlatl.

What really caught his eye, however, was the assortment of swords, every shape and size. Some, such as the samurai sword hanging to his right, he was familiar with. Others he was not. While all were beautiful and precision crafted, one in particular struck his fancy. It occupied the center position in this elaborate display, which Jonathan deemed significant.

It was unique—three gold blades molded into one. He had never seen anything like it before. As his training would suggest, he walked over to the display and reached for the weapon. It was about the same size as a samurai sword, but a tad wider and longer. This sword was built for both power and speed. Its blade tip was pointed slightly upward and outward, undoubtedly handy when disarming another being. There were three gemstones inlaid in the cross guard. As Jonathan grabbed the hilt, he was surprised to see the central gemstone light up in a brilliant deep yellowish green hue. He tested his facility with the weapon as he swung it in a concise circular and figure-eight motion, with alternating hands and using a dual grip. The sword was perfectly balanced, razor sharp, and incredibly light. Jonathan was not sure what type of metal it was made of, but considering where he was, it was sure to be something he had never heard of.

Now armed with something other than the various knives he carried, he felt more at ease proceeding with his assessment of his situation. On the wall adjacent to the weapons display was what appeared to be a flow chart, except Jonathan could not read it. He assumed it to be an operational guide or command hierarchy.

Along the center of the wall, opposite to where he stood, was a sphere of amber crystal on a pedestal that closely resembled the one he was heading to study in the Puerto Rico Trench. Careful not to have any contact with the sphere, knowing that many crystals contain powers that could kill the uninitiated, he bent forward to get a better visual inspection. The whole crystalline structure, fracture lines, color, and clarity all seemed to be identical to what he had researched at the S-4 facility.

This object was huge, about the size of a medicine ball—tens of thousands of carats, he guessed. Other than the amber crystal, which he concluded was some type of control and storage device, the only objects in the room that seemed to have any practical purpose were the multicolored pools, a three-foot cubic box that was gyrating, and two capsules, one of which he had occupied. Jonathan could only assume it contained someone else, but who?

The capsule, while mostly opaque, glowed with a soft white light. Looking down, the top was translucent, allowing him to see inside. To his astonishment, he recognized the woman he was on his way, indirectly, to meet. It was Ariella Talah Marconi. "Wow!" he whispered.

Ariella was even more gorgeous in person. She possessed a simple kind of beauty that would make any man smile. She wore little makeup, and what she did wear was done sparingly, just enough to highlight her eyes and cheekbones.

Jonathan studied her face as she slept. There was a peaceful, innocent, and relaxed look on her face, which accented her smooth, wrinkle-free complexion and made her skin appear to glow. This was the type of woman Jonathan could imagine waking up next to in the morning.

After being lost in her innocence for a while, he snapped back into reality as he heard someone—or something—approaching. With a silent quickness, he and the sword returned to the pod he had awoke in. His plan was to play possum and gain some intel on the situation before he formulated a plan of action. He lay in wait, coiled like a rattlesnake, ready to strike.

CHAPTER

TWENTY TWO

ENSIGN RAHKAEL HAD been briefly reviewing the flight recording of the trip to Earth. She studied the majestic blue whales, the towering Himalayan peaks, and the sprawling cities of Hong Kong, Delhi, and Cairo. She was bewildered as to why humans could be so cavalier in destroying Yahweh's beautiful creation, their home, the Earth. She felt disgusted just thinking about being around them.

While she had seen pictures of humans and had viewed them on the display monitor on the Cruiser Rah, RahKael decided it was time to see one up close, face to face.

She stepped out of the Cruiser Rah on a mission to see the humans in the life pods. As RahKael strutted out of the hangar, she exuded confidence in herself. Her intention was to show her superiors what they did not know—a thing or two about these humans. RahKael also wanted to have another look at the frequency which only she had detected and figure out what it actually was. The others were skeptical, though. She would show them, she thought. RahKael had high aspirations and was not going to let anyone stand in her way.

As she neared the room, she was curious as to why the male repeatedly kept burning up his monitoring devices. She was going to run tests on him as well, cross-checking his frequency with the one she had discovered on her earlier flight.

Entering the room, she saw that the male's pod had been opened. RahKael walked over to see if he had been revived. He was not moving, and being too busy to check his brain activity she just figured he must have been jostled enough in his static state for the automatic slide to open.

Staring down at this human, she wondered what all the fuss was about. The young ensign was over a foot taller, undoubtedly stronger, smarter, and faster—essentially better in every way. RahKael supposed it was a fascination with lesser creatures that the others had—an interest she did not share. She knew why she was here and what she was looking for. As she turned to the crystal sphere to determine his frequency, Jonathan popped his eyes open to see a grayish, silver giant walking away from him.

Although having no real defining characteristics, he could tell this humanoid was a female by the shape of its body. Other than that, there were no features—no eyes, ears, nose, or hair. The gray silver female did have feet and hands with opposable thumbs and stood at least seven feet tall. As he watched, she worked with the crystal. *What is she doing?* he thought to himself.

RahKael was comparing Jonathan's electronic frequency to that of the earlier transmission. As she suspected, they were indeed similar, both being Dimerian in origin. Although his was not Rah, as the other wave was, he contained a pattern she was familiar with. Being fresh out of the Rah training academy, she had the most up-to-date knowledge available, information her crew mates were probably not current with.

As the data glowed in a holographic cloud, she felt a rush of excitement course through her. She was right! This human not only had a large percentage of Dimerian in him, but it was of the House of Yah. He was the God seed and she had found him. There was also something else, which she did not understand, but that was not important to her right now. She smugly said, "I knew it! My destiny marches on. I'm going to be the first female leader of the House of Rah."

Her visions of grandeur were interrupted by . . . yes, the human is awake, she sensed. Without turning around, she spoke out loud. "I know you are awake and watching me . . . human." She showed her disgust by stressing the final word.

Jonathan, being used to dealing with the Grays, was not all that surprised that this being could sense his alertness. What was a surprise to him, however, was that he heard her thoughts as she was gathering information from the amber sphere.

When RahKael finished speaking, he, more to himself than to her, thought, *You're not going to have to worry about being the head of anything, because you're about to lose yours.*

RahKael turned around swiftly, hearing what he said by reading his mind! This primitive creature just read her thoughts. How was that possible? It must be the Dimerian in him.

Jonathan rudely interrupted her thoughts again, this time with words from his mouth. "I don't know about all this Dimerian, Rah, Yah bullshit, but enough of this telepathy shit. It's giving me a headache." He leapt from the pod and quickly, with one revolution of a figure eight, brandished the tri-sword. "Let's dance."

"Ah, the little human has a toy. He wants to play. Be careful, little man, that blade you've chosen can destroy you just by you holding it wrong." RahKael was confident as she sashayed over to the wall to select a blade of her own.

She noted that only the first gemstone was illuminated on Jonathan's tri-sword, and so it posed no threat to her. Only at maximum power could her essence be forever lost, and only from a mortal wound. It was highly unlikely that an untrained Dimerian could activate or even control the god killer at full power. It would be nearly impossible for this lowly human to do so, even if he did have Yah in him.

Jonathan poised, motionless, at the ready. He always thought it foolish to go through a long, elaborate display of swordsmanship to try and intimidate an adversary. He learned in kendo, one slash, one kill, much like sniper school's one shot, one kill motto.

RahKael, after grabbing a sword, whirled it around in a lavish display of movement. There was no doubt she was remarkably familiar with the blade, but Jonathan was not easily intimidated. Hubris would be her Achilles' heel, he thought.

Ensign RahKael sensed he was not fearful of her. No matter. What was perplexing, though, was there seemed to be almost no thoughts she could actually make sense of, except for one phrase he kept repeating . . . conjunction, junction, what's your function . . . Nevertheless, she confidently stated, "I'll try not to kill you, but I can't make any promises. Accidents happen," RahKael said brazenly.

Jonathan still just stood there, both hands on the hilt of the sword, which was pointing back and down toward the ground on his left side, while repeating his mantra.

The silver female raised her blade and engaged to attack. As her blade started its downward motion toward Jonathan's head, in one fluid motion he moved forward and brought the tri-sword upward at a 45-degree angle. Just before his blade struck the arrogant female, slashing her from below the stomach upward to her right armpit, the second gemstone lit up with the same yellow green glow.

The strike, while not lethal, did give her pause as she tried to recover from the damaging blow. RahKael had noticed that prior to striking her, the second gemstone was mysteriously activated. But the human's motions were so fluid and precise, it caught her completely unprepared. How did he move that fast? How could he beat me?

Before that thought was finished, Jonathan continued the sword's motion, while rotating his wrists 180 degrees, causing the sword to face left, parallel to the ground at neck level, the third gemstone activated. As he reversed the blade's direction and cleaved her head from her neck, he answered her last question, "Because Rangers lead the way, bitch!"

RahKael knew her life was over; his words were the last ones she would hear. So much for destiny.

Suddenly, a rush of electrical energy and amber smoke billowed from the headless corpse. Jonathan backed away, not exactly sure what was about to happen. The energy seemed to be attracted to the sword. Not being one to block the natural course of things, he moved back toward the body and touched the electrical amber cloud with the blade. To his astonishment, the sword absorbed all the smoke and electricity. The only remnant of the humanoid braggart was a pool of tarnished-looking silver spreading across the floor.

Jonathan was unsure whether this swift battle had alerted others to his present condition of being awake. He had no intention of getting trapped in this room.

Quickly moving to the other pod, he poked and prodded at it until Ariella moved. The automatic slide door was activated. Slowly, Ariella opened her chocolate brown eyes to see a pair of light hazel green eyes staring down at her. Before she could react, a man's deep voice calmly informed her that he was not there to harm her, but to help and that they were in danger and needed to move, now.

"Whaaat? . . . Wh—Wh—Where am I? Uh . . . who are you?!" she asked, frightened.

Jonathan calmly said, "Miss Marconi, I am Major Jonathan Hawthorn, Delta Force. I know we haven't met, but you're going to have to trust me. We're in grave danger and must leave here yesterday."

Ariella not only loved the sound of his voice, but the quality of it was one of complete, commanding confidence. She immediately trusted what the man said, which until recently had never happened. Getting out of the pod capsule, she reached for the man who stood before her.

Major Jonathan Hawthorn was a well-built, muscular man who appeared to be in peak physical condition. He looked to be about her age, thirty-six, and stood about five feet nine inches tall. Jonathan had reddish brown hair, which was in the typical high and tight style common in the military. His facial structure was not round or rectangular, but somewhere in between. He had a short nose and thin lips. He had fair skin with some freckles, but he had a good complexion and a decent tan.

Major Hawthorn was a handsome man, not the kind of looks that a woman would go gaga over, but good looking nonetheless. The one peculiar thing she noticed, which struck her as odd, is that her savior had a dried white crusty substance on the right side of his face. Considering the situation, though, she thought it better to ignore it.

Jonathan's eyes were what made him special. They were why Ariella was listening to him now. His eyes were light hazel green, but she suspected that they changed color and intensity depending on his mood. There was also a thin yellow ring around each pupil, like that of a cat, a lion. If eyes are the windows to the soul, as is said, then Jonathan's soul was very old and wise.

While intuition told her he was an honorable, just, and kind man, she sensed the animal lying just under the surface.

When Jonathan looked at her and spoke, she could not help but trust him. He had that regal quality about him that she desperately needed as she became aware of her surroundings.

As he offered his right hand to assist her exiting the pod, she asked him, already fearfully knowing the answer, "Are we in San Francisco? You are the same Major Hawthorn that I'm supposed to meet and go to Puerto Rico with?!"

"No, ma'am, we are not in San Francisco or Puerto Rico," Jonathan answered while moving his hand in an arch, directing her to look around the room. "But I am the man you are to meet, Miss Marconi. I wish I could tell you more, but now is not the time. We need to move, and quickly."

Jonathan urged her on as he lightly tugged on her arm. At that instant, she saw a glint of light on the sword, which he had tucked under his belt on his left side. Seeing him armed and trusting he knew how to use it, offered her a little sense of security while sending a chill up her spine. Completely believing and trusting him, she obediently followed.

Although she had the feeling that this man was used to giving orders and getting his way, hence his rank, she determined his judgment was better than hers and that he would protect her. At least she hoped he would.

Jonathan braced her lower back with his left hand as she stepped to the floor, slowly getting her balance. Ariella noticed his light but firm touch and guessed that this Major Jonathan Hawthorn was an old-fashioned romantic at heart.

"Please don't call me ma'am. It makes me feel like an old woman," Ariella asked politely.

"Sorry, ma'am . . . I mean, sorry, Miss Marconi. It just comes from my upbringing," Jonathan said, smiling.

"Ariella, please call me Ariella. And should I call you Major or Jonathan?" She attempted a bit of nervous humor.

Jonathan nearly said, "You can call me anything you want, as long as you call me," but decided against it at the last second. This was not the time or place for flirtatious humor. "Yes, ma'am . . . shit!!! Yes, Jonathan would be just fine, Ariella."

Her eyes lit up and she smiled at his bit of profanity. She was right; there was an animal in there! "Good, now I don't feel like an old woman anymore."

"I doubt you're going to have to worry about that for quite some time." A tasteful compliment.

As Jonathan led her out the room, she looked around. She was obviously not on Earth anymore. Her mind started to come to the reality that she was on some sort of spacecraft. But one unlike any she had never seen in the movies.

If it was not for her brave and calm leader, she probably would have crawled back into her capsule and cried herself to sleep while wishing her ass back to Kansas, though that was not entirely true. She was a survivor and would have sooner or later stopped feeling sorry for herself and got out of the pod.

They were walking down a hallway when they came to a glowing golden circle. Jonathan looked up and noticed the contour of another circle on the ceiling. Knowing enough about alien technology from previous experience, he led Ariella to join him inside the gold ring. As they did, an amber light surrounded them, and a circular hole in the ceiling appeared. When they started to rise, Ariella grabbed Jonathan in an embrace for security. He reflexively wrapped his right arm around her waist while looking up. She felt safe in his arms.

All of Jonathan's senses were on high alert. Despite his having been in many alien craft and been into space, he was totally unaware of where they were, where they were going, or, most importantly, how they were going to get out of there.

On reaching the next level, Jonathan extended his hand for her to grab, which she did, and they exited the Golden Ring. He saw a large display screen on the opposite wall. Near it was another spherical amber crystal on a pedestal, this one twice as large. Leading her over to the screen, Jonathan whispered, "I think this is the bridge. Look here," looking at the large display. The only thing they both saw, other than empty space, was an enormous amber crystal. This one matched the dimensions of the one at the bottom of the Puerto Rico Trench.

"What the hell is that?!" Ariella said pointing at the crystal on the screen.

Jonathan merely put his index finger to his lips and respectfully but quickly shushed her without diverting his attention from the display.

The new mission, their presence here, Gilla's intuition, the reports from Abhar about the USOs coming out of the water near Puerto Rico, one amber crystal found in the trench and another here . . . ? It came to him!

After a long, uncomfortable pause, he said flatly, "It's a portal," looking directly at Ariella as if she had come to the same conclusion.

"A porthole . . . what are you talking about, Jonathan, there's no window here?!" Ariella nervously asked.

Jonathan pointed to the screen. "You see that amber crystal?"

She nodded.

"There is one just like it in the Puerto Rico Trench . . . that's why we were going there, to study it. And I said port-al, not porthole." He noticed her starting to comprehend what he was saying—portal.

"Uh . . . okay. But how does that make this a portal? And to where?"

Jonathan took a deep breath and paused. He knew she was questioning him because she did not understand and not because she doubted him. Still, it was going to take some time to get used to this behavior. It is hard for anyone to change the way they feel, including him. He asked her, "Do you see any stars or planets . . . or anything out there?" Jonathan knew she did not, because there was nothing.

She shook her head side to side.

"And that looks like space, empty space, right?" Jonathan patiently asked, spoon-feeding her the information. It was important to him that she understood. It is impossible to cope with a situation if the situation is unknown.

"Yes . . . Jonathan, you're scaring me!" Ariella said as tears were welling up in her eyes. This day had been a roller-coaster ride for sure. A very scary ride. She was overwhelmed.

Jonathan used his right thumb to wipe the first tear as it fell. He hated to see a woman cry, it pulled his heart strings . . . But he was not such a sap as to be manipulated by them, as some men are. Ariella's tears came from real fear, anxiety, and overload. He needed her to calm down if they were to have any chance of getting out of there alive.

Putting both hands on her shoulders and looking her directly in her eyes, he began, "I'm sorry, Ariella. I'm not trying to scare you, but I need you to be aware of what we're facing. I'm here with you, and I will fight to my dying breath to get you out of here and back to safety. Now . . . I need you to realize that we are not on Earth, we have been abducted by some pretty tall metallic-looking aliens, and that if they wanted us dead, we would probably be dead." Jonathan paused to see if she was grasping all he had just said. Ariella had a lost, bewildered look on her face, staring into the nothingness. *At least she's not crying anymore*, he thought.

"Ariella!" Jonathan snapped his fingers in front of her face. She was in a state of shock, but came out of it.

"I'm just having a hard time taking this all in right now," she whimpered.

"Trust me, this is really happening."

"That's the thing, Jonathan . . . I know it is. All of this is as real to me now as you are. I have dreamed of this before," Ariella said calmly, but with a crazed look in her eyes.

"What do you mean, you dreamed this before?!" Jonathan was feeling a bit scared at hearing what she had just revealed, although he did not show it.

"You know . . . like déjà vu, only much more vivid," Ariella answered, looking at Jonathan to see if he believed her. She urgently needed him to believe her, to prove to herself she was not crazy.

"It all makes sense now!" he said.

"Uh . . . you believe me?!" Ariella was relieved. She had never told anyone about her dreams, as she liked to call her premonitions, for fear she would be labeled a freak, or just plain crazy, which until now she had not ruled out.

"Not only do I believe you, but I believe both of us have been kidnapped by these beings before." Jonathan's pupils were dilated as he spoke.

Ariella was impressed with this Jonathan Hawthorn—cool under pressure, precise, confident, and positive, all the things she was not. Most importantly, he knew, at least up until now, exactly how to handle her—a contradiction surrounded by mystery and wrapped in an enigma. "Okay . . . what does it all mean . . . and what do we do now?"

Before Jonathan could answer, a voice from across the room, where they had come in, interrupted them.

"It means that you two are somewhere you shouldn't be, and what you both are going to do is return to your pods, with or without your consent."

Jonathan sprang into action, drew his sword, and positioned himself between Ariella and the being. What was in front of him was gold, over seven feet tall, a male version of the female Silver he had slain earlier. This Gold, however, was calm while patiently waiting for a reply. He must be the leader, Jonathan surmised.

Ariella was agasp. She was not sure what she was looking at, but it was very alluring with its gold form. Curious, but that is how she felt. She sensed that he meant them no harm.

Rahzu, reading the thoughts of the humans, quickly learned that the human male had beheaded his new, young pilot trainee with the same tri-sword he was holding now. The first gem was activated.

With his telepathy, Captain Rahzu contacted CheRahna and ordered her to the bridge. He slowly but methodically moved away from the entrance and toward the amber crystal. A cornered animal tends to panic; he did not want to harm them. Also, he knew CheRahna was coming to spring the trap and sneak up behind them. "You are right, Jonathan Hawthorn. I am the captain of this vessel. My name is Rahzu, and yes, Ariella Marconi, I have no intention of harming either of you." Rahzu wanted to see their reaction when they realized he was listening to their thoughts.

The male showed no response. Knowing RahKael, she tormented him and bragged about herself enough for him to know of their skills of telepathy. Ariella, even though she showed surprise, reacted with more curiosity than expected.

Jonathan circled right, as the Gold did, always careful to keep the proper distance to maintain his circle of protection. Rahzu was still far away from them. Jonathan was having no luck reading Rahzu's thoughts, though. He also realized there were too many simultaneous factors present for him to isolate his thoughts with his mantra. He not only had to listen carefully, to gain helpful intel, but to protect both Ariella and himself.

"Why are you holding us? What are we doing here?!" Ariella confidently shouted.

"It is really quite simple. We are studying and monitoring you. We have been doing this to both of you for the past thirty years. You are periodically picked up, brought to this universe; Parallel Universe 430, through our portal . . ." Rahzu pointed to the amber crystal seen in the display. "And then we return you, unharmed," Rahzu told them the truth. Not that it mattered; they would not remember any of this once they were returned to Earth.

"Parallel Universe 430. You mean there are 430 different universes!?" Ariella was questioning Rahzu as she had Jonathan earlier.

Jonathan was relieved to know he was right about her inquisitiveness.

As Rahzu picked up on Jonathan's thought, he laughed. "No, actually there are 777 universes. Your Earth is in PU 431, and we are now in PU 430. But none of this is important right now." Rahzu focused his full attention on Jonathan, who was still mimicking his movements, the sword, held with both hands, raised straight up over his right shoulder.

"Now, as for you, Major Hawthorn. What am I to do with you? I see you have been trained well. Kendo, I believe that is what it's called nowadays. But you see"—Rahzu was gone—"I do not need"—he said from behind Ariella, then disappeared—"a sword"—he whispered in Jonathan's ear and vanished—"to defeat"—he said, levitating in the middle of the room, then blinked back to his original position—"you, Major Hawthorn." Rahzu finished his blinking display.

Jonathan realized that this Rahzu could easily have killed him if he had wished to, but the warrior in him would never surrender. "Pretty good trick. What do you do for an encore?" was all he said, though.

"Ah, you liked that, did you? Then you're going to love this," Rahzu said as a sword grew out of his hand. When complete, Rahzu was armed with a golden broadsword.

"Yep, that was pretty cool too. I just bet you're the life of the party," Jonathan said curtly.

"I thought you didn't want to harm us!" Ariella yelled at Rahzu when he armed himself.

"I have no desire to harm either of you. Major Hawthorn here is a soldier, a warrior. He will never willingly surrender his weapon. Watch how he circles; see how he holds the blade. The major here has been trained very well. Surprisingly well, considering how much of the ancient teachings have been lost in your world. He has already killed one of my crew, an impressive feat." Rahzu gave Jonathan a bow of respect, then returned to answering Ariella. "No, Miss Marconi, I will have to take his sword from him."

Ariella looked at Jonathan with reverence. This man whom she barely knew, who had already defeated one of the aliens and was protecting her, gave her hope. Maybe they would escape.

"Miss Marconi, please do not let your emotions cloud your judgment. I think you know I could already have disarmed your protector without harming him if I wanted to. But I respect him, you see. For what and who he is, how he has been trained, and what he is willing to do to protect you. This man has honor, Miss Marconi. A trait that is disappearing in every universe. I hope you can see that!" Rahzu paused to let this sink into Ariella's heart. "So you see, I honor him by fighting him." Rahzu really liked those two humans, and even though Jonathan was human, he was sure he could teach more than a few Dimerians about the warrior code.

Ariella again looked at Jonathan and said, "Jonathan, thank you, but I don't want you to die." She knew not to ask him to lay down his sword.

Jonathan said defiantly, "He will have to pry this sword from my dead hands." Jonathan realized he could not defeat Rahzu using his powers. However, he would not surrender. The Japanese in World War II did not have a word for surrender. When the home island was threatened by invasion by Allied forces, they invented a form of surrender they could live with. They called it kamikaze. They died with honor. Jonathan felt the same.

"Are we going to sing kumbaya all day and bore me to death with all this talk?" Jonathan said in his typical prebattle tone. He liked to try and get into his opponent's head and make him angry. While angering an enemy can elicit powerful attacks, it usually disarms them of the most important weapon, the mind. However, with the word kumbaya, he unknowingly awoke the Yah power that had lain dormant within him.

Rahzu had heard the word before and knew what it actually meant. But to Jonathan, it was just a word he used in his banter. The Yah power was not strong enough yet for Rahzu to sense it.

"You are indeed wise, Major Hawthorn. Maybe next time you are here, we will talk more. But I agree, it's time to fight. This is going to be fun. I learned the style you are using over 500 years ago from the finest samurai in Japan. I promise you, as a fellow warrior, I will not use any of my powers, other than my physical abilities, during this session." Rahzu brandished the blade and with two successive dual handed figure eights, he brought his sword up as Jonathan held his, above his right shoulder, he then brought it forward, arms straight out, then brought it to his chest, face on the blade, and he bowed—a traditional swordsman's greeting to fight.

Jonathan, recognizing the invitation, showed his respect to Rahzu in kind. He then returned to his original pose.

The two modern samurai circled several times, and simultaneously both advanced to engage in the thrill of battle, each warrior striking, parrying, countering, turning, lunging, and spinning. Jonathan and Rahzu, again at the same time, retreated to reevaluate and wait for the right time to reengage.

"You are an impressive swordsman, Jonathan, I'll give you that." Rahzu was genuinely impressed.

"You're not too bad yourself, Rahzu. Since we're now on a first name basis," Jonathan retorted. "You hold your sword a little high, though, slows you down."

"I'll keep that in mind, thank you." Rahzu charged and struck; Jonathan blocked and countered, with no success.

That was how it went, over and over. They were at a draw when CheRahna suddenly appeared behind Ariella, grabbed her, and pushed a pressure point in her neck. Ariella weakly said, "Jonathan . . ." and fell to the floor unconscious.

Jonathan, unprepared for the sudden assault on Ariella, glanced over as she fell to the floor. He quickly realized Rahzu's blade was coming down toward the crown of his head, that he had made a foolish error, taking his eyes off his opponent while in the throes of battle.

As he turned his eyes back toward Rahzu, all he could say was, "Shit!" as the flat of Rahzu's blade hit him in the forehead, knocking him out cold.

Rahzu walked over quickly and collected the tri-sword by prying it out of Jonathan's living hand. He was unconscious, but Rahzu was not taking any chances. He then looked at CheRahna, who was just staring at him.

"Rahzu, what happened?"

He previously had telepathically told her about the humans being loose on the bridge, but he had not informed her of RahKael's death, which he did now. He explained that he wanted her here to capture the female unharmed and to spring the trap he had planned.

Even though Jonathan had a tri-sword and was an exceptional swordsman, he would soon have tired, a condition that did not affect Rahzu. He would have been defeated.

"I thought also I could use some practice," he concluded, satisfied.

"With a human? What kind of challenge could he offer?!" CheRahna did not understand or believe the human to be worthy.

"This human," he seriously stated, "Is one of the finest swordsmen that I have ever had the pleasure to spar with. Without the use of his powers and if the human were to have our physical stamina, he would be a challenge even for ShemRahya. He is an honorable warrior and will be treated as such! Is that understood?!" Rahzu said with authority.

"Yes, sir. I didn't mean any disrespect, Captain. I'm sorry." CheRahna bowed her head.

"Lift up your head, Commander, and stop apologizing for your beliefs." Rahzu was giving her some overdue tough love. "You don't have to agree with everything I do or say, and that's okay. You just have to follow my orders, which you have always done flawlessly. When you become captain, CheRahna, your beliefs will be tested and will play a critical role in how you command. There are going to be times you must stand your ground. What makes a good captain is choosing the right time to do both, for you. No one else. You will not command like me, because you are not me. You have your own convictions that you must follow." Rahzu hated preaching, but she really needed to hear this. He had all respect for her and was coming down on her so hard because she was ready—ready for the captain's chair. Rahzu was giving her one of the few lessons he could before that came.

CheRahna had a confused look on her face. She knew she was being reprimanded but sensed a lot of respect from Rahzu. *What does it mean?* she wondered.

Rahzu noticed her confusion. "CheRahna, beliefs are important, as is standing by them, which you do. So did this human," pointing at Jonathan's unconscious body. "I am proud of you and honor him, not only because it is my belief, but it is his also. Do you know what is even more important than standing up for what you believe?"

"No, sir."

"Knowing why you believe something. Tasting it. Feeling it. Taking it apart and getting to the root of its meaning."

"I think I understand," CheRahna said, seeing the wisdom in the captain's words.

"Good. Because I would like to talk with you later about some of your feelings." Rahzu waited to see what CheRahna was going to say.

"Okay, Rahzu," CheRahna was hoping it did not involve what she was thinking. He could see the fear building in her. It was important that she dealt with this. He hoped she was ready. "Yes, it is exactly what you think it is, and no, I did not read your thoughts." He paused to let her compose herself. "But it's completely up to you. You don't have to talk to me if you don't want to. Your service record will remain impeccable, and you will still receive my highest recommendation. Regardless, you will be a great captain. I just think, from knowing you and seeing how you work, that you strive to be the best that you can be. I believe you have to deal with your feelings before that can happen." Rahzu reached and grabbed her hand to comfort her as she thought, which was unusual because she and Rahzu had never had physical contact of this nature. His touch was as sincere as his words. "It really is your decision."

CheRahna felt what he said in his touch. She was not looking forward to this but believed it necessary for her evolution. There was no other Dimerian she could even imagine confiding in—her mentor and her only true friend. As he was about to let go and pull away, she grabbed his hand tightly and pulled him into a hug. CheRahna was unsure what possessed her to do that, but her words afterward were purposeful. "Yes, Rahzu. I very much need, and want, to talk with you later. I believe it has been long overdue," CheRahna said nervously. She had now committed herself, she thought.

Rahzu knew the hug was one of security, friendly respect, and thankfulness. He was pleasantly surprised by the affection, though. He was not expecting such a leap from the commander. She was an amazing Dimerian, he believed in her. "Looks like you've already taken the first step, CheRahna," referring to the hug. "I would be honored. Thank you for trusting in me."

"No, thank you, Captain, for always believing in me." She relaxed and released him.

"Now . . . get TamaRah and Rahphila up here to find out what happened with these two. Then get them implanted and back to Earth. We want their absence to go unnoticed," Rahzu ordered his commander happily, with a smile.

"Yes, sir, Captain Rahzu." CheRahna returned the smile. She already felt different.

CHAPTER

TWENTY THREE

THE ELECTRIC CAB was silent as Abhar and his wife, Sarah, headed for the maglev station. He was not driving fast, as he did at work. He never did when his beloved was the passenger, it made her uncomfortable. Abhar hated that they had to leave their home, which had been quite comfortable and private for a while now. But such was their life; peace never lasted long, not in one place anyway. They had at least got to stay here in the Groom Lake area longer than anywhere since they had left India. For that, Abhar was thankful.

Sarah was sitting quietly. She had a concerned look on her face, one that Abhar had seen many times before. He could tell she wanted to question him, but he knew she would not. She had been with him, always, no matter what, since their youth. He knew her as well as he knew himself.

Although they had been together for many years, Sarah was still a beautiful woman. She looked incredibly young, with smooth, nearly wrinkle free skin, dark brown eyes, and straight black hair. She could easily pass for a woman in her early forties. Sarah did not have to put on false pretenses as her husband did. An outsider from the secret world, she was, as she had always been, a Persian from near the ancient city of Ur, or Nasiriya of modern-day Iraq.

For her, life had been one of service, not only to her husband, but to Yahweh. She was grateful for her life and never forgot what a gift it truly was. Sarah had lived a long life, produced a son, and lived in many different places during the years of service. She had seen the wonders this world had to offer and had come to realize that humanity and Earth were more important than her comfort. This personal sacrifice for the greater good was a deep-seated belief she had. It was one of the main reasons she loved her husband. He too was willing to sacrifice everything, if necessary.

Once upon a time, in another land and another time, they had been royalty and were treated as such. Everywhere they went, they had been admired, respected, and lavishly greeted. No one dared challenge her husband's authority, which came from the most high. Anyone who did was destroyed.

Such power came at a price. It brought much attention from former allies, who sought to usurp their and their lord's position. It almost cost her her life. Sarah had been trapped in a comatose stake of nothingness for many years. Somehow, her dear husband had rescued her from the mental and physical prison she had been trapped in. He never did explain how he accomplished this feat. It did not matter, though, she trusted him fully.

Although they had relocated many times before because of the nature of his work, this time concerned her greatly. She was nervous. The confluence of all the events taking place seemed to signify the coming of the prophesied conclusion. Sarah knew there was not much time for humanity and Earth in its current state of existence; things were going to change, and drastically. She estimated it would still take a decade or two before it all came to fruition, but it was coming nonetheless. What concerned her most was that she did not know what their role was to be in these final days.

No one was directing them anymore. They were going on what her husband had been told to do so long ago, which he had done faithfully, without complaint, all in the service of Yahweh, to watch over and protect that which was most precious to him, his creation.

Abhar read what Sarah was thinking, which she was aware of. But rather than stay silent and read each other, he finally spoke aloud and asked, "Sarah, my princess"—which is what her name means in Hebrew—"tell me what's on your mind."

Sarah had waited patiently, but was ready to burst with questions. She was so glad he gave her the invitation, instead of her initiating the interrogation. "Abraham, what is happening? What have you done?" Sarah asked, not to doubt or question him, but to try and understand what was upon them and what was next. She saw the concern and uncertainty on her husband's face.

Abraham—he had not heard that name in an awfully long time. It was one that he no longer used, for it was too dangerous. But considering the circumstances, it did not matter, at least in the cab. It reminded him of a different age. An age of glory for the father. The Rahs would know he was here now. He could, however, this time keep his wife from harm's way.

As he took a deep breath, he attempted to try to formulate an order to all the events that had brought them to this moment. Sarah could tell by the sound of his inhalation that he was in deep contemplation.

With a long exhale and another deep breath, he started with a simple, concise statement. "The prophecy involving the God seed is happening." Abraham let that sink in before he continued. "I have both seen and been involved in events which have set in motion the beginning of the end. I met him and aided him, Sarah. I had to! He is worthy of my sacrifice if that is what is required of me."

"You know I trust you, dear husband, and will follow you through Armageddon if required, but are you sure he is the one the tables of destiny and the secret scrolls speak of?"

Abraham was not upset with her about her line of questioning, because she had earned that right by sacrificing everything, when the time called for it, for the success of the mission. He also knew she would do whatever he asked of her, something she had done time and time again, even if it meant her life. This time, however, it was his turn to push the sands of time.

Besides, he thought, this was not one of those decisions like, *Hey, honey, I'm painting the kitchen purple,* or *I'm buying an RV so we can travel the nation.* These things were petty. No. His actions and decisions affected everyone, everywhere. Life was literally in the balance with every move he made. Abraham continued, "After meeting him this morning and sensing his Yah energy, which was still dormant, he is the one, without any doubt."

"Oh my!" Sarah let the gravity of her husband's words flow through her mind. "Where is the God seed now?"

"The Rahs have him . . . in PU 430." He saw her fidgeting as her anxiety level steadily rose. "They don't know it's him, Sarah. I only know because I met his father, ZYah Zeh, a few years ago while he was stationed at Fort Detrick, Maryland. He was occupying the human flesh and was not consciously aware of who or what he was, much like his son now. The man I met this morning, Jonathan, is the Yah we've all been looking for." Abraham noticed her anxiety level decrease.

She sighed, "Do you know where ZYah Zeh is now?"

"No. But I do know that Johnathan Arlin Hawthorne is dead. I can only assume he is fulfilling the prophecy Yahweh set into motion at the beginning of time," Abraham concluded.

"Well, I suppose destiny is once again upon us, my love. What do we do now?" she implored.

Arriving at the maglev station, Abraham turned off the electric taxi and turned to look directly into Sarah's big beautiful dark eyes, "Princess Sarah, I promise I will tell you everything when we get on the train and behind the privacy cloud. But I must make a few calls first, my love." He grabbed her by her shoulders and pulled her in for a kiss, which she was thankful for.

"I'm not a princess anymore, Abraham," she murmured. She was impatient to continue their discussion, but knew he had to warn Rakesh, Haji, and the others about their exodus. They too could be in danger.

"You will always be my princess, my bride. But I am no longer Abraham," he said in a sincere but serious tone. "I love you." He kissed her once again.

"I love you too . . . Abraham," she replied reluctantly.

Abhar hit speed dial as the two headed for the station platform. He had just enough time to get his plans onto action before the next transit arrived. He checked the time and date. It was 12:34 a.m., Sunday, May 21, 2007. He would remember this date for the remainder of his days.

TWENTY FOUR

FEELING UNUSUALLY REFRESHED and somewhat newer, CheRahna was shining a little brighter. Even though she was nervous about her upcoming meeting with Rahzu, she was glad it was him and she was thankful it was happening now. CheRahna was ready, or so she thought.

As she walked through the passageways, CheRahna had formed a different opinion of what she had witnessed earlier between TamaRah and Rahphila. While still not condoning the behavior of anyone who had sampled fleshly experiences, she was starting to see how her own emotions had played a role in her decision making.

Captain Rahzu and she had suspected what their two science officers were up to at the time of RahKael's death. Rahzu had advised her to be understanding when she encountered the duo. He reminded CheRahna that she had never worn the flesh, and though she had no desire to do so, she could only try to understand the feelings and emotions of those who had. Rahzu asked that she exercise some empathy with all the crew, something she had never done. The captain used his recent encounter with the human male number 99985 as his case in point. He explained that even though he believed it was foolish for this human not to surrender his weapon, especially considering the god powers he had displayed, Rahzu's personal beliefs in this case did not matter. The captain empathized with his opponent's convictions and gave him the honorable exit in which he desperately required.

While making his request and offering his advice, Rahzu made it clear that he would support CheRahna in whatever she decided was necessary. It was her time to practice being captain.

Commander CheRahna knew the captain would follow her lead—he was a man of his word—but she wanted to make him proud of her. For some unknown reason, she needed his approval. Maybe she would find out why later. CheRahna did feel, however, that she could put her emotions aside and make decisions based on logic, just as a captain should.

As she turned down the corridor that led to the private living quarters, TamaRah and Rahphila appeared from around the corner. Before they noticed her, CheRahna noticed the pleasurable aura surrounding her subordinates. They were emitting a tremendous amount of positive energy as they held hands facing each other, walking and talking. *Disgusting!* she thought briefly before putting that thought out of her mind. The commander had suspected that they had been involved in some activity centered around fleshly pleasures, but decided not to be so quick to judge, as Rahzu had suggested.

Rahphila was the first to detect CheRahna standing there, arms crossed. He stopped in his tracks as soon as he saw her. *Busted!* he thought.

TamaRah, sensing the change in her lover's mood, turned her head to look in the direction he was staring, motionless. She was instantly petrified, like an arachnophobic being caught in a spider's web. TamaRah started to speak. "Commander . . . we . . ."

"Not now!" CheRahna cut her off. "Because of how happy you two appear to be, I'm willing to venture the news of the humans' escape from their life pods and RahKael's death have evaded you both." She was firm, but not berating them as TamaRah and Rahphila expected.

"No, ma'am . . . ma'am!" TamaRah sheepishly said.

"No, Commander CheRahna!" Rahphila formally followed, knowing they were in for it.

Trying to say as little as possible so as not to ignite the ridicule she thought was imminent, TamaRah mumbled, "Have the humans been apprehended?"

". . . Yes." CheRahna paused while collecting her thoughts. Their actions and demeanor had supported her initial assessment that they were up to no good. She wanted to tear into them and give them such a tongue lashing that they would have scars on their elemental forms for eternity. But why? And for what?

CheRahna realized it was not TamaRah's or Rahphila's fault that the humans woke up and caused RahKael's death. It was not against protocol to leave the life pods unattended for any number of trivial reasons. She was mad because they were acting like humans. CheRahna was confident Rahzu would help her determine why she had this deep-seated anger later, but for now she decided to use logic and look at the facts.

There was no dereliction of duty, and although these two may have pushed the limits as to what pleasures of the flesh they were allowed to experience, especially in the course of duty, CheRahna concluded she would rather have happy, satisfied crew members than miserable ones. She made her decision.

"I need you two to get back to the life pods, get the humans reimplanted, and place them back on Earth. We will figure out how and why they woke up later, after you have returned. ShemRahya and KaRah will be in the Cruiser Rahs waiting." The commander hesitated; something had to be said about TamaRah's and Rahphila's behavior. "And whatever this is"—CheRahna slightly scolded while pointing her right index finger back and forth between the two officers—"it had better not affect either of your performances, or so help me Rah, I will expel you both to Chaos myself. Is that understood?!"

Both TamaRah and Rahphila, now truly in shock at CheRahna's new-found empathetic behavior, could only nod in affirmation.

"Good. Now move it! We've got a lot of work to do."

"Yes, ma'am. Thank you, ma'am," TamaRah said professionally while grabbing Rahphila and walking away at a speed just short of a run. She felt they had just dodged a bullet and did not want to tempt their good fortune any longer.

CheRahna turned and watched the two as they departed. Both Lt. Commander TamaRah and Lt. Rahphila glanced over their shoulders at her just before turning into the next corridor. If she did not know any better, it appeared that there was a sense of respect in their gaze. It made her feel good inside, like a captain. *Maybe I will adopt this new way of thinking*, she thought.

CheRahna, embracing her new journey into self-discovery, set out to search for Rahzu. She was ready to talk.

CHAPTER

TWENTY FIVE

ARIELLA OPENED HER eyes to the sound of the two-way radio echoing throughout the bathysphere. "Miss Marconi! USS *Ronald Reagan*. Repeat . . . Miss Marconi, USS *Ronald Reagan*. Please respond!" The voice had a note of concern in it.

Feeling out of sorts, she did not know where she was, the time, or what in the hell was going on. Ariella decided to gather herself before answering the radio.

"I'm in a bathysphere. Check." Things were coming back to her. *Why am I so absentminded*, she thought? "Man, that was one hell of a nap," she said, shaking her head vigorously side to side. That had to be it. It was all that apple pie she had consumed, she presumed. "Where are the whales? And what happened to that god-awful bright light?" she questioned aloud.

Just as the radio started again, she grabbed the handle and answered before cacophony caused her to get a headache. "Ariella Marconi here, go ahead."

"Miss Marconi! We're sure glad to hear from you. We've been trying to reach you for the last fifteen minutes. We were starting to think . . . that something tragic may have happened. Is everything okay, ma'am?"

Ariella was confused as to why they were calling her anyway. Responding, after determining she was indeed fine, she said, "Yes. I guess I took a little nap. What's going on up there and how much longer before I can get out of this tin can?" She was still getting her bearings as she looked out the porthole to search for the whales. She could see quite well but could not locate the source of the lights. Maybe that is what scared the whales off, but what was it?

"Miss Marconi, we should have you on board in less than five minutes. You should be able to see our lights outside your portholes," the man on the radio said, questioning her health.

"What!" Ariella's voice echoed throughout the bathysphere. She now knew why it was nicknamed a bell. She accepted the fact that she may have succumbed to the effects of alcohol and took a nap, but for two and a half hours? No way! Also, as her head was getting rid of the cobwebs, she started to doubt, unless she had just woken from a coma, that she could have slept through the deafening volume coming from the radio. The last thing she could recall was feeling like a billiard ball being caromed off a rail between the whales. Where in the hell did they go? Her recollection was that she had been 7,500 feet below the surface. Now, looking at the depth gauge, it read 100 feet.

Thoughts were racing through her mind. What had happened? She reluctantly determined, by the way she felt now, that she had not drunk enough to totally black out, that much she was sure of. Ariella quickly checked the oxygen levels; everything was okay there. She pressed the button on the handle and answered, "Yes. I can see the lights. Did the oxygen levels drop anytime during my ascent? Apparently, I was asleep for more than two hours."

"No, ma'am, everything was okay on our end. We did notice that carbon dioxide levels were unusually low, but that's all."

"So you didn't see whales on your sonar and weren't responsible for the really bright lights when I was at a depth of 7,500 feet?" Ariella asked the communications seaman.

"No . . . ma'am. We did pick up some whales several hours ago, but that was it." The radio went quiet for a moment, enough time for Ariella to wonder if she was suffering from some sort of decompressive hysteria.

"Miss Marconi, Captain LaMarr did contact us shortly after you departed and said that you had experienced a long, stressful day, and that you were administered a sedative to help you relax while ascending in such an enclosed environment. Are you sure you're okay, Miss Marconi?"

Other than being a bit sore between her shoulder blades, she felt fine. Quite rested, actually. Maybe she did drink more than she thought, and Nancy Taylor altered the chemical formula of the apple pie enough to negate the effects associated with a hangover, which she did not have. She was also amused to hear how Justin had the forethought to concoct a story for the boys upstairs, to explain away any of the possible side effects from the alcohol that she might experience; alcohol was prohibited on any US Navy vessel. Sea Lab X was considered a Navy vessel.

"Yes, I'm fine. Thank you . . . and yes, I remember taking some meds just before I departed. It slipped my mind with me saying goodbyes and all." She considered how to continue the ruse. "It's easy to lose track of time down here. I must have been more exhausted than I thought. That's all."

"Good. Glad to hear that, ma'am. Get ready to sit back and hold on, you are about to break the surface. We'll have you on deck very shortly."

"Thank you. I can't wait," she responded. Ariella was thankful that the habitat's internal atmospheric pressure nearly matched that on the surface. Thus, she would not need to decompress, which was truly a miracle. In the civilian world, she would never even have been able to go to a third of the depth in which she had been living at for the past two months.

The aluminized windows and the material of which the Hab was constructed—Ariella did not know what it was called—were highly classified, and judging by the bathysphere's construction, with its thick steel shell and one-foot-thick quartz glass windows, even those aboard the *Ronald Reagan* were unaware of what lay beneath the surface. Without the science that went into Sea Lab X's design, she would have been forced to decompress in an iron lung, for so the decompression chamber had been coined, for over a month. And that was only the known decompression time for 1,000 fathoms, not the 2,500 where the habitat was located. Ariella was not sure it would be possible for the human body to tolerate much more.

The military always had the best gear, she thought. So unfair. But that was the way of the world. It is said that knowledge is power. But Ariella started to see that power was knowledge. The ones who had the power controlled the knowledge the rest of the world was to have. It was something for her to ponder over.

All she wanted to think about for the moment, however, was getting out of here and breathing the fresh, salty ocean air and seeing the colorful sunset. Looking out the porthole as the bell surfaced, she could see the distorted colors of purple and orange on the horizon. Beautiful. In just a few more moments, she would get to witness this colorful display in all its glory.

In another minute, Ariella was free of the prison she had spent the last several hours in and was standing on the carrier's flight deck. The sky was a magnificent display this evening, she thought. It was good to be topside, if only for a little while.

After getting to briefly look at the sky and get her sea legs, she was ushered to the ship's infirmary to get the once over. She just wanted a hot shower. After getting a clean bill of health, Ariella realized that her dream of enjoying some warm water was just that, a dream. She was given a cup of black coffee, of not such good quality, and escorted to a US Coast Guard Jayhawk helicopter, which was ready to transport her to Anderson Air force Base, near Apra Harbor, Guam. Once there, an F-15 Hornet jet fighter waited on standby to whisk her to Honolulu, Hawaii, over 3,000 miles away. She learned that they would be traveling at near Mach 1, or the speed of sound, which was 720 miles per hour. Taking into account an aerial refueling, the flight should last around five hours.

Ariella had to admit, she felt important, considering everything that was happening: the bathysphere, the aircraft carrier group, the chopper ride to Guam, and a private supersonic jet transport to Honolulu, and then on to San Francisco, all for her. Talk about making a girl feel special. *Wow!* she thought while smiling.

As the Jayhawk lifted off and she gazed out at the darkening horizon, she could not help but think to herself, *What a day!* With her security clearance upgraded to Ultra, whatever that meant, and regarding the knowledge she was already privy to, she began to wonder what would be revealed to her tomorrow. Looking at her watch, she saw it was 9:30 p.m. Sunday, and since she was going to cross the International Date Line on her way to the States, she would get to repeat the day all over again. She however, doubted the encore performance would be as memorable.

CHAPTER

TWENTY SIX

JONATHAN AWOKE WITH an awful taste in his mouth, "What the . . ." was all he could say before he cringed and stuck his tongue out to prevent himself from gagging. Reaching for his water bottle, he unscrewed the cap and poured the cool liquid into his mouth. After swishing it around, he leaned over the door and spit the water out. He took another huge series of gulps until he was sated, and then replaced the cap. Flipping the overhead visor to look in the mirror, Jonathan noticed a dried white substance splattered across the right side of his face. It was all coming back to him, slowly.

With a jolt, Jonathan quickly realized that the dried substance on his face was bird shit. He opened the Viper's door, stood up, and proceeded to wash his face with the remaining water. "Wait a minute." He abruptly stopped, water dripping from the tip of his nose. "When the fuck did I get back into the car!?"

As he wiped his face and walked around to get the blood flowing, his memory started to return. He had experienced this feeling of absentmindedness before, but it usually followed a brutal interrogation session and the use of sodium pentothal, which left him with one hell of a headache. There had been several occasions in his past that were eerily similar to what he was going through now, where things just did not make sense.

Slowly, calmly, Jonathan started reviewing the events of the evening and early morning. He had left the airport in the Viper, and it was here. He was driving, listening to Art Bell for a while until some woman started talking about abductions and such near Mammoth Cave. He remembered flooring it and rocking out to "Danger Zone" when suddenly, out of nowhere, a bird shit all over him. He recalled spinning out, thanking God for the wide wheelbase and low profile of the Viper, which made it nearly impossible to flip. He got out, fell because he was dizzy, saw the bird, and unloaded the entire clip from his Glock at it. Here is where it started getting tricky.

Jonathan distinctly remembered the stork falling from the air without his having hit it, and then being surrounded by a bright, warm light. All was silent except for the radio. "What was that song . . . 'Rocket Man'!" Which certainly seemed appropriate, considering he felt like a space cadet at that moment.

That is where his recollection ended. He grabbed his shirt and pulled it up to dry off his face. With his eyes closed, he tried to think back again to see if there was any detail he might have missed. Satisfied that his memory was correct, he pulled the sidearm from its holster and checked to see if it was indeed empty. It was. He did not, however, remember returning it to his holster. Scanning the ground, Jonathan could clearly see the nine-millimeter shell casings strewn on the pavement near the vehicle.

Still staring around at the road, unsure of what he was expecting to find, it finally dawned on him. "Where's the fucking bird?!" He knew he did not hit the thing, but it had dropped from the sky like a steel anvil. It was dead, he remembered.

Jonathan put both hands out, like he was getting ready to take flight. This was done to steady himself, not physically, but mentally. Determining that he needed a reality check and, since it was a clear night, he looked to the stars for the answers.

"Find the Big Dipper," he said aloud while locating it. "Use the pointer . . . five times the space between . . . cool . . . there is Polaris, north." Using the widths of his fingers and fists as a ruler, he calculated that he was at 36 degrees, 30 minutes north latitude, roughly. "Okay, that seems about right. Now what time is it?" Looking again at the North Star and drawing an imaginary line from it back through the pointers, representing reversed twenty-four-hour clock's hand, he added the thirty minutes necessary to match the star and solar times. "Zero four hundred thirty. Wait a minute," he said, doing a double take to check his math.

Since he did not wear a watch—it had something to do with the quartz drawing energy from his body, making the watch malfunction—he reached into the car and grabbed his phone from the center console. The phone screen indicated 4:37, May 21, 2007. *Not a bad guess*, he thought to himself, evaluating his star clock timing skills. But what happened to the missing two and a half hours?

Jonathan looked skyward again, just to make sure he was on Earth. A funny thought entered his mind. Humor never seemed to escape him. He had adopted a simple truth of life he had once read on a bumper sticker. Changing the words my to your and driving to life, he created his own slogan, which read *If you don't like your life, dial 1-800-EAT-SHIT!* He always thought that to be more appropriate. Even now, he has to chuckle because he actually had just eaten shit. Bird shit!

"Cassiopeia, where are you, baby . . . ? There you are, legs spread wide for daddy." Using double the distance between the W or M, depending on one's perspective, and drawing a perpendicular E to the line created between the first and last stars of the constellation, he found the North Star again. Just as expected.

The Big Dipper, part of Ursa Major, and Cassiopeia consist of circumpolar stars, which means they always travel counterclockwise around the North Star, Polaris. The two formations are on opposite sides of the bright North Star; if one is high in the sky, the other is low and vice versa.

Thankfully, these little checks assured him that he was indeed sane, even though he had seemingly been afflicted by a temporary bout of amnesia. "What now? I guess it's time to step back and punt," he said, dumbfounded.

Fresh out of ideas, Jonathan returned to the car. As he sat down, he remembered having Abhar's encrypted scrambler phone in his pocket. "Dead!" The phone was lifeless. Luckily, the charging cord he had for his personal phone matched Abhar's, so he plugged it in and waited. After about a minute, the phone had still failed to come to life.

Jonathan tapped the phone on the dash. His thinking was that he could shock it back to life, much like a paramedic armed with a defibrillator, except his method was cheaper and more readily available. It might work, he guessed.

Manufacturers, especially those that make electronics, do not recommend tapping, hitting, or shaking electrical devices to make them work. However, silly as it sounds, it had always seemed to work for Jonathan.

He applied this logic to many things in life. If his right hip felt out of place, he would just straight leg kick the hell out of something with his left leg. Voilà, just saved a visit to the chiropractor. If the left side of the car seemed to be out of alignment, go find a pothole and run over it on the right. Problem solved. While not being particularly good for the ball and CV joints, it usually corrected the misalignment.

After several unsatisfactory attempts, before he was ready to call time and announce the time of death, he unplugged the phone from the charger and removed the back cover. To his surprise, the batteries' copper connections were burned. He looked at the visible circuit board; it too was fried.

While not an electronics expert, Jonathan fancied himself as knowing a little about almost everything and a lot about a good number of things. He was famous for being able to hold a conversation with anyone, from a bricklayer to a biochemist.

His initial observation of the device pointed to one thing, an EMP. But the only electromagnetic pulse he had been exposed to was at S-4, and even then, the phone was placed in a protective bin and not exposed to the damaging pulse. Besides, the phone was working when he left the airport in Nashville. The memory of that bright, warm light returned to him again. *Something is not right about all of this*, he quietly pondered.

Turning around and looking to the southwest, Jonathan located Leo, just prior to its disappearance over the horizon. "See you another time, buddy." He cranked the car, pushed the button to close the roof—he had been shit on enough already today—and it was once down, he hit the highway. With more than 300 miles to go, he figured he would arrive sometime around 0800 if he did the speed limit, which was fine. It was Sunday morning, and for most people, the weekend meant rest and relaxation. But in Jonathan's world, there was no such thing; he was always on call. Everyone in his office would be hopping today, expecting his arrival. He had been gone for nearly a week, during which everyone took most of it off, even Ashley. Therefore, he did not feel so bad for everyone having to be there.

***

The remainder of the drive went well, and other than a nagging pain between his shoulders, he felt surprisingly rested. He still had not come up with any solid answers concerning the missing stork, the bright lights, and the missing time. And although there were a few possible explanations that could explain what happened—food poisoning, a chemical imbalance, a hidden brain tumor, or some sort of exotic bird shit virus—none of these seemed viable. He felt perfectly healthy.

As stubborn as he was, Jonathan was not ready to admit to the only explanation that made sense. There was no way he was abducted, not him. He would know, remember, wouldn't he? Could Gilla have been right all this time?

Jonathan was beginning to think all the events that have happened—the USOs, the trenches, the amber crystal, his vision, and now the missing time—all had to be connected. He was not one to believe in coincidences. He had been hit with and had used the flash gun in paralytic mode. It will erase the hell out of someone's short-term memory, he recalled. He knew the CIA used a method termed EDOM—electronic dissolution of memory—but that was more for long-term memory and mind wiping.

Trying to answer a question that had no apparent answer, at least right now, was only going to frustrate him again. Jonathan was going to talk with Haji Patel and see what his take was on all of this. Besides, he needed to contact Abhar, and Haji was his only link since the phone was fried.

Pulling up to the front gate at Wright-Patterson Air Force Base, Major Hawthorn presented his ID, even though the guard at the gate knew who he was. After a brief exchange of good mornings and how was your weekend so far, Jonathan headed for the office. He was sure his secretary, Ashley Butler, was already there.

Ashley usually showed up between 0700 and 0730 hours most mornings, and since it was 0736, he figured she would have the coffee made, which he was looking forward to, by the time he got up there. Jonathan anticipated a busy morning. He had several things that must be taken care of before the next leg of his journey. Time was running out. He would need to use the maglev for the rest of his trip if he ever expected to meet Miss Marconi on time, tomorrow afternoon.

Quickly calculating in his head, he expected her to arrive at Alameda Naval Air Station by 1300 hours and transfer to San Francisco Naval Shipyard no later than 1400. Considering she would probably want a shower, a bite to eat, and possibly a nap, Jonathan speculated he could stretch the meeting time until 1800 or so. He was confident she would be thankful for the rest, though he was fairly sure she would have something curt to say about tardiness. Jonathan just smiled; knowing what to expect made things go a lot smoother.

As he pulled into his spot near the front door—he loved assigned parking; at least now that he was a major he did—he saw the familiar black Saturn Outlook parked one row back. The crossover was covered with various University of South Carolina Gamecock stickers, license plate covers, and magnets, plastered everywhere possible, while not being tacky. The garnet and black mixed together, the Gamecocks colors, really was eye-popping. Looking more closely at the vehicle, Jonathan noticed a new sticker in the lower right-hand corner of the hatch windows, a pink Carolina Girl sticker.

Ashley Butler was a Carolina girl through and through. She lived and breathed the University of South Carolina sports program, and not just football. She watched and followed them all through thick and thin. Jonathan was quite sure if USC—the real one and not that pretender from Southern California, as Ashley would say—had curling, she would follow that too. Many people claim to be fans, and to the normal person they are, but once meeting Ashley during a sporting event, they would quickly realize that they fell way short when representing their teams.

Jonathan loved her as one of his most trusted friends. To further deepen her southern roots, her husband's name was Rhett Butler. Coincidently, although never married to a Scarlett, Rhett Butler did not "give a damn." He was also one of Jonathan's oldest friends, and they had served together many years ago in the same Ranger unit.

Rhett was a man who spoke his mind and stood up for what he believed in. Though not big in stature, he was completely capable of backing up his words and making someone see his point, if tested. He had one of the deadliest spinning back kicks Jonathan had ever seen.

Rhett was not a violent man; to the contrary, he was very peaceful and good at avoiding conflict. Surprisingly, while not really liking people in general, he led a team of call representatives for a nationwide company. He was simply the best.

Jonathan knew he could always count on his friend if needed; however, he knew Rhett's priorities lay with his family, where they should. Jonathan would never do anything that put his surrogate family at risk.

Opening the building door and heading to the elevator, Jonathan wondered what information he would share with Ashley. Of all the people he could have picked for a secretary and assistant, Ashley was the best. They were already friends due to her husband Rhett before she started working for him.

She had just given birth to a daughter, Callie, and wanted to work while watching her little one. At the time, Jonathan was working predominantly out of his home, which she was familiar with.

On one evening, when Jonathan was having a small get-together, Ashley told him that he needed a secretary. The thought had never really occurred to him before, but he figured, *Why not?* He bought her a desk, a nice chair, and set up an office in the spare bedroom. After getting the military to run a direct hard phone line to the house, they were in business.

He remembered her first day on the job, when he was so unprepared. Jonathan was unsure of what he needed to do until he saw the boxes in the corner. Inside the three-foot cubic boxes were receipts, invoices, bills, and various other office memos he had been accumulating for more than eight months. He needed them categorized, duplicated, and recorded so that he could get refunded for his expenditures dealing with work on his tax returns. No one can hide from the tax man for long.

Jonathan assumed the sea of little bits of paper would keep her busy for at least a week. He was wrong. At the end of the second day, Ashley had announced that she was done and requested something else to work on. Jonathan at the time, flabbergasted, just told her to do something to keep busy.

By the end of the week, she had developed a spreadsheet that efficiently organized and tabulated credits and debits, a program that allowed him to cross-reference his contacts with different categories of information, while straightening up around the house. He remembered how happy she was to be working and for allowing her to bring young Callie along, who also appeared to be thankful, with her cute little smile. From that day forward, Ashley became his most valuable asset. Jonathan would keep her employed if all she did was filter his calls, which she was a master at.

Jonathan pulled open the glass door and was greeted with a smile. Ashley walked over, gave him a hug and a peck on the lips, like a sister would give a brother, then said, "Hey. I thought you were going to be here early. I stopped by and got you a chicken cheese biscuit and some hash browns, but they're probably cold," she stated, cocking her head and with her hands on her hips, smiling at him. Before he could answer, she added, "How was your trip? Productive, I hope."

Looking over at the coffee pot, which was full of black gold, Jonathan responded, "Oh . . . long. Thank you. Got some things done I needed to get done, only to pick up a few more things that I now have to do. You know how it is for me. I'll tell you about it later."

"You should really slow down and find you a good woman," Ashley preached.

"You have anyone in mind?"

"No, that's the problem. Of all the girls I know, none of them are good enough for you," she said.

"I guess I'm cursed then. Always the wrong woman at the right time or the right woman at the wrong time," Jonathan sighed.

"It'll change soon, I can feel it. You just watch . . . and I want to meet her right off too. Don't wait till you've been seeing her for a month before you bring her around. I'll save you a lot of troubles, and you know it."

"You're awful peppy this morning. What time did you get here?"

"Five thirty. I figured you'd be hungry, and after three days, I was ready to get out of the house anyways, before Rhett got up," she said matter-of-factly.

"Is it more that Rhett was driving you crazy or that you just needed some Jonny time?" he said, pointing to himself by placing both palms on his chest.

"A little of both. I love that man, but sometimes . . ."

While Jonathan drank some coffee and ate his food, which he had zapped in the microwave, Ashley filled him in on the latest Gamecock baseball scores and stats, how Callie was doing in school and karate, how the boys, Jay and Logan, were doing, and what Rhett had recently been pestering her about.

Ashley essentially used Jonathan for the next few minutes to vent her problems and as a sounding board. She too, being a Pisces, tended to get flighty in thought at times. Jonathan gave her some grounding and would tell her the truth while putting a positive spin on things. Much of what her husband Rhett would do, except the positive spin bit. Even Ashley would have to admit, and has, that there was a huge difference in the levels and types of honesty concerning sexual versus platonic relationships. Jonathan supposed that was why he was still single—he had not been good with all the deception and mind games included in relationships, which is a contradiction, considering his work. He was learning, though. Thanks to his friend here.

After finishing his meal, Jonathan thanked Ashley for the food; the little things meant a lot to him. He asked her to let him know when Haji arrived. Unsure of the danger level he was in, Jonathan decided not to divulge any unnecessary information to Ashley, or anyone else. No more people needed to be in the crosshairs, unless they had to be.

As he turned, once he finished speaking, Ashley chimed in, "Haji is already here. He was getting out of his car when I arrived. He said he had a lot of work to do," Ashley said while shuffling through some paperwork.

"Hmm." Jonathan pondered Haji's early arrival.

"Something wrong?"

"No. I'll call him from the office. Thanks." Jonathan continued walking toward his desk, closing the door behind him.

As he took a seat, he spun toward the window, sipping his coffee. There it was, the infamous Hangar 18. *If they only knew*, he mused. "Oh yeah!" he said aloud, reaching for a positive note. He wanted to write down the name and model of the Broyhill chair he sat in during his remote viewing session in the tachyonic chamber at Dulce.

After that was done, he again thought about how much he was going to tell Ashley. She had an Ultra security clearance, and he could reveal almost anything to her in confidence. He decided that, with all the mysteries involved with the trenches and the amber crystal, he would tell her just enough to do her job. She would know he was holding back but understood that was the nature of his job. Secrecy. Plus, with all these little Gray fuckers walking around in the underground, the less she knew the better.

While finishing his coffee, he checked the calendar to review all the appointments he was going to miss. Some for the second and third time. *Thank God for Ashley; she has to deal with those people*, he grinned. With nothing else demanding his immediate attention, he picked up the secure base phone and called the research and development department. After a few rings, a man with a thick Indian accent answered, "R and D, Haji Patel speaking."

"Hey, Haji, it's Jonathan Hawthorn. You busy?" Jonathan asked, knowing he was. Why else would he have come in at 0530 in the morning? He wondered what he was working so diligently on, since Jonathan's list of items was not too complicated or demanding.

"Always, Major Hawthorn. When can you come by the lab? I can give you the items you requested then and show you how they work," Haji said, knowing Jonathan was quite capable of operating the devices on his list. He needed to talk to the major.

Jonathan picked up on Haji's play and went along. In a relaxed, jovial tone, he responded, "Sure, Haji, let me get one more cup of mud and I'll be right down. You want one?"

"No, thank you, Major. I'm having a spot of pekoe tea at the moment. It's quite refreshing."

"Okay, see you in about ten minutes then."

"Very good, Major." Haji hung up.

Getting up from his desk and walking out of his office, Jonathan gave Ashley the Post-it note about the chair, asked her to clear his calendar until further notice, and told her that he was going to R&D to meet with Haji. He went over to the coffee pot, filled his cup, and as he was about to leave, Ashley asked, "Jonathan, are you okay? Is there anything I can do for you?"

"Just keep being my guardian angel," he said affectionately. "I'll talk to you later. I need to figure a few things out first. Hold my calls, except those dealing with my new assignment. Forward those to my cell, please."

Ashley was looking at him with doubt. She knew that once he got to talking, he hated to be interrupted and rarely answered calls, even important ones. He had explained to her how rude he thought it was to stop a conversation with an actual, present person for a conversation with someone who was not even there.

"I'll answer it." Jonathan's response signified that there was a fifty-fifty chance that he would.

"I'll forward only the ones that absolutely can't wait. How's that?" She was the one who always had to deal with the flak when she forwarded a call and he failed to answer.

"Okay, I promise. If this phone rings, I'll answer it. Satisfied?!" he said, putting both hands up as a sign of surrender.

"Satisfied," she smiled.

"You're the best," he finished.

"You know it."

Jonathan snapped to attention, cut an about face, and walked out of the office. He was now headed for Hangar 18, or more precisely, under it.

CHAPTER
TWENTY SEVEN

CAPTAIN RAHZU SUSPECTED that Ensign RahKael was hand-picked by YetziRah to infiltrate his ship and remain under his tutelage. As to the reason why, that remained a mystery.

After repeatedly trying to contact his protégé with no success, Fleet Admiral YetziRah flashed there personally to have a discussion with the captain. During the meeting, Rahzu felt as if he was under some sort of interrogation by the way YetziRah was grilling him with questions.

Once he was satisfied that Captain Rahzu was not involved in the young ensign's death, the admiral proceeded to accuse him of not doing his job and being derelict in his duties as a Rah Jump Craft commander.

At that point, Rahzu had had enough. He would not let the admiral question his character or his dedication to the Rahs' mission here in PU 430, damn the consequences. The captain presented a plethora of evidence that YetziRah's pupil acted insubordinately toward fellow crewman who outranked her, and many times had performed her duties as if they were beneath her. Rahzu went on to suggest that her own pompous and careless attitude was the true cause of her death, and that the negative traits she possessed were not cultivated aboard his ship.

The admiral, caught completely off guard, was not used to subordinates talking to him in such a manner or questioning his authority. He retaliated by saying, "Captain Rahzu, are you insinuating that I instilled this sort of behavior in my young recruit and that my teachings had something to do with her death?!" He growled as he awaited the captain's response.

Admiral YetziRah, probing, asked, "So, Captain, if you believe that Ensign RahKael had other reasons for being aboard this ship, what do you suppose they might be?" he asked, trying to find out what knowledge Rahzu may or may not have had about RahKael's actual mission.

Being a crafty, intelligent, and ruthless leader, YetziRah had a notoriously bad temper and a propensity for violence. Many times in the past, he had shown that he would use these to accomplish his agenda. Blackmail, theft, and torture were just a few of the tools he employed to ascend to his current position as head of all Rah interests, including PUs 78, 430, and 431.

YetziRah's student, RahKael, was a newer version of himself. In time, she would have sought to usurp her master's position of power. He was secretly working to become the leader of the House of Rah, believing their current leader, Xanix Rah, was being manipulated by some unknown master. YetziRah considered Xanix unworthy to lead, but had neither the backing nor the evidence to support his coup d'état. Therefore, he had sent RahKael on a mission to specifically find the God seed and bring the human to him, dead or alive. YetziRah could then place the human's essence in a special, gold-platinum-electroplated amber crystal sphere, which he had secretly created and which would extract and alter the host's DNA sequences. Then he, YetziRah, would have the most powerful source of energy known in existence, the white enhanced Dimerian energy crystal, or WEDEC.

Only the House of Yah, the most powerful group of Dimeria, had the ability to access and use this mineral crystal's power. The God seed's DNA, while in human flesh, was vulnerable to genetic alteration at the elemental level. YetziRah believed he had found a way to combine these genes with his own to make him one of the most powerful beings in the realm of the gods.

He also knew where an incredibly large deposit of Dimerian crystal, which was relatively unguarded, could be found. It made up the inner core of the planet Earth in PU 431.

Xanix Rah too was looking into using the God seed's genetics to gain the ability to use the WEDEC, but he was many decades away from anything viable. YetziRah was ready now. He just needed the DNA, which, unbeknownst to him, his fallen protégé had found.

Listening carefully to Captain Rahzu's answer, YetziRah needed to be extremely cautious at this stage in his plan. Any hint that pointed to knowledge of his intended coup would have to be dealt with swiftly and brutally.

Rahzu, realizing the delicacy of the situation and sensing that he was being coerced into revealing his true thoughts about the current situation, avoided the trap by saying, "For me to make a statement concerning the nature of Ensign RahKael's true mission would merely be speculation at this time." Rahzu said this while studying his superior's reaction to his words. "I would first need to conduct a thorough investigation to determine how and why the human male gained consciousness. Then, in order to ascertain whether or not the ensign had an alternative assignment aboard this ship, it would be necessary for me to abandon my crew, leave my post here, and return to Dimeria. After visiting the Rah Academy to question known acquaintances and connections, it may then be possible to formulate a theory as to what she was really doing here in PU 430. Only then would I be able to begin to accumulate a list of motivated suspects." Rahzu could see that what he was saying began to make YetziRah anxious. He knew that the admiral was up to something nefarious, but was also smart enough not to poke at a vicious animal. YetziRah was dangerous, and if threatened he was powerful and cunning enough to destroy him and place the blame for the ensign's death on him.

Besides, Rahzu now knew, judging by YetziRah's actions, what he needed to know; the admiral, though ever so slightly, revealed his tell. The captain, in a calculated manner, continued his proposal. "I believe, sir, that my going to Dimeria to investigate this incident would be a misappropriation of resources and is beyond my purview."

"What do you suggest, Captain?"

"Sir, I feel that any investigation in Dimeria would be best handled by you. With your connections in the political arena, as well as your tenacity, you will undoubtedly get to the truth of this matter," Rahzu said using a bit of flattery.

YetziRah was silent at first, thinking. He had been trying to probe Rahzu, ever so slightly, to determine if the captain's feelings matched his words. However, he was unable to get a clear read without being detected. *Captain Rahzu is a very accomplished and capable officer, but does he know anything?* YetziRah thought.

Finally, deciding that Rahzu was unaware of his plans, he responded. "Captain, you have made some very valid points." He paused while walking around, with his arms behind his back and looking down as he talked. "Go ahead and conduct your investigation here. Get to the bottom of the human's escape and how Ensign RahKael died. I tend to agree with you that her own hubris was the cause of her death. Whatever you uncover, I want you to report directly to me. No one else. Is that understood, Captain?"

"Yes, sir."

"I will return to Dimeria and conduct a probe personally into the ensign's activities. Remember, Captain, we don't know who is involved or how high up the ladder this conspiracy may go, so be careful."

"Yes, sir, I will. Brilliant plan, sir." Rahzu continued his flattery to deflect any possible suspicion YetziRah might have toward him.

"Keep me posted. We want be vigilant in these most important of times if we as Rahs are going to claim our proper place among our fellow Dimerians."

"I completely agree, Admiral YetziRah. I will let you know what I discover," Rahzu said before YetziRah flashed out.

The admiral, before he left, realized he had a great opportunity to further his plans for domination. He would, of course, need to establish a connection between RahKael and Xanix Rah, which he felt would not be too difficult.

The wheels of his twisted mind turned. YetziRah could see the beginnings of his devious plot. Then, as fast as he arrived, he flashed back to Dimeria, the center hub of all the universes.

Rahzu, having dealt with Admiral YetziRah before, knew how close he had come to death; after the encounter, however, Rahzu had no further doubts about YetziRah being RahKael's puppet master. He pulled the strings to get her on board this ship and set her to working on some devious scheme he was concocting. What that was, though, Rahzu did not know.

While quite obnoxious, Ensign RahKael was thorough, methodical, and brilliant. She was looking for something specific when she visited the life pods alone. The captain was determined to find out what that was. She was trained by YetziRah, though, and would likely have covered her tracks well. Rahzu was counting on her arrogance, however. *That was her fatal flaw*, he thought.

As the Cruiser Rahs returned from PU 431 after dropping off the two human subjects, Captain Rahzu ordered both crews to the place where the incident occurred. He also contacted Commander CheRahna and requested her presence on the bridge to talk privately with her before they met the others.

It had appeared to Rahzu that she was ready to bare her soul when YetziRah arrived. Even though he had had no choice, he still wanted to apologize for not being able to talk with her at that moment.

Rahzu also, in time, wanted to tell her what his encounter with YetziRah revealed. But now he needed to focus on his investigation.

As TamaRah and the other junior officers arrived in the lab, conversation was abuzz about the humans' escape and RahKael's death. The crew were still, as of yet, unaware of Fleet Admiral YetziRah's surprise visit. This was the first time they had all been together to discuss the recent tragedy.

TamaRah and Rahphila calmed their budding love affair down and focused on the tests involving the avian. They also studied the biofeedback data they had collected from the human subjects.

ShemRahya and KaRah, in typical fashion, being the security officers, were busy looking for clues concerning the silver remains of the ensign, which were pooled on the floor, and the life pod mechanisms, respectively.

Everyone was individually working very diligently on particular bits of evidence when the captain and commander entered the room. Rahzu was glad to see his crew of officers taking the investigation seriously, even though no love was lost with RahKael's passing.

Looking at CheRahna, Rahzu asked, "Commander"—he was much more formal when around the other crew members—"I want you to give me an assessment of what you see!"

"Captain? I don't understand?!" CheRahna replied.

"Look at the crew, the environment, and describe what is happening and your impression of what they are doing," Rahzu explained.

"Oh, I see. Well . . . the first thing that stands out to me is the pool of tarnished silver that ShemRahya is testing. Then I see KaRah inspecting the life pods to determine if there was some sort of mechanical defect involved in the escape. TamaRah is studying the results of the tests of the ciconine avian, while Rahphila is examining the data collected from the humans. They all appear to be vigorously working while doing an in-depth analysis of the data," CheRahna said, feeling as if she was stating the obvious.

"Yes, all of what you just said is quite accurate. Well done. However, I want you to tell me what's wrong with the situation. How would you improve what they are doing to better facilitate solving the case?" Rahzu challenged.

Pausing momentarily, CheRahna looked out over the room. She saw that the things being done were all vital to the investigation. She again noticed how each person was working hard, individually putting together information. The room was silent; there was no talk among the crew.

As if a light bulb went off in her head, she was suddenly illuminated by what she believed the captain wanted her to see. Excitedly, CheRahna blurted out, "They're not communicating their findings in real time. They should be working together as they compile evidence so that each opinion or theory is tested and discussed."

Rahzu was beaming. He was proud of his commander and told her as much. "Excellent, CheRahna. That's the exact assessment I would have come to. What do you recommend be done then?" The captain extended his arm in an arching motion to signify that he wanted her to take charge of the situation.

CheRahna happily accepted; it was a sign of great respect for the captain to allow her to call the shots on this important task, especially with him present.

"Everyone, listen up!" Commander CheRahna said in a loud, official voice.

The crew stopped what they were doing and gave her their complete attention.

"You are all doing a great job and working very hard. The captain and I thank you for your diligence in this matter. However, in order for us to get to the bottom of this more quickly, we feel that you need to work together as one group, in one area at a time. This will allow each person's expert opinion in his or her respective field to assess the data as it is revealed."

Everyone looked at each other and seemed to agree that this was a good plan of action. Also, they all noticed the change in CheRahna's demeanor, as TamaRah and Rahphila had earlier.

CheRahna, sensing their approval, asked, "Are there any questions or suggestions? Any way to improve what we are doing here?"

"Commander, I think if we start where the problem originated, at the life pods, and work our way forward as the events happened, we may best be able to piece together the information chronologically," TamaRah concluded, unsure how CheRahna would react.

"What do you think, ShemRahya?" the commander charged.

ShemRahya, as half of the security duo, was actually in charge of the investigation team in principle; although no one was throwing titles or rank around under these circumstances. He thought the plan was sound and efficient, and he responded, "I believe that both your and TamaRah's assessments are accurate and are the optimal ways to facilitate the solving of this case. We should begin immediately."

"Good. If there are no other recommendations or questions . . ." CheRahna waited for any, but none came. "Then let's get to work and see what we can find. Again, thank you for all your hard work dealing with this matter."

After snapping to attention, the crew began to gather around the life pods. There was a low chatter among them, which she could not hear. The vibe was a positive one, though. CheRahna believed she had made the correct decisions and motivated the crew positively.

Turning back to the captain for the first time since addressing the group, she could feel the approval radiating from his golden form.

Rahzu was utterly amazed by how quickly she had transformed. It was almost as if he had a new commander. She was really taking this empathy thing seriously. It was time, he thought, for them to talk. Not about YetziRah, though—that could be done later, after the investigation was over—but about her. He wanted to ride this wave of positivity in his commander while it lasted. Rahzu signaled her to follow him as they left the area. "CheRahna, let's have that talk now. Your place or mine?" he asked jokingly.

CHAPTER TWENTY EIGHT

WHILE ON HIS way to the R&D division, under Hangar 18, Jonathan glanced at his phone to check the time. The display showed in a light green glow, 8:30, May 21, 2007. Exiting the elevator, once again he was in the underground world. This time, however, he was much more relaxed, being on his own turf.

Below Wright-Patterson Air Force Base, though security was extremely stringent, with several biometric and coded measures needing to be successfully passed in order to proceed, once under the surface, no one would ever question his presence. It was assumed that if you could get through the security and enter this secret world, then you belonged there—a theory that was essentially correct.

As he walked, a feeling of nostalgia came over him. The Hangar 18 facility was the place it all started. The thought of being here in 1947, when the Roswell spacecraft and its occupants were brought in for study, gave him goose bumps. The men in those days were on the cutting edge of discovery, when all was new. The atom, just two years earlier, had been split. Amazing scientific discoveries in rocketry, jet propulsion, and antigravity craft were coming to the forefront with the end of World War II, especially with the competition with the Soviets for German scientists. Jonathan could not help but wonder, if these walls could talk, all the stories they could tell.

Back then, Hangar 18 at Wright-Patterson was the place to be if you were in the know. It was the home to the Air Technology Intelligence Center (ATIC), now called the National Air Intelligence Center (NAIC). All exotic terrestrial and extraterrestrial research were brought here, to the Foreign Technology Division.

Allegations of dead aliens, and even live ones freely walking around, strangely enough, even today, are true. Jonathan believed that at times information was leaked to the general public in order to desensitize them to the inevitable truth, that humans were not alone in the universe. Even the current chief of the FTD, Air Force Colonel George Weinbrenner, leaked classified information about the presence of live aliens and the existence of film footage showing several types of UFOs.

Apparently, all the cloak-and-dagger tactics surrounding the data leaks, along with knowledge gleaned from the Freedom of Information Act, had been successful, because the general population believed in ETs and UFOS.

Following the Roswell crash, the most well-known incident involving visitors from another world, the craft, as well as its occupants, were studied extensively.

One of the aliens, named EBE, for extraterrestrial biological entity, claimed to be from a planet in the Zeta Reticuli star system, approximately thirty-nine light years away. EBE, once the language barrier was broken, was quite helpful in providing scientists with explanations, so that now the engineers had at least a layman's knowledge concerning the processes of the ship's operation and much of the equipment aboard.

The Eben presence, as they were called, and the acquisition and visitation of other worldly beings with their technologies, prompted the government to begin Project Silver Bug, the sole function of which was the development of flying disc-type aircraft and other vertical takeoff craft. Through reverse engineering of the Eben vehicle, and with the help of scientist Townsend Brown's electrokinetic thrusters, the United States was able to develop superluminal aircraft capable of traveling to the stars.

Project Silver Bug stimulated a greater understanding of the influx of technological advancements that came not only from afar, but from those developed here on Earth. Gravity beam projection and microbeam technologies now were better understood as means of propulsion. Scientists gained insight and understanding about the Nazi Haunebu flying discs, which in 1947 caused Admiral Richard Byrd's Operation Highjump to be prematurely terminated. While in Antarctica, one ship, the USS *Pine Island*, was sunk and several aircraft were blown out of the sky by flying discs traveling over 8,000 mph. They all displayed the Nazi swastika and used the KraftStrahlKanone phased energy rectifiers as weaponry.

Nazi Germany, at the end of the World War II, was decades ahead of the rest of the world in the fields of rocketry and ballistics. Luckily, Wernher von Braun, Walter and Reimer Horten, and other Nazi scientists were acquired from Germany through Operation Paperclip. They quickly advanced not only the public NASA space program, but the secret one as well.

As Jonathan headed north through the underground passages, he focused on what he could experience through his senses. Although his thoughts could be stolen here as well, he found that this method of focus worked just as effectively as chanting his mantra. Plus, it allowed him to live in the present, which was hard enough when living between two worlds, the public and the secret. While he continued to take in the wonders of his environment, an antigravity transport containing two Pleiadeans passed by. Since Wright-Patterson has been alien friendly for many years, the sight of beings from other worlds was commonplace.

The Pleiadeans were a humanoid race that stood around seven feet in height. They usually had long blond hair and blue eyes. Their skin was fair but tanned well. They were always in excellent shape. If one had to describe them, they most resembled people of Scandinavia on steroids and were closely related to the Nordics and the Anshar civilizations which lived in Antarctica. Surprisingly, many alien entities are genetically akin to humans—one big melting pot.

While the Pleiadeans currently occupied four planets that orbit the star Tangeta, or M45 as denoted by scientists, which is forty-two light years away, it is not their home. Their origins are traced back to the planet ERRA, some 500 light years away, where they too, though industrialization and war, nearly destroyed it. The Pleiadean presence on Earth is one of guidance and assistance. They are part of the Galactic Federation of Light that wishes to guide humanity into the future.

The transport, a land speeder as it was jokingly called, operated using microwave phase conjunction. Basically, a dispersed high-energy microwave was fired downward into the ground and reflected back to the craft. Then a metamaterial, such as barium titanate, reflected the wave between the ground and the craft repeatedly, providing levitation. By varying the angle of the microwave beam, propulsion is also achieved. The process is quite similar as to a microwave heating food, except that where the microwaves penetrate the food, they are reflected off the metamaterial making up the craft.

The microwave beam, if not dispersed but concentrated and focused, was also used as a weapon in the Strategic Defense Initiative (SDI), or Star Wars defense platform. This antimissile weapons system has been in space since the 1960s, decades before President Reagan even alluded to its existence in the 1980s. Such is the information that reaches the public. Incredibly enough, though, the innovation for SDI was not of alien origin, just one more pearl of technology that has been suppressed under the guise of national security.

Jonathan smiled as he entered the research laboratory. He felt privileged to be among the select few who had some idea what was really happening in the world, or at least he thought he did. Also, the R&D lab had enough gadgets to excite any soldier. From the TALOS (tactical assault light operator suit), which enhanced a soldier's combat performance in the field, to various arrays of nanomachines that performed myriad functions, ranging from regenerative kinetics to adaptive sensing and control, the R&D was as futuristic as it gets.

Sitting in front of his computer monitor, busily typing, was Haji Patel. Haji was originally from Saharanpur, India, in the Punjab region just north of Delhi. He had married Sarah's sister Myrah over thirty-five years ago. They had met when Myrah was attempting to settle a dispute between two people involved in a traffic accident. The situation started to get out of control, but before it escalated any further, Haji, believing Myrah was in danger, stepped in to her defense. Though she was more than capable of defending herself, the gesture made her instantly fall in love with him.

Haji Patel was a driven man. Born in poverty, from the lower caste of Varnas, called Shudras, he sacrificed much to change his karma. Meeting

Myrah was the best thing to ever happen to him. Through her, he found the confidence within himself to leave India, move to England, and get an education. Luckily, Myrah, although not part of the caste, or jatis, system, a Persian, had come from a family of means. Haji attended Cambridge and received his master's in both physics and chemistry. After graduation, he and Myrah picked up again and moved to the United States, where Haji earned his doctorate in both fields of study from MIT. It was only natural, with Abhar's connections and Haji's own exceptional intellect, that he would also come to work at Wright-Patterson, in the secret world.

As Jonathan approached, Haji stood to greet him with a handshake. Though not a muscular man, he had a remarkably strong grip and exhibited well-defined muscle tone, all undoubtedly due to his years of practicing the discipline of yoga.

Since he was of the Shudras, he had the characteristically dark skin of the people of that caste. His hair was jet black, with only traces of gray; Haji looked quite young for a man approaching sixty years of age. As with anyone who reads a lot, since the eyes were not designed for that purpose, he wore thin, circular wire-framed silver glasses.

Though Haji was slightly taller, because of his boots, Jonathan was able to look directly into his dark brown eyes. While considered disrespectful in many parts of the world, especially in the Middle and Far Eastern cultures, Haji had become Americanized long ago and suffered from no such feelings about eye contact.

"Good morning, Major Hawthorn," Haji said semiformally. He could not bring himself to just call him by his first name.

Jonathan had countless times given Haji permission to be less formal and call him Jonathan, but he knew it was no use. Haji was a man of conviction. "Hello, Haji. What are you working on now?" Jonathan looked intently at him as he explained his latest project. Currently Haji was creating a computer program that would autonomously alter physics equations in the CERN computer system in order to hinder the project from achieving a mini-Big Bang.

CERN was Europe's large hadron super collider, located on the French-Swiss border. It smashes protons together at near light speed while using the Higgs boson, or "God particle," to re-create the events just after the beginning of the universe. The problem is, with its current calculations and if the collider were allowed to operate at full capacity, it would create a black hole under the town, which would destroy the planet.

Haji had successfully stalled CERN to date; however, the scientists working there were getting better and faster at correcting his purposely placed glitches. He needed a program that adjusted, in real time, to automatically install a new safeguard equation as soon as its predecessor was solved. Besides, here in the FTD, the knowledge CERN was attempting to learn was already known.

Jonathan always allowed Haji to ramble on a little before getting to business. He knew that not many people came to visit, and those that did wanted whatever they came for quickly, without a lot of chatter. Also, Jonathan, being educated himself in geology and civil engineering, had a working knowledge of what Haji was attempting to explain.

As Haji moved back toward his computer to show his latest physics equations and computer program, Jonathan could not help but notice that he was unusually jittery. When Haji had finished with his explanation, Jonathan now told him, "Haji, I need you to look at the phone that your brother-in-law gave me. It's fried."

Grabbing the phone, Haji pulled out the battery and inspected the device. He already knew that the circuitry was destroyed by the mini-EMP that Abhar had programmed into the phone but was stalling because he was unsure how to begin explaining it to the major.

"Yes, it is indeed . . . how would you say . . . burnt to a crisp. Do you have any idea how it happened?" Haji asked in order to see how insightful Major Hawthorn was. Abhar had told him to use his judgment as to what to reveal, but Haji felt sure Jonathan could handle any information he wished to divulge.

"Well, Haji, if I had to guess, I'd say it had to be some sort of an electrical pulse, like an EMP . . . but if that was the case, everything else would have been destroyed too. The rental car, my other phone . . . It doesn't make any sense."

"Major Hawthorn, may I see your other phone?" Haji asked, holding out his hand. He looked at it and quickly came to the conclusion that Jonathan did not have the phone on his person at the time of his abduction. Again, probing Jonathan's mind to determine what he actually remembered and how he processed the events of his recent experience, Haji asked, "Major Hawthorn, last night . . . did you experience . . . something unusual?"

Jonathan had not made up his mind whether he was going to tell about his missing time when he arrived, but Haji's line of questioning insinuated that he knew something, so Jonathan merely said, "I think you know something unusual happened." He paused to study Haji's reaction to his statement. It was stoic. "Last night, I had two and a half hours that I cannot account for, I shot at a stork, and it fell from the sky dead, or least that's how it appeared to me."

"Major Hawthorn, you are an excellent shot, I'm sure. It does not sound so unusual that you were able to shoot a bird from the sky. Especially one as large as a stork."

"Yeah, but the thing is . . . I missed. I shot an entire clip at it and hit nothing but air. The damn bird still fell from the sky. It was dead. I'm sure of it," Jonathan said scratching his head.

"Tell me what you remember," Haji said earnestly.

Jonathan went on to tell Haji about his experience: getting the Viper at the rental place, listening to the radio program and what was said, his high-speed drive through the Mammoth Cave area, the subsequent spin-out, getting out of the car, shooting at the stork, and then crawling over to inspect it, only to see it had not died from being shot. "The next thing I remember is waking up in the car, two and half hours later, with bird shit smeared on my face and in my mouth, shell casings all over the ground, and no fucking bird to be found!" Jonathan threw both hands in the air, exasperated, something very uncommon for him. He typically did not get frazzled, even under the most stressful conditions. "Then I went to check Abhar's encrypted phone . . . and there you have it! That's what I got!"

Jonathan looked at Haji with a lost look on his face. Haji could tell that the major was not used to being in a situation that offered no reasonable explanation, or at least one he was willing to believe. Noticing this, Haji asked, "What do you think happened to you, Major Hawthorn?"

Jonathan had already come to the obvious conclusion, the only possible explanation, but until now he was reluctant to admit it. "The only thing that makes any sense is that I was drugged and kidnapped."

"Kidnapped or abducted? There is a difference, Major Hawthorn." Haji pressed him to answer. He needed Jonathan to accept what happened if he was going to tell him more.

Jonathan, with a furrowed forehead, snapped, "Okay, fine, abducted!"

"Major Hawthorn, considering your type of work, the beings you associate with, your best friend is a lizard! Look around! Does it really seem so unbelievable that you too could fall victim to one of these beings?!"

"Well . . . no . . . but I don't remember anything, not a blurb. Nothing!"

"Haven't you yourself been on the other side of this and left people feeling similar to how you are feeling now? With no memory of anything?"

"Yes, but that's different."

"Why? Are you some sort of god?!" Haji asked him to see if he knew who his father actually was.

"Damn it! No, Haji, I'm not!" Jonathan looked down and paced as he finally accepted what he suspected. Gilla was right all along. Jonathan knew he would have to admit that to him and eat crow. The hissing that would ensue! He could not help but smile at how he thought his Reptilian friend would react.

Haji studied Jonathan as he processed the information. Considering what he had just got him to admit, he thought the major was handling all of this quite well. Well enough to smile.

"All right Haji, what now? You seem to have all the answers." Jonathan asked, completely flabbergasted. He had been captured and drugged before, been tortured and had moments he could not remember, but nothing like this.

Haji, seeing the confusion on his face, decided to only reveal what was necessary to the major. He would let Abhar enlighten him more later. Baby steps, he thought. "How do you feel? Any aches or unexplainable pains?"

Jonathan could not think of anything that stood out to him. He did have a slight ache between his shoulder blades as he explained, but he attributed that to muscle strain from his spinning out at high speed.

Haji walked over to a cabinet on the other side of the lab, reached for a drawer, and pulled out an electromagnetic detection wand. Jonathan had seen these many times before and knew exactly what they were used for. As Haji approached, Jonathan asked, "You don't think I'm bugged, do you?"

"I'm not sure, Major Jonathan, but it's best to be safe and check anyway." Haji was sure Jonathan had some sort of device implanted in him.

Haji started waving the wand at Jonathan's feet and moved it all over his body, purposely avoiding the area between his shoulders. When this was done, Haji walked over to his lab counter, where a powerful electromagnet was located. He turned it on and waved the wand near it. The wand beeped each time it passed the magnet. After showing Jonathan that this wand indeed worked, Haji returned to where his friend was standing. He looked Jonathan directly in the eyes, grabbed his right shoulder with his right hand, and pulled him forward, turning him slightly. With his left hand, Haji then brought the wand up between the major's shoulders.

To Jonathan's surprise, the wand sang in displeasure. Haji waved it a second time; and once again it chirped to life.

"Major Hawthorn, you have been chipped."

"Shit! Get this fucking thing out of me!"

"Major Jonathan, I'm not a doctor. I . . ."

"I don't give two shits about that. I want this thing out and I want it out now! I'll cut it out myself if I have to." Jonathan was completely serious. "Look, you operate on these gadgets all the time," he said, waving his hand around signifying the location of equipment, which was everywhere. "You can do it on me. I know it. Please, Haji!" Jonathan asked passionately.

Haji, looking at the spot where the device was located, had been informed by Abhar as to what to look for, where it would be, and how to safely remove it. "Major Jonathan, I believe I can remove the device, but it could be extremely painful." Haji paused while trying to find a solution to the pain problem. Walking back over to the counter, Haji pulled out several foot-long, extremely thin sticks of hardened silver solder, which he used to repair or make circuitry in transistors no larger than a droplet of water.

"I can use these to perform a nerve block, like acupuncture, to at least mitigate the pain while I remove the implant. We'll need to deal with your pain afterward, though." Haji showed Jonathan the silver sticks, which were sharp and fine enough to do the job.

Jonathan took a deep breath and studied Haji for a moment to determine if he indeed planned on sticking those needle-like objects in him. Satisfied that Haji was completely serious and looked as if he knew what he was about to do, Jonathan agreed. "Okay. Where do you want to do this?"

Haji motioned for Jonathan to come over to the island, in the middle of the lab, while he went around collecting the supplies he needed for this impromptu surgery. Jonathan did as he was told and looked around the lab trying to find something to focus on while Haji would be cutting into his back.

Haji, besides working on the physics program to deter CERN from destroying the planet, had several projects he was working on. This was not the first time Jonathan had been in here, so he was familiar with some of them.

At the opposite side of the room, Haji was searching through drawers and cabinets for anything he felt would be helpful in removing the implant. Thanks to Abhar, he knew exactly what to expect. Hopefully, no complications would occur that might put Major Hawthorn's life in jeopardy.

Other than beakers, pipettes, flasks, Bunsen burners, cylinders, and various other glass apparatuses, the lab had every measuring device that a chemist or physicist would require: balances, calorimeters, barometers, vernier calibers, potentiometers, mass spectrometers; it even had a Geiger counter. Needless to say, the laboratory was exceptionally well equipped, even for a military installation.

Just above Jonathan's head was a retractable light with a built-in magnifying glass. Several different hoses with which Haji could hook up various air tools or vacuums, and what appeared to be some sort of laser cutter. Haji found all these tools invaluable when working on his various projects.

Jonathan was familiar with and had used much of the equipment around the room. None of them, however, kept his attention for very long. He noticed that a TALOS suit, along with all its size variations, was in the northwest corner of the laboratory. The suits were used to increase a soldier's strength, speed, and stamina. Jonathan had used then in combat before, in Kosovo, and while seeing their necessity for the common grunt, he formed the opinion that elite forces that employed them too much would come to rely on them. The machines currently were not hard to disable, if one knew where to hit them. They were also easily detectable. Because of these faults, they had only limited use in the covert world.

But as much as he hated to admit it, even the secret world was changing. Biomedical implants for increased senses and performances; mini-electrode brain and nasal chips that monitored, advised, and even triggered the release of hormones. There were super drugs that increased stamina and awareness while suppressing empathy. There now was even an Integrated Individual Constellation System that contained low-orbit, smart satellites that allowed an implanted soldier to interface with resource materials while generating a personal, computer-generated, neural visualization of the battlefield.

On the far western wall of the R&D lab was where all the nanotech was located. Nanomachines, more commonly called nanobots, were performing tasks ranging from building bridges to repairing capillaries. Nanotechnology was already being utilized commercially in swimsuits or wetsuits. The fabrics created are friction resistant, waterproof, and are thermoregulatory. Jonathan was sure Haji had much more advanced gear than the typical swimmer or diver could purchase. Other than using some aerogel socks and thermals, which adjusted temperature as needed, he was not current on the field.

Haji returned with a stainless steel cart loaded with supplies. An emesis basin, which contained the silver solder needles, an Exacto knife, and several pairs of adjustable clamps, was filled with enough isopropyl alcohol to cover all the items. Curiously, on the cart there was also a soldering iron, a jar of honey, a fine wire thread with a needle, both in the alcohol; and a tube of some sort of unknown substance. Haji even had a dozen or so sterile cloths and a few pairs of sterile gloves, which he used to repair advanced computer circuits and other experiments that required a sterile environment, along with a vial of silver nitrate for bleeding. There was even a Rife ray tube, much like the one at S-4, which would kill any pathogens before and after his surgery.

"Remove your shirt, Major Jonathan, as I prepare the equipment and get started."

Jonathan did as instructed, and while viewing what Haji had brought, he could not help asking him a few questions. "What's the soldering iron and honey for, Haji?" Jonathan asked with a nervous look on his face, especially concerning the soldering iron.

"Well, sir, they are both prophylactics," Haji said matter-of-factly.

"Whoa, buddy . . . I like you and all, but we're not going there." Jonathan held both hands up, gesturing as if he was pushing him away. Haji showed no reaction. Jonathan still did not know what Haji had meant though, and asked him to explain.

"The soldering iron is here in the event that I cut an artery. If that happens, I will be able to cauterize it immediately. The honey is to apply to your wound after everything else is done, creating an impenetrable barrier which will protect you from infection as you heal."

"Really! Cool . . . and I'll taste sweet too, right!" Jonathan tried some humor again.

Haji caught on to this reference, did a double take, and responded while smiling, "Yes, Major, as sweet as sugarcane."

"And the tube of goo?" Jonathan pointed at the five-inch-long tube.

"This," he said, picking up the tube, "Major Jonathan, is a substance that was given to me by an Asharian named Lanah. It has a rather undescriptive name in English, but suffice it to say, it fuses your skin together so that you will heal scar free in about three hours," Haji said as if he was revealing the cure for cancer, which they already had.

"Wow! I bet this stuff would fly off the shelves at the local drug store," Jonathan pronounced.

"Unlikely, Major Hawthorn. The salve has iridium in it. As I'm sure you know, iridium is one of the rarest substances in the universe. This tube would cost the manufacturer around twelve thousand dollars to make. You can only imagine how much they would charge the public," Haji quipped as he continued getting ready. "I need one more thing, Major Jonathan," Haji said while walking toward his desk. He was searching for his adjustable magnifying spectacles.

Still looking for something to focus on, Jonathan looked toward the northeast corner of the room. There were two objects he had never seen before and that seemed particularly odd to be in this environment.

One was a mask of gold that showed some resemblance to the ancient gods seen on Sumerian clay tablets. It had a roundish face, two nose holes, a slight opening for the mouth, and a helmet that covered the wearer's head. The mask was simply carved, but flawless.

The other object was what appeared to be a beautiful harp carved completely in gold. It was almost three feet in height had silver strings with white crystal beads; it was also exquisitely made. Many of the markings looked similar to those on the mask; Jonathan assumed they were from the same area as well as the same time period. Having some knowledge of ancient relics, he was confident that they were indeed from Sumer.

"Haji, what are those doing here?" he asked, pointing at the mask and harp.

Haji, looking at what Jonathan was referring to, had not considered that the major might ask him about them. He knew he was not going to tell him that they were Abhar's and he was told to bring them here for safe keeping. He also was not going to tell Jonathan what they were really called and that they were both enormously powerful devices.

The Mask of Warka was used to not only read the most trained mind, but also protected others from viewing the wearer's thoughts. It had traditionally been worn by judges and kings when conducting trials or matters of state. Subjects would not, or more accurately could not, hide the truth or their intentions from whoever wore the mask. King Solomon had a similar object, which was why he was so wise. Abhar Am acquired the object from his father, Terah, because he was the eldest son, as was his birthright.

Abhar's other possession was the Harp of Haran, one of the most powerful sonic weapons ever to exist. It was similar in technology to the device that was used to topple the walls of Jericho thousands of years later. Even though it produced a beautiful sound, it could mesmerize, hypnotize, or pulverize, depending on the intensity and intention of the harpist. It could be focused with pinpoint accuracy or broadcast over a large area. This was one of several ancient weapons with otherworldly powers.

Knowing the truce history of these relics, Haji also knew of the existence of their decoys. They were created to replace these that were now in his possession, to slowly, over time, let their fabled power disappear into legend and lore. The plan was to give Jonathan the names of the decoys. Hopefully, this ruse would work, because he did not feel it was his place to let him too far into Abhar's life, even though Abhar gave him permission. Haji himself was not one of them and was only related through marriage.

"That is the Mask of Warka," he said, pointing at it with his right index finger. "And that is the Harp of Ur, Major Jonathan," Haji lied convincingly.

"So they are Sumerian, yes?" Jonathan asked, but was sure they were.

"Yes, they are both over five thousand years old. The mask was made in the city of Sippar and the harp, obviously, was made in Ur. They were a gift from the Anunnaki god Ninurta to the keeper of the holy of holies, the MEs."

"I vaguely remember hearing something about both of those a few years ago. Where was it . . . oh yeah! They were stolen from the Iraq National Museum just after the war started in 2003. Right?"

"Yes, Major Jonathan, they are the very same." Haji was impressed with Jonathan's memory.

"I thought the harp was destroyed for its gold and the mask returned to the museum, though. What are they doing here?" Jonathan asked inquisitively, knowing how replicas are passed off as originals in many public places.

"Well, Major Jonathan, let's just say that these are not the same as those," Haji whispered. "These are the real ones."

While Haji got everything prepared, Jonathan closed his eyes and imagined being in the time of the ziggurat, the days of Sumer, at the dawn of modern civilization. He imagined watching spacecraft coming down from the heavens and being in the bird city, the ancient spaceport of Sippar. It was a time of gods and men living together. The gods were an actual physical presence. Yahweh talked to Adam, Enoch, Noah, and later Abraham. Many other gods were present in those days too, trying to impress their wills on humanity. A larger number were not gods at all, just technologically advanced enough to appear godlike. Jonathan, like most people, was very confused about this period in human history. He had heard so many different versions from various beings; he did not know what to believe. He was confident, however, that there was an all-powerful God, and his name was Yahweh.

Haji could see that Jonathan was deep in meditative thought and decided to start the procedure without interrupting him. He knew precisely how and where to place the silver needles so that Jonathan would not even feel them penetrating his skin.

Once this was done, Haji pricked Jonathan with another needle, directly in the area he was getting ready to incise, to see if he felt anything. Jonathan did not flinch. Satisfied that his nerve block was successful, using sterile technique, Haji laid out all his operating equipment on a sterile cloth to the right of his patient. Haji, being right handed, always used his right hand as the clean hand and the left as the dirty one, if the procedure allowed. With his left hand, he reached for the magnifying spectacles pushed up on his head.

After he finished cleaning the area with alcohol and performed a quick wave of the Rife ray tube to kill any remaining bacteria—a bit of overkill— Haji was ready to begin cutting. Abhar had informed him that the device would be just beneath the epidermis, about one-half centimeter inside the adipose tissue. It was surrounded by muscles. He was looking for an object that was only three millimeters in size, which he had located using a smaller, more precise electromagnetic detector. This is a very sensitive region of the body and one of its major energy centers. He knew he had to be careful not to disrupt the natural energy flow, or future complications could arise.

Jonathan was lost in his thoughts about the days of yore when he heard Haji tell him to remain still. Thankfully, Haji's slight interruption did not wake him from his semiconscious state. He pictured himself being in the holy of holies, looking at the star charts, plotting courses through the universe. when suddenly he was in a spaceship standing over a woman in some sort of pod, sleeping. It was Ariella Marconi.

Just prior to Jonathan's abrupt meditative scenery change, Haji had performed his incision and exposed the device, which was vascularized like a spider web in Jonathan's back. *Fascinating*, he thought as he grabbed a set of hemostats with his left hand and attached them to the device.

Although pleasurable to look at her while in her sleep-like state, Jonathan could not help but wonder why she was in his dream. None of this was real! He quickly let his thoughts go and allowed things to unfold without concentrating on them, as he should while meditating. His mind shifted again to a seven-foot-tall silver-looking humanoid figure. It was talking to him, but not with its mouth. He realized it was female, but how? His mind drifted again to a wall of weapons. He now had an odd, triple-bladed sword in his hand. Although his thoughts were jumping to different events, they all appeared to be from the same place.

Haji was cutting away arteriole-like appendages from the implant. Luckily, there was little bleeding. He could see the object well and knew what it was made of. "Incredible," he whispered. It was an amber crystal, exactly like the one Abhar possessed and had shown him many years ago. Just a few more cuts and he would have it out. Thus far, he had been very careful not to damage the spherical crystal, which, judging by his potentiometer, was still functioning.

Jonathan's mind now had him standing in front of a worried-looking Ariella Marconi as they both were looking out some sort of huge porthole, through the darkness of what appeared to be a starless space. There it was, a massive amber crystal, floating in oblivion! Again, his senses shifted, and he was face to face with a golden figure which he knew to be male. A sense of respect came over him as they appeared to circle, as if in the throes of battle. He heard a scream, turned his head to see another silver female holding Ariella, then a flash of light.

Haji had a firm grip on the hemostats as he cut off the last of the crystal's vascular appendages. Suddenly, Jonathan jerked. Haji reflexively pulled both hands back to avoid cutting Jonathan with his Exacto knife, and to keep hold of the implant as Jonathan appeared to be waking. Haji looked at the hemostats, which verified that he had successfully removed the amber crystal device. Seconds later, however, the arteriole appendages encompassing the device started to melt away into nothingness, as if they had never existed. Looking again at his potentiometer, which now read zero, Haji knew that the implant was no longer functioning. He was hoping that after removing it from its power source, the human body, it would retain enough residual charge to function until he could hook it up to an alternate power source.

Jonathan, waking up, heard Haji fidgeting behind him. Coming out of his dream state, he was unaware of what stage of the surgery he was in.

"Are you all right, Major Jonathan? I hope I haven't hurt you."

"I'm fine. I just got lost in a very bizarre dream. I'm glad I snapped out of it. How are we coming? Are you ready to start cutting yet?" Jonathan asked, not having felt a thing.

Haji chuckled a little as he informed Jonathan that he had already removed the implant and all that was left was to sew and bandage him up.

"Wow, either I was so deep in mediation, or you are truly a master acupuncturist, because I didn't feel a thing."

"I believe it had more to do with your meditation, Major Hawthorn," Haji said modestly. Judging from Jonathan's comment, as Haji was severing the synaptic and arteriole connections from the crystal, as predicted, the device, in an attempt to remain connected to the neural network, started to alter Jonathan's state of consciousness and ingrained patterns of memory. The major was remembering events that had been purposely blocked. Haji had studied implants before and knew that is how most of them operated. Much like electricity flowing through power lines, if one line goes down, the electrical current finds an alternative path. Haji was curious, though, as to what Jonathan was seeing during the operation.

As he was stitching the major up, Haji inquired, "Major Jonathan, you said you experienced some bizarre visions under meditation. Would you care to share them with me?" Haji paused, realizing that his request may have seemed odd to Jonathan, but continued, saying, "I only ask you because the device was still transmitting during the surgery and immediately stopped functioning upon removal. It may help me determine what its purpose was."

Still a little groggy from his meditative state, Jonathan responded, "Ah . . . okay." It took him a few more seconds to process the request; but after a moment he realized what Haji was getting at. "Oh, I get it now!" Jonathan said upon his understanding of the question.

"Sir?" Haji was unsure what Jonathan meant.

"Never mind." Jonathan jumped right in and told Haji of his visions during his surgery. It struck him as odd that Ms. Marconi was in his thoughts, because he had not met her face to face. He told Haji of the silver and golden elementals and the amber crystal that was perched in the void. He explained, briefly, about the same crystal in the Puerto Rico Trench. "I guess that implant really pumped up the imagination hormones, huh, because that was some strange shit," Jonathan said laughing.

Haji remained silent, understanding that the events Jonathan had just told him about were of his recent abduction. Because Jonathan had already accepted the fact that he had been kidnapped by otherworldly beings, Haji did not think it too big a leap for Major Hawthorn to be enlightened further.

"So you say you have never met this Ariella Marconi before, correct?"

"Yep, positive I haven't. I'm supposed to meet her later this afternoon for the first time in San Francisco for my new assignment."

Haji was aware of the major's assignment and what Jonathan would be studying. He had just removed a small piece of the same substance from Jonathan's back moments ago. "Ok, Major Jonathan. I know this may seem a strange question, but when you first looked at Ms. Marconi's picture . . . did she seem . . . familiar to you?"

Jonathan, unsure of where this line of questioning was going, was intrigued. "As a matter of fact, she did. I felt like I somehow knew this woman."

"Did the Ms. Marconi in your vision match the Ms. Marconi of the picture?"

"No, she did not," Jonathan answered with a confused look on his face. "What's going on here, Haji?"

"One moment, sir, while I finish up," Haji said as he rubbed on the iridium salve, sealed the wound with a layer of honey, waved the Rife ray tube, and applied the bandage. "All done! You will be as good as new in several hours, minus some pain, of course. I'll have Ashley requisition a few Percocets from medical for you."

"Thanks." Jonathan, back to task, asked again, "Haji . . . what's going on?" A little more impatiently this time.

While Major Hawthorn put on his shirt, Haji refreshed Jonathan on how biological monitoring and control devices worked and how they mimicked the human nervous system, making them virtually undetectable. They connect to a person's neural network and predominantly monitor or record events that happen in real time. Occasionally they are used to control behavior. Haji went on to say that due to the amount of energy the implant he removed was using, it was only in monitoring mode. Therefore, the events Jonathan saw in his meditative visions were likely real.

"Wait a minute. You're saying that shit really happened. I was on a space-ship with not only a woman I can't remember meeting, but with gold and silver gods?!" Jonathan cried out, exasperated. He was being more sarcastic and stubborn than doubting Haji's theory.

"Well, Major Jonathan . . . I believe this happened during your abduction, and apparently, Ms. Marconi was also abducted," Haji answered. "I also do not think it was the first time for either of you."

Jonathan was having a hard time thinking that all of these recent events were just coincidence; Haji's rationalization was the only thing that made sense. "Let's just say I believe everything you just said . . . my question now is, why me? What makes me so damn important?"

Haji motioned for Jonathan to look down at the hemostats lying on the tray. He moved the magnifying light so Jonathan could get a better look. "I believe it may have something to do with this, Major Jonathan," Haji asserted, referring to the amber crystal he had pulled out of the major's back.

Peering through the lens of the magnifying glass, Jonathan's mouth dropped open as he grasped what he was looking at. It appeared not only to be the same material as the amber crystal he was going to study in Puerto Rico, but the same one he saw while meditating, both here and at Dulce. Jonathan was starting to sense that something far more sinister was going on underneath the surface than he previously thought.

After seeing Jonathan's revelation, Haji added, "Judging by your scar tissue, this was not the first time you have been implanted."

"How is that possible? I go through electromagnetic scanners almost daily; it would have been zapped and I would have been alerted if one was in me," Jonathan said, questioning Haji's latest assumption.

"Not if it had already stopped functioning," Haji revealed as he reached for the potentiometer and pointed it at Jonathan. The meter jumped to life.

Jonathan, seeing the movement of the meter's needle, stared blankly. He then looked at Haji, pointing at the meter. "That's not normal, is it?" He knew it was not.

"No, sir, Major Jonathan, it is not normal."

"Well . . . what does it mean? Is there something wrong with me?"

To calm Jonathan down, Haji said, "What I meant to say was that it's not normal for most people. You, however, are among a small percentage of people who generate a measurable amount of energy through biological processes."

"What does that mean? You can hook jumper cables to me and start your car?"

"Essentially, with enough time, yes!"

"Well, how many more people are there out there like me, one to two percent of the population?" Jonathan asked.

"No, sir, it's more like two thousandths of a percent. I would say somewhere around 100,000 people."

"In the United States?"

"No, sir, Major. In the world," Haji seriously said.

Jonathan had always thought of himself as something special, but just figured this was his Leo ego. It actually did not bother him that he was different, but that was still no explanation for how the implants that were supposedly in him before went undetected. "I guess I'm special then," Jonathan said jokingly. "But tell me what this means and how come no device has ever been detected on me."

"I believe that your individual magnetic resonance and electrical frequency actually short circuits the implants within weeks, perhaps even days after the insertion." Haji went on to say that he had already noticed electrical scarring on many of the large synaptic clusters just prior to removing Jonathan's device. He then made the assumption that if Jonathan had been implanted, it would be safe to guess that Ms. Marconi had as well.

After hearing this, Jonathan knew it was time for him to go. He had planned on going more into depth about his vision at Dulce, but that would have to wait. He had enough information for now. He did, though, need to contact Abhar. "Haji, do you have a message for me or another phone from Abhar?"

"Yes, Major Jonathan, Abhar said he would see you in Puerto Rico."

"How does he know . . . ?" Jonathan went on to say before Haji interrupted. Something very uncommon for him.

"Abhar said he would know how to find you . . . I think you know my brother-in-law well enough to know he is a man of many talents and means. If he says something, he will do it, Major Jonathan."

"Yeah, you're right. I only met him yesterday and I already trust him with my life. I know there is more to his story than he is letting on, though."

"Most certainly, Major Hawthorn, and I'm sure he'll tell you in time," Haji said, signifying that he was going to be tight-lipped when it came to Abhar's life.

Jonathan admired him for that. Loyalty was something hard to find these days. Haji just jumped a few points on Jonathan's list of important people.

"I'll send the supplies you requested by vacuum tube up to your office, Major Hawthorn. I will also call Ashley about the pain meds. You'll need them soon."

"Thank you, Haji. For everything," he said, looking him directly in the eyes. Haji knew, at that moment, all his actions to that point had been what his karma wanted. The implant was removed, Jonathan was informed that he had been abducted, not just once but on several occasions, Abhar would meet him in Puerto Rico, and there was a sinister Rah presence in the universe, even if he did not name them.

"Take care of yourself, Major Jonathan, and remember, things are not as they seem," Haji finished as Jonathan was walking to the door.

"I will, Haji. If I need anything, I'll contact you," Jonathan said as he exited the laboratory. He picked up on Haji's cryptic warning and sensed that he knew more than he was telling. But, as things go in the military as well as the secret world, information was given on a need-to-know basis. Apparently, at this time, he did not need to know. His mind wondered anyway.

Before arriving back at his office, Jonathan had been reflecting on recent events and formulating a plan of action. He sensed that things were about to come to some sort of climax. But what that would be, he had no idea. He did know he wanted one of his best men there with him, and Gilla too. He had texted Ashley and told her to get the base provost marshal to his office ASAP, before he arrived. Recent revelations had forced him to alter his plans. He was getting short on time.

As he entered his office, Ashley was sitting at her desk talking to the base Provost Marshal while he drank a cup of coffee. He knew he could count on her. Seeing him enter, the captain stood at attention and waited for Jonathan's lead. Dispensing with formalities, Jonathan looked at both of them and in one terse statement demanded, "Somebody get me Haney!"

CHAPTER

TWENTY NINE

WHILE ABHAR SAT on the dock bench awaiting his ride, he allowed himself to use senses that were once so foreign to him. He gazed upon the crystal-clear blue water, smelled the jasmine growing near the beach, felt the warm spring breeze on his skin, and heard the song of a male frigatebird calling for a mate.

Although originally only meant to serve under Yahweh as a spy, Abhar found him to be wise, honorable, and loving, something he had never experienced in his own house. Little did he know at the time that his defection had been predicted in the very prophecy he was now struggling to fulfill. There were a great many things he still did not understand or was unsure of, but his trust and obedience to his master Yahweh was not among them.

Abhar, trying to relax while waiting for his train, closed his eyes and released all thoughts he had about the future. Instead, he focused on his bride Sarah—her beautiful smile, the enchantment of her eyes, her smooth brown skin. She too had given all her loyalty to him and the father. Even though living here, in a foreign world, in the service of the lord had taken its toll on them both, they each had retained much of their former youth. Much of what they had experienced in life, especially after siding with Yahweh, was tragic, but their service was what had made all the difference. All his efforts had led him here, to this moment, closer to the father than he has been in a very long time.

He quietly revisited his actions of the past several hours to ensure he had done all that was necessary.

Just as the maglev arrived, he was talking with Rakesh and advising him to close up shop, collect his family, and make his way to the rendez-vous point. Once he and Sarah boarded the train in their own cabin, he immediately turned on the privacy cloud and hit speed dial again, this time calling Haji.

After informing Haji of Jonathan's probable abduction, he explained everything Haji needed to know about locating and removing the Rah crystal implant. He then directed Haji to call Myrah and get her prepared for travel. He was sending Sarah there to meet her. They would leave together.

As the two men discussed what they thought might happen in the near future, Abhar noticed the tips of Sarah's ears turning very red. She had gotten angry, as he knew she would. Thinking back, he wondered that if he had paid closer attention, he might have seen steam actually emanating from the top of her head. Strangely, the thought amused him.

Once he had hung up on Haji, Abhar was braced for the verbal assault that followed. Sarah barked at him for a full five minutes, using multiple languages, and with some words that even he was unfamiliar with.

After her tirade abated, Abhar looked at his wife blankly and said, "Are you through?"

"Yes!" she snapped. Brooding.

"Feel better?" Abhar asked with the same, stoic tone.

"Yes." Sarah felt guilty about how she had spoken treated this man she trusted, the man she loved. Sarah knew Abhar served the father, Yahweh, and only did what he felt necessary and right to see that his will would be done. She would have had it no other way. Whatever his plans were, whatever he asked her to do, she would honor follow him. Sarah just absolutely abhorred being on the sidelines, away from the action and her beloved.

"Abraham, I'm so very . . ." She was trying to apologize to her husband when he stopped her by placing two fingers gently over her mouth.

"You never have to say sorry with me, my princess. Your passion for what you believe in is one of your most endearing qualities," Abhar soothed her.

"I just want to be with you Abraham, by your side. I need to see this through to the end, my love. We have sacrificed so much together. I want to be there with you, to celebrate in his glory," Sarah pleaded with her husband.

"Sarah, I will not allow you to be trapped in the sands unnecessarily again! This is not the end, not yet. I promise . . . if it is within my power, I will have you there with me, with the father, when the reaping begins. But until then, you need to go to Myrah's, not just for your protection, but for hers. Together, there is not a force on Earth that can harm the two of you."

"What about Jambres and Jannes?" Sarah asked, still fearful of her past imprisoners.

"Those magicians caught us off guard last time. That won't happen again," Abhar offered as a rebuttal, though, when it came to the brothers, he knew anything was possible. He was pretty sure they were again behind the scenes, manipulating people and events, but he could not focus on them at the present. Abhar went on to tell Sarah that traveling with Myrah, away from him, offered him the best chance to further their cause.

Sarah knew he was right. His love for her could be used against him, cause him to zig when he should zag; every move they made now was critical. She grabbed Abhar's hand and kissed it gently, passionately. It was her way of showing her love, trust, and obedience not only to him, but to Yahweh. "What do you want me to do, Brahmin?"

"I need you and your sister to contact the rest of our clan and have them go to Bharat, to our old home in Harappa," he told her distinctly and clearly.

As he continued to give her detailed instructions, she could see that this was not one of his spur-of-the-moment solutions. It was clear he had been planning this for quite some time.

"Forgive me for asking, but how long are we to wait in Harappa for you," Sarah asked with her head down, but her eyes up.

"Don't wait for me. Once the clan is assembled, go to Peetah's house in Dwarka. I'll meet you there soon enough." He could see the worry developing on her face. Reaching forward and grabbing her by the chin, he raised her head and told her not to worry. "I have this," Abhar said, referring to the tri-sword in his nag.

"Don't you have to give that to the God seed, though?" Sarah asked, still fearful for her husband's life.

"Yes, my princess, but at that time, my life will become secondary to his. Besides, I know where to find all three pieces of the other sword."

"You know where the Spear of Destiny is!?" It was more of a statement than a question. Sarah was surprised by Abhar's revelation, though. She had not heard a word about the spear since World War II. Hitler reportedly held one of the three blades, and he nearly took over the entire world. He may have succeeded if his hubris had not of gotten in his way. It was the same spear that was used to pierce Yahweh's son.

Luckily, at that time, the Romans, who had the complete sword with all three blades, had no idea how to activate its full power. However, as Abraham had told her long ago, it was no accident that they had the sword, and that they were not fully instructed on how to utilize its true power.

The Rahs' time to usurp the father's power had long passed, and they had no intention of instigating him to use his full wrath upon them. Nonetheless, they did kill Yahshua's flesh to see if he was the God seed they were in search of. He was not, and their actions merely fulfilled Yahweh's prophecy for his only begotten son to sit by his father's side awaiting mankind's judgment.

"Where are the blades to the spear now?" Sarah asked.

"Don't you worry about that. But I'll have at least one piece before I see Jonathan in Puerto Rico." He smiled, sensing her approval of his plans. "If things work out the way I believe they may, I will have all three pieces of the Spear of Destiny, the Schefa Crystal, and the Ark of the Covenant when I meet you in Dwarka," Abhar said proudly. He was much more confident when Sarah believed in what he was doing. She truly had provided him with the strength to continue as they had.

"It's a good thing you're setting your goals low, my love," she said with a sassy grin and puppy dog eyes. Sarah knew her husband was a man of many means and that once he set his mind on a goal, especially one for the father, rarely did he fail to achieve it.

They both knew that their successes were all possible due to Yahweh's power flowing through them—endeavors that nowadays were concealed from everyone. The honor of being chosen to fulfill the prophecy for the Lord supplied them with all the thanks they required.

Abhar, picking up on Sarah's playful banter, felt an urge he had not had for an awfully long time, to be completely human. "Have I told you how much I love you lately?" Abhar said flirtingly.

"Why don't you show me instead, Brahmin," Sarah sighed as she desperately awaited his warm embrace.

———⌣———

Sensing eyes upon him, Abhar awoke from his reflective trance to see a Wilson's petrel sitting on the handrail, inspecting him and looking very much like a black swallow; a distinctive patch of white above the base of the tail was its only distinguishing characteristic. Although a little late in the season, the bird was undoubtably resting from its long migration from Antarctica up the Atlantic coast to its spawning grounds farther north, in the Artic.

Abhar extended his hand to supply the bird with a perch and wished it to him. Instantly, the petrel flew to him. Abhar then puckered his lips and blew cool air all over the bird's body. The avian ruffled its feathers, chirped approvingly at Abhar's kindness, and took to the air to continue its journey.

Watching the bird fade into the distance, Abhar sat back and basked in the sun. He had reached Bimini Island, Bahamas, in good time, just six hours. After making passionate love to his wife, he and Sarah had parted ways when the maglev arrived in Atlanta. He was then able to contact his source in Puerto Rico to inform him of his impending arrival.

A few moments later, the sound of a propeller to the south caught his attention. In the distance, he could see the white Cessna Corvalis TTX seaplane he had called for making its way up from Nassau. Abhar would have preferred to have just chartered the flight he arrived here on, but it was already fully booked. There was too much to be done, to think about, to waste a lot of time and energy haggling. He also did not want to bring unnecessary attention to himself. That is why he chose to travel with a small, private company in the first place instead of taking a commercial flight out of Miami. Besides, he had a little time to spare.

Abhar raised his hand to act as a visor while he watched the plane successfully land. It slowly approached the dock. Upon arrival, the pilot throttled down, opened the sliding door, and threw Abhar a bow line. He quickly jumped off with the stern line in hand and anchored the craft to the cleave. After the plane was secure, the pilot extended his hand and introduced himself.

"G'day, mate. Jack Dresher's the name. Please to serve ya on this fine spring morning." The man had a thick Australian accent and firm handshake.

"Abhar Am. The pleasure is all mine."

"Well, sir, times a wastin', and seeing that the weather is good, let's get ya boarded and we'll act like a Joey in its mother's pouch and head out." He certainly had his own unique way of communicating.

Abhar agreed, and they quickly boarded and were on their way.

Jack Dresher was a blond-haired, brown-eyed Aussie from the town of Pine Creek in the Northern Territory of Australia. The nearest city was Darwin, to the north-northwest, over 125 miles away. His tanned skin was cracked and leathery from all his years in the sun. It was hard to determine his age by looking at him, but Abhar guessed he was a man in his late fifties.

"How long do you think it will take us to get to San Juan, Jack?" Abhar turned to ask the pilot. He sat in the front next to Jack, which provided an amazing view.

"If I had a hankerin' ta guess, with two refuel stops, ya see. That should put us thar, crikey, in ten hours. About four thirty ta five o'clock in the afternoon, I'd say."

Abhar could see that his pilot was quite an animated fellow. As they flew over the turquoise waters, Abhar swiftly realized that Jack enjoyed talking.

He had originally come to the Caribbean for the sole purpose of removing and relocating crocodiles from newly developed resort areas. Growing up in Pine Creek, near the Daly River, where swamps and crocs were prevalent, there were limited options for fun growing up. Playing with crocodiles helped youngsters pass the time.

Once he got older, the land being too wet to farm and having no desire to work in the mines, croc hunting supplied him with food, fun, and finances, as Jack said humorously.

For a bit of adventure, Jack enlisted in the Australian Air Force and was soon conscripted to serve in the US Army Air Corp in Vietnam as a cargo pilot. Because he had been flying planes in the bush and over various terrains most of his life, his skills in maneuvering and landing planes in the jungle were exceptional. He was given a field commission and attained the rank of lieutenant.

It did not take long for another pseudo-military branch to take notice of his unique skill set. Jack Dresher was recruited and flew for the CIA under the cover of Air America. After several years of running guns and drugs under the guise of humanitarian aid, the war was ending and Jack, feeling the scars of war in his body, mind, and soul, no longer had the desire to return to his childhood home.

As fate would have it, one of his cobbers—Australian for friend—who was from Miami, Florida, told Jack of the growing resort industry in the Caribbean. With the soldiers who returned home after World War II, Korea, and now Vietnam, more Americans were starting to see the beauty of the tropics. Because of the advances in air and sea travel, it was no longer just a playground for the rich.

Jack, having saved up a little nest egg during the war, bought a plane, traipsed across the globe, and ended up in San Juan, Puerto Rico. Seeing the resort boom in progress, Jack promoted himself as the on-call crocodile wrangler. Since he had no competition and could travel to almost any location on a few hours' notice, Jack quickly gained a reputation as a man who could get things done. He did his job, just as he did in Vietnam, quickly, quietly, and without a lot of questions. This eventually attracted the attention of some very unsavory characters, who wanted to retain Jack's services to move more than just crocodiles.

Fortunately for Jack, the war on drugs by the US Coast Guard and the American government in the Bahamas and Puerto Rico made his potential employers look elsewhere for their business venture. Jack, knowing they were Mafia, was planning to leave town anyway. He had experienced enough working for the CIA to realize that he wanted nothing they had to offer.

Abhar, who usually had no problem getting information out of people when he wanted it, was amazed at how much this man revealed about himself in the first hour alone. Usually, this much talking would have irritated him, but under the circumstances, he found Jack Dresher quite refreshing—an open, honest, and genuine fellow who flew his plane and loved people. Abhar was under the impression that everything Dresher said was true. He also started to wonder if he and Jack knew some of the same people, since Jack lived in the San Juan area.

"Have you done work in the Sierra de Luquillo? The Laguna Cartagena Wildlife Refuge to be more precise?" Abhar asked, since that was where he received information from his source.

"Sure . . . but that's farther west from my normal digs, mate. Pulled two crocs from the Playa de Fajardo several months back and relocated them thar on the Grande Rio. They were some big-uns too, one was about 14 feet and the other was every bit of 18 feet long," Jack responded. "I've moved crocs all over the Karibbeean. Anywhere they were building something that was not croc friendly, ya see."

"Eighteen feet!? They really get that big here?" Abhar had seen Nile crocodiles that could swallow a wildebeest, and they rarely were that long.

"Ya betcha, mate. It's not that they're that wide, mind ya. Not very girthy creatures here, no big prey if ya know what I mean. But there's plenty of fish and they get real long. I saw one in San Pedro, Belize, on Ambergris Caye that was 22 feet long. And although it ate the occasional dog or cat, the locals thought of it as a kind of tourist attraction." Jack smiled as he took a deep breath. He always got a little excited when discussing the ancient reptiles.

"Have you ever seen the crocodiles that live on the Nile River in Africa?" Abhar, seeing how much he enjoyed the topic, entertained Jack with another such question.

"Let me put it this way, mate. When I was a digger in the army, one of my survival courses took me to Afrika to work with the French Foreign Legion. I saw one of them monsters take out a zebra, blam! As quick as ya please. Thar is no man alive that could wrestle with one of them. Maybe ten, no never one." Jack Dresher shook his head, doubting that ten men could do the job.

At that moment, Abhar's phone began to ring. He could not believe that he and Jack had been talking for almost four hours. It was now approaching ten a.m. He had been expecting Haji's call, but had uncharacteristically not thought about the privacy issue, being in the plane with another person, until now.

"Oh crikey, mate, ya have one of them satellite phones too. My mate Binah had one also," Jack said with delight. "Maybe ya get ta meet him when we land in San Juan."

With what Jack had just told him, the mention of his friend along with past experiences with the CIA, Abhar threw caution to the wind, went with his gut instinct, and answered the phone.

All seemed to be going smoothly for Haji. He informed Abhar that Jonathan had arrived safely at Wright-Patterson and that, as predicted, he had indeed been abducted. The implant he was carrying was removed without incident. Unfortunately, as Haji explained, he was unable to prevent the chip from shutting down after its extraction. Abhar thanked him anyway and informed him that it would have been practically impossible to keep the Rah crystal chip functioning once it was removed from its power source, Jonathan. Abhar told Haji that conventional electrical power would have had no effect and therefore would have been useless.

When Haji was asked about Jonathan's insight and knowledge, though, he paused. Abhar again assured him that he did not expect miracles from him but needed to know the facts. Haji told him what Jonathan knew before entering the R&D lab and what he was told about while there. Abhar understood why his brother-in-law felt uncomfortable telling Jonathan the details of his life. Haji knew how important he was to the prophecy and did not want to put too much on him or distort the facts. Abhar was pleased with all that Myrah's husband had done. He had always liked Haji and, in the past, had used him from time to time in a limited capacity; but he had never relied on him this much. Haji had performed above and beyond what he had expected. Abhar could now see what Myrah saw in him all those years ago when she fell in love with him. His decisive intelligence and quick thinking had put them in a most auspicious position. Jonathan was now aware that he was part of something otherworldly in origin.

After showering him with praise for his service to the mission, Abhar, having been briefed on Jonathan's plans, instructed Haji to pack the Mask of Warka and the Harp of Haran among Jonathan's things. Because of their size, Haji explained that he would have to hand deliver these items to the major. Abhar merely told Haji to tell Jonathan that he was bringing them to him.

With that settled, Abhar asked Haji to remain there, at least until he and Jonathan had made contact. He did, however, tell him to send Myrah and Sarah to the rendezvous point in India. Hopefully, if everything went as expected, Haji might very well remain there to work behind the scenes.

Glad to be of service and happy that he had made Abhar proud, Haji wished him good luck and told him he would be ready for his next assignment, whenever and whatever it might be.

For the first time in hours, the cockpit was silent. Captain Dresher was aware that most people who reserved his services did so discreetly and valued their privacy. This was not what concerned him, though. Jack having been around the secret world picked up on the little nuances that Abhar was using when talking on the sat phone. Additionally, his just having a satellite phone was a bit suspect since they were very expensive and fairly hard to come by. The uninitiated would have missed most of this.

Abhar, too, noticed the eerie silence that had come over the plane. Just the fact that Jack mentioned Binah's name told him all he needed to know about the man's character. While not sure what Jack actually knew about Abhar's old acquaintance, he was confident that Binah would not let him see his satellite phone if he did not trust the man. Also, as Binah was Abhar's contact and quite resourceful in his own right, he may have arranged Jack Dresher to pick him up in the first place.

Not sensing anything nefarious in Captain Dresher, Abhar decided to break the uncomfortable silence by asking him about his cobber, Binah.

Thankful for the break in silence, Jack went on to tell Abhar how Binah was one of the "good eggs." He was a man who always kept his word and treated everyone with respect. They worked together from time to time and occasionally enjoyed a can of Foster's. While Jack knew much more about Binah and was closer to him than he was telling, he did not feel uncomfortable sharing the information that he did, since they were likely to meet when they landed anyway. Binah, although very private, would not be disappointed either.

Abhar, realizing that Jack was giving him just superficial information about Binah, stuff anyone with a computer could look up if they decided to search for it, was impressed with how easily he maneuvered, without hesitation, from one topic to another, as if he was telling all and omitting nothing. Abhar decided to pry a little further and test Jack's resolve.

"So, Jack, seen any USOs lately coming out of the Puerto Rico Trench area?" Abhar asked matter-of-factly.

Jack was caught a bit off guard by what his passenger had just asked him, but, in typical fashion, he remained calm as he responded to the question.

Although he knew exactly what Abhar was asking him about, he answered with a ruse instead. "USOs . . . sure . . . thar's a few more in the Keys and another near Andros Island, but I was unaware thar was one in the trench. That crack is deeper them da holes they drill in the billabong for oil back home, which I'm here to tell ya, are deep, mate." Jack was truly a master at the gift of gab.

"Interesting . . . so you haven't seen anything of interest lately? Anything that would seem otherworldly?" Abhar now just wanted to see what Jack could come up with next. He was enjoying this more than the improv shows in Vegas.

"Well, mate, ta tell ya the truth"—Jack was whispering and looking around as if he was checking to see if someone else was listening—"a few weeks ago while I was prospecting down near the Loiza River . . ."—he paused again for effect—"I'm pretty sure I saw a chupacabra!"

Ah, this is fresh, Abhar thought. He smiled, patiently awaiting the story behind this deflection. "A chupacabra! What in the world is a Chupacabra, Jack?" Abhar knew exactly what the devilish creature was, but he had to hear Jack's description and story in full.

"Crikey, mate. It's a cross between a dingo, a wombat, and a koala bear, but with evil red eyes, big kangaroo-like ears, and horribly long fangs, ya see." Jack used his fingers near his mouth to signify fangs. His description was quite accurate, Abhar noticed, as if he had actually seen one. "I was getting a little pickish, ya see, so I decided ta go down ta the river and catch me a fish. That was when I saw it, lying on a boulder, slurping water from the river with its forked tongue. Now mind ya, old Jack has seen a lot of strange things in my day, especially in the bush; but nothing prepared me for what happened next." Jack had Abhar's full attention. He had missed his calling in life and should have been a storyteller or narrator.

"What happened, Jack!?" Though aware of how Jack had completely changed the subject, Abhar was now engrossed in his companion's story, which seemed to be real.

"The little bugger looked right at me, let out a blood-curly screech, and charged. Just as I was about ta brain the beast with my boomerang—I'm a nature lover, ya see, and don't ever want ta harm animals if I can help it—the little devil leapt into the air, cleared my head by at least five feet, and ran off into the jungle. I've had saltwater crocs and snakes chase me down trying ta get a bite out of me, ya see. And . . . I've gotta tell ya, that little bugger scared me so much that I had to actually check my trousers ta see if I messed myself." Jack was as serious as he could be.

Abhar was laughing quite audibly now. He had to ask—he just could not help himself. "Well, did you mess yourself?"

"Nah, mate . . . thankfully, I was scarred shitless." Jack now had to join his passenger laughing. The plane's cockpit echoed with joy. Abhar was crying, he was laughing so hard. He felt truly blessed to have Jack as his pilot on this day. He needed the distraction more than he thought he did. Abhar could not remember the last time he laughed so hard.

They still had a few hours before they needed to stop to refuel. For the remainder of this leg of the trip, Abhar decided to relax and enjoy the company of his traveling companion. After a brief check of the instruments and gauges, the Jack Dresher comedy show, act two, continued.

CHAPTER / **THIRTY**

NATURE TRULY IS *beautiful*, Ariella thought as she witnessed the sun rising in the eastern sky. The brilliant shades of purple, orange, red, and blue that scattered across the horizon resembled an artist's palette just prior to starting the next masterpiece.

The flight, thus far, had been quite pleasant. Flying at an altitude of 30,000 feet across the middle of the Pacific Ocean, in quite possibly the most remote place on the planet, was the best view of God's creation Ariella was ever going to get.

With the moon waning and nearly invisible, the bands of the Milky Way were spiraling for inspection. Ariella had been in isolated places on Earth before, but none could hold a candle to the light show she was experiencing now.

Even though they were cruising through the clear night sky at nearly 700 mph, it felt as if they were traveling on a cushion of air. In the distance, she noticed several brownish dots projecting out of an otherwise azure ocean.

"Is that Hawaii?" Ariella asked the pilot.

As he throttled down the jet for their approach to Hickam Air Force Base, the pilot responded, "Yes, ma'am. We are heading to the third island, Oahu. Once we land in Honolulu for a quick refuel and leg stretch, we'll be on our way shortly," the lieutenant finished as he contacted the flight tower.

"Wow, I never realized there were so many islands that make up the chain. What is the first one called?" Ariella asked, sort of embarrassed about her ignorance.

"Oh," the pilot snickered, "that's Niihau. It's privately owned. Don't worry, Ms. Marconi. When I first flew into Hawaii, I didn't know there were that many islands either," he said reassuringly. "As a matter of fact, if you look just to the east of Niihau, you can make out another island forming just under the surface of the ocean."

"What's that one called?"

"Nothing yet, ma'am. Hawaiians believe it would be cursed if they named it before it revealed itself."

"I guess that makes sense." Ariella agreed.

Looking out through the canopy, she could see the whole Hawaiian Islands chain, which stretched 350 miles east to west and 230 miles north to south. Hawaii was considered the crossroads of the Pacific. It services seventeen shipping lines and thirteen oversea airlines. Almost everything that travels from North and South America on its way to Asia or Australia has to transit through this hub. Due to its strategic location, it is also the center of all US military activity in the Pacific, with bases from each of the four branches of the armed services along with multiple Coast Guard installations.

As they circled, making their final approach to the air base, Ariella could see the beautiful white sand and coral beach of Waikiki and the iconic extinct volcano, Diamond Head. Oahu, much older than the islands to the east, did not have the colossal, world renowned volcanic features of the other islands. For example, the entire big island, Hawaii, was actually one huge volcano with two peaks, Mauna Kea and Mauna Loa, with an elevation of about 13,680 feet that made up the base of the island. Most of the volcano was located up to 22,000 feet below the surface of the ocean. In fact, if all the mountains of the world were stacked side by side, base to summit, Mauna Loa would preside over Mt. Everest by over 6,000 feet.

Dropping lower and lower, Ariella could now distinguish Pearl Harbor and caught a glimpse of the USS *Arizona* Memorial, which was located on Ford Island. Pearl Harbor has almost the shape of a person's hand, starting at the wrist and splayed out in all directions. Fingerlets of water canals surrounded by extensions of land provided ample room for the various military, commercial, and civilian complexes. She could easily see how this haven truly provided sanctuary from the savage Pacific in times of need. Not surprisingly, the name Honolulu means "Sheltered Bay" in Hawaiian.

After landing, as they taxied down the tarmac toward the flight line, the pilot informed her, "Ms. Marconi, it's 0627 now, we've got thirty minutes to stretch our legs, hit the head, and grab a quick bite to eat before we take off for San Fran."

"Thank God. I've had to pee for the past several hours. What do you do if you just can't hold it?" Ariella asked.

"Well, ma'am, I just go in my flight suit. There's really no other option," he said comically.

She cringed as she said, "Gross."

"My recommendation, ma'am, is to go light on the fluids and no coffee. But that's just a suggestion," the lieutenant advised.

"That sounds like a pretty sound idea, thanks."

The F-15 came to a stop and the ground crew attended to the fighter. After disembarking, Ariella confirmed, "Thirty minutes, right?"

"Yes, ma'am, 0700, give or take. I'll be here when you return," the pilot said with a smile.

"Great!" Looking at the ground's crewman, she said, "Point me to the ladies' room, pleeease."

Once she had taken care of her needs, she quickly got a sandwich and a small glass of pineapple juice. She was amazed at how good and fresh the juice tasted, though she should not have been, since much of the islands had been cultivated to produce pineapples, one of Hawaii's major exports. Sitting on a sofa and looking out a huge rectangular window, Ariella could see that even though she was amid a jungle of concrete, some care had been given to ensuring nature was not totally extinct. Planters containing yellow hibiscus, the state flower, were quite prevalent as well as palm trees, which dotted the base to provide shade for benches and entryways.

Finishing her sandwich and juice, Ariella decided that it might be a good idea to try and relieve herself once again, just to make sure. They still had roughly five hours and 2,400 miles before they reached San Francisco, and she had no intention of peeing in her flight suit.

Walking back to the F-15, she felt quite comfortable. The temperature outside this morning was near 70 degrees, songbirds were chirping, and a slight offshore breeze from the south was spreading the sweet scent of hibiscus. All in all, it was starting out to be a good day.

The pilot had already arrived back at the fighter and was doing the final preflight inspections as she approached. Looking down at his watch and back up at her, he commented, "Five minutes early, I see."

"I don't like being late, it's just how I was brought up," she replied.

"It's a good character trait, don't lose it." Slapping the jet with his palm, the lieutenant asked, "Ready to go, Ms. Marconi?"

"Yes," she said with a sigh. "But I'm going to have to come back here someday. When I can enjoy what I've seen."

"That's a big affirmative. It's worth it," the pilot said as he offered her assistance boarding the fighter jet.

While moving into position for takeoff, the thought struck her again—it was Sunday once more. Thus far the day was looking pretty good; however, she wished Justin was here with her. She doubted that the rest of the morning would be as memorable as yesterday, but, not being one to read the last page of a book first just to see the ending, Ariella decided to wait until day's end before she formed her final opinion.

With the approval for takeoff coming from flight control, they were quickly airborne and headed for the next destination, Alameda Naval Air Station, near San Francisco. *Maybe I could take a nap*, she thought. Ariella flipped the shade visor down on her helmet and told the lieutenant to wake her if anything exciting happened. As she slowly drifted off to sleep, her thoughts returned to Captain LaMarr and the crew of Sea Lab X. She sensed something ominous in their future, which bothered her. Little did she know how prophetic her foresight actually was.

CHAPTER

THIRTY ONE

ALTHOUGH RAHZU WAS not known for being overly formal, he did adhere to certain standards when it came to fraternizing with his subordinates. On this occasion, however, he felt it appropriate to converse with the commander in his quarters, for privacy.

Surprisingly, in all the tours they had served together in Parallel Universe 430, this was only the second time she had been invited into the captain's stateroom; the first was when she initially arrived to serve under his command. CheRahna, though, on that occasion, was too nervous to notice anything of significance. This time, however, under much less stressful conditions, she was able to let her eyes rove around the room, providing even more insight about her trusted mentor.

On the wall opposite the entrance was a display of the various awards and medals Rahzu had received throughout his illustrious career. Three of these, positioned on an onyx backdrop in the shape of a triangle, immediately caught her eye. In fact, with their central positioning, she was astonished she had not noticed them before.

In the lower right of the triangular array was the sparkling Ordo du Jurat, the silver Order of Bravery. On the left was the Bellum Tempus Vous Cruis, the Golden Wartime Service Cross. Finally, at the apex of the display was the Custos du Virtute Medallous, the Multielemental Guardian of Valor Medal, the most prestigious award any Dimerian could receive. The latter two were awarded for Rahzu's bravery and courage during the PU 4 uprising. This one incident, the most traumatic in Dimerian history, resulted in the halting of creation and beginning of the Blade Wars.

Although strictly forbidden, the House of Yah, under the direction of Yahweh, took it upon itself to create life in PU 431 on planet Earth. Currently, due to Toyah Veh, the leader of the Yah house, and his position on the council, the issue of illegality was still unresolved. Fortunately for the Yahs, the councilmen were too preoccupied with attempting to collect universes in the Blade Wars to trifle with Yahweh's crime, at least for now.

Currently, 435 of the 777 inhabitable universes, thanks to the God of the Blades, the current champion, ZYah Zeh, were owned and under the control of the House of Yah. All houses of Dimeria, except the Rahs, had all their energies focused on producing a warrior who could defeat the champion in the Golden Ring.

The Rahs, however, were determined to seize the vast collection of universes through legal or secret, illegal means. That was the main reason they were here in PU 430, to build evidence against Yahweh in order to present it to the Dimerian Council. The other reason, a more nefarious one, was to gather any information to aid in their own illegal endeavors on ET Rah in PU 78.

From the onset of the Blade Wars, the remaining Dimerian houses gambled universes to increase or decrease their standing within the community.

Toyah Veh, having no interest in participating in the Blade Wars, was under tremendous pressure to produce an entrant for the event, lest all his universes be legally confiscated. In response to this pressure, he created another son, ZYah Zeh, whose specific purpose was to fight and win in the Golden Ring. His oldest son, Yahweh, had no intention of participating in the arena. ZYah Zeh quickly ran through the rank and file of all the best fighters, until only one remained, the champion, ThundoRah.

The warrior ThundoRah, from the House of Rah, was an impressive champion and had collected many universes for his clan, making them very powerful. With his legendary fame and ZYah Zeh's growing reputation, the stage was set for the most epic battle in Blade War history, a day on which many fortunes would be won and lost.

From the outset of the contest to the death, the two gladiators mesmerized the audience with their superior skills in the throes of battle. They were so evenly matched, both gaining and losing ground throughout the match, that everyone in attendance was on the edge of their seats. In the end, ZYah Zeh won and beheaded the warrior to become the best fighter of Dimeria, the God of the Blades.

Since that day, ZYah Zeh had been unstoppable, even fighting more than one opponent at a time. And though nearly destitute at the time of his creation, the House of Yah had become the richest in all Dimeria, gobbling up universes from those houses that were foolish enough to challenge him or bet against him. Because of ZYah Zeh's success, the Rahs, wanting to return to their former glory, were pursuing any and all means necessary to seize power and property from the Yahs.

CheRahna, continuing to study the artifacts in Captain Rahzu's private sanctuary, noticed the flowing crystallized display of ThundoRah swinging his sword in preparation for battle. The image, while looking much like a video from Earth, was an imprinted memory recorded on a flat sheet of quartz crystal. Although these quartz sheets were also used as a medium for imaginary creations, this one was from an actual event Rahzu had attended.

Upon further investigation, she saw another crystal display featuring the pyramidal spires of the Temple of the High Seats, the seat of government on Dimeria.

Aware of CheRahna's wandering eyes, Rahzu saw the moment her focus fixed on his samurai sword, his most prized possession. Though many of the other swords on the display wall in the pod area were stronger and made with superior technology, he cherished this one because it was given to him by a real samurai.

In the year 1473, Yoshido Nakamura of feudal Japan taught him the many nuances involved in the art of swordfighting, now called kendo. He was indeed a master with the blade, and if not for his fatal weakness, that of being human, he too would have been able to defeat many of the combatants in the Golden Ring of the Blade Wars.

It was a sad day for Rahzu when Nakamura's fleshly existence ended, especially because he had the power to heal his master and evolve his life. Yoshido, however, knowing of Rahzu's power, still wanted to die as he had lived, as a human, his honor intact.

Since Dimerians, while not immortal because they could be killed, were eternal, the experience of witnessing Nakamura's final breaths of life was very trying for Rahzu. Although he would be reluctant to admit it, and never in certain circles, Rahzu had been so influenced by his sensei's life and death that he began to develop an admiration and understanding of what Yahweh was attempting to accomplish; the creation of a sentient being.

After all, the envy of Xanix Rah and YetziRah, who both saw the success Yahweh was having with his creation, was the initial reason for this mission. They were here to learn what worked and what did not work, so that they too could create and improve on Yahweh's model. Now, however, Rahzu was no longer sure what the mission was.

While CheRahna gazed at the sword's simple beauty, Rahzu stated, "It was a gift from a human who taught me more about swordsmanship than any Dimerian ever had."

CheRahna, who had not been with Rahzu when he was training with Nakamura, gasped. "I had no idea you allowed yourself to be subservient to a mortal." Quickly realizing how bad that had sounded, CheRahna rebounded, "Rahzu, I didn't mean that as an insult. I just don't have any experience in dealing with humans."

Rahzu, seeing that she was sincere in her apology, was still amazed at her apparent transformation. She went from being a somewhat overbearing tyrant to the crew, to being a more calm, understanding, and rational leader. He now knew that his decision to bring her here to talk was a prudent one.

"The humans are not innately evil, CheRahna. There are many of them who have much to offer us with their knowledge, faith, and loyalty." Rahzu's comments confused his protégé. Holding his hand up to signify he was not finished, he continued, "You were about to ask me what a human could teach us, right?"

"Well . . .yes, sir. But I didn't feel you probe my mind, so how did you know?"

"Because I had the same question myself, long ago. We are not as different as you might think. I was once headstrong, career focused, and rigid in my thinking," the captain continued on with a more nostalgic tone. "I have come to believe that humans, due to their mortality, have a unique perspective on very many things."

"How so, Captain?"

"Because we are elemental beings, that's how we perceive things, as elements . . . atoms . . . chemicals." He paused to be sure what he was saying was being absorbed by the commander. Rahzu said further, "Those sensual, human feelings you abhor so much are how their kind connect to the world around them. They cannot discern things as they truly are, as we see them."

"But, Captain, I fail to see the point of having all these senses. What are their purposes?" she interrupted. CheRahna, puzzled, had just asked a very pertinent question.

Pausing to collect his thoughts, Rahzu simply replied, "They are necessary experiences for their lives."

CheRahna was now totally baffled by what her captain was saying. She had always seen things only one way, her own. It has not been until coming under Rahzu's command that she had been learning to adopt another way of thinking. "Sorry, I don't understand, Captain."

Rahzu, knowing she had never occupied human flesh, slowly came to the conclusion that explaining this concept might be more challenging than he had initially thought. Thinking on his feet, he leaned forward and with his right hand slapped her upside her head.

"What the HELL was that for?" she said angrily.

"Oh! Did I hurt you!?" Rahzu egged on her anger.

"NO!" she said snidely. Her emotions had clouded her thinking so that she had no compunction about how she was responding to her superior officer, which is what Rahzu had intended.

"Are you mad?" he questioned.

"Yes . . . I'm furious!"

"But why?"

This was not a question she expected. Being unprepared caused her to stutter as she began to answer. "Bbecccause ittt was uncalled for. I did nothing to deserve it!" She was still spitting venom.

"But I didn't hurt you and you didn't feel anything." Rahzu glowed as he was now about to explain his epiphany to her. "You are mad, so much so that you are talking to me like I was one of your subordinates . . ."

CheRahna, suddenly sensing what she had done, started to speak, but Rahzu continued.

"It's all right, CheRahna . . . that's what I wanted. You are mad over an experience you deemed unjust because you think it to be. Your emotions consumed you and you tossed out all standard protocol and responded in anger." He paused, showing by his expressive tone that he was not upset. "Humans would not only be angry for the same reasons that you are, but because it also physically hurts them."

"With all due respect, Captain, I fail to see your point," CheRahna impatiently said. "My being injured or not should have nothing to do with it."

"Precisely!" Rahzu's gold glowed even brighter now.

"Huh?"

"With our kind, in our form, our emotions, as you well know, control how we act, not our physical feelings . . . Even if my slap had caused you injury, you would not have registered it as a human, as pain." Rahzu now reached out and caressed her arm. "How would you describe what I just did?"

"You touched me softly?" She was unsure if that was the answer he was looking for.

"Yes . . . but was there any pleasurable feeling in it for you?"

CheRahna shook her head from side to side in an unspoken response.

"Of course not," Rahzu said. "To us, the physicality of contact is merely analyzed as injury versus noninjury, because we don't feel pleasure."

"You're talking about the duality principle, right?" CheRahna was starting to understand. "You can't have an up without a down, a good without a bad, or a right without a wrong."

"Exactly!" Rahzu was glad she was grasping why he did what he did. Secretly, though, he was amused by her reaction when he popped her. "The pain humans feel is equally matched by the pleasure they experience. Things can taste either delicious or horrible, smell good or bad, be loud or quiet. These, in varying degrees, are how the humans navigate through life. When they feel pain, they recoil from the source of it. If they feel hungry, they eat; the smell of flowers may be pleasing, while the odor of a dead animal carcass repulses them."

CheRahna clearly understood the principle, but still could not see the significance. "But why are these feelings important?" she said, feeling flustered.

"These senses are their survival mechanisms. Remember, they are mortal. Things that taste and smell good are typically safe to eat. Stimuli that are painful could kill them. And there is not only the internal drive to procreate, because it is in their DNA, but it feels wonderful. It's hard to explain," Rahzu finished, unsure himself if he had gotten his point across.

"Is that why almost every one of our own agents that has impersonated a human ends up acting at times . . . a little crazy." She could not come up with a better way to describe the behavior she had witnessed on many occasions.

"Yes. We Dimerians typically become exhilarated by these new, foreign experiences. So much so that, for some, pain even feels good. It can all be quite addicting," he answered.

"I think I sort of get what you are saying, Captain, but it's hard for me; I've never been human," CheRahna said and then posed another excellent question. "Is this addictive pleasure you speak of the reason why TamaRah and Rahphila were acting so bizarre earlier?" She suspected it was.

"Probably. Is it affecting their performances?" he asked seriously.

"Not that I am aware of, Captain. I have been watching. They just seem . . . happy."

"Good. If that changes and their duties suffer, handle it!"

Captain Rahzu felt that at this time this was all he had to offer on the subject. Since she had never been human, further discussion of the matter would be frivolous. In fact, he found it difficult to convey mortal feelings to anyone who had not experienced them firsthand. The only way CheRahna was going to truly understand what they had just spoken of was for her to wear the flesh. At this time, however, he did not think she was ready, at least not yet.

The reason they were meeting in the first place was to help her deal with her own personal feelings concerning her past. Throwing new and strange stimuli at her now could be too much for her to handle and might stall, if not reverse, all the progress she had recently made.

"Ponder on this thought for a while . . . you"—pointing at her—"do the things that you do because you want to succeed, to be proud of a job well done. Correct?"

"Yes, sir! Absolutely." she proudly responded.

"And when something does not go your way"—Rahzu could not help but chuckle—"it makes you angry."

CheRahna started to speak in response of the captain's snickering, but Rahzu continued speaking.

"Try and think of physical feelings in the same respect, except they are much more . . . shall we say . . . intense. So powerful that at times they can dominate human logic and completely control their lives."

CheRahna stood silent while contemplating the question Rahzu had just posed. After digesting the thought a little longer, she looked at him and spoke. "I will Rahzu. I'll try to understand as best as I can."

"That's all I can expect of you, Commander. Later, we can talk about this more." He paused, trying to determine how best to segue into talking about her past. How he started was critical to whether she would respond favorably toward their next topic.

"Remember when I said that I too questioned what I could learn from a human?" Rahzu started slowly, leading CheRahna toward a desired response.

She nodded. "Yes, Captain."

"A powerful Gold, a trusted mentor, a leader and dear friend helped me discover all that I've explained to you now. I miss him very much," Rahzu explained, reminiscing.

"He sounds very wise, Captain, but I am unaware of who your mentor was or what happened to him."

"Actually, CheRahna, you know exactly who my mentor was and what happened to him," he said cautiously.

Upon hearing this, her mind began working, using all known dates, history, and activities her leader had been involved in, until she began to discern who he was referring to. "No . . . that just can't be!?" CheRahna pleaded, hoping she was not right.

"Yes, CheRahna. It was Abraham, your uncle. He was my mentor and friend . . . before he made a decision and sided with Yahweh for the humans," Rahzu said calmly.

She was livid. "He's a traitor, an embarrassment to me and my family!!! I have struggled all my life to make up for his treachery!" She was so mad she was almost at the point of a breakdown, but Rahzu decided to let her vent her rage, her anger. They needed to start fresh.

As CheRahna continued to rant and rave for the next several minutes, Rahzu could see she had been holding on to this pain and had probably never shared her true feelings with anyone. Listening to her, the captain surmised that she and Abraham had once had a very close relationship, and that his defection was the root of many of her problems.

Soon after speaking her into creation, her father, ZoRah, had been killed in the PU 4 uprising while defending their home. His brother Abraham picked up his mantle and raised her; he was the only father she ever knew.

"Why did he choose the human flesh over his own kind, over the House of Rah . . . over me? If these human feelings are that addictive, why would anyone tempt themselves with it?!" She looked at Rahzu, defeated, pleading for guidance.

Rahzu paused to see if she had finished. Seeing she had, he began by stating the facts first.

"I know this may be hard to believe, but no matter how primitive the humans may be, they are quite intuitive. None of our agents has ever been successful for long when mingling among them unless they donned the flesh. It is a necessity and has been approved at the highest levels."

That said, he now had to attempt to deal with the more subjective portion of her grievance, the one concerning her uncle. Knowing he was about to reveal more than he wanted to, fearing he might express his true feelings and doubts about their mission here, while exposing the new direction the Rah dynasty was heading, Rahzu felt it a necessary risk for CheRahna to at least know the facts about Abraham. Her uncle's past had been distorted to fit the current ruling class's rendition of the events, which led to his defection.

Keeping this in mind, Rahzu decided to ask her what her version, the popular version of the tale, was before he informed her about the true story.

"Five thousand years ago, your uncle and aunt defected to the House of Yah. What have you been told as to the reason and the events that followed?" Rahzu asked, knowing exactly what had happened.

Seeing a copy of the Dimerian Codex on the captain's corner table, CheRahna pointed toward it as she spoke. "The Codex tells us that Abraham was sent to Earth to collect evidence concerning Yahweh's illegal creation. But in his own quest for personal power and being seduced by the rewards he received from Yahweh, Abraham seized the Ark of Power from the Great Pyramid at Giza, attacked all Rah strongholds, and banished Amon Rah to Chaos. He then methodically searched out and destroyed any remaining peaceful Rah settlements that had been chartered by Yahweh himself. Yahweh used

Abraham in his plan to weaken the House of Rah by destroying many of our clan through deception, allowing them to live in peace, luring them into a false sense of security. Then, when all was perceived to be well, he sent the defector to attack." She paused. CheRahna was disgusted by her ancestor's actions. "Luckily, two of Pharaoh's sorcerers were able to halt his progress before he accomplished the complete genocide of our people on Earth, by trapping my aunt, Sarah, in myriad atomic quartz prisons while she was in elemental form. Although nearly tricking Abraham into killing his own son, Isaac, Yahweh sent one of his angelic creations, just in time, to stop him. Using the imprisonment of Sarah as leverage, my uncle was ordered to relinquish control of the Ark, except through a treacherous act of deception he only gave us a replica." She paused again, making sure she had the story right. Rahzu sat silently, waiting for her to finish.

Continuing her tale, she said, "Because of previous strategic planning, however, Xanix Rah and YetziRah had formulated an alternative plan to terminate Abraham's terrorist control. In my uncle's moment of weakness, trying to free my aunt from the desert sands of the Sahara, YetziRah moved in with his forces and all but destroyed the traitor and his army; Abraham was forced to go into hiding." CheRahna had a particular energy emanating from her, one of joy mixed with pain. "After that, the Codex doesn't refer to him much. He has become no more than a nuisance, and my aunt is still trapped in the sands of the Sahara. At least that was what we were taught at the Rah Academy."

Hearing the rendition of what the commander had been taught, Captain Rahzu was not surprised by its propagandistic rhetoric and misinformed nature of the story.

"So you were taught your aunt is still trapped, split into molecules in the Sahara Desert?" Rahzu's question was stated as a fact, as if thinking out loud. "And that your uncle defected to the House of Yah because of his quest for power." He knew that this is what the Codex she had read said, which was completely fictitious. His Codex, while also distorting many facts, had a slightly different version of the historical events, one she might find startling.

CheRahna responded, "Yes, sir. That's what the historical codex says," still referring to Rahzu's copy in the corner.

The Dimerian Codex, although not like a standard book, recorded information within a quartz crystallized matrix. It could be accessed, much like a computer, for its stored information, which was immense.

Rahzu, seeing an opportunity to enlighten the commander, pointed to his Codex and said, "My Codex . . . does not contain the version of events you have been taught, CheRahna."

CheRahna, like a deer staring into headlights of an approaching car, had no answer. She stood there speechless.

Walking over to the corner table, Rahzu grabbed his Crystal Codex and handed it to CheRahna. "You are more than welcome to take my copy with you and browse through it in your own time, but I can assure you that the story you just told me is not accurate," Rahzu stated factually. "Your aunt and uncle were not sent to PU 431, to Earth, as spies, but with Yahweh's permission as ambassadors from the House of Rah, in order to learn about his creations. Whether you know it or not, the House of Rah has the desire to create, and in fact, has done so in another parallel universe."

At this, she was taken completely aback. CheRahna was still naïve enough to believe everything, to the letter, that she was told and taught by her superiors. She was now having trouble comprehending what Rahzu was saying—that all her anger and pain had been supported by lies. *Could that be possible?* she thought.

The young commander accepted the Codex and studied its exterior surface. It was indeed older than any version she had ever seen concerning the historical events on Earth.

Rahzu, watching his subordinate inspect his historical matrix, turned and added, "Your Uncle Abraham's is older than that one." He turned in the other direction, walked a few steps, then turned again and began earnestly. "CheRahna . . . no matter what you have been taught about your uncle, I can assure you that he was, and is, an honorable man. He always stood up for what he believed in, regardless of the consequences. And whether or not I agree with, or even understand the events leading to his and your aunt's defection, he would have done so with the belief that he was doing right, not only for the House of Rah, but for all Dimeria."

She was listening intently, not only trying to grasp the importance of what he was saying, but to interpret the energy with which it was being said. As far as she could tell, everything Rahzu had told her was completely true, or he believed it to be. She was completely frazzled, not knowing what to think.

He began speaking again, this time focusing the discussion on her. "Look, regardless of what your relatives did or did not do, that has nothing to do with you, especially now. You are your own entity and have proven your value and loyalty. You cannot hold yourself responsible for their actions!" he said passionately. Turning his fervor down a few notches, Rahzu went on to say, "I realize you have lived under a dark cloud of scrutiny, but just look at yourself. You are one of the finest commanders in the fleet, intelligent, loyal, and as far as I can see, destined for great things . . . soon, you will have your own command, and do you know why?" Rahzu faced her squarely.

"No, no, sir," she responded, emotionally spent and flustered.

"Because you have earned it! Despite what people's perception of you is or has been, you've earned it. No one can take it from you. Remember that!" Rahzu voiced with convincing authority. "You are the finest commander I have ever seen and have, and will continue to have, my highest recommendation."

Her mood, though still confused, began to lighten somewhat. The shame and anger she had been carrying for so long had blinded her to the fact that she was a successful, industrious, valuable, and trusted member of her house.

Noticing the positive effects of his words, Rahzu kept pouring on the flattering remarks. "Just here of late, you have become more empathetic with the crew and more confident in making the hard decisions. And, in general . . . much more pleasant to be around. You have arrived! . . . I'm sure you have felt it from the crew also." He was not really asking but stating. "There is one thing that is for certain with you, CheRahna. The intensity and energy of your mood is directly expressed in your presence."

She was feeling much better about herself. So much so that she giggled a little when speaking. "Yes, I have noticed that too; I wish I wasn't so easy to read."

"No! Absolutely not! That is one of your greatest assets. You exhibit genuine truthfulness and honest feelings. People may not like or agree with that you do or say, but at least it's real. They know what they are getting. What you are about. Never lose that!" Rahzu begged her.

"Ookay . . . I mean, yes, sir!" she finished with pride.

"Now I want you to go and relax for a change. I want you to know that you are respected, trusted, and needed by all of us. By me," said Rahzu, building on the wave of positive ions flowing around his quarters. 'So squash the anger and resentment, because you have overcome any reason for them, especially on this RJC."

Feeling pride and love, though a bit embarrassed by all the praise from her mentor, she again laughed a little. "Is that an order, Captain, sir?"

Captain Rahzu, too, could not help but laugh. "Yes, ma'am . . . it is. Now get out of here," he finished, without telling her about his meeting with YetziRah. But she had had enough for now. He would use this time to talk with ShemRahya, his trusted confidant, and check in on the investigation. He needed to piece together the events leading to RahKael's death.

When CheRahna reached the door to the passageway, she turned and faced her superior. "Thank you, Captain Rahzu. For your patience and for believing in me. It's made all the difference." Looking at the Codex in her hand, "I'll look at this later too."

"You make it easy, CheRahna."

She turned and headed down the passage, still confused about Abraham's past, but happy with her own.

CHAPTER / THIRTY TWO

FEELING THE PAIN from his surgical site building, Jonathan reluctantly swallowed another Percocet 10/325 along with a 25 mg Phenergan. He always got nauseous when taking narcotics and needed the promethazine to combat this. At the moment, he did not have the time to sleep either, which the medication cocktail he had just consumed was likely to induce; he had Ashley give him a handful of 200 mg caffeine tablets.

After ingesting two of these, a sandwich, half a jug of orange juice, and another cup of coffee, Jonathan felt the need to visit the men's room. Once relieved, he returned to his office with the hope that Ashley or the provost marshal had located Haney. Because of all the coffee he had consumed this morning, nature was going to call again, and soon.

"Ashley, what you got for me?" Jonathan asked slangily.

"Damn it, Jon, you know it's nearly impossible to find Haney when he goes off the reservation." She was irritated, busily trying to locate his comrade in arms.

"Where's the police?" he said, referring to the base provost marshal, who was no longer present.

"He went back to his office, but had his people send this over," handing Jonathan a fax. "It's all he could come up with at this time, but he's still looking."

Jonathan was scanning the fax but knew that Ashley would tell him what it said. They had a brother-sister type of relationship, and even though he was older than Ashley by several years, she acted like the elder sibling, always looking after him. If not for her, he would be lost most of the time as to what he was doing or where he was going. She was his right-hand woman.

"He's disappeared again, somewhere near Mount Shasta this time," Ashley said, sort of exasperated. "You know him; he's removed his tracking chip again. Probably dug this one out of his ass with his knife. Crazy son of a bitch."

Jonathan laughed; all Delta Force personnel are required to be chipped to facilitate locating them if they went missing during a mission. "I always take mine out too; I just get Mark at medical to do it."

"Yeah, hahaha, I know. I'd like to kick all your Special Forces asses. Do you know how hard it is to find you guys? I don't see how ya'll can get away with it." Ashley just shook her head while looking at the map of the Klamath Cascades and Sierra Nevada regions of Northern California. She knew soldiers qualified enough to be selected for Delta Force were very rare, which is why they were given such leeway. Ashley was not mad, she embraced taking care of those she loved, but it was in her nature to nag, just a little.

Jonathan was smiling, though he already had a rather good idea where Haney was going. But he was not through picking on Ashley, not yet anyway. "So where is he . . . geez, come on Ashley."

No words were said; she just cut her eyes at him like two lasers looking for a target. The gaze was priceless.

"Whhaaat?" he picked a little more.

"You do realize that I make your coffee in the mornings. One day, I swear, I'm going to mix laxatives in it and watch you shit your life away."

"I love you too," Jonathan retorted, getting her to grin. "I think I know where he is anyway."

"Oh really, where?" she said in a playfully condescending tone.

"Think about it. Where's he always talking about going?" he asked.

"How the hell should I know? He's your friend," Ashley said as if it was obvious. "I only tolerate him because of you. He annoys the shit out of me."

"He only picks on you because he likes you, you know," Jonathan explained.

"I know. I wouldn't want to be his enemy if he treats his friends the way he does."

"No . . . you wouldn't," Jonathan agreed, thinking of some of the scrapes he and Haney had been in. "He's always talking about going to the 'Enchanted Forest.'"

As this sank in, Ashley slapped her own forehead and said, "Duh!" Punching a few keys on the keyboard and using the mouse, she quickly pulled up two of the possible locations for Haney's 'Enchanted Forest.' Turning the monitor, which was positioned on a swivel stand, toward him, she said, "Bam! Redwood and Sequoia National Parks. Take your pick . . . My bet is on Redwood," Ashley said with confidence.

"Been watching the Food Channel again, I see," he said, referring to the saying made world famous by a Louisiana chef. "Why . . ." Jonathan almost continued with a wisecrack but decided not to at the last second.

"Why what?"

"Never mind . . . what made you choose Redwood National Park?"

"Well, he's got Indian in him, right? I mean, that's why you call him chief sometimes. So I figured he wanted to be near a reservation too. Hoopla Valley Indian Reservation is right here," she said, pointing to it on the screen with the mouse. "What do you think?" Her thinking was sound.

Jonathan had heard his friend talk about General Sherman, the world's largest tree at 103 feet in circumference, and saw that the Tulle River Indian Reservation was just south of Sequoia National Park. He could have used the same logic as Ashley had just done to argue for this location, but knowing his friend; the allure of the ocean in such close proximity to the trees made Redwood National Park his pick also.

"I agree. I'll start looking in the city of Trinidad. It shouldn't be too difficult to find someone who has seen a bald headed, six foot two, 230 lbs. half Indian, half hillbilly lumbering around. I just need to get within a few miles of him and he'll know I'm there," Jonathan confirmed.

"How's that?" Ashley genuinely asked.

"The voices will tell him I'm there," Jonathan informed her, expecting her inevitable question.

"The voices?! What the . . ."

He interrupted. "Don't ask"—holding up his hand—"but trust me, they are real, and if he's not being too stubborn, he'll listen to them and find me," he assured her.

"Whatever you say, you're the boss."

"Look . . . the coffee is running through me again; I need to go and pop a squat," he said, being purposely vulgar.

"Gross! You boys and your military slang."

"Anyway, I'm waiting on Haji to send me a few things, so if you could, check the vacuum tube, please."

"Oh, I almost forgot. Haji called while you were on your way back here. He said he would have a courier bring your things," Ashley added.

"Huh. Did he say why?"

"Nope. But you know him, there must be a good reason or he would have done as you asked."

"Yeah, you're right as usual," Jonathan said.

"Damn right! You remember that when you're in wine country. A nice bottle of pinot noir would show your appreciation quite nicely, don't you think?" Ashley pined for the wine.

"I'll see what I can do. I'll bring Callie back something too. How about an Indian turquoise necklace and earrings?"

"Oh God! Like the girl doesn't love you enough."

"That's right. I'm Disneyland. Tell Rhett I'll get him a rock," Jonathan mused.

"You guys and your rocks. You know he's got a rock from every place he's been since you brought him back that meteorite from Wyoming," she sighed.

"Yes, there's power in the Earth and things from beyond." He had tried explaining the metaphysical properties of rocks to her before, but discovered he would have a better chance of getting cats to enjoy swimming.

"I'm just saying, his man cave has rocks, tools, and baseball equipment, everywhere. In some kind of Rhett Butler type of order. I can't figure the man out."

"And you probably don't really want to," he figured.

"No, you got that one right," she agreed.

"Look, I gotta go, Ashley," Jonathan said, squeezing his legs. "Get my stuff from Haji . . . I'll be back soon." Grabbing a crossword puzzle off her desk, he started to leave the office.

"Okay . . . I'll get on it . . . Oh, and a rental car too," Ashley added while Jonathan exited the office.

As he made his way to the men's room, he remembered not having such a pleasant experience the last time someone rented a car for him. Maybe this time he would handle it himself, he thought.

When he arrived back to his office, Jonathan noticed a full green duffel bag on the floor in front of Ashley's desk.

"Well, I hope you're feeling better. I was about to send in a rescue team for you." Ashley laughed with amusement. She knew that Jonathan's life was busy and that he used his restroom breaks to do crossword puzzles, to keep the mind sharp and to have some "me time."

"How long have I been MIA?" he quipped.

"Thirty minutes. Haji had your things brought up," she said, pointing to the bag.

"Yeah, I see that." Jonathan picked up the bag and set it on the armchair next to Ashley's desk. Luckily, whatever was in it, it was not too heavy.

"Haji said that there were two things in there that Abhar requested. Who's Abhar?" she asked while working on the computer.

"Yeah . . . let's just say he's my new best friend. I'll explain more another time, when this is all over." He continued to inspect the contents of the bag so that he could inventory what he had. Just inside was a note listing the contents and offering detailed instruction for their use. The two items listed for Abhar were the Mask of Warka and the Harp of Ur, or at least that's what he thought they were. *Why would Abhar want these now?* he pondered.

First things first, he thought. He gathered the few items he had requested and the others that Haji had bagged up for him. A zero-point energy power supply was the first thing on his list. This small device, no bigger than his BlackBerry, had no moving parts, never wore out, never needed recharging, and could supply enough power to run a city block. It operated using a Casimir force engine, gathering energy from fluctuating electrons, which are held in a gravity field between two parallel metal plates in a dielectric material. Essentially, it's the same force that allows a gecko to stick to a wall.

The second thing he expected and found was several sets of tactical digital contacts. These lenses allowed the user to interact with a global network of satellite data to rapidly access any information required. They also provided a computerized, digital view of the environment, in real time, to determine temperature, distance, and the chemical composition of objects. They also acted as binoculars and night vision lenses. Since they were not implants, the user maintained complete autonomy with regard to decision making and choice of action. Though an implanted soldier, rather than one wearing these contacts, could react and process information much like a computer, Jonathan felt that the natural instincts that were lost were unquantifiable. He refused to be implanted, which is why he had flipped out earlier when Haji found one in him.

The last two items he had requested were for more serious situations, when niceties have been exhausted. One was a tungsten dart gun, a handheld kinetic energy weapon. It was shaped much like a French horn but fit neatly around the shooter's thumb and ended in a two-inch barrel. Surprisingly, this weapon, no larger than a soup can lid, held twenty-four needle-sized tungsten rods, which, propelled by electromagnets, left the device at an astonishing 20,000 feet per second. The impact could potentially blast a five-foot-diameter hole through a six-inch carbon steel plate within an accurate range of 200 feet. It could shoot much farther, however, due to atmospheric friction, temperature, and wind; its trajectory became erratic at greater distances, making the dart unpredictable.

The other weapon was another miracle of engineering. This handheld particle beam, a scaled-down version of the ones in space as part of SDI. It could put a precise hole in any known substance. Because of its size, it was easy to conceal. Although not having the range of functions of the flashgun at times, being designed to resemble a fountain pin, it was far more appropriate item to have on one's person.

It also went without saying that Jonathan would still be carrying his two pistols and vast array of knives.

The only items he had requested that he did not plan on using himself were the mercury-filled tungsten pellets and arrowheads. These were for Haney's slingshot and bow, respectively; the man was part Indian and loved his primitive weapons. He was deadly with both, as well as a master with any blade.

Continuing to rifle through the contents, Jonathan pulled out two items that looked like hooded wetsuits, except he knew they were not. As Haji explained in his letter, these were among the newest technologies available in combat apparel.

These suits were made of nitinol carbon steel nanofibers mixed with billions of nanobots. They offered the wearer increased performance by increasing reaction times, stamina, and strength, much like a TALOS suit, while providing protection from injury similar to Kevlar. Additionally, some of the nanobots were specifically dedicated to injury mitigation, to repair damage tissue, to stimulate the body to secrete a variety of hormones during times of stress. The nanomachines also contained medications such as antibiotics, painkillers, clotting factors, and virtually every drug one would expect to find on a crash cart. Essentially, these suits eliminated the need for first-aid kits and field medics.

The final, and newest upgrade, was the wearer's ability to operate in stealth mode, using the latest in cloaking technology, to become harder to detect on reconnaissance and in combat theaters. While this gear did not make a person invisible, it did significantly enhance one's abilities, putting a human on a more even keel with the other humanoid species operating on the planet.

After reading the details of the suits, Jonathan was impressed. He began to wonder what something like this might cost, but then decided it was undoubtedly some astronomical amount, so there was no need to know; he would never be able to afford one; not on his salary. The plan was to put one on just before meeting Haney, to show off.

"Those look cool," Ashley said.

"Yeah, mine's going to make me look and feel like Superman. All I need now is a cape," Jonathan said as he held up his all-black suit. "Good thing the hood is detachable, or I wouldn't be able to wear it in too many places."

"She'll love you in that," she said, smiling.

"Who will?"

"Ms. Marconi, who else?"

"Wait a minute. This is a sophisticated piece of military equipment," Jonathan said, feigning embarrassment.

"Oh, I'm sure! You'll definitely get to show off . . . your equipment," she said, waving her hand at him, referring to his physique.

"Stop that! I'm on a serious mission. It could be dangerous," he pleaded.

"You're always on a serious mission. It's always dangerous. But all work and no play makes Jonathan a dull lay." Ashley's tone was like than of someone dictating a memo.

"You're bad. Where is your mind at?"

"Where yours should be." Ashley pulled out the picture of Ariella from the dossier on her desk and held it up for Jonathan to see. "Look at her, she's beautiful, smart, in shape, and . . . SINGLE."

"Yes, so?"

"I'm just saying . . . when was the last time you got laid?" Ashley asked.

"I dunno, a few months," he said sheepishly, although he knew it was longer.

"Yeah, uh huh. Think again, Casanova." Ashley knew. "Look . . . just be open to the possibility, that's all I ask."

"Why do you care?"

"Really?!" Ashley said in a manner that signified her care for him. "Because you are a thirty-six-year-old man with no wife, no kids, no girlfriend, and no PROSPECTS! When was the last time you even had a date?! Hell, Jonathan, I love you and care about you, but you have to slow down, lighten up, and enjoy life. No man's an island, you know," she preached.

"But I have you to take care of me," Jonathan deflected.

"You know what I mean," she groaned. "Plus, I want you to have a child so I can spoil the hell out of it just like you've done with Callie." Her tone had lightened.

"Sooo, the true reason comes out, Revenge. And since you don't know anyone to introduce me to, here we are, me single, without any prospects and you out of answers," he fired back.

"I just provided you with an answer," she said, holding up the picture again. "I'm going to call Dawn, though, just in case you screw this opportunity up. We'll come up with something, you'll see."

Shaking his head and smiling, he said, "I'm sure ya'll will." Jonathan ceded this round to her.

With the inquisition into his sex life over, he delved further into the bag and pulled out the mask and then the harp. After setting them down on Ashley's desk, he proceeded to inspect them further. The harp was plated with real gold and had strings made of pure silver. They were connected to the body of the instrument by white crystals that he could not readily identify.

"That is beautiful. You look so cute holding that harp, like a big cupid," Ashley cooed.

Jonathan, playing along, picked up his right leg, bent it at the knee so it was parallel to the ground, put the harp under his arm, and like cupid, lightly strummed the instrument. The sound was captivating. They were both frozen and speechless until the rhythm ended.

"What the hell just happened?" Jonathan asked, wondering if Ashley just experienced the same thing he had.

"I don't know. That was weird. I couldn't move."

Jonathan strummed it again, this time harder. Suddenly the computer screen cracked, the flowerpot in the corner exploded, and both his and her coffee mugs crumbled; luckily, they were empty. The coffee pot, however, was not, and coffee went everywhere.

When the rhythm released its grip on them, Jonathan cried, "Holy shit!"

"Don't play that thing again . . . What the hell is that thing?" Ashley asked as she got up to go mop up the spilled coffee.

"It's the Harp of Ur . . . a five-thousand-year-old artifact from ancient Sumeria," Jonathan explained.

"Somehow, I don't think it was used to entertain people. You said that's Sumerian?" Ashley questioned.

"That's where it comes from . . . I'm just going to put this up." He placed the harp in the duffel bag.

"Good idea," she agreed.

Picking up the mask, he was timid about handling it because he was unsure what it might do. It too was covered in gold. The inside, however, was molded with the same type of white crystal that he could not identify on the harp. Despite wanting to try it on, he decided it best to repack it also.

"Look, Ashley. Just call janitorial and have them send someone up here to clean up the mess."

"And what should I tell them?" she asked sarcastically, because her prized South Carolina Gamecock coffee mug lay in pieces.

"I'll tell them we had a tuning experiment that went haywire and that the pitch frequency broke this shit." Which was not that far from the truth.

Ashley stopped and smiled. "Actually, that sounds pretty good. You know . . . for an honest guy, you're pretty good at making shit up." Ashley walked back by him and lightly patted him on the back between the shoulders.

"Ouch!" he winced. She had unknowingly hit his surgical site. Luckily for him, the painkillers had kicked in, and it was more a reaction to being touched there rather than pain.

"Sorry, are you all right?" she asked. "What did you do to yourself anyway?"

"Just a little sore from my spin-out last night,' he lied.

"It must have been pretty bad for you to take narcotics," Ashley said worriedly, trying to see if he'd tell her what really happened.

"I'll be all right. Just a strain."

"Allll right."

Looking at the computer and holding both hands out toward it as if she was a game show model presenting a potential prize, she whined, "I had a car reservation for you in Redding, but I obviously can't pull it up right now."

"That's okay. I'm not having much luck with rental reservations lately. I'll just get my own ride . . . thank you, though," he said without further explanation.

Ashley had a confused look on her face but brushed off what he just said and started thumbing through the rolodex for janitorial services and maintenance.

Jonathan had not told her about his vision, his abduction, or what he and Haji had uncovered. Other than his going to California to find Haney, pick up Miss Marconi in San Francisco, and going to Puerto Rico, she had no knowledge that could put her in jeopardy.

"I'll explain later, when I get back," he said, satisfying her for now. She knew he would tell her what he could and did not press him any further for answers. "What time is the next train?'

"Let me see . . . 11:30, heading west, nonstop to Denver." Looking at the clock, she continued, "You've got time, but you need to get a move on," Ashley warned.

"Send a message to San Francisco and tell them I'll be there around 1800 hours," Jonathan ordered as he gathered up the equipment.

"Were they expecting you sooner?"

"Yes, but I have to find Haney. There's something more to all of this." He was preparing for the future.

"He's not going with you, is he?" Ashley asked warily.

"No, no, I'm going to get him to meet with Gilla in Los Alamos," Jonathan explained. "He's with Jen."

"See, even a lizard needs to get laid every once in a while." She had to pick at him again.

"Yeah, yeah, yeah. Once I find Chief, I'll call you," He retorted as he retreated to his office for his backpack.

"I packed ten 2,500-calorie food bars for you just in case; I know how you get when you're busy." She always made sure he was fed.

Jonathan, packed and ready, walked over to Ashley and kissed her on the forehead. "Love you, babe."

"You too."

Grabbing the duffel bag, he looked back at her while heading toward the door and said, "Tell Callie I love her and tell Rhett 'Hooah.' I'll come by with some steaks and beer—oh, and some more rocks for his collection."

"Greeaat. He'll be thrilled." Ashley rolled her eyes. "Bring a date," she harped again.

"I'm going to tell Haney that you miss him and secretly want him," Jonathan volleyed back.

"You better not." She knew he was kidding. They both laughed as he reached the glass door.

With a left fist bump, Jonathan cheered, "Go Gamecocks!"

"Go Cocks!" she echoed back.

With that said, he turned and left the office heading for the elevator. On the way down to the transportation level, he could not help but wonder what powers the mask possessed, if any. Maybe he would put it on once he found Haney, in the woods; less likely he could do as much damage there.

He arrived at the platform just as the maglev arrived. After getting on board, he quickly sealed his cabin and turned on his cloud—one could never be too safe in the underworld. Besides, he needed to get a little peace and quiet without any stress. Although the train would be traveling near Mach 2 for much of the trip, even with stops in Denver, Colorado, and Dugway Proving Ground, Utah, before getting to Shasta, California, Jonathan still felt he could get a few hours shuteye.

Pulling out his phone, which read Sunday, May 21, 11:30, taking into account the time changes, he set the alarm for two hours, which was 10:30 the same day. He figured that would wake him up just prior to arrival at the Mount Shasta Interplanetary Complex. Once that was done, he shut off the overhead light, reclined his seat, and slowly drifted into his thoughts. Hopefully, he could find Haney quickly and enlist his aid.

CHAPTER THIRTY THREE

THANKFULLY, THE ALARM went off just as the maglev came to a stop and woke Jonathan out of his drug-induced sleep. He had taken one more of the Percocet/Phenergan pill combination so that he would have no chance of being disturbed by pain. "Ahh . . . completely healed," he said aloud. "That salve really worked." He would need to procure some of that for the future. Quickly reaching into his pack, he grabbed the spandex-like black nanosuit and put it on. Realizing that here he needed to be particularly aware of his thoughts, he decided to do a few quick deep knee bends and pushups to get the blood flowing. Being frosty was a necessity in this underworld.

Unlike Dulce, Los Alamos, or Wright-Patterson, this facility was under the total control of an ancient Reptilian race who long ago had defected from their ancestors, the Alpha Draconians and Sirian Wolfen, in order to live a more peaceful life with humanity. Contrary to what many of the other, more hostile, Reptilian races' objectives were, these Earthbound, cold-blooded creatures sought to rule not by force, but through economics, and they had fostered influence worldwide.

Telos City, under Mount Shasta, was among the 200 or so deep underground military bases (DUMBs) located all over North America. Under the Treaty of Grenada, the US government, along with a coalition of alien races, jointly constructed these bases for research and activity. According to Jonathan's latest estimates, the annual black budget for this project was around $1.5 trillion, more than double what it had been a decade ago. A financial collapse, dwarfing Black Friday of 1929, was imminent and would probably happen sooner rather than later.

With the opening of the cabin door, Jonathan took a deep breath, cleared his mind, and began his mantra: conjunction, junction, what's your function . . . Once out the door, he quickly surveyed his environment. Despite it being Sunday, he noticed that the terminal was abuzz with activity. He recognized beings representing numerous star systems, humanoids, Reptilians, and of course the cursed Grays, which Jonathan despised.

Although not always on the best of terms, every race here existed in a state of forced peace. The Mount Shasta Interplanetary Complex at Telos City was neutral ground for all beings. It was also one of the largest secret structures in North America, encompassing thousands of square miles and several cities. It is also a well-guarded fact that much of the hydroelectric power generated by the Shasta Dam, near Redding, California, was secretly diverted by the US Department of Energy to power the massive complex.

Although he had not been to Telos City in a long while and longed to visit some old contacts, Jonathan was pressed for time and needed to get to the surface; finding Haney was the priority.

Chanting his mantra and moving with purpose, he headed directly toward the elevator that exited the complex. Unrepentantly, a voice from his past echoed in his ears.

"Major Jonathan Arlin Hawthorn, you sexy man toy. Where have you been hiding?" The words came from a distinctly female voice, one with a raspy Bostonian accent. Immediately and to his delight, Jonathan recognized who it was. Cynthia Ryland was a stunning, thirty-two-year-old, five foot two, 105 pound, blonde-haired, blue-eyed bombshell he had met two years ago while attending a three-day seminar on the significance of geologic formations and the location of ancient megalithic structures. They were seated next to one another and spontaneously hit it off. It ended as one of the greatest weekends in Jonathan's life. Unfortunately, as much as he would hate to admit it, it was also the last time he had been intimate with anyone.

Even before he turned to look at his past lover, he could smell the hint of jasmine perfume she was wearing. Instinctively, he felt an erection beginning to develop, so much so that he had to readjust in order to avoid embarrassment.

Turning with a smile, he returned the greeting. "I've been searching for anyone who could compare to you."

"How's that been working for you?" she asked confidently, batting her baby blues at him.

"Not too well, still single. God broke the mold when he created you, Cynthia," he flirted back.

Cynthia was wearing a tight, bright red turtleneck cashmere sweater that displayed her supple breasts, and a pair of bleached Levi's jeans that perfectly accented the curves of her ass. She had her hair pulled back in a braided ponytail that exposed her soft jawline and small, round ears. As always, she wore scant makeup to enhance her eyes and lips. Her naturally olive skin needed nothing more. On a scale of one to ten, Cynthia was an eleven, a woman most men would generally consider out of their league. She had it all: the personality, looks, brains, and kindness to make anyone lucky enough to be with her feel like they had died and gone to heaven.

"I know you're a busy man, Jonathan, traveling all over the world, but I'm disappointed that you never called me. I've missed you," Cynthia cooed.

"Oh! So you're saying that I'm a hard act to follow also?" Jonathan blushed confidently.

"Well . . . let's just say that no other man occupies my dreams at night." Her response was seductively devilish.

While their flirtatious banter continued, Jonathan could not help but think about his current situation, which was typical for him. He really did not have time for this. It's always right girl, wrong time or wrong girl, right time, with the latter usually dominating. He just could never catch a break.

The disjoined couple was as compatible as each was ever likely to find. They were not only matched in their educations, beliefs, and astrological signs—she was a Sagittarius, a perfect match for his Leo—they were also phenomenal together in the bedroom. Jonathan could definitely see himself spending more time with her, if he had it. He did believe, however, that he might be able to make time for her in the future.

"Cynthia," he said, grabbing her by her arms, pulling her closer, and looking into her eyes.

She quivered with expectation.

With this, he lost all his inhibition, latched onto a tress of hair, gently pulled it downward, and kissed her passionately.

As they embraced, she moaned with excitement, and if it had not been for their realizing where they were at the same time, they might very well have ended up on the ground, humping like rabbits.

"I've missed you too!" Jonathan said, breathing deeply, a little lightheaded from the short reunion.

"Please tell me you have a little time. I want you so bad that I'm wet," Cynthia gasped, pupils dilated, lips full and red.

As these words flowed from her lips, Jonathan threw caution to the wind; he could no longer help himself, his animal instinct had just been freed. Looking around, Jonathan quickly found a maintenance closet. They rushed over and entered, slamming the door behind them.

She pounced on him like prey while scratching and growling in pleasure. Jonathan was sure that if anyone was near the janitor's closet, they would have heard them and probably investigated. However, at that moment, he did not care.

Although it did not take long for both of them to climax, which occurred at the same time, the intensity of their lovemaking drained them. Cynthia just lay on top of him, her head on his chest, and giggled girlishly.

"My God, Jonathan, what have you been feeding this thing," she said, referring to his penis.

"Brunettes," he quickly answered, prompting her to playfully slap his chest.

While lying there with Cynthia in his arms, Jonathan began to ponder a future, one that included her. He had never met anyone he felt so kindred with before, and the thought not only intrigued him, but aroused him as well.

Feeling the urge again to carnally unite with his lover, Jonathan gently rolled her over and began to make love to her. This pleased her much more that the first time, which was purely an animalistic necessity. Each got lost again in the passion of the moment.

After what seemed like only minutes, Jonathan checked his watch and realized that they had been in the closet for almost an hour. The reality sank in as they both hurriedly began to get dressed.

Once fully clothed, they looked into each other's eyes, which were just visible in the small amount of light emanating from the cracks in the door and laughed at what they had just done.

"Let's get outta here before we get caught," Jonathan whispered. "You first, I'll follow in a few seconds so that we don't draw attention to ourselves," he continued.

"How about we just go out together," Cynthia challenged. "I'm not embarrassed by what just happened and don't really care who sees us."

"Yeess, ma'am." He opened the door.

Back in the terminal, the lights seemed brighter than before, causing them to squint. Once their eyes adjusted, they turned to one another again. Without a word, they just stared at each other, mesmerized by the deep connection they felt.

Cynthia was the first to break the silence. "Jonathan, I know our lives are complicated . . . and there will be times when we will be apart, but I think it would be a mistake for us if we don't try to make this work and see where this could go." Using her index finger, she pointed at him and herself. "I have feelings for you, I always have," Cynthia nervously admitted. She felt exposed and vulnerable, emotions she rarely experienced. "I hope . . ."

Jonathan, hearing the frailty in her voice, went into protection mode and interrupted her. "I feel the same way, Cynthia. I'm captivated by you and would love nothing more than to get lost in life . . . with you. Forever how long that turns out to be."

Apparently, this was the perfect sentiment, because she at once embraced him tightly, placing her head on his shoulder.

"Promise me . . . we will see each other again as soon as possible," Cynthia implored.

"I'll tell you what . . . ," he said, pulling away from her embrace to retrieve his phone. He quickly took her picture and stored it as his wallpaper and checked her phone number, which he still had. "As soon as this assignment is completed, I'm calling for you."

"What's the picture for?" she said, enjoying being photographed.

"I want to always remember the way you look right now. It will be a reminder of how wonderful life could be."

She started to blush, nearly matching the color of her sweater. Everything he was saying struck a chord in her heart. She knew that, more than anyone before, he would be good for her. Her thoughts turned into a wonderful tingling in her stomach, but she would not let it get out of control. Cynthia knew she needed to leave before an Act III commenced. The next maglev for Boston left in fifteen minutes, and she had to be on it. She was a guest speaker at a symposium discussing Reptilians and lodestone collection, myths versus facts.

The chemistry between the two star-crossed lovers was palpable, making it difficult to separate. Reluctantly, however, they said their goodbyes and agreed to contact each other again in several days. Though they had had the same intention years ago, this time Cynthia was going to fulfill her part of the bargain; she already knew Jonathan juggled many responsibilities at a time, many of them life-threatening. These, understandably, made him scatter-brained at times.

With a final goodbye kiss, Cynthia headed toward the train while Jonathan went to the elevator. As he pressed the up button, he turned to look at her one last time. At that same instant, she too, feeling the same as he, turned and met his gaze.

The elevator door beeped and opened. Luckily, it was empty, because Jonathan, not wanting to break eye contact, backed into the elevator car. Once the door closed, his thoughts quickly shifted to speculating how long this assignment might take and how he could see Cynthia again. Though not usually one to place timelines on the future, he now found himself doing so.

Laughing under his breath, Jonathan was surprised just how fast everything happened. In a matter of an hour, he went from a man who had not had sex in two years or even had a date in months, had no prospects or hopes for either, to one that had just had amazing sex with a woman he genuinely cared for and who could possibly turn out to be the love of his life; his soul mate. He was not sure what he had done to deserve this good fortune, but he was thankful karma saw fit for him to experience it.

At the very least, Ashley would get off his case. She would be proud of him. Always telling him *carpe diem*—seize the day, which he had. He was sure, too, that she would approve of Cynthia. Visions of bonfires and cookouts started to filter into his thoughts when the chimes of the elevator pulled him back to reality.

"Ding . . . ding . . . ding . . ." The door opened. He needed to lock it in, collect his thoughts, and focus. Hesitation has killed many a soldier. The task at hand was getting on the road and finding Haney.

This particular exit, which was near the very spot where he rescued Gilla years earlier, was located inside an ancient lava tube that protruded from the base of the dormant volcano. Stepping out of the car, he headed toward the light, about 100 feet away. The elevator door; which was made to look like a rock; closed behind him, concealing itself amid the rest of the rock.

Jonathan made a quick study of the camouflaged door and determined that it would take more than a glance to identify the entrance. Additionally, signs posted outside the lava tube provided another layer of deterrence for the curious hiker.

Outside, he called for a cab, and after a short trek arrived at the ranger's station. Instead of waiting for his ride outside, he decided to walk in and inquire about any information concerning Redwood National Park. Park rangers were always excited to help guests and could usually supply information that was not available on maps or in brochures.

After buying a topographic map and discussing the park's various hidden treasures and lesser-known trails, Jonathan was confident that he had a fairly good idea where Haney frequented. He thanked the ranger for his help and went outside to wait for his cab. Sitting on a bench and drinking some water, he closed his eyes so that he could listen to nature—the rustle of the trees, the songs of the birds, the buzz of the bees collecting nectar from spring's wildflowers. All of this offered a calming, almost intoxicating effect to his auditory sense. He could even hear the bugle of a bull elk, off in the distance, calling a mate.

This chorus of natural bliss lasted for about forty-five minutes until his taxi arrived. Wanting to be on his way, he gave the driver some quick instructions and they were off—next stop, the city of Shasta.

Once there, he rented a truck in the hope that his luck would be better than the last time. With little time to spare, he headed west toward the coastal city of Trinidad, some 125 miles away. He estimated that it could take him as long as two and a half hours to make the trip, depending on weather. Jonathan prayed that Haney was in tune with the voices today, because his little sexcapade had cost him valuable time.

While he drove past and away from Mount Shasta, he got to see the snow-capped volcano in all its glory. At more than 14,000 feet above sea level, the peak seemed much taller. This illusion was enhanced because it rose nearly 10,000 feet above the surrounding plain, making it an ideal location for a massive underground spaceport.

He drove rapidly, exceeding the speed limit where he seemed it safe, and arrived in Trinidad at 1444. After stopping to top off the gas tank and get a cup of coffee, Jonathan started inquiring about his friend. The convenience store employee knew of Haney and directed Jonathan to the local gift shop, where Haney made Indian necklaces that were sold on consignment.

Fortunately, the owner, who was an elder of the Hoopla Indians, knew Haney well and was expecting the bald-headed Indian-hillbilly any time. He invited Jonathan to stay and browse while he waited, which he did. Perusing the merchandise up and down the aisles, Jonathan came upon a jewelry display case and instantly recognized his friend's work. Wanting not only to support his friend, but to get a gift for Ashley's daughter Callie, he picked out a short necklace made from elk bone, jasper, and hematite. The center pendant was an Adena point arrowhead chipped from obsidian. It was quite beautiful; Callie would love it.

Pleased with his choice, Jonathan walked back to the front and placed the necklace on the counter. The owner smiled and confirmed that it was indeed Haney's work. Jonathan gave the elder a $100-dollar bill and told him to place the change in the collection jar on the counter; apparently a young woman had lost her husband while he was fighting a forest fire just south of town. With a gracious bow, the owner dropped the change, which amounted to nearly sixty dollars, into the jar. Jonathan said a quick prayer for the widow, touched the picture of the deceased husband on the jar, and wished him safe journey. He grabbed his package, wished the Indian owner a farewell and headed for the door; he decided he would wait outside. Just before grabbing the door handle, a peculiar but familiar feeling came over him, which caused him to pause. Unable to determine the cause of this sensation, he proceeded out the door.

From out of nowhere, he felt a poke in his side followed by someone making a squishy sound with their mouth. Like a cat, Jonathan instinctively jumped, retreating several feet from his unknown assailant.

Once he gathered himself and decided that there was no danger, he only then saw his friend, who immediately began laughing, panting, and pointing in amusement.

"I knew you were here, and I still let you get me! Damn it!" Jonathan shouted, pissed off but at the same time amused.

Holding his hand to his heart and snorting while he continued laughing, Haney could only manage to say, "Oh, hee hee hee, it hurts, oh it hurts, hee . . ."

Looking up at the sky, Jonathan sighed. "Thank God the simple things amuse him, or we'd all be in trouble." Looking back at Haney, who was starting to calm down, he said, "Damn, I've missed you, Chief. How'd you know I was here?"

"The voices told me to come here. Then I saw you in the window, tee hee hee. Boy, I sure got your ass good." Haney started laughing again.

"I knew you were here."

"Yet you did nothing. I told you a long time ago that you needed to start listening to the voices too," Haney said with his left eyebrow raised.

"Yeah, yeah, yeah, come here, you big oaf and show me some love," Jonathan said as he opened his arms and gave his friend a hug, after which Jonathan jestingly warned, "One day, you're going to do that and I am going to knock the hell out of you."

"This is my world; you're just a squirrel trying to get a nut," Chief countered.

"Oh no! You're mistaken, my friend. I don't want any of the nuts in your world. I don't believe you can afford to lose any more."

"What are you insinuating?" Haney said with a grin.

"I'm not insinuating anything; I'm saying it, you're nuts," Jonathan retorted.

"Oh . . . okay . . . I do enjoy talking to myself quite often. Tee hee hee hee."

After Haney finished his fit of laughter, Jonathan asked if they could go somewhere private to talk. At once, Haney knew that his friend wanted to talk to him about a mission, probably something dangerous. He was instantly locked-in, and the fun and games were tabled. Haney had been itching for some action for quite some time. While he enjoyed making necklaces, and they supplied him income, it was not overly exciting or the best use of his skills. He was a hunter, a tracker, and, as the military saw it, a natural-born killer.

Jimmy Haney, aka Chief or Jimbo, was six foot two, 250 pounds—he had put on 20 pounds since Jonathan had last seen him—half hillbilly, half Cherokee Indian who had a mostly bald head with a long ponytail. He was the type of man who would give his life for his friends just as easily as he would take the life of an enemy. The word quit was not in his vocabulary, a characteristic that helped him become and Army Ranger as well as a sniper, despite not being well educated.

Jonathan had learned long ago that when Chief picked on someone, he liked that person. Conversely, those he did not care for were sent a clear message—stay away or else.

Even though they had eaten the same dirt in Ranger and sniper schools, in Bosnia and Kosovo, which reinforced the initial impression of the grit Haney possessed, Jonathan's memory always returned to the bar they went to to celebrate after graduating and becoming Army Rangers.

Haney, who had drunk about enough to kill a horse that evening, was still standing. He had been watching a group of five young football players from the local university progressively hound a small drunk man who was shooting billiards. Haney hated bullies, so his agitation level grew.

Jonathan was just sober enough to realize what was about to befall the young collegians, and he tried to warn them. However, when one of them said, "Sit your ass down or we'll make an example of you," Jonathan decided to let them eat the shit sandwich they had created. He walked over to Haney, patted him on the shoulder and told him not to kill them. He giggled with an evil grin, smiled at the one who had spoken to Jonathan, and challenged, "Enough of this talk, swing motherfucker!"

What these boys would soon learn was the Chief would never give in. After each of them had their turn hitting him, which he allowed; Haney got up, blood dripping from his nose, lips, and ear. His gait was steady, pupils dilated and clear, and his gaze heart stopping. In a calm voice, he merely said, "My turn."

The ass-kicking that commenced is still talked about to this day. Haney had taught those boys a lesson they would never forget. So much so that, if not for the army needed him more than the sheriff, he might have very well have ended up in prison.

Upon Jonathan's suggestion for privacy, Haney insisted that they go to his place to talk. He wanted to show his old friend his lair anyway.

On the drive over, Jonathan presented Haney with the tungsten pellets and arrowheads for his slingshot and bow, which pleased Chief greatly. Haney was deadly with both primitive weapons.

Jonathan then went on to explain what had happened with the Harp of Ur and his reluctance to put the Mask of Warka on at that time. Haney assured him that he knew the perfect spot to test this ancient veil.

Driving west toward the Hoopla Indian Reservation and through Redwood National Park, Jonathan was surprised when Haney asked him to pull over within the park boundary and explained that they would walk from here. Jonathan always knew his friend loved the "Enchanted Forest" and would want to be close. He did not, however, consider him actually living in it. This should not have come as a surprise, though. Haney always did what he wanted, regardless of the rules. This was one of the reasons that after eighteen years of military service, he never could get past the rank of sergeant, despite having received the Purple Heart, Silver Star, and Distinguished Service Cross.

After walking 100 yards down a game trail, Jonathan figured this might be a good spot to try out the mask. Digging through his pack, he retrieved the relic and showed it to Haney.

"Looks like the face on Mars," he said flatly.

Jonathan had not made that connection as of yet, but once Chief said it, he agreed. He also knew that the layout of the pyramids on Mars and the ones found on the Giza Plateau, in New Mexico, and the ancient Hopi cities all shared a common link: the Orion constellation. Studying the mask further and considering what the harp could do, he started to wonder about its true origins.

"Well, try it on. My head is too big for it. Too much brain matter. Hee hee, I'm a beast," Haney chuckled.

At his suggestion, Jonathan held up the mask of gold and slowly lowered it onto his head. As soon as the inside touched his crown, the mask tightened to a snug fit. It wore so well that Jonathan was no longer aware of its presence.

"Hey, Chief, did you see this thing shrink to fit my head?" But Haney was just staring, agog, in total amazement. "What's wrong with you?"

"The mask . . . it's gone, Jonathan."

"What do you mean gone?" Jonathan asked.

Haney pulled out his hunting knife, which looked more like a shiny machete, and handed it hilt first to his companion.

"Look at yourself" was all he said as Jonathan took the shiny, polished blade.

To his surprise, the mask was gone. He immediately reached for his face. Although he could not see it, he could feel it. "What the . . ." he wondered.

"Well, other than disappearing when you wear it, what does it do?" Haney asked.

"I have no idea."

For the next few minutes, Jonathan tried to yell, concentrate, and even tried to use ESP to read Haney's mind. Nothing special seemed to happen. Haney had offered to punch Jonathan in the head, just to see if that was what was needed to activate its hidden power. But Jonathan was sure it was more than just a simple helmet for protection, and he did not want Haney hitting him in the head, killing more brain cells.

Grabbing the mask by both ears, he pulled it upward. It easily came off his head, and once off it reappeared. Since this was Abhar's mask, he would just have to wait until he met him in Puerto Rico to find out what its purpose was.

Once the mask was securely packed away, they continued another several hundred yards until they came upon a massive, looming trio of redwoods. Though not as big, circumference-wise, as its cousins the sequoias of the Sierra Nevadas, these trees were taller. The tallest of the three stood around 300 feet, while its sisters skied some 250 feet upward. With their canopies spread out like a large parachute, barely a ray of sunshine reached the ground.

Walking around to the north side of the tree, which was covered with moss, Haney bent down and grabbed what appeared to be a small root. With a quick tug, a door covered with moss opened, exposing a hidden staircase.

"Welcome to my kingdom," he said proudly. Leading the way, Haney entered and hit the light switch, illuminating his subterranean world. The Chief had ingeniously placed solar panels above the lower trees' canopy, providing ample energy while remaining hidden from the ground. He had also tapped into the main root of the largest tree to supply all his water needs.

His living space, which did not include his hydroponics room, being about 300 square feet, gave him plenty of room to suit one person's needs.

What surprised Jonathan the most, though, was the array of books and literature stacked on a shelf near the grow room.

"What is this, have you become a scholar now?" Jonathan jested.

"I just wanted to edgimacate myself so I could rap with them dumb asses who use big words to make themselves seem smart," he said, mispronouncing the word educate purposely.

Looking again at the library, Jonathan pointed. "Which one of these is your favorite?"

Haney paused with a look of contemplation on his face. He then walked to the shelf, scanned its contents, reached down, pulled out a book, and handed it to Jonathan.

"*Seven Reasons to Believe in the Afterlife*," Jonathan read. "That makes sense with the voices and all," he laughed, shaking his head.

"What's wrong with that, huh?" Haney said.

"Nothing. I think it's great. I'm just used to you shooting guns and drinking beer. Not reading."

"I still drink beer. I just read while I'm doing it, hee hee. I'm multi . . . tasking," Haney said, slapping his stomach with both hands.

"Speaking of beer, you got one?"

Haney looked at Jonathan with his head cocked; as if that was the stupidest question he had ever heard. He then walked over to his mini-fridge and pulled out two cans of Pabst Blue Ribbon.

Opening the cans and handing one to his friend, Haney asked, "Okay, Bro, what you got for me?" He was bright-eyed and excited.

While Jonathan brought Chief up to speed about his vision, the crystal amber sphere, his apparent abduction, and his new friend Abhar, he could see the intensity build in Haney's aura. He was all in.

After telling him of his mission in Puerto Rico and of Ariella Marconi, Jonathan explained that he needed him to go to Los Alamos to meet Gilla. Though he was not sure what he wanted them to do yet, his instincts told him it was time to assemble his team. As an extra, unneeded incentive, Jonathan gave the Chief a wad of cash totaling $25,000, which was just an initial payment.

Haney all the while remained silent, but eager. Of course he would accept the mission, but he wanted to at least try to play hard to get.

"Hmm, you are giving me 25k to go play with a big lizard and wait, whether I'm needed or not, with the potential of more money and great danger, and leave all this excitement behind, right?"

Jonathan played along. "Yep, that's it in a nutshell."

"Hell yeah! When do I leave? I'm a beast, hee hee hee." Haney was exuberant. He also felt honored that Jonathan came all this way just to get him. "I won't let you down, whatever you need."

"I know that, Bro, that's why I'm here. Plus, with your looks, if all else fails we can just scare the hell outta whoever is causing all this!" Jonathan playfully punched him in the shoulder. "Plus, you look like you put on some weight, you need the exercise."

"My brains getting bigger from all the books."

They both paused for a moment, then laughed aloud together before Jonathan finally asked, "What time do you have, so we can synchronize our watches."

"It's time that all dogs are dead, ain't you's glad you's a puppy?" Haney could not help himself, and Jonathan should have expected it.

"Yep!" Jonathan had to play along. It's 1532 in five, four, three, two, one, set." Haney and Jonathan synced their devices. "Man, I'm going to be late as hell," Jonathan stated, only mildly concerned. He was rarely on time for anything.

"You have to be in San Fran at 1800 . . . It'll be close," Haney said while thinking of an alternative.

"It'll be fine. I half expected to get bitched out by this Ariella chick anyways. I heard she wasn't happy about being pulled from her assignment."

Without a word, Jonathan tossed his friend the keys. On the way back toward Trinidad, Haney called a friend who had a crop duster and owed him a favor. He would take Jonathan back to Shasta, the nearest maglev, and he would drive the rental car back. Both agreed it was a good plan.

When they arrived, the plane was fueled and ready. Jonathan gave Haney a hug and gave him Gilla's contact information so they could get in touch. He then boarded the plane and was off.

In about an hour, Jonathan was once again in the underworld maglev system traveling toward San Francisco. He expected to arrive only a little late, thanks to Haney. Considering the logistics of two people traveling from opposite sides of the globe, he thought he was doing pretty well.

Now he decided to rest. Cynthia Ryland occupied his thoughts. He only wondered how that could become a reality.

CHAPTER

THIRTY FOUR

ARIELLA, ALTHOUGH FEELING special and enjoying her private jet fighter flight, was ready for a shower, a bite to eat, and some sleep. She had taken a little nap during the flight, but she had been up for more than twenty-five hours. This normally would not have bothered her, but sixteen hours earlier she had been 6,200 miles away on the other side of the Pacific Ocean. The jet lag was definitely kicking in.

Upon landing at Alameda Naval Air Station, just southwest of Oakland, California, a small black unmarked chopper was waiting to whisk her five miles to the San Francisco Bay Naval Shipyard.

On the short flight, Ariella had an incredible view of the eight-mile-long Bay Bridge and San Francisco Bay. They landed mere minutes after leaving Alameda. Upon landing, a Humvee picked her up at the chopper pad and continued west down Spear Avenue toward the waterfront. Ariella could see four ships docked at the pier—a destroyer, two frigates, and an aircraft carrier. There was also a Trident submarine, one of the largest in the fleet.

At the administrative building, a lieutenant commander ushered her inside, where she was quickly debriefed and offered some food, a shower, and a quiet place to get some sleep. It was now two p.m. and her contact, Major Jonathan Hawthorn, was not expected to arrive until late afternoon, around six p.m.

Though she was thankful for the meal, the hot shower, and the chance to get four hours of needed rest, Ariella was a little peeved that she was rushed here from the other side of the ocean, and the major was not. She would give him an earful when he finally decided to show up.

Now, though, the cot, which was not particularly comfortable, was a welcome change from the bathysphere and the jet fighter's stark accommodations. It had been a long, tiring day.

Ariella's thoughts drifted to the Ultra Secret file Justin LaMarr shared with her back at the Hab. What was going on in the trench? Why was she going to Puerto Rico? Who was this Jonathan Hawthorn? Hopefully, she would get some answers when he arrived.

CHAPTER

THIRTY FIVE

THE INVESTIGATION INTO Ensign RahKael's death had now been going on for quite some time. All the evidence was being scrutinized, as ordered by CheRahna, in a coordinated team approach. They had been scouring through RahKael's remains—a mere pool of tarnished silver—the fallen stork from Earth, the life pod and why it opened, and the record contained in the amber crystal sphere.

Lt. ShemRahya was amazed at how well the team worked together. He had always had a close relationship with his CO and head of security, Lt. KaRah, but had only recently worked on missions with the two science officers, Lt. Commander TamaRah and Lt. Rahphila.

Although he and KaRah had never disguised themselves as humans and only went through the portal to PU 431 to perform abductions, ShemRahya could easily distinguish how TamaRah's and Rahphila's interpersonal relations differed from his and his partner's. The two science officers had worn the flesh, and recently at that. However, despite how they and related to one another within their respective fields, they worked quite well together, explaining every possibility from multiple angles.

Since they were used to the investigatory process, ShemRahya and KaRah furnished the direction the team needed in collecting evidence, while TamaRah and Rahphila performed the tests to uncover the facts. They were the forensic team per se.

Systematically, the group went through all the evidence before forming any conclusions. They looked for motives and discussed possible outcomes.

They started with RahKael's pool of silver. After collecting and testing samples, it was discovered, as shown by the crystal's internal codex, that the young Silver had indeed been eliminated by a god killer, the tri-sword welded by the human male subject number 99985.

The next question involved the mechanical operation of the life pod and why it had opened in the first place. Rahphila showed that the device was functioning properly and was in perfect working order. The only reason the pod would have unlatched would have been if someone deactivated it from the outside or if its occupant awoke, which the codex's recording showed later.

Third, the evidence that was studied the most and tied all the facts together was the amber crystal sphere's codex. It recorded and stored all the events and could only be altered by the captain, or so they thought. By tracing the steps taken by RahKael, TamaRah was able to determine that the decreased ensign had discovered a frequency that had been tracking the Cruiser Rahs on Earth. it was of Rah origin.

Additionally, the sphere detected an energy spike in the human male's pod, which was what awoke him from his suspended animation. The energy also matched the one that tracked the ships, also of Rah origin.

That left the question of the source of the Rah vibration frequency and how it was transmitted through the portal into the life pod. This would require further investigation by the captain. He was the only one with the clearance to access the crystal's files, which contained frequencies of all known Dimerians.

Last, and most controversial, was the mysterious death of the ciconine, or stork, which ShemRahya and KaRah had personally witnessed. There was no apparent reason for the avian's premature death, other than the fact that it fell lifeless from the sky.

Although ShemRahya believed that the stork's death was unconnected to RahKael's death and that it was different from the Rah energy used to open the life pod and track the ships, he was convinced that the unknown force warranted further investigation.

TamaRah, however, swayed the others with her explanation of what she believed happened. She, having lived in the flesh, and having been in charge of several spies currently in PU 431 on Earth, had witnessed the phenomenon by which some humans could manipulate the concrete world around them using only their will. This power had been described by various names—telekinesis, possession, chi projection, and even faith, all of which were applicable and could supply an acceptable explanation for the bird's death.

Much like Dimerians, since they were created in Yahweh's image, humans had enormous mental potential to manipulate the world around them. There were select groups who, through a lifetime of training, could tap into such forces at will, although the species as a whole is too unevolved to effectively rise to its full potential. Only on rare occasions, usually those involving intense stress or danger, do these creatures summon the powers within them.

TamaRah, following the description of events as related by ShemRahya and KaRah and the records kept about the human male's past training, concluded that this was one of those rare occurrences and that any further investigation by the group would be a waste of resources. Since she had given a practical explanation for the bird's death, had much more knowledge in the scientific field than he, and outranked him, ShemRahya accepted her explanation and the group's conclusions without any negative feelings. He agreed that it would be a misuse of manpower to have the team continue with this aspect of the investigation. He would, however, continue to investigate the matter on his own, feeling there was more to this than some transient instance of one human achieving clarity with the universe.

At the conclusion of the investigation, he and KaRah left TamaRah and Rahphila to their flirting. Although he found it oddly distracting and did not completely understand, ShemRahya did not have any issues with their behavior. They both performed their duties exceptionally, without letting their emotions direct their actions.

Walking sown the long corridor, away from the science area, KaRah also had more questions about TamaRah's explanation. "ShemRahya, have you ever seen humans do what she described? Because I haven't," she asked him in a way that in no way suggested TamaRah was wrong or twisting the facts. On the contrary, she knew the chief science officer to be very credible and likely correct, which was why she agreed with her conclusion. But she herself had never seen anything like what they had witnessed back on Earth. Having been around her partner enough, KaRah could sense that ShemRahya did not agree with the team's conclusions concerning the avian. But why?

A long pause followed, as was characteristic of him. ShemRahya was a warrior, and as in battle, he was not one to rush into speech before carefully considering his options, his opponent's motivations and his own, and their joint assets and weaknesses.

Seeing her patiently waiting as they walked, ShemRahya collected his thoughts and answered. "In studying the Shaolin and Tibetan monks, I do know that they have both developed some of the abilities TamaRah was talking about. I personally have seen a Shaolin master ring a gong from a great distance by merely projecting his chi and pointing at it. They also use their life force to heal themselves but others by channeling the powers of the cosmos. The forces they can weld are quite impressive, for humans."

"They can extend their life force, like we do?" KaRah was amazed at how similar the Earthlings were to them.

"Yes, but these individuals are exceptional even in their areas of practice. It can take an entire lifetime to achieve these abilities, and most never will," ShemRahya added.

"What of the telekinetic powers or possession? Have you ever seen someone who uses these?"

ShemRahya paused for a moment before speaking. "I have seen video signals, while monitoring the airwaves, that show people who can control objects with their mind. I have no doubt that many of the practitioners are charlatans, but a few are entirely genuine. They are very uncommon even among their own people." ShemRahya took another few moments to allow KaRah to absorb this information. He continued, "As you know, we can also slip behind the veil of a human mind and occupy the space within."

"Yes, but neither you nor I have experienced that," KaRah interjected.

"No, you're right. But the powers of the possessed are akin to one of us entering a human."

"Oh . . . okay, I remember something about how Yahweh's creations . . . the angels and demons can do this—control human beings," KaRah said as her silver glow increased in intensity.

ShemRahya persisted; there was something important still to be brought up. "We must remember that those who possess these powers from birth are typically deficient in some other area of development or have evolved from an ancient Dimerian bloodline that still exists in their genes."

Listening silently, KaRah considered what her partner had just shared. She was smart, and like him, she liked to slowly digest a thought before formulating a conclusion. She also had a good knowledge of the history of Earth and how the human species came into existence. "Yes, I see it now. Yahweh used DNA from JahVeh's creations after the House of Yah obtained PU 4 and the planet Rheta in the Blade Wars. He then added a unique blend of his own genes to create mankind." KaRah too liked to think deeply in order to be accurate.

"And then what happened?" ShemRahya knew the history but thought it respectful to allow his partner to finish. He also, at times, thought aloud and would state the obvious.

KaRah's ideas, decompressing like a huge data file, started revealing information. "So then the other Dimerian houses, whether invited or not, started to wear the flesh, mate with humans, and produce offspring. The human bloodline became completely intermixed with various strands of Dimerian DNA. That was the reason Yahweh flooded the Earth before, to kill off the offspring whose bloodlines were not purely of his own."

"But he didn't get them all," said ShemRahya, advancing the discussion. "And our kind still inhabited the planet. At least for a time . . . Most humans today have only recombined Rheta DNA, with only a trace of Yahweh's. Over time, as they have gotten further from the creator's initial genetic matter, less and less of his genes remain. The same goes for those from other Dimerian houses."

"The last scion that I remember hearing about was Yahshua, and he was executed over two thousand years ago. I seriously doubt there are others close to Yahweh's line that have gone unnoticed," KaRah said with confidence.

ShemRahya, who rarely spoke in absolutes, cautioned his silver companion. "Perhaps . . . but never say never, KaRah. Let's not forget who we're talking about. Yahweh is very powerful and he's ZYah Zeh's elder brother. If not for his love of life and desire to create, he would have fought in the Golden Ring for the Yah clan. And from what I gather, he too is exceptional with a sword. Never underestimate him, or any opponent. Just ask RahKael."

"I see your point," she said, feeling a bit foolish for jumping to such a conclusion without thinking it through. The ensign's arrogance and misjudgment of the human had led to her downfall. KaRah did not want the same fate to befall her. "So why do you not agree with TamaRah's findings about the stork?"

"What makes you ask that?"

"ShemRahya, I may not be the philosopher and warrior that you are, but I do know you," she said as if she had been insulted.

"I'm sorry. Of course you do. I wasn't trying to hide anything, but . . . something doesn't make sense about the bird falling dead from the sky. There has to be more to it, I just know it!" He was starting to get a little frustrated, and KaRah could see it.

"You'll figure it out, you always do," she calmed him quickly. "Just talk with Rahzu. He'll provide you all the information you need."

Thanking KaRah for her kindness, ShemRahya wanted to impress one final thought. "What we must consider is that these feats humans perform from time to time, whether from stress, danger, possession, or even because of us . . . the power is innately within them. When our kind wears the human flesh, they become human."

"What are you saying?" KaRah was lost.

"That the human species, coming from Yahweh, already possesses these forces. They just don't know it. Our kind, when human, can only call upon and manipulate powers that are already present," ShemRahya said, unsure whether he was making any sense.

"I understand, I think. When Dimerians wear the flesh as humans, they become, very simply, human, nothing more," KaRah stated, looking for confirmation.

"Yes! Thank you! They can only use powers that are already present." He sighed in relief. Thankfully, she understood.

On that final thought, which would require some reflection, KaRah left ShemRahya and headed for her quarters. She needed some time to assimilate all they had discussed.

ShemRahya headed toward the captain's chambers to report the team's findings. As he walked the halls, he felt, as KaRah had said, that Rahzu would be sympathetic to his need to delve further into the matter. As he got closer, his outlook became more positive and his radiance glowed a little brighter.

———⌣———

Rahzu, sitting in his chair looking out his porthole, was reflecting on his earlier run-in with YetziRah and the ramifications it could have for his future. He realized that by standing up to him, he had exposed his true nature, one of truth and honor. YetziRah, being subversive and power hungry, now knew that Rahzu would never be an ally in his quest for supremacy. He would be his enemy.

Still believing he had chosen the correct course of action—it was hard to tell when dealing with a megalomaniac—Rahzu had some major decisions to make. His young commander, CheRahna, who had recently shown much growth within herself, had also just been awakened to a confusing insight about history and her past. All these new facts, and the emotions associated with them, would take her time to accept. Bringing her into this conflict with YetziRah might be too much of a burden on her at this time. Plus, he did not want to put her in danger at such a critical time in her development. He decided that the conspiracy involving her uncle, Abraham, was all she could handle at the moment.

The only subordinate Rahzu felt he could confide in, and who would be sympathetic to his plight, was Lt. ShemRahya. He too was a warrior Gold, one of truth and honor. ShemRahya would be able to offer insight, as he was wise beyond his years, as to what course of action would need to be taken.

The captain had worked and trained with the younger security officer for some time now. Although ShemRahya's swordsmanship had always been better than his own, Rahzu was able to help him refine his skills both in and out of the ring.

Rahzu, in his own right, was also constantly refining himself. He found it particularly helpful to adopt combat techniques and strategies to deal with day-to-day situations. Whether or not most would care to admit it, every existence seeks to preserve itself; it is, as it has always been, a struggle between life and death.

By first accepting this way of thinking, at a simple, primal level, ShemRahya had learned to incorporate it into his thoughts, actions, and emotions for use in the protection of the Rah Jump Craft, as well as the House of Rah. Rahzu knew him well enough to chance that he too, would see the treacherous actions of their senior officer.

Fortunately, ShemRahya was on his way to see him with the results from the investigation. Rahzu hoped they had turned up information to explain what Ensign RahKael was doing in the pod area in the first place. YetziRah's protégé had been as cunning and deceptive as he. She had to have security codes to the amber crystal codex, which the admiral had supplied. There was no other way she could have gained access to the data files. Additionally, because RahKael was well trained, she was likely to have covered her tracks, at least partially, before her unexpected demise. He was optimistic, though, that the team would have found something, a lead he could follow. Rahzu was desperate to uncover YetziRah's plans.

When Lt. ShemRahya arrived, Captain Rahzu was lost in thought. He had an awkward aura about him, shiny but not the usual golden sheen Rahzu was accustomed to. Ignoring that for the time being, Rahzu motioned for ShemRahya to enter. He was excited to get to the bottom of everything. While his security officer filled him in on what the team had concluded, Rahzu uncovered the reason for his officer's strange appearance.

"Thank you for your report and conclusions. We need to access the data files to determine the exact origin of the Rah vibrational frequency," Rahzu said, waiting to see if his fellow warrior would tell him his doubts.

"It does appear that Ensign RahKael was onto something. I too felt the vibrations by happenstance. One question I have is how did she know what to look for and why was she looking for them to begin with?" he said in earnest.

"I too am wondering about her purpose aboard this ship. I fear it was a bit more seditious than we could have known."

"What do you mean, Captain?"

"We'll get to that in a moment. First, you said that was one question you had; do you have any others?" In the interest of time, Rahzu thought it best to press his lieutenant on what troubled him.

ShemRahya, almost always hesitant to commit himself when he was not sure of himself, felt comfortable enough with his leader to tell him his doubts.

As he explained, he did not agree with the group's explanation for the avian's death, but there was nothing more to examine at this time. He was also bewildered at how RahKael, not only just an ensign but new to the crew, could gain access to the restricted files.

Rahzu, sensing his subordinate's confusion, quelled the warrior's reservations and assured him that a solution would present itself in time. Changing his tone to a more positive one, Rahzu invited the lieutenant to join him and together they would search the data contained in the crystal for the unknown Rah vibration.

During their search, a moment of insight came to ShemRahya, but, just as he was about to relate his epiphany, Rahzu asked him a question that pertained to exactly what he was thinking.

"ShemRahya, you said that the vibrations you and RahKael noticed originated near coordinates 19 degrees, 30 minutes north, 64 degrees west, and only when the ship breached the surface of the ocean, correct?"

"Yes, Captain, that's right." ShemRahya did a double take, looking at his captain. Since he was not reading his thoughts, it amazed him how much in sync they were together without outside interference.

"And that you picked up Jonathan Hawthorn at 37 degrees, 15 minutes north, 85 degrees, 52 minutes east, is that correct?" Since he had met the human in battle, Rahzu felt he had earned enough respect to at least call him by name.

"I believe we are seeing the same thing here, Captain," ShemRahya cautiously ventured.

"And that is what?" Rahzu asked as he brightened. He too sensed their connection when they worked together in private. It was only logical, since they used the same philosophies and had compatible value systems, that they would arrive at similar conclusions on many things.

"That even though the vibratory tones are a match, it is highly unlikely, if not impossible, that they were sent by a single entity, since they happened simultaneously, so far apart." ShemRahya also glowed brighter.

"Precisely what I was thinking." Rahzu then asked, "Do you suspect who might be responsible for the signal?" Rahzu himself already believed it was his old mentor, but wanted to see where his cohort's thoughts lie.

"Well . . . without reviewing the frequency lists in the data banks . . . I can't be sure, but . . . my bet is on Abraham. He's really the only one on Earth whose vibrations have been long forgotten. Also, we keep track of almost everyone else." ShemRahya was fairly confident that it was the ancient defector.

"Interesting assumption . . . let's see if you're right." Rahzu got up from his chair and the two golden godlike beings exited his quarters.

On the way to the command bridge, the two warriors talked about Rahzu's encounter with Major Hawthorn. Rahzu explained how well trained the human was and that ShemRahya also would have enjoyed a duel with him.

Lt. ShemRahya, who had never had the opportunity to spar with a human because he had never worn the flesh, envied his captain's stories about the epic duels he had experienced when working with the Japanese samurai. So, as the captain described his battle with the human abductee, he listened intently. Even though ShemRahya typically bested him in training, Rahzu was an excellent swordsman and a master tactician. The captain still had much to offer in the way of wisdom and experience.

"One day, you too may have the opportunity to spar with Major Hawthorn," Rahzu commented.

"How is that possible? As you well know, I have never disguised myself as a human, and it would be a conflict of interest for me to do so as security officer." ShemRahya was taken aback, puzzled by Rahzu's suggestion. The captain knew that protocol prohibited him from wearing the flesh, both in the past and in the present.

"That's why I trust you ShemRahya, your honor." Rahzu meant every word. "But the next time we pick up Mr. Hawthorn, we might just have to wake him up . . . as an experiment, of course. You know the effectiveness of interdimensional fighting styles." Rahzu was justifying for his plan with a bit of cynicism.

"Oh . . . an experiment, of course, Captain," said ShemRahya, noticing the captain's ploy. It made him feel valued that Rahzu would be willing to do that for him.

Once they arrived at the bridge, Rahzu went directly to the amber crystal sphere, which was situated on top of a pedestal, and placed both his hands on the sides. The sphere came to life.

Accessing the secure data files, he and ShemRahya were able to confirm their suspicion. It was indeed Abraham's vibrational tone. That in itself, though, did not explain who was helping him or how they were able to use Abraham's frequency to mask that of his accomplice.

Because Rahzu's mentor had always kept him informed of his history, things he had learned, information about his assets on Earth, even those from other Dimerian houses, Rahzu had a good idea who Abraham's accomplice was—Binah.

Currently, however, the captain did not feel it necessary to focus on this old Anunnaki, because Binah was only a minor player in a much larger game. What was Abraham thinking, haphazardly exposing himself after all these years? What was so important as to risk his and his family's safety?

Whatever it was, Rahzu speculated that it was extremely important. He started to wonder it YetziRah's recent actions in Earth's two deepest trenches had spurred his mentor into action. Or was it something else? Why did Jonathan Hawthorn's pod have an electrical spike from Abraham's frequency? What does this human have to do with his old friend?

Although Rahzu trusted his security officer with his life, he did not feel it prudent to burden him with this information at that time. It would serve no purpose until he was sure. Rahzu needed, though, to confide in ShemRahya about his meeting with YetziRah, and the possible negative implications. His own and the crew's safety depended on it. The lieutenant would be able to offer another viewpoint and help him decide what to do next.

"ShemRahya, while you and the others were returning our guests to Earth, I had a visit from Admiral YetziRah." The captain had a serious tone in his voice.

The young officer's aura faded slightly with the mere mention of the admiral's name. He had always had an eerie sense when it came to the admiral, and therefore never trusted him. "Oh, I was unaware he had been here, Captain."

"No one knows about it, my friend. He blinked onto the bridge and essentially accused me of being incompetent for allowing Ensign RahKael's death."

"What!? RahKael's own arrogance is what caused her death! The evidence shows that!" ShemRahya was a little heated over the accusation, something that had not occurred often.

"Don't worry, I stood up for myself and explained that Ensign RahKael had been an insubordinate snob and that she was likely sent here for some ulterior motive," Rahzu said, calming his lieutenant.

"Looking at the recording, it does look as if she was searching for something specific. She did discover Abraham's frequency before anyone else. However, we were unable to ascertain exactly what else she found. Part of the record had been wiped clean. Do you know who she was working for?" ShemRahya too suspected that she was a plant.

"It all looks legitimate. She graduated from the Rah Academy, went to advanced training for reconnaissance, and then was sent to us. All pretty standard," Rahzu answered sarcastically, doubting the official records.

"I don't believe it, except the part about the recon training. I think we can both agree she passed that with flying colors. But do you believe the rest of it?"

Rahzu shook his head side to side, indicating that he did not.

"Who taught her advanced recon techniques?" ShemRahya asked.

"Take a guess," Rahzu challenged.

"Admiral YetziRah."

"Correct, and his unannounced visit makes me suspect he is the one who sent her here on a secret mission. Why else would the supreme commander of operations be so upset over the loss of a lowly, insignificant ensign?"

"Unless, of course, he had a vested interest in what she was doing," the lieutenant finished for him.

"That's exactly what I'm thinking. However, I'm not totally sure what they are trying to find." Rahzu stated, not telling ShemRahya of his other suspicions, at least not now. "Whatever YetziRah is planning, you can bet it's not with the approval of Xanix Rah or the other Rah clans."

Both Golds paused for a moment to review what they had come up with. ShemRahya, who had always followed Rahzu's orders without question, had no idea what their mission here in PU 430 was all about. Until now, that was not important. He was ordered, from time to time, to abduct various humans, get them chipped, and return them. For what purpose, he did not know. However, he was starting to realize that if he was going to be of any further assistance to the captain, he would need more information.

Unsure of whether or not he was overstepping his bounds, ShemRahya cautiously said, "Captain Rahzu, I have always done my duty to the best of my ability, without question, and will continue to do so if that is what is required of me. But, with the recent developments, not only am I finding it difficult to adequately do my job as security officer, protecting those aboard this ship, but . . . and providing you with any more useful information until I know what we are actually doing here."

Rahzu listened calmly to his lieutenant's request. He agreed with everything he had just said. The captain knew he needed to trust someone, so that the knowledge he had obtained would not be lost with him in the event of his untimely death. All he had been waiting for was for ShemRahya to volunteer, which he had just done.

Knowing the pitfalls of idle talk, Rahzu had always been very reserved when it came to sharing information. It was not that he was untrusting. On the contrary, he usually gave individuals the benefit of the doubt when it came to issues of trust and honor, allowing each to either build a bridge or burn it. However, most, not having come up through the ranks or being closely associated with the political powers, did not understand how everything that was said or done could someday be turned by others for their own purposes. All too often, he had seen idle, innocent chatter destroy careers.

Of all the members of his crew, though, ShemRahya was the only one he felt a kindred spirit with. He was also the only one who was mentally strong enough to handle the information he was about to unload on him. Seeing that his long silence was causing the lieutenant anxiety, Rahzu replied tersely, "You're right."

Undecided as to what he was actually going to say to his new confidant, the captain started circling around ShemRahya.

"Okay." Rahzu stopped circling in front of the warrior and faced him. "Are you sure you want to know what's really going on?"

The matter was put to ShemRahya with great seriousness, causing him to pause before he answered. "Yes, sir. I have to," he responded vigorously.

"Once I tell you what I have to say, you'll have to guard your thoughts, especially around the political elite. You will have to do much of your work in secret, trusting no one; not even KaRah." Rahzu emphasized the significance of his request again.

Although ShemRahya trusted KaRah with his life, and in many ways considered her his equal, she did not think or act as he did in regard to many things. Perhaps that is why they made such a good team. Though he would have preferred to have her assistance, ShemRahya would defer to the captain's judgment on this matter. "I understand, Rahzu."

"What I am about to divulge to you will contradict everything you have been taught, my friend." Rahzu studied the lieutenant's reaction again to be sure he was still willing to be involved. He was. "I want you to pay attention not only to what I'm telling you, but to my energies displayed when I'm telling it. There can be no doubts, no distrust between us, if we are to be successful."

"I will, Rahzu."

"Do you believe that I am loyal to the House of Rah and that I work not only to achieve what benefits us, but all of Dimeria," Rahzu asked, already knowing what the answer would be.

"Yes! Of course I do."

"Good . . . because I fear what is coming is going to tear our house, as well as all Dimeria, apart."

"I am ready, Captain."

CHAPTER

THIRTY SIX

THE FINAL LEG of the flight was just as enjoyable as the first. After a brief stop on Caicos Island to refuel, Jack Dresher continued to entertain with stories from his childhood, Vietnam, and his many adventures wrangling crocs throughout the West Indies. It had been one of the most pleasurable flights Abhar had ever taken.

As they came in to land in San Juan Bay, the plane flew directly over El Morro Fortress. It was built on the western end of a bluff by the Spanish in 1539 to protect one of the best harbors in the new world from foreign navies, as well as from potential pirate attacks, which had become rampant throughout the Caribbean.

Abhar reminisced about the island, where, before Ponce de Leon and the Spaniards, lush vegetation crept right up to the edge of the waters and the now polluted and dammed rivers flowed freely and cleanly into the sea. The only inhabitants then were the Arawak Indians; who today are all but extinct, killed off by the Spanish through slavery, war, and disease. *How could such a beautiful paradise be transformed in such a short time*, he thought. Before deplaning, Abhar asked Jack if he could meet his friend Binah. Jack agreed.

Once the single-prop Cessna was successfully docked and moored, both Jack and Abhar walked toward town. Old San Juan was alive with activity. The Puerto Rican Theater Festival, which was ending in just over a week, was at its peak. It was just after five p.m. on a Sunday afternoon, and siesta was over as the heat of the day gave way to the cool of the night.

Music filled the air. Beautiful dancers, adorned in colorful, pleated dresses, waved *panuelos* over their heads and stomped the ground vigorously as they performed traditional dances. Other exhibitioners were found near the docks, including fire twirlers, puppeteers, musicians, fortune tellers, and contortionists, all there to join in the celebrations.

Along the narrow streets, which had been blocked for the weekend's event, vendors were lined up along the curbs to sell their wares. Santeros selling miniature nativity scenes; palm frond weavers making baskets, hats, and mats; young *floristas* selling bouquets of hibiscus, poinsettia, and jasmine mixed with the red and purple flowers from the bougainvillea vine. It was a tourist Mecca, and another excuse for Puerto Ricans to have a fiesta—not that they needed one.

Leading the way, Jack, like a racecar driver, bobbed and weaved through the crowd. Abhar could only imagine how Jack would have fared driving a cab on the streets of Delhi. Moving away from the dockside area and into town, Jack made a beeline toward a familiar refreshment stand, turned around, and smiled. "Over here, mate," he said, waving his hand to Abhar. "This here is my cobber Carlos Grandos. Ya see, he makes the best rum on the island."

Grabbing two shot glasses, which Carlos had filled to the brim with his golden-brown elixir, Jack, without asking, handed one to Abhar.

"Bottoms up, *omigo*." Jack's Spanish sounded strange with his Australian accent. He brought the glass to his lips, tossed his head back, and downed the beverage in a single gulp.

Abhar, who had no aversion to consuming fine spirits, followed in kind. "Wow! That's incredible!" Abhar stared, inspecting the remaining rum on the glass. "I've tasted good rum before, but nothing like this."

Carlos smiled a satisfied grin and responded to the compliment. "The secret, señor, is the temperature. Rum should never be left in *el sol* and never, *nunca*, served *frío*. That ruins the . . . flavor."

Jack looked a bit satisfied himself. "Ya gonna love this one too," he said, looking at Abhar. "Give us some of the rocket fuel."

"*¿Blanco o negro, mi amigo?*" Carlos asked with delight.

"Let's go with the *blanco*. It's a little smoother than the *nagro*, especially on an empty stomach. I'm startin' to feel a little pickish, ya see."

Slamming this shot down as they had done with the first, both men stood breathless momentarily, until the effects of the rum dissipated.

"Crikey, Carlos, that's gotta be over 160 proof. Ya've outdone yourself this time. What's that new flavor I'm tasten', sorta smoky . . . peppery?" Jack inquired.

"*Sí*, I've added some charred tansy. *¿Muy bueno, no?*" Carlos asked Abhar.

"It's strong, but also one of the finest blends I've had the pleasure of drinking." He held out his glass to Carlos. "We might as we try the *negro* while we're here."

Jack was happily surprised at Abhar's request. "Ya see, Carlos, I always bring ya the good ones."

All three men laughed as Jack and Abhar enjoyed another splash of spirits.

After saying "good day," Jack directed them deeper into the constricted corridors of the old city. Though the music faded, the number of people did not. Turning a corner and heading south, aromas of various foods stimulated the gastric juices in their stomachs, which up to this point had remained quiet. The smell of *arroz con pollo*, *cabrito estofado*, and *lechon asado* hit their nasal passages like ammonia, awakening the salivary glands with the expectation of a satisfying meal. Traditional dishes were being served by various vendors, each with their own cooking methods and flavors.

Not wanting to get too weighed down before their meeting, Jack led them to a stand and suggested that they treat themselves to a few *empanadas*. After consuming several of the meat-filled pastries, which were lightly covered with jalapeño jelly, they purchased some fresh fruit juice and continued on their way.

Jack explained that they would be at Binah's in the next five minutes. He ran a quaint smoke shop on the edge of old San Juan, near the cruise ship terminals. Business at this locale was good. People coming off the cruise ships, from all walks of life, visited his shop, bought various cigars, many times in bulk, and took them back to their home countries. Binah had done so well, he had even grown quite a large mail-order business from customers worldwide.

With people from various cultures and countries visiting him constantly, his shop provided the perfect cover for his other, more discreet operation, the information business. There was little that happened on the island, or in the Caribbean, that Binah was unaware of.

Because of the information he had acquired, Binah could at any time be the puppet master pulling the strings, which on occasion he did, though, by and large, he chose to live a life of relative anonymity, keeping his affairs, especially his history, private.

Like Abraham, Binah had been around for millennia. In fact, he had arrived on Earth, from Nahbirrhu, just after the last great galactic alignment some 25,000 years ago. His people, the Anunnaki, were once the House of Nah from Dimeria. After the PU 4 uprising, suffering tremendous losses and weary of the political encroachments upon the clans, they transformed their water wheel, the energy of their house, into a spaceship, the Nahbirrhu, and left Dimeria forever. With Yahweh's permission, the Nahs settled on Earth.

In time, most of his house had either returned to Nahbirrhu or been eliminated in the Great Purge, which followed Yahweh's deluge of Earth, but Binah choose to stay on the planet, which he had grown to love. Since his presence was in no way subversive, Yahweh allowed it.

Fortunately, Binah, seeing the past mistakes of his people, had formed a lasting and mutually beneficial agreement with another one of Yahweh's converts, Abraham. Together, the two estranged sons of Dimeria traded secrets, aided each other in data collection, and on occasion met to ensure that Yahweh's prophesies were fulfilled.

Currently, Binah, through his network of spies, had been Abraham's eyes and ears, monitoring the movements of the Cruiser Rahs in and out of the Puerto Rico Trench. They were well aware of the portal that led to PU 430. However, for fear of being discovered, Binah was unable to go near it to see what was happening.

Judging by the increase in volcanic activity, something cataclysmic loomed just over the horizon. If his intelligence and suspicions were indeed correct, he could come to only one logical conclusion: the Rahs were planning to destroy the planet. For what reason, he did not know.

Abraham's coming San Juan confirmed Binah's hunch and signified an escalation in the seriousness of the situation. They only met face to face when things were important.

At the edge of old town, the pungent odor of burning tobacco permeated the air. Looking for the source of the scent, Abhar's keen eyes instinctively locked onto a sign reading Fuma y Vete, or "Smoke 'n' Go" in English. Brazenly hiding in the name of the shop was the ancient runic letter *N*, the symbol of the House of Nah.

As Jack opened the glass door, a chorus of wind chimes echoed throughout the shop. Abhar at once surveyed his environment, assessing the safety of the situation. Though he and Binah had known each other for eons and had built a trusting relationship based on mutual respect, one could never be too careful, especially now. Binah too had always remained loyal to his house. Helping Yahweh was what was best for him to do; even though his own people could not see it.

Sensing his old companion's presence, Abhar detected no negative energy or ill will. Abhar switched from alert, combat mode back into a calmer, more serene state.

Jack, noticing Abhar's reaction on entering the shop, chuckled a bit. "Relax, mate. Old Jack Dresher has never got a cobber caught in an ambush." Jack feigned a cough and smiled. "I mean *amigo*. When in Rome . . ." He left the rest unsaid.

The Smoke 'n' Go had a regal sort of atmosphere. The shop walls were covered with hunter green velvet, with solid red mahogany trim. Huge crystal chandeliers hung from the twelve-foot, copper-tiled ceiling. The long counter and bar were dark walnut inlaid with ancient Spanish gold and silver coins from colonial times. If Abhar had to guess, there was at least a million dollars' worth of coinage covered by over an inch of clear urethane finish. The massive humidor room, which took up over a quarter of the 2,500 square feet of public space, was state of the art. It contained copious amounts of some the finest tobacco that the West Indies and the world had to offer. Cigars and cigarillos from Cuba, Dominica, Haiti, and, of course, Puerto Rico were featured. Brands from Turkey, India, and Southern Africa were also on hand. The shop had a plethora of various blends and strengths.

For the more discerning smoker, the shop offered patrons a chance to relax on one of its many antique leather sofas while enjoying a fine cigar and their choice of favorite spirits. At the bar, a patron could choose from quality brandies, cognacs, rums, scotches, liquors, and whiskeys. However, these were strictly for the customers who wished to stay and enjoy their purchases. The barely audible exhaust fans kept the air fresh, while not taking away from the ambient atmosphere.

Abhar was truly impressed, which did not happen often. Binah had created a unique niche in a part of the world where such places did not normally exist. His smoke shop, along with his side job, had helped make him wealthy.

Sensing his friend's presence and mood, Binah telepathically invited Abhar to have a seat on the far sofa while waiting.

As Abhar headed toward the rear of the shop, Jack signaled that he was going to find his friend. Abhar liked Jack and wanted to tell him that Binah was on his way, but that would produce more questions than answers. It was not his place to expose his longtime cohort. Besides, maybe Jack Dresher already knew about Binah's . . . abilities.

Though he could read Jack's mind to find out exactly what he knew, Abhar was worried that in doing so he would expose himself to any Rahs that were probing for his frequency. Too much was at stake to risk being discovered. Also, he thought Jack was a good man and that Binah had also recognized that. He already knew, from his previous inquiries, that Jack was aware of more than he let on.

While waiting for his fellow Dimerian to arrive, Abhar studied how Binah had covered the shop with gold, silver, and copper. The windows were made of clear aluminized panes, while the floor was made of slabs of granite, which contained high concentrations of quartz. He had created an environment that blocked out all wavelengths of electronic, X-ray, and ultraviolet surveillance. In this space, no one could pick up on his presence. *That's why Binah communicated by telepathy*, he thought with a smile.

At that moment, Jack was leading six-and-a-half-foot-tall, blond-haired, blue-eyed, middle-aged man toward him. The man had a salty look about him, with a two-inch-long scar on his right cheek. As he approached, Abhar could hear the clinking of the three glasses and bottle of alcohol he carried.

Jack extended his hand toward Abhar as he made the introductions. "Binah, this is the guy I was telling ya 'bout, Abhar Am. Abhar"—Jack now shifting his hand toward the owner—"this is my *omigo*, Binah." Jack winked at Abhar to show him he was doing as a Roman would do in Rome.

"Abhar Am, huh. Well, it's a pleasure to meet you. I see that you have the fine pleasure of getting to know one of my most trusted companions." Binah looked at Abraham with a sly grin. He then telepathically told Abhar that Jack Dresher, although unaware of who he was, was very aware of who he was not—not a being from Earth.

Abraham telepathically acknowledged what he had said and thanked him for creating this haven. The two them collaborated on a plan to have a little fun at old Jack's expense.

With the plot hatched, Binah signaled the group to have a seat. Abhar sat on one sofa and Binah another. Jack sat facing the two on a Victorian armchair. Binah handed Jack the bottle, as he was better positioned to serve the group, and asked him to fill the three glasses.

Jack, looking at the aged spirits, asked Binah if he had intended on opening a 100-year-old bottle of Chivas Regal scotch. "Binah . . . is this the bottle ya meant ta grab?" He held it out for him to see.

"Absolutely. I want our new friend here to feel welcome. I also believe our gathering today is more than just a coincidence."

After Jack poured the golden-brown liquid, Binah took a glass and offered it personally to Abhar. Abhar smiled graciously and nodded as he accepted the offering.

Reaching into his pocket, Binah then presented each man and himself a fine-quality, medium *robusto* Puerto Rican blended cigar. After trimming the ends, the men lit their smokes while enjoying a sip of scotch. For a moment, all was silent as they savored the experience.

Binah broke the silence. "So, Abhar, what brings you to Puerto Rico?"

"I'm here to see an old friend. He's been holding a relic of mine for quite some time, and I really need it back," Abhar said, as the two set up the unsuspecting Aussie.

"Really . . . hmmm, maybe I know him. What does he look like?" Binah replied, adding to the charade.

Jack, unaware as yet, sat and enjoyed his scotch and cigar, while Abhar and Binah conversed.

"Perhaps," Abhar added as he studied Binah's features. "He's about six foot five, blond-haired, blue-eyed, a little on in age, but not too old, and has a scar"—Abhar held his hand up and touched his right cheek—"about right here. As a matter of fact, it's exactly like the one on your face."

At the end of Abhar's description, Jack began coughing. Some scotch had gone down his windpipe when he suspected that Abhar may very well be referring to Binah.

"Very interesting . . . When was the last time you have seen this friend of yours?" Binah asked, continuing this ruse.

Jack forced himself into the conversation, "You guys are screwin' with old Jack, aren't ya?" He looked back and forth at the two men, who for the time remained stoic. "C'mon, mate!" Jack pleaded to Binah.

Unable to contain himself any longer, Binah burst into laughter, followed by Abhar.

"I knew it! It's hard to get one past me for long. I knew ya were a generous cobber, Binah, but when ya broke out thousand-dollar bottle of scotch for some bloke ya just met . . . well, right then I figured something wasn't right."

All three men were now laughing at Jack's expense, and he did not mind. Jack Dresher enjoyed laughter, especially considering all the horror he had seen in his life.

"It's good to see you again, old friend." Abhar spoke first. "And thanks for the scotch and cigar. Both are excellent."

"I've been holding that bottle since just after the last time we saw each other." Binah watched Abhar as he counted the years in his head. He continued, "Yes my friend, it's been fifty-two years. Right after all that Hitler business."

Jack, as sharp minded as he was quick witted, surmised that Abhar was probably not of this world either. "Ya guys haven't seen each other in fifty-two years. Crikey, I was so young, I was still suckin' on my mother's tit," Jack said as he smiled, having a brief oedipal moment.

Having confirmed that Binah trusted Jack and he could speak freely, Abhar began filling them in on the events that had transpired over the past day.

After being told about Jonathan, Binah asked Abhar if his potential God seed had been marked by the Yahs.

Although Abhar was unaware of its location, he was sure he had been, being the son of ZYah Zeh. It was curious, though, that the Rahs had not located it during their abductions. They were normally quite thorough.

Now that he understood the importance of Abhar's visit, Binah offered himself to the cause. "What are your plans, and how can I help?"

"If Major Hawthorn is who I think he is, he'll need a tri-sword for protection," Abhar explained, already knowing Jonathan was the prophetic one.

Understanding what Abhar was getting at, Binah said, "I had Jack hide my piece of the tri-sword in the Sierra de Luquillo, near El Yungue. He'll be more than happy to take you to it." Looking over at Jack, Binah expectantly asked, "Won't you, jack?"

Up to then, Jack had been intrigued by the yarn the two Dimerians spun. Having been involved with black ops for a good part of his life, Jack had thought he had heard it all. He was wrong—this was all new to him. It appeared, at least to him, that Binah had been working with Abhar to spy on another group of aliens, the Rahs, who came to Earth from time to time. While doing recon for Binah, he himself had seen UFOs breaching the surface of the ocean over the Puerto Rico Trench. Though unaware of who or what these two beings really were, Jack began to realize that whatever was happening was of the gravest importance and that all humanity was at risk.

Deep in thought, digesting what he had heard, he barely heard Binah; stupefied, Jack nodded in acceptance.

With Jack's agreement, even though he knew the Aussie was a bit overwhelmed, Binah returned his attention to Abhar. "I only know the location of one of the other two parts of the Spear of Destiny. It's in Neuschwabenland, Antarctica. The Nazis had it in the city of New Berlin, which is located some two miles under the ice. Although aware that Abhar knew the spear's history and its location, Binah continued for Jack's benefit. "Hitler originally took it with him to Bariloche, Argentina, when he fled during the last days of the war. Following his death in Estancia San Ramon, his piece of the spear was taken by submarine from Tierra del Fuego to Queen Maud Land. The Nazis have created a colony, with many cities there, encompassing some 360,000 square miles."

Jack was actually not too surprised by the news he was hearing. He always knew that history was written by the victors and that knowledge did not always mean power, because those in power always controlled the knowledge. Besides, he was in the company of two aliens who had been here on Earth longer than he'd been alive; at this point, almost anything was possible.

"My other sources tell me the same information, my old friend." Abhar nodded in agreement.

"Where's the other piece? Come to think of it, I haven't heard a whisper about it since . . . yes, since it pierced Yahshua." Binah was surprised that it had been kept hidden all these years and because he had not even thought about it. "Abraham . . . you have it, don't you!" Binah cried.

With a sly grin, Abhar answered. "Not on my person. I hid it in the ziggurat that still lies under the sand in Nineveh. It's safe."

"That place is a war zone!" Jack howled, getting involved in the conversation. "I tell ya, mate, it's not going to be easy getting in and outta thar unnoticed."

"You're right, Jack." Abhar looked at him with a gaze that could stop time. "It's going to require some inventive thinking on our parts to get to it undetected."

"You have special powers, like *omigo* Binah, right?" Jack asked seriously. "I've seen him disappear and reappear elsewhere in the shop before. I think he called it . . . blinking? Anyway, you can do that?"

Abhar looked at Binah with a surprised smile.

Binah just shrugged his shoulders. "We got a little drunk on tequila one night and I bet him that I could go from one end of the bar to the other without him seeing me." He then faced the croc hunter. "Damn, Jack, you really don't miss a thing, even when you're drunk."

"Naw, mate, in the bush and in the jungle, situational awareness means survival. Crocs, snakes, and the Viet Cong, yep, all have tried to take a bite outta old Jack's ass." His levity provided some needed stress release, which had been building up during this tense discussion. Each man took a moment to puff on their stogie and enjoy another sip of scotch before Abhar continued.

"Yes, Jack, I have the ability to do that, as well as other things. However . . . the problem is, when those powers are used, the inhuman ones, others from our home, can sense our presence and ascertain our precise location."

Jack was slightly confused, because Binah had used telekinesis, telepathy, and teleportation on a number of occasions here at the Smoke 'n' Go.

Abhar, seeing the conflicting information and understanding Jack's confusion, pointed out that Binah had created a virtually impenetrable electro-vibrational fortress that blocked out their harmonies to eavesdroppers.

Noticing that the conversation had started to go into an unnecessary direction, Binah focused the questioning back to Abhar. "What else do you need from me?"

Abhar spoke hesitantly. "I need the transponder that I gave you to track the Cruiser Rahs. Because I activated the device I gave ZYah Zeh's son, I'm now confident that the Rahs suspect our clandestine operation. They'll be scouring the planet looking for me."

The Anunnakian realized that since the device used the Rah amber crystal for power, only Abhar, or another Rah, could mask its location; he could not. Still, wanting to be helpful, Binah offered again. "What else? Please let me do something Abraham!" he pleaded.

The Rah defector was very keen on the challenges that lay before him. It was imperative that he collect the three pieces that made up the Spear of Destiny. It would be the only viable weapon at his disposal that could even the odds in the event of an attack.

However, recognizing that successful short-term tactics without long-term strategies would inevitably lead to failure, Abhar insisted that Binah remained here, at the Smoke 'n' Go, where it was safe. If he was successful in obtaining the pieces of the spear and containing whatever destructive force the Rahs had activated in the abyssal trenches, then Binah would be of more use.

Long ago, Abhar had taken the Ark of the Covenant, along with the Tables of Destiny, to an Anunnaki colony on Mars in order to keep them from falling into Xanix Rah's or YetziRah's hands. Since Binah's vibrational frequency was needed to access the Gateway of the Sun portal, located at Tiahuanaco, Bolivia; his safety was critical. It was the only means for Abhar to return to Mars and retrieve the relic in secrecy.

Binah, although unhappy with his present uselessness, agreed with Abhar's assessment of the situation. It was in all of their best interests to ensure that Yahweh's prophecy be fulfilled.

The Rahs, a tyrannical clan since Xanix Rah's rise to power, sought to control and manipulate all 777 universes. They had no respect or regard for any other house of Dimeria, let alone the less evolved Earthlings. Thus, any plan of action initiated by them would be detrimental to the relative peace existing among the realms.

Knowing that his longtime companion not only wanted, but needed a purpose in this quest, Abhar gave him some encouragement. "Binah, I assume with your businesses you have developed a communication network that encompasses the globe, all of which uses nothing but common human technology and ingenuity as its driving force."

Binah nodded in confirmation.

Abhar went on to say, "Your resources will be invaluable if we are to succeed in getting the sword back together, reacquiring the Ark, and retrieving the Schefa crystal. I sense that we have much more to worry ourselves with than just the Rahs," Abhar apprehensively said.

Binah, who was also very familiar with the other nonhuman players in the game, responded with trepidation. "I too am troubled by the past activities of the two sorcerers, but I haven't heard anything about the magicians since the Great War." Binah pondered a moment before finishing his thought. "Do you think they are involved with what the Rahs are doing?"

"I'm not certain. But if they are not part of this now, you can bet they soon will be. That much, I'm sure about." Abhar took a long drag from his cigar, blew out the smoke, and took another swig of his scotch. "PandoRah's whereabouts are also unsettling. She is too devious not to be part of this . . . Remember the last time she was reunited with her brothers . . . That sorceress unleashed the bubonic plague on the world, nearly eradicating humanity," Abhar warned.

Jack again found it impossible to remain silent. "Magicians . . . PandoRah, really?" Seeing they were telling the truth—Jack prided himself on having a good bullshit meter—he sighed, "Wow! I tell ya, old Jack is as lost as a platypus in the desert." Once more, Jack's comical nature broke the tension.

Binah consoled his trusted friend by informing him that he was now part of a very small group of people who had some knowledge of a part of Earth's true history.

Satisfied by his cobber's encouraging words, Jack fell speechless, soaking up all the information being presented. He already figured that he too would be playing his part in shaping the future. The more he knew, the better, a practice that had always served him well. Luckily for Jack, he remembered most things, especially when he concentrated on doing so.

Looking at Binah and then at Jack, Abhar said, "My old and new friends, we need a lot to go our way for all of these things to be accomplished."

"Where is the chosen one?" Binah asked.

"My brother-in-law, Haji, informs me that he and another abductee are on their way here now, as we speak." Checking the wall clock, which read 7:30 p.m., he said, "I expect they'll be arriving here tomorrow sometime around one a.m.," Abhar finished while still studying the clock as if planning ahead.

"Where will they be arriving?" Binah questioned.

"San Juan Naval Air Station on a C-117 out of Miami."

"Splendid! I know the base commander. I'll get passes for you and Jack so that you can meet them there," Binah offered.

Abhar graciously bowed his head toward his friend, thanking him for his assistance. It was awfully nice being around others who had connections. It certainly made getting things done less tedious.

For the next few minutes, the three men sat and enjoyed their cigars. They pledged to finish off the rare, aged scotch before continuing to formulate their plans. It was unusual for Abhar to find comfortable silence so peaceful, but in the present company, it felt natural. Seeing that Jack Dresher was an intelligent, entertaining Australian, he was mildly surprised by his ability to sit back and not be the center of attention. Abhar was glad to have him as a member of the team, for however long that lasted.

Thus far, with the addition of Binah and Jack, Abhar was pleased with the team that was being assembled, as if it had been predestined. Not one to rely on fate, particularly his own, to control his actions, he was glad for all the help he could get. It was certainly going to be needed in the very near future.

CHAPTER THIRTY SEVEN

JONATHAN OPENED HIS eyes to the pulsating hum of the maglev train as it traveled toward its next destination. Wiping the sleep from the corners of his eyes, he focused on the digital display, which showed time, location, and speed.

To his surprise, he had only nodded off for forty-five minutes. As the display showed, they were approaching Sacramento; the train slowed. Calculating that the remainder of the trip would take at least another forty-five minutes, he relished the thought that he would be late for his appointment in San Francisco. At least now Ms. Marconi would have something legitimate to bitch about, he thought to himself. Looking at her file previously and judging by the way she had been rushed across the Pacific, he had already predicted she would anyway.

Deciding that it would be pointless to nod off again, Jonathan reached for his backpack, which was stowed under the seat, and retrieved Ariella Marconi's dossier. Thumbing through its pages, he came upon her photograph again. All he could do was stare. His mind wandered.

Yes, this woman was beautiful, but not a knockout like Cynthia Ryland. Hers was a classic, raw beauty, the kind without a lot of makeup. No, that wasn't it. There was something about this woman Jonathan could not put his finger on, as if he knew her. The feeling was palpable. But that was impossible; he would have remembered her, unless, of course, he had met he during one of his abductions.

Choosing not to dwell on that any longer, at least for now, he turned his attention to her history and credentials. Notwithstanding her family's background and achievements, the academic and professional accomplishments she had amassed at such a young age, meant that Ariella Marconi was brilliant in her own right. Jonathan was relieved that he would not have to dumb down the conversation when speaking with her. Also, judging by her assignment at Sea lab X, he surmised that she was familiar with taking orders, which was a plus. Working with civilians who were unaware of military protocols could be challenging, to say the least. Things needed to have order, although he himself was guilty of spontaneity on occasion.

Ms. Marconi's qualifications were impeccable, and he planned on using every one of them, if necessary, to figure out what the hell was going on in the trench.

As Jonathan closed the file and started to put it away, her picture fell to the floor. Picking it up, he found himself mesmerized once more, staring into her chocolate brown eyes. There was something more about this girl, more than the feeling of knowing her. His heart began to flutter, his pupils began to widen, he felt a nervousness begin to develop in the pit of his stomach, and then . . . "No!" he cried out loud, jamming the picture of her back into the file.

For the remainder of the trip, Jonathan tried to focus on Cynthia Ryland, to no avail. His thoughts always wound up returning to Ariella. In his mind's eye, he pictured the rest of her body, her mannerisms, and the sound of her voice. He even envisioned how she smelled, like powdery honeysuckle.

Something was amiss, and in time it would be discovered; he was confident about that. Instead of fighting it, which never worked for him anyway, he just went with it. Soon enough, they would be face to face and all this business could be sorted out.

CHAPTER
THIRTY EIGHT

AT PRECISELY THE same time, 5:45 p.m., Jonathan Hawthorn had awakened on the maglev, Ariella woke from her slumber. Feeling a little groggy, she let out a long yawn before looking at the clock. Lying back down, she could not help but have a smile plastered across her face. Her dreams had taken her back to the Mariana Trench. She giggled slightly as she reached for the glass of water on the nightstand next to the cot. As she took hold of the glass, Ariella noticed an envelope that had not been there before. *Someone must have brought it in while I slept,* she deduced.

Assuming the envelope was for her to read, she picked it up and sat cross-legged on the bed. Putting the pillow on her lap, forming a makeshift desk, she studied the sealed package. The name Hawthorn II, Jonathan A. was all that was visible, except of course for the paper seal labeled Top Secret.

Ripping through the paper barrier with ease, Ariella looked inside the envelope and pulled out a green file folder. Opening it and seeing Major Hawthorn's photograph, she found herself uncharacteristically struck with a moment of stupor. All thoughts ceased. Only the chemical reactions involving sight and eroticism seemed to function.

Before she could get control of herself, her pupils dilated, her pulse quickened, and her breathing intensified. She could not understand what was happening. It was as if nothing else mattered. Her mind was blank, and without realizing it she had dropped the picture.

Suddenly, with a groan, she snapped out of it. "What the fuck?" she managed to whisper aloud. As her senses returned, she became beet red as embarrassment overcame her. Hurriedly, she scanned the room to see if anyone had witnessed what had just happened. "Thank God," she sighed. There was no one there but her. Realizing that she needed to be more alert, Ariella opted for another shower.

With the warmth of the water caressing her skin, she attempted to come up with an explanation for what had just taken place. Strangely, she felt a bond with this mystery man, someone she was sure she had never met. Could they have met in a past life, star-crossed lovers continuously reuniting throughout the ages? Ariella was not averse to such occult beliefs, but nothing of that nature had ever happened to her before. Maybe they had run into each other in passing.

Out of the shower, Ariella again had a look at Jonathan Hawthorn's Top Secret file. Although she was able to contain herself this time, the strange feeling did not change within her, which vexed her.

After reviewing the file and getting dressed, she decided to return to the administration building and wait for Major Hawthorn there. It was five minutes past six; either he was here and they had failed to inform her, or he was late! She was betting on the latter.

Unfortunately, she had met men of this type, gung-ho and self-absorbed. Everything they did or were involved in was the most important thing in the world. They were typically egotistical, to the point of being vomitously obnoxious.

She paused, thinking it better not to judge someone before meeting them. Maybe she was wrong. Maybe this guy would at least be bearable. He certainly had the academic qualifications of a man with some sort of culture, and he had risen quickly through the military to his current rank. Additionally, to her pleasant surprise, she had just left a man hours before whom she had originally categorized in much the same way as she was doing to the major now. Ariella was confident, however, that Justin LaMarr was the exception to the rule. She had never met a man like him before.

Impatiently entering the administration building, she notified the secretary of her presence. Ariella still could not shake the feeling she had for the stranger. As the minutes ticked away, so did her control over her anger. "I knew this asshole would be late. I was right! No fucking respect for anyone but himself," Ariella mumbled to herself. As she sat on the sofa, waiting for him to arrive, a voice in the back of her mind told her she was being unreasonable, that there was something more, something endearing about this man—that this anger was a defense mechanism trying to block out feelings she did not understand. *No matter*, she thought. This Major Hawthorn was going to get an earful soon enough. She would expose him, and his true colors would come to light.

CHAPTER

THIRTY NINE

WHILE EVERYONE ELSE was recovering from the farewell celebration in honor of Ariella, Captain Justin LaMarr was alone on the bridge listening to satellite radio. The song "Here I Go Again" by Whitesnake was playing. How fitting, he thought.

Most of the crew, understandably, had enjoyed the celebration way too much. Nancy Taylor's apple pie moonshine was not only tasty, but quite potent as well. Thankfully, she had chemically lowered the alcohol content just enough so no one got totally out of control.

The captain suspected that Robert Washington and Dr. Deborah Walker slept together following the party, unless, of course, Dr. Walker was now making house calls at the crack of dawn. He had seen her leaving Robert's room this morning, dressing as she walked toward her quarters. Hopefully, this escapade would loosen Robert up a bit. He was wound a little too tight, always consumed in his work.

After ensuring that the bathysphere was off safely, Roger Sealy and Steven Barett decided it would be prudent to get into an eating/drinking contest. The challenge, issued by Roger, required the participants to slam a Red Bull, down a shot glass of Nancy's smoking apple pie moonshine, eat a slice of pizza, and repeat. To everyone's shock, Roger held up for eleven rounds. Inevitably, however, the acidic mixture of tomato sauce, alcohol, and energy drink became too much for his stomach to contain. He succumbed to a violent episode of projectile vomiting, of which Lt. Barett ended up being the unfortunate recipient.

Apart from being covered in Roger's stomach contents, Steven felt no ill effects following his gorging, at least none that would affect his duties. This was partially due to the fact that he had a cast iron stomach. He still managed to finish his double quarter pounder meal before turning in for the evening.

Thankfully for Roger, Dr. Walker was on hand and prepared. After administering some electrolytes and Pepto Bismol, Nancy Taylor helped clean him up. Like a mother tending to a sick child, she placed Roger's head on her lap and dabbed his face and forehead with a cold, moist cloth. Captain LaMarr, as well as everyone else, could see that Nancy had a crush on Roger, and he on her, but both had been too scared to act on it as yet.

To Justin's shock, Frank Gilmore, the hippie and free spirit of the team, actually acted the most responsibly. He enjoyed the moonshine as much everyone else had, but never got drunk. Also, other than ordering two dozen ranch-covered chicken wings and an order of french fries, the remainder of Frank's food order consisted of fresh fish, particularly sushi and sashimi. Being in such an isolated part of the Pacific Ocean, the ahi and toro tuna, as well as the maguro and hamachi, were among the finest in the world. Justin, with his sophisticated palate, also recognized this and had ordered some sashimi for himself.

Ariella's sudden departure had hit him much harder than he had anticipated. After she entered the bathysphere, he opted to monitor her journey to the surface from the bridge. Captain LaMarr also decided to relieve everyone else of any further obligations for the evening. He wanted them to enjoy themselves; they had definitely earned it. Additionally, with the new data they had just received in the classified file, it might be quite some time before they got another break.

The large amber-colored, crystal-like anomaly located at the bottom of the trench appeared to be expanding. Its very existence was the reason the Sea Lab team was here in the first place, although up until yesterday only he and Steven Barett were privy to the full scope of the operation.

With the new discovery of another such object in the deepest trench in the Atlantic Ocean, half a world away, the powers that be decided it best that Ariella's security clearance be upgraded and that she be relocated in order to spearhead the investigation.

Once in San Francisco, she would be escorted to Sea Lab XIII, located some 25,000 feet below the surface in the Puerto Rico Trench. The man chosen for the job was a Major Jonathan Hawthorn.

Viewing Jonathan Hawthorn's military file, it came as no surprise to him that much of it was either classified or missing. Major Hawthorn had graduated from West Point with honors, was an Army Ranger, SpecOps sniper, and had served in Bosnia and Kosovo early in his career. More recently, he had been deployed to Iraq and Afghanistan and apparently was used in several other theaters around the globe. Jonathan Hawthorn was also well educated, with a double master's in geology and geotechnical engineering. Judging by his age, he, like himself, had been groomed for greater things. Looking deeper into the major's assignments, deployments, and their corresponding dates, Justin soon realized that the file had been altered.

Undoubtably, because of his training and qualifications, the major was, or once was, a member of an elite Delta Force unit, most likely in the late 1990s or early 2000s. Now the major was stationed at Wright-Patterson Air Force Base in the National Air Intelligence Center under the wing of the Foreign Technology Division. This meant only one thing—Jonathan Hawthorn investigated exotic, secret, unknown, and sometimes extraterrestrial phenomenon. He was the ultimate spook.

Whatever was happening in the abysses definitely fell into the realm of the unknown and super top secret. If the general populace was made aware of even a percentage of the happenings that occurred in secret, world governments and religions would collapse. The globe would be thrown into complete chaos. Secrecy was necessary for peace, at least a perceived one.

Surprisingly, though, despite the captain's feeling a bit jealous, Major Hawthorn was smart, young, fit, and handsome; Captain LaMarr was more concerned with Ariella's safety and the success of the mission, both of which the young major was more than qualified to handle. He knew, being Special Forces himself, that this man would give his life to protect an asset, especially a female one. That was just the way he was built. Satisfied that Ariella's new protector was more than capable of doing his job, Justin closed the Ultra Secret file and contemplated all the events that had taken place since she had departed.

Daydreaming, he pictured how much Ariella enjoyed the whales that had surrounded the bell during her ascent. Knowing her, she would be as giddy as a schoolgirl receiving her first kiss. Justin also predicted that due to the importance of the mission, Ariella would have been jetted across the Pacific at supersonic speeds, probably in a fighter. The stars over the ocean at night, he envisioned, would have been on full display for her pleasure—a view through the jet's canopy that one would never be able to experience on a MAC or commercial flight.

"Man, I miss her," he mumbled aloud as he snapped back to reality.

As much as he would have loved to sit there all day and dream of the past and of things to come, there was work to be done. The one downside, or in his case a plus, to letting everyone relax was that someone had to pick up the slack. That someone was Justin. He was actually looking forward to getting his hands dirty, so to speak, and doing some of the work he usually delegated to others. It would also keep his mind off of her, or so that was his plan.

The first order of business was to do some diagnostic checks on some of the equipment to ensure proper operation. Yesterday, Lt. Barett had detected an unusual energy spike at about the same time as the whales had surrounded the bathysphere.

Additionally, the on-board timing system was out of sync by more than a few seconds with the atomic clock located at the National Institute of Standards and Technology in Boulder, Colorado.

Last, the seismographs had been registering an increase in the number and intensity of the tremors which were originating from deep within the abyss. A systems check would determine if the recorded effects of current differentials and entropic changes in the water temperature gradient were caused by heat escaping from the volcanic fissures in the trench floor or by the increased pressure due to the anomaly expansion.

With all the recent seismic activity, Captain LaMarr suspected some of the increased readings would be attributed to magma seeping out from the mantle, but how much he was unsure. While quite capable of running the diagnostic tests and calculating data, he was no expert in the fields of seismology or fluid dynamics. That was Ariella Marconi's job. With her background in physics and geology, combined with her vast knowledge as one of the world's premier oceanographers, she would have been able to instantly identify any deviations in the readings for the area—if there was such a thing as normal readings at a depth of more than 35,000 feet.

As Justin started to run the first series of checks, Steven arrived on the bridge, seemingly ready for work. He was, though, walking in a weird sort of way, almost as if he had something shoved up his ass!

Captain LaMarr, noticing his lieutenant's stride, knew exactly why his subordinate was behaving in such a manner.

"Good morning, Steven," he said, shaking his head side to side with a smirky sort of smile.

"Good morning, sir. I planned on being here sooner, but something un-expected came up. With all the work that needs to be done, I wasn't about to let you have all the fun by yourself."

Although, the alcohol, the Red Bulls, and the unfamiliar greasy food did not make the young officer sick to his stomach, it did wreak havoc on his di-gestive system. Lt. Barett had spent most of the morning on the toilet. Steven, being young, dumb, and full of cum, as Dr. Walker described him, had ada-mantly refused anything she had to offer him last night for his digestion. He claimed that he would be fine and that he never got sick. Steven now wished he had let his brains override his bravado, because he was certainly paying for it this morning.

Captain LaMarr, impressed that the young man still showed up even after being given the day off, could not help but have some fun at the lieu-tenant's expense.

"Oh! Really . . . well, I appreciate your help, but are you sure you're okay?" Justin mimicked how Steven had walked in as he headed for the coffee pot.

"I should have taken some Pepto last night when Deborah offered it to me," he explained, laughing slightly at his hardheadedness.

"From the looks of it, the baby wipes would have helped too," Captain LaMarr added as both men now had a hearty laugh.

Steven gingerly walked to his chair and sat down. It was obvious that he was in pain.

"I really do appreciate you coming in this morning; I definitely could use your help." Holding up the coffee pot, he motioned to Steven. "Can I get you some coffee?" As much as he tried to keep from picking on the lieutenant any further, Justin could not help himself. "I hear that coffee can get the digestive juices flowing. It might help . . . you know . . . clean you out."

"Nooo, sir. I'm pretty sure my colon is quite clean, thank you very much." Lt. Barett put up his hand and cringed at the mere mention of coffee. "I'm afraid that if drink any coffee, it'll make me shit again. My ass can't handle that right now!" He was jokingly serious.

With that, the captain showed him some mercy and let him off the hook.

After pouring himself some more of the brew, Justin briefly went over the plan for the day and what he intended to accomplish. Justin and Steven complemented each other very well in everything that they did together. This was the main reason he had taken the young lieutenant under his wing. Where he was strong, Lt. Barett was weak, and where he was weak, Lt. Barett was strong. It was rare, not only in the armed services but in life in general, that people ever get the opportunity to work with a true complement of themselves. Once Captain LaMarr discovered that he and Lt. Barett possessed this connection, he made sure to never let the occasion escape him. Luckily, he had the rank and connections to see it through. Another added bonus was that Steven Barett's family also had some pull. After meeting the senior Barett some years ago, following Steven's successful completion of his SEAL training, Justin had discussed with Mr. Barett, in detail, what he had thought of his son. While not knowing then how well he and his young officer would end up meshing or what his immediate future held, he promised the father to keep him abreast of Steven's progress. Once Justin put all the pieces together, Mr. Barett was happy to offer his assistance; he liked Justin LaMarr and knew his son would grow and excel under his command.

Now, back at his desk amid the array of LED screens, Lt. Barett checked on the progress of ARES. Captain LaMarr had sent the automatic submersible down into the depths before Steven's arrival in order to perform a visual inspection of the crystalline anomaly. By collecting its own data, ARES would either support or refute the measurements of the sensors that were located on site.

"Captain, ARES still has about an hour before reaching the site. It's already measuring a number of tremors that exceed 2.0 on the Richter scale."

"Good job, lieutenant. Let's finish the system checks; then we might be able to figure out what the hell is going on down there." The captain was becoming concerned about the crew's safety. The Hab was in a hazardous environment to start with, some 15,000 feet below the surface on the edge of an abyssal cliff. Even though the Sea Lab was designed to handle earthquakes up to 9.0 magnitude, that was not what Captain LaMarr was worried about. The greatest threat to the Hab was not from below, but from above.

Situated on a thin, flat ridge, precariously close to a 20,000-foot sheer drop on the front and a 1,500-foot vertical wall to the rear, it was easy to imagine a scenario where the habitat was pelted by falling debris. While it was made of some of the strongest materials known, at such depths, any damage to the structure's hull would spell certain disaster.

Another major factor to be considered was that if the tremors got strong enough, the Sea Lab could snap its anchors and be shaken right off the ledge and into the chasm. By the time it finally slammed into the bottom, the structure's deflection could cause it to be compressed to the size of a car.

Unfortunately for the crew, if the volcanic activity was indeed becoming more constant and intense, their day off would be cut short. For now, however, they were all still safe to sleep in.

As Lt. Barett continued running checks on the seismograph, the electromagnetic and atomic spectrometers, the Geiger tubes, and the various other devices used to measure practically everything, Captain LaMarr decided as a precaution to venture to the sub bay in order to inspect the PRIEST and the exosuits. It was better to be safe than sorry. No one could ever accuse Justin of not being thorough. "Chance favors the prepared mind," he would always say to Lt. Barett when the younger officer commented on his anal retentiveness.

The Hab was eerily quiet this morning as Captain LaMarr descended toward the sub bay. Unsurprisingly, medical was empty. Dr. Walker must have gone back to sleep following last night's caper. Looking through the porthole on the western wall, he noticed that only the service lights were on in the living quarters. *Good, everyone is still sleeping*, he thought.

Once Justin reached the terrarium, he was pleased to find Frank Gilmore was awake and chipper as usual. He refused to take time off for fear of neglecting his plants. This morning, he was adding nutrients to their hydroponic spray mixture, while exposing them to some morning music. He had tuned into a classic rock station that was now playing "Come Monday" by Jimmy Buffett. *What a comparison*, he thought. It was Monday, but he was not at all sure that "it'll be all right" as the song suggested.

"Top of the mornin' to ya, Cap'n," Frank smiled, feigning a British accent.

"Why am I not surprised to see you up, Frank? I guess our old biological clocks make it impossible for us to sleep in, huh?"

"We're not old, Justin; like fine wine, we're just aged to perfection."

"I can go with that. How are the babies doing this morning?"

Frank often called his plants his babies, since he had no children of his own. He had been conducting experiments subjecting two groups of green beans to different styles of music. For this particular bunch, he played only classic rock, while the other, positioned on the opposite side of the grow room, was exposed to traditional classic works. Frank had read a book by Dr. Masaru Emoto about the effects of music, thought, and prayer on water molecules, as viewed through an electron microscope. So far, the beans under the influence of classic rock grew faster but did not taste as good. At least that was Frank's subjective opinion. He still needed to analyze the chemical compositions of each group in order to present some credible scientific results.

"They're doing great! This group has grown over two inches since yesterday. In a few more generations, I'll be able to gather some accurate data." Frank was always excited to talk about his plants.

"I truly admire a man who loves his work. We need more men like you in the world."

"Thank you, Justin. That means a lot." Frank balled his fists and double pounded his chest over his heart. "But I'm just a humble man trying to spread the love."

"You most certainly do that."

"Speaking of love, how are you doing?" He was obviously referring to the captain's feelings toward Ariella.

"I'm all right. She'll be back soon," Justin said, more to convince himself than Frank.

"She's definitely a keeper. You're a lucky man."

"Yes, she is." The captain started to daydream about her again before realizing that he wanted to make Frank aware of what was happening. The problem was that his security clearance did not warrant it. For all the crew knew, they were here to study volcanic activity and its effects in the abyssal oceans. Justin was able, though, to drop a subtle hint to the botanist.

Frank Gilmore, being very observant, picked up on the captain's body language. "Is everything all right, Captain?" he asked with his head tilted forward and down while looking Justin directly in the eyes.

"I'm not sure. Just be attentive, okay, Frank? I may need your assistance later."

"Anything you need, I'll be there."

Still having much to accomplish before the real work began, Captain LaMarr left Frank perplexed, but alert to the possibility of complications. If a situation were to develop, Frank Gilmore would be critical in assisting with the crew's evacuation. Justin had already witnessed the botanist's grace under pressure when he had skillfully handled several minor incidents over the past few months. The captain felt certain he would react the same way under more stressful circumstances; Frank was always cool as a cucumber.

Entering the multilevel submarine bay, Captain LaMarr headed directly for the exosuits. While the mini-sub, PRIEST, was more important if they needed to abandon the station, the exosuits, while used for exploration, were essential if the need arose for emergency repairs—so much so that each crew member had at least forty hours of simulator training along with at least one four-hour extra-vehicular activity. Everyone loved it, except, of course, Robert Washington. It took away from his work.

As he approached the hollow, white metallic objects, the childhood memory of the TV series *Lost in Space* and its robot came to mind, only these "robots" were much cooler.

The suit's hull was made of the same nickel titanium zirconium alloy mixture that formed the Sea Lab's external shell. Extremely strong and light compared to the commercially available versions, the 200-pound exosuits were easily maneuverable at great depths. Theoretically, they could go anywhere in the ocean. Thus far, however, they had proven to be successful to at least 30,000 feet.

Like an automobile, the passenger entered the exosuits by swinging open the front door. A person as short as five feet and as tall as six feet five could be accommodated within the adjustable cavity. Once sealed inside, the helmet, which was made mostly of clear compressed aluminized glass, offered a

270-degree field of view. It also featured an eyes-on digital display that would make any jet pilot or submarine captain jealous.

Its bionic arms and legs, made of nitinol fabric woven between multitudes of rigid, boronic titanium rings and composed of forty joints, allowed for a nearly 90 percent flexible range of motion compared to natural movements.

At the end of each arm was a prehensor device consisting of three plier-like fingers and a thumb. These not only offered the diver 95 percent of normal dexterity, but could also provide sensory feedback pertaining to grip pressure. With a little training, the wearer could pick up an egg.

On the distal ends of the legs, each boot held a three-horsepower, foot-controlled thruster, which could allow the diver to "fly" through the water like a caped superhero. The larger thruster pack, located on the exosuit's back, much like those worn by astronauts, could propel the suit at speeds up to fifteen knots.

Understandably, these twenty-million-dollar suits used a tremendous amount of energy for both their functional and life-support systems. Traditional power supplies would be quickly drained, especially during increased activity, and would therefore be inadequate at these depths. A solid-state, zero-point energy generator, similar to a Casimir engine, only with resonating dielectric spheres, charged the battery used to supply all the exosuit's power demands.

While seeing and using many different types of super-secret devices, and hearing of still others, the exosuits were the most advanced pieces of equipment Captain LaMarr had ever had the pleasure to work with.

After inspecting all eight suits, the captain moved toward the mini-sub. The PRIEST was also quite an amazing feat of engineering. At 20 feet long, 12 feet wide, and 8 feet high, it provided adequate room for four crewmen and one pilot. In an emergency, seven of the eight-man crew could be stuffed into the submarine, while one would have to don an exosuit and be held between the PREIST's two forward clawed arms for the ride to the surface.

Weighing in at 15,000 pounds, much lighter than the unclassified model because of its special alloy hull, the mini-sub could carry an additional 2,500-pound payload at a maximum speed of twenty knots.

Fortunately, the PRIEST's life-support system could be functional for up to ninety-six hours and the exosuits for seventy-two hours. Both provided ample time to get to the surface, which could happen in as little as an hour and a half if necessary.

Tapping into the submarine's computer screen remotely, Justin determined it too was in perfect operating order. It could be ready to launch in under ten minutes if needed. He had an overwhelming premonition that both the exo-suits and the sub would be effectively field tested before the mission was over, especially if ARES went on the fritz.

Captain LaMarr, satisfied that all the equipment was up and ready if required, began to wander around the Hab. His thoughts were alternating between Ariella and the amber crystal anomaly. One second, he found himself missing his newfound love, and then he was engrossed with what was happening in the trench. This led him to be thankful that Ariella was not here, but made him worry about where she was going.

Justin knew that all the money spent to place the highly classified Sea Lab, with all its components, and man it with a crew was not just for the hell of it. For the powers that be to say, "Look what we can do, whoopee!" No, they were here to study an anomalous amber crystal of unknown origin, made of an unknown substance, and with no known purpose except to apparently grow and expand; putting even more pressure on the fissures in the Mariana Trench.

Then, without warning, the team's only qualified oceanographer capable of interpreting the data was whisked away to investigate another identical crystal, in another abyssal trench, and positioned almost precisely on the opposite side of the globe. Coincidence? He did not think so. With all the activity starting to happen here, he could only imagine the hell breaking loose in Puerto Rico.

Back in business mode, Captain LaMarr decided to pick up the pace and make a beeline to the bridge. He was normally a man who dealt with facts more than speculation. Right now, that was what he needed to bring order back to his mind. With luck, he would soon have some answers.

CHAPTER

FORTY

STILL REELING FROM the revelations that Captain Rahzu had told her about her Uncle Abraham's history, Commander CheRahna found herself wandering aimlessly around the RJC. While she felt good about her recent progress, she sensed that her lack of knowledge wearing the flesh was becoming too much of a hindrance for her to ignore.

How was she to lead others when she had no experience or commonality with which to give credence to her orders or directives. CheRahna knew what she had to do, but with whom, and when?

Thus far, the only one she would even consider copulating with was Rahzu. However, that would be a huge conflict of interest for the captain because he was her direct superior. Likewise, everyone else on board was subordinate to her. Besides, she was not comfortable or friendly enough with any of them. Neither scenario would be very ethical. Since there was no logical candidate with whom she could share the experience of being human, at least not one who would not ruin her integrity as a Rah commander, CheRahna tabled the desire for the time being.

Instead, she turned her focus toward another dilemma, which if unraveled might provide her with something a bit more concrete to latch onto. In her confusion, she had forgotten that Rahzu had given her his codex. Now, as her senses returned, CheRahna headed directly to her quarters. It was time to uncover who her uncle really was.

Reaching her stateroom unnoticed, she felt fortunate that she was not forced to put on a false front of composure for any of the crew. Apparently, she was not adept at doing that anyway; everyone always knew how she felt.

Opting to recharge her energy while she read, CheRahna climbed into her private amber pleasure pool, which was located in a room attached to her quarters. Immediately upon entering the pool, she could sense the elemental amber energy of the Rah return to her essence. While not needing to eat or sleep, Dimerians did require, from time to time, nutrients, just as all beings do. Here in the Rah Jump Craft, the pool provided the elemental necessities to maintain peak performance. If not on a ship, stationed in such a barren universe as PU 430, she would have just acquired the elements needed from the surrounding ether.

Understandably, CheRahna was starting to see how life on Dimeria, which was much simpler and without the distractions of being so near to Earth, was appealing to many of its inhabitants. Other than the political ramifications of the various houses jockeying for power, which was usually associated with the Blade Wars, things were such that one could tend to more utopian pursuits.

As soon as the feelings of nostalgia passed, the commander opened Rahzu's codex and began to read. To her shock, Rahzu's claim was accurate—this manuscript, which was much older than any she had seen, was different than the codex issued at the academy.

Right from the beginning, Abraham's purpose on Earth, just as Rahzu had stated, was to be an envoy for the House of Rah, on a mission of peace and scientific exploration. Arriving on Earth some 35,000 years ago, her uncle had been stationed at the city of Dwarka, southeast of the modern-day Indus River Delta.

Though various cleansings were performed periodically to eliminate the existence of parasitic Dimerians, Abraham, the House of Rah, as well as a small contingency of Anunnaki were welcome to stay.

Just prior to Yahweh's decision to ethnically cleanse the Earth of all life some 11,000 years ago with a Herculean deluge, Abraham was alerted and decided to move his family to Harappa, in modern-day Pakistan. Since

Dimerians were essentially godlike compared with humans, and did not die from ordinary things, Yahweh's warning was more of a convenience. His goal was to eliminate any genetic variants that were not 100 percent pure human.

Continuing to read, CheRahna thus far could identify with most of the story in Rahzu's codex, except for Abraham's initial purpose in being there. Now, however, she was starting to enter some unfamiliar territory within the tale—things she had not been taught.

According to the ancient account, the Rahs and Nahs, otherwise known as the Anunnahki, started creating more and more problems with the growing number of humans on the planet. The issues were due to both parties' increasing need for resources and land.

She had never heard of anything like this before. She had been told that the Rahs had always been welcomed on Earth and performed a service for Yahweh by keeping order among his creation.

The codex went on to say that, for reasons unknown or not mentioned, Yahweh chose no longer to utilize or negotiate with the other houses that were on his planet and ordered them to leave. His ultimatum was simple: Leave or be destroyed. Ample time was given for everyone to depart safely.

The Creator then formulated a plan to seed the air with a secret compound that, once activated, would eliminate any remaining Dimerian or other offspring not of the House of Yah.

Knowing that the Anunnaki used the various pyramids that had been constructed all over the globe to power their planet-sized Nahbirrhu, as well as their smaller craft, Yahweh patiently waited, allowing those wishing to leave to do so. Once enough time had passed—many years in fact—the sky would be seeded. The only thing that remained was for their energy beam to be shot toward the heavens, activating the compound and initiating the attack. Most Dimerians departed as ordered. Abraham, as well as a few others, went underground in order to avoid the aerial attacks. Little did they know—at least that's what the codex infers—this decision to dig in saved their lives.

As predicted, the Anunnahki fired up the pyramids with their arks to charge up their ships. Instantly, the combination of the microwave energy beams and Yahweh's secret compound selectively destroyed any Dimerians and their offspring left on the surface. This all supposedly occurred almost 9,000 years ago.

Once again, none of this history was ever taught at the academy—especially the part about most Dimerians leaving as ordered. "If this were true, where did they go? They certainly returned to Dimeria," she whispered to herself.

CheRahna kept reading, realizing that this version was very different from what she had been led to believe.

Following the Great Purge, Yahweh was ruthless in hunting down any Dimerians who remained on Earth. This was the point where Rahzu's codex started to somewhat match the one she read as a recruit.

Abraham, for reasons unknown, then defected and started taking orders from Yahweh. He left Harappa, where he and many Rahs had taken refuge underground, and moved to Ur of the Chaldeans. Once relocated, Harappa and Mohenjo Daro were devastated by what could be best described as a nuclear blast. At the same time, the space port of the Anunnahki, located on the Sinai Peninsula, was also leveled.

Moving from Ur, to Haran, to Bethel, and then into Egypt, as ordered, Abraham, given special weapons by Yahweh, patiently and methodically hunted and eliminated any Rahs who remained.

Finally, after his spy, Lot, discovered the secret hideouts of the last vestiges of Rahs on the planet, Sodom and Gomorrah were destroyed in a series of massive explosions of which the smoke plumes could be seen from anywhere in the region. The destruction was so thorough that the inland sea that the cities were near was left poisoned and devoid of life. To this day, the Dead Sea's shoreline soil is too acidic and its water too salty to support vegetation or marine life. In fact, anyone exposed to its waters for any length of time will develop the symptoms of radiation sickness.

Although in the rendition of history which she remembered, Abraham's reasons for defection were well known, the majority of the events conformed to what she already knew. The rest of the codex talked about how Pharaoh's magicians nearly fooled Abraham into sacrificing his own son and how they captured her Aunt Sarah in what is now the Sahara Desert, her current prison. It went on to explain how Xanix Rah and YetziRah then destroyed Abraham's elite 318 Naharai troops, all defectors from the Houses of Rah and Nah. This, along with Sarah's capture, effectively ended the reign of death and destruction, all of which was repeated, verbatim, in what she studied at the academy.

Finished reading and feeling quite recharged from her soaking in the amber pleasure pool, CheRahna returned to her quarters just as confused as she had been before she had started reading. Was she that naïve to think that the political elite would not resort to altering history to accomplish their agenda? Of course not! But to be so thorough that no Dimerian Rah even knew about this version of history in Rahzu's codex? That would not be as difficult as she had initially thought. This was as it was told, a secret mission that only a few important Rah leaders even knew was underway. She herself did not even have all the details involved in their campaign.

CheRahna wholeheartedly trusted her captain, Rahzu. He had always been an understanding, caring, and wise mentor who had challenged her to be the best that she could be. But so had her uncle. He would periodically visit her for a vacation, even after being stationed on Earth, at least until he defected.

Still, CheRahna had to believe in her leader. Under Rahzu, she had evolved from a dull gray silver ensign, to an enlightened, nearly platinum-colored silver Rah commander. "This has to be the truth; why would he lie to me!" She uttered.

Calmly pausing for a moment, reflecting on all her interactions with Rahzu, all of his interactions with the crew, and his known history, CheRahna decided that she would have noticed by now if he was attempting to deceive her. His energies would have given him away long ago. No one, she thought, was that good at lying for so long as to fool her. It did not matter how good the story was or the facts presented; she would be able to tell.

Happily concluding to trust Rahzu and his codex as factual, many questions arose about her uncle and their purpose here. These needed to be answered. The only way that was going to happen was for her to go and talk to her beloved captain, which she planned on doing immediately.

As she opened the door and headed toward the command bridge, CheRahna felt a feeling of exhilaration she had never experienced before, as if something within her had changed. Could it be that her Uncle Abraham was not the evil traitor that she thought him to be?

For the first time in a long time, she was not only looking forward to reviewing her past but was cautiously optimistic about what she might find.

CHAPTER

FORTY ONE

UPON RETURNING TO the Rah Academy on Dimeria, YetziRah immediately began plotting. He needed to formulate a scenario with he could blame Ensign RahKael's tragic death on Xanix Rah's incompetence and treachery. He understood that, even with his political connections, his ability to sway opinion, and the shared hatred of his clan for their house leader, ousting such a polarizing member of the Dimerian Council would be no easy task.

Xanix Rah, who owned nearly a third of the 312 universes controlled by the House of Rah, was the second most powerful member of the Council; only JahVeh outranked him as chairman.

For many years, despite his domineering bravado and sociopathic tendencies toward violence, YetziRah believed Xanix Rah was being influenced by some unknown puppeteer. But who and why—that remained a mystery.

All he was sure about was that he, YetziRah, was the last of the HooRahs, a warrior class that was created for leadership and bred for battle. The previous leader of the House of Rah was a HooRah named ThundoRah. He was one the greatest warriors in Dimeria's entire history. His fame and prominence were born out of the calamitous PU 4 uprising during which he singlehandedly beheaded over a thousand of the god-killing beasts. ThundoRah's fame morphed into legend when he became champion within the Golden Rings. With him as God of the Blades, the House of Rah experienced a period of magnificence, a model all the other houses strove to emulate.

Unfortunately, the day came when ThundoRah lost his title and his head to ZYah Zeh, from the House of Yah. With his loss, the House of Rah was also obligated to forfeit the properties ThundoRah had wagered, which were many. Only by betting for ZYah Zeh against ThundoRah, using his own properties and those he controlled by proxy as collateral, did Xanix Rah acquire the necessary universes to assume control of their house.

This justification for leadership still perplexed YetziRah. If rule was indeed to be based on property holdings, especially for Council positions, then Toyah Veh, the founding leader of the House of Yah, should be chairman. The Yahs, since ZYah Zeh had risen to be God of the Blades, now had control of 433 of the 777 universes, more than all the other houses combined. Therefore, leadership based on property was a political ruse and was merely bent to the wishes of an unknown master of manipulation. Whoever that was, he had found the perfect front man!

Xanix Rah had no honor, no loyalty, and, most importantly, no trusted allies. What he did have was a charismatic ruthlessness and hunger for power that was insatiable. He cared little about who he had to use and crush on his way to the top, especially those of his own house.

YetziRah, although not known for his love or tenderness, and being quite comfortable with cruelty when he deemed it necessary, had always remained loyal to his house. He too, admittedly, wanted to reign supreme, leading the House of Rah back to greatness. However, and not for just selfish reasons, he genuinely believed he was the most fit to lead and the best chance for the Rahs to once again control Dimeria.

Instead of wasting too much time thinking about the way things were, he turned his concentration to the way things should be. To take down such a big player in the political game, he was going to need some help, primarily from those in his own clan and house.

First, he needed to communicate his wishes to his son, Arin Rah, who was the sole heir to his fifty-two universes. It was imperative for him to work behind the scenes to recruit other major universe holders within their house. Without them, there could be no successful plan to oust Xanix Rah.

When he met with his son, he would direct Arin Rah to focus his energies on Ku Ton Rah, owner of thirty-nine properties, and Shante-Ori-N-Rah, owner of twenty-two universes. Both had fought for and won the majority of their universes while in the Golden Rings. In fact, Shante-Ori-N-Rah had won all his properties in the Blade Wars. These two Rahs were warriors who had little respect for Xanix Rah. If his son could bring them into the fold, that would give him voting right of 113 of the 312 Rah holdings. Though this was more than Xanix Rah's 102, it was not enough to gain the proxy of the other fourteen various scattered properties, bringing the total to 127 universes.

While it might be enough, particularly if he could prove treason against the Council, he would feel more at ease if he could get more. Mor Rah Svyn, with forty-three universes, and El Zyen Rah, with forty universes, were the only Rahs left who owned property. El Zyen Rah was loyal to Xanix Rah, so much so that he would have to be taken down during the coup d'état. Mor Rah Svyn, on the other hand, was a gambling man and had won all his properties betting on ZYah Zeh in the Blade Wars. He was an opportunist who showed no real loyalty to the house. This could actually prove to be extremely helpful if YetziRah's conspiracy were to prove to be successful. Mor Rah Svyn would bet on the sure winner, and the winner would be YetziRah.

Since he knew Arin Rah would do as instructed, YetziRah could discuss his plot with him later. For now, he needed to formulate the initial and most important part of the hostile takeover, the political ruination of Xanix Rah. That was the key to getting the support of the other clans. Without a properly designed scheme, no one would stand against their leader, and he, not Xanix Rah, would be in danger.

What he needed here was a political ally, someone who would do his bidding in Dimeria. Overseeing the illegal clandestine operation in PU 430, the admiral had to be careful not to incriminate himself while he worked to expose Xanix Rah. He also had no intention of alerting the Council to their own forbidden experiment with creation on Planet ET Rah, in the Biord Rah galaxy in PU 78. This would be catastrophic to his house and to his plans for complete domination.

Auspiciously, he already had the perfect accomplice in mind. The present lead instructor at the Rah Academy, Suda Rahma, was just as subversive as he. Together, back when he was lead instructor, they had altered the history of PU 431 being taught to recruits in order to present the Rahs' mission in a more positive light. Although Suda Rahma took orders from Xanix Rah on how and what to teach, he like YetziRah had no love for their house leader. On several occasions, scenarios had been discussed in which it would be appropriate to facilitate a changing of the guard.

Suda Rahma's knowledge of subterfuge, which was essentially what he taught at the academy, would be instrumental in twisting the facts to not only convince the Council members and the clans of Rah, but to alter history for future generations. This would be vital for their coup to stand up legally and be recognized once the smoke settled. It would be foolish to succeed in his quest to attain power just to have it later stripped away.

A meeting with Suda Rahma could also be put aside for the moment. The most crucial aspect of his plan was to get control of the situation in PU 430. Following the run-in with the captain of the RJC, YetziRah was certain that Rahzu would have no part of this conspiracy. If he was not muzzled, YetziRah would have no chance of achieving his goals and would likely be eliminated himself. He knew he could not challenge Rahzu to a duel out-right. It was not that he feared the captain; to the contrary, he was bred for battle, and he had a better than average chance of besting him in combat. It was more a matter of justification for such a duel. With Rahzu's service record, his medals and awards, no one would believe any story he conjured to end the captain's life.

Knowing this, YetziRah needed a patsy, someone already aboard the ship, to do his bidding. But who? After looking at the ship's roster, a nefarious wave of energy flooded his very being. "Aw . . . My darling CheRahna, I almost forgot about you. You, my dear, are perfection," he happily cooed aloud.

At the time CheRahna was attending the Academy, YetziRah had been the lead instructor. She had arrived at the Academy young and cocky, as if she had something to prove.

Although the young recruit had negative feelings about her uncle's sudden disappearance, she had coped well. The details of Abraham's defection had long been altered and deemed secret; she had no knowledge of it as of yet.

Being the master manipulator that he was, YetziRah used this alternative history to poke and prod at the proud recruit's persona every opportunity he got. As a result, CheRahna developed such insecurity within herself that even when she excelled, which she did in every aspect of her training, she still felt inadequate. He was sure, at that time, he could have caused her to have a psychic break if he had had a mind to do so. While remembering the experience to be enjoyable, his madness had a purpose: he needed to get the only remaining relative of Abraham living on Dimeria to believe the story he and Suda Rahma had concocted, and she did! CheRahna believed in their deception wholeheartedly—so much so that the mere mention of her uncle's name generated such an intense combination of rage and shame that she would lash out vehemently, separating herself from her treacherous uncle's past.

To YetziRah, this all seemed like providence, as if the One Father, Zenith, had bestowed the gift of foresight upon him. All the work he had done to ensure Abraham was the scapegoat for the mistakes of the past was still paying dividends.

He realized that Rahzu, who knew a different version of history than what his commander had been taught, would undoubtedly have attempted to inform her of his version by now. Rahzu was, regardless of his moral stiffness, an excellent captain, and an exceptional mentor. He would have told CheRahna about Abraham, not to break her down, but to build her up. Too bad he had to go; YetziRah hated to lose such a fine leader.

However, because even Rahzu was not privy to what had really happened on Earth, YetziRah was sure that the seed of doubt, the one he had planted in her psyche so long ago, was still alive and well in Commander CheRahna.

Now he just needed to get her to turn on her beloved mentor. "Hmm . . . what could get her to go against Rahzu?" He stood motionless, hand on his golden chin. "Ah ha!" he yelled in triumph. YetziRah now knew his angle, how to break her to do his will. In a flash, he blinked away, returning to PU 430 and to the pawn who would lead him to his destiny.

CHAPTER

FORTY TWO

ΛS TH∃ MΛGL∃V pulled into the station beneath the San Francisco Bay Naval Shipyard, Jonathan found himself uncharacteristically nervous. *But why?* he wondered, though the answer was clear. Who was this Ariella Talia Marconi that she could have this much influence over his emotions before his even meeting her, other than in a dream? He still was not fully buying that he had met her during one of his abductions.

Bullets of sweat started to develop over his upper lip as he departed the train. Looking down at the glowing green LCD of his phone, Jonathan noticed the time, 1837, May 21, 2007. "Holy shit, I'm late!" he exclaimed aloud followed by a slight laugh.

At least his nervous tension would be masked by Ms. Marconi's inevitable verbal assault due to his tardiness, for which, at this point, he could hardly blame her. It was almost as if it was a self-fulfilling prophecy. As a civilian, Ariella Marconi was not attuned to the regimen of military life, particularly one involving her being moved to the opposite side of the globe in such a short period of time.

Still, even with her rapid redeployment and his delayed arrival as distractions, he was not certain his bewildered feelings toward her would go unnoticed. Jonathan was rarely nervous around women, especially with those whose bios he had read. She was different, though. From the instant he first saw her photograph, Jonathan could not shake the feeling that he knew her and that their connection was of grave importance.

Sensing the need to get his emotions in check, he started to recite his mantra. Though it was unnecessary here—San Francisco station was a strictly human facility—Jonathan found solace in his chant. The more he repeated the phrase from his childhood, the more relaxed he became. This repetitious mind training had other benefits too. It allowed him to focus strictly on the facts, without a cloud of emotional entanglement. He had used this technique many times in the past, when under no threat of his thoughts being stolen, in order to calm his anxieties.

After he punched in the code and the floor number, the elevator began to rise. This station, although still classified above Top Secret, required only a personalized access code and a hidden biometric scan for admittance. Sites such as this were mainly used for the rapid transportation of influential politicians and critical military personnel, neither of whom had access to any other "nonhuman" facilities.

By the time the elevator door opened, Jonathan was feeling much more at peace with himself, which was a blessing considering the past few days had been so stressful. In the past thirty-six hours, he had experienced a prodigious vision, which could possibly have worldwide implications; met a mysterious man from India, who was proving to be much more than what he had initially appeared to be; crossed the country twice, nearly dying in a car accident; came to the realization that he had been abducted, multiple times; been reassigned to a mission which was eerily related to his vision; had incredible sex with his potential soul mate; and was now about to meet a woman he was sure he had never met, despite the feeling and the dream that he had.

With all his training, his self-awareness, and his mantra, this was a lot even for him to handle. The moment of truth had arrived. "It's time to suck it up and drive on," he mumbled to himself. Jonathan then walked down the short hallway and turned the corner. There, sitting on the couch, was the woman who had been the source of his recent vexation.

Now, within a comfortable social distance for a handshake, as he offered his hand, he found himself paralyzed. Her physical presence was mesmerizing.

Peering deep into her chocolate brown eyes, Jonathan became lost in a torrent of emotion, one that would shake him to his very core.

⌣

Ariella was sitting quietly, coiled like a pit viper ready to lash out against this Major Jonathan Arlin Hawthorn. As the minutes ticked by, the angrier she became. Why was he late while she was on time? Why did she even have to be here? Surely there were more qualified individuals who could have fit the bill! Why was she taken away from the Hab; and finally, why was she so upset anyway? None of this was that unusual in her life. She was and had been dedicated to her work for as long as she could remember. This was not the first time she had had to drop everything she was doing to be called off to some faraway land. No, she knew exactly why she was angry, she just didn't want to admit it.

Ariella was a woman who did not mind having questions, as long as they had fathomable answers. Admittedly, sometimes that meant stretching the fabric of known reality and even entering into the mystical realm from time to time; but even then, there would be some sort of theoretical answer that could be derived.

What she had experienced earlier, while looking at this strange man's picture, had her totally flustered. What the hell was wrong with her? Ariella felt dirty, as if she had been unfaithful to a lover. However, a feeling of nervous excitement persisted. This, more than anything else, was the source of her anger. What about this man had her this enamored, so much so that she was finding it difficult to concentrate on anything else? Ariella was disgusted with herself because she had finally concluded that she was actually looking forward to meeting this mystery man.

After looking at her watch, her anticipation began to build. She was not accustomed to all these nervous emotions and wished for them to end. Ariella closed her eyes, took a deep breath, and attempted to calm herself.

Precisely upon opening her eyes, she noticed a figure approaching from around the corner, just down the hallway. Instantly, she recognized who it was—Jonathan Hawthorn. He moved briskly, with purpose, as he neared.

All her questions, anxiety, and anger dissipated into the ether once her gaze met his. She became lost in a sea of hazel green as she probed deeper into his eyes. Her thoughts stopped, heart fluttered, and the most powerful wave of emotion she had ever experienced washed over her entire body. It was a warm, compassionate feeling, one composed of safety, admiration, and love.

Why she was experiencing such things was a complete conundrum to her. She did believe, however, that there had to be a reason, even if it was an esoteric one.

Although classifying herself as a New Ager due to her present spiritual beliefs, she did believe in a supreme creator—just not the one she had been taught about in church. As a recovering Catholic, Ariella had chosen to adopt her own perception of God, with her own interpretation of the Bible. These beliefs alienated her from those who were involved in the service of the church and ultimately led to her excommunication. At first, she was devastated, but later found peace within her faith. Besides, she would rather serve a loving Creator or God than the church anyway.

Even with her open-mindedness, the tenets of Catholic school still lingered in her mind, as if she was committing some mortal sin. While unaware of how or why she had such an emotional attachment to a stranger, and despite it being contrary to her beliefs, to her consternation, Ariella had to admit, these feelings felt good.

As Ariella and Jonathan remained silent and motionless, enraptured in each other's gaze, Lt. Commander Robert Briggs, the same naval officer who originally supported Ariella on her arrival, approached the couple with a confused look on his face. He was almost reluctant to interrupt the two, who appeared to be in the throes of an epic staring contest. He supposed he could have waited to see who would blink first, but he too was a busy man.

"Huh-umm," he grunted, acting as if he was clearing his throat.

On cue, both Ariella and Jonathan snapped out of the trance that had ensnared them. Briggs, seeing that his disruption was a success, began with the introductions.

"Major Hawthorn, I am Lieutenant Commander Briggs, SFB's chief administrative officer. It's a pleasure to meet you, sir."

As they were indoors and out of uniform, saluting the naval officer would have been inappropriate, so Jonathan snapped to attention and responded, "Nice to meet you too, sir, I'm sorry about my tardiness, but it couldn't be avoided." Jonathan's apology was directed more toward Ariella than the lieutenant commander.

"That's quite understandable, Major, I know you've been busy keeping our nation safe."

Motioning toward Ariella with his right hand, the lieutenant commander now properly introduced her. "Major Hawthorn, let me introduce you to Ariella Marconi. She will be accompanying you to Puerto Rico on your new assignment." Now addressing Ariella, he presented Jonathan in the same manner. "Ms. Marconi, this is Major Jonathan Hawthorn, one of our nation's finest. You'll be in good hands as long as you're with him."

Ariella, embarrassed about her staring, gave Jonathan a quick glance and a short hello before returning her focus to Lt. Commander Briggs.

Jonathan, however, directed his complete attention toward her while offering his hand, palm up. As he looked at her, she felt compelled to reach out and take his extended hand. As soon as their skin touched, an electric charge surged up her arm and dispersed throughout her body. The feeling was exhilarating.

Once her palm was firmly in his, Jonathan gently pulled her closer; she neared without question. He then brought her limp arm upward, encircled it with both hands, and tenderly bowed.

Jonathan too felt the spark between them, as if their frequencies flowed together to be at one with the cosmos. It was truly invigorating. He had never had such a connection with anyone before, not even Cynthia Ryland. At that moment, he sensed that he and this Ariella Marconi were destined to be connected.

Jonathan, again addressing the lieutenant commander, blushed slightly as he thanked him for his warm introduction. He did, however, believe himself to be everything he was touted as. Major Hawthorn was not arrogant, or at least he did not think he was. Instead, he would describe himself as confident. Since childhood, he just knew he could accomplish anything if he put his mind to it, which at times had caused him to quit things prematurely out of boredom. Additionally, life's experiences had further reinforced this belief in himself and his abilities.

Jonathan, being fairly self-aware, realized that his self-assurance was often misconstrued, causing deep-seated envy and hatred. To combat this, on occasion he made adjustments in his presentation of himself to others. "You can catch more flies with sugar than you can with salt," his mother Cathy used to say. Most of the time, however, he was not overly concerned with pleasing people, as long as he felt justified in his actions.

In the brief moments in which the two men were stroking each other's egos, as if they were cocks, Ariella noticed several interesting things about her new companion; other than the chemistry that apparently existed between them. Major Hawthorn's presence commanded his opposite's respect. She wondered what he had done to earn such admiration.

Another quality that the major possessed was an air of confidence that radiated from him like rays from the sun. It showed in his personality, his postures, the way he moved, and, most importantly, in his smile. She, as Lt. Commander Briggs had pointed out earlier, already felt safe just being around him. It was like having a sense about him that said, "No matter what happens it will be all right. I'll take care of it." Since her own father had alienated her for choosing any career other than physics, along with the fact that he was an alcoholic, Ariella had never felt such a patriarchal presence. It was something she had longed for.

Considering herself to be an observant person, Ariella was quite aware of how Jonathan faced her when he made his apology to Lt. Commander Briggs. While not being made directly to her, Ariella felt it was for her. It did a lot to show that at least the major was sympathetic to her situation and needs. It also soothed the need to lambaste him for being so late. Maybe it was just as he said, unavoidable.

Finally, Ariella watched intently as Major Hawthorn was being complimented. When he blushed with his boyish smile, she saw a man who acted on principles rather than one who sought the acceptance of others or personal glory. She imagined this was a learned trait, probably fostered during childhood by his parents. Although having principles was an essential quality of integrity and honor, it did not necessarily mean his principles were the correct ones. It could just mean that he was a stubborn jackass who was incapable of change or compromise; such a man could be dangerous. Ariella, though, did not believe this to be true either, unless, of course, all her senses were wrong. This was not likely, since it was her one asset that she trusted so far; it had never let her down as she felt her way through life.

Actually, the more she looked at the facts and rationalized her emotions, the more she returned to the beliefs that had been formed while studying his photograph. Ariella once again began to get flustered as her heart started to race. Sweat developed on her brow and her pupils dilated. Before she could get control of herself, she whispered aloud, "Oh God, not again." *Did I actually just say that aloud?!* she wondered. Maybe I just imagined it. A few nanoseconds passed before an answer to her question came.

"Excuse me? Did you say something, Ms. Marconi?" Jonathan politely asked has he shifted his attention back toward her.

Ariella was mortified. If she could have crawled under the couch she had been sitting on earlier, she would have. She feared that Jonathan somehow knew what she was thinking, like he was some sort of mind reader. *Oh please, Lord, pleeese don't let him know what I was thinking!* she screamed inside.

Unsure how to answer Jonathan's question, Ariella's fight or flight response activated. In order to gather herself, she did what any woman in her right mind would do. "If you gentlemen would excuse me, I need to visit the ladies room."

Seeing the sweat on her reddened face, Jonathan, concerned, touched her on the shoulder and asked, "Ms. Marconi, are you okay? Is everything all right?"

Although she appreciated his caring tone and warm touch, she needed to escape, and now! Giving him a brief smile as she turned to walk away, Ariella answered, "I'm fine; it's just a female thing."

As if he was Superman and just exposed to kryptonite, Jonathan recoiled. "Oh . . . well . . . I see then . . . Okay, I'll be waiting in the lobby around the corner there."

As she expected, he said nothing more about the matter. Already walking away, Ariella offered no further explanation. She needed to refrain from having more contact with Major Hawthorn until she could get control of herself. She felt naked, totally exposed in his presence. Ariella imagined that he could not only read her every expression and nuance, but that he could see her thoughts and emotions as well, especially the ones about him.

Upon entering the ladies' restroom and after ensuring that she was alone, Ariella succumbed to her emotional stresses and burst into tears. What was happening to her and why!? As she sat down in a stall and wept, in the back of her mind she knew that it would be all right. She was with Jonathan Hawthorn.

———— ⌒ ————

Following Ariella's departure, Major Hawthorn finished his business with Lt. Commander Briggs and bid him farewell. While he waited in the lobby, he began to reflect on his initial meeting with the woman, who of late had been occupying his dreams. Jonathan was puzzled by how stunned he was upon their encounter. What was it about her that incapacitated him so thoroughly that he became a statue, unable to speak? Was she beautiful? Yes, even more so than in the photograph in her bio. There was not a single ounce of makeup on her blemish-free face. She did not need it anyway; au naturel was just fine.

Were her chocolate brown eyes mesmerizing? Of course they were; in the yellow halos that encircled her dark, wide pupils, Jonathan felt he could discover the answers of the universe. In her stare, he could see that she too experienced a profound awakening, as if she also had known him previous to this rendezvous. There was a hint of admiration, love, and trust, as well as fear located deep in her soul; they were all for him.

He was becoming increasingly perplexed by the electric jolt delivered on touching her. It was as if their combined forces were intended to be one.

Beginning to realize that he was slipping down into the rabbit hole once again, Jonathan started to concentrate on the more concrete aspects of his new partner. While the lack of makeup signified that she was not too concerned how others judged her outward appearance, the clothes she wore at least matched. They were functional too. Ariella had donned a light blue Adidas breathable long-sleeved shirt and a pair of black Nike rayon pants, both of which displayed her fine curves and athletic build. She also had on a pair of dark blue and gray Timberland boots. Lying on the couch where she was sitting was a light blue and gray Columbia Gore-tex jacket. On her head, covering her shoulder-length black hair, she wore a black cylindrical fleece hoodie that increased her height by several inches.

Judging by her choice of apparel, Jonathan ventured to guess that Ariella loved the wilderness as well as the ocean. "Damn, she was cute!" He grinned as the thought of her wearing one of the tactical suits floated through his mind. This could be interesting, having never been with a nature girl before.

Jonathan had already arrived at the conclusion they were going to be together, at least for now, and since he could not seem to think of any other woman, particularly Cynthia Ryland, he might as well, for the time being, entertain what seemed to be the will of destiny.

Being a sort of go-with-the-flow kind of guy, and being presently uncommitted, he did not have any moral issues with how he felt about what happened between them, as long as the mission came first. But he was not going to push the union either. *To be or not to be, that is the question.* He laughed at himself for thinking of Hamlet's famous soliloquy at a time like this.

What troubled him most, however, was how Ariella was going to react to the hidden world into which she was about to be thrust. Long ago, it was decided, for good reason, that all alien life and technology be kept secret. The reason was that people could not handle the truth. After Majestic Twelve gathered a group of prominent scientists, doctors, journalists, and powerful politicians decades ago and introduced them to the Ebens, based on their reactions, the policy of the world governments has been one of denial. It persists to this day, over half a century later. Now, Ariella was about to not only be shown that aliens exist, but also that humans have been working with them since well before she was born. Apparently, someone thought she could handle all of this, or she would not be here. Or the situation was so bad that they had no choice. He would find out soon enough.

Jonathan's plan was to take the maglev all the way to Homestead Air Force Base in South Florida and then fly one of the new F-22 Raptor fighter jets to San Juan Naval Air Station. Ariella would have no issues with any of this; she had already been made aware of some super tech by her mere presence on the Sea Lab X. The maglev and the Raptor would be more of the same. However, a problem may arise when they stop at Los Alamos in order to give instructions to Gilla. Jonathan was quite sure, judging by her bio and recently upgraded security clearance that this was going to be an entirely new experience for the oceanographer.

After crying for several minutes, Ariella got up, went to the sink, and looked at herself in the mirror. "Holy crap . . . I look like shit!" Though not that vain, she did care enough about her appearance to not want anyone to know that she had been sobbing. Turning on the water, she cupped her hands and buried her face in the cool liquid.

As the water relieved the inflammation and redness around her eyes, Ariella thought of how silly she was acting. She was a thirty-six-year-old woman who had earned a doctorate, enjoyed a prestigious career, and had just discovered a new species of shrimp, which she had named after herself while departing from a super-secret underwater laboratory. Surely she could behave more maturely than the average teenage girl with a crush. Although that was not what was really happening with her, it was the only way she could rationalize her actions.

Once Ariella dried her face, she felt and looked much better. The redness and puffiness were thankfully gone. While sitting in the stall, tears falling from her eyes, she had made the decision to just accept things as they came. If Justin was meant to be her man, then she needed to put on her big-girl panties and get through this as quickly as possible. For that to happen she needed to lighten up and focus on the task at hand.

Exiting the restroom, Ariella vowed to be a rational, self-controlled, and confident woman. Silently, she hoped her little self-pep talk would work because her whole attitude was much better. The crying must have released a lot of pent-up anxiety and stress, both of which she had had her share of since leaving the Hab. In fact, Ariella felt so well that she nearly started whistling "Zip-a-Dee-Doo-Dah" like Jiminy Cricket as she walked. If she had had a cane, a top hat, and an audience, she probably would have.

Soon after she turned the corner, Major Hawthorn came into view. He was pacing back and forth in front of the elevator, totally absorbed, texting on his BlackBerry. From her standpoint, although not gorgeous, he was a very handsome man in his late thirties. His reddish-brown hair was cut short in a crew cut, revealing his well-formed head. She could tell he had not shaved in a day or two because his five-o'clock shadow was now approaching midnight. It still looked good, though. Ariella noticed, too, that if he continued to let it grow, he would soon have a full, even, reddish-brown beard. She loved facial hair. Actually, she loved all body hair on a man; there was something primal about it. Sadly, though, Justin did not have as much hair as she would have liked. A girl needs to be able to hold on to something.

Although she could not see his muscular tone, due to the loose-fitting maroon and black flannel button-up shirt that he was wearing, the V shape from his waist to his broad shoulders suggested a man who was in shape. Under his flannel, Jonathan had on what appeared to be some sort of black tight-fitting undergarment. Around his neck, he wore a unique necklace that had caught her eye earlier. It seemed to be of Native American origin and contained one large piece of jasper supporting two dangling pieces of jade, which, when they met, matched his eyes. She was not sure, but believed it gave him some sort of protection from unwanted energies while projecting his own.

Continuing to look him over, she noted that, covering his well-defined rear, Jonathan had on some green Marmot khaki pants and wore a pair of Merrill hiking boots. Being an Army Ranger, he was probably a nature lover, like herself. Instinctively, Ariella was undressing him as she studied his movements.

Ariella had to laugh at herself. Earlier, with all the stress, she would have freaked out at having her current thoughts, but now she knew it was only natural. She was a single, fertile, and vibrant woman who was hunting for a mate, or at least her subconscious was. The biological clock was ticking.

At the very instant in which this fantasy popped into her mind, Ariella felt the urge to slap herself. Why did she all of a sudden go from being sort of prudish, to now becoming some sort of super slut, instantly transforming into a bipolar fucktress! No! It had to be hormones; that time of the month was nearing. Lately, it was hard to tell when the curse was going to start; with all the globe-hopping and elevation changes, she could only make a guesstimate.

Putting all these thoughts and images aside, Ariella continued forward, still approaching unnoticed from behind. Then suddenly, like an animal with a sixth sense, Jonathan pocketed his phone and abruptly turned around. Now she was once again standing face to face with the name in her dreams.

~

Jonathan, having previously been exposed to her energy, had already sensed Ariella's eyes on him even before he turned around. Life, whether it be through his experience in nature, the martial arts, or the military, had taught him to be aware of the subtle differences of frequencies in his environment.

After checking his messages and updating Ashley on his position and plans, he began to compose a text message to Cynthia. It has been the first time since studying Ariella's bio that he had the clarity of thought to do so. However, sensing Ms. Marconi's proximity, Jonathan was forced to save his draft. He flipped his phone closed and pocketed it in one fluid motion. He then cut an about face to catch her, mouth open and arm half extended, as if she was about to tap him on the shoulder to make her presence known.

Although loving his prompt attention to her arrival, she was caught aghast at how promptly he turned to meet her. Placing her hand to her chest, Ariella timidly spoke, "My . . . that was quite serendipitous of you to turn around just as I arrived."

Noticing her elaborate use of wording, Jonathan responded in kind. "It was of no mere fortuitous coincidence, Ms. Marconi; I felt you coming." Realizing how his response was unintentionally embedded with sexual innuendo, he decided to be more discrete in his choice of words in the future. "I'm glad to see you're feeling better. You were looking a little peakèd earlier."

Picking up on his rhetorical statement, Ariella elected to let it slide and dumb down the language a bit. Major Hawthorn had just shown her that he too possessed an expansive vocabulary and that perhaps she was being some-what pretentious. "Thank you for caring." Ariella then paused to determine if his concern for her was as sincere as it sounded. It was. "Ariella . . . please call me Ariella, Major Hawthorn."

"Just Jonathan. Nice to meet you again . . ." Because of how he was raised and being accustomed to military etiquette, Jonathan struggled to call her by her first name. "Ms. Mar . . . I mean Ariel-la." Looking down to break eye contact in embarrassment, he once again wished his words were not too revealing.

Seeing him labor at his communication did much to put her at ease. At least she was not the only one fumbling her words. Ariella also thoroughly enjoyed how he spoke her name, separating it as if it was a gourmet meal meant to be savored.

It became clear to each of them that the other was nervous as well. As if it had been rehearsed, Ariella and Jonathan simultaneously started to giggle at their situation. Instantly, the tension between them evaporated.

Still snickering, she said, "Okay . . . Jon-a-than," mimicking how he stresses the syllables of her name. "What's the plan?"

Already prepared for her question, he decided to test her. "San Juan ultimately, but first, let's get down to the transportation level and we'll talk more when we get on the train."

"Down!? Train!?" Ariella was flabbergasted. She had ridden the trolley before but was unaware that there was a subway system under the base.

Expecting her confusion, Jonathan smiled and calmly led her to the elevator. Once the doors opened, he punched in his key code and directed her to do the same. Ariella, exhibiting a puzzled expression, was about to speak when Jonathan intuitively interrupted. "Not everyone is allowed to go down." Damn, did it again, he thought. At least he had not said "deep inside" yet.

Stirred by his words, Ariella punched in her code as required, leaned against the wall near Jonathan, and in anticipation fell silent as the elevator descended into the unknown. When the door opened, she was astonished by what she saw.

It was a Sunday, so the terminal was not as busy as it would normally have been. Only a few commuters occupied the boarding platform of the small station. As Ariella stared in awe at the maglev and the underground facility, Jonathan explained what it was, how fast it could go, and the numerous destinations worldwide that the system serviced.

Overwhelmed by the enormity of this hidden world, Ariella shook her head and asked, "Where did they get the money for all of this?"

"Derivatives and subprime mortgage failures most likely." Jonathan answered matter-of-factly.

Ariella appreciated how he was concise with his remarks, especially considering their mutual unspoken attraction. Many times, when such chemistry had existed between her and a man in some sort of pseudo attempt to offer protection, the constant coddling or withholding of pertinent information would ruin it. She was an adult and expected to be treated as such. Furthermore, it had been her experience that most men were the ones that need protecting, constantly in search of a new mother. No, if she was going to be with a man it was going to be a partner, someone to rely on in order to cover her inadequacies while depending on her strengths; a man who was not so overbearing as to smother her, but caring enough to have real passion and emotional expression.

Someone who was comfortable with his shortcomings while not being some sort of pussy.

Ariella was under no delusion that men and women were equal. They absolutely were not. Each sex had its own strengths and weaknesses. Together, working in tandem, they were intended to become one, a complete union.

Continuing to the boarding area, Ariella and Jonathan chose a berth toward the rear of the maglev. This was of no benefit other than the fact that Jonathan believed it mitigated the slight vibrations felt during the ride. Plus, it meant there were fewer other passengers he would have to keep an eye on.

Taking her seat and looking out the window, Ariella was startled when Jonathan activated the privacy cloud. Unsure of the necessity for such security, she simply made an observation. "I know this is for privacy"—referring to the cloud—"but why do we need it? Won't we be traveling faster than the speed of sound in what is essentially a vacuum tube? Who's going to see in?"

Jonathan, still in a bit of shock over not being berated for being late, was amused by her line of questioning. It was valid, considering the information she had been given, and he could easily see from their brief time together that Ariella was an intelligent, inquisitive, and persistent woman who was ever searching for the keys to unlock the mysteries of the universe.

"No, you're right, Ariella; no one will be able to see in. The cloud, more or less, is used to block all incoming and outgoing electronic transmissions. Check your cell phone. It doesn't work, does it?"

Ariella, pulling out her cell phone, confirmed that there was no signal.

Already gathering that Ariella's quest for knowledge would lead to a never-ending barrage of questions, Jonathan elected to withhold as much information as possible, at least for now. Besides, when introducing someone to the secret world, he had found that seeing was believing. She would definitely see enough soon. "There are . . . things . . . down here that can read your thoughts. The cloud effectively negates the risks of sensitive information being hijacked. As a matter of fact, I couldn't record our conversation, even if I wanted to."

Even though she could fathom the need for and workings of such technology, Ariella was starting to build up a deep resentment for the powers that be. "Of course! The government has all the best toys. They've not only reinvented the wheel but are the only ones who get to play with it."

Appreciating the wit of her metaphor, Jonathan realized where her emotions were beginning to take her. Evading the trap of getting into this type of discussion, he began to focus on his task of preparing her for what lay ahead. With stops at Area 51 and Durango before arriving at Los Alamos, Jonathan was hoping to avoid deactivating the cloud until they reached his Reptilian friend. However, for this to happen, he would first need to get to know the woman, the one not in the dossier. With luck, they would be so distracted in conversation that there would be none until they met Gilla.

CHAPTER

FORTY THREE

EVEN THOUGH THE distance was only around 35 miles as the crow flies, the journey from the coast to the mountain rainforest would take nearly two hours. It was not much time if they were to meet Jonathan upon his arrival back in San Juan.

While Jack navigated the Jeep along the straight ocean highway and through the various switchbacks and hairpin turns of the elevated jungle, Abhar could not help but reflect on what he and Binah had discussed. The whereabouts of the two evil sorcerers, as well as their evil half-sister, vexed him greatly. They had always been at odds with the Creator's plan and wished to subjugate the Earth for their own ends.

Understandably, Abhar still wanted his revenge on the brothers for imprisoning his wife in the sands of the Sahara eons ago. But he knew that his vindictiveness, left unchecked, could jeopardize the mission. Realizing that emotion clouds judgment, even his, Abhar determined that any actions or plans would have to be formulated by someone other than himself; he was simply too personally involved. Optimistically, he believed he could get the others up to speed in what was really happening well before that time came.

Coming out of the fog caused by his thoughts, Abhar opted to stop worrying about things that were not of immediate concern and start focusing more on what lay ahead, a feat easier said than done.

———

After departing from the Smoke 'n' Go, Jack Dresher uncharacteristically refrained from his usual chitchat. He had learned much over the past several hours and was now just starting to assimilate it all.

The drive from San Juan to the city of Carolina was quiet and peaceful. As they headed south, away from the coast, the lush canopy of robust palms gave way to endless calabash and ceiba trees. The undergrowth changed from hibiscus and seagrass to tropical ferns and bamboo. The bougainvillea vines, weaving their way through the jungle, created a nearly impenetrable barrier; only the well-worn trails and windy road offered safe passage for the would-be traveler.

By this point, Jack had come to the conclusion that whatever he was involved in, his services were needed. How many people could say they not only knew aliens, but were working with them? It seemed as if the clandestine missions he knew about and those he participated in, along with the knowledge he had gleaned, all culminated in this very specific moment.

Surprisingly, he felt relaxed about the whole situation, as if it had been ordained by some unseen, higher power that he be there. Still, Jack wondered what he, an ordinary human, had to offer these beings. Sure, he had connections and knew people, but so did his cobber Binah. Also, this Abhar fellow seemed to be well traveled and would have no trouble blending in anywhere he chose to go.

Jack was comfortable with who he was and the assets he had either been born with or had acquired on his journey through life. He knew he was good with people and rarely drew negative attention to himself. In fact, his entire character, which seemed to naturally put others at ease, along with his sharp, quick wit, had provided him excellent cover when doing undercover work for the CIA back in Nam and collecting information for Binah.

Knowing his skills in the bush were second to none, Jack ventured to conclude that it was these assets that were most needed at present. Also, not one to question fate, Jack just decided to go with it. He decided to do whatever was required of him by his new friend Abhar and trusted ally Binah to complete their current assignment, which, at present, was to retrieve Binah's piece of the spear. Only two individuals on the planet could accomplish this goal, and the other was back at the Smoke 'n' Go.

———⌣———

With the changing altitude, Jack could smell the thick moistness of the air. He and Abhar were now about to begin the more adventurous part of the trip, the part he lived for. Jack had been driving over rain-washed, mud-filled, potholed, rutted roads all his life. Everyone considered him to be an expert. He just loved doing it; driving in the jungle was second nature to him, which was probably why he was so good at it.

Being his usual considerate self, Jack felt obliged to alert his passenger to the upcoming perils. With a glow on his face and excitement in his voice, Jack turned to Abhar and broke the silence. "It's time ta empty ya bladder and stow away any loose gear, mate. We're about ta enter my world, the bush." Like a child waiting to get on a roller-coaster ride, Jack continued with zeal, "Yes siree! Thar'll be no more asphalt from here on out. If ya're not careful yar head will bounce around like one of them thar bobble-headed dolls, ya see." Jack, with tongue sticking out, rocked his head in all directions to provide Abhar with a visual.

Thankfully for Abhar, Jack's interruption broke the monotonous symphony being performed by the tires on the highway. It also provided him with the distraction he needed to break his train of thought.

"Glad to see you're embracing the trip with such enthusiasm, Jack." Abhar pepped up as he spoke. "So it's going to get rough, huh?"

"Ya betcha, mate!" Slapping the wheel with his right palm, Jack went on. "This Sheila's gonna shake more than Elvis's hips did on *American Bandstand*. If ya're prone ta backaches or have a soft ass, ya're sure to have a crock day."

Abhar merely stared at Jack in utter amazement. His choice of words and sunny disposition could break through the darkness of the cloudiest of days.

"Thar's a turnabout up ahead. We'll stop ta get the old gal ready for the ball, if ya know what I mean. She'll be singing like a dingo howling at the moon if we don't."

After crossing the Grande de Loiza River and pulling over at the turnabout, Jack got out and locked the hubs so that he could engage the Jeep's four-wheel drive. Walking to the front of the vehicle, he went on to check the winch before asking Abhar to pop the hood. "Gotta check up under her skirt," Jack said as he laughed.

While Jack was under the hood, checking fluid levels, Abhar opened the door and got out to stretch his legs. The rainforest was beautiful this time of year. The dense canopy supplied adequate shade for wild orchids of many colors, and a home to several species of parrots.

Just to the south of the bridge, up the slope, he could see the river as it cascaded down, forming a three-tiered waterfall. With the northerly breeze, the moist ionized air filled the small valley, producing almost euphoric foglike conditions. *It's all so peaceful*, Abhar thought. He could see why so many people came here to escape.

Studying the terrain, Abhar now understood why Jack was being so thorough in preparing the Jeep for travel. The narrow dirt road, which ran like a slithery snake up the craggy slope, looked to be precariously close to the ledge. If a vehicle were to somehow go off it and fall, the passengers aboard would almost certainly perish.

Though Abhar, as a Dimerian and not worried about his life, at least not in this form, he was concerned for Jack's. However, judging by his history and the self-confidence he displayed about his abilities, Abhar was sure Jack was everything that he claimed to be. He was a bullshitter, no doubt, but he was not full of shit.

"Hey, Jack!" Abhar cried. "Is that where we're headed to?" he asked, pointing to the winding road.

Jack, finished up under the hood, slammed it shut, and started toward his companion. Smiling his salty grin, Jack replied, "That's right, mate. Up and over. I stashed the spear over on the other side of that thar hill in a ceiba tree, where no one would ever find it."

"Oh, I'm quite sure of that, my new cobber," Abhar said, parroting Jack's lingo.

Thoroughly pleased by Abhar's witty banter, Jack countered with a bit of his own. "I knew, sooner or later of course, that old Jack could get ya ta stop speaking like them bloody poms and start gabbing like the rest of us commoners."

"Bloody poms?!"

"Yea, ya know, them arrogant Brits, or if ya prefer, prisoners of her majesty. They all walk around with their 'I'm better than you attitudes.'" Looking around quickly and leaning forward, Jack whispered, "Just between ya and me, I think tha're constipated from all the pomp and circumstance. If they would all just take a laxative and relax on the crapper, the world would be a better place . . . but what do I know?"

Abhar, who knew many British people, tended to agree that many were indeed uptight, but he had never heard an explanation as descriptive as Jack's to diagnose an entire population. At that moment, Abhar, longing for a true human friend, realized that he and Jack meshed well together. The Aussie's unassuming, trustworthy nature put him at ease, offering him the kind of comfort he usually only experienced around one of his own. Abhar hoped their relationship would continue for years to come.

Sensing the hour and pointing to the sky, Jack turned around and started back to the vehicle. "We better get a move on, mate, sunlight's a wastin'. It'll be dark soon, especially on the other side of that thar mountain."

In a purposeful way, the two men climbed back into the Jeep and started the treacherous trek up the muddy, macadam road. Jack was as good a driver as Abhar had ever seen, maneuvering quickly around potholes, landslides, and washouts as if he was trying for the high score on some off-road video game. Abhar would love to take him to India one day and test his skills on the crowded streets of Delhi. Now, that would be a challenge of a different sort. *Some day perhaps*, he mused.

With the light waning and shadows increasing, the rugged vehicle came to a stop. As they reached their destination, Jack reached into the center console and grabbed two headlamps, a couple of dryer sheets, and his one-liter water jug. After getting out, he retreated to the rear of the Jeep, only to return with his trusty boomerang and a machete.

Puzzled, Abhar first asked what the dryer sheets were for.

Jack simply replied, "The masquitoes out here are as big as blowflies, mate. These dryer sheets will keep the little buggers at bay."

Never having heard of this bug repellant method, Abhar mimicked his guide, rubbing the static reducer all over his exposed body. To his surprise, it actually worked; he could see the mosquitoes, which were huge, circling as if they were bombers searching for a target, but not one landed on him.

"Pretty good trick, Jack. Where'd you learn that one, Vietnam?"

"Nah . . . I got that one from one of them Foxfire books. Ya know, the ones with all the home remedies. Fascinating stuff, I tell ya."

"I've heard of that series, but I've never read any of them." Abhar paused before posing his other question. "What's the boomerang for?"

Jack looked at Abhar with shock. "It's in case we run inta that chupacabra! This is where I saw the little red-eyed devil, right after I hid the spear." Jack was nervously serious.

"That story was all true?"

"Ya betcha it was, cobber. Old Jack here may avoid directly answering a question—hell, I even deflect sometimes—but I don't typically lie."

Abhar, unsure of whether he had hurt Jack's feelings, began to apologize. "Jack, I hope I didn't offend you, I just . . ."

Jack interrupted with a warm smile. "Ya don't owe me an apology, Abhar, my skin's tougher than that. Now let's get that spear and be quick about it before it gets any darker and that infernal beast arrives."

Satisfied with Jack's response, Abhar put on his headlamp, turned it on, and followed Jack down the overgrown animal trail. As they descended, he kept his eyes wide, secretly hoping to spot the elusive creature.

After a few minutes, the sound of flowing water became louder and louder. Upon nearing the small feeder stream, Jack cocked his head and cried, "It's just up ahead, on the other side of the creek. That's where I saw the red-eyed little monster. Keep yar eyes peeled, mate."

After successfully traversing the stream without incident, Abhar heard what he thought was a chorus of birds chirping. How odd, he thought, for birds to be making all this noise at this time of night, "What birds are singing, Jack?"

"Oh, that thar's no bird mate. That's the coqui frog. Thar's probably hundreds of the little hoppers around us as we speak. Elusive little creatures, I tell ya. Ya wouldn't even know they were here if this wasn't mating season. Thar lookin' ta do the nasty, if ya know what I mean."

Continuing up the escarpment, Jack led them away from the river and toward a huge, gnarled ceiba tree. Curiously, it was surrounded by a swarm of cucullo fireflies. Their bioluminescent light offered an eerie glow to the area.

At the tree, Jack reached high into the air with both hands, grabbed a limb, and hoisted himself up. Using his legs like vises, he hugged the knotted trunk, while reaching down into a deep hole located where the branch he was holding onto originated. Carefully feeling around, in case something had decided to make a home there, Jack finally took hold of what he was probing for. Slowly, so as not to drop the relic, he pulled out a long cardboard tube wrapped in plastic.

Scanning the surrounding area, half expecting to see someone or something, Jack whispered, "Let's get outta here, mate. I really don't want to run inta that crude creature again. It gives me the creeps," Jack worriedly admitted.

Slightly amused by his fretting behavior, Abhar consolingly agreed. "Okay, my friend, we can leave . . . lead the way."

Jack gladly spun around and briskly guided them back toward the roadway. Strangely, as they retreated back to the Jeep, a procession of cucullos joined them, lighting up the night sky in their wake. Jack, too busy putting distance between the river and himself, failed to notice the luminous display darting through the heavens.

For Abhar, however, their presence could not be ignored. The fireflies, which positioned themselves between Jack and himself, seemed to be attracted to some unknown energy; apparently being produced by what Jack was carrying.

Never having experienced this sort of phenomenon with his own triple sword, he pondered the source of this powerful attraction. He muddled the question over in his mind as he followed Jack and the glowing insects.

Back at the Jeep, Jack let out an audible sigh of relief. This was the first time Abhar had seen the old salt flustered. It was clear that his mild distress had been genuine. However, now far away from the river, Jack returned to his former, jovial self.

Finally noticing the swarm of glowing insects, Jack posed the question, "What do ya suppose is causin' these little buggers ta pile around us like we're in a football scrum?"

Although Abhar, after living in America for so many years, failed to see that his description referred to rugby, did understand the question. "I believe they're attracted to what you are holding in your hands, Jack."

After a slight pause to register what had just been said, Jack turned off his headlamp, raised the tube high, and began waving it through the darkness. His motion was similar to that of a child playing with a lit sparkler; the cucullos were much like the burning magnesium bits as they sloughed off into the air.

Abhar had been pondering the source of the spear's attractive power since he had first noticed the fireflies, but, as of yet, had failed to formulate an answer.

Being more proactive, Jack brought the package down, turned his head-lamp back on, and began to open the wrapped relic. Taking out his pock-etknife, he cut vertically down the cardboard tube's shaft and removed the plastic, discarding it in the Jeep. Carefully he turned the tube over and emptied its contents out onto the vehicle's hood.

Glistening under the headlamp's light, there it was, the first piece of the Spear of Destiny. This two-and-a-half-foot section, which had been fashioned into a Roman short sword, had been kept hidden for many years. Its golden color had blotches of what at first appeared to be tarnish, near the tip of the blade, but Abhar knew different. Otherwise, the sword was in excellent con-dition, especially since it was thousands of years old.

Upon closer inspection, there was an engraving across the top of the hilt that read "Ferus Amor, Mors Extrema, Deus Vult," meaning "Fierce Love, Extreme Death, God Wills It" in Latin.

At the bottom of the hilt, located on the ball, was an inscription that dated the sword, "Anno urbis conditae DCCLXXXVI," which in English read, "in the year of the founded city [Rome], 786," otherwise known as 33 a.d.

Taking into account the date and the blotches, it was Jack who spoke first, proposing his theory as to what was causing the insects to flock around. "See this dark discoloration here." Jack pointed to the tip and down the sides of the blade. "That thar is dried blood, mate! I betcha that is what's causing all the fuss."

Abhar stared dumbfounded at the dried blood. Although he had known what it was and who it was from, he wondered how the flies could have detected the scent while the sword was encased in cardboard and plastic. Surely their sense for blood was not that keen.

Jack, seeing Abhar's confusion, thought he was about to teach his com-panion something new. With a gleam in his eye, Jack was almost reverent as he spoke. "Thar's only one thing that I know of that happened around that time . . . that's the blood of the Messiah . . . This was the part of the spear that actually pierced his body, killing him."

As Jack finished his words, Abhar had an epiphany. It was not the scent of blood that attracted the cucullos; it was the remnants of Yahshua's powerful frequency, one so close to that of the Creator that the insects longed for.

Aware of the pride Jack felt at believing he had taught him something, Abhar kept his discovery to himself and patted Jack on the shoulder, thanking him for his insight. Briefly, as they remained still and silent, allowing for a period of homage, both men reflected on the meanings of their revelation.

After this moment of pause, Jack then picked up the other, smaller item to secure it. The mysterious object was about twice the size of a silver dollar, with a half -inch T-like prominence on one side, for holding, and a raised relief on the other. The artifact resembled an ancient intaglio, a stamp used to mark official documents or private messages. With no words inscribed in it or noticeable pattern, at least not to Jack, he wondered what the relic was and what the intaglio represented. Undoubtedly it was important, because it was made of white gold, which was not easy to process in ancient times. This artifact was made to last.

Before Jack could ask, Abhar, with a pleasant sigh, said, "Jack . . . it's a key." Pausing while he revisited the days of old, Abhar continued: "A key to a very old, secret ziggurat that has yet to be discovered."

"If the ziggurat hasn't been discovered, then how'd ya know that's what it's for, mate?" Jack asked before realizing that he and Abhar had not exactly originated from the same time. Abhar had seemingly been around for thousands of years.

Seeing that Jack had discovered error in his question, Abhar reached out and requested the key. Jack respectfully handed it to him, hoping for more answers.

Flipping the stamp over, Abhar reacquainted himself with the intaglio before speaking. "The key is very, very, old. I made this in Eridu, over 5,000 years ago, to keep the holy of holies locked away out of the wrong hands." Seeing that he had Jack's undivided attention, he continued. "When I was relocated from Ur to Haran, I took the lock and key with me; the holy of holies was no longer in danger."

Jack did not want to interrupt but was hung up on one question; he raised his hand as if he was back in primary school. Abhar motioned for him to speak.

"What is the holy of holies? They sound biblical ta me, but I somehow don't think ya're talking about what them thar preachers are referring ta," Jack said, unsure what Abhar's response might be.

Amused by Jack's trepidation, Abhar boldly stated, "I am Abraham, from the city of Ur of the Chaldeans. My father TeRah was the priest, the protector of the holy of holies, which for the most part follows the biblical text. The holy of holies, however, was the star charts used by Binah's clan to land on Earth and travel back and forth to their Nahbirrhu. In fact, the name Chaldeans means 'star gazers' in Greek. My father . . . how can I say this . . . was like a modern-day air traffic controller. Without his permission and direction, no one was allowed to come to Earth."

"Yar pop was a powerful man," Jack aid.

"He operated under an agreement my house had with Yahweh, the Creator. It was a privilege for us to be allowed here."

Jack, satisfied with Abhar's answer, fell silent once again. He was not as surprised as one might expect, but he was fascinated by what he was learning.

"When the Creator ordered the other houses off the planet, the star charts were no longer needed. Only a few of us were allowed to remain, under his service." Abhar held out the key and motioned Jack to come closer. Using his finger, Abhar began showing him what the raised relief represented. "This is a map of the first eight cities in Mesopotamia, none of which remain today. Each raised cylindrical projection represents a particular city. The two solid cylinders are the spaceport of Sippar and the mission control center at Nippur. All the rest of the hollow raised cylinders map significant positions along the flight path. I choose to keep this lock and key because few people on this planet, if any, would be able to decode what this intaglio represents. Furthermore, they would have to have knowledge of all my travels and know the location of the ziggurat and its tomb, which are both buried. It is highly unlikely that anyone but me or Binah could enter the ziggurat," Abhar confidently stated.

"I certainly have never heard of most of what ya're talking about. No siree, if old Jack has never heard of it, ya can bet it's pretty secret stuff. I'm a world traveler, ya see, and know my history, at least most of it." Jack put his finger to his lip. "Now I see that Abhar Am is just one of them thar word jumbles for yar real name, which Binah also called ya."

Abhar had to laugh out loud at Jack, who never failed to amaze. He was quick-witted, smart, and nobody's fool, that was for sure! It was just the way that he expressed himself that Abhar found so endearing, a comedic-like sureness.

"Yes, Jack, you're right about my name. Good memory."

"Should I still call ya Abhar then?"

"Yes, I prefer it. Abraham died long ago," he said with a bit of regret.

Shifting back to a more positive tone, Abhar began explaining to Jack how the key was to fit in the lock. "It must not be oriented to true north, but to the magnetic north in the age when the key was made. The lock also has 360 possible insertion positions, one for each degree in a circle. If the key is improperly inserted and then turned, the entire buried ziggurat will implode, collapsing on top of the hidden tomb, making it nearly impossible to retrieve the second piece of the Spear of Destiny. I buried it there almost 2,000 years ago."

Considering all of what Abhar had just revealed to him, Jack made an assumption. "That's whar we're goin' next, Iraq . . . yeah?"

"Well, I wasn't going to volunteer you, but I could sure use your help and would be honored by your company, if you so choose." Abhar beamed with pleasure at the mere thought of Jack's offer.

"Of course I'll go with ya! What kind of cobber would I be if I didn't help a mate in his time of need, not a good one, no sir. Plus, for all the SpecOps I've done for the bad guys, I think it's about damn time I finally get ta go on one for the good guys."

Emotionally touched, Abhar nearly started to cry. Little did Jack know that he was the first human, other than Haji, in nearly two millennia that he had shared his secret history with, and the only one to whom he had disclosed the location of the second piece of the spear. Abhar, feeling lucky to be in Jack's company, made a mental note to thank Binah for the introduction.

Since time was ticking away and they had a schedule to keep, Abhar suggested that they repack the artifact and head back to the city.

Jack, looking up at the night sky to determine the time, agreed. By his estimation, they should arrive at the air base just before midnight, giving them ample time to meet the arrivals who were due in at one a.m. Once he could get a cellular signal, he would call Binah to ensure Abhar's new arrivals stayed put until they arrived, just in case. Jack, once again, was a handy one to have around.

Arriving back at the highway safely, Abhar looked at Jack and asked him not to speak of what they had talked about or discovered, not to anyone, especially Jonathan. Though he was a decorated soldier who was destined for greatness, he was like a child and needed to be spoon-fed information as required; less, for now, was more.

Jack, his wise self, completely understood Abhar's request. It's not every day one finds out he is a god. It would be hard for even him to take it in all at once. He vowed to keep Abhar's secrets and carry them to the grave if necessary. Abhar knew he meant every word of it too.

Staring out the window at the starlit sky, Abhar sensed that the spear was already beginning to live up to its name. This felt like destiny. Hopefully, the power of the son, which remained, would be with them from here on out; they could surely use it.

CHAPTER

FORTY FOUR

ON HIS WAY back to the command bridge, Captain LaMarr, filled with anticipation, tried to predict what the diagnostic tests would reveal. He hoped all of the devices were working properly, as they should. He desperately needed to determine what was happening in the abyssal depths of the trench, and fast.

Prior to the captain's arrival, Lt. Barett was busy finishing up the systems check and recalibrating the equipment. Everything thus far was working perfectly; although he could not determine why the clock was off.

ARES had reached the site and was within minutes of taking measurements and sending its live video back to the Hab. Once that occurred, a comparison could be made between the robot's and the on-site data.

Just as Steven was about to begin the first series of measurements, Captain LaMarr entered the bridge through the sliding glass doors.

"What's the status of the diagnostic tests, Steven?"

"All diagnostics are completed, sir. I was just about to start the first series of measurements when you arrived," Lt. Barett answered smartly. He had been expecting the captain to request a status report.

"Excellent. Fire them up then . . . where's ARES? Is he on site yet?" Captain LaMarr, anxious to get some information, was terse.

"ARES just reached the site, Captain. We should have a visual any second now."

"Outstanding, Lieutenant," the captain said. Leaning forward, closer to Steven, he added, "Now let's see what we can see."

Meanwhile, at a depth of over 5,900 fathoms, the robot was busy preparing itself to perform the experiments at the site. Upon arrival, ARES, programmed to operate without direct human instruction, guided itself to an area near the amber crystal in order to mitigate any uncontrollable factors; this would provide the robotic submersible with the most accurate readings possible.

Once in position, the tubular robot started its test run. Now stationary, it switched on its onboard video relay and patched into the Sea Lab's computer. Within seconds, live images and real-time data were being streamed to the Hab.

As it hovered, nearly motionless, it measured, filmed, and sent the data it collected. Without warning, a large tremor, registering 4.7 on the Richter scale, rocked the surrounding chasm. Chunks of rock began to break away from the overhead ledges, raining debris down on both the crystal and the submersible.

Before the little robot could react to this event, a large section of basalt broke off from its perch and pulverized the propulsion system of the craft. Once its shell had been breached, the enormous pressure of over 16,000 psi crushed it into the size of a distorted football.

Just prior to ARES's death, it managed to draft one last message for transmission. "Danger . . . explosion imminent . . . evacuate immediately," although the last part of the transmission failed to be sent.

Back at the Hab, Captain LaMarr and Lt. Barett were receiving the robot's data and its first live video. Steven commented on what he saw just as the static ceased. "That thing looks like it's getting bigger to me!"

"I think you're right, Lieutenant. Check the measurements and compare them to the previous data set."

As the readings popped up on the computer screen, both Justin and Steven were baffled by the results.

First, the water temperature around the crystal, which should have been in the neighborhood of 34 degrees, was lower than expected, by more than 10 degrees. If not for the tremendous pressure, the crystal would have been encased in a block of ice. If anything, with all the volcanic activity present in the area, the temperature should be higher than the norm.

Second, the magnetism being generated in the crystal's vicinity was increasing, as if the object was being charged, like an electromagnet, from some unknown source.

Thus far, the magnetic flux density was recorded at 2,500 gauss, or .25 tesla on the magnetometer. This reading was almost half the intensity one would predict from the strongest permanent magnets.

Third, and potentially the most perplexing finding, was the massive amounts of radiation being detected by the Geiger tubes. At over 800 REM, which was concentrated enough to destroy any cell, the source or the energy appeared to be nuclear.

Looking at the on-site stress sensors, they confirmed the data they had received from ARES. The crystal had indeed increased in size by 1 percent since the last readings. Additionally, the rate of expansion seemed to be building exponentially, presently growing at an astonishing rate of 1 percent per hour. At this speed of enlargement, the trench would split wide open in a matter of hours.

Suddenly, the video image sent from ARES turned into static; then it was gone. All data being streamed ceased. One final message from the submersible appeared across the screen. "Danger . . . explosion." That was all the Sea Lab received.

"What the hell just happened?!" Captain LaMarr cried.

Almost simultaneously as the words escaped his lips, the Hab shook slightly.

Lt. Barett, frantically monitoring the LCDs, gave the captain what information he could. "The sensors on-site just measured a 4.7 magnitude seismic event originating directly blow the amber crystal, Captain!" Lt. Barett rolled his chair across the floor to another monitor, which showed a fixed image of the area. "Sir . . . ARES is gone!"

"What do you mean gone?!" Justin, none too pleased with the loss of the multi-million-dollar piece of hardware, was now more concerned about his crew.

Lt. Barett was already in the process of rewinding the video when he motioned for the captain to have a look.

After reviewing the video and taking into account ARES's final message; Justin quickly but calmly examined all the data from both the on-site sensors and the submersible. The measurements that had been transmitted were identical. *At least all is not lost, we still have time,* Justin told himself.

"Steven." Justin waited for the lieutenant to look at him in the eyes. With that connection, he could determine how his young officer was handling the situation. Steven Barett was collected, as usual. "How long do you think we have before all hell breaks loose down there?" Captain LaMarr wanted a second opinion, and Lt. Barett was quite qualified to give one.

Once he performed a few calculations on a note pad next to the computer and did a double check of the measurements, Steven answered tentatively, "Right now, sir, with the present readings and . . ."

"Just spit it out, Lieutenant."

"Six hours, sir. But that's just a guess, of course."

"Steven, your guesses are better than most people's sure things." Captain LaMarr paused for a moment to collect his thoughts. "Get on the intercom and wake the crew. Have them assemble in the mess hall for a meeting in fifteen minutes. I'm going to get on the horn to HQ and give them an update on what just happened." On second thought, while walking to the communications room, Justin hollered back, "Check to see if that tremor caused any fracturing in that fucking 15,000-foot cliff behind us. We sure as hell don't want anything to come down on us." Justin rarely cussed; he thought it was unprofessional, but on occasion he felt it was acceptable, especially when stressing a point. He had always been suspicious of the positioning the Sea Lab so close to a sheer vertical precipice. The structural integrity of the Hab was strong, no doubt, but he was quite sure that it would crack open like an egg if hit by a large enough boulder.

"Yes, sir, I'm on it." Steven too sensed the urgency of the situation.

The aftermath of last night's festivities made the crew less than cheerful when asked to assemble in the mess hall. Rarely did they get a day off. However, any anger they exhibited was overridden by their concern. They all knew and respected the captain. He would not have called this meeting if it was not important. Mumbled rumors about a recall to the surface, something tragic happening to Ariella, and even a sudden terrorist attack against another US target circulated around the room.

Frank Gilmore, discounting all this idle talk, described the tremor he felt just prior to Lt. Barett's announcement. He suspected this was the reason for the meeting and nothing more.

Deborah Walker, who was also awake and felt the tremor, agreed with Frank. Quakes were common down here.

A more nervous tone spread throughout the room once the crew learned that they may actually be in danger. However, Frank, his normal calm self, quelled their fears. "Look, everyone, if we were in mortal danger, alarms would be sounding, lights would be flashing, and we wouldn't have met here but in the submarine bay. Just relax! The Cap will be here in a few minutes." The speech worked, as everyone lightened up.

The Hab's crew were making small talk, keeping their minds off any potential danger, when Justin arrived. Immediately, silence filled the room.

Captain LaMarr, in a purposeful way to show his crew that there was nothing to get hysterical about, quietly walked over to the coffee urn and filled his mug. Still no one made a sound. He turned toward them, took a sip of his coffee, and set his mug down on the table in front of him.

"Good morning, everyone, I'm truly sorry I had to wake you all up on your day off, especially when I'm the one that suggested you take it." He looked around the room. He had everyone's attention. "It looks like no one is the worse for the wear due to last night's celebration . . . I'm glad, some of you . . . let's just say that no one can accuse any of you of not knowing how to have a good time." Justin then let out a sigh, as if to say, *here's the bad news*. "I'm sure some of you may have felt a slight tremor we experienced almost twenty minutes ago." Holding his hand up to allay the growing noise among the crew, he said, "The Hab is fine and in perfect working order. We are safe and in no danger at the present time . . . however, the tremor did occur as ARES was performing routine experiments in the trench. The earthquake, which read 4.7 on the Richter scale, dislodged a large boulder . . . we lost ARES."

A hushed whisper spread throughout the crew.

"Holy shit! There goes a few million bucks," Robert Washington said as flatly as possible. Even after getting laid, he was still a grouch.

"Yeah, the Navy's not going to be too happy about that. Poor ARES," Nancy Taylor added.

"I just lost my little buddy," Roger Sealy whined sadly.

Captain LaMarr regained control of the crew once again. "Okay, okay, calm down, everyone." Silence once again filled the mess hall. "Thank you. You're correct, Nancy, the Navy's not going to be happy about losing their state-of-the-art submersible. But, as they say, that's the breaks." Justin, pointing at Roger, said, "Not only did you lose your little buddy, Roger; the earthquake knocked most of our sensors out of whack. With ARES offline, I've been ordered to realign the sensors on-site, manually. We have to get things up and running again." The captain again paused; this was the part of his announcement he dreaded. "I've also been advised to initiate evacuation readiness protocol." Raising both hands beside his head, he continued, "Just as a precaution. We're not entirely sure what is going on down there and need to be prepared." He picked up his mug and took another sip of coffee. This time, though, he decided to hold onto it. "Two divers are going to have to put on the exosuits and go down into the trench."

"Who'd you have in mind to take the plunge, Cap?" Frank Gilmore asked.

"Well, to tell you the truth, I'm going to be one of them. I've always wanted to be famous. I suppose going deeper than any human has ever gone before qualifies." The captain's smile lightened the mood further.

"Didn't the *Trieste* go down to Challenger Deep long ago, Captain?" Robert Washington asked as if to rain on the captain's parade.

"In a 'so there' sort of way," Captain LaMarr retorted. "You're right, Robert, they did. But where we're going is over 400 feet deeper, past the 36,000-foot mark, breaking the record." The captain was actually being much more jovial than when he began the meeting. He felt it was important for crew morale to keep the mood casual. Being confined under thousands of feet of water without sunlight was stressful enough.

"So, who's number two?" Roger Sealy asked.

"I would prefer to have a volunteer . . ." Seeing Roger starting to raise his hand, Justin stopped him by saying, "No, it can't be you, Roger. Sorry, you to stay here and help Lieutenant Barett with the EVAC readiness preparations. No one knows the equipment like you."

Captain LaMarr again looked around the room, searching for the next enlistee. "Anyone?" he pleaded.

A second or two has passed when, unexpectedly, Dr. Walker, looking directly at Justin, raised her hand. "Hell, I'll join ya in the history books, darling. I've been going down all my life, there's no sense stopping now."

Everyone laughed heartily at Deborah's sexual reference. They were also relieved it was not them.

Most would contend that, while potentially one of the greatest experiences one could have, traveling to the deepest point on the planet, the exosuits were untested at those depths. No one, not even the Navy, knew for sure if they would actually withstand the pressure down there, which is more than double what they were experiencing at their present depth.

Justin too laughed. He knew her sexual reference was accurate, since he had seen her leaving Robert's room that morning. Whether it was fate or good fortune, Deborah was probably the best person for the job. She was smart, enjoyed wearing the suit, and was good under pressure. Under the circumstances, her assignment as ship's physician was one of the least critical positions during an emergency evacuation. Another asset the doctor possessed was her trustworthiness. At least Justin thought so, which was critical considering what she was about to see. Deborah was about to become privy to a secret only a few people on Earth were aware of. *She's ready*, he thought. She had to be.

Adjourning the meeting, the captain asked Deborah to follow him to the bridge. He needed to brief her on what was happening and what they would be doing. Justin had already been authorized to raise anyone's security clearance as he deemed necessary, so showing her this classified information presented no sort of dilemma to him.

While he presented the information concerning the amber crystal sphere, Steven was continuing to monitor the situation in the trench. There were a few devices still operating correctly, among them the Geiger tubes and the seismometers. Thankfully, the earthquake activity had abated for the time being.

Because of his multitasking abilities, Lt. Barett was also working on the EVAC readiness protocols as ordered. SEALs worked well under pressure—that was their job. This involved keeping the PRIEST ready, shutting down nonessential systems to conserve power, and through video surveillance and the intercom, directing the crew as necessary. If the order to evacuate was given, they all could be in the PRIEST and out of the Hab in less than ten minutes. Hopefully, none of this would be needed.

Once the captain finished with Deborah, they agreed to meet in the sub bay in thirty minutes. This would give each of them time to get their things ready and to visit the head before suiting up.

"How's Doctor Walker taking it all in, sir?" Lt. Barett asked.

"You know her, she's fine with all of it . . . funny thing, though, I expected her to be at least a little surprised, but nothing. It was almost like I was telling her we were having chicken for dinner and instead I switched it to fish."

"It could be that's just the way she handles shock. With a flat affect," Lt. Barett offered casually, continuing his work.

"Maybe you're right, Steven, maybe you're right." Justin patted him on the shoulder and started to leave for his cabin. "Are you good here?" he asked, sticking out his hand with a thumbs-up.

"All good, sir, go and get ready to make history."

"Hell yeah. I'll buzz you when I get to the sub bay."

"Aye aye, Captain."

Turning away from his young protégé and walking toward the sliding door, Justin experienced a gut-wrenching pain, one of utter dread. Without a thought, he instinctively turned around and looked at the lieutenant once again.

"Is there anything else, sir?" Steven asked when he noticed his commanders about face.

"No . . . never mind. I'll see you in a while." As he turned and walked through the door, he remembered the last time he had felt this particular sensation and what he believed it meant. It was when the hatch had closed on the bathysphere, the last time he laid eyes on Ariella. Then, as now, he felt it was the last time he would look upon Steven Barett. The feeling was so powerful it made him nauseous; he needed to get to his cabin and fast.

This is so unlike me, he thought. Although not normally too nervous over situations due to his SEAL training, he had to admit, he had never been on an assignment quite like this. Maybe he was feeling the effects of having been trapped under the water for months. It could also be that he was about to make history as the deepest man alive; though it was likely no one would ever hear of it, not while he was alive anyway. Maybe it was the small amount of apple pie moonshine he had consumed last night. All of these things would make anyone nervous, nauseous, and paranoid. *Yeah, that's the answer*; at least that is what he told himself.

FORTY FIVE

THE CONVERSATION RAHZU had with ShemRahya went well, as expected. The captain was fairly confident that his security officer, after hearing what he had to say, would be on board with whatever plan he chose to orchestrate.

As the Captain explained the situation, although angry at the deception and treachery of YetziRah, ShemRahya's concern for the crew grew with each passing minute. Rahzu's revelation had not only put himself in danger, but also the whole crew. He knew too well that the admiral's quest for power would never be satisfied with being the mere overseer of the empty PU 430 universe and head of operations in PU 431. No, he had much higher aspirations than that.

From his experiences in battle and through his extensive studies of history, though it might be a distorted one, ShemRahya knew coups d'états tended to be vicious in nature and typically led to the elimination of the ruling regime. Such changes almost always filtered down through the clans, often causing chaos within families. Many times, such takeovers were used as justification for assassinating rivals or grabbing property and power. This caused ShemRahya to worry, as YetziRah's actions seemed to suggest just this.

Consequently, the result of their discussion was that the lieutenant was now aware of the plot Captain Rahzu had stumbled upon. He was also enlightened as to the alternate version of history and what was happening on the planet ET Rah, in PU 78.

As predicted, ShemRahya had no issues digesting any of this new information. In fact, he knew too well that history was written by the victors and that not everyone, including himself, was aware of the many happenings that occurred in secret.

Listening patiently, he silently concurred with Rahzu's assessment concerning the ship's former ensign; there was little doubt, even though her purpose still eluded them. Neither officer was naïve enough to believe it was simply Abraham's frequency she was sent to search for. Nor was she a simple ensign who had just graduated from the Rah Academy and completed her primary training, as she had claimed. RahKael was much more.

ShemRahya, although never having met YetziRah, had heard rumors of his ruthless tactics and ruling style. He understood why Rahzu was fretful about possible repercussions, especially when considering his recent run-in with this new adversary.

When ShemRahya questioned his captain as to whether Commander CheRahna, the second in command, had been informed of his suspicions, Captain Rahzu gave him the short version of what his executive officer was dealing with at present and his decision to keep her out of this business. ShemRahya could easily empathize with Rahzu's reasoning.

Even though his security officer was taking in all this information with an open mind, Rahzu had to make sure, once again, that the lieutenant was aware of how critical his silence was. As he faced him, studying his every energy variation, Rahzu asked, "ShemRahya, so you understand why only you and I can know about all of this?"

"I understand fully why you've decided to keep the commander out of the loop, but . . ." He paused, thinking of how to proceed without being disrespectful.

"But?"

"I think KaRah would be an asset, Captain!" ShemRahya cried. "With me at your side, she would not only do whatever you asked of her out of duty and respect for you, but out of loyalty to me!" He was emphatic with his words.

Rahzu, sensing his young officer's passion, knew he needed to explain his reasoning to him in another way. "This is like a battle, a battle of wits, where a warrior's senses take over not only to defeat an opponent, but to discover the enemy's intentions. We are YetziRah's opponents and he ours." Rahzu, with hands folded behind his back, walked back and forth in front of his companion. He then started with a fact. "ShemRahya, you and I operate on similar energy frequencies, have similar beliefs, and practice nearly identical philosophies. Would you agree?"

"Yes . . . sir," he answered, unsure where the captain was going with this.

"Good. Because of our similarities, we, as if we were one, will stand a good chance of hiding our thoughts and intentions while being in close proximity to one another. YetziRah, or one of his minions, would be none the wiser."

Rahzu could see that his words were starting to make sense. He continued, "How would you describe KaRah and your energies together? Are they the same?"

"No, sir, they're not. We're as different as two Dimerians can be! That's why we work so well together. She's the yin to my yang, taking a line from your Master Nakomura."

"Yes, very good, Lieutenant. That's why I chose to make you and her partners, instead of opting to place one over the other. You and she together are a great asset, the perfect team."

"Then why not use that asset now?!" It was clear ShemRahya still did not understand.

"Calm down, Lieutenant, calm down," Rahzu said as he raised his hand. He did not take his lieutenant's passion as disrespect. "There is a valid reason for not including her."

"I am sorry, sir; I was out of line. It was not my intention to disrespect . . ."

Rahzu interrupted him. "Say nothing more about it. You"—he said, pointing at ShemRahya and then back at himself—"and I are fine."

ShemRahya relaxed, glad that his relationship with the captain was so close. Many leaders would not allow any dissension concerning their orders. They were to be followed without question, or else.

Seeing his subordinate's mood change, Rahzu explained his thoughts more clearly. "Because you and Lieutenant KaRah are so different, in both sex and frequency, it would be nearly impossible for you and her to keep the energy of your intentions hidden, at least to a Dimerian. In YetziRah's presence, he would sense the combined mutual disdain and distrust each of you had for him, making him probe deeper into your thoughts. I think he would have no trouble uncovering our plans; that, most likely; would lead to all of our deaths. We can't risk that, ShemRahya! Too much is at stake!"

The lieutenant faced away for a moment to gather his thoughts. Although he agreed completely with everything Rahzu had just mentioned, at least for now, he still did not like it. ShemRahya abhorred the thought of keeping secrets from KaRah, his most trusted companion. But for now, he had to accede to the captain's wish, which was the right course of action. Later, he would find a way to include her in their plans.

Following his moment of consideration, ShemRahya turned and asked, "What of Commander CheRahna? I know she's not going to be told of this; but how's she going to react when she finds out we've kept all of our plans from her?" His question was a very valid one. Even with her sudden change in attitude, she was still apt to be an emotional juggernaut under the right circumstances.

Rahzu had already thought of this and knew how he would approach her when the time came. "Don't worry, my friend. When the time comes, I'll talk with her."

ShemRahya just had to trust that Rahzu was making the right choices. The captain knew CheRahna better than anyone. Hopefully, she would see things their way and be a part of the solution rather than another problem.

———— ⌒⌒ ————

Before going to find Captain Rahzu, CheRahna decided to stop by the bridge to check on the results of the investigation. The questions she had about her uncle and their mission here would have to wait. She was too perplexed as to what Ensign RahKael had found and the chain of events that led to her demise to put it off any longer. There was also the question of the abductees' escape and the mysterious death of the avian creature. All these events seemed to signify an escalation toward some defining event, but to what was anyone's guess.

Now, in front of the amber crystal sphere, the commander reviewed the data concerning these disturbing events. Although the findings were inconclusive in many respects, one was clear—Uncle Abraham was alive and well.

A sudden rush of mixed emotions flowed through her very essence. She was excited, no doubt, but she was unsure whether to feel good or bad about this influx of energy.

It was positive in that she might be able to finally reunite with her only living relative, one she had once loved and trusted. With all the information she had acquired from Rahzu's codex, maybe it was possible to have a family again.

The negative aspect of this energy was the lingering doubt that any of this was true. The hate and embarrassment she had lived with for such a long time was her defense mechanism, her way to combat and overcome adversity. Letting her guard down had almost never happened in her life. The only being able to chip away at her shell, thus far, was her beloved captain.

While thoughts of Abraham, RahKael, Rahzu, and the amber portal spiraled through her mind; CheRahna nearly let out a scream of frustration over the confusion she felt. The only thing that stopped her was the potential embarrassment she would have to endure if someone happened along and witnessed it. She knew she needed to get herself together, and fast. This was not the way an RJC commander should act.

However, before she could collect herself, CheRahna sensed the presence of a terrifying but familiar energy. Turning around, she found herself face to face with the one Dimerian she had never wanted to see again, Admiral YetziRah.

When he blinked aboard the RJC's bridge, YetziRah half expected to find Captain Rahzu poring over evidence in an effort to discover Ensign RahKael's purpose for being aboard his ship; he never would know, though. RahKael had been trained personally by him; he was sure she had covered her tracks.

To his delight, however, he found himself behind his quarry all alone. Judging by the aura she was emitting; she was in a very unstable state. Splendid! He could not have scripted a more perfect scenario.

When CheRahna turned around, her mood changed from one of nervous distress to utter chagrin, as if she had seen an old enemy. YetziRah believed that only the appearance of Abraham himself could have elicited such a response. Speechless, his former student just stood there in silence, her wavering silver color fading quickly. She was never any good at hiding her emotions. It was what had made it so easy for him to get into her head long ago. He was glad to see that some things never change.

Commander CheRahna's hesitation troubled her greatly. She was second in command, a position she had earned through hard work and perseverance, and she needed to form some sort of response to the admiral's presence. With all the energy she could muster, CheRahna managed to speak. "Admiral YetziRah, welcome aboard, sir. Shall I contact the captain and alert him to your presence, sir?"

YetziRah was surprised how quickly the commander had recovered from her initial state of exasperation. Not only did she hail him correctly, with cheer, but it showed in her sheen. Her silver color was again shining brightly. It must be pride, he thought. Good. He could work with that. "My . . . my . . . my C-om-man-der Che-Rah-na. I must say this radiant silver suits you," he said, waving his hand as if he were a salesman showing off a display item. "I have heard good things about you back in Dimeria. Good things indeed."

CheRahna was caught off guard momentarily. YetziRah was not known for giving out compliments, especially not to her. She repeated her original question, unsure how to respond otherwise. "Sir, shall I inform Captain Rahzu of your presence?"

"That won't be necessary, Commander. Truth be told, I came here to see you."

"Me, sir?! What could you . . ." CheRahna caught herself. Questioning the admiral never turned out well for anyone. "Sorry, sir, for my . . . I mean, I'm flattered. However, I'm not sure what I have done or what you have heard about me to warrant such a visit." CheRahna stuttered a bit before finding the correct words. As far as she was concerned, his presence here further supported the crew's suspicions that Ensign RahKael was sent by him.

Recognizing that his time was limited, since Captain Rahzu or another crew member could enter the bridge at any moment, YetziRah spoke frankly. "Let's skip all the niceties, shall we, Commander?"

"Yes, Admiral, if that is your wish."

Cleverly, he then made a decision to use a ploy he had never utilized with her before—honesty. "As the kind of officer I've heard about in my briefings, I'm confident you have come to the conclusion that Ensign RahKael was working for me."

"Yes, sir, it was starting to become apparent."

"Indeed, she didn't have . . . shall we say . . . the charisma that I hoped she would have developed. No, Ensign RahKael was akin to a chisel chipping away at a stone, methodical and monotonous. However, she was still a good asset, and her death was tragic."

"May I ask the Admiral what exactly she was sent here for?" CheRahna was comfortable asking him this; it was her duty as executive officer to know all orders given to the crew.

"Of course you may, CheRahna. I expected nothing less from you." He paused to ensure her question was asked in earnest. It was. He could see that his plan was working. "Quite honestly, Commander, she was sent here to spy on this ship and its crew . . . Does this surprise you, Commander?"

She was astonished by his candor. This was not the same Rah she had come to despise back when he was lead instructor at the Rah Academy. He seemed more refined, calmer, and most noticeably, less cruel. "But why, Admiral? I'm unaware of the need for such an action."

"For a long while now, we have been aware of a frequency vibration that has been used to track our movements on Earth."

"We just discovered the signals ourselves, Admiral."

"Yes . . . well . . ." YetziRah saw an opening where he could plant a seed of doubt. "That statement is not completely accurate, Commander," he said matter-of-factly.

Feeling as if she was being accused of something, CheRahna got ready to defend herself when YetziRah held up his hand to silence her.

It's all too easy, he thought. Everything was going as planned. Soon she would be ripe for the picking. "You have done nothing wrong, Commander. Forgive me if you took it that way. As a matter of fact, Ensign RahKael reported that you were a highly competent and professional leader, one worthy of command."

CheRahna brightened at hearing this. She always thought she was doing a good job, and only recently, even Rahzu had told her so.

"She also mentioned that you were one of the few officers on board who has never worn the flesh. Congratulations, Commander." He clapped and nodded in approval.

"I was beginning to think my lack of experience as a human was a defect, a scar on my ability to properly command, especially here, so close to Earth, sir."

In a firm voice YetziRah reinforced her decision to stay pure. "Whatever led you to believe such a thing? You're exactly what this ship needs—order!" He again studied her, his prey. "Everyone else on this ship is so busy indulging themselves in carnal pleasures that they have become negligent in their duties."

On this particular point, though he was echoing many of the words she had recently spoken to Rahzu, CheRahna decided to stand up for her captain. "Admiral, with all due respect, Captain Rahzu does not wear the flesh. He is loved and respected by all of the crew, including myself, sir!"

The admiral expected no less from his former student. He knew she was loyal to her captain, but the House of Rah had always come first to her. That's what he was counting on. "No disrespect taken, Commander. I would have thought less of you if you did not stand up for your beliefs and your mentor, Captain Rahzu. However, your beliefs and feelings are not of importance. What is important are the facts." YetziRah felt it was time to slowly water the seed of doubt he had planted. He wanted to laugh out loud. Things were going much better than he had hoped. "My concern is that your beloved Captain Rahzu has had knowledge of this probing frequency, this ancient Rah frequency, long before the ensign arrived here in PU 430." The admiral let that sink in before he continued. Skillfully, he was driving in shims to widen the psychic break he had reopened. "I didn't want to bring any of this up. I know better than most what you went through before, with the knowledge of your uncle's defection. But I feel you need—no, deserve—to know the truth." He calmly moved closer. "The frequency Rahzu discovered and has kept to himself belongs to none other than his former mentor, Abraham."

CheRahna's mind and emotions were sent into a violent vortex. *What is happening?* she thought. Did she not know anything?

YetziRah clearly saw her luster start to flutter; he now set himself to his task. "Is it a coincidence that Abraham was also responsible for waking the human subjects, which led to the assassination of the very agent sent to investigate your captain. No, Commander! I don't believe in coincidences. This was a deliberate, planned attack to conceal a more diabolical scheme."

She remained silent, stunned at what she was hearing. Could all this be true? *Not again*, she begged herself. *Please, not again.*

He went on to say, "Ensign RahKael had uncovered a plot between your uncle and Rahzu to either turn or eliminate all remaining Rahs residing in or around PU 430. The House of Yah has always been wary of our presence here, and as it looks now, is trying to end it once and for all."

Though CheRahna was close to cracking, some of what YetziRah was saying did not register with her. Suddenly, she calmed down and started thinking more clearly. She had always expected that her uncle was still alive; that was no big revelation. But she started to remember the conflicting stories between what she had just recently read in Rahzu's codex, compared to what she was taught at the Rah Academy. She was also having trouble believing Rahzu was a traitor. She would have felt it.

To his surprise, the admiral now truly saw the officer she had become. Her brilliant, radiant silver color returned, and she stood with confidence. He had definitely struck a nerve. This was not going to be as easy as he had first thought, which would make it even more pleasurable.

As a result of the contradictions, along with her loyalty to Rahzu, CheRahna now began to speak less formally. "Wait one minute, sir." Later she would be amazed that she had gotten away with speaking to one of the most powerful Dimerians alive in such a tone. 'You're telling me that not only did Captain Rahzu know of my uncle's activities, but was aiding him. I just don't buy that, Admiral. What proof do you have, the word of an insubordinate twit." The commander was on a roll now and would not be stopped. She was making a stand, a stand that could very well cost her her life. "I have also learned an alternate version of Earth's history that makes much more sense than the fabrication you taught me back at school. It explains how you and Xanix Rah broke the agreement with the Yahs, which led to our house getting expelled from the planet in the first place. And you, having worn the flesh, are telling me not to. Rahzu believes it would help me grow and become a better leader. Finally, that my uncle, the one I knew and loved, was faithful to our house and an honorable Dimerian, doing only what he believed was right!" Upon finishing her statement, she felt the electrons in her form start to evolve. She knew she was in mortal danger but did not care. If it was her time to be banished to chaos, at least she would go with honor.

YetziRah, though furious at her display, was impressed. He did not think she had it in her. Normally, if someone had addressed him in the manner she just had, he would have instantly, without compunction, obliterated that being's existence, sending the shattered remains into the void of chaos. However, he needed her. CheRahna was the key if his plan had any chance of success. Her display of strength made him more determined than ever to bring her into the fold. She would be a powerful ally indeed.

Keeping his true intentions hidden, Admiral YetziRah knew that the best way to sway opinion and to present a rebuttal was to start with a confirmation of truths. He was a master at manipulation. "You're absolutely right, CheRahna." He could already see that this approach had taken her by surprise. "I did at one point in my young career, regretfully, don the flesh and choose to experience all of its addictive pleasures. If it wasn't for my mentor Ruach Rah, I too would have strayed further from my duties and ultimately defected; much like your Uncle Abraham, who had no one." He had her complete attention; she hung on his every word. "I wasn't trying to mislead you earlier when I said this ship needs order." YetziRah meant it too; that is why she had believed it in the first place. However, his vision of order was a bit more tyrannical. "I know from personal experience how the flesh can warp one's mind. It caused the defection of a great man, a confidant and friend, Abraham. It almost took control of me, and now I fear it has taken control of Captain Rahzu."

Now the skillful manipulator decided to direct all his attention toward her trusted captain. "Did Captain Rahzu tell you that I visited him, right on this very ship, immediately following RahKael's murder?" He had hoped he had not. It was a risk that paid off.

"No, sir, he didn't."

"I didn't think so. Another question, Commander. Were you present when Rahzu fought the human?"

CheRahna, in shock that she was still alive and unsure of what and how to respond, merely nodded silently.

"Would you say he fought like a Dimerian or like a human?"

"Like . . . a . . . human, sir." Her senses were starting to return to her, but she was still confused as to what he was inferring.

"This is what I'm talking about, Commander. Little slips in his character, such as this, show how much he still enjoys the experience the flesh provided him. Why else would he fight like a human? What possible good could it accomplish, other than to fulfill his longing for carnal pleasure?!"

"Uh . . . none, I suppose." CheRahna had totally forgotten about Rahzu's explanation of honor. YetziRah was very convincing.

"Does he allow crew members, against regulations, to experiment with such debauchery on board this very ship?" This he had heard from his fallen spy.

"Well . . . yes, sir, he does."

"Don't you see, Commander? Little by little, he is conditioning and grooming the crew for defection." YetziRah could see she was in conflict. But rather than letting her respond, allowing her to regain some of the control she had lost, he continued. "As far as the distortions in history you mentioned, much of what you said is true. But not for the reasons you've been led to believe." He was now about to drop a proverbial bombshell on her, one that he would use to win her over. "We have altered all the history books, even Captain Rahzu's, for one simple reason." He could tell he had her on the hook. "We too have created a planet with the beginnings of life. It is called ET Rah and it's located in PU 78. Captain Rahzu knows about it; however, because of his association with Abraham, he has only been given the most basic information." He paused to allow this to sink in and to switch ploys. "Judging by your reaction, you were unaware that such a planet existed, weren't you?"

"Yes, sir, this is the first I've heard about it. But if it's such a secret, why tell me?" CheRahna did believe what he was telling her, despite her question.

"Captain Rahzu was ordered at the beginning of this deployment to inform all of his officers about its existence. That is why we came here in the first place, CheRahna, to study Yahweh's creation in order to develop our own. No wonder you are so confused. You don't even know what you're doing here!" He had regained control.

To CheRahna's dismay, this was making perfect sense, all of it. *Why has Rahzu withheld this information?* she wondered. "Admiral, why were we exiled from Earth?"

He realized the seed of doubt had now sprouted. "I'm not sure whether it was jealousy over what we were trying to accomplish on ET Rah or something else; but all of a sudden, we were ordered to leave Earth at a most critical period in our planet's history. We were about to start creating complex life forms, but we did not want to make the same mistakes that occurred on Earth. That's the reason for the abductions, to help us find a way to eliminate the problems associated with the flesh."

YetziRah was sure he had her ensnared, but did not want to push too hard. Now came the apology. "CheRahna, I am sorry about the way I treated you at the Academy. I was still fighting my own carnal desires. I saw greatness in you but had to ensure you would never be tempted like both myself and your uncle . . . It appears that it worked, though. Just look at you, pure. Furthermore, I am sorry now for having to bring this nasty family history back into your life again, I really am." He was using his sincerest voice. It was working. "But I need your help. There is no one else aboard this ship that I can trust to do their duty. Can I trust you to do your duty, Commander?"

After a moment, the commander responded firmly, "I will always do my duty, Admiral YetziRah, always. What do you ask of me?"

"All I ask is that you pay attention to details. Through simple observation, you'll be able to verify that what I'm saying to you is true. I hope this is not too much to ask, Commander. I know this is all shocking. But I want you to make your own decision. You must, because you hold the future to the House of Rah."

Aghast at everything she had just heard, CheRahna was reluctant to answer. Her word was her bond, and she did not want to commit to anything unwittily. But what YetziRah was suggesting was nothing more than her duty to the House of Rah. It presented no moral dilemmas. In a voice that began timidly, but finished with strength, CheRahna responded, "Yes, Admiral. I will do as you ask."

CHAPTER

FORTY SIX

AFTER MATING WITH his female Reptilian, Jen, Gilla felt much more at peace and was once again able to think clearly. Even though his ritual usually only happened once annually, the instinctual drive to fulfill it was uncomfortable. If he failed to mate, he would become the ravenous beast he appeared to be. Now, however, with his lust sated, Gilla bid his life partner farewell and boarded a shuttle headed for Los Alamos, as instructed.

A sprawling facility located near Santa Fe, New Mexico, Los Alamos National Laboratory consisted of numerous above-ground and subterranean buildings, as well as a vast system of tunnels. With only one surface access road leading to the base, which was nestled inside a canyon, the complex was one of the most secure sites known. This was the place, during the Manhattan Project, where the first atomic bomb was created.

Little do people know, it was also fundamental in establishing SDI, Project Solar Warden, and the secret space program. It not only manages numerous military satellites, which encircle the globe in their geosynchronous orbits; it also operates a fleet of manned space vehicles and space platforms, many of which are located throughout the solar system.

Although classified Top Secret and unknown to the world, the lab currently contains the most powerful computer system on the planet, called the Cielo. It is capable of performing more than a quadrillion floating-point operations per second.

Open to both terrestrial and nonterrestrial entities, it offered a much safer environment for Gilla to wait until Jonathan arrived. Unlike Groom Lake and Nellis AFB, only races allied with humanity were allowed access here.

Upon reaching the base, Gilla received a message via courier from Jonathan. Since he would be there soon, instead of leaving the terminal, he just sat there and waited patiently. Reptilians, unlike warm-blooded humans, found it easy to sit still, unmoving at times for hours on end. Although being underground for millennia had caused them to lose their chameleonic traits, the ability to remain silent and unmoving, along with incredible senses and strength, still made them one of nature's most lethally evolved predators.

Additionally, sitting on the bench reflecting on his recent rendezvous was exactly what the lizard needed, a calm before the storm. Gilla knew Jonathan well enough to realize that the time for planning was nearly over. He and whoever else was to join him were surely in for an adventure. It had been a long time; Gilla welcomed the action.

***

Luckily, the hour and twenty-minute ride from San Francisco to Los Alamos went by quickly. Jonathan and Ariella, in an attempt to get more acquainted with one another, found themselves totally enrapt in conversation. Finding common roots in their mutual love of nature, education, and places visited or wanting to visit, they both could envision being on an extended adventure in the wilderness together.

Jonathan was quite surprised to discover that Ariella had been to Machu Picchu and seen the Nazca Lines in Peru, floated down the Nile touring the sites of ancient Egypt, and visited the archaeological digs going on in Pakistan at Mohenjo Daro. Though she appreciated the knowledge of the ancient cultures, she suspected that man was not alone in the world when these structures were erected.

This all sat well with Jonathan, especially considering who she was about to meet. He too, though he had much knowledge about the true origins and uses of the ancient ruins, still wanted to travel to them someday. One bonus to being single with no children is that he was free to travel when the urge struck him, except, of course, when he was too busy saving the world, which seemed to be consuming all of his time of late.

Ariella too was enthralled with Jonathan and his adventures around the world, though he was typically occupied doing whatever work the government had him doing. However, he did occasionally get to take in the sights.

With his fluency in several languages and proficiency in many others due to his training and extensive travels, he would be a handy partner when it came to logistics. Nothing could be worse than wasting countless hours trying to get to a place you want to go.

From the outset of their conversation, Ariella could see that Jonathan Hawthorn was a man of action, while she was a bit of a dreamer. No matter, though, at least he was not a bore. In fact, as the maglev pulled into the station under Los Alamos, she found herself disappointed at the interruption.

With the stopping of the train, in an attempt to calmly talk with her, Jonathan reached out for Ariella's hand, which without thought she gave him. Somewhere deep inside, she trusted him implicitly. Jonathan now took on the task of preparing her for what was about to happen. With a smile on his face, a caring stare, and a relaxing touch, he began to tell her about his friend who she was about to meet.

Once the transport arrived, Gilla snapped out of his trance-like state and stood, anticipating Jonathan's disembarkation. It was a Sunday evening, and the maglev platform was nearly deserted, making it easier for them to locate one another. However, Gilla, knowing Jonathan's mannerisms, predicted that he would be seated toward the rear of the train, which he was.

When the doors slid open, Jonathan and Ariella stepped out onto the platform. With a slight scream of terror escaping from her lips, Ariella put her hand to her chest and cried, "What the . . . !" She fell silent before finishing her outburst.

Amused at her reaction, Jonathan made the introductions. "Ariella, this is my trusted friend Gilla; Gilla, this is Ms. Ariella Marconi." He waved his hand between the two as he spoke.

Gilla, always polite, bowed and, with his left hand balled in a fist, pounded his chest as he spoke. "Nicsh sho meesh yoush, Ms. Marconi." He smiled at the shock on her face.

Though Jonathan had told her that his friend was unique and that she had never met anyone like him, Gilla was not what she expected. As Gilla bowed and greeted her, startled that the overgrown lizard spoke, Ariella nervously looked at Jonathan, who motioned her to respond.

"Hellooo . . . I'mmm . . . glad to meet you?" she finally said.

"I told you he was different!" Jonathan laughed out loud.

Gilla also hissed in approval, which put Ariella more at ease.

Following her initial shock, she calmed down as her mind went to work. Seeing this huge, seven-foot-tall, walking and talking Reptilian confirmed her suspicions that they were not alone. Ariella had a thousand questions, none of which she could manage to ask at the moment. She was too busy looking at him in awe to talk.

Instead of standing on the platform, Jonathan led the group over to the waiting area, where they could sit and talk. "Coffee?" Jonathan asked Ariella.

"Uh-huh" was all she managed to respond with.

"You good, Gil? They have some of that insect slurry you like."

"No shank yoush, Jonashon."

"Try not to eat her while I'm gone then." Jonathan had to mess with Ariella; he could not help himself.

The look of surprise was priceless. This caused Gilla to follow Jonathan in laughter, all of it at her expense.

Ariella just gave Jonathan an "eat shit" look as he left. She had to admit, however, the levity broke her nervous tension.

"Hesh such a kishsher, hiss, hiss, hiss." Gilla too sensed that Jonathan's humor had eased her fear. Additionally, he could predict what her first question was going to be. So he answered it before she spoke, which also helped to relieve her anxiety. "I'm nosh an esh [ET]. My knish have been undergrounsh since before yoush were mashe [made]."

"Well, that explains a lot," she gasped. Still in awe of him, she asked, "Are there other . . . I mean . . . different kinds of . . . beings?" Ariella was finding it difficult to choose the correct words.

"Yesh, some from here, some nosh."

With a twinkle in her eyes, Ariella pepped up. "You mean aliens, don't you?" she asked, pointing toward the heavens.

"Yesh."

"How many are you? Sorry, I mean, how many different groups are there?"

Pointing down toward the Earth, Gilla answered, "Only a few." Then pointing up, he finished, "Fifsheen . . . shenshy, no one knowsh?" He raised both hands in speculation.

As Ariella and Gilla continued getting acquainted, Jonathan contacted Ashley with an update. Though it was two hours ahead in Dayton, Ohio, and it was now after ten p.m., Ashley was anticipating the call. As expected, she wanted to know all the details about Ariella: was she as pretty as her picture suggested, did they get along, did he like her, etc. . . . Jonathan went on to inform her about his run-in with Cynthia Ryland, who he had totally forgotten about, until her ribbing began, and that this was a business trip, not a sexual escapade; but she was happy for him. However, Ashley was inquisitive and still wanted her questions about Ariella answered.

After another minute of chit-chat, he hung up, purchased two coffees and some bug juice for Gilla, just in case. He then headed back to where his companions were seated. Before sitting down, he paused to watch how Ariella was interacting with his Reptilian friend. To his astonishment, she was already well acclimated to Gilla's presence. She looked alive, as if the world was new, which to her it essentially was. He hated to interrupt, but they had work to do.

"Ariella, here's your coffee. I guessed on how you wanted it . . . light on the cream with a drizzle of honey?"

With a smile, Ariella pried her attention away from Gilla and cut her eyes upward. Looking directly at his, she cooed, "Perfect. Thank you." She was starstruck. Who was this rock star of a man, and what would he show her next? *The possibilities are truly endless*, she mused.

Now focusing his attention on Gilla, Jonathan presented his offering. "Here's some blood and guts anyway. I know you were just being polite."

With a nod and a grin, Gilla gladly accepted.

"So, Gil . . . I'm still not quite sure what I need you to do yet, but I'vs found you a traveling partner." Looking down at his phone to check the time, he continued. "In fact, he should be here in a few hours."

"Promish, promish," Gilla responded sarcastically.

"Well, I had to find someone who was willing to work with your scale-shedding ass."

"Ash long ah ish nosh yoush, hiss, hiss, hiss."

Ariella was enjoying the banter between the two. It was apparent that they were very dear to one another, which pulled at her emotions even more .

To Gilla's delight, Jonathan informed him of who he had recruited to aid him in his upcoming assignment. Jimmy Haney was not only a trusted, a well-seasoned soldier, but he was one of the few humans, other than Jonathan, who Gilla considered a friend. He was someone he would die for if necessary, and vice versa.

Pleased that Gilla approved of his choice, which he had known he would, Jonathan then briefed him on what he had learned, which was not much. Although Ariella, as of yet, was unaware of everything concerning the mission, he was now comfortable enough to speak frankly with Gilla in her presence.

Jonathan told the Reptilian about the Harp of Ur, the Mask of Warka, although still unsure if its power, and about the tactical suit. He made the boast that if Gilla wanted to get physical; he "best prepare for an ass kicking," especially wearing his new duds.

Gilla, of course, laughed at his folly.

Though he did not want to, during their discussion, Jonathan withheld the discovery of the implant and the fact that he had been abducted, something Gilla had always suspected. It was not that he could not trust him, because he did. But as far as Ariella was concerned, he could not allow her to see any weakness or, more importantly, any uncertainty. Her ability to cope with this new world, one she had been thrust into, was directly dependent on her perception of him as her protector. As long as that situation continued, he felt confident that Ariella would be more of an asset than a debit.

After his briefing, the three of them enjoyed their drinks and spent the rest of the time in light conversation, which Ariella dominated with questions. Understandably, she wanted to know everything; however, time did not allow it. Her excitement was good, though; it gave both Jonathan and Gilla the jolt they needed. This world had become common to them.

About the time they finished their beverages, a bell rang, followed shortly by an announcement informing them of the arrival of the maglev they had been waiting for, which traveled nonstop to Atlanta, Georgia. From there they would continue on to Miami, Florida.

Getting up from the table, Ariella and Gilla said their goodbyes. Jonathan, unsure when he would see his friend again, leaned forward and gave him a big hug. Gilla responded in kind. After separating, Jonathan told Gilla that he would call him soon with instructions and invited him to "give Haney hell"—he deserved it.

With the train pulling up to a stop, Jonathan and Ariella headed toward the platform. Once there, he looked back one last time at his Reptilian friend to wave goodbye. He somehow sensed that the next time they met, things would be different. He and Ariella then boarded, engaged the cloak, and waited for the trip to begin. The feeling he had, however, remained; everything was about to change.

CHAPTER

FORTY SEVEN

ONCE HE FINISHED packing his things, in preparation for a possible evacuation, Justin headed toward the submarine bay. Despite being excited about being part of history, he still could not shake the feeling of doom seeping from his every pore. Nonetheless, the show must go on.

The Sea Lab was alive with activity. Nancy was working furiously to securely store all the chemicals in the research lab. If a large earthquake were to occur, the random mixing of falling solutions would not help matters. It was the last thing they needed to deal with under those circumstances.

In his office, Robert was none too pleased at having to spend the rest of his morning scanning his many notes into the computer for storage. He had been working on an equation he believed described the relationship between geomagnetism and subterranean volcanism. With all the recent seismic events, he felt he was extremely close to a breakthrough. The last thing he wanted to do was evacuate.

Deciding to take the long way down to the bay, Captain LaMarr walked across the catwalk leading to the terrarium. As he did, he could not help noticing Roger busily working on getting the exosuits prepared for the dive. To his surprise, Dr. Walker was already there. Apparently, she was eager to get things underway. Maybe she too was excited about making history?

As he entered the grow room, Captain LaMarr recognized the beautiful music of Tchaikovsky's *Swan Lake* filling the air. Frank was not only ensuring that the automatic hydroponic plant feeders were filled to capacity but had also made a compilation of the world's greatest classical works: Mozart's *The Magic Flute*, Schubert's Symphony in C Major, Beethoven's *Eroica* and Chopin's *Fantasia*, to name a few. He wanted his "babies" to be at peace if he were forced to leave.

Continuing down the stairwell, Justin quietly entered the sub bay. As he walked past the PRIEST, which was up and ready, he saw that Roger and Deborah were performing final inspections of the suits. Dr. Walker was actually humming.

"Good to see you're in such great spirits, Dr. Walker." Justin was usually more professional with Deborah in public; she *was* an MD.

"Well, darling, at my age, new adventures are few and far between. So when the chance to experience one comes along, ya just got ta grab it by the horns and ride it, honey." Deborah's mood was light and cheerful, despite the inherent danger in what they were about to do.

"What's our ETD, Roger?" the captain asked.

"Let's see . . . seven minutes to get both of you secure in the suits, another three minutes or so to get you into the pool, and another minute to close the chamber and pop the lock. Then voilà! You're free." Roger was also in good spirits, probably because he loved getting his hands dirty and physically working with the equipment.

"Great! Good work, you two. Let's get to it then; we need to be out of the Hab in fifteen."

"No problem," Roger responded.

Considering the circumstances, Justin was grateful for the positive attitude displayed by Roger and Deborah. It seemed, with the exception of Robert Washington, who was always miserable, that everyone else was also hopeful, which made his stress level recede.

Once securely enclosed in their suits, Justin patched into the bridge for a final systems check. With all the biometrics and sensors functioning properly, Captain LaMarr called, "Coms check, Dr. Walker, can you hear me?"

"I hear you, Justin, but you're coming in a little staticky," Deborah responded. "Steven, adjust the squelch, would you?"

He did as instructed. "How's that, Dr. Walker?"

"Much better, thank you, dear."

"How's everything on the bridge, Lieutenant?" Captain LaMarr wanted no problems.

"Everything's shipshape up here, Captain. All systems are go." Steven did notice that the captain's heart rate was a little elevated, but considering his responsibilities, it was well within normal range.

"Good to see you're calm in tight spaces, Dr. Walker. Judging by your heart rate, if I didn't know any better, I'd think you were asleep," Steven said to see if Deborah was actually still awake.

"I'm as snug as a bug in a rug." Dr. Walker never failed to bring her southern wit with her.

Roger, instead of using the squawk box every time he wanted to speak, put on a headset. "Are we ready, Steven?"

"Roger, Roger." Lt. Barett had to chuckle a little at how that sounded. "Get 'em in the drink."

"Will do, good buddy," Roger said.

"Nice CB lingo, Roger. Makes me feel like I'm back home on a dirt track date, hon, sooo romantic," Deborah chimed in.

"Alright, everyone, enough of the chatter," Captain LaMarr ordered.

Swiftly but methodically, Roger operated the crane with precision and maneuvered both of the occupied exosuits into the pool. Once in position, Roger asked for one final systems check from the bridge before sealing them in the air lock.

"A few nominal issues, but nothing to worry about. Air lock is a go," Steven confirmed.

"Last chance, Dr. Walker. You ready to take the plunge?" Justin asked.

"Hell ya! After three marriages, this is going to be a snap." She laughed slightly. "This is goin' to be more fun than a pig pickin' on the Fourth of July."

"All righty then, let's kick this pig." Captain LaMarr gave the order with a bit of humor of his own.

"Aye aye, Captain, sealing the pool. Watch your heads, kiddies." Roger then began the process of closing the hatch.

Within a minute, the flood pool was sealed, and the air lock was ready to open. Moving toward the exterior wall, Justin looked at Deborah and said, "Here goes nothing." He hit the button and the hatch slowly slid open, allowing them access to the abyssal ocean.

Immediately, a slight wave hit them while still in the air lock. This was to be expected due to the vast pressure differences.

In preparation for their adventures, all of Sea Lab's exterior illumination had been turned on, lighting up the entire area. The darkness was no more, at least immediately surrounding the Hab.

Successfully out of the air lock and onto the ledge's floor, Captain LaMarr asked, "Everything good with you, Deborah?"

"Perfect, Justin, just perfect." She was spellbound by the silent beauty she was witnessing.

"Good. Hey, Steven, everything's a go down here. We're going to start our descent. Go ahead and get the crew ready with the EVAC precautions. Roger can keep an eye on us and give any necessary updates, over."

"Yes, sir, Captain, I'm on it. Be careful." Lt. Barett got to work.

"Roger," Justin called out. "We're going to use the foot thrusters at half power to increase our rate of descent. I figure it'll take us about twenty-six minutes to make it to the bottom and another few minutes to reach the site. Does that sound right to you?"

"Let me check . . . That's what I get, Captain," Roger confirmed.

Approaching the sheer vertical drop-off of the shelf, Justin activated several liquid chemical weighted lights and threw them over the edge into the darkness.

Both he and Deborah peered down and then looked at each other.

"Man, that's deep." It was the first sign of nervousness Deborah had displayed.

"Let's go make history, on three?" Justin asked.

"On three."

In harmony, they both counted, and on three, leapt into the abyss. After a few seconds of freefall, they positioned downward and activated the foot thrusters, speeding toward the bottom, toward the amber crystal.

Roughly twenty-six minutes later, Captain LaMarr and Deborah touched down. It was now official; this was the deepest dive in human history. The depth gauge read 36,437 feet, almost seven miles below the surface of the ocean.

Thankfully, ARES had thoroughly mapped the entire area, so getting their bearings was not a problem. The three chemical lights Justin had dropped significantly aided in illuminating the area. Although they were still a few hundred yards from the crystal anomaly, its teardrop shape was clearly visible.

Looking around, both Deborah and Justin pirouetted in wonder. All the video and pictures from ARES and the on-site camera did little justice to the panoramic view they were experiencing. Thermal vents billowed out scalding water, which nourished the reddish extremophiles surrounding them. Jagged, nearly vertical cliff walls rose as far as the eye could see. Various forms of phytoplankton, attracted by the lights, wafted effortlessly through the depths. Everything was happening in complete, eerie silence.

Captain LaMarr was the first to disturb the mood. "What do you think, Doctor, worth the trip?"

Deborah responded in awe, "Heavens, darling, how could I have ever imagined." For once, she was at a loss for words.

Following a brief check-in with the Hab, Captain LaMarr suggested that they slowly hover over to where the amber crystal was located. Walking around on the fine silt-filled bottom would cloud things up quickly, destroying their visibility, especially if they planned to move with purpose. Once there, they could afford to move more slowly, keeping the turbidity to a minimum.

Within seconds, they were afloat and again propelling themselves toward their destination, only this time slower. Several minutes later, it was Deborah who first noticed it. "There it is, Justin. That thing is huge." This was Deborah's first sight of the crystal.

Though Justin had seen it many times before, from the safety of the Sea Lab, being on site offered a completely unique perspective on the size of the crystal. Deborah was right, this thing was massive; it dwarfed them. Strangely, though, even with all the lighting from the exosuits' illumination, not one photon was reflected or refracted off the crystal, a property that simply did not happen in nature. Since the amber crystal had little translucence, light particles should be bouncing everywhere, but there was nothing.

Looking around, visualizing its boundaries, Justin could easily see the numerous chunks of rubble near the base of the cliff. He quickly determined where the pressure was greatest, posing the most danger for future cleavages.

Fortunately, only a few of the video cameras and sensors were in the fracture zone. If they were quick about it, Justin felt they could be done and out of the area before the next expansion occurred. Calling up the readout of all the malfunctioning systems, the captain thought it best for them to work separately, but within sight of one another, in order to fix the problems more expediently. As beautiful as it was down here, this place was dangerous. There would be plenty of time for visual inspection of the crystal, from a safer location once they had completed their task.

With the plan in motion, they both got to work realigning the lasers, installing new stress gauges, and replacing any damaged components. Of course, Justin placed Deborah out of harm's way, if there was such a thing 6,000 fathoms down, far from the towering sides of the trench. If anyone was going to be crushed by a falling boulder, it was going to be him; but so far so good. At the moment, all was well.

Constant updates from Lt. Barett showed that the environment was unusually stable; not even minor tremors were detected. Captain LaMarr felt that this meant one of two things. Either the expansion had slowed and the environment had indeed stabilized, or the pressure was building and this place was about to erupt.

Moving around smartly, he believed the latter to be the case. Careful not stir up too much silt, Justin and Deborah made quick work of the repairs. Even Steven was amazed by the expeditiousness of their work. As far as he was concerned, if there was an opening for a Navy deep-sea diver, she was hired.

Even the captain agreed with his young lieutenant's assessment. Deborah turned out to be quite capable in the suit, much better than he had hoped for.

Now that the repairs had been accomplished, it was time for a more up-close and personal viewing of the crystal. After moving closer to the center of the trench, approximately 125 feet from either towering wall, Justin felt much more comfortable performing a more in-depth visual inspection. First, however, he wanted to check the new readings.

Pausing for a few moments to double-check his calculations, Lt. Barett answered, "All the equipment is working correctly, Captain, but we're getting some wacky readings up here."

"How so, Lieutenant?" Justin asked calmly.

"For starters, the temperature of the surrounding area has returned to normal. It's currently at 34.3 degrees Fahrenheit." Lt. Barett's confusion could be heard in his voice.

Justin checked the temperature on his heads-up display, which he had not been paying attention to. It verified the temperature he gave. "Steven, are you also reading a REM level of 200?"

"Yes, sir, and that's also strange since just over an hour ago, it was near 800 REMS. What's going on, Captain?" Steven was unusually flustered.

"Slow down, Lieutenant. Let me think this through. What's the magnetometer's latest measurement?"

"This too is baffling, Captain; the magnetism of the object has nearly doubled to 4,900 gauss. If anything, metal gets too close to that thing, it's going to grab on tight."

"Thanks, Steven, we'll keep that in mind down here." Captain LaMarr remained silent briefly, in order to ascertain what the next course of action should be. Still unsure, he asked, "Give me the current predicted expansion rate."

"Sir . . . it is zero."

"What do you mean zero?"

"I mean, it has stopped growing. It just stopped!" Steven was adamant in his assessment.

"Okay, okay, Lieutenant, put a lid on it . . . Roger, got any ideas?" Captain LaMarr was open for any answers he could get.

Roger, not confident in what he was about to say, answered nervously. "Well, Captain, this is just a theory, and it's a little out there, but I think the crystal somehow absorbs energy from nearby power sources and uses it to expand."

"What do you mean, Roger? What other power sources are you referring to?"

"ARES, Captain. ARES was the power source," Roger stated.

"Explain, Roger, please." Captain LaMarr, though clueless, remained calm. He actually thrived under pressure; his heart rate was normal.

"All right, I'll try . . . ARES has an almost inexhaustible energy supply. Its batteries can essentially power a city block with its Searle engines recharging by movement. It's basically a dynamo, Captain!" Roger was onto something.

"So what makes you think the crystal was absorbing ARES's power?"

"When ARES imploded, its energy reservoir should have caused an explosion, but there was nothing. Look, Captain, ARES has sensors located all over its shell; it should never have been hit by a falling boulder in the first place! The only explanation why it didn't motor out of there at the first sign of trouble was that . . ."

The captain interrupted, finishing his though for him. "Its batteries had been drained and it couldn't move fast enough when the tremor hit."

Roger's theory was starting to make sense. "Exactly, Captain! It really is the only thing that seems to make sense." Roger sighed, as if he had just taken his final breath.

"What do you think about Roger's theory, Steven?" Justin respected his opinion.

"It sounds entirely plausible, sir. That would at least explain the lack of an expansion—it ran out of power. But what about the decreased radiation levels and rise in magnetism?" Both were good points brought up by the lieutenant.

Rarely getting one over on Steven, Roger was amazed. "Really, Steven, Physics 101, electromagnetism produces radiation. If ARES's electromagnetically powered batteries were being drained . . ." Roger purposely stopped to allow Steven to answer.

"Then that would account for the increase in ambient radiation levels . . . Holy shit, Roger, you are amazing!" Steven was truly impressed, which did not happen often.

Captain LaMarr, realizing that the reading of increased magnetism remained unexplained, decided to table that question for the time being. Besides, the mere presence of this crystal was one huge question in itself. What was it made of, who put it here, and, most importantly, why?

Instead on dwelling on things had no answer for, Captain LaMarr dealt with what he could. "Great job, Roger. You're definitely one in a million." Justin felt a little pride himself in the moment. He was the one responsible for assembling his crew; and thus far they had all exceeded his expectations, even Robert Washington.

"It's your call, Captain, but I think you and Deborah are safe enough to get a closer look at the crystal, sir, as long as you don't touch it," Lt. Barett said.

"I believe Steven is correct also, Captain. Your ZPEs are not magnetic and shouldn't present any problems, especially with their casings," Roger added.

Captain LaMarr contemplated all that he had heard and performed a risk assessment. He knew that it was still possible, by Physics 101 as Roger so simply put it, that their ZPEs, while not magnetic per se, produced electricity. This in itself meant that it innately produced a magnetic field. What was even more disconcerting was that these little devices generated enough energy to power a small city. If the crystal, however unlikely, were to somehow drain even one of their power supplies, the result would be catastrophic.

In the end, however, Captain LaMarr decided that the risks were far out-weighed by the potential rewards. They were already down here and needed to get all the answers they could. He realized, though, that he needed to ask Dr. Walker, who had remained silent for quite some time, what she thought. She too was at risk, and therefore should have a say in the decision. "What do you want to do, Deborah? Mind you, we have completed what we came here to do—what I asked you to do, and what you volunteered for. The decision is yours to make."

With only a brief pause, Deborah answered. "Let me put it this way, Captain, I got all dressed up and went to the ball with you. I think I deserve to get at least one dance before ya take me home, don't you?" Dr. Walker was completely serious. She too wanted a closer look.

The captain spoke up, "All right guys, you heard the lady, start the music, we're going in." Looking at Dr. Walker, he said, "But, Deborah, if anything, and I do mean anything changes, we're gone. Agreed?"

"Agreed, Justin."

"Steven, Roger?"

"Yes, sir," Steven responded.

"Yes, Captain," Roger also answered.

"You two are to keep a close eye on the gauges and the monitors. If anything changes, let us know."

"We will, Captain," Steven and Roger answered simultaneously.

Justin, now turning toward Dr. Walker, bent forward, extended his mechanical hand in a gesture, and asked, "Deborah Walker, may I have this dance?"

"I thought you'd never ask."

FORTY EIGHT

FOLLOWING YETZIRAH'S VISIT, unnoticed again by the rest of the crew, CheRahna was left disoriented by the admiral's accusations against Captain Rahzu. Before this meeting, she would never have allowed herself to believe such allegations, especially coming from such a power-hungry, cruel, and abrasive leader. Now, however, after listening to his account of history and the reasoning behind his actions, she was finding it difficult not to consider that YetziRah's story was true.

What was Rahzu's reason for not following orders and informing the officers of the planet ET Rah? It would certainly have helped them understand why they had been sent here, so far from home.

Why did he not tell her, until recently, about his relationship with her uncle? Was he fearful that his past with Abraham might drive an impenetrable wedge between them? Maybe he was attempting to coax her into following him when he defected, as YetziRah alleged?

Finally, did Rahzu have prior knowledge that Abraham's energy frequency was being used to track the movements of their ships on Earth, while also being instrumental in RahKael's death, which now seemed more like an assassination.

Obviously, the question still remained; what was Rahzu's plan? What was the end game? Surely it was not for political gain. The Rahzu she knew abhorred politics and had not made any significant ties with those in the Rah leadership, at least none she was aware of. However, if he were to follow Abraham and align with the Yahs, anything was possible.

After considering these questions, CheRahna concluded that she would find no answers in isolation. By putting herself in the captain's presence, she expected to be able to study his essence; possibly helping her determined the reasons for many of these inconsistencies. Hopefully, there was an explanation, other than the treasonous one given by YetziRah, to account for his actions. Deep inside, though, the seed of doubt YetziRah had planted long ago and had recently fostered was firmly rooted.

After his debriefing of ShemRahya, taking into account the investigative conclusions, Captain Rahzu made the decision to study the many frequency variations in an attempt to discover what Ensign RahKael was really searching for. He was not convinced that she had merely discovered Abraham's frequency and that its discovery precipitated the events that led to her death. No, there had to be something much more profound.

Just as CheRahna entered the lab, Rahzu believed he had found what he was looking for. A nearly undetectable, immensely powerful Yah frequency emanating from male subject number 99985, known as Jonathan Hawthorn. A force potentially so strong that it could only signify one thing: the prophesied God seed had been located.

Sensing the commander's presence, Rahzu quickly ended his session on the amber crystal and erased his search results. He was not sure what the this finding meant for the future, but he was sure he was not ready to share this revelation with anyone, especially not with his overstressed commander.

Curiously, when CheRahna finally found the captain, he was accessing the crystal sphere in the science lab, poring over what appeared to be Dimerian energy frequencies. Immediately following her entrance, Rahzu abruptly ended his search and turned to greet her. He was hiding something, she thought.

"Commander, good to see you're out and about. What can I help you with?" Rahzu asked innocently enough.

"After reviewing the investigation results, I just have a few questions, Captain," CheRahna said, not sure what she was going to ask yet.

"That's all? No questions about the codex?" Rahzu knew she had been reading it.

Unable to refrain from talking about the codex, CheRahna, however, was aware of how and what she was asking. "Well . . . Sir, I do have a few questions I suppose." She tactfully continued. "I understand we initially came to Earth to study Yahweh's life forms, with his permission; that much is clear. And at some point, for whatever reason, we left. Surely, no matter what version of history one chooses to research, we did not come here merely to collect evidence about an act that the Council was already well aware of. No! We were here and compliant in Yahweh's illegal act. But what was the point?" She fell silent for a moment to gather her thoughts. "The only logical explanation is that we have, or are planning to have, a planet of our own and are attempting to create life ourselves without the knowledge or consent of the Council."

"And your question is, CheRahna?" Rahzu knew where she was going but was surprised that she came to this conclusion on her own.

"Have we created a planet and started experimenting with life?" she asked bluntly.

Rahzu was still reluctant to confirm the existence of ET Rah, but did not want to lie to her either. With skillful evasiveness, he answered, though he still felt guilty doing so. "I have personally never seen any planet or created life that can be claimed by the House of Rah. If such a place does exist, it would be amazing, I'm sure." Everything he said was essentially the truth; Rahzu had never seen ET Rah.

CheRahna noticed the cryptic answer and sensed his guilt. She was now convinced that YetziRah was telling the truth about the creation of a Rah planet and Rahzu's knowledge of it.

She felt such ambivalence over the situation; she was not sure how to act. The respect and admiration she had for her mentor was now being challenged by a feeling of betrayal. This was all perversely reminiscent of her long-lost relationship with her uncle, a reenactment of one of the worst periods of her life—one in which she had loved and trusted a mentor only to be abandoned when she needed him most.

Luckily, though, before allowing her anger to get the best of her, CheRahna remembered what the admiral had asked of her—to be attentive. For her to accomplish this successfully, she would have to control her feelings better.

Therefore, instead of dwelling on her own thoughts and perceptions, she would ask him another question, one she expected the captain to answer truthfully. CheRahna was attempting to create a baseline in order to compare truthful answers against lies. She asked him something to which she knew the correct answer. "What was the name of the Japanese human that you used to spar with?"

Although an unusual question, Rahzu answered. "Yoshido Nakamura. Why do you ask?"

"I was just speculating whether or not the human was also trained by such a great sword master; he was quite skilled with a blade."

"He was trained in the Japanese art of kendo, there is no doubt about that. But I do not believe he learned from a kendo master. This Jonathan Hawthorn is a soldier and not skilled in the other, nonviolent aspects, which are displayed by all the true masters. But I agree, his skill was impressive." He was still perplexed by why she would ask such a thing.

Satisfied she now had enough to work with, CheRahna proceeded. "Before all of this unpleasantness began, did you know that Abraham was keeping tabs on what we were doing?"

Picking up on her tension and still realizing how delicate a subject this was for the commander, Rahzu chose his words carefully. Despite her subtly accusatory questioning, he answered truthfully. "I have always suspected that he was. But since the search for him was ended long before I arrived here, I saw no point in digging into to it any further." Rahzu paced back and forth in front of her.

"And now, Captain?"

"I think the answer is quite obvious, Commander." Rahzu was slightly irritated by her tone but decided to ignore it. "I will say, however, that even though Abraham's signal has been tracking our Cruiser Rahs and was somehow used to arouse the male subject, it was Ensign RahKael's own arrogance that led to her demise and not the abilities of some human."

Rahzu was not actually trying to defend Abraham, which was how CheRahna took it; he was trying not to have her jump to conclusions in order to wrap up the investigation, while putting all the blame on her uncle, his former mentor. There was more to these events than just a fallen Rah's actions.

Though the captain was being completely truthful in his explanation, CheRahna's ability, at this point, to determine what was the truth or fiction was completely unreliable. Because of Rahzu's deception involving ET Rah and her own feelings about her uncle, she was hypersensitive to any tension in his answers, which, to her disappointment, was present in this case.

Regardless, she still needed to ask one more question so that she could solidify her suspicions. "Captain, while reviewing the results of the investigation in the ship's records, I noticed the appearance of an unknown energy surge following the ensign's death. Did we receive a visit that I am unaware of, sir?"

Tentatively talking about Abraham and skirting around the questions involving ET Rah with her was one thing; having a conversation concerning YetziRah with her was quite another. Rahzu had no intention, at this time, to subject her to anything involving her former instructor. He could see she was still at odds with her uncle's alterative history. Before answering, Rahzu made a mental note to erase the record of his visit from the amber crystal's memory. "We have received no visitors that I am aware of. I'm sure it was probably a reverberation coming from our Cruiser Rahs as they pierced the veil of the portal while returning the humans to Earth." Rahzu's explanation sounded convincing, even to himself. "I'll check on it later, though. Good work, CheRahna. You never fail to amaze me." He knew she was thorough, but right now he did not need her looking too deeply into this energy surge. "Is there anything else, Commander? I need to meet with Lieutenant ShemRahya in order to prevent our craft from being tracked. You're more than welcome to join me if you like." Rahzu was being polite, though he did not really want her to come.

CheRahna, crushed by the deception of her trusted mentor, was doing a remarkable job of hiding her true feelings. She wanted to scream! She was also aware that he was uncomfortable at her line of questioning and wanted nothing more but for her to take her leave, in which she obliged him. Besides, she was unsure of how much longer she could keep up the act. "No, that's all right, Captain. I want to go back to my cabin and research more in the codex. I've got thousands of years to catch up on."

"Very well, CheRahna. If you have any more questions, I'll be glad to answer them."

"Thank you, sir. I'm sure I will," she said as she turned and departed. Unfortunately, her tone had a hint of sarcasm in it, which Rahzu noticed. He let it slide, though.

Consequently, Rahzu began to worry about whether she would be mentally stable enough to handle the information he was hiding from her; it was nearing the time to act. He would meet with her later to decide how much he would reveal to her. Rahzu hated not having her by his side, where she belonged. CheRahna was the future and needed to be part of its creation.

CHAPTER

FORTY NINE

ONCE JACK AND Abhar descended from the mountain and left the switch-back roads behind, Jack called Binah and updated him on their progress. Luckily, Binah had already contacted the San Juan base commander and found that Major Hawthorn would not arrive until sometime after two in the morning.

Therefore, instead of heading directly to the base and sitting idle for several hours, they decided to take a slight detour to a small, late-night café for a quick recharge. After ordering huevos rancheros, coffee, and various fresh local fruits; Jack probed Abhar about Jonathan's purpose in coming to Puerto Rico.

Although Abhar did not know the specifics of Major Hawthorn's assignment, he knew enough to know that he would need their help. Knowing the Rahs, they would now have their agents everywhere.

Since Jack was already aware of Abhar's true identity and certain facts about the world, as well as Jonathan Hawthorn's secret history, Abhar felt it only prudent to fill him in on the details concerning the amber crystal. Not only was it a portal to another universe, and being used by his old clan to conduct missions here on Earth; it also, as Abhar feared, had a much more nefarious purpose—the destruction of this planet.

As Abhar spoke, Jack remained silent, patiently absorbing all that he heard. Jack was a natural strategist. Thus far, following closely, he only had two questions enter his mind: Why would the "others," as he referred to the Rahs, want to destroy the Earth, and how were they going to stop them?

Abhar was confident he could enlighten Jack as to the why. The Rahs wanted to take possession of the large piece of white enhanced Dimerian energy crystal in Earth's core, although he was unsure of what they planned to do with it. Only a Yah could even touch the WEDEC.

The other question—how they were going to stop them—was a bit trickier. Not wanting to start an all-out war, one they were not prepared for, Abhar explained how they needed Jonathan to place a containment field around the crystal, one that the Rahs could not break. This would effectively render the amber crystal useless.

Being a Yah, the God seed, Jonathan had the power within him to perform such a feat. The problem was getting him to do it without alerting him to the powers he already possessed. They would need a ruse, a good one.

As Abhar paused to sip his coffee, he contemplated how they were going to accomplish such a task. This gave Jack an opportunity to ask some questions. "If I heard ya correctly, mate, ya and Binah were talking about majik. Right?"

Though constantly amazed by Jack's ability to recall information, Abhar was more intrigued by where Jack was going with this question. "Yes, Jack, as usual, you're correct."

"Well, the way old Jack sees it, ya could give yar cobber a few fancy words to say and tell him it's a majik trick?" He threw his hand up, unsure if this would work.

Though Abhar was not ready to introduce Jonathan into that world either, he did see the value in Jack's solution. It certainly gave him an idea, one he felt would work. "Jack Dresher, you've inspired me. I've got a great idea!"

"What can I tell ya, mate, when ya gat a problem, old Jack's gotta solution," he said with a salty grin and a chuckle.

CHAPTER

FIFTY

THE TRIP FROM Los Alamos to Miami was animated, to say the least. Ariella's excitement and barrage of questions, while intelligent and appropriate, were eerily reminiscent of a child continuously asking "why" after each answer, leading to a never-ending question and answer session.

Though, at times, he could feel his patience being tested by her search for knowledge, Jonathan was grateful that she was approaching all of this with enthusiasm rather than apprehension. Most people would simply either slip into a state of clinical depression, due to the fact that their whole belief system would now come into question, as well as their place in the universe; or they would be in denial, choosing not to believe what they had seen with their own eyes. Not Ariella Marconi, though, she was a trouper indeed.

Still, until he figured out what had actually happened, Jonathan neglected to tell her about their abduction. While this would help explain how she too knew him, it would present more questions; ones he could not answer. He could allow nothing to break the illusion she had of him being her all-powerful, all-knowing guardian; at least not yet.

Upon reaching the Miami maglev station, they transferred to a shuttle bus that traveled the subterranean highway on its way to Homestead Air Force Base. On their arrival topside, to Jonathan's pleasure, thanks to Ashley, there was a new F-22 Raptor waiting for them, fueled and ready for takeoff. As it was the highly classified pride and joy of the Air force, he felt fortunate to get to fly in this amazing machine. In fact, if it were earlier in the evening, or if their flight path was over US soil instead of international waters, Jonathan knew this aircraft would not even be seen on the tarmac. Granted, any other supersonic jet would have served the same purpose, but Ashley always made sure he got to enjoy the finer things the military had to offer. *Rank definitely has its privileges*, he thought.

As Jonathan and Ariella approached the fighter jet, Ariella could not help but notice the childish look of excitement plastered all over Jonathan's face. *Damn, he's cute*, she thought.

While Ariella walked and gazed upon her new protector, Jonathan just smiled and laughed. "What!?"

Shaking her head, Ariella responded, "Boys and their toys."

"Well, we're already late; at least we'll arrive in style."

"Okay, so where's the pilot then?"

With a growing smirk on his face, he answered pridefully, "You're looking at him."

While he continued to mumble about how fast the aircraft could go, the multiple targets it could lock onto, etc. . . . All Ariella could do was gawk at this man of action, this modern-day Superman. Who was this guy?

Jonathan, of course, noticed her look of desire, but it was time to get a move on, so they boarded the fighter and taxied down the runway. Although he was always late, he rarely intended to be; things just always happened that way.

Shortly after takeoff, Jonathan eagerly informed Ariella to put on her mask because "We're about to go supersonic."

Ariella thought this was the second time in as many days that she was in a fighter jet traveling at night and at great speeds. While typically not one who liked all the attention and adrenaline, she had to admit that she could get used to this, particularly if Jonathan was around. "My, how things can change in a day . . . I wonder what will happen tomorrow?" She whispered aloud.

It was 0242 when Jonathan and Ariella arrived at San Juan Naval Air Station. As expected, the base was virtually abandoned, which played out well for keeping the fighter's existence under the veil of secrecy.

Almost immediately after they deplaned, the ground crew arrived and rushed the Raptor off the flight line and into a small hangar, and then quickly shut the doors.

Crossing the tarmac, walking toward the control center, Jonathan locked onto two distant figures standing just outside the buildings. He recognized one of them. It was, to his surprise, Abhar. Though he had been instructed by Haji that Abhar would meet him in Puerto Rico, Jonathan was impressed by his ability to gain access to the base. This was not the underworld.

Once he and Ariella were within earshot, Jonathan called out, "Abhar, you are a most resourceful man, I'll give you that much,"

Abhar, keeping with the persona which Jonathan knew as more of a jest than a necessity, responded, "Oh yes, sir, it's not what you know but who you know, sir."

Jack, never having heard Abhar talk in this manner, immediately cut his eyes at him in awe. For the first time, he realized that Abhar was indeed a master of deception. *Good thing he's on our side*, Jack thought.

Jonathan, seeing Jack's reaction to Abhar's speech, extended his hand to-ward Abhar for a handshake and said, "Now you can drop that sir shit, I know you're much more than what you seem to be. So let's drop the false pretenses, shall we?"

"Well . . . I suppose I could, but you enjoyed my ploy, didn't you?" Abhar asked humorously.

"That I did, Abhar, immensely."

Releasing his hand from Abhar's firm handshake, Jonathan introduced his new traveling partner to the two men. "Ariella Marconi, I want you to meet my trusted confidant Abhar Am and his friend . . ." He ended there, not knowing who Jack was.

Removing and tipping his hat, he said, "Jack, Jack Dresher's the name. It's a pleasure to meet ya, ma'am."

"It's nice to meet both of you," Ariella said softly.

Jack then quickly extended his hand toward Jonathan, who took it. "I've heard a lot about ya, mate, Abhar here thinks mighty highly of ya, I'll tell ya that much."

In a jesting way, while shaking Jack's hand, Jonathan retorted, "It's all lies, don't believe a word this guy says." Jonathan gave Abhar a wink. "So, Jack, what racetrack, uh . . . I mean road did you find old Abhar here driving on?"

Abhar answered for Jack. "I'll have you know, Major Hawthorn, that Jack found me on a dock on Bimini Island."

"What were you doing on a dock?" Jonathan continued the banter.

"I was taking in some sun in the salt air when this plane showed up out of nowhere." Abhar said, pointing, "Jack here is a pilot and if I'm correct, the only on-call crocodile wrangler in the Caribbean."

"Really! I've heard of you before." Ariella, being quite familiar with the West Indies, had heard of occasions when Jack's unique services were required.

Looking at Abhar, Jack smiled. "Told you, cobber, I'm world famous. Even the Sheila knows me." They all laughed jubilantly while entering the control center.

Once he and Ariella had changed out of their flight suits, Jonathan suggested that they find a quiet, private nook where they could talk. He and Abhar had much to discuss. Though it had only been two days, so many things had transpired that it felt like months.

———

While Jonathan and Abhar slipped off to talk in private, Ariella and Jack got better acquainted. Jack, as she soon discovered, was quite a spirited Aussie who lived for adventure and loved life. It became apparent, as Abhar too had noticed, that Jack was a natural-born storyteller. She almost felt like she was present as he spun his yarns, which she would later learn were absolutely true.

As he continued to entertain the oceanographer with some of his more interesting escapades while crocodile wrangling, Ariella studied his appearance.

Although his facial features and leathery skin, which had taken their toll from the years of salt and sun, showed a man of age, his mind and energy were still those of a much younger man.

His brown leather hat, formed perfectly to divert rain off his back, made him look more like an archaeologist than a man of the sea; it was completely inappropriate for his line of work. Salt and leather just do not mix. Though she could detect a slight coat of mink oil, judging by its wear and discoloration, this cover could very well be as old as Jack.

Deceptively, the tattered clothing he wore suggested a man of limited means to the average observer. However, Ariella noticed subtle hints, such as his Vasque boots, Seiko Marine diving watch, and K Bar style knife, all of which indicated that Jack was a man of substance, not concerned with the frivolities of life.

After relating a few adventures of her own, which she had experienced while traveling the world's oceans, Ariella asked Jack if he knew what she and Jonathan were doing here. She assumed he had been somewhat informed about her and Jonathan's assignment prior to their arrival.

It was not an unexpected question, but the timing of it caught Jack slightly off guard. Ariella tended to do that to people. Quick to recover from the initial shock, he determined that at this time, less was more.

"What I've been told, ma'am, is that you and the major thar are ta be driven ta the far end of the island so that ya both can go under the deep blue ta the north. Now old Jack here is not scared ta go under the water, ya see, but whar ya're going, it's mighty deep, yes, ma'am . . . this bloke's got no business being down thar."

Judging by her reaction, his plea of ignorance, as expected, worked well enough to quell any questions that dealt with topics of a more sensitive nature.

Although she did not like being called ma'am—it made her feel old, or at least older than she wanted—Ariella knew that a man like Jack, with his culture and his upbringing, only used the term out of respect. It would be difficult, if not impossible, for him to omit it from his vocabulary, even if he wanted to. Ariella liked Jack and did not want to alienate him. Because she rarely related well to what other people thought or felt, she tended to do that. "It is deep, yes; but it's really quite beautiful down there. Things are so peaceful and . . . less complicated." Even as the words escaped her mouth, she recognized that the past few days had contradicted what she had just asserted.

Just being in Jack's presence, to Ariella's relief, she began to feel the tension dissipate from her tired body. Apparently, this light conversation was exactly what she needed; her entire worldview had just recently been destroyed. Under the circumstances, though, she felt she was doing quite well.

Jack too felt at ease while in Ariella Marconi's presence. Yes, his life experiences had helped him to rapidly adapt to change, but they did not make him immune from its side effects. Jack, on occasion, had trouble sleeping. All the years spent in the employ of the CIA had trained him to dissect the subtle nuances in every situation. Determining the what, when, why, how, and, most importantly; the level of danger had all become second nature, a habit not easily broken.

Often, he would lie awake at night reviewing the events of the day, thinking of various scenarios of how things would later play out, formulating plans for how to react, and then coming up with contingencies in case his initial plans failed to achieve the results he desired. "Plan and prepare to properly perform" was his mantra, and it had served him well. Luckily, though, through his use of Eastern meditative practices, along with the occasional nightcap, Jack could usually alleviate his periodic insomnia.

Since they enjoyed the other's conversation, as well as the feeling of being in one another's company, Ariella and Jack continued to swap tales of undersea explorations and jungle expeditions. Little did they know that they naturally acted as energy recharger and tension relievers for the other.

Meanwhile, Jonathan and Abhar had some tales of their own to swap. Once they were far enough away from the others, Jonathan started the conversation. "So, Abhar, if that is your real name, I think I've been a pretty good sport about all of this." Jonathan was speaking with conviction. "I've trusted you and done as you've asked, but I need to know who you are and what the hell is going on!"

Without giving him too much information, Abhar answered his question. "My name is really Abraham, but I have gone by Abhar Am for more years than I care to remember. I have been fighting all my life against a powerful cabal, who for thousands of years have been secretly working to take control of this planet. They are everywhere, and yet they are nowhere . . . I believe you have met a few of them."

Jonathan stood there dumbfounded for a moment. It was not Abhar's admission of his identity that perplexed him—he expected as much. It was that he had met them, the ones causing all this trouble. "What do you mean I've met them?! Who are you talking about, Abhar?"

Seeing that he had not yet put two and two together, Abhar clued him in. "The implant, your abduction . . . you met them during your abduction."

This revelation hit Jonathan like a stiff jab. Fortunately, he had already been accustomed to the many other beings who occupied this planet. Even Gilla's race, which predated humanity by epochs, wished to return to the days when they ruled the Earth. However, the elemental gods he had seen while meditating were something new, and seemingly much more powerful. "The beings I remember seeing were featureless. They were gold and silver, masculine and feminine; at least that's what I sensed they were . . . who or what the hell are they?" Jonathan pleaded for an answer.

Again, without revealing information that was not pertinent at this time, Abhar responded. "They are essentially shape shifters and can assume any form, even becoming human. They came from a place called Dimeria, located in another . . . well, another dimension, Major Hawthorn." Although he dodged the complete story, Abhar was telling Jonathan the truth.

"If these things have been here for thousands of years, why haven't I ever heard of them before now? Their existence would surely have come up in conversation at some point." Jonathan did not doubt Abhar's claims; he was simply having a hard time understanding how this supremely powerful group could have remained hidden from all the other entities in the universe.

"As I said, Jonathan, they can be anyone or anything. They can assume the form of a Reptilian, a Gray, a Pleiadean . . . they could even be you. Their kind are able to disappear in an instant and suddenly appear elsewhere . . ."

Jonathan interrupted. "Yeah, I remember that gold fucker doing that."

"They can travel at speeds that are, quite frankly, incomprehensible. They are the closest things to gods that you're likely to ever meet."

"Really! The God I believe in can't die, and I killed one of those silver bitches!" Jonathan proudly stated.

Although Abhar had talked with Haji about the implant and Jonathan's abduction, he did not recall his brother-in-law mentioning the fact that Jonathan had exterminated a Rah. *How did he accomplish such a feat?* he wondered. Nevertheless, now was not the time.

"I'll have to hear that story sometime."

As Abhar was in contemplation over the abduction, Jonathan reached into his pack and produced several pictures of the amber crystals, which were in both the Mariana and Puerto Rico Trenches.

"Since it's obvious that you and Haji have talked, maybe you can tell me what this is. These are the objects located in the trenches." Jonathan closely studied Abhar's reaction as he fanned through the pictures.

As Abhar handed him back the photos, he replied, "They have been traditionally used as portals."

Jonathan, catching on to Abhar's words, cried, "You said traditionally . . . what are they used for now?"

"Oh, they're still being used as portals, that's where they entered when they abducted you."

Jonathan cringed as a tingle went up his spine.

"But lately . . ." Abhar paused. "They seem to have another purpose." He had no intention of telling Jonathan what he believed they were being used for. He needed him to stay focused. It was not that the major could not handle the information; no, he was constantly involved in operations that had worldwide consequences. It was that a proper explanation would lead to a never-ending series of questions, some of which could not be answered with words alone; they had to be seen.

"What other purpose?" Jonathan interrupted Abhar's thoughts.

"I'm not entirely sure, Major Hawthorn, but I know they're growing."

"If they keep growing, Abhar, there's going to be a cataclysm of biblical proportions. What can we do to stop them, or at least slow them down? I'd really prefer going down there with something other than a hope and a prayer, if you know what I mean."

Abhar noted that this was his attempt to mask his nervous frustration. It was predictable. Reflecting on what he and Jack had talked about, Abhar decided it was the perfect time to put his plan into action. "Jonathan, did you bring the items I requested—the mask and the harp?"

Shuffling through his duffel bag to locate one of the items in question, Jonathan said, "Yes, the mask is in here. The harp is in this box," he said, pointing to the cardboard box he had brought. "I have to tell you, Abhar, there should be some sort of warning plastered all over that harp. I nearly destroyed my office playing that thing." His mood brightened at the memory of the event, which on reflection was hilarious.

Abhar also had to laugh slightly. He could imagine the havoc that must have caused. "What if I had instructed Haji to wrap warning tape all around the harp that said 'Danger, Do Not Play' in big bold letters, would it has made any difference?"

"Nope, I suppose it wouldn't. I would have strummed it anyway," Jonathan admitted sheepishly.

Abhar just displayed a grin of satisfaction. He already knew Jonathan all too well. "You're lucky you didn't strum it even harder; you would have brought the entire building down." Abhar was serious.

Though he suspected the harp held great power, it did not actually sink in, until that very moment, how close he had been to death. But, being inquisitive by nature, he asked, "It's some sort of sonic weapon, isn't it?"

"Among other things." It was unnecessary to explain its use as a hypnotic device.

"What does the mask do?"

"I can assume you tried that out as well?" Abhar's eyebrow lifted as his head dropped.

"Yeah, but other than it shrinking to fit my head and disappearing, which was awesome by the way, I have no idea what it is used for. Haney wanted to hit me in the head to see if it was some sort of armor, but I gave him the big No on that one."

"Who's Haney?" Abhar asked.

"He's one of my most trusted allies. I have him headed to Los Alamos to meet Gilla, who told me to tell you hello. He's probably there now."

Feeling he needed to explain himself, although he was unsure why, Jonathan stated that he had put Gilla and Haney on standby, just in case. He had a sense they would be needed, and in this case, he was right.

Realizing that those two would come in handy, he merely nodded and told Jonathan, "Good idea. I think we can find something for them to do." He already had a job for them, but first things first. "To answer your question, the mask has several uses. The first, which you will undoubtably find quite applicable in your line of work, protects the wearer's thoughts from being read. Nothing, not even the Grays, can peer into your mind while you have this on."

Jonathan, though he enjoyed chanting his Schoolhouse Rock mantra—it was his conscious meditation—was eager to discover what else the mask could do.

Abhar continued, "The user can also instantly determine whether someone, anyone, is lying or telling the truth. It was traditionally worn by the judges and royalty of Sumer. As you can guess, it made negotiations and the enforcement of law much more efficient; wouldn't you agree?"

"Oh, hell yes. I can think of numerous situations where this baby would have come in handy."

There was a long pause while Abhar paced. He was contemplating how to introduce his plan. It lasted so long that Jonathan nearly asked him if he was all right; but just before the words came out of his mouth, Abhar spoke. "The mask has another, more sensitive, function. With the mask on, along with a magical Incantation, which I will teach you, you, Major Hawthorn, will be able to stop the crystal's expansion and render the portal useless."

Holding the mask up to get a better look at it, Jonathan cried, "Holy shit, this thing has magic powers?" It was not so much as a question as a statement. He was not all that surprised that the mask had magical properties; he knew it disappeared and changed sizes.

"Not exactly, Jonathan, but it will help you do what is necessary to bind the crystal."

"Coooool . . . so . . . so do I need a wand or something?" Jonathan said jokingly. At times he could be quite childish, a trait that would keep him young.

Abhar realized that by using the mask, a ploy of magic, and some ritualistic type of hand gesture, he could manipulate Jonathan into summoning the power that resided within him, all the while keeping the true nature of its source hidden.

"No, Major." Abhar just shook his head. "No wand will be required, but I will need to show you how to hold your hand so you can project the spell correctly." Holding his right hand out, Abhar pointed forward with his middle and index finders. With them extended, he touched the other two fingers to his thumb. After Jonathan successfully mimicked what Abhar had shown him, he explained, "Then you say 'Yah anan Yah,' three times. Getting progressively louder each time. As so: 'Yah anan Yah, Yah anan Yah, Yah anan Yah.'"

"Okah, 'Yah anan Yah,' three times, got it."

As Jonathan echoed the words softly, over and over again, Abhar worried that something might actually start to happen if he continued. Therefore, he instructed only to say the words only with the mask on and with the special hand gesture. He needed Jonathan to believe that the spell only worked properly according to his instructions.

After a few moments, Abhar was convinced that his ruse was successful. It was a fairly good plan, Abhar thought. He had effectively controlled the situation without lying, which might have been detected, and judging by the way Jonathan was repetitiously practicing throwing his hand gesture as if it were a pistol, had persuaded him into believing that all the elements of the spell were essential for it to work.

"What's going to happen when I use the spell, Abhar? Will lightning bolts come out of my hands?"

Abhar thought for a moment about how close to the mark the young major was. With a little chuckle, he answered, "Almost, Jonathan . . . It will actually look more like a ribbon of white fire bordered by two bands of blue, but good guess."

Although he was glad Jonathan remained relaxed, especially considering the severity of the situation, he needed to reinforce the fact that he was the only one in the world that could accomplish the task before them.

"Just remember, Jonathan, there is only one mask, and you have it. Without it . . ." Abhar's warning was interrupted.

"Don't worry, I got it."

The problem was, Abhar had to worry. The Rahs were not going to just let some arbitrary human come in and ruin their plans. It would only make sense that they would have someone monitoring the situation on Earth, probably on the Sea Lab. Any action taken against the crystal would likely be met with fierce resistance, placing Jonathan's life in danger; however, it was the only way.

"You said before that you killed one of the Dimerians during your abduction, correct?" Abhar asked, already knowing he had.

"Yes, at least I think I did. It's all still sorta hazy," Jonathan responded.

"Do you remember how you did it?" Abhar delved.

"I remember this room, with weapons all over the wall." He paused while trying to piece together the events from his clouded memory. "I remember grabbing a sword, which was in the center of a display. I couldn't help but think that that this was significant somehow, like it must be special to be there. I recall a silver being with a feminine voice, taunting me, but only in my head. It had no mouth, ears, eyes, lips, nothing; it was just a form and tall. This bitch had to be at least seven feet tall." He again stopped to gather his thoughts. "For obvious reasons, I got pissed off and goaded this thing into a fight. The rest is history. I won." Scratching his head, he added, "That's all I really remember about her."

Abhar brought his right arm up and pinched his chin between his finger and thumb as he posed his next question. "Do you remember what the sword looked like? Was there anything special about it that you noticed?" He was already convinced that Jonathan had welded a tri-sword during his duel; it was the only way to actually kill one of his kind. However, Abhar felt that if Jonathan could recall the finer details of the weapon on his own, he stood to a better chance of getting the sword to work for him again.

Before responding, Jonathan thought for a few seconds. "It had a golden tipped blade made up of three pieces, which struck me as odd. At first, I thought it might be bronze, but it was feather light when I grabbed it. Bronze swords are obsolete anyway . . ." Jonathan continued, "The handle had three inlaid jewels; one of them glowed greenish yellow or yellowish green." He shrugged his shoulders, unsure. "I distinctly remember it being longer than a samurai sword, razor sharp, and perfectly balanced . . . come to think of it, I've never held such a precisely made weapon in my entire life."

"Sounds like that whoever crafted it knew what they were doing. Though you know what they say, it's not the sword, but the swordsman."

"Yeah, uh-huh, and guns don't kill people, bullets do," Jonathan wittily added as they both laughed. "All things considered, Abhar, I'd still rather be the kid with the best toys."

"I agree with you completely. Sometimes it's even essential." Abhar said this while pointing to the mask. He also was indicating the importance of the sword. However, this was not the time to talk about this. Later, after Jonathan and Ariella had been escorted to the other end of the island, Abhar would determine whether to reveal his sword and instruct Jonathan in its use. For now, a change of subject was needed.

"Did you inform Ms. Marconi that she too had been abducted?" Abhar asked.

"Hell no. Don't get me wrong, she's handling all this like a champ, better than most of the seasoned soldiers I've introduced into our world, but I think Ariella's got enough on her plate right now," Jonathan said.

"I think you're right. No sense complicating things any further." Although Abhar agreed, he saw strength in Ariella, a strength that would later be needed by her protector.

"So, what's Jack Dresher's story?" Jonathan asked.

Just the thought of Jack made Abhar smile. "He's quite a character, that's for sure. I actually just met him through a trusted friend of mine."

"Do you trust him?"

"Unquestionably," Abhar responded seriously.

"Good, then I do too. Does he have any skills?" Jonathan's training made assessing situations second nature.

"Let's put it this way . . . it would be easier telling you what Jack couldn't do rather than what he could. He's an old CIA agent from the Vietnam era, we're lucky to have him."

"A spook?! Uh, I would never have guessed that," Jonathan said with a look of astonishment. "What does he know about what we're doing?"

"He knows enough that you don't have to monitor what you say around him. He's highly intelligent, extremely personable, remembers practically everything, and assimilates new information quickly." Taking a jab at Jonathan, Abhar added, "I would suspect that in his younger days, Jack was among the elite, maybe even better than you."

Graciously accepting the comparison, Jonathan nodded in approval. He could not help but wonder, though, what Abhar's motives were in all of this. Sure, he said he had been fighting these Dimerians all of his life, but why? Though he did not suspect anything nefarious in his actions, Jonathan had rarely met, or even heard of, anyone who fought against tyranny out of sheer benevolence; there was always an underlying reason, and it was usually personal.

Looking down at his phone, with the time constraints before him, Jonathan knew he would not learn much more about his companion at this juncture.

He motioned that they should return. Agreeing that they should get back to Ariella and Jack, Abhar led the way.

Evidently, at least to Jonathan, Abhar had more knowledge about what needed to be done than any of his superiors. *Typical*, he thought to himself. "At least this time I have some legitimate help," he muttered in his mind. Though he was sure there was still much more to the story, his trust in Abhar grew. If nothing else, Jonathan had learned to trust his instincts, and at this moment they were giving Abhar a big thumbs up.

Still, he had to wonder, was their initial meeting, as fortuitous as it has turned out to be, a mere coincidence; or was it destined by the will of fate? This question would continue to puzzle him for years to come. But for now it didn't matter. This Abhar Am, Abraham, or whoever he was, was the only one with a feasible plan. A plan that appeared to facilitate his own goals.

As Abhar walked away, Jonathan, usually the one leading, uncharacteristically followed him back to the others.

<hr />

Approaching Ariella and Jack, Jonathan was glad to see that the two had made the best of their time together. They were still in deep conversation when he and Abhar arrived—something about swimming with crocodiles off the northern coast of Australia. Not being particularly fond of the prehistoric creatures, especially before meeting Gilla, Jonathan's only use for the beasts would have been material for a good pair of boots or a nice belt. *But to each his own*, he thought.

Noticing her companion's arrival, Ariella turned toward them and smiled directly at Jonathan, which would have not been so unexpected if not for her appearance. Ariella was radiant, as if she had just been recharged by the best night's sleep in her life. At that moment, she was more beautiful and angelic than Jonathan could ever have imagined. All her stress lines, which were few, had completely vanished. The look in her eyes was one of blissful content. It left him speechless, thinking of how happy he would be to wake up to that face every morning.

Abhar too saw the change in Ariella's, as well as Jack's, auras. Instantly, he surmised that they must be synergistically connected, each recharging the other, truly a rare occurrence. While never a successful mating couple—symbiotic energies were too strong to allow for the creation of offspring—their continuous contact, in small doses, would greatly lengthen their lives.

Like a statue, Jonathan stood motionless, in a trance, until Ariella broke the silence. "Hey, Jonathan, hey, Abhar. I hope you boys had a nice talk." She blushingly smiled while visibly biting her tongue; she noticed how Jonathan was looking at her. His stare made her feel like a little girl whose object of affection had finally taken notice, but without the pressures and contrived notions normally associated with such emotions.

Seeing that Jonathan was entranced by Ariella's rejuvenated glow, and not wanting to spoil the pleasant mood, Abhar responded, "We did, thank you Ms. Marconi. And by the looks of it, so did the two of you."

"Please, it's Ariella, just plain Ariella," she said with a soft smile.

"Oh, I seriously doubt there is anything plain about you, Ariella," Abhar commented. Ariella's eyes lit up.

Jack then spoke up, "Yeah, mate, this Shelia's got more stories than an aboriginal elder; we could go on for hours. Yes, sir, if old Jack was a tad younger, ya'd have ta fight me for her, cobber. Ya better hold on ta this one."

Ariella coyly blushed even more as the compliments continued. Jonathan finally snapped out of his trance, having heard nothing.

"Huh?" was all he managed to say. Everyone burst into laughter. "What's so funny?" Jonathan asked.

"Never mind," Ariella answered while still giggling. "So what's the plan, Jonathan?"

Clearing his throat, Jonathan responded, "Since Abhar and Jack know the island, they have graciously volunteered to escort us to the old naval base just outside Ceiba. Then we'll go solo to Vieques Island, get geared up, and head into the drink."

"Ya mean the old Roosevelt Roads Naval Station?" Jack curiously asked.

"Yes," Jonathan said. "Why?"

"That thar base has been abandoned for years, mate, though from time ta time, old Jack's noticed a few Army types headed that way."

"Sounds like an ideal spot to me," Ariella pronounced.

"How so?" Jonathan asked.

"Jonathan, we're going to a super secretive high-tech underwater laboratory; it's probably best that the place is abandoned," she said matter-of-factly.

Slapping his hand to his forehead, Jonathan said, "Duh!" Sometimes Ashley would call him the stupidest smart person she knew, and on occasions such as this he had to agree. Luckily, he was comfortable enough with himself that it did not bother him too much.

"How long will it take us to get to the base, Jack?" Jonathan asked.

"A couple of hours, I reckon. If we were ta leave right now, we should get thar by first light."

Looking at his phone, Jonathan said, "Its 0400 now, we're to be there by 0700. I suggest we hit the road, so at least I can be on time for something."

"Yeah, that seems to be a problem of yours," Ariella said humorously, but with a little sass.

Picking up on the sauciness in her statement, Jonathan thought it best to ignore it. She had earned it. Ariella could have berated him earlier, when they first met, but had not. Besides, she was so damn cute when she said it; Jonathan began to wonder what he would purposely do next to press her buttons. *No time for that sort of thinking now*, he thought. There would be plenty of time later for foreplay.

As they all loaded into Jack's Jeep, apparently the foreplay started sooner than he had planned. Ariella, feeling comfortable with Jonathan, especially after allowing her to bitch without rebuttal, sat just a little closer to him than normal.

Of course, Jonathan did not object. He too felt something profound developing between them. That was something he and Cynthia lacked, a shared experience, perhaps. Although not sure exactly what it was, he was positive about one thing—that this woman was growing on him.

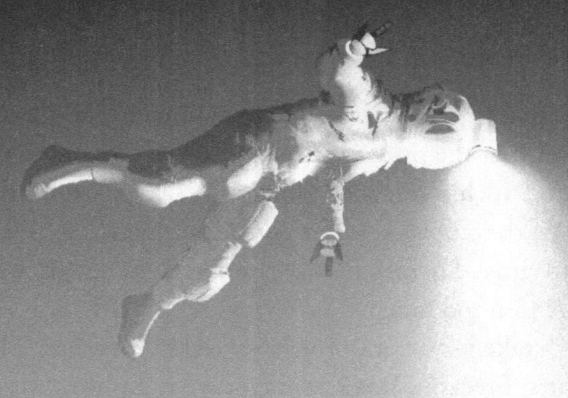

CHAPTER

FIFTY ONE

TOTALLY DISCOMBOBULATED, CHERAHNA found herself wandering aimlessly through the corridors of the Rah Jump Craft. She was still unable to come to grips with everything that was happening. In her eyes, Rahzu was doing to her now what her Uncle Abraham had done to her. Except coming from Rahzu, she considered it much more devious. He knew about her past and the torment it had caused. Even though his actions were not personal, she still felt that they were.

Maybe she was just being overdramatic about everything, and the captain had good reasons for keeping information from the crew; she, as a commander, understood that things were explained on a need-to-know basis.

CheRahna also realized that in the past, she had not been the master of her own emotions. Without Rahzu's help, some member of the crew would undoubtably have been the target of her wrath long ago. The kindness and understanding which he had shown her during her time here was the only reason she was even contemplating these questions. If it had been any other officer, she would immediately have had him or her arrested and brought up on charges of treason.

Just as she turned the corner to head to her stateroom, CheRahna detected an eerie but familiar presence. While still not particularly comfortable with the energy she experienced, it was growing on her.

⌣

Although not on board the ship, YetziRah had not ventured far. He had silently kept tabs on CheRahna's frequency as he remained just outside anyone's awareness, a trick he had learned long ago. By staying on the exterior of the ship, adjacent to one of the pleasure pools, he masked his presence by expanding elementally, melding his own energy signature with that of the pools. While not completely undetectable, it was enough for him to go unnoticed; no one was scanning for frequencies originating in this dark, lifeless universe.

Consequently, from listening in on her conversation with Captain Rahzu, the admiral, for the first time, witnessed his plan coming to fruition. The seed of doubt that he had planted in CheRahna's naïve consciousness was working even better than he could have predicted. With one more gentle nudge, he was sure she would go over the edge and be his.

This was an extremely critical time. YetziRah not only needed to facilitate the thoughts of treasonous activity that CheRahna was developing about Rahzu, he also had to make her believe that her captain was so potentially dangerous to the House of Rah that his immediate termination was a necessity. Admiral YetziRah was going to trick CheRahna into killing her captain.

It's perfect, he thought with a grin. Since she was the only one who was aware that he had visited both her and Rahzu, he could have plausible deniability concerning the entire situation. If things went awry, CheRahna, wretched with guilt over killing her captain and mentor, in an act of despair, would end up taking her own life. Hopefully, though, things would not come to that; he needed her.

With Captain Rahzu, a major threat to his plans, eliminated and framed for treason, he would then take personal control of the operation on Earth. Normally, when an admiral takes over this type of operation, red flags are thrown up, signifying a changing of the guard. In this case, however, it would not only be legitimate, but expected that he would assume command.

Ultimately, the success of this move was the most critical aspect of his plan. It needed to be effective in order to convince the Rah property holders that a coup was feasible. Without their support, he stood no chance of dethroning Xanix Rah.

Knowing that his relationship with CheRahna, while growing, was tentative at best, he decided to materialize slowly in front of her. This allowed her to feel his presence well in advance of his complete arrival. He did not need her any more jumpy than she already was, at least not with him.

———⁓———

"Admiral YetziRah, I didn't expect to see you so soon." CheRahna said as he solidified in front of her.

"Very perceptive and alert of you, Commander." He was feeding her ego. "To be honest, I was worried about you."

"Worried? No disrespect, sir, but I never pictured you as someone who 'worries' about anyone, especially not me," she said doubtfully.

YetziRah could sense that there was a battle raging inside her—a fight over her loyalty to Rahzu, the mentor she had believed him to be, against the deception that had been created. YetziRah was winning.

"That's simply not true, Commander. Here"—he said, extending his hand—"take my hand and feel my energy. Determine for yourself if I am being truthful or not," he said confidently.

CheRahna cautiously took hold of his extended golden hand, unsure what to expect.

"I told you before I left that you are very important to me and the future of the House of Rah. I am worried about you because I am concerned that your loyalties, understandably, are being put to the test." YetziRah was adroit with his words, so as not to actually lie. Holding his hand, she would sense it. He actually did care about her, though, before now, she would have never believed it to be so.

She acknowledged that she believed him, and, still holding her hand, he continued. "Are you now convinced that Rahzu is lying to you and the crew?"

"Yes, sir." She responded in a dismal tone.

"Under the circumstances, you couldn't have known. It's not normal for any officer to question a superior's word without great cause. Until now, you had no such cause." He could feel her relief over that simple statement. "But now that you do know, I think you should know some more . . . don't you?"

"Yes, Admiral, tell me everything. I need to know it all."

"Yesss . . . I thought you might." Trying to figure out how to proceed, he cautiously paused.

CheRahna, sensing his reservations, spoke firmly. "Admiral, I'm a Rah commander and do not need to be coddled. Just tell me, sir!"

YetziRah was caught completely off guard by her moxie. It pleased him so much, he did as she asked. "Rahzu has erased precious bits of information from the control crystal's memory." However, he did not tell her exactly what the captain had deleted. The admiral planned to use this to push further blame on Rahzu for the data that went missing just prior to Ensign RahKael's death.

CheRahna, shocked by the captain's deceptive activities, gasped and pulled away from YetziRah, dropping his hand.

He consoled her, saying, "I know this is hard for you to hear, but I believe he was also responsible for deleting the data Ensign RahKael had uncovered, which implicated him in the clandestine plan happening on Earth."

"Why didn't you tell me that earlier?!" CheRahna was beginning to become unhinged.

"Because I didn't have proof then! I do now!"

"What proof, sir? Tell me, I beg you. I have to know," she pleaded.

While outside the ship, YetziRah had witnessed Rahzu delete the record of his visit. Unaware of YetziRah's visit with his commander, he foolishly erased all of the admiral's frequencies from the more recent records. So, until now, he had never been here.

"If you check the crystal's data banks, there will be no record of my visits," YetziRah explained.

CheRahna knew for a fact that he had come to talk with her. "Why would he do such a thing? I don't understand his motivation." At this point, she fully believed the admiral.

"I'm not sure, but I surmise that he is going to try to frame me for RahKael's death and then accuse me of collusion with Abraham." Thus YetziRah planted another seed, one he could later use against Xanix Rah too, but first things first.

"That's ridiculous! No one is going to believe you're conspiring with my uncle." CheRahna was disgusted by the mere insinuation of such an allegation.

"I'm afraid, my dear, that you don't understand politics and power very well. Remember, my dear, an accusation is all that is needed to ruin someone."

If CheRahna had not been so emotionally wrecked, she might have picked up on the ominous statement YetziRah had just made. But at this point the perceived deception of her mentor had turned to anger. That anger was now consuming her, clouding her judgment, and manifesting itself in revenge. Her thoughts were now YetziRah's to control.

Seeing that she had cracked, the admiral realized that he needed to assume the role of trusted mentor and quiet her down. "Commander, I want you to calm down. I know this is trying; I've been through this myself, but you need to get a hold of yourself." YetziRah was stern, but with a caring tone.

"I'm sorry, sir; this is just all so unbelievable . . . Okay . . . I'm better now . . . thank you, sir."

"Look, in all fairness to you, Commander, I don't expect you just to blindly believe me in this. After I leave, I want you to check the crystal sphere's memory yourself. I need you to trust me."

"You're leaving?!" CheRahna said.

"I won't be far away. But for you to trust me, I cannot be around to influence your decisions."

"I do . . . trust you, Admiral," she stated nervously.

"Not wholeheartedly, you don't. I can hear the doubt in your voice," YetziRah said with compassion. He could see her conflict. "It's fine, my dear, it really is. That's why you must see the evidence for yourself, alone. Then there will be no doubt." He paused to let this sink in. "There can be no mistrust between us if we are both to survive this and stop Rahzu." This was his coup de grâce, how he finally won her over.

"Why would I be in danger?" CheRahna asked.

"Do you plan on defecting or framing me?"

"Absolutely not, sir!" She was furious that he would question her loyalty. She realized, though, that he was not actually accusing her; it just felt that way.

Finally, with all his seeds of deception firmly planted, YetziRah believed she was now ready. Cautiously controlling his thoughts and emotions, he pulled out a crystal vial and presented it to her.

"What's this for, Admiral?" she asked as she studied the multicolored vessel.

As he began to inform her about what the vial contained and what he used it for, YetziRah cunningly avoided revealing what the substance truly was. He had to be careful not to lie. CheRahna, though confused, might sense it. Inside the crystal vial was a copious amount of the same mixture of elements Yahweh had used in the Great Purge, monatomic gold and white enhanced Dimerian crystal (WEDEC). Dimerians not of the House of Yah exposed to this compound would slowly dissolve into their elemental form, forever vaporizing and becoming part of the cosmos.

"This vial, my dear, contains a special compound that was developed long ago. I have used it many times during interrogations to extract information from less than willing participants. It's quite effective."

"What am I to do with it, sir?" the commander asked, though she already knew the answer.

Matter-of-factly, YetziRah replied, "Use it on Captain Rahzu, of course. We need to find out what he knows and what his plans are, Commander."

CheRahna retreated a few steps. She knew that if she went through with this, the relationship she had built with Rahzu would be over. *Is this the right thing to do?* she wondered. "What will this do to him?" she reluctantly asked, taking hold of the vial.

Feeling her inner struggle, YetziRah knew he had to be extremely careful if he had any chance of her following through. "It's going to slowly start to separate him." He needed to be quick with his words, so that she could not respond. "He'll think it's killing him; that's what makes this stuff work so well. Then, with any luck, he'll tell you everything we need to know."

Since Dimerians do not feel pain, games of the psyche were among the few tools used that were effective during interrogations.

"With any luck?" she snapped, still uncomfortable about this plan.

"I have found that most who believe that they are at their end will usually come clean about the wrongs they have done. A cleansing of the soul, if you will." He skillfully kept the focus of his answers on what those exposed to the compound would think or believe, which allowed him to be cryptic, but truthful. He did not need to include the fact that they were actually being destroyed. "Nothing, though, is a sure thing."

"And this stuff won't destroy him?"

The admiral had already prepared himself for this question. He used a technique that allowed him to speak truthfully about almost any subject, as long as he thought about it from the right perspective.

YetziRah knew that there were very few things that could completely eradicate a Dimerian's elemental existence; this powder was not one of them. It would, however, successfully separate the elements from one's essence, which would then be consumed by the vacuum of chaos. But, technically, the soul was not destroyed, only trapped. "He definitely will think he's dying." He decided to take a chance and avoid answering her question directly.

CheRahna, so upset about how fast things had changed, did not pick up on the vagueness of his response. Looking at the vial, she asked, "All right, Admiral, tell me what to do."

Splendid! he thought to himself. "It's simple, my dear. Remove the top, pour it into the air in front of him, and will it toward him . . . Now CheRahna, be careful not to expose yourself to the compound or you'll suffer its effects also. It's not pleasant, I assure you." He had been exposed to a minute amount before, but not enough to permanently disaggregate him.

"I understand, Admiral. I'll be careful." She was still unsure whether she was going to actually use the powder. She would decide after checking the crystal's data files.

Feeling confident that she would do as he asked, the admiral only needed to leave her with one final thought. "With what you know now and what you will learn, you and I will become Rahzu's biggest threats. There's a simple rule of combat you will learn to adopt, Commander—eliminate threats before they eliminate you . . . Think about what I have said, CheRahna. It could save your life." Turning to leave, he said one last thing, "I will not be far away."

YetziRah then disappeared. Nothing more needed to be said. CheRahna would do as he suggested, he knew that much. She would find out that Rahzu had indeed erased the crystal's data files and then she would use the powder on him. After that, he was not sure what she would do; he could only watch and wait.

CHAPTER

FIFTY TWO

AFTER DROPPING JONATHAN off, instead of returning the rental car—he would later use it to get to the maglev station at Shasta—Haney went back to his hidden lair and proceeded to pack his gear.

Among his things, he always carried specific items anywhere he traveled. "Necessities," the Chief claimed. These included his slingshot, an adjustable compound bow, and his father's Old Henry lever-action .22-caliber rifle, an assortment of cutlery, and perhaps the most important item, super glue. Haney professed that he used "that shit" on everything, from setting traps and snares to repairing weapons. It could even be used in the combat theater sealing wounds, a remedy that worked much better than stitches. In fact, it worked so well and had so many uses that even Jonathan added it to his survival kit.

Additionally, he carried Bertha, his large fifteen-inch turquoise and opal inlaid, single-edged, serrated hunting knife. This was another one of the Chief's necessities, since he never went anywhere without it. Besides being a weapon, it served as his razor, ax, saw, back scratcher, eating utensil, hammer, and on occasion grabbling hook. Besides, it was such an intimidating weapon, what surprised people the most was how nimbly and precisely

Haney was able to manipulate the blade, as if he were a surgeon cutting out a tumor.

Haney finished packing and began to prepare his home for his extended absence. While methodically tending to his plants, checking his lithium battery array, his solar cells, and turning off various other systems in his abode, which were unnecessary when he was away, he could not help but try to visualize the many different scenarios in which he could encounter; the possibilities were endless, especially considering who he was working for. Chief knew he could end up anywhere on the planet, or quite possibly off it.

Once he completed his departure checklist, Haney grabbed his pack and headed for Mt. Shasta. He was ready. It had been nearly a year since his services were last required and he was itching for an adventure. A Native American, it was in his blood.

After boarding the maglev—to his chagrin, since he had already missed the last nonstop train to Los Alamos—Haney decided to use this turn of events to his advantage; he boarded, sat down, crossed his legs, and began meditating. It had been a while since he had communed with the spirits. Hopefully, they would provide him with some much-needed insight that could aid in the upcoming mission.

As the train cruised along, the repetitious hum it made as it traversed each section of the tunnel helped lull him deeper and deeper into a trance-like state. Before long, he would be in Los Alamos, but until then he would just sit and listen.

Accustomed to the solitude that his normal subterranean habitat provided, Gilla was waiting comfortably for Haney's maglev to arrive. Though it was Monday, it was still far too early for the station to be crowded, particularly considering the number of basketball fans who worked here. The San Antonio Spurs, the closet thing that many folks here had to a home team, had just clinched a spot in the NBA finals. Gilla knew how humans could be so distracted by sporting events and that many would likely call in sick due to over celebrating.

Though he saw the folly of humans, Gilla had always supported the idea of a world based on their cohabitation with his own kind; many of his species did not. Collectively, they were tired of mankind's reckless abuse of the planet, polluting the environment with no consideration for other species. The ramifications of human activities were already starting to infiltrate into the underground realm. The air they breathed and the water they drank were becoming more and more toxic. Their sensitive biology had not evolved to handle such contaminants; sickness and disease, which had previously been nonexistent, were now becoming commonplace among his people.

Although the technology to cure many of these ailments was available to his kind as well, much like their counterparts on the surface, only the Reptilian elite had access to such advances. Overpopulation, though not as big a problem as it was to humanity, still had to be contended with from time to time.

Since Gilla was born into royalty and groomed to be a leader, he was more aware of the complex geopolitical considerations than the majority of his species. They too, like the humans, were easy to manipulate through disinformation, distraction, and propaganda.

Long ago—many years before Jonathan had saved his life—Gilla had been a champion of the concept of sharing the planet with humanity, working together to create a better, cleaner world. A war to exterminate mankind, though there was a moderate chance of success, would greatly damage the planet in the process. The massive stockpiles of nuclear weapons that the humans had amassed were produced for this very purpose. Mutually assured destruction had little to do with mankind destroying itself. It was a strategy employed to deter any entity, terrestrial or not, from invading the surface of Earth. So far, it had worked, too, at least on the large scale.

Additionally, it would be nearly impossible to eradicate the entire human race, inevitably leading to a baby boom and a resurgence in their population. Humans multiply extremely quickly, compared to other higher life forms; being able to produce offspring every nine months. In fact, one human male in his prime could be set aside for stud, impregnating hundreds of females yearly. His own race was fortunate if copulation produced offspring every two years; unlike humans, Reptilian males adhered to a biannual cycle. The struggle for resources and survival underground caused them to evolve that way. This was another reason to avoid war. Though confident that his race would win, the population loss that his kind would suffer could take thousands of years to rebuild. Humanity, which had largely forgotten the Reptilians' existence millennia ago, would again be alerted to their presence. In just over a few hundred years following a war, his species would likely be bred out of existence.

Plus, if the human earthlings were destroyed, his people would sooner or later be forced to contend with something even more dangerous to their survival. Something so voracious that in just a few generations the Reptilians would also cease to exist. The original, non-Earth humanoids had been created for a more nourishing, secretive purpose. Only a select few Reptilians and humans were aware of what that purpose was; Gilla happened to be one of them.

However, none of these issues seemed to matter to the opponents of peace. They wanted the humans exterminated, at any cost. This ideology was what allowed Philoraptor, the current ruler, to overthrow Gilla in the first place, nearly costing him his life. Gilla has been living in exile ever since.

Since Reptilians were extremely sensitive to environmental changes, Gilla was aware of the approaching maglev even before the loudspeaker announced its arrival. He was excited about seeing Haney again, who, like himself, used his instincts more than his thoughts when reacting to situations. This was one of the reasons why Haney, despite being a big man, appeared to move with such quickness.

Now, with the train nearing, Gilla stood prepared, on guard for whatever shenanigans Haney intended to come at him with. Gilla knew it was just Chief's way of showing his affection.

As the train doors opened, instead of rushing him, as Gilla expected, Haney slowly exited, inching toward him. It was quite apparent that something was wrong because of the way Haney bent forward as he walked. Concerned for his friend's well-being, Gilla was the first to speak. "Yoush okay? Yoush look like yoush in pain, Haney."

Responding in his typical smartass manner, Haney said, "I ain't too sure what's worse, this damn back spasm or that ugly mug of yours . . . woof!"

"Yoush one sho shalk, melon head. When yoush wash born, yoush Mosher said yoush was a gifsh. So yoush fasher wrapped yoush up and gave yoush away. Hiss, hiss, hiss," Gilla countered.

"Yeah, yeah, yeah, at least I had a mother and father, ya hatchling." Haney was referring to the fact that Reptilians came out of eggs and were alone at birth.

As Haney put his bag down, Gilla braced for an attack. To his surprise, none came. Instead, Haney spoke with all the earnestness he could muster. "Seriously, Gilla . . . my back is killing me. Can I get you to crack it for me?"

Sensing that his old friend was serious and was actually in pain, Gilla motioned for him to turn around. He then wrapped his long, muscular arms around the hillbilly Indian, lifted him up, and gently applied pressure. Two things happened simultaneously. This first the repetitive cracking sounds as the vertebrae popped back into place. The second, more unpleasant sound was Haney passing gas. The fart was long and loud, so that it echoed throughout the nearly vacant train station.

After being set down, Haney began to laugh. "Man, I feel better. Thanks, Gilla, you just squeezed the shit outta me. Heh, heh, heh."

To Gilla's delight, his companion appeared to be back to his old self. Understanding human etiquette, he too thought the whole situation was rather humorous—until, of course, the smell hit him.

"Yoush smell bad!" Gilla stated, covering his nostrils with his hand while backing away.

"Yep, that musta been dem egg and corn beef hash biscuits I are earlier." Haney took a long, deep breath, "Can't ya smell the onions?" Haney used both hands to waft the odor.

While blood and guts smell like a gourmet dish to a Reptilian, human excrement was one of the foulest odors they would ever encounter. Thankfully, it was not like that of a skunk's and dissipated rapidly, with no lasting effects.

Seeing that Gilla was plainly disgusted with the smell of his flatulence, Haney chuckled. "I love my job, heh, heh, heh." Picking up his bag to follow his retreating friend, Haney then asked, "Where can a man get a drink around here? I'm kinda hungry too."

Gilla shook his head back and forth in disbelief as he led Haney to the food court. Some things never change, he thought. It was sure good to be back with his old friend again. Together they were what Jonathan referred to as his "wrecking team."

As they sat, eating and drinking, the two warriors caught up and reminisced over old times. They also discussed the significance of their reunion and what Gilla knew about their mission thus far. At this point, all they could do was speculate. Whatever Jonathan needed them for, it had to be serious. He never would have brought them back together unless it was.

CHAPTER FIFTY THREE

IMMEDIATELY AFTER CHERAHNA'S departure, Rahzu deleted all the data having anything to do with frequencies and of YetziRah's surprise inquiry. To be on the safe side, he also included the records of their activities on Earth, all the way back to the admiral's last visit. The captain could not afford to miss any information that could later be used to frame him.

Rahzu was troubled by the conversation he had just had with his commander. Under different circumstances, he would have been more patient, slowly feeding her information, so that she too would be privy to what was really occurring around them. However, there was not enough time for that. Things were happening quickly now—too quickly.

Although he knew her to be intelligent, hardworking, and skillful, Rahzu never pictured her being insightful. Why was she all of a sudden becoming suspicious of his actions? How did she conclude that the House of Rah had created a planet with life? He had not divulged that information to anyone on board except ShemRahya, whom he trusted. Surely this revelation was not derived from the codex he had given her; it suggested nothing.

Additionally, in their previous conversation, back in his office, he had been led to believe that CheRahna's outlook on her uncle had changed for the better, especially after he had revealed his own relationship with the defected Rah; though her recent tone, mannerisms, and color suggested just the opposite. But why? Even her line of questioning, which at times was accusatory and bordered on insubordination, seemed to have a purpose; of this much he was sure. It was as if the commander was testing him, as if she no longer trusted him.

So what if he had withheld information about Abraham, ET Rah's existence, and YetziRah's visit from her and the crew. It was his job as captain to determine what was best for those he led. Even if his commander had uncovered something that showed that the admiral had indeed come here, she would have to know that as her mentor, he withheld the fact of his visit in an attempt to protect her from her former tormentor.

Maybe all this new information was too much, too fast. Maybe she was not as strong-minded as he thought. No, that wasn't it. Something was afoot, something devious, he just knew it.

Instead of wasting any more time trying to figure out what was going on in CheRahna's head, Rahzu decided to take council with his protégé, ShemRahya. Hopefully, the two of them could determine the reason for the commander's behavior, and what to do about it.

Still brooding a bit over the realization that he could not tell KaRah about what was happening, ShemRahya had decided to return to his quarters. Though he was in control of his emotions and thoughts, he was not ready to lie to her if she started asking questions, at least not yet.

The security officer completely understood the captain's reasoning for excluding her from their plans, so he could not be angry. It had been quite insightful of Rahzu to pair them up in the first place. KaRah was not ShemRahya's vision of the perfect partner. Now, however, he could not dream of ever having another.

While ShemRahya was sharp-minded, quick-witted, and performed exceptionally on every assignment he had ever had, his one deficiency was that he was too preoccupied with himself, or more accurately, his self-presentation—the typical mindset of a warrior. He needed more work on being empathetic toward other's thoughts and emotions. Seeing the big picture was not one of his strengths either, an attribute his mentor, Captain Rahzu, had been helping him improve on.

It was not that Lt. ShemRahya was uncaring or blind to the needs of others. On the contrary, he was kind, forgiving, and never held others to his own personal standards. Also, he was excellent at reading another's intentions, a skill necessary in a successful security officer.

The young lieutenant had spent his life focused on self-improvement, trying to fulfill what was expected of someone of his lineage. It was his destiny to achieve greatness, even if it was not to be in the Blade Wars. Although bred for war, like the current champion of the Golden Rings, ZYah Zeh, ShemRahya thought that his existence could offer so much more than that of a warrior, who merely claimed his spoils after victory in battle.

He had actually met the famous Yah champion once, and though he was the epitome of a swordsman in battle, ZYah Zeh was quick-tempered, confidently arrogant, and seemed to possess little tact. Though not unfair or outright cruel, and very respectful toward others who acted in kind, he had no compunction about sending anyone to chaos who crossed him or his family. In fact, the only respect he received was from those who feared him or had won property betting on him.

This was not the life ShemRahya wanted. He had envisioned himself as a leader, someone who was respected more for the wisdom of his rule rather than his prowess with a sword. Though his skill with a blade had already instilled fear in some, he wanted peace in Dimeria, something that had been missing since even before the PU 4 uprising.

While one may look at these aspirations as his just being power-hungry and arrogant, he perceived them as events in his inevitable future. They were destined to happen sooner or later, no rush. ShemRahya lived by a simple motto, one that never failed him: "I think, therefore I am."

***

While still in his room contemplating the fact of having to withhold information from his trusted security partner, KaRah, ShemRahya sensed someone approaching. Just as he turned to face the doorway, Captain Rahzu appeared. He was projecting a peculiar energy, one ShemRahya had not noticed in him before. At once, the lieutenant rose to his feet to greet his captain.

"ShemRahya, may I have a moment of your time? We really need to talk," Rahzu said in an uneasy, stressful tone.

Rahzu's behavior caught the security officer completely off guard. He had never seen him so flustered before. It made him nervous because his mentor always had an answer or explanation for everything. "Yea . . . yes, sir." ShemRahya looked around his quarters to ensure they were presentable. "Come in, Captain."

Not one to waste time with words, Rahzu started talking about Commander CheRahna's recent inquisition. Carefully explaining the events as they had occurred, Rahzu refrained from inserting his opinion as to what all this might mean. He realized that he was too emotionally involved with the well-being of his commander to formulate a rational explanation for her actions.

Rahzu's plan was to tell his side of the story and to allow his fellow warrior to derive his own conclusions. Hopefully, he could offer a fresh perspective on the increasingly difficult, evolving situation.

Silently absorbing the information, Lt. ShemRahya not only took into account the facts, but also the captain's emotional energy as he spoke to them. Being somewhat more disconnected from the situation, he was sure he could gain some insight by studying Rahzu's feelings.

Once Rahzu was finished, ShemRahya began to delve further into CheRahna's activities. Although he did not know her as well as the captain did, he had formed a reliable baseline of behaviors and knew what to expect from her. She wore her emotions on her sleeve, making it easy to predict how she was going to act given a particular situation. Recently, however, he had noticed a negative residue surrounding the second in command. The source of this negativity, while not unfamiliar, eluded him. He was sure, though, that this cloud of energy did not belong to her.

Carefully considering the timeline of recent events, ShemRahya started to see things more clearly, but he needed a few more details before solidifying a theory.

"What was CheRahna's energy like after you gave her the codex, Captain?" he asked.

After reflecting for a moment, Rahzu answered, "She was obviously confused, but largely relieved . . . I think it was the first time in a long time she had heard anything good involving her uncle. Yeah . . . she had a tentative but positive glow about her."

"The next time you saw her, what did her energy projection look like?"

"It was dark. She was accusatory, insolent, and overall negative. There was something devious about her demeanor . . . I just can't figure it out." Rahzu was still showing his frustration.

"If I'm hearing you correctly, after you told her about Abraham and gave her the codex, she was fine, things were looking positive?"

"Yes," Rahzu replied.

"Then the next time you saw her, she is essentially the exact opposite, correct?"

"Yes, that's correct, Lieutenant." Rahzu, though still unable to form a rational explanation, could see what his trainee was doing, leading him to the answer.

After pausing for a moment to collect his thoughts, ShemRahya informed Rahzu what he himself had witnessed. "On my way back here, after our earlier conversation, I saw the commander talking to herself. While this in itself was not that unusual—she's always thinking out loud—it was the nature of the talk that troubled me...She was heatedly arguing with herself. As if there were two different CheRahnas inside her, each taking a position . . . At the time, I didn't think that much about it, but now . . ." ShemRahya changed the direction of his questions. "You said you erased the data recordings containing the variant frequencies and Admiral YetziRah's visit, correct?"

"I did."

"Is there any way CheRahna could have accessed that data prior to you deleting it?"

Rahzu distinctly remembered checking the crystal's logins, which only he, CheRahna, and the security team had access to. "No one but me accessed that information. What are you getting at, Lieutenant?"

"Well, sir, if we know that the commander received no additional information other than that which was in the codex or that you specifically told her, then that leaves only one other explanation for her change in attitude." ShemRahya left the captain hanging on purpose, seeing if he would come to the same conclusion.

Rahzu, though following the lieutenant's thinking, was still lost as to what it all meant. He was too close to the situation to be of any use. Sensing Rahzu's confusion, ShemRahya spoke his mind. "Commander CheRahna is being fed information by someone else."

"But who?! No one aboard this ship, other than myself, had any of the information about Abraham, ET Rah, or . . ." Suddenly it hit him. There were actually, at one time, three individuals who had been aboard his ship who did have this information: Lt. ShemRahya, Ensign RahKael, and Admiral YetziRah.

Rahzu quickly ruled out the ensign as being the source of the leak since she had expired before all the turmoil began. ShemRahya, though completely loyal, could unknowingly have had his thoughts read by the commander. Rahzu realized that he stood more of a chance of becoming the ruler of all Dimeria than that happening, especially since he had told him to guard his thoughts. No, that only left one. "YetziRah!" He spoke out loud.

"Precisely," ShemRahya confirmed.

"But how is that possible, she abhors him!" Rahzu was baffled but knew this theory had merit.

ShemRahya let out a worried chuckle. "I can't believe I didn't put it together sooner."

"Put what together?"

"That foreign energy that has attached itself to CheRahna was the same energy that was attached to you. It was right after the investigation began into the ensign's death when I first noticed it. At the time, I didn't put much stock in it. I had no business questioning you or your affairs. Later, when you told me of the admiral's surprise visit, I assumed it was his energy residue . . . Sorry, Captain, I should have paid closer attention to the details." ShemRahya, as security officer, felt that he had not done his job.

Rahzu immediately stifled the lieutenant's self-criticism. "Look, ShemRahya, we're not used to dealing with such subterfuge. YetziRah's a master of deception and manipulation; we never had a chance . . . Fooling us, though, is not what concerns me most!"

"Oh?" ShemRahya asked.

"How did he meet with CheRahna, and how did he manage to influence her? What did he say? That's what bothers me."

"I agree, sir. I don't understand either; her hatred and distrust of him is well known," the lieutenant agreed.

Both Golds were silent as they digested this new predicament. Rahzu, exasperated, finally said, "Unfortunately, there's not a lot we can do about this right now. There are several matters that are more pressing."

As Rahzu informed ShemRahya about the unexpected expansion of one of the amber crystal portals on Earth, the lieutenant could not help but wonder if YetziRah was responsible for that also. Although the admiral had placed the portals there millennia ago, the captain doubted if that was his intention at this time.

"He's still not ready," Rahzu said cryptically.

"Not ready! What does that mean, Captain?" ShemRahya asked empathically.

Although he had not originally planned on sharing some of this information with anyone, especially his discovery about the God seed, Rahzu knew that YetziRah's apparent manipulation of his commander meant that he was in more danger than he had thought. Though he did not have all the facts, he could not let what he knew lie; if the worst came to pass, it was too important.

Rahzu started out slowly, making sure he chose his words carefully. "ShemRahya, there are a few more things I need to tell you about. Things that could get you sent to chaos, right alongside me."

ShemRahya's reaction was stoically silent, as if he expected as much.

Rahzu continued, "While I was conducting my own investigation into Ensign RahKael's tragic end, I came upon a variant energy frequency I had not encountered before; it's not even registered in the data files. As it turns out, it has never existed before."

"An unknown energy, hmm . . . What could it be?" ShemRahya wondered.

"Not a what, my friend, but a who . . ."

ShemRahya remained speechless, paying attention to every detail. *I knew there was something not quite right about those energy frequencies*, he thought to himself.

Rahzu added, "I can't believe it myself, but the prophecy seems to have begun."

"Prophecy?! What prophecy?! I've never heard of . . ."

The captain quieted his security officer. He spoke slowly as he recited the tale as it had been told to him. "Long before we came to PU 431, eons before the Great Purge, a humanoid race occupied the Earth. They had evolved to be at one with the cosmos, able to see the past and the future while occupying the present. They had existed for millions of years, charting the stars, uncovering the mysteries of creation, and forecasting future events. I think you will agree that being able to see future events is a remarkable, but dangerous gift, for anyone."

"Yes, sir, it is . . .What happened to them?" ShemRahya asked.

Rahzu saw that his young officer was mesmerized by the tale, hanging on his every word, just as he was when he first learned of it. "No one knows for sure. Some say they became so preoccupied with other timelines and different dimensions that they failed to take care of their basic needs in the present. Others say they went extinct after some Earthly cataclysm. Some even believe they transcended their physical bodies and escaped to a more ethereal existence . . . It's all just conjecture, though."

ShemRahya impatiently dug further. "What did they foretell, Captain?"

"Patience, Lieutenant. Patience," Rahzu calmed his friend. "About six millennia ago, two Egyptian magicians, while searching for lost energy crystals deep within an abandoned mine in South Africa, discovered several buried coffers. Inside one of them was a copper scroll, which was written in a forgotten, ancient language. Because of their resourcefulness, they were able to decipher the cryptic writings." Here he paused for effect. The captain, although his mood was serious, enjoyed sharing this tale with his mentee, just as his mentor had shared it with him. "Though the scrolls contained many predictions, there's one that is extremely pertinent to our current situation... It has been foretold that a Yah God seed would be born when the Yahs were close to supremacy. He would sire seven sons, and that those sons would someday rule."

"Rule what?" ShemRahya asked, a little more calmly than before.

"I'm not entirely sure. That was all that was passed along through the ages. But if I had to guess, it's more than just the Earth," Rahzu speculated.

"Forgive me, Captain, but what does this have to do with us, in the now?" ShemRahya was not one who enjoyed long, drawn-out stories. He was a straight-to-the-point kind of Dimerian.

While Rahzu again ruminated on what he was about to disclose, he could not help but remember the prophetic warning Abraham had issued to him. Though he still had no idea what it meant, he knew Abraham would not have made him memorize it if it was of no importance.

> "A mysterious box, once well hid
> Ultimate Evil contained, under its lid.
> Destruction, pain, torment do hold.
> An unwanted soul, not bought but sold.
> For whosoever shall open to look and see?
> Will set free its wrath for eternity."

Rahzu decided he would tell ShemRahya about this cryptic riddle only if he took the other, more pressing predication seriously.

"I believe that the unknown energy frequency I detected belongs to none other than this prophesied God seed, the very same human male, Jonathan Arlin Hawthorn, number 99985, who was on board this ship. I think that's significant."

ShemRahya stood astonished; surprised he had never heard any of this before. He still, however, failed to see what this had to do with the expanding portal.

As if reading his mind, Rahzu raised his hand to halt the lieutenant's question. "I know what you're about to ask, but let me finish . . . It has been uncovered that the Earth contains the largest piece of WEDEC outside of Dimeria. It is located deep within the Earth's core and provides it with its unique, protective magnetic fields. YetziRah and Xanix Rah have long been exploring ways in which they can utilize the Yah crystal, but thus far have had little success. My guess is that they want to somehow use this Yah in human form in order to unlock the secrets to manipulating the WEDEC's power. I think that's why the portals have expansive properties to begin with." Rahzu now was looking for his lieutenant's input.

After a long sigh, ShemRahya started to understand the significance of Rahzu's findings. He still had a few questions, though. "Sir, why don't you think that the admiral is responsible for the portal's growth? You said 'he's still not ready,' but why?"

"Because he doesn't know that the God seed is alive and has been located."

"What about Ensign RahKael, I thought she was working for him?" ShemRahya asked.

"She was. It appears that, although she stumbled upon the God seed's frequency too, she was, thankfully, unable to pass this information on."

Recounting all these recent events, ShemRahya needed some clarity to ensure he was understanding Rahzu correctly. "So you're telling me that, somehow, Abraham used his frequency, while in another universe, to revive the human male on board this ship, and then that same male, who turns out to be this prophesied God seed, killed RahKael just before she could inform her master of her discovery. He battled you and then got a ride back to Earth, none of us any of the wiser?" He was not finished, and Rahzu allowed him to continue. "And it just so happens that around the same time, the humans back on Earth decided to begin investigating the portals, and they started to somehow, accidentally, expand. Is that what you're telling me?"

Admittedly, it all sounded pretty unlikely once put into words. However, that is just how prophecies work—a series of events tied together by the strings of the cosmos, only to wind up at some predicted end.

Responding to ShemRahya's questions still gave him no answers. Rahzu kept it simple, though. "I'm not telling you any of that, even though that is how it appears to have happened. All I'm saying is that the prophecy has begun and that Jonathan Hawthorn, the Yah God seed, has yet to sire any sons." Accounting for the vagueness of his retort, Rahzu said, "I'm sorry, I don't have the answers at this time. That's why I came to you. I need your advice, your trusted council as to what we should do."

Taken aback, not so much by the captain not having an answer as by his asking for his help, ShemRahya calmly thought more objectively about the recent chain of events. It all started to make sense: the dead bird, human male number 99985 blowing his implant, Ensign Ra Kael's mission, YetziRah's surprise visits, CheRahna's radical change in behavior, the two different energy variations, one old and the other new; and finally, the existence of a prophesied God seed. Something epic was happening, of that much he was sure. The intricate web of lies, deceit, and manipulation was starting to unravel, at least for the captain and himself.

While always loyal to the House of Rah, ShemRahya cared about all of Dimeria. He knew that because of their evil nature and unrelenting lust for power, neither YetziRah nor Xanix Rah could ever learn of the God seed's existence. Keeping this information hidden was of the utmost importance.

Once he was through collecting his thoughts, the security officer faced and addressed his captain. "Rahzu, I'm honored that you have asked for my help. I hope I don't disappoint you." With that, he continued. "This situation is extremely complex and sensitive, one that I am not totally unfamiliar with. I have seen similar tactics and ploys by those gambling properties in the Blade Wars; that's why I left. I wanted no part of it. I fear that by the end of this we will be either praised as heroes, saviors of our House and Dimeria, or tortured and killed as treacherous traitors. And as you said, sent together to chaos . . . Regardless of the consequences, there is nothing good that can be had by telling the current Rah leadership. The less we divulge, the safer things will be."

Glad that the lieutenant believed him and was willing to help, Rahzu presented another dilemma. "We'll have to come up with a good way to keep the Yah's energy frequency masked even from the sensors. If we don't, sooner or later, he'll be discovered."

ShemRahya quickly piped in. "I've got that taken care of, sir. I've seen every trick in the book about how to mask one's energy profile and even came up with a few of my own. Only someone who is incredibly detail-oriented in the methods of energy manipulation and who is actually looking for his specific frequency would be able to detect him after I get through." To some, this might sound like arrogance or cockiness, but the fact was Lt. ShemRahya excelled at everything he did. He was not one who issued idle boasts.

"Good. What should we do about Commander CheRahna?" Rahzu knew this was a much more fragile situation.

"Sir, as much as I don't like it, I think you're going to have to talk to her, and fast. If YetziRah is manipulating her, we need to find out what he's done to her and what she knows. Everything rides on her, Rahzu." ShemRahya knew how emotionally tangled this meeting was apt to be but saw no way around it. Rahzu was the only one aboard who outranked her, and likely the only Rah alive who could bring her back to reality.

Rahzu agreed. There was just no way around dealing with her. Although he knew that this was going to be difficult, he still clung to the hope that

CheRahna had not retreated to her former, untrusting self, and that he could still include her in what was happening now. An uneasy thought passed through Rahzu's mind—CheRahna was going to become either a powerful ally or a dangerous foe. This absolutely left him with a feeling of dread and despair, one he could not shake. Now, perhaps, was a good time to have ShemRahya memorize the cryptic riddle. Maybe he could make some sense of it.

CHAPTER

FIFTY FOUR

STANDING IN FRONT of the immense amber crystal was truly an awe-inspiring experience. It resembled a large piece of smoky quartz, only without the multitudes of terminal gem points. Not even taking into account what the oddity was or what it was made of, Justin could still not imagine how such a large object came to be in one of the remotest places on the planet.

Realizing the uncertainty of their situation, Captain LaMarr looked at Dr. Walker and issued a warning. "Deborah, be careful not to get too close to the crystal. We still don't know what it is." He paused momentarily while looking up at the towering face. "I still suspect that if its magnetic pull grabs either of us, it will somehow absorb the energy from our ZPEs."

She responded with perplexity. "I thought our suits would be safe. At least that's what I gathered from Steven and Roger's explanation. Are you now saying they're not?!"

Without giving her a physics lesson, Justin merely expressed his fears that they may not be correct and that it might be best to err on the side of caution. Also, considering the necessity to expedite their assignment, Captain LaMarr determined that they could cover more ground if they split up. He was confident that Deborah was keen to the real danger they were in and would keep her distance. Additionally, since everything was being recorded by the exosuit's video cameras, Justin could have the Hab link to Deborah's video feed if necessary and view things in real time from her perspective if the need arose.

The one other factor that helped him decide to split up became apparent when they first touched down on the bottom. The ocean floor, made up of largely of dead, decayed marine life, was easily disturbed, creating a fine particulate cloud. Two exosuits working together in such proximity would likely stir up this silt-like material, reducing visibility to near zero.

As they separated, Deborah toward the west side of the chasm and Justin toward the east, he gave one final warning. "Be careful not to get to close to that cliff," he said, pointing to the rubble field near its base.

"Oh, don't you worry. I have no intention of going anywhere near that mess," Dr. Walker said.

"If you see anything unusual, just patch me into your video feed, understood?"

She knew that the captain was being cautious for a reason, which in this environment was the prudent thing to do, but she wanted to get to it. There was work to be done. "I will, darling, you can count on it. I'll be okay, I promise," she responded.

"You better. I've already lost one of my best girls, I don't want to lose another," he said, referring to Ariella.

After separating, both Justin and Deborah made a sweep of their respective areas, taking note of anything unusual—that is, anything unusual in an environment 6,000 fathoms underwater.

Everything was eerily calm and deadly silent. All sea life, other than the bacteria around the thermal vents, appeared to be nonexistent. Not even the current, which normally flowed due to changing temperatures, was noticeable.

Shining the LED lighting attached to his exosuit toward the crystal, Captain LaMarr was still baffled how there could be absolutely no transference of light. It was as if the amber object absorbed it, like it was a black hole.

Now, pointing a laser at the ocean floor perpendicular to the base of the crystal, he was able to gather temperature, pressure, radiation, and magnetic flux readings. While only negligible changes in temperature, pressure, and radiation were noted, the magnetism had again increased substantially. It was now at 5,900 gauss, which was odd since he could not detect any energy source responsible for the increase. It was not coming from his suit, at least not that he could measure.

Quickly, in the interest of safety, Justin began to think about how close to this object he could get before the magnetic attraction grabbed him. At present, he was about 10 feet away.

Turning westward and looking down the vertical face of the crystal, the captain saw Dr. Walker, who was almost half a football field away. She had heeded his warning and remained safely distant from the crystal. She too, as well as the Hab, then verified the reading he was getting.

Concerned that the magnetic attraction might continue to rise, presenting a potentially serious problem for an up-close observation, Justin ordered Deborah to continue to observe and scan the crystal, but to keep her distance. The last thing he needed was to have to pry her off the magnetically charged object. He, however, was going in for a closer look.

Determining that he was in even more danger than Deborah, Justin methodically surveyed the area for a safe solution, which he found. As he moved carefully toward the eastern cliff wall, so as not to stir up too much silt, he pulled out his tethering line. He wedged a piton into a small but stable crack, and attached his line to it. As he retreated from the cliff face, carefully releasing the tension back toward the crystal, Justin was now on his own secured line. He felt confident that if he did get into any trouble, he would be able to use the suit's winch to free himself. The plan was, of course, to get a sample of the mysterious object. Those were his orders.

Although not a gemologist and having no experience in the proper fracturing of crystalline objects, Captain LaMarr had the next best thing—a plasma torch. This amazing tool of modern design, which generated temperatures greater than those found on the surface of the sun, could essentially cut through anything, quickly and precisely. Considering that the Sea Lab's external shell, as well as those of the exosuits, was composed of nickel titanium zirconium alloy, which could withstand incredible amounts of heat before melting, this tool was necessary for repairs or in the event of a situation where cutting was required. Hopefully, if he could get close enough, he would be able to collect the small sample required for study.

Tentatively, as he approached the anomaly, Justin increased the tension on his tether. Though most of the suit's functions operated by voice command, he cautiously programmed the computer to automatically retract in the event that the magnetism readings approached the winch's pulling capacity. Luckily, too, the exosuit's motorized appendages gave the wearer the strength of twenty men, which could aid him in making this assignment a success.

With torch in hand, he slowly crept toward the object. When he was within five feet, he darkened his visor and turned on the cutter. A bright lightning-like glow illuminated the area as the plasma beam extended nearly a foot out from the torch. After adjusting the tool to cut no more than around four inches, Justin was ready. Expecting to make quick work of this task, he was not prepared for what happened next.

Moving the torch closer to perform the extraction, as predicted, he felt the magnetic pull that the crystal was emitting. After the initial tug, he was able to adjust his approach so that, once again, he directed the torch smoothly toward the target. Holding the plasma cutter at a 45-degree angle, he began moving it in a slanted, rotational motion, hoping to remove a conical sample. Several seconds later, a problem became apparent—the torch was not cutting. Also, the light produced by the plasma beam was absent, absorbed by the crystal. "How is this possible?" Justin whispered aloud. There was not even a scratch on the amber object's surface.

To inspect the torch to see if it was indeed functioning correctly, Captain LaMarr, with much more effort than expected, was able to successfully pull the plasma tool away from the object. Once more, the beam lit up the area.

Although he would have liked to determine what was causing this phenomenon, events more pressing began to occur. Alarms programmed in the exosuit's computer started to ring, alerting him to a massive increase in magnetism being detected. Suddenly, at the same instant that Steven announced the change in readings, Justin's winch activated, pulling him rapidly away from the crystal's faceted face.

Now at a safer distance, some 50 feet away, he stopped the winch and responded to the Hab. "Steven, locate the source of the magnetic spike while I . . ." Before he could finish, Deborah screamed his name. "Juusstinnn!"

With even more alarms sounding, he turned to Deborah's last known location, only to see her being pulled across the ocean floor toward the crystal. The stirred-up white silt behind her looked much like the spray of water produced by a water skier. And though this was all happening very quickly, to Justin, thanks to his training, everything appeared to be happening in slow motion.

Even before Dr. Walker violently collided with the crystal, the veteran SEAL had activated his thruster and was rapidly heading her way. Firmly but calmly, Justin called out, "I see you, Deborah. I'm on my way. Brace for impact!" he yelled at the last second, to no avail. Deborah hit the object hard. "Deborah!" Justin yelled. There was no answer. "Steven, the magnetic force of the crystal has got hold of Doctor Walker. I'm heading to her right now. I think she's unconscious. What are her vitals?"

Lt. Barett responded smartly, "Doctor Walker is stable. But, Captain, I'm getting gauss readings over 10,000 and climbing. Plus . . ." He paused, calculating the remaining data. "Yes . . . the temperature is dropping; radiation is increasing, and the tension sensors indicate . . ."

Captain LaMarr interrupted. "The crystal's growing again."

"Yes, sir, that's affirmative." Before Lt. Barett could identify the source of the magnetic spike, Captain LaMarr already suspected the cause. It was the plasma torch. However, now he feared that the crystal was attempting to draw energy from Dr. Walker's exosuit.

Once within sight of her, Justin asked, "Steven, check the status of Doctor Walker's ZPE."

"Holy shit, Captain!" Lt. Barett uncharacteristically exclaimed. "The ZPE is operating at near full capacity . . . What the hell is that thing?!" he finished with more of a statement than a question.

Since Dr. Walker was unconscious, Captain LaMarr had to inspect her carefully from a distance, so as not to get pulled into the object as she had. Though he could feel the magnetic pull, Justin had wisely extended the crampons located on the bottom of his feet, allowing him to keep his distance.

Understanding that sooner or later the growing object would cause more massive tremors, dislodging boulders from the surrounding chasm walls, anchoring himself to the cliffside was out of the question. There was only one solution.

"Steven, I want you to override Doctor Walker's computer and remote fire her grappling hook toward my location. Can you do that?" Captain LaMarr knew it was possible, but did they have time to perform the task?

Lt. Barett answered after a long pause. "I've got Roger on it now, Captain. He needs thirty seconds."

Before he could respond, the Earth started to shake violently. Boulders fell from the cliff walls, crashing into the crystal and onto the surrounding ocean floor. It caught Justin so off guard that he found himself flat on his back. As he got up, he pleaded, "Roger, you have to hurry and shoot that thing while I can still see her." The silt continued to disperse into the surrounding waters. In a few more seconds, he was going to lose sight of Dr. Walker. "Roger?!"

"Firing in three, two, one," Roger shouted.

From a compartment located just over the dorsal thruster, a tethered grappling hook shot out toward the captain. Luckily, he had played third base for his local church softball team, or the hook would likely have brained him.

With hook in hand, Justin attached it to the tow hitch situated on the lower rear of his suit. "I've got it, Roger. Take up the slack. I'm going to fire up my thrusters and try to pull her free." Retracting the excess line, Roger gave Captain LaMarr the go-ahead.

In engaging his thrusters, Justin was now floating, no longer subject to the jostling effects of the surrounding area. He could now see just how serious the quake was. In an attempt to prevent nausea, which typically occurred when one tried to focus on a single shaking object, he blankly stared across the abyss.

"Thrusters at half power, and still nothing," Justin radioed the Hab. "Increasing to maximum power." Still nothing happened.

Determining that his present course of action was futile, Justin turned off his thrusters and fell to the ocean floor. He had one more trick he wanted to try.

"Roger, feed me another 50 feet of line."

"Yes, Captain, but what are you planning?"

"I'm thinking that if I take off at maximum thrust, when the extra line tightens, I might have built up enough momentum to jerk Doctor Walker off that damn thing."

Doing a few quick calculations, Steven said, "That's going to put a force of almost 75,000 psi on that cable, Captain. It's only rated for fifty!"

"We don't have a choice, Lieutenant. Hopefully, the engineers who designed the limits included a factor of safety of at least 1.5 or we're screwed," Captain LaMarr said.

"It'll work," Roger chimed in.

"Here goes nothing." Captain LaMarr took off.

The 50 feet of cable proved to be just enough, because Justin reached maximum velocity after traveling 48 feet. At the instant the line tightened, fear that the tether would snap or that he would tear their suits apart engulfed him. He could not stand the thought of losing Dr. Walker. Thankfully, that is not what happened. Instead of the line snapping, Captain LaMarr felt a strong backward jerk, then nothing. With thrusters still operating at maximum capacity, the cable became taut again. He had done it; Dr. Walker was free.

"It worked!" he yelled triumphantly.

"Hell yes!" Roger shouted.

"Good job, Captain, quick thinking!" Lt. Barett added.

"Roger, activate the doctor's thrusters at three-quarter power or it'll take us an hour to get back up," Captain LaMarr said.

"You betcha, Captain." Roger answered.

With Deborah's thrusters activated, they were rapidly ascending. All Justin needed to do was to avoid any falling boulders; the Earth was still shaking in the depths.

"Steven, prepare the crew for the shock wave. It should be there any second now," Captain LaMarr warned.

"Already done, sir." Lt. Barett had been watching the screen, taking note of the wave as it propagated up from the chasm depths. The quake registered 6.9 on the Richter scale.

Over the loudspeaker, Lt. Barett alerted the crew. "Everyone, here it comes. Ten seconds . . . five, four, three, brace for impact!"

The wave hit with tremendous effect, causing alarms to sound as the Hab shook forcefully. Thanks to the crew's preparation, however, and the fact that the Sea Lab's footings rested atop high-tension springs, which were designed for this specific purpose, the damage to the underwater laboratory was minimal.

After the initial shock wave had subsided, Steven silenced the alarms and performed a quick systems check.

"How's everything up there, Steven?" Captain LaMarr asked.

"A-okay, sir. A couple of overturned chairs, a broken table, and, sir . . . We're going to have to deep six your coffee mug. She cracked right down the middle. But other than that, all systems are go."

"Damn, that was my favorite mug . . . oh well. What are the readings at the crystal? Are we still up and running?"

"The magnetism and radiation levels are rapidly receding, but the temperature is still lower than normal."

"What about the size? Is it still growing?" Captain LaMarr asked, fearing the answer.

"Yes, sir, it is," Lt. Barett answered nervously. "And if my calculations are correct, there'll be another tremor within the next few minutes. It's going to be bigger than the last one, Captain," he added.

"All right, Steven." Justin paused to think. "I want you to get Frank to assemble the crew in the sub bay, just as a precaution. The Hab is tough, Lieutenant; she'll be able to handle the quake. I'm more concerned with the boulders falling on her from that damn cliff. The sub bay is the strongest part of the structure. Get everyone in there. Are we clear?"

"Yes, sir, I got it."

"Good. After that, get on the horn to control and let them know what's going on down here. I'll be there as fast as I can," Captain LaMarr directed.

"I'm on it, sir."

"Roger." Captain LaMarr now focused his attention on his technician.

"Yes, Captain?"

"At present velocity, we won't be there for another twenty minutes. What can you do to speed things up?"

Roger briefly studied how the captain was dragging Dr. Walker through the water when the idea came to him. "Captain, I think by retracting Dr. Walker's cable, I can increase your speed." Roger said.

"Okay, how so?"

"Well, you know I like NASCAR, and . . ."

Captain LaMarr calmly broke in. "Roger . . . give me the short version, we are in a bit of a crisis here."

"Oh . . . yeah . . . okay, well, just like race cars, you and Doctor Walker are creating drag while you move through the water. If we can get you closer, we can largely reduce that friction and the two of you together will be able to travel faster than apart," Roger finished joyfully, finally justifying the endless hours spent watching the races.

"Roger, you will always have a job working for me. Do it."

"Yes, sir," Roger said with pride.

As Roger retracted the tether, Justin thought how lucky he was to have him aboard. Now, as he clutched onto Deborah's legs, lining up on her ventral side opposite of the dorsal thruster, he immediately noticed the speed increase. He was, as Roger referred to it, drafting behind Deborah. "It's working Roger, you're a genius."

"Smart, brilliant . . . I suppose I can handle being called a genius."

"Well, Mister Edison, do you think it'll be safe if we increase our thruster jets to maximum power?" Captain LaMarr asked with a touch of humor. Considering the stressful situation they were in, he was using humor to relax himself, hopefully assisting in his performance.

"As long as you hold on tight and avoid the backwash of her and the thrusters, everything should be fine, Captain."

Giving the order to both Roger and his exosuit's computer, Justin said, "Increasing thrusters to maximum power." Now traveling like two race cars down the track, the captain recalculated his estimated arrival time and was astonished to discover he had shaved off another five minutes.

"Hell yeah! Roger, I'll be on site in thirteen minutes. Prepare the air lock and get the med cart ready for Doctor Walker. We need to get her revived and quick."

From out of nowhere, a weak, southern voice echoed over the air waves. "I'm awake, darling. Feelin' like I just came in last in an ass kickin' contest, but I'm awake."

"I am so glad to hear your voice, Deborah. I'll have you on board and out of that suit ASAP," Justin happily stated.

"What in the hell happened? The last thing I remember was that I was being pulled toward that amber thingee." It was obvious that Deborah was suffering from a slight concussion; she sounded like she was drunk.

"I'll explain it later, I promise. For now, let's just say that you took a hard hit and we're all glad you're okay," Justin empathically said.

"Why are you holding my legs . . . and why are we going so fast? Are we in danger, Justin?" She was becoming more lucid. Unfortunately, Justin did not have to answer her question.

The cliffside walls around them started to shake as large chunks of its façade fell into the abyss. The wave was moving with so much force that it actually deflected the cliff face as it traveled upward, toward the Hab.

"Steven! Another aftershock is on its way . . . and by the looks of it, it's going to be stronger than the last."

"Affirmative, sir, at the epicenter, sensors registered this one at . . . 7.4. It should be her in . . . just over two minutes, Captain."

"Is the crew in the sub bay yet?"

Looking at the video monitor, Steven answered, "Looks like Frank is arriving with the rest of them now, sir."

"Good. Get them to start loading all the essentials into the PRIEST in case we have to evacuate."

"I read you, sir, but do you really think that's necessary right now?" Lt. Barett rarely questioned his captain's orders; he knew the strength of the Hab and thought this to be a bit of overkill.

With a hint of agitation in his voice, Justin squawked, "Lieutenant, have you forgot your training? You know how we operate. We need to be prepared for all contingencies . . . and right now, I'm worried that the fucking world is going to come crashing down on our happy little home. Is that clear?"

"Yes, sir, Captain, I wasn't questioning . . ."

"Stifle that shit, soldier! Just get it done!" Captain LaMarr was rarely so terse giving orders and seldom used profanity, but he had a bad feeling welling up in the pit of his stomach. He was also upset that there was absolutely nothing more he could do at that moment; he and Deborah were still almost ten minutes away.

Back at the Sea Lab, Frank Gilmore was efficiently directing everyone in the sub bay and the loading of the mini-sub. Although fear was plastered across all of their faces, Frank's laid-back demeanor kept the rest of the crew calm enough to prepare for evacuation, if that was indeed what was needed. Even Robert Washington, who was normally against anything that distracted him from his work, was being receptive to Frank's direction. Nancy and Roger worked together as if they were a precision drill team, quickly getting the airlock and med cart ready for the captain and Deborah's arrival. Roger also performed the final preparation on the PRIEST'S computer system. If they had to leave, it was ready.

While everyone was preoccupied with EVAC procedures, they all were aware of the severity of their situation. Steven was on the bridge monitoring the readings at the site and watching the shock wave as it approached the research facility. Instead of getting caught off guard again, which was how he felt during the last tremor, he was going to ensure that he and the crew were more prepared this time.

Grasping the intercom, he announced, "Everyone, put everything not secure on the deck now. We've got another tremor approaching rapidly. It'll be here in less than two minutes. I want everyone to gather in the center of the sub bay, away from everything, and huddle together, tightly." Steven watched them through the onboard video monitor. Seeing that they were all staring at each other, unmoving, as if in a state of shock, he ordered, "Move it, people, now!" With that, everyone snapped into action.

Luckily, everything other than what they were loading onto the PRIEST had already been secured. The remaining items were quickly thrown together and covered with a cargo net, which was then attached to hitches located in the deck. After that was complete, they all assembled in the center of the bay as directed. They were only there a few seconds when the apocalypse began.

Outside the Sea Lab, some 500 feet up the abyssal precipice, was a large basaltic outcropping protruding to form a ledge; it stuck out approximately 25 feet. Already precariously cantilevered, the first tremor caused the immense slab to develop a shallow fissure along its top and a quarter of the way down both sides. When the shock wave finally took hold of the Hab, it was only a nanosecond before it reached the ledge.

The Earth trembled, bubbles rose from the depths, and boulders from above fell all around, many pelting the outcropping and others, the Hab. Part of the lab's foundation, under the eastern wing, which contained the offices, science and medical labs, and living quarters; partially collapsed into the chasm. But so far, all was well. The Sea Lab was safe.

When the worst of the shaking, which lasted several minutes, was over, it appeared that they had dodged the proverbial bullet. They were wrong. High above, over the projecting rock, the last of the shock waves subsided. The tremors had been so violent that a large rectangular section of diorite, located on the ocean floor near the top edge of the trench, had slid down a mound of silt and teetered dangerously over the abyss. Seesawing back and forth for a few minutes, it looked as if the large rock was slowly starting to settle. That was until the sandy bottom on which it rested, like an hourglass, started draining into the ancient fault.

It only took a few moments before the large rock became unbalanced and plunged into the trench. Since it was so dense and heavy, its shape had little effect on its trajectory as it rapidly descended through the water. It was headed directly for the large outcropping, almost 1,000 feet below. Forty seconds later, it would reach its target.

Andesitic basalt, very dense and particularly heavy, is a strong material. It is commonly used in railroad beds because of its high compression strength and the fact that it is so widespread. However, once a crack develops, it cleaves fairly easily. Since the earthquake had already caused the cantilevered stone to fissure, it would only be a matter of time before it would fail under its own weight. The massive piece of falling diorite merely sped up the process.

The instant the falling object hit the basalt, a twenty-foot chunk of stone sheared off at the fissure. Now, two large pieces of rock plummeted toward the Hab's location.

The crew of the Sea Lab was beginning to relax, as the worst of the quake appeared to be over. As designed, the habitat had withstood the 7.4-magnitude jolt with only minimal damage. Even the area where the foundation had partially collapsed was in no structural danger.

Silencing the alarms, Steven now checked the measurements at the crystal. It seemed that it had once again, with the removal of any significant power source, ceased its growth spurt. Temperature and radiation readings started returning to expected levels. He was just about to contact the captain with an update when it happened.

The two large falling chunks of igneous rock, although they did not land directly on the top of the Hab, caromed off the cliff's face and hit the facility on its north side with such force that the jolt knocked it off its support columns. The structure fell some 15 feet before hitting bottom.

As the Hab fell, the crew was thrown into the air. Once it landed, they crashed violently onto the sub bay floor. Even though it was unpredicted, and no one was prepared, the episode caused no serious injuries, only a few bumps and bruises. But now, with the flood pool resting on the ocean bottom, it would be impossible for them to escape in the PRIEST. Another problem was that the air lock hatch too rested against the silty floor.

Slowly getting to his feet, Lt. Barett got his bearings before starting to figure out what had happened. Looking at the external cameras and checking the Hab GPS coordinates; he quickly determined that whatever had hit them had knocked the facility clear of its footings. What were they going to do now, was the first thought that came to the young SEAL's mind? But that would have to wait; he needed to check on the crew.

Looking into the video monitor tasked to watch the sub bay, Steven clutched the intercom and asked, "Is everyone all right?" As the crew moved and started getting up, he could see that no one was any the worse for wear.

Roger, who was already on his way to perform a systems check on the equipment, responded, "We're all okay down here. A little shaken up, but okay." He then looked around and inquired, "Steven . . . are we on the bottom?"

It took a moment for Steven to respond; he did not want to break the bad news to the crew. However, knowing that he must, the lieutenant affirmed, "Yes, Roger . . . we are." Silence filled the Hab as the words echoed throughout the sub bay. Everyone knew what that meant; they were trapped, deep under the ocean.

Roger, not forgetting about the crew members who were not on board, asked, "What are we going to do about the captain and Doctor Walker? How are they going to get back in?"

Lt. Barett had already been thinking about that very question. It popped into his head the instant he discovered that the facility was resting on the bottom. Thankfully, he had a solution. "Roger, I need you to go to the rec room.

We're going to use the bell's docking chamber to get the captain and Deborah back inside."

Obviously still shaken, literally, from the earthquake and subsequent jolt from the falling rocks, Roger was clueless as to how they were going to accomplish this feat. "How are we going . . ." he started to say, but Steven broke in.

"You need to seal the docking chamber, fill it with water, and then pressurize the damn thing. All you have to do then is open the docking ring and presto, they're in. Since the doc is now conscious, it shouldn't be a problem."

Roger thought for a second and then said, "Since the chamber is not big enough, we'll have to bring them in one at a time, but it should work. Quick thinking, Steve." Roger again looked around the sub bay, seeing the med cart overturned and its supplies strewn everywhere, he had to ask, "Is the rest of the Hab okay, are we safe?" It was a question to which everyone bent an ear to hear.

"So far, I can see nothing that is currently posing any danger to any of us," Steven voiced over the intercom.

An audible sound of relief was heard throughout the sub bay. Nancy, still quite frazzled from the whole experience, began to sob with joy. Frank, though silent, smiled and gave two thumbs up to the camera. Robert joined in too with a loud, "Hell yeah!"

Although he sensed that the worst was over, Lt. Barett did not want the crew to relax too much; there could still be more unexpected aftershocks. Also, since they were positioned essentially within a large fault, where the tectonic plates met, regular quakes could and did happen frequently. There was no telling what else the massive tremors jarred loose.

Lt Barett realized that until they could survey not only the damage to the Hab, but the surrounding area, they could ill afford to let their guards down. Lt. Barett grabbed the mic again. "Let's everyone stay alert. Remember where we are and what just happened. We have no idea the damage done to the trench wall behind us or to the ledge sitting below us. We need to keep focus and get the captain and Doctor Walker back safely inside. Then we can start to figure out what to do next."

Seeing that his words were received, he continued, saying, "For right now, everyone travels in twos. Roger, you and Nancy head to the docking bay and get it ready. Frank, you and Robert start walking around, performing an eyes-on inspection, just in case the sensors are missing something. I'm goin' to stay here in the bridge and try to figure out if everything is still working. Sound like a plan, everyone?"

"Sounds good, Steven, me and Robert need to stretch our legs anyway," Frank answered.

"I want to check my experiments too," Robert said in his usual snobbish tone. But, as he and Frank started to leave; he graciously said, "Thank you, Steven."

Surprised, Steven laughed a little, saying, "You're welcome, Robert."

As everyone departed the sub bay, heading out on their respective assignments, Steven got to work determining what was working and what was not. Hopefully, he would have some answers before the captain arrived.

CHAPTER

FIFTY FIVE

DESPITE THE LONG drive along the winding road, the ride was a pleasant one. The continuous hum of the Jeep's knobby tires on the pavement, while not conducive for conversation, did allow everyone time to reflect on recent events.

Even Jack, who was never at a loss for words, remained silently fixated on the road as he navigated the vehicle past El Yunque, commonly called the Anvil; it had been a long time since he had been part of a mission of such importance.

In fact, Jack had not even been that busy wrangling crocs as of late. The Caribbean had, for the most part, already grown up, being extensively developed. Other than the occasional relocation call or charter flight, the only adventures he had been involved in recently were of his own making.

Once again, his interpersonal skills had placed him a position to be part of something epic, something that could have worldwide ramifications. He was loving every minute of it. The bonus was that he got to work side by side with an extraterrestrial who at one time had been a biblical juggernaut, kicking ass and taking names for the true God, Yahweh. How many boys from the bush could say that? None! *It's good to have purpose again*, he thought as he clutched the steering wheel a bit tighter. He needed to stay focused on the road.

———⌣———

Taking advantage of the jostling caused by the endless switchbacks and hairpin turns, Ariella moved closer to Jonathan, who quietly obliged. She was captivated by his presence; this man of mystery who had introduced her into this world. She had to admit, just the anticipation of seeing what could be next was enough motivation to fall for such a man. But there was more, an unknown force that seemed to bind them together. Like Jonathan, Ariella began to suspect that they were destined to be together, as if they were kindred spirits. Only time would tell.

For now, she smiled, because she was having the experience of a lifetime. All other thoughts—Justin, the trench, the mysterious crystal—all faded into the recesses of her mind. At that moment, she was happy and content, sitting close to Jonathan as the sunrise beamed through the mist-filled jungle.

———⌣———

Peering at the ceiba trees as they traveled toward their destination, Jonathan, while enjoying Ariella's proximity, was preoccupied with the conversation he and Abhar had had earlier.

He was particularly concerned with the part dealing with the ancient cabal. If he believed his new friend, which he did, there was a strong likelihood that this organization had already placed an operative in Sea Lab XIII. Once there, he would use the Mask of Warka to uncover the mole.

Furthermore, since the cabal was responsible for placing the amber crystal portals in their respective positions in the first place, it would also be safe to assume that an agent was on board the facility located in the Mariana Trench. Ariella would have known and had contact with the spy.

Although highly unlikely, Jonathan had to entertain the thought that the oceanographer had been turned—that she was working with them. Maybe she herself was the mole. Other than the portals themselves, Ariella was the only remaining common denominator between the two sites—at least she would be once they arrived.

Though he knew deep in his core that Ariella had nothing to do with this, he had to be sure. Being methodical was his modus operandi. It was one of the reasons he was still alive. Once they arrived at Vieques Island, he would get to the bottom of her involvement by stealthily testing the mask on her first—a dry run if you will. "That's going to be fun," he thought to himself. All the questions he might ask.

Pulling his head out of the clouds, Jonathan began to focus on the problem that was most pertinent at this time—the implant Ariella was still carrying. At the very least, she was being tracked and her biological functions monitored, just as his were before his own implant was removed by Haji.

Since removing hers in the field was not an option, Jonathan was certain that the tactical suit's nanobots could be programmed to locate and disable the device. This could easily be done without alerting her to the fact that she too had been abducted. "Man, she is going to look so hot in that suit," he mouthed silently, allowing his mind to slip off once again. He just couldn't help himself. He was smitten.

Shaking his head, he returned his thoughts to the mole and how he planned to deal with that situation—assuming Ariella's innocence. Discovering the hidden asset's identity was only part of the problem. Another facet to consider was how to neutralize the agent without alerting the cabal that he was onto them. Jonathan, as an agent himself, still had to report to his superiors from time to time, no matter how deep under cover he was. It would only be natural that this mole did too.

Additionally, the spy was not likely to stand idly by while he decommissioned their portal. Unfortunately, the agent would have to be eliminated. It was the only way to ensure the portals remained out of commission while protecting his anonymity. After this was accomplished, and since both his and Ariella's chips would no longer be functioning, the ancient organization would have no knowledge of who disrupted their operation, or how.

Due to the secrecy surrounding the mission, Jonathan would need to take operational command of the Sea Lab once on board, no matter who was in charge or what rank he or she held. This was essential so that all sensitive information remained compartmentalized, allowing him to perform essential tasks with little or no scrutiny. As the old adage goes "loose lips sink ships." Being in charge would also afford him the privilege of doing whatever he deemed necessary in order to ensure the mission's success, which, in this case, meant liquidating the mole. This bit of wet work, undoubtably, would not be popular with the crew and they would demand an explanation.

With only vague evidence of the spy's guilt, everything in the military was on a "need to know" basis; with the imminent danger the unrestrained portals presented, Jonathan was confident that everyone would accept his actions.

With his plans set for what needed to happen concerning both Ariella and the mole, Jonathan now turned his attention to Abhar himself. The interest Abhar seemed to have in how he had dispatched that silver elemental bitch—Jonathan took it personal when others tried to kill him—still bothered him. What was the big deal? He cut off the damn thing's head, end of story.

Granted, after seeing their golden leader's teleportation abilities, he himself concluded that luck had been on his side. If it had not been for this silver opponent's cocky decision to underestimate him, he would probably have met his own end instead.

However, he did not live in the world of luck and always went into a fight, or any challenge, with a mindset focused on victory. "I will" were two simple but powerful words in his arsenal. Even the Bible says, "If man had the faith of a mustard seed, he could move mountains." But it never says faith in what. Jonathan chose to have faith not only in the Creator God Yahweh, but also in himself and the abilities he had been blessed with. Thus far, this outlook had served him well.

Something, though, was still not adding up. Abhar had been more than simply curious about how he had accomplished this feat; he wanted to know every detail, especially those concerning the weapon employed. What made that particular sword so significant? Was there something needed to properly utilize it, and that he happened to stumble upon? And what of the yellow-green glowing crystals? Weird.

Although at the time, Jonathan did not think this the most pressing matter, at some point, Abhar would need to discuss his interest in the matter. More importantly, though, why was Abhar involved in fighting this cabal in the first place? What is his angle, his motivation? Even if Jonathan sensed nothing sinister in his actions and trusted his new friend and ally, he still needed to know.

Suddenly, he heard a low voice echoing in his head. It was Abhar's! Looking in the direction of the front passenger seat, all Jonathan could see was the back of Abhar's head. He quickly adjusted his gaze to peer into the side view mirror. To his surprise, Abhar was staring back at him, mouth closed, wearing a sheepish grin. "I sense your confusion. Be patient, my friend, all will be revealed in time, I promise," the voice softly said.

What the . . . ? Jonathan thought. Apparently, like the silver and gold elementals he had met during his abduction, telepathy was just another hidden skill Abhar possessed. "Who are you?" he silently asked back.

Abhar merely smiled and said, "We'll talk in Ceiba, okay?"

"We sure will," Jonathan answered back.

Moments of tranquility over the past few days had been few and far between. Though the drive through the rainforest at dawn was captivatingly beautiful, Abhar had other things on his mind. He badly wanted to contact his wife Sarah to see if she and Myrah had arrived safely; but he knew not to risk it. Abhar was sure that since coming to Jonathan's aid, his frequency vibration was now being closely monitored. There was no way he was going to put his beloved in danger again if he could help it. He would just have to wait until he could get in contact with Haji, which should be soon enough.

Seemingly, to his relief, the Rahs were still unaware of Jonathan's true lineage, or else they would not have returned him to Earth. This fact, however, troubled him. Did he really need to expose himself to the Rahs when he decided to wake the God seed? Maybe it was unnecessary to do so. Little did he know, though, that Ensign RahKael had discovered Major Hawthorn's secret identity and had no intention of setting him free. Yahweh works in mysterious ways.

Thus far, with the crystals' expansion in both trenches, thereby threatening the stability of the entire planet, Abraham was starting to believe that he had made a wise decision. The major's role was just too important to be left to chance. With his help, Jonathan could stop the growth of both the crystals and effectively render the two portals useless. This would allow Abraham to continue to operate from behind the scenes, out of direct involvement. The last thing he wanted was to fully expose himself. While powerful in his own right, he would stand little chance against the Rah contingent that awaited just a universe away, in PU 430—for a Dimerian, a very short distance indeed.

Instead of continuing to dwell on things that had already occurred or those he had no control over, Abhar decided to center his thoughts on something he could manage. The dilemma remained whether to arm Major Hawthorn with his triple sword or not. Either decision presented its own dangers, neither of which could be ignored.

Giving Jonathan the sword would be like giving a child a toy and expecting the kid not to play with it. It was a foregone conclusion he would use the sword upon identifying the Rah agent. However, what would bring even more attention was his having a sword; especially a tri-sword; aboard an underwater facility in the first place. This in itself would expose Jonathan to the Rah agent before he had a chance to learn who it was.

On the other hand, Jonathan needed some sort of defense, or offense, to use against the Rah in the event he was prematurely discovered or while neutralizing the portals. Abhar did not expect that the mole on board would simply watch and do nothing once Jonathan went to work.

After some thought, he came up with a plan. Fortunately, he had a perfect alternative, one that had all the benefits of both options with none of the dangers. It was a substance he had been saving for millennia. It was very rare and extremely effective at eliminating any Dimerian that was not a Yah. In a crystal vial, similar to the one owned by YetziRah, Abhar had managed to obtain a mixture of WEDEC—white enhanced Dimerian energy crystal—and monatomic gold. He was given the compound long ago by the last Memphite pharaoh while stationed in Egypt. Although it was a minute amount and could only be used once, it was enough to do the job. Yes, this was a better alternative; it would definitely draw less attention.

Hopefully, when the time came, the major would utilize some tact and not reveal himself too early. It was of the utmost importance that his identity remain hidden. He would talk to Jonathan more about this later. Besides, Jonathan was a military man and a secret agent; not blowing his cover was his standard operating procedure.

Interestingly enough, Abhar sensed that while he was thinking about Jonathan, Jonathan was also thinking about him. Coincidence? He did not believe in such things. The cosmos simply did not work that way. Like energies congregate, opposite ones repel; that was how it had always been.

Understandably, his human friend had many questions, especially about him, that needed to be answered. In an attempt to quell Jonathan's fears, Abhar decided to risk detection and use telepathy.

Since the amount of energy used to accomplish this was minimal, only someone in the immediate vicinity, specifically scanning for his frequency, would detect his presence. This simple action would not only strengthen the growing bond between them but would provide another clue to his true identity.

Satisfied and slightly amused at the conclusion of their telepathic communication, Abhar decided to relax and enjoy the rest of the ride. The sun was rising, revealing the colorful flora of the rainforest. Miniature rainbows were appearing everywhere, glistening off the dewy palm fronds. Things were tranquil, he was at peace.

Unfortunately, that feeling did not last. Abhar started to detect a pair of familiar but insidious frequencies, ones he had not felt in over ninety years. This was not the omen he was hoping for. These two beings were extremely dangerous, causing mayhem and devastation everywhere they went.

Although he was not exactly sure where the brothers' energies were emanating from, Abhar was convinced that they were near, and closing in. Luckily, his senses, having been honed over the years, were keen enough to determine that they were not whole, and of no immediate threat. Nevertheless, he would need to be mindful of their presence.

A pang of doubt raced through his mind. "Maybe I shouldn't have used telepathy to speak to Jonathan after all."

***

Once a quaint little village located on the western end of Puerto Rico, the town of Ceiba had grown up quickly after the US Navy moved in back in 1944. For fifty years, the Roosevelt Roads Naval Station, positioned just south of town, was one of the most important bases in the US Navy's Southern Command.

Because of its remote location, far from any large population centers, the station was utilized as a hub for the various secret facilities scattered throughout the rainforest. These hidden installations performed experiments ranging from biological warfare to genetic research. However, with rumors abound about escaped genetically altered creatures, such as Jack's chupacabra, along with the island's population and economic explosion, the majority of the programs were ultimately moved. Finally, in early 2004, the military pulled out completely, abandoning the area.

Although still mostly deserted, the far end of the base now operated as the José Aponte de la Torre Airport. From the air, it was situated on one of the points of the horns of Mt. El Toro's (the bull).

For the past several hours, everyone in the Jeep, absorbed in private thoughts, had been able to get some much needed "me time." It was rare, particularly on assignments of this nature, that one was ever afforded such an opportunity.

Despite the lingering questions and uncertain future, the group was in good spirits when they arrived in the small town. The morning sun was up, not a cloud in the sky, and the surrounding jungle was alive with activity.

———— ⌣ ————

While not her first time in a tropical rainforest, this was not the usual habitat in which Ariella operated. As an oceanographer, she was accustomed to the deep blue sea. Still, she was in an unusually good mood. Though she would never admit it, Ariella liked not being the one in control. She actually preferred it, especially when those around her seemed so capable.

Once the Jeep came to a stop, Ariella, having spotted a food shack, jumped out. She was hungry and needed to stretch. "Huevos, anyone!?" she said joyously, looking at Jonathan and motioning both arms toward her intended destination.

Before the words had fully escaped her mouth, Jonathan looked up to see her dark brown hair billowing in the light morning breeze. Her radiant glow was accented by the rising sun, which was slightly behind her. In that moment, he was speechless.

"What?" she said coyishly, knowing exactly how Jonathan was looking at her.

Not waiting for anyone else to answer, Jack spoke up. "I'll have a coffee nagro if ya please, ma'am. After that knuckle-buster of a drive, old Jack could use a little pick me up, if ya know what I mean."

"Anything for you, Abhar? Some fruit perhaps?" she asked.

"Thank you, I would like some milk if you please."

"Yum, that sounds good . . . now what about you, Major Hawthorn, what'll it be?" Ariella was jokingly picking on him, acting like an inpatient waitress.

Coming out of his trance-like stare, Jonathan smiled and responded, "Yes, ma'am if you could get me some fresh fruit and a coffee, that'd be great. Thank you, Ariella."

"I'll see what I can do. Be back in a minute, boys," she said as she happily skipped away.

Realizing that their time together was short, Jonathan seized the opportunity in Ariella's absence to ask Abhar a few questions.

"All right, Abhar, what the hell is going on?!"

Before he could respond, Jack looked up at Abhar with a "huh-oh, the gig is up" sort of look.

Smiling, Abhar slowly turned around to face the soldier. Not one to assume anything or to give out information unnecessarily, Abhar asked, "What precisely do you want to know, Jonathan?"

Shaking his head, expecting that type of response, Jonathan began his interrogation with a series of questions. "Who are you really? I know what you said earlier . . . Abraham . . . but that isn't telling me squat. For instance, how did you talk to me before, telepathy? And why are you so interested in the sword I used to kill that silver"—he put his two hands up and, using his fingers, signaled dual quotation marks in the air—"Dimerian? Is there something special about the blade I should know?"

Pausing to see that Ariella was still at the food shack, he continued before Abhar could answer. "Why are you fighting this cabal . . . and don't tell me it's an act of benevolence, because I'm not going to buy that. No one fights for something as long as you have claimed without some personal motive or agenda . . . Just level with me, Abhar," he pleaded.

Looking around at the beautiful landscape, Abhar was trying to decide how much he should reveal to the God seed at this point. He knew he did not have the luxury of time to provide an in-depth explanation. But he also realized that superficial or ambiguous answers would not satisfy the major. No, he needed to give him more than he had originally planned. Still, it was imperative that Jonathan's true heritage remained concealed. He was simply not ready to find out that he was more than just an ordinary home-grown human.

While contemplating how to begin, an ingenious solution came to his mind—one that would not only provide his interrogator answers in an effective and efficient manner, but one that would also be believable. "Jack, tell the major here who I am."

Although caught off guard momentarily, Jack quickly rebounded, understanding what Abhar was trying to accomplish. By allowing him to interpret the question, it would provide more validity to the answers. No one had ever mistaken Jack for a liar.

Tipping his hat up and looking directly at Jonathan, Jack smiled. "Well, ya see, this here is Abraham from Ur of the Chaldeans." As Jack spoke the words, he could see the wheels turning in Jonathan's mind and the question he was about to ask. "That's right, mate, the one from the Bible." Jack chuckled on seeing the reaction. "I think old Abraham looks pretty good for being thousands of years old, don't ya too?"

Quickly interjecting, Abhar added, "True, Jack, all true. But who am I really?" Abhar was surprised that Jack's answer did not turn into some long, drawn-out monologue.

"Yar one of them thar Dimerians! But I ain't really got a clue where that is at."

Taking a few seconds to process this, Jonathan asked, "Do you trust him, Jack?"

"With my life, mate."

Switching his attention between his two companions, Jonathan could sense that Jack was being truthful. Remembering what Abhar had told him about Dimerians before, he focused on him and scoffed, "Shape shifters, huh?"

With an innocent smile, Abhar merely shrugged his shoulders.

This revelation of Abhar's true identity also answered how he was able to read Jonathan's thoughts and use telepathy to communicate, although it also led to still more questions, and time was of the essence. Ariella would be back soon. "What about the sword?"

"Jack, could you get the artifact from out of the back?" Abhar asked, referring to the spear. As Jack exited and moved to the rear of the Jeep, Abhar attempted to answer the question.

"As you may have surmised, we Dimerians live a long, long time and are extremely difficult to kill, especially in our elemental form. Yet you managed to do so."

"You mean you're really like that cocky, golden prick I met on that UFO?!" He did not mean any disrespect toward Abhar with this outburst.

Sensing this, Abhar said, "Yes, but that's not what's really important right now. That sword you used during your abduction is one of the few things in existence that can actually eliminate one of my kind."

Jonathan let this percolate for a second before replying. "So if I pull out my pistol and shoot you square in the head, you're not going to die?"

"Well, right now, Jonathan, I'm occupying a human shell, which can be killed, just as any human can. But my essence, or soul, will live on. The difference being, though, that I could return in my elemental form in the blink of an eye if I so choose."

As part of the secret world, Jonathan had met a variety of life forms that possessed incredible abilities. They included: long life spans, regeneration, super strength and intelligence, mind melding, ESP—especially those little, big-eyed Gray fuckers—and while defeating their various technologies might present a challenge, he had never met a species that could not be killed with a bullet, or multiple bullets.

What Abhar was suggesting was something completely new. In his experience, each life form that occupied the Earth was eventually affected by the same mortality that all humans inevitably succumbed to. As Jonathan pondered what this new knowledge meant, Jack returned and handed Abhar a tubular, plastic-wrapped package.

"Here ya go, Abhar, minus the flies, of course," the Aussie said.

Jonathan continued, "So let me get this straight . . . your name is Abraham, the one of the Bible, who with 300 men . . ."

Abhar corrected him to add a bit of humor to the situation. "Three hundred eighteen to be precise, all good men too."

"Okay; you and 318 men went around and kicked ass all over the ancient world some four millennia ago. But in reality, you're not even human, you're Dimerian, and your reason for doing all this is . . . ?"

"Because I was asked to, Jonathan."

"Asked to by whom?"

Abhar pointed to the sky, certain Jonathan would comprehend the meaning. "God?!"

"God, Yahweh; which is his true name. But yes." He ended there as if no further explanation was needed. He was right.

Visibly shaken by what Abhar had just said, Jonathan said no more on the subject. Despite all he had seen and learned, he still believed in the Creator and was not about to question his intentions. Meanwhile, during the silence, Abhar had unwrapped the tubular cardboard package and pulled out its contents.

Seeing that Ariella was on her way back to the Jeep, Jonathan asked the others to be mindful of what they said. He did not want her to know too much at this time. All agreed, but Abhar offered a bit of wisdom. "She can handle whatever you tell her, Jonathan. She's stronger than you give her credit for."

Arriving back with her arms full, Ariella graciously started handing out the orders. "Here's your coffee, Jack, freshly brewed and unsoiled."

"You are an angel, Ariella."

"I hope you like goat's milk Abhar, it's all they had."

"That's wonderful, thank you very much."

"And, Jonathan, some coffee leche with a touch of cane sugar . . . and here's some freshly sliced pineapple."

"Wow! Thanks, Ariella."

Waving her hand in the air, Ariella said, "Enjoy, everyone." She then proceeded to drink half a cup of goat's milk in one long chug. When she removed the cup from her lips, she had acquired the typical milk mustache one would expect to see on a child.

"Ummm, would you like some, Jonathan? It does a body good," she said as she innocently offered her cup.

Hearing the Freudian slip, Jonathan responded without thinking, "It certainly does." Upon realizing what he had said, he rebounded by saying, "No, no thank you."

Although it had not been her intention to be so flirtatious, she was merely in a great mood; Ariella was most definitely enjoying how it was affecting Jonathan. *What girl wouldn't?* she thought.

After finishing his drink, Abhar pulled out what appeared to be a Roman short sword. It was old and stained, but otherwise seemed to be in good condition.

"This sword is old and very, very special. It was fashioned, along with two others, out of a much longer blade. This was the tip of the weapon, the final piece, and it contains great power," Abhar said as he brandished the object for all to see.

Before Abhar could continue, Ariella, who had been intrigued by the artifact, figured out what it was. "That looks like a piece of the Spear of Destiny," she said matter-of-factly. Abhar and Jack both looked at each other with eyebrows arched and grins plastered across their faces. They then gave her a look of approval.

"My grandfather used to tell me stories about it. How the Nazis scoured the planet looking for all the pieces . . . I think he said that Hitler had one piece, but I'm not sure. I was just a little girl when he told me," she added.

Staring at Jonathan, Abhar ribbed, "You see, I told you she would surprise you."

"Come on, really?! That's part of the Spear of Destiny? The one used to pierce Christ?" Jonathan asked.

Abhar nodded and presented him with the sword for inspection. "Here, take a look."

Although it was a little risky—Jonathan would feel the energy the weapon possessed—Abhar was confident he would not realize his connection to its power. Besides, not to offer it up for him to look at would cast undue suspicion on himself, something that he could ill afford at this time.

Immediately upon taking hold of the hilt, Jonathan felt the energy rush up his arm, filling his body. It was so intense that he nearly dropped it.

"You feel the power?" Abhar asked rhetorically, seeing that he did.

Jack too was in awe at how Jonathan reacted to the blade. He had held it several times with no such effect. At that moment, he was convinced of Abhar's assessment of the young major—he was indeed the God seed.

With this strange but somehow familiar energy flowing throughout his body, while not uncomfortable, Jonathan began to fear what he was feeling. Since he could not rationalize what was happening nor control it, he wanted nothing more to do with it.

"Here! Take this thing!" He indiscriminately extended the sword for anyone to take it.

Ariella, seeing how it affected him, grabbed it. She wanted a closer look anyway. She took it by the hilt and slowly waved it around, feeling . . . nothing. Though she did not have the experience Jonathan had had, Ariella maintained that different people were in tune to different types of energies and frequencies. Therefore, she believed Jonathan's experience to be genuine. Nevertheless, she continued to carefully study the blade. Turning it over, she noticed the Latin inscription and the date. "Fierce love, extreme death, God wills it; 786 . . . How appropriate."

"786, what does that mean?" Jonathan asked, still irritated slightly.

"It's the date, Jonathan," Ariella answered.

"But I thought . . ."

"It's the date from . . . ," Abhar started to say before Ariella butted in. She was starting to get a little peeved herself. Jonathan's mood was infectious.

"It's the number of years from the founding of Rome . . . or if you prefer, Anno Domini 33!"

Picking up on the snide nature of her response, Jonathan realized he was acting like an ass. Instead of apologizing for his behavior, which would have forced her to look at her own actions, he deflected. "Hey, what's that stain?" His voice was calm, without agitation.

With her anger abated, she once again looked at the blade. Looking at Abhar, she asked, "That stain is dried blood, isn't it?" She handed it back to him.

Putting it back in the cardboard tube, he answered, "Very perceptive, Ariella, you never cease to amaze me."

With that comment, Ariella glowed with delight. She was thankful for the compliment and smiled as if she were a daughter getting approval from a father, something that had rarely happened to her as a child. It was most likely the main reason that she had remained single and had been so driven in her life—ever seeking approval from her father, which she would never get.

"Jonathan, remember that sword you used during your last . . . sparring match?" Abhar asked, referring to the duel that had occurred during the recent abduction. "This blade is composed of the same material."

Jonathan understood what his companion was inferring.

"We need the other two pieces before they fall into the wrong hands. Luckily, I know exactly where one piece is. As for the other"—he said, stopping to smile at Ariella—"Once again the lady is correct; the Nazis did find one piece, and they still have it."

Taken aback by how he had reacted while holding the spear, Jonathan could not deny its power. He knew the history of the blade and the men who had possessed it. Constantine, Charlemagne, Napoleon, and Hitler all were rumored to have had it, or part of it. They all nearly conquered the known world. If the Nazis indeed controlled a piece of the ancient spear, it would be only a matter of time before they utilized its power; if they were not doing so already.

"Okay, I'll bite. Where is the Nazi piece located?" Jonathan asked with sense of urgency.

Ariella spoke up. "My guess would be Argentina or Antarctica. The Nazis were in both places during and after the war." Jonathan looked at her in awe. She certainly was full of surprises. He began to wonder what else she knew, the stuff not in her bio. She just shrugged he shoulders and smiled, as if this was all common knowledge.

"I agree with the fine Shelia here. But them Nazis are a particular sort and it's my guess that ain't a one of them gunna tell us a thing," Jack added.

"Don't worry about that, Jack. I've got the perfect team for the job. They've been on standby back at Los Alamos . . . I need to know what direction to point them in."

"If it were me, mate, I'd start in Bariloche, Argentina, and work my way south. I know in the past, it was certainly a hot spot of postwar Nazi activity. A lot of people down thar speak German too."

"Outstanding—that sounds like a plan. I'll provide them with a sit rep and direct them there ASAP." Jonathan was in military mode now.

Jack, a former spook and very familiar with the lingo, offered some of his own. "I've got a cobber who used to be a GSG9 asset; maybe he could provide your team with some actionable intel?"

"Is your source reliable?"

"He's never failed me in the past. Plus, anyone's reliable for the right price."

"Understood. We'll get your asset to find out what he can and then meet my team in Bariloche. They'll have more than enough money to buy his loyalty. Does he happen to have blond hair and blue eyes?"

"Ya, mate . . . he does." Jack well knew what Jonathan was getting at. "He could definitely pass for a Nazi."

"That may be very helpful. Keep him on a need-to-know basis, though. There's one member of my team who wished to remain . . . anonymous."

"Will do," Jack said as he pulled out a notepad to retrieve his contact's information.

Ariella, who had been intently watching Jonathan take control of the situation, immediately knew who he was referring to—Gilla. Before she could say anything, Jonathan shook his head side to side, signaling her to remain silent. Luckily, Jack was too busy rummaging through his pad to notice.

It was not that he did not trust Jack, he did. Jonathan was just honoring Gilla's wishes to keep his identity hidden if at all possible. Plus, Gilla's role in this would be covert anyway, working his way through the underground Nazi world.

With that bit of business taken care of, he now turned his attention back to Abhar. "What about the other piece? The one you have its location."

"Jack and I have that well in hand. We have to make a stop in Mosul first, though," Abhar said cautiously, knowing where that was located and the turmoil happening there.

"Iraq!! Well, I suppose you know what you're doing, you are . . ." Jonathan caught himself. He was about to say, "You're thousands of years older than I and practically invincible!"

"I can assure you, Major Hawthorn, that the other piece of the spear is safe. No one on this planet will find it." Abhar said.

"I trust you, Abhar, but for Jack's sake, be careful. Iraq is hell on Earth right now, especially where you two are headed."

"Hell is whar I go on vacation, mate," Jack squawked. "Don't worry about old Jack here; I'm a chameleon, ya see. I'll blend right in."

Jonathan had to laugh a little at Jack's outlook on life. Even in times of adversity, he was able to find something funny to say. Jonathan would love to have met him in his prime, back in the days of Vietnam and Air America.

"Found it," Jack cried, locating his asset's contact information. "We have to get closer ta the airport to get a good signal."

Pulling out his cell phone, Jonathan saw that he only had one bar. "Good idea, Jack. I need to check in and see about our transport. I'll also contact my team at Los Alamos and get them on the move."

Seeing that everyone was in agreement, they piled back into the Jeep and headed toward the airport. Within moments Jonathan's phone beeped, indicating that he had a message. Unlocking his phone, he could see that Ashley had left him a text message. It informed him where and what time to catch his ride. He and Ariella were to go to Point Puerca, at the end of Roosevelt Roads, where a Zodiac would be waiting. They would then ferry themselves to the east end of Vieques Island to would meet a contact at the secret facility located in the Playa Grande Lagoon. This would be the launching point that will finally take them approximately 100 miles northwest to Sea Lab XIII. This laboratory, situated somewhere in the Nares Abyssal Plain under the Atlantic, deep within the Puerto Rico Trench, was positioned even deeper than the one located near Guam, some 30,000 feet down.

Satisfied with the travel arrangements, Jonathan contacted Haney and directed him and Gilla to travel to Bariloche, via the South American line of the underground transit system, which ran under the Andes Mountains. After giving him a quick briefing and explaining the mission's parameters, they ended the call in typical Ranger fashion. "Rangers lead the way, Haney."

"All the way, Major. Hooah!"

"Hooah. See you soon, my friend."

At about the same time that Jonathan finished talking with Haney, Jack finished talking with his asset. He signified to Jonathan that everything was go and that he had passed on Haney's contact location and the password they had discussed. Luckily, he was already in Brazil working on assignment. Jack was sure that his asset could help the team gain some ground in tracking down the other piece of the spear.

Before time completely slipped away, Abhar motioned for Jonathan to step away from the others. They still needed to go over a few things in private, away from Ariella's ears. Although he had instructed Major Hawthorn in how to uncover the Rah spy and contain the expanding amber crystal, the issue of how to dispatch the mole remained. Having already made the decision that carrying a tri-sword was not the best or safest option, Abhar pulled out the crystal vial he had been carrying and presented it to Jonathan.

"What is this?" he asked, studying the multifaceted crystal vial while casually turning it end over end.

"It contains a toxin that will eliminate the Dimerian agent on board the Sea Lab, assuming there is one there." The look on Jonathan's face at that moment was priceless, as if he were handling the Ebola or anthrax agent. He instantly froze.

Abhar laughed heartedly. "Don't worry, it's harmless to humans."

The worry in his face instantly drained away. Now, only furrows of purposeful thought remained. "How do I administer the toxin?"

"You can blow it into the air, place it in food or drink, or simply sprinkle it on the spy's head; it really doesn't matter.

"How much of it do I need to use for it to be effective?" Jonathan asked as he opened the vial.

Reflexively, Abhar blinked away with such speed that it reminded Jonathan of the Gold he had fought aboard the UFO. Nervously, Abhar explained, "I said it posed no harm to humans. I'm not human! Please cap the vial."

"Oh shit! Sorry, Abhar." He resealed the toxic container.

"Thank you." Abhar was visibly relieved and moved back within speaking distance. "It is only enough for one dose, I'm afraid. That substance was hard to come by and nearly impossible to obtain in this day and age. But I assure you, it is 100 percent lethal upon exposure."

"And this stuff will kill the . . . Dimerian spy?"

"It will not only eliminate the threat but erase the mole's entire existence. Remember, this spy is not human; it's just occupying a human body, as I am. If you just kill the human body by conventional means, the mole will return to its elemental form and report back to its superiors. This would expose you and endanger the mission. The consequences would be catastrophic."

Nodding in comprehension, Jonathan again made sure the vial's cap was secure before putting it away. Abhar then gave him some words of encouragement before they returned to the company of Ariella and Jack. It was time to part ways.

Since they were within walking distance of their departure point, only about a mile, Jonathan thought it would be a good idea for him and Ariella to stretch their legs and go on foot the rest of the way. She happily agreed. It was a beautiful morning for a stroll.

As they said their goodbyes, uncharacteristically, Abhar gave Jonathan a hug. Before pulling away, he whispered some final words in his ear, which sent chills down Jonathan's spine. "Good luck, Jonathan, and be careful. The world needs you."

CHAPTER

FIFTY SIX

APPREHENSIVELY, CHERAHNA HEADED for the science lab, the place where all this chaos had begun. There she would be able to access the amber crystal's data records in privacy. Although she was convinced that Rahzu was involved in some sort of subversive activity, despite what she had learned, she was still having difficulty believing that he was a traitor.

Could she have really been so naïve as not to have noticed any of this? Was it possible that her deep-seated need for emotional acceptance by Rahzu as a father figure caused her to be unable to see his actions and intentions? She had to admit, it was possible.

Evidently, she had misjudged Admiral YetziRah also, because before this, she would have never put faith in anything he claimed to be true. Now, however, she found that she not only trusted him, but began to respect him. An almost overwhelming anxiety filled her elemental silver form as she approached the crystal's pedestal. All her questions would soon be answered, for better or worse, she thought. "Please be here," she said aloud, almost begging as she explored the data files.

At the instant she recognized that what YetziRah had claimed was true—Rahzu had erased the frequencies discovered during the investigation and all evidence pertaining to the admiral's visits—she nearly collapsed to the deck, landing on one knee. Her radiant silver color faded. "It's all true!" she gasped. Her anger began to grow. "How could I have been such a fool . . . How could he have done this to me?"

Although she was upset and wanted revenge, most of her ire was directed at herself; she wanted redemption. CheRahna had never had trouble taking responsibility for her faults; it was why she had been so successful in spite of her tainted lineage.

As she picked herself up, returning to her fully erect stature of seven feet, the commander knew what needed to be done. It was now a fact that Rahzu had erased vital records and lied about it, disobeyed orders by not informing the crew of planet ET Rah's existence as instructed, and hid his past relationship with her Uncle Abraham. Furthermore, it was likely that he had falsified Earth's history in his codex in order to manipulate her into doing his bidding, whatever that was to be. He could no longer be trusted, that much was obvious.

It was all just a test, she decided. A test she planned on passing. There was only one way she was going to get the truth; and the means to do so was contained in a small crystal vial.

With the brightness of her silver restored, CheRahna, now confident and determined, would not be swayed from her duty. Leaving the lab, she set out to confront her once trusted mentor, her captain and now her enemy, Rahzu.

FIFTY SEVEN

THANKFULLY FOR GILLA, the call from Jonathan came sooner than expected. While it was good to see Haney again, he was not the most pleasant human to pass time with. The ill-natured half-breed's idea of entertainment under these circumstances was a constant barrage of insults and incessant badgering. He loved getting under people's skin. Gilla knew his behavior wasn't personal, Haney was an equal opportunity "agimatator" and would usually cease when his friends had had enough. Getting to that point, however, was often quite irritating.

To be fair, the Chief too loathed idle time, at least when it served him no purpose. This was an unusual trait for a Ranger sniper, who at times was required to patiently wait, sometimes days, in order to successfully eliminate a target. Under those conditions, however, he could see a purpose to what he did. Plus, in the solitude, he did not have to associate with others, which had never been his strongest attribute. No, Haney was much better at conversing with the voices of his ancestors; who never left him alone.

After hanging up his satellite phone, Haney got up, looked at Gilla, who was anxiously awaiting the news, made a gesture much like a hitchhiker thumbing a ride, and in a businesslike tone said, "We've got our orders. Let's move."

"Wheresh sho?" Gilla was up and ready.

"Argentina. San Carlos de la Bariloche . . . never heard of it. 'Bout you?"

"Mounshianous. A losh of Dracos and my kindsh. Nosh a safe plash. Losh of secreshs," he warned.

"Lots of what?" Haney knew perfectly well what Gilla was saying.

"Seacresshhs!!"

"Oh, secrets . . . heh, heh, heh. You really need to learn to speaka the English gooder."

Gilla remained silent and glared. Haney had got him to play his game again.

Luckily, the banter ended with the ringing of the station's bell, which signified the an approaching train. Fortunately, as if the forces of the universe were with them, it was the exact one they needed to catch.

Because the underground maglev system was an extensive, worldwide transportation network, important sites, such as Los Alamos, had numerous connecting lines fanning out in a multitude of directions. This line traveled due south, tunneling under the Sierra Madres to Mexico City, through Central America, under the Panama Canal, and terminating in the main South American hub under Bogotá, Colombia. From there it went under the Andes, all the way down to Cape Horn, the southern tip of the continent. Bariloche was near a very secret station, just outside of town.

Although their destination was nearly 6,700 miles away, with stops in several important Central American cities, once in South America and on its southern line, the delays would be few and far between. It was one of only a handful of sections worldwide where the maglev could flex its mechanical muscle and travel at maximum speed for an extended period of time.

Looking at the wall clock, Gilla determined that in about six hours, just before the sun set behind the Andean peaks, they would arrive in the small German ski town. As briefed, their contact would either be there or not far behind. In the meantime, the train stopped, and the misfit duo boarded. Haney would fill Gilla in on the details of the mission along the way, under the cloak of secrecy the cabin provided. Hopefully, Gilla could maintain his usual calm nature and be goaded into playing Chief's senseless game again.

FIFTY EIGHT

AFTER SEVERAL MINUTES had passed, Justin began to wonder why he had not heard from the Hab yet. His mind raced, trying to ascertain what could possibly have happened. Deciding that his speculation no longer served any purpose, he radioed in.

"Sea Lab X, progress report, over." Nothing. "Sea Lab X, progress report, over." Still nothing. "Steven, come in!"

The absence of any response could mean only one of two things: the first that the Hab was destroyed, and everyone was dead. Though not an impossible scenario, he seriously doubted that was the case. The second, more probable, cause was that something occurred that damaged the communications network. Unfortunately, if anything, this was the one defect in design that Justin had not noticed when he took command. The communication antennas, one for the clandestine HAARP array and the other two for short- and long-range radio, while small and fairly well protected, were located on the top of the structure. This flaw left them vulnerable to objects falling from above, which, due to the Sea Lab's location, was a realistic possibility. Hopefully, this was all it was, and once he and Dr. Walker got closer, Captain LaMarr would be able to contact his crew.

Sensing the captain's frustration, Dr. Walker, despite having a concussion and suffering from a painful headache, attempted to comfort him. In a soft voice, she said, "Steven's fine, darling, you've trained him well. I'm sure he's got it all under control."

While her words did little to diminish his concerns, he did appreciate her positive attitude. "I'm sure you're right, Deborah. It's just frustrating not knowing what the hell is happening." Now, focusing his attention to her condition, Justin asked, "How are you doing? How's the head?"

"It hurts . . . Have you ever drunk too much of that cheap boxed wine?"

"Unfortunately, a couple of times."

"Let's just say you can take that hangover you got from drinking that shit and multiply it by ten. That's what my head feels like."

"I wish there was something I could do."

"You're doing it, hun. Just keep steering. The less I move the better."

"Will do, Doc. I got you," Justin said with a smile. Several more minutes passed as they continued their ascent. As they approached, the illumination from the habitat's light began cutting through the darkness above.

Thank God, Captain LaMarr thought. At least they have power. This meant that the Hab was still largely operational.

All Deborah could think of was getting some aspirin for her aching head.

"Almost there, Deb," Captain LaMarr whispered. Once again he tried to contact the crew. "Sea Lab X, this is Captain LaMarr, can you read me, over?"

There was a brief pause before a voice pierced through the silence. It was Lt. Barett. "Captain, it's sure good to hear your voice. I've been trying to reach you for the past several minutes and was beginning to think the worst. How's the Doc?"

The captain let out a quite sigh of relief.

"I'm fine, Steven, just a little shaken up, that's all," she said. Now, speaking to Justin, she said, "Told ya he'd be fine."

"It's good to hear from you too, Steven. What happened up there?" Justin asked in an uneasy but thankful tone.

"Well, sir, it's just as you feared. It appears that a large chunk of rock fell from somewhere up above and not only damaged our comms but has knocked the Hab off its foundation. We're lying flat on our ass, sir."

Captain LaMarr remained quiet as he processed this bit of information.

Lt. Barett continued, "Other than a few possible exterior concerns, all other systems seem to be operating properly, Captain."

Captain LaMarr asked, "How's the crew, any injuries?"

"Nothing serious. They're all functioning well, sir."

"Good. We're approaching your position right now. Then we'll see what we can see," Captain LaMarr responded.

Continuing to rise, the captain could see the shadow being cast over the ledge by the Hab's west section, where the foundation had collapsed.

Upon arrival, Justin and Deborah separated. While she remained still, next to the fallen Hab, Justin conducted a survey in order to discover any additional damage. Immediately, his eyes locked on the sub bay, which was lying flat on the silt-covered bottom, just as his young lieutenant had described. Continuing his inspection, he noted the large rock that had caused the calamity; and although the Hab itself was still structurally sound, even after the blow, he could not help but wonder if they would have been so lucky if the facility had taken a direct hit.

After circling around the perimeter for a cursory inspection, only noticing a few broken lights and some damaged cameras, Captain LaMarr reunited with Dr. Walker. She too had noticed that the Hab's collapsed position presented them with a problem. In a worried voice, she asked, "Justin, how are we going to get back inside?"

Though all the members of the crew were trained to deal with such contingencies, as the military was famous for having multiple backup plans, under the circumstances he understood her forgetfulness; she was not a trained solider. Pointing up toward the spot where the bathysphere had docked hours earlier, he merely said, "Up there."

———⟨⟩———

Once inside the Sea Lab, Captain LaMarr and Lt. Barett discussed, at length, what needed to happen. Although the Hab was, at the moment, safe, there was no way to ensure that it would remain that way. Another quake could easily dislodge more rock and debris from above—or even worse, cause the Hab to fall into the abyss. Neither scenario offered a positive outcome for the crew. They needed to evacuate and fast. But with the sub bay's exit pool lying flat on the bottom, they needed to get creative if they planned on returning to the surface alive.

After much debate, the crew knew what needed to happen; it was how they were to do it that remained to be solved. Because the comms were down, the only viable means of escape remained with the PRIEST. It was simply too dangerous to leave anyone behind and wait for a surface ship to arrive.

The plan they concocted was simple. Captain LaMarr would once again put on his exosuit, return to the frigid exterior waters, and use the plasma torch to cut a hole in the sub bay. This in itself presented several potentially dangerous problems that needed to be addressed if the plan was to succeed.

The first and undoubtedly the most critical had to do with the extreme pressure experienced at these depths. The moment the integrity of the Hab's exterior became compromised; the ocean would flood in, bringing its pressure into the bay; everything not designed for the exterior environment would be crushed.

Though the Sea Lab was essentially composed of separate, self-contained modules—and like a ship, each section was designed to be sealed to withstand exposure to the harsh exterior environment—there was always the risk of a breach in one of the sections. Nothing could be taken for granted at these depths.

Also, in order to mitigate the effects of the compression wave, which was always felt when transitioning from the air lock or flood pool to the abyssal ocean, the sub compartment itself would have to be flooded prior to any cutting. Without that, everything, including the PRIEST, would likely implode due to the rapid change in pressure.

Another unavoidable issue was that all the sub bay's computers, equipment controls, storage lockers, and so forth that were not intended for deep water exposure would either be destroyed or rendered useless. Anything that was too valuable to lose would need to be moved. The goal was to escape the Sea Lab while causing as little damage as possible to the multi-billion-dollar facility, which, in sections, could later be hauled to the surface for repairs.

The sudden change of pressure posed additional problems. Anything that could not be removed had to be safely secured, so as not to accidentally shift, which could cause damage to the mini-sub, and since the PRIEST itself was not immune to the inevitable compression wave, it too, just as if it were in the flood pool, would have to be secured before being exposed to the pressures of the deep ocean.

The final problem was that though the sub, with Ariella's departure, could now accommodate the entire crew, once the Hab's shell was broken and the hole cut, there would no way for Captain LaMarr to board the sub. The docking bay air lock and the PRIEST's hatch were not positionally compatible; another design flaw, one that would need to be changed. However, Captain LaMarr would, as if they had been operating with a full crew, ride out his trip to the surface safely in the sub's clawed arms.

Because all the other EVAC preparations had already been completed, Captain LaMarr gave the crew twenty minutes to remove any loose gear, batten down the hatches, and secure the equipment and the sub before he commenced flooding the compartment.

Fortunately, the docking bay air lock was designed to be operated by a single individual by remote, if necessary. Justin would be the one to flood the sub bay before letting himself out. According to Roger, it would take the compartment approximately ten minutes to fill, just about the amount of time it would take him to get to the bathysphere's docking ring and exit the facility.

Everyone worked furiously, but with attention to detail, as if their lives depended on it, which in this case they did. Everything that could be removed was, and all other items were safely secured. Even the sub was tautly tethered on each of its four sides, as well as its top and bottom, all of which Justin would have to cut later with the plasma torch.

With all the tasks coming to completion, Captain LaMarr addressed his crew. "I know this is not the way any of us wanted to leave our home . . . but under the circumstances, it's the only way. I want to tell you that this group has performed way above any expectations that I could possibly have had . . . It's been an honor working with each and every one of you. Thank you." He paused for a moment to look at the faces of his crew before continuing. They were all alert, poised for his orders. "Now let's everyone load up. In a few hours, we'll be sipping mai tais in the afternoon sun."

A loud cheer went up in the sub bay as the crew began boarding the mini-sub.

"Steven!" Captain LaMarr called. "Make sure to bring the PRIEST out slowly; we can't afford for anything to happen to it."

"You just be careful out there. If that wall were to fall . . . ," Steven cautioned.

"Don't worry about me, Steven, I'm frosty. Let's just get these civilians to safety, hooah?"

"Hooah, Captain."

With that, Steven climbed the ladder, entered the sub bay and closed the hatch. On his way out, Justin hit the button that operated the pumps; water rapidly started filling the sub bay. Before making his exit, he turned around to get a view of the PRIEST one last time. Through the large bow porthole, he could see Roger and Steven giving him the thumbs up. All systems were go.

CHAPTER

FIFTY NINE

TOGETHER, ABHAR AND Jack watched as Jonathan and Ariella walked away; however, they each felt quite differently about it. Although it was hard for Abhar to send his wife, Sarah, away, especially considering what had happened to her so long ago, watching Jonathan leave to face this challenge without his help was harder.

At least with his beloved Sarah, since they had both occupied countless different human shells over the thousands of years they had been on Earth, it was almost a certainty that he would reunite with her again at some point in the future. It really did not matter if it was in this form or another. With Jonathan, though, being human and having not yet evolved into his destined state, Abhar felt no such comfort. If the God seed were to be struck down now, not only would the balance of power shift on Earth and in PU 431, but throughout the cosmos. Until he was fully trained and mature, his safety and anonymity were of the utmost importance.

Unfortunately, to openly reveal himself to the Rahs now would expose Jonathan, placing the major in even more peril. While the danger that awaited the God seed was real, it had become apparent that his true identity had remained concealed. This, along with the Mask of Warka, at a minimum provided him with the element of surprise. Abhar was betting that these would be enough.

At present, though, Abhar's attention needed to be focused on gathering the remaining pieces of the spear. Not until recently had he understood why the Spear of Destiny was so significant. While he already possessed a tri-sword, which he could later give to Jonathan if needed, it was just a weapon. Remembering how the cucullos swarmed around the blade back in the jungle, it all became clear.

Not being a Yah himself, Abhar's abilities, while providing a powerful ally and great assistance, were unable to bring about the maturation of Jonathan's true self. Because there was no other Dimerian Yah on the planet, or at least none that he was aware of, the spear was the only option.

Though it too was a tri-sword, a very powerful weapon capable of dispatching any of his kind, it possessed the energy required to complete the God seed's transformation. The Yah energy needed was in the dried blood, which had once belonged to Yahshua himself. It stained every part of the ancient blade. At present, this appeared to be the only option to fulfill Jonathan's destiny.

A sense of urgency engulfed him. The time to collect the remaining pieces under the relative secrecy they had thus far enjoyed, was coming to an end. Sooner or later, the Rahs would discover that his role concerning the changing events was not a minor one. They would then become much more proficient at finding and monitoring his movements. Until then, he would continue to take advantage of his good fortune.

Also feeling unsettled by the group's split, Jack too recognized the significance of Jonathan and Ariella's departure. His concern, however, was not centered on the God seed. Having once been part of the clandestine world himself, surrounded by elite soldiers, Jack could tell that Major Hawthorn was the real deal. Jonathan would adhere to his training and keep his cover in order to make the mission a success. Of this, Jack had no doubt.

No, Jack's concern had everything to do with his new friend, Miss Marconi. He questioned whether it was wise to send her into a situation where she was blind to what was about to happen. Will Jonathan tell her what he is planning, especially concerning the mole? Not likely. How will she feel when her trusted protector mysteriously produces an energy field that encapsulates the expanding crystal portal? Betrayed, perhaps. What will be her reaction about being kept in the dark about all these aspects of the mission? Pissed off, probably.

Though Ariella had worked under military authority before and understood compartmentalization, it was highly unlikely that her life had ever been this close to being in the line of fire. And although this happens often in this line of work, Jack could not help but think that she should have been told more. That Ariella was more than just a pawn on a chess board. Not only did he feel that she would have been able to handle the truth—that much was obvious to him—but that she would be an asset in the event things went awry.

Abhar too, on several occasions, had told Jonathan that Ariella was more resilient and capable than he was giving her credit for, that he should trust in her more drawing on her strengths. But, in the end, it was not their call to make, it was Major Hawthorn's. It was his cross to bear, and they had to abide by his wishes. Hopefully, for all their sakes, he would make the correct decision.

Although Jack had his worries, not unfounded, he knew they were quite trivial in the big scheme of things. He calculated that the major had a high percent chance of success. Therefore, he was not overly upset over the situation. He could tell that Abhar, however, felt much differently. Seeing the grimace on Abhar's face, Jack attempted to allay his fears. "See here, mate. I know yar not happy over our present predicament; but just trust old Jack, yar boy thar will do just fine."

"Yeah . . . I know he will. It's just . . ." He started to recall the pair of energies he felt earlier.

"What is it, Abhar? I get the feeling there's more ta it than just them leaving."

"You're right, Jack, there is . . . A little while back, I sensed we were being followed."

"Followed! Crikey, mate, by who!?"

"Two conjurors who are notorious for stirring up trouble," Abhar sighed.

"Oh, ya mean the pharaoh's mates?"

With a look of surprise on his face, Abhar stared speechless at his Aussie companion. But before he could say anything in response, Jack continued.

"I remember what ya and my cobber Binah were talking about back at his shop."

"Of course you do, Jack, of course you do." It had slipped his mind that Jack seemed to have an uncanny ability to remember practically everything. "And yes, those are the two I was referring to."

With an intense gaze, Jack scanned the surrounding area. "Where are they now?"

"I can't see them, but they're not far away, at least part of them anyway."

Displaying a puzzled look, Jack did not say a word.

"The brothers have learned how to divide their individual energies, allowing them to be in two places at once. Unfortunately, their two totems are very keen at detecting various frequencies, especially those they are familiar with."

"Ya mean you." It was more of a statement from Jack than a question.

"It could be me or the spear, my friend." Abhar was unsure.

"Should we be worried?"

"I don't think so. They are not working with the Rahs, that much is sure. But we do need to leave here as soon as possible. We cannot afford to bring any undue attention to Jonathan and Ariella. Either they are onto me or the spear; regardless, we are their quarry, and they will follow. We will regroup at Binah's and stash this piece of the spear there while booking a flight to Damascus. At least at the Smoke 'n' Go, my frequency and the spear's energy will be effectively blocked. Maybe then we'll be able to shake them."

CHAPTER

SIXTY

SOMETIMES, WITHOUT CAUSE or provocation, the strangest thoughts appear in one's mind. For Jonathan, they always seemed to be associated with a song or familiar jingle. As he and Ariella were walking to their pickup location, out of the blue, one such melody popped into this head. The realization of its meaning came to him so quickly he nearly burst out laughing.

Though he could not remember the exact title of the song, or which name the band who sang it was going by at the time of its release, either Jefferson Airplane or Jefferson Starship, he would have bet on the latter. Part of the refrain was quire memorable and kept repeating in his head: "Marconi plays the mamba, listen to the radio, don't you remember . . ." That was all he could recall as he silently sang.

It was such a well-known song in its day, he was sure that someone else had also made the connection with Ariella. It was referring to her great-grandfather. Unsure how she would react if he started ribbing her about it, he decided to table the thought for now. She was in such a good mood that he did not want to spoil it. Time would take care of that.

Jonathan could not help but take note of how Ariella bobbed slightly up and down she walked. It sort of resembled someone skipping along in slow motion, only that was not what was actually happening.

With all of his training in the martial arts and having completed various courses in profiling, he had become extremely adept at deriving people's intentions through body language—so much so that it had become almost second nature. At least it did in the theater of combat or in the covert world, not so much in dealing with interpersonal relationships.

Despite not being used more, watching how people move can tell a lot about them. For instance, someone who walks heel to toe and upright, with shoulders back and down, had probably been trained to march, usually in the military or in a school band. Those that slouch slightly and walk more flat-footed tend to do manual labor, carrying loads, or are from areas of varying elevation.

In Ariella's case, her walking on the balls of her feet, making her appear to bob up and down like a buoy in the ocean was directly caused by all the time she had spent on the water. This type of mobility gave her balance while moving around on a boat or ship, especially during rough seas.

Still, even with this knowledge, Jonathan thought that some of her spring stemmed for her lust for life and her present altitude, which was refreshing. At that moment, he decided to hold off on briefing her about what was happening. Ever since Abhar had pointed out the strength within her and how capable she had already proven to be, Jonathan had been trying to decide how much he should tell Ariella about what lay ahead.

Indeed, she had surprised him by how readily she transitioned into his world; he had not expected her to be so calm at meeting Gilla. Sure, she was highly educated, her degrees showed that; but she was also quick-witted, able to process information rapidly and arrive at relevant conclusions. Though hard to tell because of her clothing, she appeared to be of athletic build, which never hurt in times of danger. Admittedly, all these assets were definite reasons to support including her more in his plans, but several critical aspects of her character were still unknown.

The first, the less important of the two, was how she would react under fire. Would she be able to keep her composure, think quickly and clearly, and do what was necessary to complete the mission? Or would she freeze, potentially getting them both killed? Although this trait remained to be seen, judging by how she has handled things so far, Jonathan believed she would perform well when the time came.

Additionally, she had been intensely vetted and not only chosen by the powers that be to be part of the Mariana Trench team, but to also join him in Puerto Rico. Granted, they were not privy to all the current details and have surely never heard of Abhar or the Rah cabal before, but nonetheless, they selected her for a reason, and that was good enough for him.

Another, more concerning unknown about Ariella was something that had taken Jonathan many years to master. It involved hiding and blocking his thoughts from prying minds while still being able to think himself—the practice of brain compartmentalization, if you will. This aspect of one's being, regardless of any other impressive assets, was the most important trait anyone needed to possess; it could potentially determine mission failure or success.

Jonathan could guide her, teaching her some methods which that been proven to work; but with his time frame, he doubted she would be able to utilize any of them with any measure of success. On the other hand, she could be a natural, with little to no training required. She was kind of flighty, which shows multiple levels of thought occurring simultaneously.

Unfortunately, the only way he was going to find the answers to these questions was to put her to the test, in real time. To trust or not to trust, that is the question. One he would have to stew over a little longer.

<hr>

Moving along with an almost serendipitous attitude, Ariella, for the first time in as long as she could remember, had totally lost control of her life. She was loving every minute of it. In fact, she was so happy she nearly started whistling the "Supercalifragilisticexpialidocious" song from Disney's *Mary Poppins*, a favorite melody from her childhood, which is exactly what she felt like—a child again. All of life now seemed new, dangerous, exciting, and fun. She had a new purpose, one of real importance.

As she reflected, Ariella was able to pinpoint the event that started all of this in motion. Accepting the position aboard the Sea Lab those few months ago had made all the difference, and made all this possible. The dull days of classrooms filled with overprivileged, ungrateful students was over. She could never go back to that life. Her string of dead-end relationships seemed to be coming to an end as well. While not vain and never having been overly concerned with how men thought of her, for the first time in her life, thanks to two men, she felt beautiful. Justin touched her heart and Jonathan excited her, a feeling she was unable to explain.

"Enough!" she said to herself. Ariella refused to overthink things this time, trying to fit everything into its own neat little box. Instead, she was going to go with the flow and do what she felt was right, come what may. That is what she had done of late, and so far so good.

Now it was time to clear her mind, to take in all the energy flowing through nature, and to open herself to the will of the universe. Prepared to experience all that was, she started taking long, deep breaths while she walked. She was ready, open, and waiting for the energy to flow. When it did, she sighed and squawked, "Jonathan! Stop it!"

⌣

Deep in thought over what to do concerning his companion, Jonathan was caught off guard by Ariella's demand. Unsure what she was talking about, he defensively asked, "Stop what? I'm not doing anything."

Ariella stopped walking, turned around, and pointed to her own head, "You're thinking too much, Jonathan. Sometimes you just have to let go, trust your gut, and go with the flow," she answered while spreading her arms wide through the air. "Breathe!" She inhaled deeply while smiling widely. "The universe will give you the answers you seek, if you ask."

"What!!!" *Who is this woman, Guru Marconi?* he thought.

"I'm trying to be one with the universe here, and you're screwing it up with all of your conflict," she said bluntly.

He almost reflexively asked her how she knew he was in conflict but decided that her answer would likely be just as cryptic as her last statement. However, his question still remained. Was she reading his mind? Doubtful, or she would have acted with more hostility. But it was plain to see that she was picking up on his thought energy. Maybe she had ESP and did not know it; it was possible. That would certainly help explain the absence of any lasting personal relationships. It's never easy being around others when you can read their thoughts.

Little did either of them know that Ariella and Jack's relationship, besides boosting their energies and mood, had activated each other's latent psychic abilities. In time, though its strength would dissipate, a permanent channel was opened in the pineal gland, allowing for psychic energy to flow. At present, however, her psychic energy was very active, causing her to more easily accept the totality of things.

Instead of questioning her, though, Jonathan changed tactics and began reciting his mantra. He wanted to see if she could pick up on that also. Oddly enough, Ariella began to laugh. This time, however, it was Jonathan pushing out his thoughts rather than her merely reading them—a gift he had no knowledge of possessing.

"What's so funny?" he asked.

"Just how things pop into your head."

"What do you mean?"

"For some reason, I started thinking about the Schoolhouse Rock commercials that used to come on with Saturday morning cartoons." She saw that Jonathan had no reaction, as if he did not know what she was talking about. "Come on, you know: 'I'm just a bill, yes I'm only a bill, and I'm sitting here on Capitol Hill.' Ooh, ooh, ooh, and the '3, 6, 9 . . . 12, 15, 18 . . . 21, 24, 27 . . . 30' . . . Oh, and my favorite, 'conjunction junction, what's your function and but, and or, will get you very far.'"

Jonathan was stupefied and kept staring blankly. He really did not know what to say.

Ariella, against her new and better judgment—old habits die hard—took his silence and stare to mean he thought she was crazy. "It's all your fault I'm acting this way," she stated.

Did she really know he was reciting his mantra? No way, he thought. But he needed to find out. "My fault! How do you figure?"

"Yes, your fault." Her eyes widened and she smiled as she turned to look out over the ocean. "You've shown me a whole new world, one I can't wait to explore, new friends, new beginnings. I feel like a little girl again, where everything is new . . . no wonder I'm remembering my childhood memories." She squinted as she looked into the sun in the east. "So yes! It is your fault I'm so giddy," she said in a sassy but joking manner.

"Yeah . . . okay, my bad. I'm such an asshole, I know! Forgive me, Ariella, I'll try and be more careful in the future." He went with it as she had suggested. But he had learned that she was sensing his thoughts, even if she was not searching for them. At that instant, he made the decision to give her a little more information once they arrived on Vieques Island. Until then, they needed to push on.

Upon reaching the rendezvous point, Jonathan noticed a small, abandoned building adjacent to a path that led downward, over a small seawall. Once they reached the building, he could see the unmanned Zodiac awaiting them at the end of the concrete pier.

Looking inside the structure, he decided it was the perfect time to give Ariella her tactical suit. She could go into the building and change in privacy while he prepped their ride.

Pulling open his tote bag, he pulled out her suit and handed it to her. "Here, go in there and put this on," he directed. He then wondered how she would look in the skintight suit—something he had been curious about since they first met. The only problem was, he had forgotten that Ariella was able to pick up on his thoughts.

Holding it up inspecting it, she tersely said, "I have my own wetsuit, thank you very much."

"That's not a wetsuit."

"Well, whatever it is, it looks to be a few sizes too small." She looked at him with a devilish smile, sensing what he was thinking. She had to admit that she was loving every minute of it.

"That, my dear, is the most advanced tactical suit the world has ever known. I'm wearing one too." He took off his shirt and showed her, exposing his muscular physique. muscular arms, sizable fully developed chest, and chiseled abs; everything that a girl would want. Ariella gawked. She too had been wondering what lay under his clothing. She decided to play along.

"You want me to put this on?" She held it up to her body while looking at him.

"Yeess, just trust me. It'll fit and could save your life."

Ariella could tell he was being sincere despite his lustful thoughts, so she put up no further resistance and walked into the building. However, she planned on giving him a bit more than he was expecting.

As she went off to change, Jonathan proceeded down the pier toward the boat. After checking the fuel level, priming the intake line, and lowering the motor, he located and studied the map. By his estimation, they were some 30 miles from their final stop; the Playa Grande Laguna on the far end of Vieques. It would take them about an hour to get there, if present conditions held.

While he was conducting a final inspection of the craft, Ariella approached unnoticed. "Well, I hope you're happy!" Her voice came from above.

When he looked up, Jonathan could not help himself. He merely stared, mouth partly open, without a word. It lasted more than just a few seconds. What stood before him was a goddess, or what he thought a goddess would look like. Yes siree! His question about her fitness was answered! She was most definitely in shape. From her well-defined legs, up to her muscularly firm butt, to her flat stomach, and upward to her perfectly developed, perky breasts, Ariella Marconi was the perfect specimen of a woman. *Statues should be modeled after her*, Jonathan thought.

Seeing his reaction and somehow knowing his thoughts caused Ariella to blush. She had never been so boisterous before, but she went with it anyway. "Sooo . . . what do you think?" She turned around, and like a model who had reached the end of the runway, paused, looking over her shoulder while biting her lip for added effect, and then spun her head back, as if she were going to walk away before turning back around to face him fully.

Jonathan, finally able to get hold of himself, smiled while shaking his head. "I think you're beautiful, but you better put something more on or I'm not going to be able to concentrate."

"Are you surrre?" she coyly toyed. But before he could respond, she was already grabbing her other clothes to put them back on. "You know I'm just fucking with you . . . I hope I didn't offend you." She knew she had not.

"No, Ariella, you didn't offend me. But I feel it's my duty as a man to warn you. If you keep up with that sort of behavior, you might wake up the animal that resides inside me, and then . . . well . . . rooaarr! Once the lion starts the hunt, he always gets his prey." He hoped to give her a bit of her own medicine. Judging by the look on her face, it worked. As the growling sound of the roar finished, shivers rapidly moved down her spine, exciting her.

While putting her clothes back on, though, Ariella began to question her newfound abilities. How was she suddenly able to pick up on Jonathan's thoughts and feelings? It was almost as if she was in his head. This talent only appeared after meeting Jack and Abhar. Had something happened to her that she was unaware of? She had to admit she felt recharged after their encounter. Maybe she was so relaxed, not concentrating on the deeper meaning of things, as she tended to do, that she was open to such an experience. *Exactly the opposite of what I'm doing now*, she thought. She made a conscious decision not to think about it any longer and to go with it. "What will be will be" was going to be her new mantra.

As Ariella hopped on the Zodiac, Jonathan handed her a life vest, showed her their destination on the map, and cranked up the motor. After untying the mooring lines and stowing them away, they were on their way, both doing their best not to think about the other.

As the boat pulled away, Jonathan turned toward the pier for one final look, when suddenly he spotted something. A red hawk and a black raven, two natural enemies, perched peacefully side by side. *That's something you don't see every day*, he thought before turning back around to the waters ahead. Next stop, Playa Grande Laguna.

CHAPTER

SIXTY ONE

THOUGH BOTH RAHZU and CheRahna were confused by the other's apparent activities, while Rahzu was under the belief that his commander might still be trusted, CheRahna had lost all faith that her captain had ever been honest.

Walking the corridors of the RJC, it was only a matter of time before they found each other. It happened to be that they finally met in the place where all the trouble had started, the science lab. Entering from opposite sides of the ship, Rahzu spoke first. "CheRahna, I'm glad to see you. I've been wanting to speak with you."

"And I have been looking to speak with you also, sir," she said.

In an attempt to feel her out, Rahzu decided it was better not to be direct in his line of questioning, at least not at first. Not only did he not want to put her on the defensive, as if he was attacking her, but he was concerned for her well-being. He genuinely cared and was worried about her.

"I couldn't help but notice how disturbed you were at the conclusion of our last conversation. How are you doing?"

Evasively, she responded, "Disturbed?! What gave you the impression I was disturbed, Captain?"

Sensing her reluctance to open up and speak frankly, Captain Rahzu tried harder; still not being too direct. "Well . . . considering all the conflicting information you have been given lately involving your uncle's history, along with the stress of the investigation, it would be reasonable for anyone to be experiencing some anxiety."

"Forgive me, Captain, but I'm not anxious either. In fact, I'm seeing things clearer than I have in a long time," she calmly stated.

Unfortunately for Rahzu, nothing he said at this point mattered; CheRahna had already made up her mind concerning what needed to happen in order to ensure she was getting the truth. Unknowingly, Rahzu pressed on, this time with more directness. "So . . . what have you concluded, Commander?"

She was very aware that the captain had detected her cynicism, but she could tell he had no clue as to the cause. Instead of bursting out with a volley of accusations and insults, which would offer him the opportunity of rebuttal—Rahzu was very persuasive when he wanted to be—CheRahna paused before she spoke again.

Being as vague as possible while building up the courage to use the compound in the crystal vial, she said in a calculated tone, "I have learned that things are rarely what they seem. That deceit and manipulation instead of truth and honor are not the exception but the norm . . . and that trust is just an illusion sold to beings so they can be made to feel better about the lies they are being forced to swallow. Even when, in actuality, they are choking on them."

While not coming right out and saying it, CheRahna was mainly referring to him. Since he and ShemRahya had already concluded that she had been in contact with YetziRah and that he had likely poisoned her mind, manipulating her, as her recent protest suggested, Rahzu could no longer afford to be passive. With precious time slipping away and the politeness in their conversation seemingly over, he came out and asked what she suspected. "CheRahna, do you not trust me anymore?"

Perhaps her last response was a bit too much. She had not quite built up the fortitude to face him confidently. Fearfully, or in an attempt to gain some time to open the vial secretly—this is what she would tell herself later—she turned her back on him and sheepishly said, "Why would I? Haven't you been lying to me all along?" Her voice faded as she finished speaking, almost like someone afraid and unsure of herself.

Up to this point in their relationship, Rahzu had always remained objective and understanding; taking into account all of her quirks, no matter how intolerable and adolescent some of them were. He believed in her and saw greatness in her future. Now, however, he had had enough. This was an outright display of disrespect, a behavior which he tolerated from no one. In a loud, commanding tone, his voice echoing throughout the science lab, he said, "Commander CheRahna!!! How dare you turn your back on me when speaking!"

The entire lab shuddered with the roar of his voice. A couple of weapons actually fell from their displays while the life pods rolled into the walls. Even the amber crystal's pedestal teetered momentarily. The captain was a powerful Rah Gold, and CheRahna knew it. Unconsciously, it reminded her of the days back at the Rah Academy when she was being berated by YetziRah. Nervously, her fingers moved quickly to unscrew the vial.

"I don't care what your issues are; I will not tolerate this disrespectful and insubordinate behavior!" He was more intense than she had ever thought he could be. His energy nearly incapacitated her, causing her to rethink what she was doing.

"You will turn around this minute"—he was furious—"and start acting like a Rah officer instead of some insolent child! Is that understood, Commander?!" Though Rahzu was angry and had never reacted well when being falsely accused, he wished he had not been so abrasive in his tone.

As CheRahna began to turn around, however, it did appear to him that his chiding produced the desired effect. He was wrong. Just as she was about to crumble, collapse to her knees, and cry out for forgiveness in her confusion, Rahzu's final words rang in her head. They gave her the strength to carry on, to start acting like a Rah officer . . . The truth and power in those few words were why she was here, in front of him now, in the first place. It was to fulfill her duty as a Rah commander, putting her personal feelings, fears, and insecurities aside. The time had come to do as her captain commanded. It was her duty to find out the truth.

Before beginning her about face, softly, with an eerie calmness in her voice, CheRahna said, "You're right, Captain Rahzu, forgive me. I do need to start acting like a Rah officer."

Even before the final sound escaped her silver tongue, she had begun to rapidly spin around. With the open vial in her left hand and moving to face him in a counterclockwise motion, she extended her left arm, dispersing the contents into the air directly in front of Rahzu.

Although Rahzu knew his commander to be emotionally unstable at times and apt to say just about anything, he was certainly not expecting a physical attack, as her movement suggested. The problem was, however, he was still unsure of what she was actually doing—what her rapid movement was for.

Surprisingly, the dust made up of WEDEC and monatomic gold flew quickly toward its intended target. It stuck readily to Rahzu's golden head, torso, and arms, as if it had an affinity for him. At first, nothing appeared to be happening. Rahzu just stood there in a stupor, trying to figure out what had occurred. Then suddenly, it started to take effect.

Since Dimerians do not feel pain as humans do, the onset of symptoms that Rahzu began to experience was not as traumatic as one might expect. At first, upon contact, his golden exterior began to boil, much like the bubbling seen in a carbonated soda. Then, white wisps of steam-like gases appeared as the boils popped.

As these symptoms increased in number and intensity, he clued into what was happening. In a distressed voice, he cried; "CheRahna . . . what have you done!?"

Oddly enough, a sense of prideful accomplishment filled CheRahna's very essence. She had been able to overcome her fear and indecisiveness while successfully administering the ancient vial's contents. *I did it!* she thought to herself. *Now he'll tell me what he's really doing.* Little did she know, that is exactly what was about to happen.

Unsure of what to expect after the powder's dispersal, CheRahna remained silent. She had no intention of offering him any response until she was certain that the captain believed he was dying; this, according to YetziRah, was how it was supposed to work. It did not take very long for her to see the results she desired.

Although Rahzu was unfamiliar with the particular compound that was now eating away at him and digesting his very existence, he did know that it contained WEDEC. As his thoughts raced through his mind, dealing with unanswered questions of the past, present, and future, he could not help but focus on how things had gone so wrong, so fast. Had he really failed CheRahna so badly that she would want him dead? That is certainly how it seemed, since that was exactly what was occurring. Still, he was not convinced she was aware of what her actions had wrought.

The question of why she was doing this was not as important to him as who told her to do it. All the evidence pointed to one being, perhaps the only Dimerian capable of this level of manipulation so quickly—YetziRah. To Rahzu, it was clear why he wanted him dead; his assassination would eliminate any opposition to his plans here in PU 430. Rahzu, knowing now that he should have been more careful, was the only one who suspected his treacherous activities; that was, of course, until he had informed ShemRahya.

With his death imminent and approaching rapidly, he still felt there may be time to save CheRahna from the clutches of the evil admiral. In a wise, accepting tone, he told her, "I doubt you know what you have done here. Very soon, I will be no more, and you will be in charge. You have killed me."

Since the captain thought he was dying, this presented the perfect time for her to begin her interrogation. "Well, if that is the case, Captain, you should probably come clean and confess your sins." She was still under the delusion that her longtime mentor was in no real danger.

Rahzu was expecting this sort of indifference toward his situation—she did not know. "I suppose you're right, my dear Commander. I am soooo sorry, I have totally failed you." He meant every word he said.

"You're damn right you did!! All these years . . . all the tales of duty, loyalty, and service, and you . . . the one I trusted the most, turn out to be just another traitor in cahoots with my estranged uncle. How could you, Rahzu?! You meant everything to me!" She was so upset that her voice cracked.

"So that is what you think of me, hmmm? That I could be so subversive and for such a long time, that no one picked up on it. Either I am the greatest manipulator in Rah history or you have been made a fool of. I mean, you have killed the only Dimerian who truly had your best interest in mind."

So far, this was not going as she expected. Yes, Rahzu was talking, but he was admitting nothing. She needed to probe harder. "I'm no fool, Captain. Not only did you lie to me about our houses and my uncle's history on Earth by giving me this fake codex . . ." She threw it down on the deck at his feet. "But you kept your relationship with him hidden!" she said smugly. "You also failed to inform the crew, as you were ordered, about the planet we Rahs have created in PU 78. You even lied to me when I asked you about it!"

Condescendingly, Rahzu retorted, "Who gave you this information . . . let me see . . . ah yes, it was Admiral YetziRah, right, Commander?"

"Well, according to you, sir"—she was being sarcastic as well—"that would be impossible since he was never here aboard this ship. In fact, according to the records, he neither met with you nor with me; he hasn't been here in quite some time."

Rahzu had heard what he needed to in order to confirm his worst fear. YetziRah had turned his second in command against him. How and why it all happened was no longer important; time was running out. With some quick thinking, in a calm tone of understanding, he said, "CheRahna, whatever that stuff is, it's destroying me as we speak. Therefore, I have nothing to gain by lying to you. Go ahead and read my thoughts if you like, I won't try to block you." He paused to let her in before continuing. "Everything I have done or said was to help you cope in a very stressful time. I wanted you to evolve slowly, healthily. Yes! I hid YetziRah's visit from you. I know how he tormented you and I have seen the effects he had on you firsthand, enough to realize that his presence would severely damage your psyche. With the alternative history I laid on you, which is all true by the way, as well as the investigation we are all involved in, I felt it better not to put that stress on you too."

She sat silently, sensing the truth and sincerity of his words, or at least what he thought the truth was. He was not finished yet. "As far as the planet, ET Rah, I was never ordered to tell anyone about it. Its existence is so secret that only the most powerful Rahs have knowledge of it. And I did not lie to you; I said I have never seen a Rah planet, which is true."

"Oh, that is just pure deception, Captain!" she snapped. "You knew very well it was there." Her silver color began to fluctuate as she began to realize that she may have made a mistake.

"But you didn't need to know about it, especially right then!" He gazed intently at her. "Just look at yourself, you are barely keeping it together, wondering what to do. How could you trust him over me?! After all that we have been through." He fell quiet to let his hurt sink in. "So now that you've killed me, what's your plan?" he asked matter-of-factly.

Still under the impression that the powder was not fatal and that it only made him think he was dying, she made a terse response while she attempted to make sense of his thoughts, feelings, and words. "Stop being so dramatic,

Captain; it doesn't suit you. You're not dying. The powder just makes you think that you are."

Knowing that his time was coming to an end, and fast, he made one last-ditch effort to bring her back to the side of truth. "CheRahna, just look at me! This is not an illusion. I am wasting away here. Believe it!"

She could only stare at him blankly, unable to process what was happening. At that moment, she felt as if she knew nothing.

Although he noticed her utterly confused state, his time was up. Rahzu cleared his mind of any negative thoughts and feelings; smiled, and then left her with one final thought. "CheRahna"—he struggled not only to find the right words but to get them out—"I forgive you and am proud of you for doing what you believed to be right. Never stop being who you are." He fell silent as he smiled one last time.

CheRahna finally understood. "Rahzuuu!" she cried out while reaching for him. But it was too late, he was already gone.

CHAPTER

SIXTY TWO

AFTER EXITING THE docking chamber, which was located atop of the western section of the Hab, Captain LaMarr propelled himself down to the exterior southern wall of the sub bay. Under normal conditions, when properly resting on its fifteen-foot support columns, the exit pool found on the belly of the facility provided the crew access to the abyssal ocean. However, with the structure resting on the bottom, this was no longer an option.

As discussed, Justin would remove a section of the sub bay's shell with the plasma torch, offering an avenue for the mini-sub's exit. Once the section was cut away, he would enter the bay, disconnect the stabilizing wires attached to the sub, and provide guidance to the pilot, Lt. Barett, in maneuvering the PRIEST safely into the open water.

The plan was well conceived and sound, with only a few, but potentially dangerous, sources of uncertainty. The first was the unpredictability of subsequent tremors, the last of which, along with a falling slab of rock, had dislodged the Sea Lab from its footings and placed it in its current position. Another falling chunk of debris, striking either the sub or Captain

LaMarr, could lead to catastrophic results, costing everyone their lives. Neither the PRIEST nor the exosuits were designed to withstand such a blunt force blow.

The second fear was whether the detached section would fall inward or outward. If it fell inward, into the sub bay, the vibrations caused by its collapse could reverberate through the chamber, potentially causing damage to the Hab or the sub itself. If it were to drop outward, Captain LaMarr himself could be crushed.

Since the danger of allowing the wall to fall inward presented too much risk, steps were taken to ensure it fell outward. By fastening multiple tethering cables, attached to torsional springs winched to the section to be removed, both the captain and the tech Roger Sealy were confident that the direction of the wall's fall could be controlled. Justin would just have to remain alert, avoiding the wall as it fell.

The last and perhaps most crucial risk was the cutting of the hole in the Hab's wall in the first place. Though the Sea Lab was designed and connected in individual modules, each division's structural integrity was strengthened by the others. Once the wall of the sub bay was compromised, the effects caused by the deep ocean's pressure on the weakened façade were unknown. It could collapse, crushing the mini-sub and the crew.

Still, after taking into account the pressure at this depth, the estimated structural strength of the wall after the cut, and the elasticity of the external shell, Roger thought everything would be fine, as long as nothing hit them from above. Only time would tell.

Surveying the exterior wall, Justin visualized the pattern in which he would perform his plasma cuts. As discussed with Roger, he would start at the bottom, burning a dashed line pattern, ensuring that the wall would retain as much compression strength as possible until the top was cut.

After accomplishing this, he would work his way across the top and up each side, leaving about a foot untouched on the lateral surfaces. The goal, of course, was to be as safe as possible while allowing the structure to retain some of its strength.

Unsure what was going to happen, Captain LaMarr thought it best to wait until the last minute to find out. With more time, the exterior wall could be braced, offering stability. Unfortunately, with the looming threat of more aftershocks, they needed to move, and quickly.

With the plan set in motion, Justin grabbed his torch and, using the suit's four-foot retractable extension cable, connected it to his ZPE power source. The blue plasma flame illuminated the area even more as he fired up the tool and began to cut.

———⌣———

Inside the cramped mini-sub, the entire crew, except Roger, was nervous, awaiting their fate as the luminescent blue glow of the torch radiated through the sub's porthole. He, sitting up front beside Lt. Barett, was curiously staring at the wall; he had never seen a plasma torch in use before. "Beautiful," he whispered at the glow.

Knowing how fast the torch would do its work, cutting through the nitinol shell, and how quickly the propagation of the ocean's compression wave would strike, Roger said, "Hold on, everyone, here it comes!" Staring out at the wall he continued, "Wait for it . . . wait for it."

All of a sudden, with a flood of blue light, a whirling vortex wave entered through the rapidly expanding cut. Almost instantly it impacted everything inside the bay, shattering computer monitors, crushing lights, and toppling everything that was not tied down. The sub and its occupants, while shaken, survived the ordeal undamaged.

"So far so good!" Steven spoke up first.

The rest of the crew remained silent, waiting to see if the wall would hold up. None of them would feel safe until they were out of the Hab, heading for the surface.

To everyone's surprise, the captain made quick work of slicing through the hull; in a matter of minutes the job was nearly done, with no apparent negative effects on the structure as a whole. Only the last two foot-long sections remained. These final cuts were critical; this was where much of the potential danger lay.

Carefully studying his completed work, Justin, trying to be as safe as possible while using the torch, positioned himself to the side of the wall while cutting. Once he finished burning the final portion of the top right side, the severed section, due to the pulling power of the winches, started to flex outward. The high-pitched, screeching sound of twisting metal pierced through the water. Everyone in the PRIEST shuddered.

Justin saw this as a good thing, at least for now; he knew which way the wall was going to fall. Hopefully, the rest of work would go as smoothly, the hull falling safely as predicted.

Propelling himself upward and to the left to avoid being crushed if the wall suddenly broke loose and fell, he quickly approached the last remaining section to be removed. "Steven, I'm about to make the final cut as soon as I can get the lines, so be ready. I want the sub out of there ASAP. Is that understood?"

"Aye aye, Captain, we're ready," Steven said joyously, sensing that the end of this ordeal was near.

Making his cuts, Justin was quite surprised at how strong the nickel titanium metal was. He had read the specs and knew it was an amazing material, but he did not expect it to still be holding, especially considering the tension being applied by the winches. He knew, though, that once he made his final cut, the wall would come crashing down, and fast. "Making the final cut now."

"Good luck, Captain, and be careful," Lt. Barett replied.

Just as the torch was about to melt the final remaining strands of metal, under the enormous tension the wall failed. A loud, echoing pop caused a powerful vibratory wave that radiated outward in all directions. It nearly caused Justin to drop the torch. The severed hull section, now completely detached from the Hab on three sides, deflected toward the open ocean. The screeching of contorting metal was practically deafening.

Inside the PRIEST, Roger looked back, gave Nancy an encouraging smile, and then returned his focus to the lowering hull. "Aren't you glad we decided to leave the bottom partially attached?" he asked proudly, since it was his idea in the first place.

Although it came as a surprise to the captain, Roger had correctly predicted that the wall's descent to the sea floor to be much slower and more controlled than he had. "Hell yeah, Roger! It did scare the shit out of me when it failed, but you were right. Good call."

As soon as the opening in the bending hull was large enough, Captain LaMarr entered the sub bay, rapidly moving to free the PRIEST from its tethering lines. After making quick work of the job, the sub was ready for departure.

Little did the crew know, however, that the concussion wave, traveling at more than 4,700 mph, had reached the same outcropping where the large slab that had damaged the Hab previously, had originated. This time, the propagated sound dislodged a smaller, but still dangerous, rock from its already precarious position. It was headed straight for the Hab.

As the silent projectile plummeted through the darkness toward its target, Justin moved into position and, like a flight deck signal man directing an aircraft on a carrier, provided guidance to the sub and its occupants.

While Lt. Barett, following his captain's directions, nimbly operated the controls, propelling the submersible through the opening; Roger monitored the sub's onboard peripheral cameras, which provided a 360-degree view of the PRIEST'S exterior. The rest of the crew remained quietly optimistic, especially now that they were in motion.

Although the size of the removed hull section was adequate for the mini-sub to escape, it was not so large as to eliminate all danger. It still required, as Steven was experiencing, some finesse in order to maneuver the vessel toward the open water. Much like an astronaut in a capsule moving in the vacuum of space, he used the sub's directional yaw jets to stabilize the craft and gently guide it through the tight opening.

"Halfway there, Steven. It's all over but the cryin'," Roger said as he studied their trajectory.

"Good job, Steven. Keep it slow and steady. Another few seconds . . . ," Justin said as he counted down. "Five, four, three . . ."

Suddenly, without warning, the falling boulder from above struck the Sea Lab, producing a sound resembling that of two semis in a head-on collision. Unfortunately, it could not have landed in a worse place, striking the facility precisely above where the hull section had been removed. The force of the impact was so great it caused the already weakened structure to deflect even more. It deformed to such a degree that the catwalk, located on the wall above the sub's current position, broke loose and came crashing down, caroming off the underwater transport. The crew's silence ended as the sub's emergency buzzers and lighting came to life. Gasps and screams filled the now red-lit submersible.

"We're going to die!!" cried Robert Washington.

"Oh, shut the hell up, Robert, and grow a pair," Dr. Walker scolded.

"That didn't sound good, fellas," Frank Gilmore added as his usually sunny disposition turned to one of gloom.

Nancy Rogers just cried, whimpering like a scared child.

"Damage report!" Steven yelled at Roger, who was already working on it.

Luckily, if one could call it luck, the catwalk was not heavy enough to pin the PRIEST down or significantly alter its current glide path. Realizing that it would be easier to assess the damage once the vessel was clear of the Hab, Justin took control. "Hit the gas, Steven. Get outta there, now!"

Without a word, Lt. Barett did as he was told, and while not a smooth transition, safely propelled the craft into the open ocean. "What's our status, Roger?"

"We're losing power, Steven, and fast. I think our battery's electrical relay must have been damaged. We're only operating at just over 10 percent capacity."

"Any way to reroute power, Roger?"

"Not from here . . . Maybe from outside, maybe."

"Captain . . ." Lt. Barett began.

"I'm already on it, Steven," Captain LaMarr answered as he moved in for a closer look. "It looks to me like . . ." He stopped speaking.

"Like what, sir? Over." Steven could hear the sound of doom in Justin's voice, even if no one else could.

Upon inspection of the mini-sub's destroyed power relay and its batteries, Justin knew that before long the submersible would be dead in the water. Looking back into the sub bay, he briefly wondered if he could safely reenter the facility in order to retrieve the tools and equipment needed to replace the broken devices. His hopes, however, were quickly dashed as the rest of the catwalk fell, causing the hull to further collapse, closing off his point of entry. He simply did not have enough time to clear a path, at least one that would be safe.

Thoughts raced through his mind as he rapidly searched for answers. This was a life-and-death situation, with something needing to be done before his entire crew perished. As unemotionally as he could, Justin described what he saw. "The power core and electrical relay are all but destroyed."

"What does that mean?!" Nancy cried out.

"Calm down, darling, I'm sure the boys will come up with somethin'," Deborah consoled the young chemist.

"How long before we lose propulsion power, Roger?" Steven asked quietly, looking directly at him.

In the same tone, Roger answered, "Ten minutes at best."

"And life support systems?"

"If we don't use any more power and just float . . . turning off the heating system . . . the oxygen scrubbers should work for . . ." Roger calculated.

"How long?" Steven asked impatiently.

"Thirty minutes before complete systems shut down. We'll have another thirty minutes of air, tops, after that before we start to suffocate."

A deafening silence filled the submersible. Even Nancy's whimpering had ceased. Everyone, including Lt. Barett, was in shock. Not one to throw in the towel though, Steven, unaware of what had happened to the sub bay, called out, "Captain, if you could go back into the bay and . . ."

"That's impossible, Steven. The way is blocked. Entry is inaccessible," the captain replied, cutting off his lieutenant.

"Well . . . you could enter the Hab back through the bathysphere's docking chamber . . ."

"Do the math, Lieutenant, there's not enough time. I would have to flood the entire western module and then burn a hole in the bulkhead in order to reenter the lab anyway. You would all be long dead by the time I finished."

"We can . . ." Steven's words trailed off as he came to the bitter conclusion that they were going to die. While the crew silently began to accept their mortality, Captain LaMarr was contemplating his own. He had found a way to save his crew.

Although Justin never classified himself as a hero—heroes, in their quest for glory, usually got those around them killed—he did consider himself a warrior. Warriors sought battle, took risks, and offered themselves up for sacrifice only when absolutely necessary. Like a captain going down with his ship, he considered it more of a duty than a responsibility to ensure his crew's safety. Regrettably, this happened to be one of those times.

With the PRIEST'S power relay and batteries damaged beyond repair, it really became a matter of simple logic; the lives of six people versus the life of one. He knew what needed to be done.

"Lieutenant Barett."

The airwaves remained silent.

"Steven!"

Snapping out of his self-pity, Lt. Barett answered, "Yes, Captain."

"I think I have an idea. I'm going to try something. On my mark, I need you to throw the main power switch. You read me?"

"Yes, sir, I read you. What are you going to do?"

"Don't worry about it. If it works . . ." Justin paused as the reality of what he was about to do hit him. "Since the comms will also go down once you kill the power, when I rap on the hull with double taps, three times in succession, flip the switch back on. Is that clear, over?"

With excitement in his voice, Steven responded, "Loud and clear, Captain. Our fingers are crossed."

Gathering up all the intestinal fortitude he could muster, Justin gave the order. 'Hit it, Steven." The sub went dark, dead in the water, for now.

Working quickly, Justin disconnected the power cable attached to his plasma torch and ZPE, plugging it directly into the mini-sub, bypassing the relay. Satisfied that the connections were secure, he then began to remove his ZPE generator, which was located on the ventral side of the exosuit, just above the waist. After methodically unsnapping the four retention clamps, he carefully pulled the power source away from the suit.

With the connections now exposed, the moment of truth had arrived. Though he knew he could always reconnect the ZPE back into his suit if this did not work, it was time to make a choice, his life or theirs. Surprisingly, as quickly as the doubt entered his mind, it went away. Justin pulled the plug.

Inside the sub, only the glow radiating from the Sea Lab's exterior illumination cut through the darkness. No one said a word. Most were busy praying. Sort of ironic, since they were inside a submersible named the PRIEST. The only sound, which was coming from outside the sub where the captain was working, was the clinking of metal. All else was quiet.

After what seemed like an eternity, three successive double taps echoed through the submersible. "Here goes nothing; I hope this works," Steven said as he flipped the power switch.

An audible sound of relief was heard through the mini-sub as the controls and overhead lights came to life.

"See, Nancy, I told you things would be just fine," Deborah said calmly.

"So far so good, Steven, everything appears to be operational. Whatever the captain did, it's holding," Roger said, breathing a sigh of relief.

"Captain, whatever you did, the PRIEST has been resurrected from the dead. We are fully operational and ready for departure, sir," Lt. Barett called out to his mentor.

CHAPTER

SIXTY THREE

THE AIR WAS unusually brisk as the maglev pulled into Bariloche station. Typically, most underground facilities maintained a constant temperature of around 58 degrees, but, as Haney suspected, the mercury here fell much lower.

Another oddity was how bright and white everything was. It seemed as if the architect's vision was to use a style that projected the exterior environment into the interior's décor. With the station's alpine setting and winter rapidly approaching, the snowy, mountainous theme was clearly evident.

Among the abnormally high concentration of subterranean creatures, particularly the Nagas, a snake-like Reptilian race from the Tibetan plateau, was a short, stocky blond-haired man who appeared to be in his mid-forties. He stood about five foot six and sported a finely cropped crew cut and a neatly trimmed, slightly gray goatee. He wore the standard alpine garb and, if not for his intense stare, would have likely gone unnoticed, blending in with the rest of the humans scurrying about.

Instinctively, after quickly surveying the environment, Gilla raised his right arm and pointed a talon toward the now approaching stranger. "Shish mush be our conshacsh," the large Reptilian announced.

"You know, you really shouldn't use words you can't pronounce, dummy." Haney, upon exiting the train seemed to be in good spirits. "Maybe if you stitched up that ass licker you call a tongue, us common folk wouldn't have to translate everything you say . . . Do you understand the words coming out of my mouth?"

Because he had worked with Haney for many years, Gilla was used to his offensive but endearing insults. He remained composed and just stared straight ahead as if nothing had been said. Now was not the time for senseless banter. In fact, as soon as they had detrained, his olfactory center detected something dangerous—a faint, but musty, septic odor was in the air, one Gilla knew well.

"What! . . . No speaka Español?" Haney continued to jest until finally cluing in on what his companion was looking at. Due to his size and general disposition toward life and death, the large Indian hillbilly was not as quick to sense danger as his counterpart. He, like most men his size, had never had a problem with people picking a fight with him, especially if they wanted to live. Therefore, the stranger was almost upon them when the Chief acknowledged his presence.

"God evening, gentlemen, it's an ehre [honor] to meet you," the man said in a thick Germanic accent as he extended his hand in greeting to the large green creature. "Mein name is Rudolph Siemens von Clause, aber [but] friends call me Von. I was sent by Jack Dresher, a friend of your Major Hawthorn's. He said to tell you that the weather is fine in the tropics."

That was the password they were waiting for.

While appreciating the introductory gesture, Gilla merely raised his large muscular green arm and wiggled his long taloned fingers. Dexterity was not an asset possessed by his kind, especially when it came to shaking hands. Noting immediately what the Reptilian meant, Von quickly offered his hand to Haney, who just stared, studying him.

"Who in the hell named you that? Sounds like you did more for old Santa Claus than lead his sleigh, heh, heh, heh."

Not one to take an insult without rebuttal, Von Clause fired back, being careful not to overtly offend the large American. "Mein apologies. Aber I do not spriche der Scheisskopf [speak shithead]."

Gilla, who understood almost every known language, burst into a fit of hissing laughter. Haney, however, was not so amused. Though knowing almost no German, or any other language for that matter, he did pick up on the hint of sarcasm in the agent's tone. That is not what bothered him. He loved it when bits of witty verbal assault came his way. What ate at him was that he had no idea what had been said, and hence no way to properly respond.

"Listen here, ya little sawed-off turd, you'd better start speakin' English or I'm gonna stomp on your head so many times yous gonna think you was in a tap-dancing contest. Sprechen Sie that! Huh!?"

Recognizing the volatility of his large counterpart, particularly when it concerned his intellect, Rudolph smartly made it a point to use more English when speaking to Haney; always leaving in some German on purpose, just for spite. "I said I do not speak, how would you say, shithead."

This was a crucial moment; not even Gilla knew how Haney was going to react. Standing poised, ready to move at the slightest sign of an attack, Von Clause dug in with the balls of his feet. He had no intention of taking a blow from such a large opponent.

Von Clause remained silent, continuing his thousand-yard stare. The atmosphere was tense as Haney sized up the smaller man, who appeared to be preparing for a fight; his respect for him grew. It was not too often that someone had the balls to speak to him in that manner and then to stand his ground when threatened. *The little guy has balls*, he thought.

Extending his hand, he grabbed hold of the German's and squeezed tightly. One can always judge a man by how he shakes hands. Surprisingly, even though Haney's hand engulfed the smaller German's, Rudolph possessed a powerful grip. The two men remained clutched, each trying to crush the other into submission. At that moment, the Chief knew he was going to get along fine with old Von, just as long as he did not cross him.

"Staff Sergeant Jimmy Haney. Call me Haney." With a boyish smile, one more relaxed than earlier, he turned toward Gilla. "Gil, I kinda like the little fella. We'll have to find ya somethin' else to eat." The seven-foot lizard just shook his head, relieved that Haney did not go off the reservation on him.

As Gilla introduced himself, Haney, being his usual rude self, made the introductions for him! "This here's Gilla. As you might guess, he's a meat eater. But I wouldn't worry much if I were you. He's more of a blood and guts kinda guy, if you know what I mean. Just call him dummy . . . dummy, heh, heh, hee . . . Did you hear that? That's why I should've been a comedian, my shit rhymes, and it's natural."

"Gilla, you are from the Unterwelt [underworld], yes?"

"Yesh." He always admired humans who could tell the difference.

"Wunderbar, you should be quite comfortable down here while Haney and I go into the Stadt [city]." Von pointed upward to let the Chief know they were going topside, to the city.

Looking around, Gilla welcomed the privacy. He had been cooped up in a cabin for the better part of the day and needed to stretch. He also wanted to explore the area; this was his first trip to San Carlos de Bariloche. Also, he could not shake the scent of the two Grays, Trick and Treat, whom he had detected as soon as the door opened. Whatever they were up to did not bode well for them. They could expose his team, further complicating their mission.

Seeing his longtime companion was tuned into something, Haney asked, "Everything all right Gil?"

"Yoush shwo go ahead. Ish not safe sho shalk here," he said, waving his arm around and pointing toward the crowded facility. "I needsh sho check on someshing anywaysh."

"Okay . . . see what you can turn up. We'll be back shortly . . . And Gil, try not to get into a fight. I know how territorial your kind can get."

"No worrsih. I jush saw Jen, hiss, hiss, hiss."

With no further words, Von Clause led Haney to the nearest elevator and to the surface. Gilla started his quest to track the source of the scent.

———

Arriving at the surface, the odd-looking duo stepped out of the elevator into the lobby of a large motel, which was originally built as a plastic surgery clinic in order to assist fleeing Nazis escaping their fate following World War II. Although crowded and with twilight rapidly approaching, combined with the ambience of a sixteenth-century German castle, the pair exited the vestibule unnoticed. Drawing too much attention to oneself was not advisable in a town such as this; spies were everywhere.

Though it was not common knowledge, many if not all of the US presidents, beginning with Eisenhower and continuing to the present day, along with several Russian premiers, various foreign dignitaries, and many of the world's elite have visited the sleepy little Swiss-style ski town situated on the eastern slopes of the Andes Mountains in the Rio Negro district of Argentina. Bariloche was far away from everything and everyone. It was indeed interesting why such a place had received such international attention.

Could it be that this was indeed the base of operations for the notorious Martin Bormann, the leader of the Nazi party in the final days of the war? Could it be that just six and a half miles away, on Huemul Island, set in the middle of Lake Nahuel Huapi, that Dr. Ronald Richter, on February 16, 1951, with the backing of then Argentine President Juan Peron, reportedly achieved a controlled thermonuclear reaction without the use of either uranium or plutonium; a feat thought to be impossible at the time. Maybe it was just because the skiing was world class, offering a more remote experience than that provided by the bustling tourist centers of Europe. It may never be known.

All Haney knew was that he was here to find a piece of a mystical spear and that—after walking through the sliding glass doors and taking a long, deep breath of the clean, mountain air—it was cold. Damn cold!

Back in the States, summer was near; but here, at the forty-first parallel in the Southern Hemisphere, winter was upon them. Haney, though wearing a pair of heavy camouflaged BTUs and a black turtleneck sweater, was ill prepared for this sort of climate change. He had been so excited and in such a rush to leave that he had failed to pack even a jacket.

On the other hand, Von Clause, born near the city of Füssen, located in the Bavarian Alps along the German-Austrian border, felt completely at home. Not only was he accustomed to the temperature and altitude, but also to the repetitive play of shadows, which was performed nightly as the sun exited the western stage behind the Andes.

Though Rudolph, a typical German, could be crude and harsh when speaking with others, he usually displayed a gentler disposition and generally cared about others' needs. This was one of those times. Upon hearing the chattering of Haney's teeth, Von Clause quickly altered their course, directing them to a trusted outfitter. Plus, he needed a few supplies himself. "I think we need to get you a parka and a hood. I know a little place just around der corner which will have precisely what we need."

"What makes you think I need a jacket, huh? I'm not cold," Haney said, refusing to admit that he was shivering.

Skillfully, Von Clause, rather than pointing out the obvious, got Haney to see the other reasons a jacket could be beneficial. "For one, Mein Herr, your appearance alone already makes you stand out. You are much larger than most here. Plus, having a bald head and ponytail does not help you blend in either. Second, everyone except you has a coat on."

Haney was silently stroking his goatee as Von Clause continued.

"And finally, it might be good to have something on that covers your Messer there," pointing to his large knife. "That might intimidate a few people."

"Ooh, heh, heh, heh . . . Bertha here," he said as his hand instinctively found its way to his trusted third appendage. "Yeah, she's been known to turn a head or two in her day."

"It's also close to the local Speismart. I want to introduce you to some of the Stadt's wurst and kraut. After washing it down with a stein of beer, I think you will agree, it's the best you'll ever have, outside of Bavaria, of course."

Though not particularly hungry, the Chief never turned down an opportunity to enjoy the local cuisine, especially when it would likely produce a large amount of flatulence. Fermented cabbage would do just that. Haney was a connoisseur of passing gas and took his farting seriously. Different foods, as well as species, produced distinct aromas, which could all be classified according to smell, volume, depth, and longevity. Rarely had he met anyone who could match his skill.

Additionally, the promise of a cold brew only sweetened the deal. With an anticipatory gurgle in his stomach and a twinkle in his eye, Haney gladly accepted the invitation. "Okay, ya little red-nosed reindeer, let's go pimp my ride and fill up the tank." Secretly, in order to achieve maximum effect, he had already begun to plot how, when, and where to release his inevitable noxious buildup. The thought made him feel warm and fuzzy inside.

Meanwhile, back underground, almost precisely below his human companion's feet, Gilla was cautiously following the scent of the two Grays. *What are they doing here, so far from Dulce, away from their master,* he thought. Surely this was a mere coincidence, but he had to be sure.

Normally, he would not have put much stock in this seemingly random event; the two Alpha Draconian slaves posed him little physical threat. However, considering what Jonathan had told him thus far about their mission, nothing could be left to chance.

As he meandered through the crowd of humans and Reptilians, he too decided it would be better to alter his appearance. Since he, like all reptiles, was cold-blooded and extremely sensitive to variations in temperature, an effect he was experiencing here in this unfamiliarly cold environment, Gilla made a beeline toward the nearest vendor and purchased a woolen poncho. Since many of his kind, coming from warmer climate, occupied the station and suffered from the conditions, ponchos were in high demand and worn by many. He blended in perfectly.

Continuing his quest, which to him seemed to last longer than it actually did—Reptilians, once engaged in a primal activity such as scent tracking—lost all concept of time, Gilla finally came upon his quarry. Standing innocuously among a variety of beings involved in various conversations, Trick and Treat were otherwise occupied, seemingly unaware of his presence. Moving closer to get a better look, he quickly discovered the focus of their attention.

Sitting relaxed, slightly reclined with one leg propped up on the other, in what resembled an Adirondack-style chair, was an elegant-looking human female. Gilla, despite thinking that all humans were grotesque-looking creatures, thought of this woman as beautiful, at least by human standards. She had long, flowing, amber-colored hair; olive tanned skin, like that of Egyptian royalty; and greenish, yellow haloed eyes, which bore into the two Grays as she calmly spoke. Although well proportioned and not overly muscular, she possessed an aura of power that Gilla immediately noticed.

Like a queen issuing orders to her servants from a throne, her silken amber robe rose and fell with each hand gesture. While her facial expressions alluded to nothing in particular, her mere actions did. It was a very rare occurrence to witness a human, any human, issue orders in this environment, especially to a couple of Grays. Something odd was definitely afoot, but what?

As the large Reptilian continued to study the unusual trio's interactions, suddenly and before he could turn away, the woman stopped talking and focused her gaze upon him. Her intense stare quickly softened as pursed lips gave way to a warm, innocent smile. For a moment, it almost appeared as if she was blushing.

Just as unexpectedly, with a quick nod of appreciation, she returned her concentration to the Gray duo. Gilla realized that while enjoying his attention, she had no idea who he was. The two Grays, never taking their large black eyes off her, were still unaware of his presence. Thankfully, reading a Reptilian's thoughts required much more focus than reading a human or he would likely have been discovered.

After some time, it became obvious that their presence here had nothing to do with him. Now satisfied that the pair posed no immediate threat, Gilla made his way to the nearest food cart. He was famished—mating takes a lot of energy. It would take him some time to fully recuperate. Nevertheless, he would need to remain vigilant in avoiding the trio as he continued to explore the Bariloche underworld. No sense in creating controversy where there was none. Still, the image of the woman lingered in his mind.

Since this was not Von Clause's first trip to the alpine city—he had been there many times conducting operations for his West German GSG9 unit or as a liaison to the East German Stasi—he understood the internal hierarchy of the town and knew who to talk to in order to get things done. Luckily, his missions rarely involved wet work, which always left the locals a bit skittish.

Although the hour was waning and lamps began to light up the salt-covered streets and sidewalks, Rudolph knew his old friend's shop would still be open at this hour. Because Bariloche was a ski town, meaning that much of the daytime activity centered on the slopes, the rest of the town relaxed until later in the day. In late afternoon, with couples returning from their day's adventures, along with their patient but tired guides; the atmosphere came to life. Everyone shopped, ate, or drank—often a combination of all three.

It only took a few minutes to arrive at their destination. Positioned beside two shimmering gas lamps was a sign that read "Das Patagonia Haus, Est. 1947." If not for the antique skis, sleds, and climbing gear that adorned the exterior wall, one would have had a hard time distinguishing this building from any other.

As they entered through the dark, wooden, walnut door; a partially cracked brass bell, shined to perfection, issued a sickly ring. Haney, quickly scanning the room, spotted a short, thin, nearly bald, white-haired man standing behind the counter, applying price stickers to various articles of merchandise. He wore silver-colored, circular, wire-framed glasses that rested on his nose, and though not particularly good at guessing age, Haney believed the man to be at least eighty, maybe older.

On hearing the bell, the man behind the counter looked up, tilted his head forward as he squinted, and then threw his hands up in glee. "Rudolph!! O ho ho. It has been such a lange Zeit [long time] . . . I was beginning to think etwas [something] bad had befallen you."

"Fritz! You old Geizhals [miser]. I thought surely you would be kaput by now," Von jested in return.

While the two men got reacquainted, speaking mostly in German, Haney thought to himself, "Great, some kind of reunion. At least I could have had a beer or two first."

As if being granted a wish by a genie itself, Von Clause showed up at his side with a huge mug of dark, hearty German Hefeweizen. "Here you are, mein Herr. Compliments of the Haus [house]. My colleague, Fritz, says life and happiness . . . Go on, have a taste."

Joyously taking the large foam-topped beverage, Haney was pleased not only with the amount of beer offered, which was more than a couple of pints, but also with the rich flavor. After several long, guttural chugs, he pulled his foam-covered face away from the mug to let out a loud, deep belch. This, apparently being acceptable, elicited a bit of laughter.

"I think that means he likes it, Fritz!"

"Of course he does, Schweinhold. Those watered-down American beers are for Fräuleins und Kinder [women and children]. This is a man's drink, and your friend here is definitely männlich [manly]," the old man said as he exuberantly beat his chest.

Haney was enjoying the rich, peppery, roasted, hoppy flavor of his lager, completely oblivious to Fritz's comments. Miraculously, the storeowner's brew bounced off his taste buds to warm his entire body. Though Chief was not accustomed to being polite or thankful, he found it necessary to express his gratitude for such a fine beverage with all the congeniality he could muster. Haney raised his mug high and said, "This here is some good shit," before burping once again.

"Mein Vergnügen [my pleasure] . . . ha ha ha." Looking to Von, Fritz continued, "I like your friend, he's got Schmecken [taste]." Laughter again filled the air; even Haney joined in.

Deciding to savor the rest of his beer alone, Haney left the two men to their business. Walking aimlessly around the shop, periodically checking price tags, he whispered aloud, "Who the hell can afford this stuff?" He did not realize that the prices listed were in australs, not US dollars, and that the current exchange rate was over hundred to one.

As he continued to browse, nothing much caught his eye, until he reached the shooting section. Although the merchandise on offer consisted mainly of the types used in competitions, such as Nordic biathlons, to Haney, rifles were rifles. As a Ranger sniper, he possessed a passion for anything that launched projectiles.

While Haney occupied himself with the multitude of targets, sights, scopes, and shooting devices; Von Clause and Fritz scoured the racks looking for a parka and a hood that would fit the large American. This presented the perfect opportunity to acquire something else Von needed—information.

A former German submariner, one of the ones lucky enough to catch a ride aboard the last of the U-boats fleeing the homeland, Fritz was well connected and knew almost everything that went on in Bariloche. Although not a follower of Hitler, or the Nazis for that matter, he had kept close ties with those who were. Information, flowing both ways, was always a valuable commodity. His neutrality and tactful information sharing had earned him trust on both sides of the aisle. This allowed him to operate his business and affairs with relative impunity from both the Argentine Government and the local German aristocracy.

"So, Rudolph, what brings you to Bariloche?" Fritz finally asked, pulling up his glasses as he did.

Looking around the room to make sure no one else was present—and he knew there was not—Von Clause leaned toward his old friend, and in a hushed voice said, "Mein Freund there"—he said, pointing at Haney—"suche (is searching) for a Schwert [sword]."

"Ein Schwert?!" Fritz responded in quiet but reverent astonishment. "Ach, mein Gott [Oh my God]!"

Slowly reaching under the counter, the old German pushed a secret button, which immediately locked the front door. Haney, at the sound of the bolt clicking into place, ducked into a crouch, spun around, and, using his right hand with cat-like reflexes, brought Bertha up horizontally, stopping just under his eye line. With the knife situated across his face, hilt toward the thumb, the hillbilly, Indian, Ranger, sniper homed in on the source of the sound.

Von Clause, though not too surprised by the large man's reaction—he was a soldier—was taken aback by his quickness and agility. Calmly raising one of his hands while taking a sip of beer with the other, he silently let Haney know that everything was fine.

Fortunately for Von, Haney was mindful and did not spill any of his frothy beverage, or he would not have been so easily coaxed out of combat mode. As rapidly and easily as he had transitioned into an elite killing machine, he returned to his typical relaxed, unsocial self. Taking his cue from Von, he too decided to enjoy another sip of brew. Without taking his eyes off the front door, and only after a succession of huge gulps that nearly emptied his mug, he eventually returned to his browsing.

Seeing that his companion was once again preoccupied, at least while the beer held out, Von Clause continued with his questions. "Do you zurückrufen [recall] Jack Dresher?"

"Ja, ja, I do! Mein Korper (my body) may be succumbing to Zeit [time], but mein Kopf"—Fritz said, tapping his head—"is still as jung [young] as ever."

"Well, he is back to seine alten Wege [his old ways], versuche die Welt zu retten [trying to save the world]." Von paused for a moment as he chose his next words carefully. "Er stellt die Heilige Lanze zusammen [he's putting together the Holy Lance]!"

As Von spoke, Fritz's eyes got wider and wider. He knew the ramifications of what Jack was attempting to do, especially if the spear got into the wrong hands.

"Genug [enough]!" was the last sensible thing Fritz said as he went off into a tirade of spitting and cussing. He was so intense that even Haney took notice.

"Beruhige dich, mein Freund, beruhige dich [calm down my friend, calm down]. You are going to have a Schlaganfall [stroke]!" Von warned.

"What is that Dummkopf doing? Er weiß, dass der Mensch niemals eine solche Macht besitzen wird [he knows that man is never to possess such power]!"

"Ich weiß, ich weiß [I know, I know], Fritz. Aber Jack versicherte mir, dass es notwendig war [but Jack assured me that it was necessary]."

"Nichts ist so wichtig, mein Herr, nichts. Es bringt die ganze Welt in Gefahr [Nothing is that important, sir, nothing. It puts the whole world in danger]."

Slightly overwhelmed by his harangue, Fritz sat down, pulled out a hand-kerchief from his back pocket, and wiped the beads of sweat that had developed on his forehead. Regaining his composure, he sadly looked at Von and pro-claimed, "Es tut mir leid, mein Freund, da kann ich nicht helfen [I am sorry my friend, I cannot help with this].

"You can't or you won't?" Von said in English, which shocked Fritz.

He too switched to the king's language, just as Von had done. "Rudolph, I love you like a Sohn, and I think the Welt of you, but I cannot agree to this. It is too dangerous."

Still hoping he could convince his colleague to help, Von tried again. "Jack is brilliant, Fritz, and would not have undertaken such a task unless he had too…I trust his instincts."

"I do not!" Fritz said stubbornly.

While the men argued, Haney quietly moved in, eavesdropping on the conversation. Finally, after hearing enough to realize that the two Germans were having a heated disagreement, he decided to add to the discussion. "I don't know half of what you two dummies are talking about, but you"—he said, pointing at Fritz—"are going to start telling us what we need to know or I'm going to have to beat it out of ya."

"You do not intimidate me, you Schweinhold!" As the words left his mouth, Fritz noticed a devilish gleam of delight developing in Haney's eyes. He had seen this look before, in the eyes of the Waffen SS. At that moment, he knew this adversaries would do whatever was necessary to get what they came for.

For an instant, no words were spoken; none were needed. Haney's piercing glare said it all. Then, uncharacteristically, because he liked Fritz, Haney pulled out Bertha, stuck it in the counter, and then placed his now empty beer mug beside it. Peacefully, in a low calm voice, Haney issued his ultimatum. "I like you, Fritzy, so I'm gonna make this simple . . . We can either talk over another mug of this delicious beer, or . . . we can talk while I skin you like a deer with this," pointing to his large inlaid knife. "What's it going to be?"

Beads of sweat again appeared on Fritz's wrinkled forehead as he weighed his options.

Although Von Clause did not like Haney's tactics—Fritz was an old and trusted friend—they proved to be quite effective. It only took a second before beer was being poured and information shared. "Wise decision," Haney said as he took a gulp from the full mug.

<hr />

Once the mugs were empty, Haney and Von had acquired all the information the old submariner had possessed. Their next stop was the seemingly abandoned Huemul facility island; located in the Nahuel Huapi National Park. From there they could pick up some more appropriate weaponry and make their way to the spear piece's current resting place.

As for Von, although it was good to see his old friend again, the moment was bittersweet. Because of the methods used to get him to talk, he knew that this bridge was forever burned, and any further contact between them would likely end in one or the other's death.

Gathering up the solid blue-lined parka and black hood, and then handing it to Haney, who gave a reluctant sigh; Von looked at Fritz and said his good-byes. "Lebe wohl, mein alter Freund. Es tut mir leid für all diese Geschäfte [Farewell, my old friend. I am sorry for all of this business]."

"Es spielt keine Rolle. Geh mit Gott und bleib in Sicherheit, mein Bruder [It doesn't matter. Go with God and remain safe, my brother]."

Looking at Fritz one last time before he followed Haney out the door, Von spoke to his friend one last time. "Auf Wiedersehen."

"Auf Wiedersehen," Fritz returned. Both men knew they would never speak again.

<hr />

Outside in the night air, the unlikely duo was ready for the next stop on their adventure. Von paused to look at Haney, who was now sporting his blue parka and black wool hoodie. He looked much more comfortable, and although Von expected no gratitude, Haney surprised him. "Thank you for the coat and skull cap, dummy."

"You are wilkommen," he gasped. 'It looks like it fits well."

"Yea, I do make this shit look good, don't I . . . heh, heh, heh."

With a bit of a giggle of his own, Von said, "Yes, mein Freund, you do; that you do."

"Let's go find that big lizard and make our way to . . . what was that place called again?" Haney had forgotten. He figured Von would take care of the heavy lifting.

"Nahuel Huapi," Von sighed humorously. "However, my large Freund, we will have to wait till morning. I know a nice, private Inn just around der corner with beds big enough for you," he added.

"Yea, that sounds peachy, but we need to tell the overgrown iguana," Haney said with a grin. Von was growing on him, especially since he had picked him and the mission over his friend. A lesser man would have caved in. Unfortunately, he feared that this would not be the last test of their respective loyalties; but for now, all was well.

"This way to the station, mein Haney." With a nod of approval, Haney followed. He kind of liked the sound of his name in broken German. It sounded more sophisticated. With an impish smile on his face, Haney gave the order. "Mush, Rudolph, ya little red-nosed reindeer, mush."

Von had to laugh as he led the way.

CHAPTER

SIXTY FOUR

BACK AT THE Smoke 'n' Go, while Abhar and Binah discussed recent events and future plans, Jack got busy booking a flight to Damascus, Syria. Since they needed a more immediate departure, using the phone and the personalized assistance that it offered provided more up to date access to flight data, much more than Binah's PC.

Though the underground transit system had a station in San Juan, as do most major US military installations worldwide, Abhar thought it better to use a more conventional means of travel. Understanding that this decision would expose him to the more traditional set of eyes that were watching, he was more concerned with whether the brothers were tracking his movements.

By traveling in a commercial jet, which in itself produced a huge magnetic signature, Abhar was hoping to camouflage his unique energy frequency. It also gave him the opportunity to recharge, slowly absorbing elemental energy from the ethereal wind. Additionally, though he would likely never admit it, Jack, not having slept the previous night, was probably in need of some rest.

Once preparations were complete, the time came for Abhar and Jack to depart. After Jack went over their itinerary, explaining that they had short layovers in both Miami and Cairo, putting them in Damascus some eighteen hours from now, Abhar thanked him for his hard work. "God job, Jack. I'm glad you're coming with me," he said sincerely. In fact, without Jack's assistance, things so far would have been much more difficult, if not impossible. Thanks to his asset in Bariloche, Jonathan's team stood a good chance of success in locating the second piece of the Spear of Destiny.

"Binah, I'm so grateful you sent Jack to pick me up. I don't know what I would have done without him," Abhar said, looking back at his newest friend. "Sorry I have to steal him away from you again."

Binah nodded, with a smile of recognition. "That's all right, my old friend. Although old Jack here has been invaluable to me for many years, I fear you need him much more than I do."

Jack, feeling a bit uncomfortable with all the compliments directed at him, wanted it to end. "That's very gracious and all, but that thar's enough. Ya two are startin' to sound like a couple of Shelias cuddling up to a little tyke. If old Jack had wanted all this attention, I got me one of them thar mamacita's long time ago."

Binah added, "Maria down at the market would certainly like the job. She's always asking about you." The response from Binah triggered a group laugh.

"I'll tell ya what, mate. If I make it back from this trip alive, I'll look her up. I might need a bit of TLC after this here is over."

As the group stepped through the glass doors of the shop, leaving the pleasant scent of cigar smoke behind, Abhar said, "Give us four days . . . with any luck, we'll get across the Iraqi border without incident. Getting to Mosul may present a challenge . . . but I have a plan," Abhar finished, looking at Jack.

"Be patient, Abraham, don't rush things. The prophecy has yet to be fulfilled, and we both know how these things work," Binah cautioned.

After a moment of silent thought, the former Rah agreed. "You're right, I know you're right."

Loading the Jeep, Abhar announced, "Watch out for Jambres and Jannes. Those two are up to something . . . and that's never a good thing." Hopping in the passenger seat, Abhar finished, "We'll contact you as soon as we get the power supply."

"I'll be waiting for you in Cusco, my friend. Good luck and be safe," Binah replied.

In a thick Aussie accent, Jack wished Binah farewell. "Adios, my cobber."

With a contrived accent, a show of endearment, Binah responded, "G'day, mate."

Parting words completed, Jack fired up the Jeep and shifted it into drive. As the two men departed, he checked his watch. "Plenty of time," he said to Abhar.

It was not long before they arrived at Puerto Rico International Airport and boarded their flight. Abhar, who before meeting Jack had rarely been surprised, was once again left amazed, this time by their seating arrangements. "First class!"

"Surre, mate, only the best for my new cobber." They both smiled. "I just figured we might as well be comfortable since we're gonna be on dis baby for a while." Jack, noticing the flight attendant, flagged her down. "Stewardess . . may I have a cocktail?"

The beautiful black-haired, brown-eyed attendant smiled and with a deep southern accent responded, "Well, of course you can, honey. What can I get you today?"

"A rum and Coke if you please, and light on the Coke."

"Certainly, sir . . . and anything for you, sir?" she asked Abhar.

"I'll have the same, thank you."

"Excellent . . . I'll be right back with your drinks."

It only took a minute before the flight attendant returned with their orders. "Now, will there be anything else I can get you gentlemen before we depart?"

"No, ma'am," Jack spoke up as Abhar shook his head.

"Okay then, my name is Jill. If there is anything else you need, I'll be just a call button away. Okay . . . if there's nothing else, I'll check back in after we take off," Jill said before moving toward her seat near the cockpit.

With a smile on his face, Jack raised his glass, "Cheers ta ya, mate."

"Cheers to you, Jack."

Each man then took a swig of their beverage. As Abhar studied the condensation developing on the exterior of his glass, he said aloud, "Not too bad . . . not too bad at all."

After the short flight to Miami and the even shorter layover were behind them, both men settled into their seats for the longest leg of their flight. Once again, thanks to Jack's resourceful negotiation skills, they remained on the same plane during their brief stay in Miami.

Jill, making her short rounds in first class, brought each of them another cocktail, as requested, and a pair of noise-canceling headphones. It was not long before each man was resting peacefully. Next stop, Cairo.

———~———

Although it had been ages, literally, since he had been to the Egyptian metropolis—his last visit had been in the time of the pharaohs—Abhar had no interest in seeing it now. The city, as well as the country, now were a sad reminder of a once glorious empire, one whose grandeur had been buried beneath the sands of the desert. Abhar wanted to remember it as it had been, back when he was young and new to this world. At the present, instead of spending time reminiscing about days gone by, he needed to focus his thoughts on the matters at hand.

First, how were they going to get into Iraq and to the ancient city of Nineveh safely? Second, once there, how were they going to not only locate, but uncover the still-buried entrance to the lost ziggurat? Last, and most importantly, once they found the power source, the Ark, how were they going to get it out without anyone noticing? A feat that was not going to be easy. All of these issues ran through his mind as he tried to rest and recharge. However, his spirits were good as he let all these problems go. Just as he had told Binah, he had a plan, a secret weapon that he was sure would work. It was none other than Jack Dresher.

CHAPTER

SIXTY FIVE

WHEN JUSTIN HEARD the exuberant cries coming from within the PRIEST, his emotions spiraled in many directions. A wave of prideful relief washed over him as he now knew that his crew was safe. Though it had cost him his own life in the process, he had carried out what needed to be done; no captain could wish for a better way to go.

Another, more subtle feeling that invaded his thoughts was one of deep sadness. In Ariella Marconi, he had finally found the intimacy that for all his life had eluded him. He would never hear her tender voice, see her radiant smile, or feel the touch of her warm skin against his, ever again. He could not even say goodbye properly, which under the circumstances was probably best.

The most profound feeling, though, was the fear that was building inside. It was not so much his impending physical death that scared him so, but the thought of what comes next. What happened to his soul? Although not a religious man, Justin did believe in a Creator God and the afterlife. Even basic physics states that matter is neither created nor destroyed, merely transformed. What that transition was to be, however, remained a mystery.

Captain LaMarr lived by a code, dominated by his morals as well as by the military's standards of conduct. He tried to help his fellow man, and even when dealing with subordinates, tried to incorporate their well-being when administering military orders or protocols.

If asked, he would have described his belief system as more akin to an esoterically spiritual practice, absorbing information from all cultures and religions. Now, however, at the end, he had his doubts. Before he could venture too far down into the rabbit hole of uncertainty, the ring of Steven's excited voice filled the comms. Instinctively, without answering, Justin popped out of his trance and entered survival mode. He rapidly, but hawkishly, searched the area for a solution to his mortal dilemma.

After a thorough survey, he looked at his battery power indicator and quickly calculated how much time he had left. Finally it was clear, and he began to accept his fate. He was going to die and there was absolutely nothing that could be done to save him.

"Captain . . . can you read me, over!" Steven said, anxiously expecting a reply.

With a knot welling up in his throat, Captain LaMarr, unsure how to reply, paused a moment before answering. No matter what, he needed to remain calm for the crew's sake. Panic kills, especially at these depths.

"Captain!"

"I'm here, Steven . . . glad you're all safe."

"Thanks to you, sir. What the hell did you do!?"

"I gave the PRIEST some holy water." The captain was trying to delay telling him the truth.

"Huh?"

"I gave it a new power supply. One that will provide you all the energy needed to get topside, Lieutenant."

Still confused, Lt. Barett began to ask, "Where did you get another power s . . ." before realizing what his mentor meant. "Captain, please tell me you didn't do what I think you did."

"It was the only solution, Steven."

"What are you talking about?" Roger Sealy interrupted, confused by the emotions being exhibited by the young SEAL.

Tersely, Lt. Barett squawked, "The captain used his ZPE to power the PRIEST."

"How is that possible?" The words slipped from Roger's mouth just before he grasped the severity of the situation.

Steven, reverting to his training, entered motto-military mode even before Roger's words echoed off the sub's interior hull. He quickly began processing options, looking for alternatives; desperately trying to find a solution, any solution, that did not involve his captain becoming a casualty. So far, only fragmented bits of possible scenarios came to mind.

From the rear of the sub, Nancy Rogers, timidly looking at Dr. Walker, asked, "Deborah, what is happening? I thought everything was all right."

"I don't know, dear, but I'm gonna find out." Deborah moved forward, positioning herself between Roger and Steven, and decided to go straight to the source of the apparent confusion and talk to the captain directly. "Justin, hun, what the hell have you done?"

"I just gave ya'll a jump, that's all." He purposely used a little southern drawl himself to add levity to the situation.

"While that sounds like fun and all, that's a bullshit answer. I'm going to be on you like stink on a possum when we get to the surface if you don't do better than that, darling."

After an uncomfortable pause, he responded, "I'm not going to the surface, Deborah." His words were calm, almost reverent.

Before Dr. Walker could ask any more questions, Roger butted in. "Captain, you could use your portable power cable and tie into the PRIEST's exterior power outlet."

"I've already used it to bypass the sub's damaged electrical relay."

"You could splice the cable and . . ." Roger started to offer until he realized that while in the exosuit, the fine motor skills required to do the job were all but nonexistent.

"How much time do you have left before you've depleted your battery power?" Steven asked, still searching for a solution.

"At current energy consumption . . . about thirty minutes," Captain LaMarr said in a matter-of-fact tone. He was pleased, though, with his subordinate's persistence.

"That's plenty of time to get your ass back to the Hab. You can then just wait it out till help arrives!" Lt. Barett hopefully replied. Unfortunately, the young officer had failed to take into account just how much power the exosuit required, especially while in motion. That is why it was powered by a ZPE in the first place.

"That's at current energy consumption levels, Lieutenant. I'm not moving. For me to get into the Hab, I'd have to propel myself to the top of the western module; that'll take several minutes. If I fire up the foot thrusters, I'll run out of power in under a minute. Just ask Roger."

Steven looked at Roger, who merely gave him a dismal nod of agreement.

"Did the fuckin' Navy not have a contingency for this!? Is there really nothing more we can do!?" Steven cried as a tear fell down his cheek.

"Yes, Lieutenant, there is." Justin was firm in his tone. "You can fire up the engine and get your ass to the surface. The crew is your responsibility now."

"But, Captain . . ."

"That's an order, Steven. Don't make this harder than it already is."

Reluctantly, the lieutenant obeyed. "Roger, fire up the engines and prepare for out ascent."

"We're leaving him!?" Nancy began to weep.

In a consoling voice, Frank Gilmore, who himself was in a bit of shock, put his hand on her shoulder and explained, "It was him or us, Nancy. He chose us." Now speaking to Justin, he said, "Thank you, Captain, you're truly a man among men and a better man than I. Safe journey."

"You would have done the same, Frank, if it had been your decision to make. I'll see you in the next life."

"If you bring the wine, I'll supply the tunes."

"Hell yeah, we'll rock out and strap one on." Captain LaMarr laughed. "Safe journey, my friend."

Although not one for many words, Robert Washington felt obligated to express his gratitude. "Captain LaMarr, may wherever you end up be pleasant. Go in peace." This uncharacteristically positive disposition caught everyone off guard, even the captain, who thanked him for his caring words.

Still sobbing uncontrollably, Nancy too said her goodbyes before promptly burying her face in Deborah's bosom.

"It was a pleasure being part of history with you Justin. I couldn't envision myself going down with anyone else," Deborah said, continuing to use the sexual innuendo to which the crew had become so accustomed.

"I've been meaning to ask you this as long as I've known you . . . Are you always thinking about sex?"

"Hell yes. When you're as old as I am, what else is there to live for?"

Justin had to laugh. Then he pleaded, "Please tell Ariella that I love her."

"I sure will, darling. You can count on it."

"And Roger."

"Yes, Captain."

"Stop wasting time. Take Nancy into your arms and never let her go." Roger looked back at Nancy. She peeled her wet, puffy face off Deborah's chest to meet his gaze. Justin continued, "Don't wind up like me and wait till it's too late to find love."

Still looking directly into Nancy's eyes, Roger, without blinking, replied, "I will, Captain, I certainly will." With these words and the twinkle in his eyes, Nancy's crying ceased.

Steven, who had been silent; with tears flowing freely down his cheeks, finally got his turn to say farewell. "Thank you, Captain, for believing that a spoiled rich boy had something to offer, sir."

"Steven, I'm proud to have known you. You're an exceptional soldier and the son I never had. The world needs more like you, kid . . . Now get outta here before I start crying."

"It has been an honor, sir." Lt. Barett, looking through the PRIEST'S forward glass observation port, saluted his captain one final time. "Roger, blow the tanks, 20 degree up bubble . . . We're getting the hell out of dodge."

"Blowing the tanks, 20 degree up bubble," Air immediately filled the ballast tanks, causing the PRIEST to rise. "Here we go," Roger relayed. Within minutes, lights from both the captain's exosuit and the Sea Lab were no longer visible, lost in the abyssal darkness. Not another word was spoken, by anyone, until they neared the surface.

———

Watching the crew's departure was difficult. However, rather than dwell on how things were, or how they could have been, Justin decided to take another trip to the bottom, to his nemesis, the amber crystalline anomaly.

After performing a few simple calculations, he determined that if he turned off the suit's heating system, powered down all the nonessential biometrical, robotic, and computer functions, and intermittently operated his rebreathers, he could buy himself enough time, approximately another ten minutes, to reach his goal. All he needed was a ten-second blast directly over his target. Gravity would do the rest.

Once prepared, he looked back toward the Hab, scanning the area to see if there was anything he might have missed, anything that could save his life. Nothing. With a sigh, he turned back to the chasm, took a few steps forward, said aloud, "Here goes nothing," and took the leap.

Exactly thirty-six minutes and ten seconds later, Captain LaMarr landed exactly where he had intended. He promptly lay down so that he could look up into the darkness. As expected, the amber crystal absorbed all the remaining power the exosuit had to offer. Since he had shut the heat off before his descent, the interior temperature had already plummeted to a chilly 45 degrees. Only his contained body heat kept it from going any lower. Realizing that he only had what oxygen remained inside the suit, a few moments at best before he passed out, Justin stared up and whispered, "God . . . if you're there, please watch over Ariella and keep her safe. Thank you for allowing me to have the time with her that I did." Finished with his prayer, he took his last breath and, while expiring, said, "Ariella Marconi, I love you." Those were Captain Justin LaMarr's last words on planet Earth. His time was up.

CHAPTER

SIXTY SIX

WHILE HIS VISIT from Captain Rahzu had been quite informative and gave him a sense of honor for being so well trusted, Lt. ShemRahya could not help feeling a bit inept. Notwithstanding he was merely a junior officer and not privy to some of the more sensitive aspects of their mission, the young Dimerian warrior was stunned that he had not deduced what was happening on his own. All the evidence was present, if not readily apparent.

As a Rah security officer, it was his job to investigate thoroughly every irregularity, no matter how insignificant it might seem—something that, in this case, he had failed to do. It would be easy to blame his performance on the relative ease of the mission. Until recently, nothing of any consequence had occurred. He could even get away with offering the importance of investigating Ensign RahKael's mysterious death as a reasonable excuse for his ineptitude; although that was really not the case either, since her murder was linked to all that Rahzu had revealed to him in the first place. No, there was actually no justification for his incompetence; at least none that would satisfy him.

Fortunately, though, ShemRahya looked at failures such as these as opportunities for improvement and growth; he was far from perfect. He had determined long ago that brooding over setbacks too long solved nothing. Next time, he vowed to be better prepared. In fact, he had already begun to make plans.

After Rahzu's departure, besides reciting the cryptic riddle he had been told a multitude of times, ShemRahya devised a plot to mask the God seed's—human male number 99985—frequency from inquiring minds. The subject was burning out his biological monitor on a regular basis, undoubtedly due to his latent Yah energy, and was normally picked up twice as other as any other Earthling. Because of this, ShemRahya determined that an unscheduled pickup to repair the device would be warranted and would not draw any undue attention.

When the opportunity presented itself, he could then replace the malfunctioning implant with one of his own design. Not only would this new monitor assign the subject another energy frequency; it also contained a separate resistor that would effectively block his Yah energy from detection. This ingenious piece of hidden hardware could possibly even retard the deterioration of the new implant, further deflecting attention away from the God seed. But that remained to be seen.

All he needed now to put his plan into action was a reason to travel back to PU 431. He could then seek out his quarry and perform the switch on site. Just in case. Nonetheless, there was one slight problem, one that had to be dealt with. What about his partner, Lt. KaRah? She would likely accompany him back to Earth—she always did. What would he say when she questioned him about breaking protocol? Could he lie to her successfully, even if he wanted to and the cause was just?

At this point, the security officer was unsure how this was all going to turn out; KaRah was very good at reading him. He was sure, though, that a solution to the problem would present itself when the time was right; it always had. That was just how things worked for him—positive attitude, positive outcome.

Dealing with YetziRah, however, was an entirely different matter. The admiral was not one to be trifled with. The lieutenant was confident that he could best YetziRah, the last HooRah, in one-on-one combat, but he knew it would never come to that! Powerful leaders almost always used their cunning and influence over others to fight their battles for them. YetziRah had the political clout to rival even the most highly positioned Dimerians.

Additionally, if Rahzu's suspicions about the admiral's aspirations to overthrow Xanix Rah were indeed correct, then he would have to be extra careful. Any slip in character, any unusual activity, any negativity, aside from the normal disdain which he and almost everyone on board the RJS felt, would likely end in his taking one-way trip to chaos.

Sadly, the lieutenant also concluded that until it was determined where Commander CheRahna's loyalties lay, she too could not be trusted. He would need to be mindful of his words, actions, and energy while in her presence as well. Hopefully, this would not be the case, and she would be an ally. He would know soon enough, when Rahzu returned from his meeting with her.

As ShemRahya rose to leave his quarters, satisfied with his plans, he instinctively detected a vacuum-like void in the surrounding energy field. He had experienced this sensation many times before, but only while involved in close order combat. It was the life force of a fallen Dimerian being absorbed by chaos. Because he had seldom sensed this and was not in the immediate area when the death occurred, it could mean only one thing. His trusted mentor had been slain!

<hr />

Following the path of the escaping energy, ShemRahya quickly found himself back in the science lab, which was rapidly becoming a kill zone. There on the floor, not far from the amber crystal sphere, was a decomposing golden body. Gingerly moving forward, so as not to disturb any evidence, it readily became obvious that his initial instincts were correct; it was his beloved captain.

Interestingly, the corpse did not leak any golden fluid onto the surrounding floor, as one would expect. Instead, it seemed to have been eaten away, vaporized, as if some sort of acid were at work. He could think of only one substance that could have caused this: white enhanced Dimerian energy crystal.

But how did it get on board the ship without tripping the sensors, and how was it dispersed? Only a Yah could touch the stuff without suffering any damage, and by the looks of it, a substantial quantity was used—enough to kill.

Carefully looking at the surrounding floor, he noticed a fine residue of white powder near the body. Extending his hand, he touched the substance with his finger. Immediately the tip of his golden appendage was vaporized.

It was as he suspected—WEDEC, only it was mixed with some other unknown compound. That could explain why it was not detected by the RJS's security system.

Continuing his survey, he also noted, by studying the dust, that there appeared to have been no struggle. Whoever did this; Rahzu knew them and was likely caught completely off guard.

As Rahzu's body performed its final disappearing act, ShemRahya had little doubt that the killer was Commander CheRahna. But how was he going to prove it, and was it in his and the God seed's best interest to do so? While deciding what course of action to take, he thought it prudent not to be seen anywhere near the body, lest he somehow he be blamed for the tragedy. He retraced his steps, careful not to disturb anything, and exited the lab.

As he entered the hall corridor, still contemplating what to do, the ship's alarm sounded. This was quickly followed by Commander CheRahna's voice. "All crew members are to report to the hangar deck immediately." As she restated her order, ShemRahya concluded that it might be best if he let this play out. Hopefully, this strategy would work to his advantage, and he could learn what was really happening.

SIXTY SEVEN

SHORTLY AFTER THEIR departure from the main island, Jonathan's senses returned as his focus drifted back to the amber crystal sphere and the mission. Ariella's pseudo modeling performance hit him hard. He had seen and been with beautiful women before without this sort of reaction. No matter how hard he tried, his thoughts continued to dwell on Ariella.

When the fog of emotion cleared from his mind, Jonathan remembered that he had failed to issue Ariella her set of tactical contacts. After the craft momentarily stopped and was allowed to drift, he popped in his own set of eyewear and gave Ariella hers. As he selected the options he needed displayed—Jonathan did not want the world to look like a fighter pilot's screen, at least not yet—he instructed his cohort on what the contacts were for and what they could do.

While Ariella was oohing and ahhing like a child, she did not find the digital readouts, which were located in her upper field of vision, to be a distraction. Jonathan, though, convinced her that they could potentially divert her attention from the living, changing environment and should only be activated as needed.

"Jonathan, these are the coolest things I have ever seen." Ariella had to giggle at this because she was actually using them to see. She went on, "They show the air and water temperature, depth and altitude, speed and distance . . ." Her voice trailed off as she continued to explore the functions.

"They also have an X-ray vision mode. I'm turning mine on right now," he said to her in jest, although there was such a function buried deep within the menu. Ariella blushed, but she liked the thought of Jonathan checking her out. Without taking her gaze away from the various readouts, she mocked, "Don't tell me . . . you're some sort of perv, aren't you." It was more of a playful statement than a question.

Quick in his comeback, he thought little about the words coming out of his mouth until it was too late. "If looking at a beautiful woman in tight clothing is perverted, then I stand guilty as charged." He wished he could take that one back.

Sensing the nervous regret as he finished speaking, Ariella remained fixated on her new toy. "I know these are government property and all," she said coyly. "But when this mission is over . . . can I keep them, please?! Jonathan, I could get so much more accomplished with a pair of these for eyes."

"We'll see . . . depends on how much paperwork you're willing to do." Jonathan, though in good spirits, was not far from the truth. This hardware was expensive, very expensive, and was on the cutting edge of technology. The powers that be would expect the return of both the tactical suits and contacts upon the completion of the mission.

With time continuing to tick away, Jonathan suggested that Ariella hold on and enjoy the ride. The sun was beaming, and the seas were calm. They had spent enough time playing with gadgets.

As Ariella turned off most of the display readouts, she left the ones dealing with the ocean on. Jonathan revved up the Zodiac's outboard and engaged the throttle. Just over an hour later they arrived at the mouth of the lagoon.

Protected by a shallowly submerged barrier reef, the inflatable craft safely and easily navigated over the sharp, jagged outcropping of coral. The Playa Grande Laguna itself was really large, hence the name. Situated at the far end of Vieques Island, there was virtually no sign of civilization. Other than a rickety-looking wooden dock, which was opposite and to the right of where they entered, the teal green water was surrounded by lush jungle growth.

As they neared the dock, a flock of birds squawked as they took flight. They were none too pleased about strangers coming to their tranquil sanctuary. Jonathan, understanding that this was the access point to some sort of secret base, still could see nothing that pointed to an entrance. Judging by the growth of foliage near and around the dock, it certainly appeared that no one had visited here in quite some time.

As he tied up to the dock, he surveyed the structure's integrity to ensure it would support his and Ariella's weight. Besides a few boards of rotten decking and some pretty extensive weathering, the grayish platform looked stable.

Jonathan disembarked from the Zodiac and promptly aided Ariella in doing the same. Before walking any further, however, the soldier paused to have another look around, this time with the use of his contacts on X-ray mode. He was confident the hidden entrance was here, somewhere.

Scouring the terrain, Jonathan was surprised he was able to resist the urge to look at Ariella's exposed body. He wanted to, but she would have known somehow, especially after he informed her of what he was up to.

Almost simultaneously, the moment he spotted a secret guard shack, completely camouflaged with vegetation, a voice rang out from a loudspeaker hidden in one of the dock's piles. "Major Hawthorn, Miss Marconi, please remain right where you are. Our sensors are performing the necessary biometric scans as we speak."

As he turned off the X-ray mode, Jonathan started to reply but knew it would be of no use. The owner of the mysterious voice would not say anything further until the scan was complete. Once that was done, he would either offer more instructions or vaporize them.

"Very well . . . you both check out. Major Hawthorn, Miss Marconi, move to the middle of the dock now, please," the hidden man ordered. After they had both done as instructed, the voice barked again. "Closer, please." Apparently, they were not close enough, because this time the tone was a little harsher. "Closer! This is for your own safety." Again, they moved closer. Now only about a foot separated them.

"Damnit man, just grab hold of her!" the man behind the microphone had clearly lost his patience with the duo. Though they failed to understand why they had to be so close, Jonathan and Ariella did as they were told. Initially, neither was uncomfortable with their close proximity. It felt natural being in each other's arms, like it was meant to be.

Suddenly and without another word, a railing rose from the dock platform and surrounded them. The water around the dock mysteriously disappeared as it drained away, exposing a submerged, square-shaped cofferdam.

Ariella, seeing why they needed to be centered on the dock, was beginning to get nervously uncomfortable in Jonathan's arms. She needed to remain in control of her emotions, something she was finding difficult to do. Jonathan, on the other hand, felt as if the mystery man was just messing with them. Normally, he would have been pissed off by now, but holding on to Ariella kept him at ease.

At about the time they began to pull apart, the dock platform jostled beneath their feet. Once again, they fell back into each other's arms. Slowly, the dock began to descend into the black unknown.

Only five seconds had elapsed before the blue sky above them began to disappear. They had gone down almost 20 feet when the retractable roof finished closing, briefly leaving them in pitch black darkness. At the instant the mechanical clang of moving metal ceased, the elevator shaft's soft white illumination flickered on. It was at that moment that their acceleration downward began to rapidly increase.

Nearly thirty seconds passed before the individual vertical lights began to blur into one. Judging by this, Jonathan calculated that they were nearing terminal velocity. Just as he started to feel the anticipated anti-gravity-like sensation develop beneath his feet, the elevator's descent began to slow.

Ariella too had been aware of the change in speed—not because she had never experienced a freefall before. All her concentration was focused on not vomiting, which until now had seemed unlikely.

Once the platform came to an abrupt, jerky stop, opening into a shallow, perpendicular tunnel, the rails lowered. Immediately, lights came on, revealing a small transport resembling an oblong capsule. It was encased in a clear tubular tunnel. As the doors of the vehicle opened, a hissing sound, which was produced by several white plumes of pressurized air, escaped into the cavernous grotto.

"Cool, this is going to be fun." Jonathan said upon seeing the transport.

Realizing that Jonathan's definition of fun probably involved moving at nauseatingly high speeds, Ariella, who was still recovering from the effects of their descent, responded with irritation. "Cool? What does that mean? Cool?"

Jumping off the dock platform with a childlike expression on his face, Jonathan turned back toward her and explained what the vehicle was. "This is a vacuum tube transport . . . once we get in, the doors will close, the air will be sucked out, and we will be shot, literally, like a bullet through a barrel, to wherever this thing ends!"

"Oh joy," she sarcastically replied.

"Aw, c'mon . . . it's going to be fun."

His puppy dog eyes and drooping lips were too much; she had to crack a smile. "You are such a child," Ariella said as she stepped off the elevator platform, following Jonathan into the capsule and into the unknown.

Although she did not actually care for the ride herself—speed was just not her thing—Ariella did enjoy watching how much Jonathan did. He whooped and hollered the entire way, like he was on an amusement park ride. Thankfully, though, the trip was short, only lasting about five minutes before they began to slow.

Considering the decline and speed at which they traveled, she wondered how far they had gone and how deep they were. "Jonathan, where are we?" she asked.

As the vehicle continued its deceleration, at this question, Jonathan bit his lip while squinting his eyes. 'Let me see . . .' Using his hands like planes flying on various trajectories, he performed some mental calculation. "Yes," he whispered. "No, that's not right," he silently muttered again. "Yeah, that's it . . . I figure we're 30 miles into the Atlantic and about 10,000 or so feet down."

Ariella did not doubt him, but her mind did not work like his. She needed some clarification. "How'd you come up with that?" Her tone was a bit harsh, which happened at times when she could not wrap her mind around something. Jonathan merely shrugged his shoulders and spread both hands outward as if to say, "Why ask me then?" He did not like being challenged, especially when he knew he was right.

Usually, she would not have stopped there; but before she could launch into a barrage of questions, the capsule came to a full stop. Even before the doors opened, a tall lean black man, smartly dressed in Marine-issued BTUs, sashayed over to greet them. "Miss Marconi, Major Hawthorn, I am Staff Sergeant Boyd. Welcome to the Nares Atlantic Research Complex, or NARC as we call it here," he said, waving his hand around flamboyantly.

They had arrived at NARC's central hub. Fairly large, with several computer stations, desks, and adjacent offices, it was all the things one would expect to see in an above-ground office building, but without the windows. Fifteen people were moving about, obviously working, completely oblivious to their presence.

"If you two will follow me, I'll take you to the break room where you can freshen up and relax," Boyd said as he led them down a hallway.

Jonathan asked, "Break room? Sergeant, aren't we going . . ."

Boyd interrupted with a roll of his eyes and a smile. "Of course, sir, but the captain figured with all the traveling you two have done over the last several days, a little 'me time' was in order." He said this while flashing peace signs. Now seeing them both in the brighter lights of the hallway, Sgt. Boyd halted and placed his hand to his chin. "Oh, my goodness . . . by the looks if it, he was right. You two look dreadful." Looking directly at Ariella, he could not help himself. "Dear, I've got this facial cream with witch hazel that'll take those bags out"—he said with a snap of his fingers—"just like that." He then turned to Jonathan. "And, Major, um, um, um, even though you look scrumptious, you yourself need a seltzer water wash and a catnap. I make this chamomile tea with honey that'll . . ."

Looking at Ariella, who was smiling, Jonathan shook his head and laughed as he broke in. "Thank you, Sergeant . . . Just take us to the break room, please, then, if you wish, you can tend to Miss Marconi. I'll be fine."

With his right hand on his cocked-up hip and eyes cut up and to the left, Boyd contemplated the major's request. "Um . . . very well then. I suppose that would be best." He started walking again. "This way, please."

The break room couches were not large, but were quite comfortable. After they showered, Staff Sgt Boyd, true to his word, brought Ariella some of his touted facial cream. She loved it. He also left a rag soaking in warm seltzer water along with a mug of freshly brewed chamomile tea. A little TLC was exactly what was needed.

Several hours into his nap, Jonathan awoke. Never one to sleep too deeply, he heard Boyd even before he entered the room. He lay there awake with his eyes shut.

"Major Hawthorn . . ." Boyd said in a whisper. "Major Hawthorn," he said, a little louder.

"Yes, Boyd . . . what is it?" Jonathan answered.

"I'm really sorry to wake you, sir, you looked so peaceful and . . ."

"That's okay, Boyd. What is it?"

With a concerned look on his face, Boyd said, "The captain needs to speak with you ASAP, sir. Something happened to the Sea Lab X.

Without another word, Jonathan sprang from the couch, put on his boots, and followed Boyd to central command.

CHAPTER

SIXTY EIGHT

ΛS SHΞ STOOϽ on the dais-like platform located on the middle of the hangar, waiting for the crew to assemble, CheRahna's thoughts spiraled down into a whirlpool of apathetic numbness. It was the only way she could cope with all that had transpired.

Following Captain Rahzu's forced departure to the realm of chaos and beyond, the young commander promptly sought council with her new master, YetziRah; who, true to his word, was not far away.

Feigning remorse over the loss, the admiral, to his secret delight, was basking in glory over his conquest. A major adversary to his devious plot to seize control of the House of Rah was dead, and he had had no hand in it, at least not a physical one. The only question that remained now was what he was going to do with Commander CheRahna. She was obviously riveted by what she had done. He needed to determine whether her usefulness had come to an end, or if he could continue to manipulate her into doing his bidding—a question that would soon be answered.

Confused, angry, and completely in doubt of herself, without thinking or caring about the consequences, CheRahna lashed out at her superior officer.

"Captain Rahzu is dead! And I killed him!" she yelled. "This was your plan all along, wasn't it?! Wasn't it!? You narcissistic piece of Voracian dung!" Her dull silver color rapidly brightened into a more reddish hue.

Encouraged by what he was witnessing; he would much rather have her angrily ranting, out of control, than for her to be calm, cool, and collected. YetziRah ignored her insubordination. *I can work with this*, he thought to himself. Under the circumstances, though he knew it to be risky, he answered her honestly, confidently, with a single, concise word. "Yes!" he said flatly.

Taken aback by his emotionless response, she stuttered, "Yes!!! Wha . . . wha . . . what do you mean yes!!? How could . . . why would . . ."

"It's all quite simple, my dear. Captain Rahzu had to die. He was in the way." He let this sink in a moment before continuing. "You cannot be so naïve as not to recognize that our house is sick, dying. I am simply the cure." He spoke calmly as he began circling her. "You see, Commander, since ThundoRah's death in the Golden Rings, the House of Rah has steadily declined. According to tradition, while it was his line's turn to lead, Xanix Rah's leadership has offered no discernible plan that will lead us back to the greatness we so rightfully deserve. It was our house that fought the hardest and suffered the greatest losses during the PU 4 uprising. We were the leaders then, and all of Dimeria benefited from it. So shall it be again."

CheRahna had never heard any of this.

"Xanix Rah's quest for personal glory has been used against him. Without an inkling of suspicion, he has become a tool, a puppet. Someone else, and not a Rah, is pulling his strings."

"Bu . . . bu . . . but . . ." CheRahna was still confused, but intrigued.

"Let me finish, Commander, all will become clear." Again, he was calm, but this time a bit sterner. He needed her to understand that his cause was just, that he was the best hope the Rahs had. He also knew that in time she would make a powerful ally.

Stopping directly in front of her, he brought his right hand up to his puffed-out chest, stood proudly, and, as if reciting a practiced monologue, continued. "I am YetziRah, last of the HooRahs, born and bred for command and battle. I fear no Dimerian and welcome a warrior's death . . . but I refuse to let our house sink into obscurity, to become just another weak, meaningless tumor of existence that so floods our reality . . . Everything! Everything I have done, every friend or enemy I have used or killed, has been for this one purpose and this one purpose only."

Almost frantically, CheRahna screamed, "But I have killed Rahzu! How am I going to explain that to the crew!? What is going to happen to me?!"

Pompously, but with skill, he calmed her fears. "I will handle it, my dear. Trust me, when all of this is over, you will be seen as a hero—a pioneer in our struggle to return to greatness. The acts of your service will be forever recorded in the annals of our house's codex. Poems will be written about your loyalty. Songs of your brave sacrifice will echo throughout the Temple of the High Seats, where you, CheRahna, will almost assuredly sit, right by my side."

Although anger, shame, guilt, all the universal emotions associated with the grieving process, still afflicted her, some clarity concerning the admiral's actions, and her part in them, started to emerge. "What about Captain Rahzu? How is he going to be remembered in all of this?" she snidely asked.

Hearing the commander's concern over her fallen leader's legacy, once again, he simply told her the truth. "He was a necessary casualty of war. Nothing more, nothing less."

"So, his death means nothing to you?"

"I live to serve the House of Rah. I cannot be concerned with such trivial matters."

Unsettled by his apparent lack of caring or compassion, she feebly asked, "So what about me? Am I just another one of your trivial matters too?" She was almost afraid to hear his answer.

YetziRah now had her, and he knew it. "Of course not, my dear, dear CheRahna. You are, and have always been, essential to my plans to restore us to glory." He paced while he continued with his flattery. "I have always, even before you came to the Academy—you, Commander stem from a powerful line of Rahs. It is only now that you are coming to accept it. One day, I will be gone—who will lead our House then?"

She stood dumbfounded, unable to answer.

Sensing that his words were striking a positive chord in her young, malleable mind, he determined that this was the perfect time to test her loyalty and question her resolve. "Commander CheRahna . . . future leader of the House of Rah, ruler of all Dimeria, what are you willing to do to help us be great again?"

With all the crew now present, patiently awaiting the reason for their assembly, it was Commander CheRahna's unfortunate responsibility to inform them why. Though she abhorred lying, Admiral YetziRah had come up with a pretty convincing story to explain the captain's death.

One thing she had learned while being a Rah commander was that everyone, including herself, was on a need-to-know basis. No one, especially not Lt. ShemRahya, needed to know what had really happened. Not only would her credibility be destroyed, but she herself would likely be killed by the crew. Rahzu was loved by everyone.

Admittedly, though the admiral suffered from the same egotistic visions of grandeur that plagued their current leader, and his methods, while at times ruthlessly harsh, were proving to be effective, she believed him. He, she began to realize, was a necessary evil. The House of Rah indeed deserved more, and YetziRah could and, with her help, would provide it.

Raising her hands to silence the murmur of the crowd, CheRahna nervously began. Hopefully, she could be as convincing selling the ruse to her shipmates as the admiral was to her.

As she began her announcement, one crew member in particular paid close attention not only to her story and how she told it, but to her mannerisms as well. ShemRahya, knowing the commander probably better than she knew herself, picked up on every lie, every deviation from the truth. The thing that upset him most was that she seemed to be speaking with purpose, as if she was promoting some new kind of ideology. Zealots are dangerous, always.

ShemRahya was smart, though. He would patiently remain silent as he attempted to discover what was really happening. Besides, secrets and security were his profession, something he was very good at.

Once the explanation of Rahzu's death sank in, Commander CheRahna began a rally to find the responsible party, Abraham, on whom the blame was laid, at all costs. Orders were issued for every available Cruiser Rah to prepare for departure. They were to scour the Earth, find the treacherous Rah, and bring him to justice. For ShemRahya, this provided the perfect opportunity to put his own plans into action.

After a quick stop at his cabin to retrieve his specially designed, secret implant, he headed for his ship as ordered. Fortunately, since they were short on seasoned pilots and stealth was still a necessity, he and Lt. KaRah were assigned separate ships. He whispered a sigh of relief; he was not ready to start lying to her, at least not yet.

His first priority was to protect the God seed by masking his frequency. After that, he would reevaluate the situation to determine who he could trust and how much to tell them. Locating the male subject Jonathan Hawthorn was not going to be easy, though. According to his latest data, the human's implant had already ceased to function.

Since he needed to keep his activities as secret as possible, lest he charged with treason, ShemRahya avoided using Lt. Commander TamaRah's mole. Although using the spy, who was already deeply embedded on Earth, could provide him with the much-needed insight as to the unknown God seed's whereabouts, this would bring up unwanted questions and arouse suspicion—two things that, coming from a spy, were never good.

As he boarded his Cruiser Rah, a thought occurred to him, one that, to his surprise, caused him to shudder. "I need to find Abraham. He is the key." Though this in itself invited a host of new problems as well as danger, it seemed logical under the circumstances. The ancient Rah appeared to be at the root of all recent developments.

Upon entering the cockpit, only one problem remained: how to keep all of this secret from his yet unknown crewmate, who was boarding now. However, being the superior officer as well as a specialist in interrogation and manipulation techniques, a security officer's best assets, Lt. ShemRahya felt confident in his ability to solve that problem too.

CHAPTER SIXTY NINE

IT WAS MIDMORNING when the Boeing 757 made its final approach to the ancient city of Damascus. The temperature in the Syrian capital, although currently a mild 74 degrees, was heating up rapidly, with highs expected to be in the lower nineties.

Prior to touchdown, Jack carefully eyed the desert-like terrain. With the Anti-Lebanon Mountains to the east blocking most of the rain coming off the Mediterranean Sea, the only source of water for the area came from the river, which ran right through the city.

Since he had never visited such a predominantly Islamic state, Jack marveled at the more than 200 mosques dotting the cityscape. They came in all sizes, and from the air, to the unfamiliar observer, they could easily be mistaken for missile command stations. This was due to the minarets always erected beside them.

Even considering the modernization of the roads, rails, and civic, public, and government buildings, as well as housing, much of the architecture and landscape had remained as it had for centuries. In fact, some mosques, along with a few other structures, were nearly a thousand years old, something not unexpected for a place that has been consistently occupied for almost five millennia.

After landing, Jack and Abhar hailed a cab and departed the airport. Their destination was the world-famous bazaars, or souks, as they were called in Syria. This was, according to Abhar, the best place for them to acquire the supplies needed for their journey to Mosul.

Though he had a long personal history with the area himself, it had been over ninety years since Abhar's last visit to the ancient capital. To his surprise, much of it was still very familiar. He had, through the years, seen the city grow from a small settlement, beginning nearly 4,000 years ago, into the heavily populated metropolis that it has become today. Just as it was long ago, it was still one of the most important trading centers in the region.

As they approached the bazaars, Abhar directed the driver to the area known as the Straight. The narrow thoroughfare was the largest, busiest, and nosiest street among the souk network. Men crowded the sidewalks, and at times the street itself, bartering back and forth to buy or sell products for the best price. This normal uproar, along with the large number of people, would make their presence go unnoticed; even if someone was watching, it would be difficult if not impossible to track them.

Indeed, as Abhar had predicted, everything they required for their trek was here. It was a one-stop shopping spree. The only question that remained was how they were going to get to their final destination, Nineveh, modern-day Mosul, Iraq.

The last time Abhar had been here, the only sensible means of travel would have been by railroad. But today, with overcrowding, breakdowns, inconsistent schedules, and the occasional robbery; traveling by rail could take them days. Although flying would have been the fastest method of travel, it was completely out of the question. In this part of the world, only important, rich people flew. This, Abhar felt, could bring unwanted attention to their activities.

The only other option was ground travel. They had the choice of going by caravan, following ancient trade routes, or by bus, the method most modern Syrians used. The primitive caravan provided the slowest and most perilous method of travel. Bandits, on occasion, would lie in wait to either rob or kidnap unsuspecting travelers. The buses, while fast and still a means of transportation on which they could remain fairly anonymous, were always overcrowded and prone to mechanical breakdowns, especially when traveling along unpaved desert highways.

Both Abhar and Jack determined that they would have to get a more private, dependable mode of transportation. They needed a vehicle, preferably a four-wheel drive. Getting a Jeep would be easy. Abraham was a man of means who always carried a sack of precious gems. They came in handy for situations such as this. The problem was deciding what route to take.

There were only two. The first was a newly paved highway, the Via Maris, which had recently been completed, connecting Damascus directly to Baghdad. This route, which would be fast and would allow them to cross the border without suspicion, went much farther south than they needed to go. It would also force them to navigate many miles of dangerous roads through war-torn country, something Abhar had no intention of doing.

No, they would need to take the second route, the northeastern track, through the desert, directly to Mosul. The long-traveled road, at times paved but mostly not, paralleled south along the country's central mountain ranges all the way to the village of Ash Shaddadi, which was roughly 40 miles from the border. Used for thousands of years, this would be their gateway into Iraq.

With their plan finalized, the duo went to work gathering the provisions necessary for their journey. Once that was done, Abhar, doing a bit of bartering himself, purchased a Jeep.

Once underway, it was not long before the paved roads of the city slowly gave way to the sands of the desert. With the top down, as it traversed the arid landscape, the loaded Jeep left a trail of dust in its wake. As usual, Jack drove while Abhar navigated. The pair, dressed for desert conditions, could almost pass as locals, which, oddly enough, one of them was. Their appearance, and the fact that Abhar was fluent in all the local Arabic dialects, would later be helpful when passing through the smaller villages.

According to Abhar, considering terrain, distance, refueling stops, and good weather, they should reach the town of Ash Shaddadi shortly after nightfall—that is, of course, assuming that everything goes as planned.

CHAPTER

SEVENTY

REUNITED WITH GILLA, the trio boarded the maglev and made their way to Huemul Island. Fritz had told them about an old Nazi counterfeiter who now called the mostly abandoned research facility home. For a price, he would be able to supply them with the proper identification and documents required for the next leg of the journey.

As Gilla and Haney discussed the origin of the scent the Reptilian's nose had detected, Von Clause, who was still upset about how things had ended with his old friend, wondered what fate would befall the next person they were to meet.

He knew Jack Dresher would never have asked him for his help if it were not of the utmost importance. Anything involving the Holy Lance was. Also, the method by which Haney extracted information from Fritz made Von realize that even his life was secondary to the mission. Since his emotions were still torn over the encounter, he thought it best to let the large American decide how things would end for their next contact.

Though the former submariner was initially reluctant to offer any useful information and was now, essentially, an adversary who would no longer help them, Haney wisely let him remain among the living. Killing the old man, especially in a place like Bariloche, would have threatened not only the mission, but their own lives. He was a trusted resource to many. Besides, Fritz would not inform on them or expose the purpose of their quest; he had the reputation of a man of neutrality to maintain—a kind of code he followed.

Similarly, the intelligence shared about the man they were headed to see now was not a secret. He was well known around town, and it was not uncommon for people to employ his services.

⁓

Once they arrived at their destination, the three, following the directions Haney had acquired, moved rapidly through the maze of dimly lit corridors toward the abandoned nuclear research lab. Because no actual uranium or plutonium was ever actually experimented on here, hence there was no threat of latent radiation exposure, the Nazi counterfeiter chose this location for its privacy.

No sooner had they turned the final corner, arriving at a large metal door, than a flood of blinding light engulfed them, causing Gilla to hiss in pain. It was so bright that Haney and Von, despite shielding their eyes, had to turn away and face the other direction. Gilla started to flee when suddenly an iron gate fell, crushing to the ground. The metallic boom echoed throughout the corridors; the sound was deafening. They were trapped. The fallen barrier closed off the way they had come.

"Szate you buszineszs and be quick about it!" an unseen voice demanded.

Von, even with the intense throb of pain behind his eyes, remained composed enough to answer tactfully.

"Mein Herr Gerling, we have come to purchase papers and identification!"

After a brief pause, the voice spoke again. "I szee . . . Who sent you?!"

"Fritz Hommell, mein Herr. He owns the outfitter shop in town!"

As the word "town" left Von's lips, the light switched off and the door swung open. Temporarily blinded by the light, at least until their eyes could catch up, the group remained motionless, frozen where they stood.

"Vell, come in! I haven't got all night!" Gerling snapped.

Still unsure of their surroundings, the three cautiously entered.

⁓

Despite his initial rudeness, Herr Gerling turned out to be quite pleasant. The whole lighting and gate demonstration was meant to chase away any foolhardy Nazi hunters looking to make a seemingly easy capture.

After taking their pictures, the elderly gentleman presented them some wine and a snack while he worked on the documents. He promised it would not take long.

Haney did not particularly care for the wine—his palate enjoyed the less refined tastes of life—but he did appreciate the bratwurst, kraut, and mustard sandwich that the counterfeiter had offered. It was perfect timing too; Haney's stomach had begun to rumble audibly. The smoked, peppery, fat-filled caraway-flavored sausages left him completely satisfied and much more cordial.

This kind of treatment made Von consider whether Fritz had contacted Gerling before their arrival or whether the old Nazi was just lonely and enjoyed their company. No matter, though, Haney did not seem to sense anything wrong, so why should he?

As if ordained, at about the same time they were polishing off the food and wine, Gerling returned with their papers. They were flawless.

After the counterfeiter had been paid and the company said their good-byes, Haney, Von Clause, and Gilla left as quickly as they had come. They boarded the maglev and headed due south, toward Tierra del Fuego and the tip of South America.

Once there, they would need to resupply, regear, and figure out the best way to get to their next destination—Queen Maud Land, Antarctica, the location of Neu Berlin and home to the second piece of the Spear of Destiny.

CHAPTER

SEVENTY ONE

ALTHOUGH THE NEWS relayed by the base commander concerning Sea Lab X and Captain LaMarr was unexpectedly tragic, Jonathan could not help but feel a sense of normality wash over his body. His fast-paced lifestyle was filled with danger, controversy, and very often death. The tranquil, relatively safe routine that most civilians enjoyed had never sat well with him.

It was not as if the major was some sort of sadomasochist or suffering from one of the many diagnosable sociopathic disorders. On the contrary, he was a kindhearted, caring individual who was emotionally capable of having healthy, fulfilling relationships. In fact, he thought so much of others, that, rather than introducing them to the hazards that surrounded his life, he chose, more often than not, to remain alone; trapped in his solitude.

Since birth, he had been educated, trained, and exposed to a way of living that taught him not only to survive under stress and extreme conditions, but to thrive. Jonathan could quickly transform from being a completely normal, compassionate man playing with his dog at the beach, into an emotionless, methodical, and merciless soldier, prepared to do whatever was necessary to complete his objective.

Naturally, his career, as well as his relationship status, reflected his mother Cathy's conditioning. But why did she guide him down this path of a warrior? It was a question that always occupied space in his mind.

As he ambled down the corridors, making his way back to the officers' break room, a dismal feeling rushed through him. Even the lights dimmed in reaction to his mood. Uncharacteristically, Jonathan began to get anxious. Despite the cool subterranean temperature of the base, sweat started to bead up on his forehead and develop in his armpits.

Though unsure of Ariella's relationship with the fallen Captain LaMarr, he was quite sure that the news of his death would be painful. He was dreading being the bearer of bad news, which as a commanding officer, he had done on many occasions; not once, however, had he felt this nervous.

At that moment, Jonathan began to see how much he truly cared about this woman. Somehow, he had developed deep feelings for her, something he was ill prepared to handle at this particular time.

Upon entering the break room, the drop in temperature and lighting followed the distressed major. His eyes scanned the room and quickly locked on the beautiful oceanographer, who had just awakened from her nap. There was a glow about her, one of angelic origin, which he was about to kill.

Seeing Jonathan standing at the break room doorway staring at her made her smile. Rubbing her eyes and yawning slightly, Ariella adjusted herself, turning toward her silent observer. She then spoke. "Good morning. Boyd was right, that nap was exactly what the doctor ordered."

Suddenly, the wave of negative energy finally hit her. She knew then that something horrible had happened. "What is it, Jonathan?" she tentatively asked.

Instinctively, doing as he had been conditioned, Major Hawthorn's affect flattened. In a stoic, professional, and unemotional manner; the Army officer began to explain the events that had occurred at the Mariana Trench facility.

While Ariella's mind could logically wrap itself around what she was being told, her heart could not, which was why, at first, she had such a calm demeanor. Initially, Jonathan was surprised at how well she was taking it all in, when suddenly she lost her composure. It all happened as if someone had pushed slow-mo on a recorder.

As Ariella listened, a peculiar look of contemplation developed on her face. After a few seconds had passed, a single tear formed and fell from her left eye.

As soon as the salty solution rolled down and hit the corner of her mouth, the water works opened, flooding her face in wetness. All she could do for comfort, ironically, was to reach out to the messenger of death and hold him tightly.

Unsure what to do—this was unfamiliar territory for him—Jonathan slowly swallowed her up in his arms, providing the only support he knew how to offer.

CHAPTER

SEVENTY TWO

SAFELY ABOARD THE USS *Ronald Reagan*, which never sailed too far from the ultrasecret underwater facility when occupied, the crew of the Sea Lab X gathered together to pay their last respects to their fallen captain. Also, lined up in formation on the flight deck, adorned in dress whites, were all nonessential personnel aboard the Enterprise Class carrier. Justin LaMarr was a highly respected member of the US Navy SEALs who had earned and deserved a hero's send off.

Following the chaplain's eulogy and recitation of Psalm 23, seven armed Marines, also in dress uniform, gave the former frogman his twenty-one-gun salute. Immediately after the last shots from the M-4s echoed off into the distance, a myriad of roaring aircraft—fighter and attack jets, helicopters, and even several cargo planes out of Guam—performed a fly-by. It was quite a spectacle.

As the flag-draped coffin neared the edge of the deck, tears flowed freely among those present. Nancy, being comforted by Roger, was practically hysterical, boo-hooing loudly into his chest. Deborah Walker cried silently, mourning the loss of a dear friend. Frank, wearing a tropical floral patterned rayon shirt, seemed to be enjoying the ceremony—not surprising considering his Zen-like approach to life and death. Robert, sporting a geeky brown suit, complete with a red bow tie, stood rigidly with his face drawn in tension. He disliked most people and hated crowds, but felt it important that he show his respect for the captain, who, oddly enough, he had liked. Finally, even Steven, decked out in his Navy best, had to use his white gloved hand to wipe away the tears.

Once the procession of SEALs, including Lt. Barett, had finished pounding their trident insignias into the top of the silver coffin, "Taps" began to play in the background. The ship's adjutant then yelled, "Present arms!"

The flag covering the coffin was held fast while the empty casket was jettisoned overboard. It sank immediately. Since Justin had no living family members, at least none he had kept in touch with, once the flag was properly folded, it was presented to the only person Captain LaMarr would have deemed worthy to receive it, Steven Barett. At that moment, not even the young lieutenant could maintain his composure; the tears poured like rain.

———

Later, after the funeral was over and the deck cleared, the Sea Lab crew gathered one final time. The seas were calm, the reddish-orange sun was setting over the distant horizon, and the air was reverently silent. Only a cool, pleasant breeze was present, mostly caused by the ship's movement over the ocean. Nancy, with help from the cook, had whipped up a batch of apple pie moonshine. *A fitting send-off for such a sweet man*, she thought.

With glasses filled and raised, Lt. Barett gave a final toast. "To the captain."

"To the captain," everyone else said in unison.

Nothing more needed to be said. As soon as they finished their drinks, they launched their empty glasses overboard. They all contemplated their futures as they watched the containers hit the water and sink.

———

The coffin, which had now been falling for several hours, finally reached the murky bottom. As it came to rest, fine silt disturbed by the landing rose up to engulf the silver object.

Miles away and significantly deeper, on top of a crystalline object of unknown origin, peacefully lay a fallen American hero. He almost looked as if he was sleeping, enjoying a deep-sea nap. The exosuit, though powerless, along with the near-freezing temperatures, would preserve the captain's lifeless corpse for many years to come. All was tranquil. The perfect final resting place for such an honorable man.

Suddenly, the Earth began to shake violently. Boulders broke off from the cliffside ledges, and dust filled the abyssal depths. The amber crystal, with no apparent power source, started to glow, as if it were coming to life.

The light, water, and even the fabric of space-time seemed to warp inward, toward some sort of vortex focal point located deep within the crystal. With a low thunderous boom, the entire process reversed.

Upon the conclusion of the combustion-like wave, two things had changed: A spaceship appeared out of the crystal, rapidly heading toward the surface, and Captain Justin LaMarr was gone.

To be continued . . .

ACKNOWLEDGMENTS

This book is dedicated to all the people who believed in me and provided me with the insight, information, and, most importantly, confidence to author this book. Although too many to include, these persons deserve special mention.

Thank you, Jimmy Haney, my brother from another mother, for enduring all my writes and rewrites while providing me with the personality basis of one of my most comedic characters. You just cannot make some of this stuff up.

I especially want to thank my sister Karrie for her tireless research and supplying me with much of the information used in this book. You are a machine.

Most importantly, I want to thank my dear friend and mentor T. S. Montana, aka Johnny Rae, for allowing me to use some of his story line from the Supreme Creation series, while creating my own. I am forever grateful for the untold hours we wrote together, inspired each other, strategized, and formed a bond that will last for eternity. Without you this would have never been possible. Meeting you profoundly changed my life, and I thank God for it.

For all those not mentioned, which would require a book in itself, I want each of you to know that you are in my heart and my prayers.

ABOUT THE AUTHOR

Sidney Son was born and bred in Charleston, SC. After attending the Citadel, Class of '92, studying Civil Engineering and receiving a Nursing Degree from the Medical University of South Carolina, he opted for a career in the construction industry. Following a tragic accident, which nearly cost him his life, he was left unsure what the future would hold. After many years, trying to reclaim the life he once had, Sidney felt the need, through fiction, to share his experiences, thoughts, and imagination with others.